PRESUMED INNOCENT
&
THE BURDEN OF PROOF

SCOTT TUROW

GUILD PUBLISHING

LONDON · NEW YORK · SYDNEY · TORONTO

This is a work of fiction. All names, places, characters and incidents are entirely imaginary, and any resemblance to actual events, or to persons living or dead, is coincidental.

This omnibus edition published 1991 by
BCA
by arrangement with Bloomsbury Publishing Ltd

Presumed Innocent © 1987 by Scott Turow
The Burden of Proof © 1990 by Scott Turow

CN 1408

Typeset by The Design Team, Ascot, Berks
Printed in England by Clays Ltd, St Ives plc

A NOTE ON THE AUTHOR

Scott Turow was a Stegner Fellow in creative writing at Stanford before attending Harvard Law School. He served with distinction as an assistant U.S. attorney in his native Chicago, trying and winning a number of important cases involving corruption in the Illinois legal system, and is now a partner in the Chicago law firm of Sonnenschein Carlin Nath and Rosenthal.

Contents

PRESUMED INNOCENT

For my Mother

Opening
Statement

This is how I always start:

"I am the prosecutor.

"I represent the state. I am here to present to you the evidence of a crime. Together you will weigh this evidence. You will deliberate upon it. You will decide if it proves the defendant's guilt.

"This man—" And here I point.

You must always point, Rusty, I was told by John White. That was the day I started in the office. The sheriff took my fingerprints, the chief judge swore me in, and John White brought me up to watch the first jury trial I'd ever seen. Ned Halsey was making the opening statement for the state, and as he gestured across the courtroom, John, in his generous, avuncular way, with the humid scent of alcohol on his breath at ten in the morning, whispered my initial lesson. He was the chief deputy P.A. then, a hale Irishman with white hair wild as cornsilk. It was almost a dozen years ago, long before I had formed even the most secret ambition to hold John's job myself. If you don't have the courage to point, John White whispered, you can't expect them to have the courage to convict.

And so I point. I extend my hand across the courtroom. I hold one finger straight. I seek the defendant's eye. I say:

"This man has been accused."

He turns away. Or blinks. Or shows nothing at all.

In the beginning, I was often preoccupied, imagining how it would feel to sit there, held at the focus of scrutiny, ardently denounced before all who cared to listen, knowing that the most ordinary privileges of a decent life—common trust, personal respect, and even liberty—were now like some cloak you had checked at the door and might never retrieve. I could feel the fear, the hot frustration, the haunted separateness.

Now, like ore deposits, the harder stuff of duty and obligation has settled in the veins where those softer feelings moved. I have a job to do. It is not that I have grown uncaring. Believe me. But this business of accusing, judging, punishing had gone on always; it is one of the great wheels turning beneath everything we do. I play my part. I am a functionary of our only universally recognized system of telling wrong from right, a bureaucrat of good and evil. This must be prohibited; not that. One would expect that after all these years of making charges, trying cases, watching defendants come and go, it might have all becoming a jumble. Somehow, it has not.

I turn back to face the jury.

"Today you—all of you—have taken on one of the most solemn obligations of citizenship. Your job is to find the facts. The truth. It is not an easy task, I know. Memories may fail; recollections may be shaded. The evidence might point in differing directions. You may be forced to decide about things that no one seems to know, or to be willing to say. If you were at home, at work, anywhere in your daily life, you might be ready to throw up your hands, you might not want to make the effort. Here you must.

'You must. Let me remind you. There was a real crime. No one will dispute that. There was a real victim. Real pain. You do not have to tell us why it happened. People's motives, after all, may be forever locked inside them. But you must, at least, try to determine what actually occurred. If you cannot, we will not know if this man deserves to be freed—or punished. We will have no idea who to blame. If we cannot find the truth, what is our hope of justice?"

SPRING

1

"I should feel sorrier," Raymond Horgan says.

I wonder at first if he is talking about the eulogy he is going to deliver. He has just looked over his notes again and is returning two index cards to the breast pocket of his blue serge suit. But when I catch his expression I recognize that his remark was personal. From the rear seat of the county's Buick, he stares through the auto window toward the traffic thickening as we approach the South End. His look has taken on a meditative cast. As I watch him, it strikes me that this pose would have been effective as The Picture for this year's campaign: Raymond's thick features fixed in an aspect of solemnity, courage, and a trace of sorrow. He shows something of the stoic air of this sometimes sad metropolis, like the soiled bricks and tarpaper roofs of this part of town.

It is a commonplace among those working around Raymond to say he does not look well. Twenty months ago he split with Ann, his wife of thirty years. He has picked up weight and a perpetual grimness of expression which suggests he has finally reached that time of life when he now believes that many painful things will not improve. A year ago the wagering was that Raymond did not have the stamina or interest to run again, and he waited until four months before the primary to finally announce. Some say it was addiction to power and public life that made him proceed. I believe the chief impulse was Raymond's outright hatred of his primary opponent, Nico Della Guardia, who was until last year another deputy prosecuting attorney in our office. Whatever the motivation, it has proved a difficult campaign. While the money lasted, there were agencies involved and media consultants.

Three young men of dubious sexuality dictated as to matters such as The Picture, and saw to it that this image of Raymond was applied to the backside of one in every four buses in the city. In the picture he has a coaxed smile, meant to show a toughened whimsy. I think the photograph makes him look like a kind of sap. It is one more sign that Raymond has fallen out of step. That is probably what he means when he says he should feel sorrier. He means that events seem to be slipping past him again.

Raymond goes on talking about Carolyn Polhemus's death three nights ago, on the first of April.

"It's as if I can't reach it. I have Nico on one side making out like I'm the one who murdered her. And every jackass in the world with press credentials wants to know when we're going to find the killer. And the secretaries are crying in the johns. And in the end, you know, there's this woman to think about. Christ, I knew her as a probation officer before she graduated law school. She worked for me, I hired her. A smart, sexy gal. A helluva lawyer. And you think about it eventually, you know, the actual event—I think I'm jaded, but Jesus. Some cretin breaks in there. And that's how she ends up, that's her *au revoir*? With some demented slug cracking her skull and giving her a jump. Jesus," Raymond says again. "You can't feel sorry enough."

"No one broke in," I finally say. My sudden declarative tone surprises even me. Raymond, who has momentarily resumed his consideration of a lapful of papers brought along from the office, rears his head and fixes me with an astute gray eye.

"Where do you get that from?"

I am slow to answer.

"We find the lady raped and bound," says Raymond. "Off-hand, I wouldn't be starting off my investigation with her friends and admirers."

"No broken windows," I say, "no forced doors."

At this point Cody, the thirty-year copper who is living out his last days on the force by driving Raymond's county car, breaks into the conversation from the front seat. Cody has been unusually quiet today, sparing us the customary reverie about the bum deals and good pinches he has witnessed in gross on most city avenues. Unlike Raymond—or, for that matter, me—he has no difficulty bringing himself to sorrow. He appears to have been without sleep, which gives his face an edge of roughened grief. My comment about the condition of Carolyn's apartment has stirred him for some reason.

"Every door and window in the joint was unlocked," he says. "She liked it that way. The broad was living in wonderland."

"I think somebody was being clever," I tell them both. "I think that's misdirection."

"Come on, Rusty," Raymond says. "We're looking for a bum. We don't need fucking Sherlock Holmes. Don't try to get ahead of the murder dicks. Keep your head down and walk in a straight line. Okay? Catch me a perpetrator and save my worthless ass." He smiles at me then, a warm, savvy look. Raymond wants me to know he is bearing up. Besides, there is no need to further emphasize the implications of catching Carolyn's killer.

In his reported comments about Carolyn's death, Nico has been base and exploitative and relentless. 'The prosecuting attorney's lax approach to law enforcement for the last twelve years has made him the accomplice of the city's criminal elements. Even the members of his own staff are no longer safe, as this tragedy illustrates.' Nico has not explained how his own hiring by Raymond as a deputy P.A. more than a decade ago fit into Raymond's liaison with lawlessness. But it is not the politician's lot to explain. Besides, Nico has always been shameless in his public conduct. That is one thing that made him ripe for a political career.

Ripe or not, Nico is widely expected to lose the primary, now eighteen days away. Raymond Horgan has wowed Kindle County's one and a half million registered voters for better than a decade. This year he is yet to win the party endorsement, but that is largely due to an ancient factional dispute with the mayor. Raymond's political people—a group that has never included me—believe that when the first of the public polls are published in the next week and a half, other party leaders will be able to force the mayor to reverse field, and that Raymond will be safe for another quadrennium. In this one-party town, victory in the primary is tantamount to election.

Cody turns back from the front seat and mentions that it is getting close to one. Raymond nods absently. Cody takes this for assent and reaches below the dash to let the siren go. He uses it in two brief spells, almost like punctuation in the traffic, but the cars and trucks part neatly and the dark Buick noses ahead. The neighborhood here is still marginal. Older shingle-sided houses, splintering porches. Kids with a kind of potato-y pallor play with balls and ropes at the edge of the street. I grew up about three blocks from here, in an apartment over my father's bakery. I recall them as dark years. During the day my mother and I, when I was not in school, helped my father in the shop. At night we stayed in one locked room while my father drank. There were no other children. The neighborhood today is not much different, still full of people like my father: Serbians, as he was; Ukrainians, Italians, Poles—ethnic types who keep their peace and their own dim outlook.

We are stopped dead in the heavy traffic of Friday afternoon. Cody has driven up the back end of a city bus, which emits its noxious fumes with an intestinal rumble. A Horgan campaign poster is right there, too, and Raymond looks out overhead, six feet wide, with the hapless expression of a TV talk-show host or the spokesman for some canned cat food. And I cannot help myself. Raymond Horgan is my future and my past. I have been a dozen years with him, years full of authentic loyalty and admiration. I am his second-in-command, and his fall would be my own. But there is no silencing the voice of discontent; it has its own imperatives. And it speaks now to the image overhead in a sudden forthright way. You sap, it says. You are, it says, a sap.

As we turn down Third Street, I can see that the funeral has become an important event for the police department. Half the parked cars are black-and-whites, and there are cops in pairs and threes moving up and down the walks. Killing a prosecutor is only one step short of killing a cop, and whatever the institutional interests, Carolyn had many friends on the force— the sort of loyal lieges a good P.A. develops by appreciating skilled police work and making sure it is not squandered in court. Then, of course, there is the fact that she was a beautiful woman and one of modern temperament. Carolyn, we know, got around.

Nearer the chapel the traffic is hopelessly congested. We stutter only a few feet before waiting for the cars ahead to disgorge passengers. The vehicles of the very important— limousines with official plates, press people looking for spaces nearby—clog the way with bovine indifference. The broadcast reporters in particular obey neither local ordinance nor the rules of common civility. The Minicam van of one of the stations, complete with its rooftop radar dish, is parked on the sidewalk directly in front of the open oak doors of the chapel, and a number of reporters are working the crowd as if they were at a prizefight, thrusting microphones at arriving officials.

"Afterward," Raymond says, as he bulls through the press horde that encircles the car as soon as we finally reach the curb. He explains that he is going to make some remarks in eulogy which he will repeat again outside. He pauses long enough to pet Stanley Rosenberg from Channel 5. Stanley, as usual, will get the first interview.

Paul Dry, from the mayor's staff, is motioning to me. His Honor, it seems, would like a word with Raymond before the service begins. I relay the message just as Horgan is pulling free of the reporters. He makes a face—unwisely, for Dry can certainly see it— before he walks off with Paul, disappearing into the gothic dark of the church. The mayor, Augustine Bolcarro, has the character of a tyrant. Ten years ago, when Raymond Horgan was the hot face in town, he almost ran Bolcarro out of office. Almost. Since losing that primary, Raymond has made all the appropriate gestures of fealty. But Bolcarro still feels the ache of his old wounds. Now that it is, at last, Raymond's turn to endure a contested primary, the mayor has claimed that his party role demands neutrality and he has designed to withhold the party's endorsement as well. Clearly he is enjoying watching Raymond struggle on his own toward shore. When Horgan finally hits the beach, Augie will be the first to greet him, saying he knew Raymond was a winner all along.

Inside, the pews are already largely occupied. At the front, the bier is ringed with flowers—lilies and white dahlias—and I imagine, notwithstanding all the bodies, a vague floral scent on the air. I make my way forward, nodding to various personages, and shaking hands. It is a heavyweight crowd: all the city and county pols. Most of the judges are here; most of the bright lights of the defense bar. A number of the leftish and feminist groups with whom Carolyn was sometimes aligned are also represented. The talk is appropriately low key, the expressions of shock and loss sincere.

I back into Della Guardia, who is also working the crowd.

"Nico!" I shake his hand. He has a flower in his lapel, a habit he has acquired since becoming a candidate. He asks after my wife and son, but he does not await my answer. Instead, he assumes a sudden look of tragical sobriety and begins to speak of Carolyn's death.

"She was just—" He circles his hand for the word. I realize that the dashing candidate for prosecuting attorney aspires to poetry and I cut him off.

"She was splendid," I say, and am momentarily amazed by my sudden rush of sentiment, and the force and speed with which it has wrenched itself from some hidden inner place.

"'Splendid.' That's it. Very good." Nico nods; then some mercurial shadow passes across his face. I know him well enough to recognize that he has found a thought which he believes is to his advantage. "I imagine Raymond's pressing pretty hard on that case."

"Raymond Horgan presses hard on every case. You know that."

"Oh ho. I always thought you were the one who was non-political, Rusty. You're picking up your lines now from Raymond's copywriters."

"Better than yours, Delay." Nico acquired that nickname while we were both new deputy P.A.'s working in the appellate section. Nico never could complete a brief on time. John White, the old chief deputy, called him Unavoidable Delay Guardia.

"Oh, no," he says."You fellas aren't angry with me, are you, for what I've been saying? Because I believe that. I believe that effective law enforcement starts right at the top. I believe that's true. Raymond's soft. He's tired. He doesn't have it left to be tough."

I met Nico a dozen years ago, on my first day as a deputy P.A., when we were assigned to share an office. Eleven years later I was the chief deputy and he was head of the Homicide Section and I fired him. By then he had begun overtly attempting to run Raymond out of office. There was a black physician, an abortionist, whom Nico wanted to prosecute for murder. His position made no sense as a matter of law, but it excited the passions of various interest groups whose support he sought. Nico planted news stories about his disagreements with

Raymond; he made jury arguments—for which abundant press coverage always was arranged—that were little more than campaign speeches. Raymond left the final act to me. One morning I went to K Mart and bought the cheapest pair of running shoes they had. I centered them on Nico's desk with a note: 'Goodbye. Good luck. Rusty.'

I always knew campaigning was going to suit him. He looks good. Nico Della Guardia is about forty now, a man of medium height, fastidiously trim. He has been concerned about his weight, eating red meat, things like that, as long as I've known him. Although his skin is bad and his coloring peculiar—red hair and olive skin and light eyes—he has the sort of face whose imperfections are not detected by a camera or even across a courtroom and he is uniformly regarded as handsome. Certainly he has always dressed the part. Even in the days when it required half his paycheck, his suits were tailor-made.

But far beyond good looks, Nico's most arresting aspect has always been the brassy and indiscriminate sincerity he is displaying here, reciting the elements of his platform while conversing, in the midst of a funeral, with his opponent's chief assistant. After twelve years, including two in which we shared an office, I have learned that Delay can always summon up that kind of overeager and unreflective faith in himself. The morning that I fired him nine months ago, he strolled past my office on his way out, bright as a new penny, and said simply, I'll be back.

I try to let Nico down easy now.

"It's too late, Delay. I've promised my vote to Raymond Horgan."

He is slow to get the joke, and when he does, he will not give the subject up. We go on playing a sort of lawyer's Dozens, dwelling on weaknesses. Nico admits his campaign is short of money but claims that the archbishop's unspoken support lends him "moral capital."

"That's where we're strong," he says. "Really. That's where we'll pick up votes. People have forgotten why they ever wanted to vote for Civil Rights Raymond. He's just a blur to them. A blob. I have a strong, clear message." Nico's confidence is radiant, as ever, when he speaks about himself. "You know what worried me?" Nico asks. "You know who would have been hard to beat?" He has crept a foot closer and lowered his voice. "You."

I laugh out loud, but Nico goes on: "I was relieved. I'm telling you the truth. I was relieved when Raymond announced. I'd seen it coming: Horgan holds a big press conference, says he's hanging it up, but he's asked his top assistant to carry on. Media is going to love Rusty Sabich. A non-political guy. A professional prosecutor. Stable. Mature. Somebody everyone can depend on. The man who broke up the Night Saints. They play all that stuff and Raymond brings Bolcarro in behind you. You'd've been tough, very tough."

"Ridiculous," I say, manfully pretending that like scenarios have not described themselves to my imagination on a hundred occasions in the last year. "You're really something, Delay," I tell him. "Divide and conquer. You'll just never stop."

"Hey listen, my friend," he says, "I am one of your true admirers. I mean that. There are no hard feelings here." He touches his shirt above the vest. "That is one of the few things that's going to stay the same when I get there. You'll still be in the chief deputy's office."

I tell him, affably, that's a bunch of crap.

"You'll never be P.A.," I say, "and if you were, Tommy Molto would be your guy. Everybody knows you have Tommy in the woodshed now." Tommy Molto is Nico's best friend, his former second-in-command in the Homicide Section. Molto has been a no-show in the office for three days. He hasn't called in and his desk is clean. The common belief is that when the furor over Carolyn's death abates a bit next week, Nico will stage another media occasion and announce that Tommy has joined his campaign. It will provoke a few more headlines. DISAPPOINTED HORGAN DEPUTY BACKS NICO. Delay handles these things well. Raymond has a fit whenever he hears Tommy's name.

"Molto?" Nico asks me now. His look of innocence is entirely unconvincing, but I do not get the chance to respond. At the lectern, the reverend has asked the mourners to assume their seats. Instead, I smile at Della Guardia—smirk, in fact—as we are parting, and begin buffeting my way toward the front of the chapel, where Raymond and I are supposed to sit as office representatives. But as I go, making restrained gestures of acknowledgment to the people that I know, the heat of all of Nico's forceful confidence is still upon me. It is like having come in out of the blazing sun: the skin tingles and remains tender to the touch. And it strikes me then abruptly, as I gain my first clear view of the pewter-colored casket, that Nico Della Guardia actually may win. This prophecy is announced by a small voice somewhere in my interior reaches, only loud enough, like some whining conscience, to tell me what I do not want to hear. Undeserving as Nico is, unqualified, a pygmy in his soul, something may be propelling him toward triumph, Here, in this region of the dead, I cannot help but recognize the carnal appeal of his vitality and how far it is bound to take him.

In keeping with the character of this public occasion, two rows of folding chairs have been positioned next to Carolyn's coffin. They are occupied, for the most part, by the dignitaries you would expect. The only unfamiliar figure is a boy in his late teens who is seated beside the mayor, directly at the foot of the bier. This young man has a poorly barbered tangle of blondish hair and a necktie drawn too tight, so that the collar points on his rayon shirt are lifted in the air. A cousin, I decide, perhaps a nephew, but definitely—and surprisingly—family. Carolyn's people, as I understood it, were all back East, where she meant to leave them long ago. Beside him in the front row, there are more of the mayor's people than there should be, and no room is left for me. As I pass in the row behind Horgan, Raymond leans back. He has apparently observed my talk with Della Guardia.

"What did Delay have to say for himself?"

"Nothing. Bullshit. He's running out of money."

"Who isn't?" Raymond asks.

I inquire about the meeting with the mayor, and Horgan rolls his eyes.

"He wanted to give me some advice, just in confidence, me and him, because he doesn't want to appear to be taking sides. He thinks it would help my chances a lot if we arrested Carolyn's murderer before Election Day. Can you believe that jagoff? And he said it with a straight face, too, so I couldn't walk out on him. He's having a great time." Raymond points. "Look at him up there. The chief mourner."

Raymond as usual cannot contain himself about Bolcarro. I look around, hoping we have not been overheard. I chuck my face toward the young man seated beside the mayor.

"Who is the kid?" I ask.

I do not think I have understood Horgan's answer, and I lean closer. Raymond brings his face right to my ear.

"Her son," he says again.

I stand up straight.

"Grew up with his father in New Jersey," Raymond says, "then came out here for college. He's over at the U."

Surprise seems to drive me backward. I murmur something to Raymond and push down the row toward my seat at the end, between two sizable floral arrangements on pedestals. For an instant I am certain that this lightheaded moment of shock has passed, but as an unexpectedly bold tone forges from the organ immediately behind me, and the reverend speaks his first words of address, my amazement deepens, ripples, and somehow takes on the infected hurt of real sorrow. I did not know. I feel a sort of shimmering incomprehension. It does not seem plausible that she could have kept a fact like this to herself. The husband I had long ago surmised, but she never made mention of a child, let alone one nearby, and I must stifle an immediate instinct to leave, to remove myself from this theater darkness for the sobering effect of strong light. As a matter of will, I urge myself, after a few moments, to attend to what is present.

Raymond has arrived at the podium; there has been no formal introduction. Others—the Reverend Mr. Hiller, Rita Worth from the Women's Bar Association—have spoken briefly, but now a sudden gravity and portentousness comes into the air, a current strong enough to wrest me from my sense of grievance. The hundreds here grow stiller. Raymond Horgan has his shortcomings as a politician, but he is a consummate public man, a speaker, a presence. Balding, growing stout, standing there in his fine blue suit, he broadcasts his anguish and his power like a beaconed emission.

His remarks are anecdotal. He recalls Carolyn's hiring over the objections of more hard-bitten prosecutors who regarded probation officers as social workers. He celebrates her toughness and her flint. He remembers cases that she won, judges she defied, archaic rules she took pleasure in seeing broken. From Raymond, these stories have a soulful wit, a sweet melancholy for Carolyn and all of her lost courage. He really has no equal in a setting like this, just talking to people about what he thinks and feels.

For me, though, there is no quick recovery from the disorder of the moments before. I find all of it—the hurt, the shock, the piercing force of Raymond's words, my deep, my unspeakable sorrow—welling up, pushing at the limits of tolerance and a composure I desperately need to maintain. I bargain with myself. I will not go to the interment. There is work to do, and the office will be represented. The secretaries and clerks, the older ladies who always criticized Carolyn's airs and are here now, crying in the front rows, will be pressed close at the graveside, weeping over one more of life's endless desolations. I will let them observe Carolyn's disappearance into open ground.

Raymond finishes. The impressive register of his performance, witnessed by so many who regard him as beleaguered, sets a palpable stir in the auditorium as he strides toward his seat. The reverend recites the details of the burial, but I let that pass. I am resolved: I will go back to the office. As Raymond wishes, I will resume the search for Carolyn's killer. Nobody will mind—least of all, I think, Carolyn herself. I have already paid her my respects. Too much so, she might say. Too often. She knows, I know, that I have already done my grieving over Carolyn Polhemus.

2

The office has the bizarre air of calamity, of things badly out of place. The halls are empty, but the phones are pealing in wearying succession. Two secretaries, the only ones who stayed behind, are sprinting up and down the corridors putting callers on hold.

Even in the best of times, the Office of the Kindle County Prosecuting Attorney has a dismal aspect. Most deputies work two to an office in a space of Dickensian grimness. The Kindle County Building was erected in 1897 in the emerging institutional style of factories and high schools. It is a solid red-brick block dressed up with a few Doric columns to let everybody know it is a public place. Inside, there are transoms over the doors and dour casement windows. The walls are that mossy hospital green. Worst of all is the light, a kind of yellow fluid, like old shellac. So here we are, two hundred harried individuals attempting to deal with every crime committed in a city of one million, and the surrounding county, where two million people more reside. In the summer we labor in jungle humidity, with the old window units rattling over the constant clamor of the telephones. In the winter the radiators spit and clank while the hint of darkness never seems to leave the daylight. Justice in the Middle West.

In my office, Lipranzer is waiting for me like a bad guy in a Western, hidden as he sits behind the door.

"Everybody dead and gone?" he asks.

I comment on his sentimentality and throw my coat down on a chair. "Where were you, by the way? Any copper with five years' service showed."

"I'm no funeralgoer," Lipranzer says dryly. There is, I decide, some significance in a homicide dick's distaste for funerals, but the connection does not come to me immediately and so I let the idea go. Life in the workplace: so many signs of the hidden world of meanings elude me in a day, bumps on the surface, shadows, like creatures darting by.

I attend to what is present. On my desk there are two items: a memo from MacDougall, the chief administrative deputy, and an envelope Lipranzer has placed there. Mac's memo simply says, "Where is Tommy Molto?" It occurs to me that for all of our suspicions of political intrigue, we should not ignore the obvious: someone ought to check the hospitals and Tommy's apartment. One deputy P.A. is dead already. That is the reason for Lipranzer's envelope. It bears a label typed by the police lab: OFFENDER: UNKNOWN. VICTIM: C. POLHEMUS.

"Did you know that our decedent left an heir?" I ask as I'm looking for the letter opener.

"No shit," says Lip.

"A kid. Looked to be eighteen, twenty. He was at the funeral."

"No shit," Lip says again, and considers his cigarette. "You figure one thing about goin to a funeral is at least no surprises."

"One of us ought to talk to him. He's at the U."

"Get me an address, I'll see him. 'Anything Horgan's guys want.' Morano gave me that crock again this mornin." Morano is the police chief, an ally of Bolcarro's. "He's waitin to see Raymond fall on his ass."

"Him and Nico. I bumped into Delay." I tell Lip about our visit. "Nico's really high on himself. He even made me believe it for a minute."

"He'll do better than people say. Then you'll be kickin yourself in the ass, thinkin you should have run."

I make a face: who knows? With Lip, I do not have to bother with more.

For my fifteenth college reunion I received a questionnaire which asked a lot of personal questions I found difficult to answer: What contemporary American do you admire most? What is your most important physical possession? Name your best friend and describe him. On this one, I puzzled for some time, but I finally wrote down Lipranzer's name. 'My best friend,' I wrote, 'is a cop. He is five foot eight inches tall, weighs 120 pounds after a full meal, and has a duckass hairdo and that look of lurking small-time viciousness that you've seen on every no-account kid hanging on a street corner. He smokes two packs of Camel cigarettes a day. I do not know what we have in common, but I admire him. He is very good at what he does.'

I first ran across Lip seven or eight years ago, when I was initially assigned to the Violence Section and he had just begun working Homicide. We have done a dozen cases since, but there are still ways in which I regard him as a mystery, even a danger. His father was a watch commander in a precinct in the West End, and when his old man died, Lip left college to take up a place that came to him by rights of a kind of departmental primogeniture. By now he has been placed in the P.A.'s office on direct assignment, a so-called Special Command. On paper, his job is to act as police liaison, coordinating homicide investiga-tions of special interest to our office. In practice, he is as solitary as a shooting star. He reports to a Captain Schmidt, who cares only that he has sixteen homicide collars to show at the end of every fiscal year. Lip spends most of his time alone, hanging out in bars and on loading docks, drinking shots with anybody who's got good information—hoods, reporters, queers, federal agents, anybody who can keep him up to speed on the world of big-time bad guys. Lipranzer is a scholar of the underlife. Eventually, I have come to recognize that it is the weird weight of that information that somehow accounts for his rheumy-eyed sulking look.

I still have the envelope in my hands.

"So what do we have here?" I ask.

"Path report. Three-sheet. Bunch of pictures of a naked dead lady." The three-sheet is the prosecutor's copy of the arriving officers' reports—the third leaf in the carbon layers. I have talked to these cops directly. I go on to the report of the police pathologist, Dr. Kumagai, a weird-looking little Japanese who seems to have come out of a forties propaganda piece. He is known as Painless, a notorious hack. No prosecutor calls him to the witness stand without crossing his fingers.

"And what's the scoop? Male fluids in every hole?"

"Just the main one. Lady is dead of a skull fracture and resulting hemorrhage. Pictures might make you think she was strangled, but Painless says there was air in her lungs. Anyway, the guy musta hit her with somethin. Painless has got no idea what. Heavy, he says. And real hard."

"I take it we looked for a murder weapon in the apartment?"
"Turned the place upside down."

"Anything obvious missing? Candlesticks? Bookends?"
"Nothin. I sent three separate teams through."

"So," I say, "our man showed up already thinking he'd be doing some heavy hitting."

"Could be. Or else he just took what he used with him. I'm not positive this guy came prepared. Seems like he was hittin to subdue her—didn't realize he cooled her. I figure—you can see when you look at the pictures—that the way the ropes were tied, that he put himself between her legs and was tryin to let his weight strangle her. It's all slip-knotted. I mean," Lipranzer says, "that he was sort of tryin to fuck her to death."

"Charming," I say.

"Definitely charming," says Lip. "This was a very charming type fellow." We are both quiet a moment before he goes on. "We got no bruises on the arms, hands, nothin like that," Lip says. That would mean there was no struggle before Carolyn was bound. "Contusion's rear right. It's got to be that he hit her from behind, then tied her up. Only it seems strange that he would knock her cold to start with. Most of these creeps like em to know what they're doin."

I shrug. I'm not so sure of that.

The photos are the first thing I take out of the envelope. They are clean, full-colored shots. Carolyn lived in a place on the water-front, a former warehouse parceled into "loft condominiums." She had divided the space with Chinese screens and heavy rugs. Her taste ran to the modern, with elegant touches of classical and antique. She had been killed in the space off the kitchen which she used as a living room. An overall shot of that area is first on the stack. The thick green-edged glass top of a coffee table has been tumbled off its brass props; a modular seating piece is upside down. But overall I agree with Lip that there is less sign of struggle than I have seen on other occasions, particularly if you ignore the blood-stain worked into the fiber of the flokati rug so that it has the shape of a large soft cloud. I look up. I do not feel I am ready yet to take on the photos of the corpse.

"What else does Painless tell us?" I ask.

"This guy was shootin blanks."

"Blanks?"

"Oh yeah. You'll like this." Lipranzer does his best to repeat Kumagai's analysis of the sperm deposit that was found. Little of it had seeped to the labia, which means that Carolyn could not have spent much time on her feet after sexual contact. This is another way we know that the rape and her death were roughly contemporaneous. On April 1, she had left the office a little after seven. Kumagai puts the time of death at somewhere around nine.

"That's twelve hours before the body's found," Lip says. "Painless says normally, with that kinda time span, he'd still see some of the guy's little thingies swimmin upstream in the tubes and in the womb, when he looked under the microscope. Instead, this guy's wad's all dead. Nothin went nowhere. Painless figures this guy is sterile." Lip pronounces the word so that it rhymes with pearl. "Says you can get like that from mumps."

"So we're looking for a rapist who has no children and once had the mumps?"

Lipranzer shrugs.

"Painless says he's gonna take the semen specimen and send it over to the forensic chemist. Maybe they can give him another idea of what's up."

I groan a little bit at the thought of Painless exploring the realms of higher chemistry.

"Can't we get a decent pathologist?" I ask.

"You got Painless," Lip says innocently.

I groan again, and leaf through a few more pages of Kumagai's report.

"Do we have a secreter?" I ask. People are divided not merely by blood type but by whether they secrete identifying agents into their body fluids.

Lip takes the report from me. "Yep."

"Blood type?"

"A."

"Ah," I say, "my very own."

"I thoughta that," says Lip, "but you got a kid."

I again comment on Lipranzer's sentimentality. He does not bother to respond. Instead, he lights another cigarette and shakes his head.

"I'm just not grabbin it yet," he says. "The whole goddamn deal is too weird. We're missin somethin."

So we begin again, the investigators' favorite parlor game, who and why. Lipranzer's number-one suspicion from the start has been that Carolyn was killed by someone she convicted. That is every prosecutor's worst fantasy, the long-nurtured vengeance of some dip you sent away. Shortly after I was first assigned to the jury trial section, a youth, as the papers would have it, by the name of Pancho Mercado, took exception to my closing argument, in which I had questioned the manliness of anyone who made his living by pistol-whipping seventy-seven-year-old men. Six foot four and well over 250 pounds, Pancho leaped the dock and thundered behind me through most of the courthouse before he was stopped cold in the P.A.'s lunchroom by MacDougall, wheelchair and all. The whole thing ended up on page 3 of the *Tribune*, with a grotesque headline: PANICKED PROSECUTOR SAVED BY CRIPPLE. Something like that. Barbara, my wife, likes to refer to this as my first famous case.

Carolyn worked on stranger types than Pancho. For several years she had headed what is called the office's Rape Section. The name gives a good idea of what is involved, although all forms of sexual assault tend to be prosecuted there, including child abuse and one case I can recall where an all-male *ménage à trois* had turned rough and the state's main witness had ended the evening with a light bulb up his rectum. It is Lipranzer's hypothesis, at moments, that one of the rapists Carolyn prosecuted got even.

Accordingly, we agree to go over Carolyn's docket to see if there was anybody she tried—or investigated—for a crime resembling what took place three nights ago. I promise to look through the records in Carolyn's office. The state investigative agencies also maintain a computer run of sexual offenders, and Lip will see if we can cross-match there on Carolyn's name, or the stunt with the ropes.

"What kind of leads are we running?"

Lipranzer begins to tick it off for me. The neighbors were all seen in the day following the murder, but those interviews were probably hasty and Lip will arrange for homicide investigators to make another pass at everyone in a square block. This time

they'll do it in the evening, so that the neighbors who are home
at the hour when the murder took place will be in.

"One lady says she saw a guy in a raincoat on the stairs." Lip
looks at his notebook. "Mrs. Krapotnik. Says maybe he looked
familiar, but she doesn't think he lives there."

"The Hair and Fiber guys went through first, right?" I ask.
"When do we hear from them?" To these people falls the
grotesque duty of vacuuming the corpse, picking over the crime
scene with tweezers, in order to make microscopic examinations
of any trace materials they discover. Often they can type hair,
identify an offender's clothing.

"That should be a week, ten days," Lip says. "They'll try to
come up with somethin on the rope. Only other interesting thing
they tell me is they got a lot of floor fluff. There a few hairs
around, but not what you'd find if there was any kinda fight."

"How about fingerprints?" I ask.

"They dusted everything in the place."

"Did they dust this glass table here?" I show Lip the picture.

"Yeah."

"Did they get latents?"

"Yeah."

"Report?"

"Preliminary."

"Whose prints?"

"Carolyn Polhemus."

"Super."

"It ain't all bad," says Lip. He takes the picture from me and
points. "See this bar here. See the glass?" One tall bar glass,
standing undisturbed. "There latents on that. Three fingers. And
the prints ain't the decedent's."

"Do we have any idea whose prints they are?"

"No. Identification says three weeks. They got all kinda
backlogs." The police department identification division keeps a
digit-by-digit record of every person who has ever been printed,
classified by so-called points of comparison, the ridges and
valleys on a fingertip to which numerical values are assigned. In
the old days, they were unable to identify an unknown print
unless the subject left behind latents of all ten fingers, so I.D.
could search the existing catalogue. Now, in the computer era,
the search can be done by machine. A laser mechanism reads

the print and compares to every one in memory. The process takes only a few minutes, but the department, due to budgetary constraints, does not yet own all of the equipment and must borrow pieces from the state police for special cases. "I told them to rush it up, but they're giving me all that shit about Zilogs and onloading. A call from the P.A. would really help. Tell them to compare to every known in the county. Anybody. Any dirtball who's ever been printed."

I make a note to myself.

"We need MUDs, too," Lipranzer says, and points to the pad. Although it is not well known, the telephone company keeps a computerized record of all local calls made from most exchanges: Message Unit Detail sheets. I begin writing out the grand-jury subpoena *duces tecum*, a request for documents. "And ask them for MUDs on anybody she called in the last six months," says Lip.

"They'll scream. You're probably talking about two hundred numbers."

"Anybody she called three times. I'll get back to them with a list. But ask for it now, so I'm not runnin my ass around tryin to find you to do another subpoena."

I nod. I'm thinking.

"If you're going back six months," I tell him, "you're probably going to hit this number." I nod toward the phone on my desk.

Lipranzer looks at me levelly and says, "I know."

So he knows, I think. I take a minute with this, trying to figure how. People guess, I think. They gossip. Besides, Lip would notice things that anyone else would miss. I doubt that he approves. He is single, but he is no rover. There is a Polish woman a good ten years older than he, a widow with a grown kid, who cooks a meal and sleeps with Lipranzer two or three times a week. On the phone, he calls her Momma.

"You know," I say, "as long as we're on the subject, Carolyn always locked her doors and windows." I tell him this with admirable evenness. "I mean, always. She was a little soft, but Carolyn was a grownup. She knew she lived in the city."

Lipranzer's look focuses gradually and his eyes take on a metallic gleam. He has not lost the significance of what I'm telling him or, it seems, of the fact that I delayed.

"So what do you figure?" he asks at last. "Somebody walked

around there openin the windows?"

"Could be."

"So they'd make it look like a break-in? Somebody she let in in the first place?"

"Doesn't that make sense? You're the one who's telling me there's a glass on the bar. She was entertaining. I wouldn't bet the ranch on the bad guy being some crazed parolee."

Lip stares at his cigarette. Looking through the doorway, I see that Eugenia, my secretary, has returned. There are voices now in the hallway as people filter back in from the graveside. I detect a lot of the anxious laughter of release.

"Not necessarily," he says finally. "Not with Carolyn Polhemus. She was a funny lady." He looks at me hard again.

"You mean, you think she'd open the door to some bum she sent to jail?"

"I think with Carolyn there's no tellin. Suppose she bumped into one of these characters in a bar. Or some guy called her up and said, Let's have a pop. You think there's no chance she'd say yes? We're talkin Carolyn now."

I can see where Lip is going. Lady P.A., Prosecutor of Perverts, Fucks Defendant and Lives Out Forbidden Fantasy. Lip has got her number pretty well. Carolyn Polhemus would not have minded at all the idea that some guy had dwelled with the thought of her for years. But somehow, with this discussion a seasick misery begins to ebb through me.

"You didn't like her much, did you, Lip?"

"Not much." We look at each other. Then Lipranzer reaches over and chucks me on the knee. "At least we know one thing," he says. "She had piss-poor taste in men."

That is his exit line. He tucks his Camels into his windbreaker and is gone. I call out to Eugenia to please hold anything else. With a moment's privacy I am now ready to examine the photographs. For a minute, after I begin sorting through them, my attention is mostly on myself. How well will I manage this? I urge myself to maintain professional composure.

But that, of course, begins to give way. It is like the network of crazing that sometimes seeps through glass in the wake of an impact. There is excitement at first, slow-entering and reluctant, but more than a little. In the top photographs the heavy glass of the table is canted over, compressing her shoulder, so that you might almost make the comparison to a laboratory slide. But soon it is removed. And here is Carolyn's spectacularly lithe body in a pose which, for all the agony there must have been, seems, initially, supple and athletic. Her legs are trim and graceful; her breasts are high and large. Even in death, she retains her erotic bearing. But, I slowly recognize, other experiences must influence this response. Because what is actually here is horrible, There are bruises on her face and neck, mulberry patches. A rope runs from her ankles to her knees, her waist, her wrists; then it is jerked tight around her neck, where the rim of the burn is visible. She is drawn back in an ugly tormented bow and her face is ghastly; her eyes, with the hyperthyroid look of the attempted strangulation, are enormous and protruding and her mouth is fixed in a silent scream. I watch, I study. Her look holds the same wild, disbelieving, desperate thing that so frightens me when I find the courage to let my glance fix on the wide black eye of a landed fish dying on a pier. I take it in now in the same reverential, awestruck, uncomprehending way. And then, worst of all, when all the dirt is scraped off the treasure box there is rising within, unhindered by shame, or even fear, a bubble of something light enough that I must eventually recognize it as satisfaction, and no lecture to myself about the baseness of my nature can quite discourage me. Carolyn Polhemus, that tower of grace and fortitude, lies here in my line of sight with a look she never had in life. I see it finally now. She wants my pity. She needs my help.

3

When it was all over, I went to see a psychiatrist. His name was Robinson.

"I would say she's the most exciting woman I've known," I told him.

"Sexy?" he asked after a moment.

"Sexy, yes. Very sexy. Torrents of blond hair, and almost no behind, and this very full bosom. And long red fingernails, too. I mean, definitely, deliberately, almost ironically sexy. You notice. That's the idea with Carolyn. You're supposed to notice. And I did. She's worked around our office for years. She was a probation officer before she went to law school. But that's all she was to me originally. You know: this very good-looking blonde with big tits. Every copper who came in would roll his eyes and make like he was jerking off. That's all.

"Over time, people began to talk about her. Even while she was still in the branch courts. You know: high-powered. Capable. Then for a while she was dating this newsman on Channel 3. Chet whatever his name is. And she showed up a lot of places. Very active in the bar organizations. An officer for a while in the local NOW chapter. And shrewd. She asked to be assigned out to the Rape Section when it was considered a crappy place to work. All these impossible one-on-ones where you could never figure out if it was the victim or the defendant who was closer to the truth. Hard cases. Just to find the ones that deserved to be prosecuted, let alone to win them. And she did very well out there. Eventually Raymond put her in charge of all those trials. He liked to send her on those Sunday-morning public service TV programs. Show his concern on women's issues. And Carolyn liked to go and carry the banner. She enjoyed the limelight. But she was a good prosecutor. And damn tough. The defense lawyers used to complain that she had a complex, that she was trying to prove that she had balls. But the coppers loved her.

"I'm not sure what I thought of her then. I suppose I thought she was just a little bit too much."

Robinson looked at me.

"Too much everything," I said. "You know. Too bold. Too self-impressed. Always running one gear too high. She didn't have the right sense of proportion."

"And," said Robinson, proceeding to the obvious, "you fell in love with her."

I went silent, still. When are words ever enough?

"I fell in love with her," I said.

Raymond felt she needed a partner and so she asked me. It was September of last year.

"Could you have said no?" asked Robinson.

"I suppose. The chief deputy isn't expected to try a lot of cases. I could have said no."

"But?"

But I said yes.

Because, I told myself, the case was interesting. The case was strange. Darryl McGaffen was a banker. He worked for his brother, Joey, who was a gangster, a florid personality, a hotshot type who enjoyed being the target of every law enforcement agency in town. Joey used the bank, out in McCrary, to wash a river of dirty money, mostly mob dough. But that was Joey's action. Darryl kept his head down and the accounts straight. Darryl was as mild as Joey was flamboyant. An ordinary guy. He lived out west, near McCrary. He had a wife. And a somewhat tragic life. His first child, a little girl, had died at the age of three. I knew all about that, because Joey had once testified before the grand jury about his niece's fall from a second-floor terrace at his brother's home. Joey had explained, almost convincingly, that the girl's resulting skull fracture and immediate death were large in his mind and had obstructed his judgment when four mysterious fellows delivered to his bank certain bonds which, to Joey's great chagrin, turned out to be hot. Joey wrung his hands when he talked about the girl. He touched his silk pocket hankie to both his eyes.

Darryl and his wife had another child, a boy named Wendell. When Wendell was five, his mother arrived with him at the West End Pavilion Hospital emergency room. The boy was unconscious and his mother was hysterical, for her child had taken a terrible fall, sustaining severe head injuries. The mother claimed that he had never been at the hospital before, but the emergency room physician—a young Indian woman, Dr. Narajee—had a memory of treating Wendell a year earlier, and when a medical record was summoned she found he had been there twice, once with a broken collarbone, once with a broken arm, both the results, his mother had said, of falls. The child was unconscious now and not likely in most events to speak, and so Dr. Narajee studied his injuries. When she testified later, Dr. Narajee said she realized initially that the wounds were too symmetrical and too evenly positioned laterally to be the result of a fall. She repeatedly examined the gashes, two inches by one inch on each side of the head, over more than a day, before she had it all figured out, and then she called Carolyn Polhemus at the prosecuting attorney's office to report that she was treating a child whose skull appeared to have been fractured when his mother placed his head in a vise.

Carolyn obtained a search warrant at once. They recovered the grip with skin fragments still on it from the basement of the McGaffen home. They examined the unconscious child and found healed wounds which appeared to have been cigarette burns in his anus. And then they waited to see what would happen with the boy. He lived.

By then he was in court custody. And the P.A.'s office was under siege. Darryl McGaffen came to his wife's defense. She was a loving and devoted mother. It was insanity, he said, to claim she'd hurt her child. He had seen the boy fall, McGaffen said, a terrible accident, a tragedy, marred by this nightmarish experience of doctors and lawyers madly conspiring to take their sick child away. Very emotional. Very well staged. Joey made sure the cameras were there when the brother got to the courthouse and that Darryl claimed a vendetta by Raymond Horgan against his family. In order to show forthrightness, Raymond was going to try the case himself at first. But the campaign was beginning to heat up. Raymond sent the case back to Carolyn and recommended, given the press attention, that she try it with another senior deputy, someone like me, whose presence would show the office's commitment. So she asked. And I agreed. I told myself I was doing it for Raymond.

The physicists call it Brownian movement, the action of molecules coursing against one another in the air. This activity produces a kind of hum, a high-pitched, almost screeching sound at a frequency level on the margins of human audibility. As a child I could hear this tone, if I chose to, at virtually any moment. Most often, I would ignore it, but every now and then my will eroded and I would let the pitch rise inside my ears to the point where it was almost blaring.

Apparently at puberty the bones in the inner ear harden so that the Brownian ringing can no longer be heard. Which is just as well. Because by then there are other distractions. For me, during most of my married life, the allure of other women has been like that daily hum which I willfully ignored, and when I started working around Carolyn that resolve went weak, and the pitch rose, vibrated, *sang*.

"And I can't really tell you why," I said to Robinson.

I consider myself a person of values. I had always despised my father for his philandering. On Friday nights he was emitted from the household like a wandering cat, headed for a tavern and, later, the Hotel Delaney over on Western Avenue, only a little better than a flop, with its old woolen carpets worn to the backing over the stairs, and the naphtha scent of some chemical agent used to control the infestation of pests. There he would pursue his passion with various soiled women—barroom chippies, horny divorcées, wives out on the sneak. Before he left on these outings, he had dinner with my mother and me. We both knew where he was going. He would hum, the only sound anything like music which came from him all week.

But somehow as I worked around Carolyn, with her jangling jewelry and her light perfume, her silk blouses, her red lipstick and painted nails, that large heaving bosom and her long legs, that splash of bright hair, I became overwhelmed by her—and in just that fashion, detail by detail, so that I would become excited

when I smelled her scent on another woman who passed me in
the hall.

"And I can't really tell you why. Maybe that's why I am here.
Some frequency is heard and everything begins to shatter. A
vibration sets in, a fundamental tone, and the whole interior is
shaking. We'd talk about the trial, our lives, whatever, and she
seemed such a remarkable mix of things. Symphonic. A
symphonic personality. Disciplined and glamorous. This musical
laugh. And an orthodontic wonder of a smile. She was much
wittier than I expected; tough, as they said, but she did not seem
hard."

I was affected particularly by her offhand remarks, the way
her eyes, hooded with shadow and liner, would take on this tone
of level assessment. Analyzing politics or witnesses or cops, she
showed you just how firm a purchase she had on what was going
on. And that was very exciting to me, to meet a woman who
seemed to really have the lowdown, who was moving through
the world at Carolyn's speed, and who was so many different
things to different people. Maybe it was the contrast to Barbara,
who is so deliberately none of that.

"Here was this bold, bright, handsome woman, much celebrated, with a kind of spotlight radiance. And I find I am going
down to her office—which is itself a minor wonder in a place as
stark as ours, Carolyn having taken the trouble to add a small
Oriental rug, plants, an antique bookcase, and an Empire desk
she snagged through a connection with Central Services—I'm
going down there with nothing to say. There is this heat, this
parched sensation—all the old crappy metaphors—and I start
thinking, Jesus Christ, this can't be happening. And maybe it still
wouldn't have, but about this time I begin to notice, I begin to
think she is paying attention to me. She is *looking* at me. Oh, I
know, this sounds like high school. No, worse, junior high school.
But there is this thing, people don't *look* at one another."

And when we're interviewing witnesses, I turn and Carolyn is
staring at me, watching with this placid, almost rueful smile, as I
do my stuff—or in a meeting with Raymond, all the top felony
people, I'll glance up, I'll feel the weight of her eyes on me, and
she continues watching me in such an unwavering fashion that I
do something, a wink, a smile, as a form of acknowledgment, and
she responds, usually that little cat's grin, and if I'm speaking I

stop, everything washes out of my mind, it is just Carolyn, things are unraveling right from the center of the skein.

"That was the worst part, this incredible domination of my feelings. I get in the shower, I drive down the street—it's Carolyn. Fantasies. Conversations with her. An uninterrupted movie. I see her full of relaxed amusement and appreciation—of me. Of me. I can't finish a phone call; I can't read a prosecution memo or a brief."

And all of it, this whole grand obsession, carried on in the face of a racing heart, a turning gut, a frantic sense of resistance and disbelief. I shudder at random moments. I tell myself that this has not happened. This is a juvenile episode, a mind trick like *déjà vu*. I grope around inside myself for the old reality. I say to myself that I will get up in the morning feeling unaffected, feeling right again and sane.

But I do not, of course, and the moments when I am with her, the anticipation, the appreciation is exquisite. I feel short of breath and giddy. I laugh too easily, too much. I do what I can to stay near her, show her a paper over her shoulder while she's at her desk, so that I can linger with the details of her person: her hammered golden earrings, the odors of her bathwater and her breath, the soft bluish color of her nape when her hair falls away. And then, when I'm by myself, I feel desperate and ashamed. This raging, mad obsession! Where is my world? I am departing, I am gone already.

4

In the dark, the red-and-blue figure of Spider-Man can be made out on the wall above my son's bed. Life-size, he is poised in a wrestler's crouch, prepared to take on all invaders.

I did not grow up reading the comics—it was too lighthearted an activity for the home I was raised in. But when Nat was two or three we began, each Sunday, to explore the funny papers together. While Barbara slept, I made Nat breakfast. Then, with my son very close beside me, we sat on the sofa in the sunroom as we discussed and recollected the weekly progress in each strip. All the random little-boy fury of that age would leave him, and he was reduced to a more essential self, small and full of a transport I could feel through his body. So it was that I came to establish my rapport with the Web Slinger. Now Nat, in second grade and almost brittlely self-sufficient, reads the funnies by himself. I must await a moment when I will not be noticed to check on Peter Parker's fate. They really are funny, I explained to Barbara a few weeks ago when I was observed with the comics in my hands. Oh, for crying out loud, muttered my wife, the almost Ph.D.

Now I touch the fine hair, so thin against Nat's scalp. If I fuss long enough, Nat, accustomed by the years to my late arrivals, will probably rouse himself to murmur some gentle appreciation. I stop here first each evening. I have an almost physical craving for the reassurance. Right before Nat's birth we moved out here, to Nearing, a former ferry port to which the city dwellers fled long enough ago that it is called a town rather than a suburb. Although it was Barbara who initially favored this move, by now she would eagerly forsake Nearing, which she sometimes blames for her isolation. I'm the one who needs the distance from the city, the gap in time and space, to manufacture in myself a sense that some perimeter protects us against what I see each day. I suppose that is another reason I was happy to see Spider-Man assume his place here. I take comfort in Spidey's agile vigilance.

I find Barbara face down on our bed, largely unclothed. She is breathless, the tight muscles of her narrow back lustrous with sweat. The VCR hums in rewind. On the set, the news has just begun.

"Exercise?" I ask.

"Masturbation," Barbara answers. "Refuge of the lonely housewife.'

She does not bother a backward glance. Instead, I advance and kiss her quickly on the neck.

"I called from the bus station when I missed the 8:35. You weren't here. I left a message on the tape."

"I got it," she says. "I was picking up Nat. He had dinner with Mom. I tried to get in some extra time on the mainframe."

"Productive?"

"A waste." She rolls over and back, breasts girdled in her sports bra.

As I undress, I receive a laconic report from Barbara on the day's occurrences. A neighbor's illness. The bill from the mechanic. The latest with her mother. Barbara delivers all this information lying face down on the coverlet in a tone of weariness. This her drear offensive, a bitterness too tired even to be regret, against which I defend in the simplest fashion, by seeming not to notice. I show interest in each remark, enthusiasm for every detail. And in the meantime, an inner density gathers, a known sensation, as if my veins have become clogged with lead. I am home.

About five years ago, just when I thought we were getting ready to have another child, Barbara announced that she was going back to school, entering a Ph.D. program in mathematics. She had filed the application and taken the exams without a word to me. My surprise was taken as disapproval, and my protests to the contrary have always been disparaged. But I did not disapprove. I never thought Barbara was obligated to be homebound. My reaction was to something else. Not so much that I was not consulted, but that I really never could have guessed. In college, Barbara had been a math whiz, taking graduate division classes of two or three students with renowned professors, all of them hermit-like creatures with wild-grown beards. But she had been cavalier about her abilities. Now, I learned, mathematics was a calling. A consuming interest. About which I had not heard a word in more than half a decade.

At the moment Barbara is facing her dissertation. When she started, she told me that projects like hers—I could not possibly explain it—are sometimes set out in a space as small as a dozen pages. Whether those were words of hope or illusion, the dissertation has lingered like a chronic disease, one more source of her painful melancholy. Whenever I pass by the study, she is looking pitifully over her desk, out the window toward a single dwarf cherry tree that has failed to thrive in the clay landfill in our back yard.

Waiting for inspiration, she reads. Nothing so much of this world as newspapers and magazines. Instead, she carts in from the university library armloads of heavy texts on arcane subjects. Psycholinguistics. Semiotics. Braille and sign language for the deaf. She is a devotee of facts. She reclines at night on her brocade living-room sofa, eating Belgian chocolates, and finds out about the operation of the world she never visits. She reads, literally, about life on Mars, the biographies of men and women whom most people would find boring, and certainly obscure. Then there will be a spate of medical reading. Last month she spent with books that seemed to be about cryogenics, artificial insemination, and the history of lenses. What is occurring on these galaxian visits to other planets of human learning is unknown to me. No doubt she would share her newfound knowledge if I asked. But over time I have lost the ability even to pretend high interest, and Barbara regards my dullness to these matters as a failing. It is easier to maintain my own counsel, while Barbara roams the far-off realms.

Not long ago it occurred to me that my wife, with her abrupt social mannerisms, her general aversion to most human beings, her dark taciturn side, and her virtual armory of private and largely uncommunicated passions could be described only as weird. She has virtually no serious friendships aside from her relationship with her mother, to whom, when I met her, Barbara barely spoke, and whom she still regards with cynicism and suspicion. Like my own mother, when she was alive, Barbara seems largely a willing captive within the walls of her own home, flawlessly keeping our house, tending our child, and toiling endlessly with her formulae and computer algorithms.

Without really noticing at first, I become aware that both of us have ceased comment, even motion, and are facing the television set, where the screen has filled with images of today's service for Carolyn. Raymond's car arrives and the back of my head is briefly shown. The son is escorted up to the doors of the chapel. The newsreader is doing a voice-over: Eight hundred persons, including many city leaders, gathered at First Presbyterian Church for final rites for Carolyn Polhemus, a deputy prosecuting attorney slain three nights ago in a brutal rape-murder. Now people are emerging. The mayor and Raymond are both depicted speaking to reporters, but only Nico gets audio. He employs the quietest voice he knows and deflects questions about the investigation of the murder. "I came to remember a colleague," he tells the camera, with one foot in his car.

It is Barbara who speaks first.

"How was it?" She has wrapped herself now in a red silk robe.

"Gala," I answer. "In a way. A meeting of all the luminaries."

"Did you cry?"

"Come on, Barbara."

"I'm serious." She is leaning forward. Her jaw is set and there is a savage deadness in her eye. I always marvel that Barbara's anger remains so near at hand. Over the years, her superior access has become a source of intimidation. She knows I am slower to respond, restrained by archaic fears, the dark weight of memory. My parents often fell into robust shouting matches, even occasional brawls. I have such a vivid recollection of one night when I awoke to their disturbance and found that my mother had taken hold of a handful of my father's Brillo-y red hair while she slapped him with a rolled-up newspaper, as if he were a dog. The aftermath of these quarrels would send my mother to bed for days, where she would lie spent, dwelling with the sensational pain of enormous migraine headaches that required her to remain in a darkened room and left me under an injunction to make no sound.

Lacking that kind of refuge now, I move over to a basket of clean laundry Barbara has brought up and begin matching the socks. For a moment we are silent, left to the burbling of the TV and the nighttime noises of the house. A tiny finger of the river runs behind the homes half a block away, and without the traffic you can hear it licking. The furnace kicks in two floors below. On for the first time today, it will spill up through the ducts a kind of oily effluvium.

"Nico was trying hard enough to look unhappy," Barbara finally tells me.

"He wasn't very successful if you saw him up close. He was positively radiant. He thinks he's got a shot at Raymond now."

"Is that possible?"

I sort the socks and shrug. "He's gained a lot of ground with this thing."

Barbara, a witness all these years to Raymond's invincibility, is obviously surprised, but the mathematician in her shows, for I can see that she is quickly factoring the new possibilities. She grabs at her hair, gray-flecked and curly, worn in a fashionable shag, and her pretty face takes on the light of curiosity.

"What would you do, Rusty, if that happened? If Raymond lost?"

"Accept it. What else could I do?"

"I mean for a living."

Blue with blue, Black with black. It is not easy with only incandescent light. Some years ago I used to talk about leaving the office. That was when I could still imagine myself as a defense lawyer. But I never got around to making that move, and it has been some time since we have spoken at all about my future.

"I don't know what I'd do," I tell her honestly. "I'm a lawyer. I'd practice law. Teach. I don't know. Delay says he's going to keep me on as chief deputy."

"Do you believe that?"

"No." I take my stockings to my drawer. "He was a river of bullshit today. Told me, in a very serious tone, that the only real primary opponent he had been afraid of was me. You know, as if I would talk Raymond into stepping aside and anointing me successor."

"You should have," Barbara says.

I look back at her.

"Really." Her enthusiasm, in a way, is not surprising. Barbara has always felt a spouse's disdain for the boss. And besides, all of this comes, somewhat, at my expense. I'm the one who lacked the nerve to do what everybody else could see was obvious.

"I am not a politician."

"Oh, you'd make do," says Barbara. "You'd love to be P.A." As I figured: I am tweaked by wife's superior knowledge of my nature. I decide to sidestep and tell Barbara that this is all academic. Raymond will pull through.

"Bolcarro will finally endorse him. Or we'll catch the killer"—I nod toward the TV set—"and he'll ride into Election Day with all the media murmuring his name."

"How's he going to do that?" asks Barbara. "Do they have a suspect?"

"We have shit."

"So?"

"So Dan Lipranzer and Rusty Sabich will work day and night for the next two weeks and catch Raymond a killer. That's the strategy. Carefully devised."

The remote snaps and the TV shrinks to a star. Behind me, I hear from Barbara a whinny, a snort. It is not a pleasant sound. When I look back, her eyes, fixed upon me, are stilled to a zero point, an absolute in hatred.

"You are so predictable," she says, low and mean. "You're in charge of this investigation?"

"Of course."

"'Of course'?"

"Barbara, I'm the chief deputy prosecuting attorney and Raymond's running for his life. Who else would handle the investigation? Raymond would do it himself if he weren't campaigning fourteen hours a day."

It was the prospect of a moment just like this that left me in a state of excruciating unease a couple of days ago when I realized that I would have to phone Barbara to tell her what had happened. I could not ignore it; that would pretend too much. My call was for the announced purpose of telling Barbara I would be late. The office, I explained, was in an uproar.

Carolyn Polhemus is dead, I added.

Huh, said Barbara. Her tone was one of detached wonder. An overdose? she asked.

I stared at the receiver in my hand, marveling at the depth of this misunderstanding.

But I cannot divert her now. Barbara's rage is gathering.

"Tell me the truth," she says. "Isn't that a conflict of interest or something?"

"Barbara—"

"No," she says, standing now. "Answer me. Is that professional—for you to be doing this? There are 120 lawyers down there. Can't they find anybody who didn't sleep with her?"

I am familiar with this rise in pitch and descent in tactics. I strive to remain even.

"Barbara, Raymond asked me to do it."

"Oh, spare me, Rusty. Spare me the high purpose, noble crap. You could explain to Raymond why you shouldn't do this."

"I don't care to, I would be letting him down. And it happens to be none of his business."

At this evidence of my embarrassment, Barbara hoots. That I realize was poor strategy, a bad moment to tell the truth. Barbara has little sympathy for my secret; if it would not pain her equally, she would put it all on billboards. During the short time that I was actually seeing Carolyn, I did not have whatever it is—the courage or the decency or the willingness to be disturbed—to confess anything to Barbara. That awaited the end, a week or two after I had become resolved it all was past. I was home for an early dinner, atoning for the month before when I had been absent almost every evening, my liberty procured with the phony excuse of preparation for a trial, which I ultimately claimed had been continued. Nat had just gone off to his permitted half hour with the television set. And I, somehow, became unglued. The moon. The moon. A drink. The psychologists would say a fugue state. I drifted, staring at the dinner table. I took my highball tumbler in my hand, just like one of Carolyn's. And I was reminded of her so powerfully that I was suddenly beyond control. I cried—wept with stormy passion as I sat there—and Barbara knew immediately. She did not think that I was ill; she did not think that it was fatigue, or trial stress, or tear-duct disease. She knew; and she knew that I was crying out of loss, not shame.

There was nothing tender about her inquisition, but it was not prolonged. Who? I told her. Was I leaving? It was over, I said. It was short, I said, it barely happened.

Oh, I was heroic. I sat there at my own dining-room table with both arms over my face, crying, almost howling, into my shirt-sleeves. I heard the dishes clank as Barbara stood and began clearing her place. 'At least I don't have to ask,' she said, 'who dropped who.'

Later, after I got Nat into bed, I wandered up, shipwrecked and still pathetic, to see her in the bedroom, where she had taken refuge. Barbara was exercising again, with the insipid music on the tape thumping loudly. I watched her bend, do her double-jointed extensions, while I was still in deep disorder, so ravaged, beaten, that my skin seemed the only thing holding me together, a tender husk. I had come in to say something prosaic, that I wanted to go on. But that never emerged. The unhindered anger with which she slammed her own body about made it obvious to me, even in my undefended state, that the effort would be wasted. I just watched, perhaps as long as five minutes. Barbara never glanced at me, but finally in the midst of some contortion she uttered an opinion. 'You could have. Done better.' There was a little more which I did not hear. The final word was 'Bimbo.'

We have gone on from there. In a way my affair with Carolyn has provided an odd kind of relief. There is a cause now for the effect, an occasion for Barbara's black anger, a reason we do not get along. There is now something to get over and, as a result, a shadowy hope that things may improve.

That is, I realize, the issue now: whether we will give up whatever progress has been made. For months Carolyn has been a demon, a spirit slowly being exorcised from this home. And death has brought her back to life. I understand Barbara's complaint. But I cannot—*cannot*—give up what she wants me to; and my reasons are sufficiently personal as to lie within the realm of the unspoken, even the unspeakable.

I try a plain and quiet appeal.

"Barbara, what difference does it make? You're talking about two and a half weeks. Until the primary. That's all. Then it's another routine police case. Unsolved homicide."

"Don't you see what you're doing? To yourself? To me?"

"Barbara," I say again.

"I knew it," she says. "I knew you'd do something like this. When you called the other day. I could hear it in your voice.

You're going to go through everything again, Rusty. You want to, that's the truth, isn't it? You want to. She's dead. And you're still obsessing."

"Barbara."

"Rusty, I have had more than I can take. I won't put up with this." Barbara does not cry on these occasions. She recedes instead into the fiery pit of a volcanic anger. She hurls herself back now to gather her will, bound, as she sits on the bed, within her wide satin sleeves. She grabs a book, the remote control, two pillows. Mount Saint Helens rumbles. And I decide to leave. I go to the closet and grope for my robe.

As I reach the threshold, she speaks behind me.

"Can I ask a question?" she says.

"Sure."

"That I always wanted to ask?"

"Sure."

"Why did she stop seeing you?"

"Carolyn?"

"No, the man in the moon." The words have so much bitterness that I wonder if she might spit. I would have thought Barbara's question would be why did I start, but she apparently decided on her own answers to that long ago.

"I don't know," I say. "I tend to think I wasn't very important to her."

She closes her eyes and opens them. Barbara shakes her head.

"You are an asshole," my wife tells me solemnly. "Just get out."

I do. Quickly. She has been known to throw things. Having nowhere else to go, and craving some form of company, I cross the hall to check once more on Nat. His breath is husky and uninterrupted in the deepest phase of sleep, and I sit down on the bed, safe in the dark beneath the protecting arms of Spider-Man.

5

Monday morning: a day in the life. The commuter coach unleashes the gray-flannel flock on the east side of the river. The terminal plaza is surrounded by willows, their skirts greening in the spring. I am in the office before 9:00. From my secretary, Eugenia Martinez, I receive the usual: mail, telephone-message slips, and a dark look. Eugenia is obese, single, middle-aged, and, it often seems, determined to get even for it all. She types reluctantly, refuses dictation, and many times of day I will find her staring with immobile droopy-eyed irritation at the telephone as it rings. Of course, she cannot be fired, or even demoted, because civil service, like concrete, has set. She remains, a curse to a decade of chief deputies, having first been stationed here by John White, who did so in order to avoid the carping that would have followed if he'd assigned her to anybody else.

On the top of what Eugenia has given me is a leave slip for Tommy Molto, whose absence remains unaccounted for. Personnel wants to dock him as Away without Leave. I make a note to talk to Mac about this and graze through my communications. The docket room has provided me with a printout naming thirteen individuals released from state custody in the last two years whose cases had been prosecuted by Carolyn. A handwritten note says that the underlying case files have been delivered to her office. I position the computer run in the center of my desk, so that I will not forget.

With Raymond out most of the day on campaign appearances, I resolve much of what the P.A. would ordinarily be faced with. I call the shots on case prosecutions, immunities, plea bargains, and deal with the investigative agencies. This morning I will

preside over a charging conference in which we will decide on
the phrasing and merits of all of this week's indictments. This
afternoon I have a meeting about last week's fiasco, in which a
police undercover bought from a Drug Enforcement Administration agent in disguise; the two drew guns and badges on each
other and demanded surrender. Their backups became involved,
too, so that in the end eleven law enforcement officers were
standing on opposite corners, shouting obscenities and waving
their pistols. Now we are having meetings. The coppers will tell
me the feds do everything in secret; the DEA agent in charge will
insinuate that any confidence the police department learns is up
for sale. In the meantime, I am supposed to find somebody to
prosecute for killing Carolyn Polhemus.

Someone else may be looking, too. Near 9:30 I get a call from
Stew Dubinsky from the *Trib*. During the campaign, Raymond
answers most press calls himself; he does not want to miss the
free ink or draw criticisms that he is losing his hold on the office.
But Stew is probably the best courthouse reporter we have. He
gets most of his facts straight and he knows the boundaries. I
can talk to him.

"So what's new on Carolyn?" he asks. The way he shorthands
the murder with her name disconcerts me. Carolyn's death is
already receding from the ranks of tragedy to become one more
ugly historic event.

I cannot, of course, tell Stew that nothing is doing. Word could
trail back to Nico, who would use the occasion to blast us again.

"Prosecuting Attorney Raymond Horgan had no comment," I
say.

"Would the P.A. care to comment on another piece of
information?" This, whatever it is, is the real motive for Stew's
call. "I hear something about a high-level defection. From the
Homicide Section? Sound familiar?"

That would be Molto. After Nico left, Tommy, his second-in-
command, became acting head of the section. Horgan refused to
give him the job permanently, suspecting that sooner or later
something like this would come to pass. I contemplate for a
moment the fact that the press is already sniffing. No good. Not
at all. I see, from the way Dubinsky has lined up the questions,
how this will run. One high-ranking deputy is killed; another,
who should be in charge of the investigation, quits. It will sound

as if the office is on the verge of chaos.

"Same response," I tell him. "Quote the P.A."

Stew makes a sound. He is bored.

"Off the record?" I ask.

"Sure."

"How good is your information?" I want to know how close we are to reading about this.

"So-so. Guy who always thinks he knows more than he does. I figure this has got to be Tommy Molto. He and Nico are hand-and-glove, right?"

Stew clearly does not have enough to run. I avoid his question. "What does Della Guardia tell you?" I ask.

"He says he has no comment. Come on, Rusty," Dubinsky says, "what gives?"

"Stew, off the record, I do not have the most fucked-up idea where Tommy Molto is. But if he's holding hands with Nico, why won't the candidate tell you that?"

"You want a theory?"

"Sure."

"Maybe Nico has him out there investigating the case on his own. Think about that one. DELLA GUARDIA CATCHES KILLER. How's that for a headline?"

The notion is absurd. A private murder investigation could too easily end up an impediment to the police. Obstruction of justice is bad politics. But as ridiculous as it is, the sheer flare of the idea makes it sound like Nico. And Stew is not the kind to float loony notions. He works off information.

"Do I take it," I ask, "that this is part of your rumor, too?"

"No comment," says Stew.

We laugh at each other, before I hang up the phone. Immediately I make some calls. I leave a message with Loretta, Raymond's secretary, that I have to speak with him whenever he phones in. I try to find Mac, the administrative deputy, to talk about Molto. Not in, I'm told. I leave another message.

Then, with a few minutes before the charging conference, I venture down the hall to Carolyn's office. This place already has a desolate air. The Empire desk which Carolyn commandeered from Central Services has been swept clean, and the contents of the drawers—two old compacts, soup mix, a package of napkins, a cable-knit sweater, a pint bottle of peppermint schnapps—

have been pitched into a cardboard box, along with Carolyn's diplomas and bar certificates, which were formerly clustered on the walls. Cartons called in from the warehouse are pyramided in the middle of the room, giving the office an air of obvious disuse, and the dust gathered in a week's inactivity has its own faintly corrupt smell. I pour a glass of water in the wilting greenery and dust some of the leaves.

Carolyn's caseload was made up primarily of sexual assaults. According to the codes on the file jackets, there are, by my count, twenty-two such cases awaiting indictment or trial which I find in the top drawers of her old oak file cabinet. Carolyn claimed a special sympathy with the victims of these crimes, and over time, I found that her commitment was more genuine than at first I had believed. When she talked about the reviving terrors these women experienced, the glittery surfaces receded from Carolyn and revealed alternating moods of tenderness and rage. But there are in these cases also an element of the bizarre: an intern at U. Hospital who gave a number of female patients a physical which ended with insertion of his own instrument; one victim received this treatment on three separate occasions before she was moved to complain. The girlfriend of a suspect who, on her second day of questioning, admitted that she had met him when he cut through the screen door to her apartment and forced himself on her. When he put the knife down, she said, he had seemed like such a nice young man.

Like many others, I suspected Carolyn of more than a passing fascination with this aspect of her work, as well, and I examine the case files with the hope that there will be a pattern I can seize on—we will be able to charge that it was actually some cultish ceremony that was duplicated six days ago in Carolyn's loft apartment, or a brutal mimicry of an offense in which Carolyn somehow displayed too obvious a voyeuristic interest. But there is none of that; the thirteen names lead nowhere. The new files disgorge no clues.

It is now time for the charging conference, but something is nagging at me. When I look again at the computer printout, I recognize that there is one case I have not come across yet—a B file, as we call it, referring to the subsection of the state criminal code addressed to bribery of law enforcement officials. Carolyn seldom handled anything outside her domain, and B files, which are so-called Special Investigation cases, were directly under my supervision when this case was assigned. At first, I assumed the B designation was the usual computer mess-up, maybe an included charge. But there is no companion case; in fact, this one is listed as an UnSub—unknown subject—which usually means a non-arrest investigation. I go through her drawers quickly, one more time, and check down in my office. I have my own printout of B cases, but this one isn't there. In fact, it seems to have been generally obliterated from the computer docketing system, except for Carolyn's call.

I make a note on my pad: B file? Polhemus?

Eugenia is standing in the doorway.

"Oh, men," she says. "Where you been? I been lookin for you. Mr. Big Cheese called back." Mr. Big Cheese, of course, is Raymond Horgan. "I was lookin all over. He left a message to meet him at the Delancey Club, 1:30." Raymond and I have many of these meetings during the campaign. I catch him after a luncheon, before a speech, to bring him up to speed on the office.

"How about Mac? Did we hear anything?"

Eugenia reads the message. " 'Be cross the street all morning.' " Observing, no doubt, watching some of the newer deputies do their stuff during the morning call in the Central Branch.

I ask Eugenia to set back the charging conference half an hour; then I head over to the courthouse to find Mac. On the second floor, the Central Branch session is held. The branch courts are where arrested persons make their first formal court appearance to set bail, where misdemeanors are tried and preliminary evidentiary hearings are held in felony cases. An assignment to one of the branches is usually the second or third stopping-off place for a deputy, after time in Appeals or the Complaint and Warrant Section. I worked this courtroom for nineteen months before I was sent to Felony Review, and I try to come back as little as possible. It is here that crime always seemed most real, the air quivering with a struggling agony at the brink of finding voice.

In the hallway outside two enormous central courtrooms, there is a churning mass, like my imaginings of the crushed poor in the steerage bowels of the old oceangoing vessels. Mothers and girlfriends and brothers are here weeping and crying out over the young men detained in the granite lockup that abuts the courtroom. Lawyers of a kind move about hustling clients in the subverted tones of scalpers, while the state defenders shout out the names of persons whom they have never met and whom they will be defending in a moment. The prosecutors are shouting, too, searching for each of the arresting officers on a dozen cases, hoping to enhance the slender knowledge provided by police reports prepared in a deliberately elliptical fashion, the better to hinder cross-examination.

Inside the vaulted courtroom, with its red marble pillars and oaken buttresses and straight-backed pews, the tumult continues, a persistent din. Situated closer to the front so they will not fail to hear their cases called, prosecutors and defense lawyers haggle amiably over prospective plea bargains. Beside the judge's bench, six or seven attorneys are clustered around the docket clerk, handing in appearance forms, examining court files, and urging the clerk to pass their case forward to be called next. The cops, most of them, are lined up in pairs against the grimy walls—many of them in from the 12-to-8 shift for the bail hearings on their nighttime collars—sipping coffee and rolling on the balls of their feet to keep themselves awake. And far to one side of the courtroom, there is a continuing clamor from the lockup, where defendants in custody await their appearance, one or two of them inevitably shouting obscenities at the bailiffs or their attorneys, complaining about the cramped conditions back there and the indecent odors from the commode. The rest moan occasionally or bang on the bars.

Now at the dead end of the morning call, the streetwalkers in their halter tops and shorts are being arraigned, tried, fined, and sent back out on the street in time for sleep and another night's work. Usually they are represented in groups by two or three lawyers, but every now and then a pimp, to economize, will take on the assignment himself. That is occurring right now as some jerk in a flamingo-colored suit goes on about police brutality.

Mac takes me into the cloakroom, where no coats are hung. No visitor would be so cavalier as to leave a valuable garment unguarded in this company. The room is completely empty, except for a court reporter's shorthand typewriter and a huge dining-room chandelier in a plastic bag which is evidence, undoubtedly, in a case that is going to be called.

She asks me what is up.

"Tell me what Carolyn Polhemus was doing with a B file," I say.

"I had no idea that Carolyn was interested in crimes above the waist," says Mac. An old line. She beams up from her wheelchair, everybody's favorite smart-ass, brassy and irreverent. She makes a number of suggestions concerning the B file, all of which I've already tried. "It doesn't figure," she finally admits.

As chief administrative deputy, Lydia MacDougall is in charge of personnel, procurement, and the deployment of staff. It is a lousy, thankless job with a nice-sounding title, but Lydia is accustomed to adversity. She has been a paraplegic since shortly after we started in this office together, nearly twelve years ago. It was one of those early winter nights where the mist is half snow. Lydia was driving. Her first husband, Tom, was killed in the plunge into the river.

In the general run of things, I would say Mac is probably the finest lawyer in this office, organized, shrewd, gifted in court. Over the years she has even learned to use the chair to advantage before a jury. There are some tragedies that run so deep that our comprehension of them is evolutionary at best. As the jurors get a couple of days to think about what it would be like to have their legs flapping around, loose as flags, as they listen to this woman, handsome, forceful, good-humored, absorb the wedding ring, the casual mention of her baby, observe the fact that she is—impossibly—normal, they are full of admiration and, as we all should be, hope.

Next September, Mac will become a judge. She already has party slating and will run in the primary unopposed. The general election will be an automatic. There are not, apparently, a lot of people who feel they can beat a lawyer with support from women's groups, the handicapped, law-and-order types, and the city's three major bar associations.

"Why don't you ask Raymond about the file?" she finally suggests.

I make a noise. Horgan is not a detail man. He is unlikely to know anything about an individual case. And these days I am reluctant to advise him of problems. He is always looking for someone to blame.

Going down the corridor to the next courtroom, where Mac is scheduled to observe, I talk to her about Tommy Molto and the problem of his unaccounted-for status. If we fire Molto, Nico will make capital, alleging that Horgan is on a witch-hunt for Delay's friends. If we keep Tommy on the staff, we increase Nico's profit from the defection. We decide, at last, that he will be placed on Unauthorized Leave, an employment category which previously did not exist. I tell Mac I would feel more comfortable about this if somebody I trusted had seen Molto alive.

"Let's get a posse out. We have one deputy P.A. dead already. If some lady finds little pieces of Molto in her trash tomorrow morning, I'd like to be able to say we'd been searching high and low."

It is Mac's turn. She makes a note.

His Honor, Larren Lyttle, his large dark face full of wiliness and majesty, is the first to notice me. A black man in a club in which only whites were members until three years ago, the judge shows no sign of yielding to the atmosphere. He is at ease among the leather club chairs and the servers in green livery.

Larren is Raymond's former law partner. In those days, they were agitators, defending draft dodgers and possessors of marijuana, and most of the local black militants, as well as a paying clientele. I tried one case against Larren before he took the bench—really just a juvenile proceeding against a very rich kid from the West Shore suburbs who liked to break into the homes of his parents' friends. Larren was an imposing figure of robust stature, shrewd and bullying with witnesses, and possessed of a rhetorical range of operatic dimension. He could adopt a refined demeanor and then move with the next utterance into the round oratory of a pork-chop preacher, or squealing ghettoese. The jury rarely noticed there was another lawyer in the courtroom.

Raymond made the break for politics first. Larren managed the campaign, quite visibly, and brought out black voters in substantial numbers. Two years later, when Raymond thought he could be mayor, Larren joined him on the ticket as a candidate for judge. Larren won and Raymond lost, and Judge Lyttle suffered for his loyalties. Bolcarro kept him quarantined in the North Branch, where Larren heard traffic cases and rumdum misdemeanors, usually the job of the appointed magistrates, until Raymond bought his freedom four years later with his early and enthusiastic endorsement of Mayor Bolcarro's re-election campaign. Larren has been a downtown felony judge ever since, a ruthless autocrat in his courtroom and, notwithstanding his friendship with Raymond, the sworn enemy of the deputy prosecuting attorneys. The saying is that there are two defense lawyers in the courtroom, and the one who's hard to beat is wearing a robe.

In spite of that, Larren remains an active force in Raymond's campaigns. The Code of Judicial Conduct now prohibits him from taking any official role. But he is still a member of Raymond's inner group, the men from Horgan's years in law school and his early time in practice whose intimacy with Raymond has filled me at moments with a kind of adolescent pining. Larren; Mike Duke, the managing partner at a massive firm downtown; Joe Reilly from the First—these are the people Raymond falls back on at these times.

To Mike Duke goes the duty of overseeing campaign financing. It has proved a more daunting task this year than in the past, when Raymond was without significant opponents. Then Raymond would not take part in a campaign solicitation of any kind, for fear that it might compromise his independence. But those scruples this year have been laid aside. Raymond has been through a number of these meetings of late, preening for the checkbook liberals, elegant-looking gentlemen like the group assembled here today, showing them that he is still the same sleek instrument of justice that he was a decade ago. Raymond delivers his campaign speech in conversational tones, awaiting the moment that first he, and then the judge, can be called away so that Mike, in their absence, can apply the squeeze.

That is my function here today. I will be Raymond's excuse to leave. He introduces me and explains that he has to catch up with the office. In this atmosphere, I am pure flunky—no one even thinks of asking me to sit down, and only Judge Lyttle bothers to stand to shake my hand. I remain behind the table and the cigar smoke, while there is a final round of handshakes and bluff jokes, then head out behind Raymond as he grabs a mint by the doorway.

"What's going on?" he asks me as soon as we are past the doorman and beneath the club's green awning. You can feel, just since the morning, that the air is starting to soften. My blood stirs. It is going to be spring.

When I tell him about Dubinsky's call, he makes no effort to hide his irritation.

"Let me just catch either one of them fucking around like that." He means Nico and Molto. We are walking briskly down the street now toward the County Building. "What kind of crap is this? An independent investigation."

"Raymond, this is a reporter thinking out loud. There is probably nothing to it."

"There better not be," he says.

I start to tell Raymond about the debacle between the police and DEA, but he does not let me finish.

"Where are we on Carolyn ourselves?" he asks. I can see that the speculation on Molto's activities has reheated Raymond's desire for results in our own investigation. He machine-guns questions. Do we have a Hair and Fiber report? How long will it be? Have we gotten any better news on fingerprints? How about a report from the state index on sexual offenders Carolyn prosecuted?

When I tell Raymond that all of this is in the offing, but that I spent the last three hours in the charging conference, he stops dead in the street. He is furious.

"Damnit, Rusty!" His color is high and his brow flexed down angrily over his eyes. "I told you the other day: Give this investigation *top* priority. That's what it deserves. Della Guardia is eating me alive with this thing. And we owe Carolyn as much. Let Mac run the office. She's more than capable. She can watch DEA and the coppers urinate all over each other. She can second-guess indictments. You stay on this. I want you to run out every ground ball, and do it in a goddamn orderly fashion. Do it! Act like a fucking professional."

I look down the street, both ways. I do not see anyone I know. I am thirty-nine years old, I think. I have been a lawyer thirteen years.

Raymond walks ahead in silence. Finally, he looks back at me, shaking his head. I expect a further complaint about my performance, but instead he says, "Man, those guys were assholes." Raymond, I see, did not enjoy lunch.

In the County Building, Goldie, the little white-haired elevator operator who sits all day with an empty car, waiting to take

Raymond and the county commissioners up and down, tosses his stool inside and folds his paper. I have begun to broach the subject of the missing B file, but I hold off while we are in the elevator. Goldie and Nico were the best of pals. I even saw Goldie break with protocol and hie Nico up and down on one or two occasions: that was the kind of touch Nico adored—the official elevator. His destiny. Nico maintained a noble poker face as Goldie scanned the lobby to be sure the coast was clear.

Once we are in the office, I trail behind. Various deputies come forward to get a word or two with Raymond, some with problems, a number who simply want the news from the campaign front. On a couple of occasions, I explain that I have been through Carolyn's docket. I do this in a desultory fashion, since I have no desire to confess to further failures, and Raymond loses the thread of what I am telling him as he moves between conversations.

"There's a file missing," I say again. "She had a case we can't account for."

This finally catches Raymond's attention. We have come through the side door to his office.

"What kind of case? Do we know anything about it?"

"We know it was logged in as a bribe case—a B. Nobody seems to know what happened to it. I asked Mac. I checked my own records."

Raymond studies me for a second: then his look becomes absent.

"Where am I supposed to be at two o'clock?" he asks me.

When I tell him that I have no idea, he shouts for Loretta, his secretary, calling her name until she appears. Raymond, it turns out, is due at a Bar Committee meeting on criminal procedure. He is supposed to outline various reforms in the state sentencing scheme that he has been calling for as part of his campaign. A press release has been issued; reporters and TV crews will be there—and he is already late.

"Shit," says Raymond. "Shit." He stomps around the office saying "Shit."

I try again.

"Anyway, the case is still in the computer system."

"Did she call Cody?" he asks me.

"Carolyn?"

"No, Loretta."

"I don't know, Raymond."

He screams again for Loretta. "Call Cody. Did you call him? For Chrissake, call him. Well, get somebody to go down there," Raymond looks at me. "Sot sits on the car phone and you can never get through. Who the hell does he talk to?"

"I thought maybe you had heard something about this case. Maybe you remember something."

Raymond is not listening. He has fallen into an easy chair, angled against what the deputies irreverently refer to as Raymond's Wall of Respect, a stretch of plaster solid with plaques and pictures and other mementos of great triumphs or honors: bar associations' awards, courtroom artists' sketches, political cartoons. Raymond has that aging look again, wandering, pensive, a man who has seen things unravel.

"God, what a fucking disaster this is. Every campaign Larren has told me to ask a deputy to take a leave so that I have somebody running things full-time, and we've always been able to scrape by without it. But this is out of control. There's too goddamn much to do and nobody in charge. Do you know that we haven't taken a poll in two months? Two weeks to the election and we have no idea where we are, with who." He folds his hand against his mouth and shakes his head. It is not anxiety he shows so much as distress. Raymond Horgan, Kindle County Prosecuting Attorney, has lost his ability to cope.

A moment passes between us, completely silent. I am not inclined, however, after the pasting I took out on the street, to be reverential. After thirteen years in government, I know how to be a bureaucrat and I want to be sure my butt is covered with Raymond on the subject of the missing file.

"Anyway," I say yet again, 'I don't know what significance to attach to it. I don't know if it's misfiled or something's sinister."

Raymond stares. "Are you talking about that file again?"

I do not get a chance to answer. Loretta announces a phone call and Raymond takes it. Alejandro Stern, the defense lawyer who is the chairman of the Bar Committee, is on the line. Raymond begs apologies, says he's been wrapped up in discussions of that bizarre episode between DEA and the local police, and is on the way. When he puts the phone down he screams again for Cody.

"I'm right here," Cody announces. He has come in the side door.

"Great." Raymond starts in one direction, then the other. "Where the hell is my coat?"

Cody already has it.

I wish Raymond luck.

Cody opens the door. Raymond goes through it and comes right back.

"Loretta! Where's my speech?"

Cody, it turns out, has that, too. Nonetheless, Raymond continues to his desk. He opens a drawer and hands me a folder on his way out again.

It is the B file.

"We'll talk," he promises me and, with Cody hard behind him, goes running down the hall.

6

"Somehow, the boy, Wendell, became important," I said to Robinson. "To us, I mean. To me, at least. It's hard to explain. But somehow he was part of this thing with Carolyn."

He was an unusual child, big for his age, and he had the ambling clumsiness of some big children, a thick, almost oafish appearance. He was not so much slow as dulled. I asked one of the psychiatrists for an explanation, as if one is needed, and he said of this five-year-old, 'He's depressed.'

Wendell McGaffen, during the pendency of his mother's case, had been moved from the County Shelter to a foster home. He saw his father every day, but never his mother. After the usual disputes in court, Carolyn and I were given permission to speak with him. Actually, at first we did not talk to him at all. We sat in on sessions he had with the psychiatrists, who introduced us to Wendell. Wendell would play with the toys and figures that the shrink had around the room, and the shrink would ask Wendell whether he had any thoughts on different topics, which, almost inevitably, Wendell did not. The shrink, named Mattingly, said that Wendell had not in his weeks there asked once about his mother. And as a result they had not raised the subject.

Wendell liked Carolyn right from the start. He brought her the dolls. He made remarks to her. He directed her attention to birds, trucks, objects passing outside the window. On our third or fourth visit Carolyn told Wendell that she wanted to talk to him about his mother. The shrink appeared alarmed, but Wendell gripped his doll with both hands and asked, 'What about?'

So it progressed, twenty, thirty minutes a day. The shrink was openly impressed and eventually asked Carolyn's permission to remain during their interviews, and over a period of weeks the story was told, in snatches and mumbled remarks, disordered offhand answers to questions Carolyn had asked, often days before. Wendell showed no real emotion other than his hesitation. Usually he would stand in front of Carolyn, with both his hands gripped hard around the midsection of a doll, at which he stared unflinchingly. Carolyn would repeat what he had told her and ask him more: Wendell would nod or shake his head or not answer at all. Now and then there were his explanations. 'It hurt.' 'I criet.' 'She set I shouldn't be quiet.'

'She wanted you to be quiet?'

'Yes. She set I shouldn't be quiet.'

From another person the repetition, particularly, might have seemed cruel, but Carolyn somehow seemed to have a need to know that was in some measure selfless. Not long before the trial, Carolyn and the shrink decided that the county would not call Wendell to the witness stand unless it was an absolute necessity. The confrontation with his mother, she said, would be too much. But even with that decision made, Carolyn continued to meet with Wendell, to draw more and more from him.

"It's hard to explain," I told Robinson, "the way she looked at this kid. Into him almost. That intense. That earnest. I never figured her to be the type to have any kind of rapport with children. And when she did, I was astounded."

It made her mystery so much larger. She seemed like some Hindu goddess, containing all feelings in creation. Whatever wild, surging, libidinal rivers Carolyn undammed in me by her manner and appearance, there was something about the tender attention she showed this needy child that drew me over the brink, that gave my emotions a melting, yearning quality that I took to be far more significant than all my priapic heat. When she took on the quiet, earnest tone and leaned toward dear, slow, hurting Wendell, I was, whatever my regrets, full of love for her.

A wild love. Desperate and obsessive and willfully blind. Love, as love at its truest is, with no sense of the future, love beguiled by the present and unable to derive the meaning of signs.

One day I talked to Mattingly about the way Carolyn had worked with the boy. It was extraordinary, wasn't it? I asked. Amazing. Inexplicable. I wanted to hear him praise her. But

Mattingly took my comments instead as a clinical inquiry, as if I
was asking what could account for this phenomenon. He drew
meditatively on his pipe. 'I've thought about that,' he said. Then
his look became troubled, recognizing, I suppose, that he was
liable to give offense or be misjudged himself. But he went on.
'And I believe,' he said, 'that in some small way she must remind
him of his mother.'

The trial went well. Mrs. McGaffen was represented by Alejandro
Stern—Sandy, outside the courtroom—an Argentinian Jew, a
Spanish gentleman, courtly combed and perfect with his soft
accent and his manicure. He is a mannerly, fastidious trial
lawyer, and we decided to follow his low-key approach. We put
in our physical evidence, the doctors' testimony and their test
results; then we offered the fruits of the search. With that, the
county rested. Sandy called a psychiatrist who described
Colleen McGaffen's gentle nature. Then he showed how good a
lawyer he was by reversing the usual order of presentation. The
defendant testified first, denying everything; then her husband
came to the stand, weeping unbearably as he described the
death of his first child; Wendell's fall, which he insisted he had
witnessed; and his wife's devotion to their son. A fine trial lawyer
always has a latent message to the jury, too prejudicial or
improper to speak aloud, whether it's a racist appeal when black
victims identify white defendants or the no-big-deal manner that
a lawyer like Stern takes when the crime is only an attempt. In
this case, Sandy wanted the jury to know that her husband
forgave Colleen McGaffen, and if *he* could, why couldn't *they* do
that, too?

In a kind of professional salvation, I found that in the
courtroom I could almost wall myself to Carolyn; I enjoyed
extended periods of concentration and would wake to her
presence beside me, and to the grip of my obsession, almost with
surprise. But this work of will came at a heavy price. Outside, I
was largely useless. To perform the most routine tasks—talking
to witnesses, gathering exhibits—required that all my energies
be directed to a frozen inattention: Do not think about her,
please do not think about her now. I did. I moved about in a
spaced-out reality, vacillating among various lurid fantasies and

moments of intense self-rebuke and instants when she was present in which I simply helplessly gawked.

"Finally," I told Robinson, "we were there one night, working in her office." The defense case was nearly over. Darryl had begun his testimony, and the pathos of this man's feckless inability to deal with anything that had happened was, in truth, terribly moving. Carolyn was going to do the cross-examination, and she was high. The courtroom was full of reporters; there were stories about the case on a couple of the TV stations most nights. And the cross itself was exciting because it required a kind of surgical skill: Darryl had to be destroyed as a witness but not as a human being. The jury's sympathy would never leave him, for he was, in the end, not doing anything less than most of us would do, trying to save what was left of his family. So Carolyn was lingering over this cross, practicing it, modulating it, talking it out, flashing in front of me like a coin turning in the air. She was in her stocking feet, and a full skirt that twirled slightly around her whenever she pivoted in the narrow space; she was pacing briskly as she worked through the tone and the questions.

"And there are wrappers from our fast-food dinner on the desk, and a scatter of various records: Darryl's time and attendance sheets from work to show that he's too busy to know what is up at home; medical reports on the child; statements from his teachers and an aunt. And we are setting up each question. 'No, no, softer, softer. "Mr. McGaffen, you couldn't know that Wendell showed his bruises at school?" Like that. Maybe three questions: "Do you know Beverley Morrison? Well, would it refresh your recollection to know that she was Wendell's teacher? Did you know that Ms. Morrison discussed Wendell's physical condition with your wife on the evening of November 7 of last year?" '

" 'Softly,' " she says.

" 'Softly, right,' I say. 'Don't come too close to him. And don't move too much in the courtroom. You don't want to seem angry.'

"And Carolyn is excited and she reaches across the desk, very high, and grabs both my hands.

" 'It's going to be so good,' she says, and then her eyes, which are quite green, stay on me a little longer, just enough so that I know we've suddenly left the trial, and I say—and I have never said a word out loud up to that moment—I just say, as hollow and pathetic as I feel, 'What the hell is going on, Carolyn?' and she smiles, for the fleetest instant, but with a stunning radiance, and says, 'Not now,' and goes right back to talking out the cross."

'Not now.' Not now. I caught the last bus back to Nearing that night and sat in the dark pondering as we flashed under the street-lights. Not now. I haven't decided? I have. It's good. It's bad. I'm uncertain. I want to let you down easy.

But at least there was something. I gradually recognized the significance of our communication. I was not mad. I was not caught up with something imaginary; something was happening. We had been talking about *something*. And that turbulent, lost unease of mine began to change. There in the bus, as I sat in the rear, in a pit of darkness, my obsessions now took on a sabering quality, and knowing that I had entered the region of the real, I began to feel, simply, fear.

7

Studio B, it says outside the door. I enter a large open space the size of a small gymnasium. There is a mustardy quality to the light in here; the walls are yellow tile and they seem vaguely luminescent. The feeling is very much like Nat's grade school: a row of sinks, floor-to-ceiling compartments of white birch that are apparently student lockers. One young man is working at his easel by the windows. I spent, of course, many years around the U.—probably, if I had to get down to this kind of dismal estimate, the happiest time of my life—but I doubt that I ever entered the Art Center before, especially if you do not count the adjacent auditorium, where Barbara, on occasion, brought me to attend some plays. For an instant, I am perplexed that I am here. Better to send Lipranzer, I think clearly. Then I speak.

"Marty Polhemus?"

The boy turns from the easel, some anxious sign working through his expression.

"Are you from the police?"

"P.A.'s office." I offer my hand and give my name. Marty tosses his brush down on a table where tubes of acrylic paint and round white bottles of gesso are randomly set; he picks up his shirttail to wipe his hand before he shakes. Marty is an art student, all right, a pimply kid, with lots and lots of hair, loose brass-colored ringlets; he has spots of paint all over his clothing and a gruel of paint and just plain dirt under his long fingernails.

"They said somebody else might like come to see me," Marty tells me. He is a nervous sort, eager to please. He asks if I want coffee and we go to a drip pot back near the door. Marty pours two foam cups full, then has to put them down to grope in his pockets for change. I, finally, toss two quarters in the kitty.

"Who was it," I ask, as we both stand blowing into our coffee cups, "who said someone else might see you? Mac?"

"Raymond. Mr. Horgan. He said."

"Ah." An awkward silence—although Marty is the kind of kid with whom it seems there would be many. I explain that I am the deputy P.A. assigned to the investigation of his mother's murder, and that I received his class schedule from the registrar. Tuesday, 1–4 p.m., Independent Art Studio.

"I just wanted to touch base in case there's something you might be able to add."

"Sure. Right. Whatever you want," Marty says. We drift back toward his easel, and he ends up sitting on the broad ledge beneath the windows. From here, beyond the university, you can see the railroad lines, dug out and gathered over the belly of the city like a large and tangible scar. The boy is looking in that direction, and I stare for a moment, too.

"I didn't know her very well," he tells me. "You heard the story, didn't you?" As he asks this, his eyes are quick, and I am not certain if he would prefer that I say yes or no. When I admit my ignorance, he nods and looks away.

"I didn't see her for like a long time," he says simply. "My father can tell you the whole thing, if you want. Just call him. He said he'd do what he could to help."

"He's in New Jersey?"

"Right. I'll give you the phone."

"I take it they were divorced."

At that Marty laughs. "God, I hope so. He's been married to my mother—I mean Muriel, but I always call her my mother. They've been married fifteen years."

He brings his legs up onto the window ledge and looks out over the clustered campus structures as he speaks. After suggesting that I call his father, the boy, in a moment, tells me himself about what's behind him. He has no particular ease about this; his hands are wound about each other in an almost crippled fashion. But he continues without prodding. The story which Marty tells in fits and starts is one of the contemporary era. His father, Kenneth, was a high school English teacher in a small town in New Jersey, and Carolyn was his pupil.

"My father said she was, you know, like real attractive. I think

he started going out with her while she was still in school. I
mean, they were sneaking around or something. Which isn't Dad.
At all. He's real quiet. I bet he didn't know two girls when he met
her. He never said that, but I'd bet. I think it was like some big
passionate thing. You know. Real romantic. On his end, anyway."
Here the boy appears confounded. His estimate of Carolyn is
clouded. He clearly does not know enough to even guess at her
emotions.

"Her," he says. "Carolyn. You know, my mother. My *real*
mother," says the boy, screwing up his face. "My father called
her Carrie. She had all these brothers. And her father. Her
mother was dead. I guess she hated all of them, I don't know.
They all hated each other. Dad said her father was always
beating the tar out of her. She was real happy to get away from
them."

The boy abruptly leaves the ledge and approaches his
painting, a swirling eye of red. He squints at it, reaches out for
one of the tubes. He intends to work while we speak.

He does not, he says, know exactly how his parents broke up.
When he was born, Carolyn was trying to go to college and was
unhappy that she had to quit. His father just says that all hell was
breaking loose in those days and Carrie got caught up in it. She
had a boyfriend, Marty says, he is pretty sure of that from the
way his father talks. But the father apparently does not dwell on
that. The way his father puts it is that because of other
dissatisfactions she stopped liking the town, his father, the life
she had.

"My father says she was too young when they got married, and
she grew up and wanted to be something else, and just like
decided to be it. Dad says it was a big mess. One day she took off.
And my father, you know, says it was probably for the best. He's
that kind of person. He says stuff like that and means it."

This father emerges in his son's words as a kind of Norman
Rockwell figure, wise and gentle, with spectacles in his hand and
the paper—the kind of man to spend long nights in thought in
the parlor, a teacher who always took his students to heart. I
have a son, I almost tell this boy. I would like to think that
someday he would feel this way about me.

"I don't have any idea who killed her," Marty Polhemus tells
me suddenly. "I mean, I assume that's why you came."

Why did I come? I wonder. To see what she was hiding, I suppose, or did not care to tell. To diminish a little further my idea of what I had thought was intimacy.

"Do you think it was somebody she knew?" he asks. "I mean, do you have like leads, or whatever you call it. Clues?"

The answer, I tell him, is no. I describe the equivocal state of the evidence: the unlocked windows, the glass. I spare him the description of the cords, the non-viable condition of the seminal fluid. This is, after all, his mother. Although my sense is that there is little need for care or solicitude. I doubt that Marty's look of nervous bewilderment has anything to do with recent events. Indeed, there is something that makes it seem as if he regards himself, largely, as an outsider to all of this.

"Carolyn tried a lot of rape cases," I say. "Some people think it might be someone like that."

"You don't?"

"Murders aren't usually mysterious. In this city these days, half of them are gang-related. In almost all the other cases, the victim and the killer knew each other well. About half of them are broken love affairs: marriage on the rocks, unhappy lovers, that kind of thing. Usually there's been some kind of breakup in the last six months. Generally, the motivation is pretty obvious."

"She had a lot of boyfriends," Marty volunteers.

"Did she?"

"I guess. I mean, there were a lot of times she didn't want me around. I'd call, you know, and I could tell somebody else was there. I couldn't always figure out what was going on with her. I think she liked having secrets, you know?" He shrugs. "I mean, I thought I'd get to know her. That's why I came out here. My dad kept trying to discourage me, but I thought it would be neat. I'm not so interested in school right now, anyway. I figured, you go to college, one place is as good as another. It turns out that I'm like flunking everything anyhow."

"Really?"

"Not everything. I can't understand physics, though. I really can't. I honestly am flunking that."

A girl with a T-shirt from the world tour of a rock group and a smart-looking set comes through the door and asks if he's seen somebody named Harley. Marty says he hasn't. You can hear a stereo on down the hallway when she goes in and out the door.

The boy changes brushes and comes within inches of the canvas as he works. His strokes are achingly small.

He goes on talking about Carolyn.

"I knew she was out here for years. I started writing her letters. Then when I could really get my courage up, I got her on the phone. It wasn't the first time I ever like talked to her or anything. She'd call up once in a while. Right after the first of the year a lot. Like she wanted to call over the holidays but she knew better than to do that. Anyway, she was nice about it. Real nice. 'Oh, well that would be lovely.' La la, ta ta. Real polite," he says, and nods to himself. "Civil. That's a word, right?"

"Right," I say.

"I'd see her. Sundays I saw her a lot. Once or twice, I met people—I guess, when it seemed to her like the right thing to do. You know, that's how she introduced me to Mr. Horgan."

The emotional currents are strong here. It is best just to let the boy go, it seems, whatever my impulse to ask questions.

"I mean, she was real busy. She had her career and all. She wanted to run for prosecuting attorney someday. Did you know that?"

I hesitate longer than I should, even in this ungainly conversation. Perhaps my own expression discloses some reflex of distress, for the boy looks at me oddly. I tell him, finally, that the P.A.'s office is full of people who see that in their future. But that does not put him off.

"Did you like know her real good? I mean, did you work with her or something?"

"Now and then," I say, but I can tell from the way his glance lingers that I have failed in my effort to be oblique. "You were telling me what happened when you saw her."

He waits a moment, but he is accustomed to cooperating with grownups, and he turns his attention to his brush, rubbing it around inside a little plastic tray. His shoulders move before he speaks.

"Not much happened," he says, then rears his head of tangled brass-colored hair and looks back at me directly. "I mean she never talked about back then," he tells me, "about when I was a kid. I suppose I expected her to. But I guess she just didn't feature that part of her life. You know? She like said nothing."

I nod, and for a moment we are silent, still looking at one

another. His eyes again take on that quickened light.

"I didn't make any difference to her. You know? She was as nice as pie. Now. But like she didn't care. That's why my old man didn't want me to come out here. I mean, he spent all those years making up for her, saying that it was a time in her life, all that. He never wanted me to feel like she left because of me. But he knew what was going on." He throws his brush down. "If you want to know the truth, Mr. Horgan had to like talk me into going to the funeral. I wasn't gonna. I just really didn't feel like it. My own mother. That's pretty terrible, isn't it?"

"I don't know," I say. He takes his canvas down and stares at it, near his feet. He seems to recognize—and welcome—my close observation of him. Young, I think. There is such a tender quality to this boy's discomfort. I speak quietly.

"My mother died while I was in law school," I say. "The next week I stopped by to see my father. I never did that, but I figured under the circumstances—" I motion. "Anyway, he was packing. Half the household was in boxes. I said, 'Pa, where you going?' He says, 'Arizona.' Turned out he'd bought a piece of land, a trailer. And he never said word one to me about it. If I hadn't come by that day, I'm sure he'd have left town without even saying goodbye. And it was always like that with us. Sometimes that's the way things are between parents and kids."

The boy looks toward me for a long moment, mystified by my candor or the things of which we speak.

"And what do you do about that, huh? Anything?"

"You try to grow up," I say. "In your own way. I have this son and he's the world to me."

"What's his name?"

"My son?"

"Right."

"Nat."

"Nat," says Carolyn's son. He looks at me again. "What was she to you, anyhow? I mean, this isn't just work, right? Was she like your girlfriend, too?"

I am sure that he has seen my wedding band. His gesture toward me with his chin as he asks this question seems almost to point in that direction, but I do not feel capable of further devices with this soft, decent boy.

"I'm afraid at one point she was my girlfriend, too. Late last year," I say. "Just a little while."

"Yeah," says the kid, and shakes his head with real disgust. He's waiting to meet somebody she didn't gull, and there is nobody here who can make that claim.

"When I flunk out," he says to me, "I'm going home." This declaration has sufficient weight that it seems to me, perhaps, this matter has just now been decided. But I do not respond. He does not need me to tell him he is correct. I smile, warmly enough, I hope, to show how much I like him. Then I leave.

8

"In the Hall, you know," says Lip, referring to McGrath Hall, the police department headquarters, "they are calling this thing Mission Impossible." He means our investigation of Carolyn's murder. "That's how the dicks are talkin. You know, 'What's new with Mission Impossible?' Like nobody'll ever figure this fuckin thing out. Not in time for Horgan. He never shoulda let the press think we could come up with somethin fast. He shoulda downplayed it, instead of givin forty fuckin interviews about how hard we're workin."

Lip's mouth is full of torn bread and red sauce, but that does not stop him from complaining. His irritation is extreme. We are standing before a vacant lot, a dump of sorts beneath the highway viaduct. Broken pieces of stressed concrete, with the snaky rusted coils of reinforcement sticking from them, litter the uneven ground, along with more ordinary refuse: bottles, newspapers, abandoned auto parts. There is also a snowfall of white wax-paper balls and crushed cups left by the many customers who have preceded us in taking a sandwich from Giaccalone's across the street. It is one of Lip's favorite places, an Italian stand where they insert an entire veal chop, laden with marinara, into a Vienna roll. Lipranzer likes heavy fare at lunchtime, the single man's answer to the anomie of dinner. Our soft drinks rest on the backless remains of a public bench on which each of us has perched one foot. Various street gangs and adolescent lovers have inscribed their names in the planks of the bench's punky seat.

Walking back to Lip's car, we trade information. I talk about my visit with the kid, and the fact that he provided no meaningful leads. Lip discusses his own recent activities. He interviewed the neighbor who said she thought she saw a stranger.

"Mrs. Krapotnik," Lip says. "She's a winner. Talk some? I'm tellin you." He shakes his head. "She'll look at mug books, but first I gotta get some earplugs."

"How about the Index?" The Index is the state file on sex offenders.

"Nothin," Lip says.

"Nothing like the ropes?"

"This lady I'm talkin to tells me she read somethin like that once in a book. No one she knows of ever done it. Christ, can you imagine that's what she's readin? You'd think she gets enough on the job."

Lip has his customary OPV—official police vehicle—a gold Aries, unmarked but for the blackwall tires and the license plates, which, like those on every other OPV, begin with ZF, thus forming a code recognized by every minor hoodlum in the city. Lip guns away from the curb. Coppers, cabbies, people who live in their cars always drive so fast. He swings through one of his many shortcuts back downtown and, because of a detour, is forced onto Kinbark, main drag of my old neighborhood. The diverted traffic is thick and we move with processional slowness down the avenue. There it is, I think, there it is. His cousin Milos, who bought the bakery when my father left, never even changed the sign. It still says SABICH'S in a heavy sea-blue script.

Even though I worked there every day, I remember only certain details of the interior—the summertime screen door that transfigured the moving shapes of the street, the racks of blue metal trays behind the counter, the heavy steel cash register with its round clang. When I was six, my presence was first demanded. I was a pair of hands, unemployed, and not requiring pay. I was taught to break and stack the smooth, white-sided cake boxes. I made them a dozen at a time and brought them from the cobwebbed basement to the store. Because the boxes were so slick and substantial, their edges had, at certain angles, the lacerating power of the finest cutlery; my knuckles and fingertips were often cut. I learned to dread this, for my father regarded a trace of blood on the outside of a cake box as a scandal. "Is not here a butcher shop." This remark would come with a look that mixed loathing and disgust in fearsome proportions. In my dreams of those times, it is always summer, when the air of this valley is as stilted as a swamp's, and the added dry heat of the ovens made it labor just to walk about the shop. I dream that my skin is slick with sweat, my father is calling, a cake has fallen, and my fear is like an acid that is corroding my veins and bones.

If I were to paint my father, he would have a gargoyle's face and a dragon's scaled heart. The channels of his emotions were too intricately wound upon themselves, too clotted, strangulated, crowded with spite to admit any feeling for a child. There was never any question of picking sides for me. Like the apartment, its walls and pictures, the furniture he broke, it was clear that my father regarded me as a possession of my mother's. And I grew up with what seemed a simple understanding: my mother loved me; my father did not.

He took his satisfaction, if you could call so arid a feeling by that name, from opening the shop, firing the oven, raising the shade, pushing the whitened dust out the back door at the end of the day. His family had been bakers for four generations and he simply did as he had been taught. His standards were unyielding and his procedures were exact. He never tried to charm his customers; he was far too humorless and insular for that. In fact, he saw every person who entered as a potential enemy, someone who would complain, chisel, wheedle, and finally settle for day-old bread. But his income was always steady: he was known to be reliable; he distrusted employees and did the work of two, at least, himself; and he did not file a tax return for more than twenty years.

He had come to this country in 1946. I was named for the town in which he had been raised, a village two hundred miles from Belgrade. Almost everyone there was a partisan. When the Nazis came through in 1941, all the adults were lined up against the schoolhouse and shot. The children were left, abandoned. My father, then barely eighteen, and soft-faced enough to have been spared, roamed with a band in the mountains for almost six months before they were captured. He spent the rest of the war in camps—first the Nazi labor camps, and the Allied DP camps after the liberation. His relatives here arranged his passage, hectoring their congressman and the congressman's local staff in a ceaseless and eccentric way. My father was one of the first of the Displaced Persons allowed to enter the United States. And after a year here, he no longer spoke to my great-aunt and my cousins who had worked so hard to save him.

Hearing the rough chorus of auto horns, I look back to make out the problem. A white man in the car behind us pounds on his steering wheel and makes a belligerent gesture in my direction, and I finally realize that Lip has stopped dead in the traffic. I take it that he has surveyed my line of sight and let the other cars move on, but when I turn to catch his expression, his eyes have shifted and he is making a determined effort to study the traffic.

"Hair and Fiber come in," Lip says finally. His gray eyes, his lined, high-cheeked face betray nothing, quiet as a pond.

"Tell me," I say, and Lip dutifully recounts the contents of the report. On Carolyn's clothes and body were minute fibers of a carpeting not found in her apartment—Zorak V is its name. It is a synthetic, milled domestically. The color is called Scottish Malt, the most popular shade. The dye lot cannot be identified and the fiber could be from either an industrial or a domestic weave. In all there are probably fifty thousand homes and offices in Kindle County from which the carpet fibers could have come. There are no hair or skin fragments in Carolyn's fingers or under her nails, confirming that there was no struggle before she was bound, and the only human hair not Carolyn's shade found anywhere near the corpse has been made as female and, thus, insignificant. The cord with which she was bound is regular clothesline, American-made, sold in every K Mart, Sears, and Walgreen's.

"That didn't get us very far," I tell Lipranzer.

"Not very," he answers. "At least we know she didn't grab anybody."

"I wonder," I say. "I keep thinking about what we said last week. How maybe this was some guy she knew. I remember when I was in law school, everyone used to pass around this case about a guy whose life insurer refused to pay out. His widow was bringing the suit, which was a real stitch, because it turned out this character had bought it whacking off while he was hanging himself. Literally. Head through a noose and everything. He cashed in when he knocked over the stool he was supposed to land on."

"No shit." Lipranzer laughs out loud. "Who won the case?"

"The insurance company, as far as I remember. The court didn't think it was a covered risk. Anyway, maybe that's what this was all about. You know, big-time kinkiness? I'm thinking that more and more. Apparently it's some weird high, coming while you're passing out."

"How does she end up dead from gettin hit?"

"Maybe her stud gets scared. *Thinks* he's cooled her. Figures it's John Belushi all over again, and starts to make it look like it was something else."

Lip shakes his head. He doesn't like it.

"You're stretchin," he says. "I don't think the path report supports it."

"I'm gonna run it by Painless, anyway."

This reminds Lipranzer of something else.

"Painless called me a couple days ago. Says he's got a report back from the forensic chemist. From the way he sounded, I take it we didn't get much, but maybe you can pick it up whenever you get there. I gotta get out west today. Show Mrs. Krapotnik some pictures." He closes his eyes and shimmies his head, like maybe, if he tries, he can stand the thought.

We are back downtown now. Lip eases into the first open space in the police lot, and we trek back through the noontime crowds toward the County Building. Out on the street, our spring, as so often happens, is turning fast to summer. You can feel some of the balminess that is a month or two away. It has inspired some of the ladies passing on the avenue to summer fashions, sleeveless tops, and those light, clingy fabrics of the season.

"Brother," I tell Lip suddenly, "we are really nowhere."

He makes a sound. "You ever get the fingerprint lab?"

I swear. "I knew I forgot something."

"You are a class A fuck—up," he says. "They ain't gonna do it for me. I asked twice already."

I promise I will do that, as well as see Painless, today or tomorrow.

When we get back to my office, I ask Eugenia to hold my calls and I close the door. I pull the B file that Horgan gave me out of my drawer.

Lip studies it a moment.

The B file, as I received it from Raymond, consists, in its

entirety, of a log-in slip, produced when the case was entered in our computer system; a single sheet of sparse notes in Carolyn's hand; and a xerox of a long letter. There is nothing in the file to indicate whether an original of this letter was received or this copy is all that came in. The letter is typewritten and clean—but it still does not look professional. The margins are narrow and there is only a single paragraph. The author is someone who knows how to type but seemingly does not do it often—a housewife, perhaps, or a professional man.

I have read the letter four or five times by now, but I read it one more time, taking each page from Lip as he finishes.

> *Dear Mr. Horgan:*
> *I am writing to you because I have been a fan of yours for many years. I am sure that you didn't know anything about the things that are making me write this letter. In fact, I think you would want to do something about them. Probably there is nothing you can do, since all this happened a long time ago. But I thought you would like to know. It happened while you were P.A. and it's kind of about somebody who worked for you, a deputy prosecuting attorney who I think was taking bribes. Nine years ago this summer a person I will call Noel got arrested. Noel was not this person's real name, but if I told you his real name you would go to him first to talk about a lot of things I am saying in this letter and he would think about it and know I turned him in. Then he would hurt me to get even. Believe me, I know him real well and I know what I am talking about. He would make me very sorry. Anyway, Noel got arrested. I happen to think that what it was for isn't real important, but I will tell you that it was something which he was very embarrassed about, because that is the kind of person he is. Noel thought that if the people he worked with and hung out with found out, they wouldn't have anything to do with him. Great friends. But that's Noel. The lawyer he got told him he should just admit it in court because nothing was going to happen and nobody would ever know about it. But Noel is a very paranoyd-type person and he ran all over the place fussing about*

*what would happen if anybody ever found out. Pretty
soon he started saying how he was going to pay
somebody off. I thought he was joking around at first.
Noel would stoop to anything, but it just didn't sound
right for him. If you knew him you would understand
why. But he kept telling me he was going to do this. And
it would cost $1500. I know all this because, to make a
long story short, I'm the one who gave him the money.
Since Noel is like he is, I thought I better be sure it was
going where he said. We went all the way out to the
North Branch at Runyon and 111th. Out there, we didn't
wait even a minute, when a secretary who seemed to
know Noel walked up and took us downstairs to the
P.A.'s office. Your name, RAYMOND HORGAN, was
written right on the door, I remember. Noel told me to
wait outside. I was too scared by then to fight about it,
which was pretty dumb since I came all the way out
there to see him give somebody the money. But anyway,
he wasn't inside two minutes and he's back out. He had
put all of this money in a sock (I'm not kidding!) and
when he came out he showed me the sock and it was
empty. I just about ran out of there, but Noel was very
cool. I asked him later what happened. Noel never liked
to talk about this thing. He said he was protecting me,
which is a laugh. I'm sure he just figured that if I didn't
forget about it, sooner or later I'd want the money back.
Anyway, he did say that the girl took him into an office
and told him to wait at a desk there. Then a man talked
behind him. He told Noel just to put what he brought in
the center drawer of the desk and to leave. Noel said he
never looked back or anything. Ten days later, Noel had
to go to court. He was just about crazy again. He kept
saying he knew he was going to get screwed over and
everything, but when we got there, the lawyer from the
prosecuting attorney told the judge that the case was
dismissed. I have tried and tried to remember this
lawyer's name, but I can't. Once or twice I asked Noel the
name of the guy he bribed, but like I said, he really never
liked to talk about this and just told me to mind my own
business. So I am writing this letter to you. I haven't seen*

*Noel in about two years. Frankly, this is not the worst
thing he ever did, by a long shot, if you believe him, but it's
really the only thing I ever saw him do myself. I'm not
really out to get Noel, but I thought that this P.A. was really
wrong for taking this money and taking advantage of
people that way, and wanted to write to you so that you
could do something about it. A couple of people who I have
told this story to without using any names said that you
couldn't do anything about something so old since the
statue of limitations is past, but I figure this couldn't have
been the only time something like this ever happened and
maybe even they're still doing the same thing. Actually, I
think that what I just wrote isn't true. I hope you get Noel
too. But I don't want him to know you got him from me.
And if you do get him from someone else, I beg you please
(Please!) not to show him this letter. I am TRUSTING YOU.*

The letter, of course, is unsigned. Our office gets letters like
this every day. Two paralegals are assigned to do pretty much
nothing but answer this kind of correspondence, and talk to the
various cranks who wander into the reception area in person.
The more serious complaints tend to get passed along, which,
presumably, is how this one found its way to Raymond. Even at
that point, a lot of what comes in is junk. But this one, for all its
funny twitches, has the ring of the real thing. It is more than
possible, of course, that our tipster was simply scammed by his
friend Noel. But the guy who wrote the letter was in the best
position to judge, and he doesn't seem to think that was the case.

Scam or not, it is easy to figure out why Raymond Horgan
would not want this file floating around in an election year. Nico
would love to have evidence of any kind of undiscovered crimes
committed during Raymond's regime. As the letter writer
surmises, it is not likely that friend Noel's case was an isolated
episode. What we have in hand is a first-class scandal: an
unnoticed—worse—unapprehended bribery ring operating in
one of the branch courts.

Lipranzer has lit a cigarette. He has been quiet a long time.

"You think it's bull?" I ask.

"Neh," he says. "Somethin's there. Maybe not what this
jamoche thinks, but it's somethin."

"Do you think it's worth looking at?"

"Can't hurt. We ain't exactly buried in leads."

"That's what I thought. Carolyn figured these guys were gay," I say. "I think she was probably on the right track." I point to her notes. She has the section number of various provisions of what is still titled the Morals chapter of the state criminal code written down, a question mark beside them. "Remember the panty raids out in the Public Forest? That would have been right about then. We were busting those guys in carloads. And the cases went to the North Branch, didn't they?"

Lip is nodding: it all fits. The embarrassing nature of the crime, the mania to conceal it. And the timing is right. Sexual crimes, involving consenting adults, were ignored as a matter of policy in Raymond's first administration. The cops brought in the cases, but we gave them the shuffle. By the time Raymond began to campaign for re-election, certain groups, prostitutes and gays particularly, were, in their more florid segments, largely beyond control. With the gays, the problem was acute in the public forests which ring the city. Families would not go there at midday on the weekends for fear of what their children would be exposed to. There were some fairly graphic complaints about what was taking place in broad daylight on the picnic tables, where, Mom tended to point out, people were supposed to eat. With the election nine months away, we made a large show of a concerted clean-up. Dozens of men were arrested every night, often in *flagrante delicto*. Their cases were usually disposed of with court supervision—a kind of expungeable guilty plea—and the defendants then disappeared.

That is the problem. Both Lip and I recognize it will be difficult to find Noel. There were probably four hundred of these cases that summer, and we don't even know his name. If Carolyn made much progress, the file does not seem to show it. The jacket date indicates she got the case about five months before her murder. Her notes reflect little investigation. "Noel" is written in an upper corner and underlined countless times. A little farther down the page she has written "Leon." The significance of this eluded me at first; then I realized that she had assumed that, like many aliases, the name chosen by the letter writer was the product of some meaningful association. Maybe the name was a rebus. Carolyn was going to suppose that she was looking for somebody named Leon. Finally, she has another name, "Kenneally," at the foot of the page, and his assignment. This is Lionel Kenneally, a good copper, now a commander. We worked the Night Saints cases together. He runs the watch in the 32nd Police District, whose cases are heard in the North Branch.

"I still don't understand why I never heard about this case," I tell Lip. I can't imagine a procedural reason for not informing me—or for the case to have ended up in the hands of Carolyn, who did not work in our public corruption unit. I have spent more than a few moments with that puzzle, full as it is with sorrowful implications about my fading romance with Raymond Horgan, and his with me.

Lip shrugs. "What's Horgan tell you?"

"I haven't been able to corner him. It's twelve days to the election. They're on a twenty-four-hour operation now."

"How about Kenneally. What'd he say?"

"He's been on leave."

"Well, you better talk to him. He ain't tellin shit to me. We ain't in each other's fan clubs."

The police department is full of people with whom Lipranzer does not get along, but I would have guessed Lip would take to Kenneally. He likes good cops. But there is something between them. He's hinted at it before.

Lip starts to leave, then steps back in the office. I am already headed out to see Eugenia, but Lip takes me by the elbow to detain me. He closes the door I just opened.

"One thing," he says. He looks right at me. "We got her MUDs back."

"And?"

"Nothin great. Only we wanted to get MUDs on any number she called more than three times in the last six months."

"Yeah?"

"I noticed as I'm goin through there, one of the numbers that comes up that way is yours."

"Here?" I ask.

An especially narrow look emerges from Lip's narrow, Slavic face.

"Home," he says. "Last October. Thereabouts."

I am about to tell him this could not possibly be right. Carolyn never tried to reach me at home. Then I realize what it is. *I* made those calls from Carolyn's place. Lying to my wife. Late again, kid. This trial's gonna be a bitch. I'll catch dinner down here.

Lip watches me calculate. His eyes are flat and gray.

"I'd just as soon you let it go," I say at last. "If Barbara sees a subpoena notice from the phone company, she'll blow a gut. Under the circumstances. If you don't mind, Lip, I'd appreciate it."

He nods, but I can see that it is still not right with him. If nothing else, we have always depended on each other to be above certain base kinds of stupidity, and Dan Lipranzer would be unfaithful to that compact if he did not take one more moment to cast his gray eyes on me harshly, so that I know I've let him down.

9

"In the end," I told Robinson, "we had to put Wendell McGaffen on the witness stand." His testimony was the only effective response to his father, and so we called the boy in rebuttal. Carolyn was splendid. She wore a dark blue suit and a beige blouse with a huge satin bow, and she stood beside Wendell, whose feet did not reach the floor from the hard oak chair in the witness box. You could not hear a thing in the courtroom.

And then what did your mother do, Wendell?

He asked for water.

When your mother took you in the basement, Wendell, what did she do?

It was bad, he said.

Was it this? Carolyn went to the vise, which had sat throughout, like an omen, at the edge of the prosecution table, grease-smeared and black, thicker in all its parts than any of Wendell's limbs.

Uh huh.

Did she hurt you?

Uh huh.

And did you cry?

Uh huh. Wendell drank some more water and then added, A lot.

Tell how it happened, said Carolyn finally, softly, and Wendell did. She said to lie down. He said he screamed and cried. He cried, Mommy don't. He begged her.

But he finally laid himself down.

And she told him not to scream.

Wendell swung his feet as he talked. He gripped his doll. And as Carolyn and Mattingly had instructed him, he never looked over at his mother. On cross Stern did what little he could, asked Wendell how many times he'd met with Carolyn and whether he loved his mother, which caused Wendell to ask for more water. There was no disputing, really. Every person there knew the child was telling the truth, not because he was practiced or particularly emotional, but because somehow in every syllable Wendell spoke there was a tone, a knowledge, a bone-hard instinct that what he was describing was wrong. Wendell convinced with his moral courage.

I delivered the closing argument for the county. My state of personal disturbance was such that when I approached the podium I had no idea of what I was going to say, and for one moment I was full of panic, convinced that I would be speechless. Instead, I found the well of all my passionate turmoil and I spoke fervently for this boy, who must have lived, I said, desperate and uncertain every moment, wanting, as we all wanted, love, and receiving instead, not just indifference or harshness, but torture.

Then we waited. Having a jury out is the closest thing in life to suspended animation. Even the simplest tasks, cleaning my desk, returning phone calls, reading prosecution reports, are beyond my attention, and I end up walking the halls, talking over the evidence and the arguments with anyone unlucky enough to ask me how the case went. About 4:00, Carolyn came by to say she was going to return something to Morton's and I volunteered to walk along. As we left the building, it began raining hard, a cold downpour driven almost sideways by the wind, which was full of winter. People dashed down the street, covering their heads. Carolyn returned her merchandise, a glass bowl whose source she did not identify, and then we headed back into the rain. She more or less shouted out as the wind came up, and I put an arm around her protectively, and she leaned against me beneath my umbrella. It was like something coming loose, and we went on that way for a few blocks, saying nothing, until I finally followed my impulse to speak.

Listen, I said. I started again. Listen.

In her heels, Carolyn was about six feet, an inch or so taller than me, so it was almost an embrace when she turned her face in my direction. In the natural light, you could see what Carolyn, with her devotion to lotions and gyms and spectacular fashions, tried to obscure—that it was an older face, past forty, the makeup clinging to the lines radiating from her eyes, a haggard roughness now part of the skin. But somehow that made her more real to me. This was my life and this was happening.

I've been wondering, I told her, about something you said. What you meant the other night when you told me, Not now.

She looked at me. She shook her head as if she did not know, but her face was full of caprice, her lips sealed to hold back her laughter.

The wind came up again then, and I drew her into the shelter of a recessed storefront. We were on Grayson Boulevard, where the shops face the stately elms of the Midway.

I mean, I said, hopeless and pitiable and small, there seems to be something going on between us. I mean, am I crazy? To think that?

I don't think so.

You don't?

No.

Ah, I said.

Still smiling wonderfully, she put her arm through mine and moved me back down the street.

The jury returned a little before 7:00. Guilty on all counts. Raymond had remained in the office awaiting the verdict, and he came downstairs with us to meet the press, cameras not being allowed above the lobby of the County Building. Then he took us out for a drink. He had a date, and so around 8:30 he left us in a back booth at Caballero's, where Carolyn and I talked and became drunk and moony. I told her that she had been magnificent. Magnificent. I don't know how many times I said that.

TV and the movies have spoiled the most intimate moments of our lives. They have given us conventions which dominate our expectations in instants whose intensity would ordinarily make them spontaneous and unique. We have conventions of grief, which we learned from the Kennedys, and ordained gestures for victory by which we imitate the athletes we see on the tube, who in turn have learned the same things from other jocks they saw on TV. Seduction, too, has got its standards now, its sloe-eyed moments, its breathless repartee.

And so we both ended up coming on smooth and wry and bravely composed, like all those gorgeous, poised movietime couples, probably because we had no other idea of how to behave. And even so, there was a gathering in the air, a racing current that made it difficult to sit in place, to move my mouth or lift my glass to drink. I don't believe we ordered dinner, but we had the menus, something to stare at, like coquettes with their silk fans. Beneath the table Carolyn's hand was laid out casually, very close to my hip.

I didn't know you when this started.

What? she asks. We are close on the plush bench, but she must lean a bit nearer because I am speaking so softly. I can smell the liquor on her breath.

I didn't know you before this case, before this started. That amazes me.

Because?

Because it just doesn't seem that way now—that I didn't know you.

Do you know me now?

Better. I think so. Don't I?

Maybe, she says. Maybe what it is, is that now you know you want to get to know me.

That's possible, I say, and she repeats it:

That's possible.

And will I get to know you?

That's possible, too, she says. If that's what you want.

I think that is, I say.

I think that's one thing, she says, that you want.

One thing?

One thing, she says. She brings her glass up to drink without looking away from me. Our faces are not very far apart at all. When she puts her glass down, the large bow on her blouse almost brushes my chin. Her face seems coarse with too much makeup, but her eyes are deep and spectacularly bright, and the air is wild with cosmetic scents, perfume, and body emanations from our closeness. It seems as if our talk has been drifting like this, circling languorously, like a hawk over the hills, for hours.

What else do I want? I ask.

I think you know, she says.

I do?

I think you do.

I think I do, I say. But there's one thing I still don't know.

There is?

I don't quite know how to get it—what I want.

You don't?

Not quite.

Not quite?

I really don't.

Her smile, so arch and delicately contained, now broadens, and she says, Just reach.

Reach?

Just reach, she says,

Right now?

Just reach.

The air between us seems so full of feeling that it is almost like a haze. Slowly I extend my hand and find the smooth edge of her bright satin bow. I do not quite touch her breast in doing that. And then, without turning my eyes away from hers, I gradually tug on that wide ribbon. It slides perfectly, and the knot breaks open so that the button at her blouse collar is exposed, and at just that moment, I feel Carolyn's hand fluttering up beneath the table like some bird and one long fingernail skates for an instant down my aching bulge. I almost scream, but instead, it all comes down to a shudder, and Carolyn says quietly that we should get a cab.

"So," I said to Robinson, "that was how my affair began. I took her back to her fashionable loft and made love to her on the soft Greek rugs. I just grabbed her the minute she set the bolt in her front door, hiked her skirt up with one hand, and put the other down her blouse. Very suave. I came like lightning. And afterward, I lay on top of her, surveying the room, the teak and walnut and the crystal figurines, thinking how much it looked like the show window of some tony shop downtown and wondering in this idle way what in the fuck I was doing with my life, or even in a life where the culmination of a long-cultivated passion passed so quickly that I could hardly believe it had happened at all. But there was not a lot of time to think about that, because we had a drink, and then went to her bedroom to watch the story about our case on the late news, and by then I was capable again, and then, that time, when I reared up over her, I knew I was lost."

10

"Whatever I can do for you, Rusty. Anything you need."

So says Lou Balistrieri, the police department's Commander of Special Services. I am sitting in his office in McGrath Hall, where the P.D.'s central operating sections are housed. I can't tell you how many Lous there are over here, fifty-five-year-old guys with gray hair and guts that hang on them like saddlebags, phlegmy voices from smoking. A gifted bureaucrat, ruthless with any person in his employ and a shameless toady to anyone, like me, who has sufficient power to harm him. He is on the phone now, calling down to the crime lab, which is under his control.

"Morris, this is Balistrieri. Get me Dickerman. Yeah, now. If he's in the can, go in there and get him off. Yeah." Balistrieri winks at me. He was a street cop for twenty years, but he works now without a uniform. His rayon shirt is sweated through under the arms. "Dickerman, yeah. On this Polhemus thing. Rusty Sabich is over here with me. Yeah. Sabich. Sabich, for Chrissake. Right, Horgan's guy. Chief deputy. We got a glass or something. Yeah, I know there latents, I know, that's why I'm calling you. Whatta you think? Right, I'm a big dumb gumba. Right, and don't fuckin forget it. This big dumb gumba can send you home with your nuts in a paper bag. Right. Right. But why I'm calling is this. Can't we do a computer scan with that laser thing against our knowns? Yeah, you got three good prints there, right? So get what you need and run them through the computer and let's figure out if they're anyone we know. I hear the cop on the case has been asking for ten days now you should do this. Murphy? Yeah, which one? Leo or Henry? Because Henry is a horse's ass. Good. Well, tell him to un-onload it. Don't give me the computer crap, I don't understand that shit anyway. No. No. Not good enough. All right. Call me back. Ten minutes. Ten. Let's figure this thing out."

The problem, as it gradually emerges, is not equipment but the fact that the computer is under another section's jurisdiction. The department owns only one machine, and the people who do things like payroll believe it should be regarded as theirs alone.

"Right. I'll ask. I'll ask," says Balistrieri when he gets the return call. He covers the receiver. "They want to know how big a field you want to run against. We can do all felons or all knowns in the county. You know, everybody who's ever been printed. County employees. Shit like that."

I pause. "Felons is probably enough. I can do the rest later if we ever need it."

Balistrieri makes a face. "Do it all. God knows if I can get back on." He takes his hand away before I get a chance to answer. "Do all of it. Yeah. How soon? What the fuck is gonna take a week? This man's runnin the biggest murder case in the city and he's got to kiss your ring? Well, fuck Murphy's statistical analysis. Yeah. Tell him I said so. Right." He puts the phone down. "A week, probably ten days. They gotta get the payroll out, then the chief needs some statistics for the LEAA"—Law Enforcement Assistance Administration. "I'll push, but I doubt you'll see it any sooner. And have your copper get the glass back out of evidence and bring it to the lab, case they need it for anything."

I thank Lou for his help and head down to the Pathology Lab. This building looks more or less like an old high school, with varnished oak trim and worn hallways. It is coppers wall to wall, men—and more than a few women these days—in deep blue shirts and black ties, bustling around and making jokes with one another. People of my generation and social stratum do not like cops. They were always beating our heads and sniffing for dope. They were unenlightened. So when I became a prosecutor I started from some distance behind which, in truth, I have never made up. I've worked with policemen for years. Some I like; more I don't. Most of them have two failings. They're hard. And they're crazy. They see too much; they live with their nose in the gutter.

Three or four weeks ago, I stayed longer than I should have on a Friday night at Gil's and began buying rounds with a street copper named Palucci. He did a beer and a shot a couple of times, and started talking about a heart he had found that morning in a Ziploc bag. That was all. Just the organ, and the major vessels, lying right next to a garbage can at the end of an alley. He picked it up; he looked at it; he drove away. But then he made himself come back. He lifted the lid of the can and stirred the rubbish. No body parts. 'That was it. I done my duty. I dropped it off downtown and told them to mark it goat.'

Crazy. They are our paid paranoids. A copper sees a conspiracy in a cloudy day; he suspects treachery when you say good morning. A grim fellowship, nurtured in our midst, thinking ill about us all.

The elevator takes me to the basement.

"Dr. Kumagai." I greet him. His office is right outside the morgue, which lies beyond, with its stainless-steel tables and the ghastly odors of open peritoneal cavities. Through the walls, I can hear a surgical saw screaming. Painless's desk is a mess, papers and journals in ramparts, overflowing wooden trays. Set at one corner, a small TV is on, the volume low, with an afternoon baseball game.

"Mr. Savage. Real important stuff, huh? We got chief deputy with us." Painless is every kind of weird, a five-foot, five-inch Japanese, with heavy brows and a small mustache divided over the middle of his lip. A kinetic type, always dodging and twisting, talking with his hands in the air. The mad scientist, except there is nothing benevolent about him. Whoever got the idea that Painless would be best off working with stiffs pushed him in the right direction. I can't imagine his bedside manner. He is the kind to throw things at you, cuss you out. Whatever bitter little notion is in his brain will find expression. He is one of those people of whom the globe at moments seems so full. I do not understand him. If I try very hard, in that sort of instinctive effort we all make at pseudo-telepathy, my screen comes up full of fuzz. I cannot imagine what is passing through his mind when he does his job, or watches TV, or turns after a woman. I know I could lose a bet even if I had ten chances to guess what he did last Saturday night.

"Actually, I just came in to pick up a report. You called Lipranzer."

"Oh yeah, oh yeah," says Painless. "Right here somewhere.

That fuckin Lipranzer. He wants you call right away with everything." Painless works two-handed, transporting the stacks of paper across his desk as he seeks the new report. "So you won't be chief deputy too much longer, huh? Della Guardia, I think, gonna kick Raymond Horgan in the ass. Huh?" He looks to me to respond. Painless is smiling, as is his custom when dealing with something that others find unpleasant.

"We'll see," I say: then I decide to be a bit more aggressive. "Delay a pal of yours, Doctor?"

"Nico's hell of a guy, *hell* of a guy. Oh yeah. We work on all kinda big murder case together. He's good, too, real good. Yeah, he get up there, he really kick those defense lawyers in the ass. This is this thing." He tosses a file folder in my direction and bends toward the TV. "That fuckin Dave Parker. Now he only got dope in one nostril, really hittin the goddamn ball."

The association between Nico and Painless had eluded me before, but it's a natural, the big-time homicide prosecutor and the police pathologist. They would need each other badly from time to time. I ask Painless if I can sit down for a minute.

"Sure sit, sit." He moves a stack of files and looks back to the television.

"Lipranzer and I have been kicking over this theory lately. Well, let's say idea. Maybe this was some weird bondage thing that got out of hand. Maybe Carolyn was living dangerously, and when her beau thought she had expired, he gave her a whack in the head to make it look like something else. Does that sound possible?"

Painless in his white lab coat rests his elbows on the turrets of papers.

"No fuckin way."

"No?"

"No fuckin way. Coppers dumb," says Painless the police department pathologist. "Somethin hard, they make easy. Somethin easy, they make hard. Read the fuckin report. I write a report, fuckin read it. Lipranzer wants me hurry up, hurry up. Then he don't read the fuckin report."

"This report?"

"Not that report." He swipes at the new report when I hold it up. "My report. Autopsy. You see anything with bruises on wrists? Bruises on ankles? Bruises on knees? This lady is dead from gettin hit, not strangled. Read the fuckin report."

"She was tied up pretty good. You can see the rope burn on the neck in the pictures."

"Oh sure, oh sure. She was tied up real tight, real good. Looked like a fuckin bow and arrow when they brought her in. But you got one mark on the neck. Somebody jerkin that rope tighter and tighter, rope's gonna move. Get a wide bruise. She got one skinny little mark on her neck."

"Meaning?" I ask.

Painless smiles. He loves to hold the cards. He pushes his face close enough to the TV that the gray gleam of the screen is reflected on his brow. "First and third," he says.

"What does it mean that there's a narrow mark?" I ask again. I wait. The TV announcer declaims over a line drive.

"Do I need a subpoena?" I ask quietly. I try to smile, but my voice has some edge.

"What?" asks Painless.

"What do you make of the bruises on her neck?"

"I make that rope was tightened there first. Okay?"

I take a moment to gather this in. As Painless knows, I'm lost.

"Time out," I say. "I thought the working theory was that somebody hit her to subdue her. The blow was lethal, but our guy doesn't realize that or care. He ties her up, and rapes her, with this bizarre slipknotting, so he's strangling her at the same time. Have I got it right or have you changed your mind?"

"Me change? Look at fuckin report. Don't say nothin like that. I'm not sayin that. *Looks* like that, maybe. Maybe that's what coppers think. Not me."

"Well, what do you think?"

Painless smiles. Painless shrugs.

I close my eyes an instant.

"Look," I say, "we're ten days into a big-deal murder investigation and I hear right now for the first time that you think the rope went around her neck first. I would have appreciated knowing that a while ago."

"Ask. Lipranzer call me up. 'Hurry up. Need a report.' Okay, he got a report. Nobody ask me what I think."

"I just did."

Painless sits back in his chair. "Maybe I don't think nothin," he says.

Either this guy is a bigger douche bag than I even remember or something is way out of line. I deliberate for a moment, working backward.

"Are you telling me you think she was raped and then tied up?"

"Tied up last, yeah. I think that. Raped? Now I'm thinkin no."

"Now?"

"Now," says Painless. We stare at each other. "Read the report," he says.

"The autopsy?"

"This report. This fuckin report." He hits the folder I'm holding. So I read the report. It is from the forensic chemist's office. Another substance in the vagina of Carolyn Polhemus has been identified. It is known as nonoxynol 9. From the concentrations, the chemist concludes that it derived from spermicidal jelly. That is why there were no viable spermatozoa.

Painless is smiling hugely, and without generosity, when I look up again.

"We're saying this woman used contraception?" I ask.

"Not sayin. She did. Contraceptive jelly. Two percent concentration. Cellulose gum base. Used with diaphragm."

"Diaphragm?" I am extremely slow. "You missed a diaphragm during an autopsy."

"Fuckin no!" Painless hits his desk. He laughs at me out loud. "You been in autopsy, Savage. Slice her right open. No diaphragm in that lady."

More time. Painless smiles and I watch him. I'll bite.

"Where'd it go?"

"My guess?"

"Please."

"Somebody took it."

"The cops?"

"Coppers ain't that dumb."

"Who?"

"Look, Mr. Savage. Ain't coppers. Ain't me. Gotta be the guy."

"The killer?"

"Fuckin-A right."

I pick up the report to read it again. When I do, I notice something else, and our conversation suddenly comes clear. I try to steady myself, but my temper is rising. I can feel the heat all the way to my ears. Perhaps Painless can see that, because after baiting me for ten minutes, he finally levels. He probably figures that sooner or later I would get it anyway.

"You want to know what I think? I think it's a setup. This man who kills her is her lover. He comes over. Has drinks. This lady has intercourse with man, okay? Real nice. But he's angry guy. Picks up somethin, kills her, tries to make it look like rape. Ties her up. Pulls out diaphragm. That's what I think."

"What does Tommy Molto think?" I ask him.

Painless Kumagai, the sadistic little shit, has finally been cornered. He smiles insipidly and tries to laugh. 'Laugh' is actually not the right word. He wheezes. His mouth moves but he does not speak.

I hand him the report back, which, I notice in passing, is dated five days ago. I point out his own handwritten note at the top. It says: "Molto 762–2225."

"Don't you want to copy this down, make sure you can reach Molto when you need him?"

Painless is gaining speed again. "Oh, Tommy." He does better at seeming genial. "Good guy. Good guy."

"How's he doing?"

"Oh, good, good."

"Tell him to give us a call sometime. Maybe I can find out what's happening in my own fucking investigation." I stand up. I point at Kumagai. I call him by the name I know he detests. "Painless, you tell Molto and Nico, too, that this is cheap. Cheap politics. And cheap police department bullshit. God better help them and you, that I can't make a case for tampering."

I snatch the report from Painless's hand and leave without waiting for an answer. My heart is hammering and my arms are weak with rage. Raymond, of course, is not in when I get back to the County Building, but I tell Loretta to have him reach me, it is urgent. I look for Mac, but she, too, is elsewhere. I sit in my office and brood. Oh, how fucking clever. Everything we asked for. And nothing more. Give the results—but not the opinion. Call when the forensic chemist reports, but don't mention what it says. Let us run as long as possible in the wrong direction. And in the meantime, leak every goddamn thing you know to Molto. That's the part that gets me worst. God, I think politics is dirty. And the police department is dirtier. The Medici did not live in a world fuller of intrigue. Every secret allegiance in the community comes to bear there. To the alderman and your bookie and your girlfriend. To in-laws, your no-account brother, the guy from the hardware store who has always cut you a deal on screws. To the rookie you have to look out for, the junkie whose base sincerity gets to you, or the snitch you've got to watch. To the licensing inspector who helped out your uncle, or to the lieutenant who you figure has got an in with Bolcarro and is going to make captain soon and maybe more. Your lodge brother, your neighbor, the guy on the beat who's just a plain good sod. Every one of them needs a break. And you give it. In a big-city police department, at least in Kindle County, there is no such thing as playing by the book. The book got trashed many years ago. Instead, all two thousand guys in blue play it for their own team. Painless was simply playing it like everybody else. Maybe Nico told him he could make him coroner.

My phone rings. Mac. I go through the connecting door.

"Well," I tell her, "we finally know what Tommy Molto is up to."

11

As I am leaving for the evening, I see lights on in Raymond's office. It is nearly 9 p.m. and my first thought is that someone is visiting who should not be. My encounter with Kumagai three days ago has left me edgy and suspicious, and I am actually somewhat surprised when I see Raymond at his desk, staring at what seems to be a computer run, and looking uncharacteristically at ease behind the wastrel fog of his pipe. At this point in the campaign this is a rare sight. Raymond is a hardworking lawyer and there have always been late nights when he was here with the stacks of prosecution reports, or indictments, or at least an upcoming speech; but with his job up for sale, most of his evenings lately are spent on the stump. When he's here, Larren and the other moguls of his campaign are with him, plotting. This moment is sufficiently unusual to be taken as private, and so I let two knuckles graze the old oak door as I am passing in.

"Tea leaves?" I ask.

"Sort of," he says, "but a lot more accurate. Unfortunately." He adopts a public tone: "The Channel 3—*Tribune* poll shows challenger Nico Della Guardia leading incumbent Raymond Horgan, with eight days remaining in the campaign."

My reaction is succinct: "Bullshit."

"Read it and weep." He shoves the computer run in my direction.

I can't make anything of the grid of figures.

"The bottom line," says Raymond.

" 'U' is undecided?" I ask. "Forty-three, thirty-nine. Eighteen percent undecided. You're still in it."

"I'm the incumbent. Once the public realizes that Delay's got a chance, they'll head his way. The new face is a showstopper in a primary." Raymond's political wisdom is usually Delphic, particularly since it represents not only his insights but Mike's and Larren's as well. Nonetheless, I try to remain upbeat.

"You've had a bad couple of weeks, Nico's played Carolyn's murder real well. You'll come back. You've just gotta let him have it. What's the margin of error on this thing, anyway?"

"Well, fortunately or unfortunately for me, it's 4 percent." Mike Duke, he tells me, is over at the TV station trying to convince them that their story should pitch the poll as reflecting a neck-and-neck race. Larren, dispatched to do the same job with the newspaper, has already gotten an agreement from the editors there, contingent on Channel 3's position. "The paper's not contradicting the TV station on the interpretation of a joint poll," Raymond explains. He puffs his pipe. "And my bet is that's the way it'll run. They'll throw me the bone. But what's the point? The numbers are the numbers. Everybody in town will smell the odor of dead meat."

"What do your own numbers look like?"

"They're crap," Raymond tells me. The campaign hasn't had the money to do a decent job. This poll is the work of a national outfit. Everybody—Larren, Mike, Raymond himself—had the impression that the situation wasn't quite this bad, but nobody can dispute it.

"You're probably right on Carolyn," he says. "It hurt. But it's the whole loss of momentum." Raymond Horgan puts down his pipe and looks straight at me. "We're gonna lose, Rusty. You heard it here first."

I look at the worn face of Raymond Horgan, my old idol, my leader. His hands are folded. He is in repose. Twelve and a half years after he got started talking about revolutionizing the idea of law enforcement, and a year too late for the best interests of us both, Raymond Horgan has finally pulled the plug. It is now all someone else's problem. And to the little incubus that argues that principles and issues are involved, there is, after twelve years, an exhausted man's reply. Ideas and principles are not foremost here. Not when you do not have the jails to hold the crooks you catch, or enough courtrooms to try them; not when the judge who hears the case is too often some hack who went to night law school because his brother already had filled the one slot available in their father's insurance agency, and who achieved his appointment by virtue of thirty years' loyal precinct work. In the administration of Nico Della Guardia there will be the same imperatives, no matter what he's saying on his TV spots: too many crimes and no sensible way to deal with them, too few lawyers, too many calls for political favors, too much misery, and too much evil that will keep on happening no matter what the ideals and principles of the prosecuting attorney. He can have his turn. Raymond's ease at the abyss becomes my own.

"What the fuck," I say.

"Right," says Raymond after he gets done laughing. He goes to the conference table in a corner of the office and pulls out the pint bottle that's always in the pencil drawer. He pours two in the little folded cups from the water cooler and I come over and join him.

"You know, when I started here I didn't drink," I say. "I mean, I don't have a bottle problem, I'm not complaining, but twelve years ago, I just never drank. Not beer, not wine, not rum-and-Coca-Cola. And now I sit here and knock back Scotches neat." I do just that; my esophagus contracts and tears come to my eyes. Raymond pours another. "Ain't time a bitch."

"You're getting middle-aged, Rusty. All this fucking looking back. One thing about getting divorced, it stopped that crap for me. You know, I leave this job, I'm not going to spend four months crying in my beer and talking about all the good times."

"You'll be sitting in one of those glass cages on the fortieth floor of the IBM building, with hot-and-cold-running secretaries and a bunch of megabuck partners asking you if thirty hours a week is too much time for the privilege of having your name on the door."

"Bullshit," says Raymond.

"Sure," I answer. In wistful moments in the last few years I have heard Raymond conjure just such a fantasy for himself—a few years to build a bankroll, then get on the bench himself, probably at the appellate level on his way to the state supreme court.

"Well, maybe," says Raymond, and we share a laugh. "Will you go?" he asks.

"I doubt I'll have much choice. Delay's going to make Tommy Molto his chief deputy. That's clearer than ever."

Raymond moves his heavy shoulders. "You can never tell with Della Guardia."

"It's about time for me to head on, anyway," I say.

"Can we get you on the bench, Rusty?"

This is a golden moment for me: here at last is loyalty's reward. Do I want to be a judge? Does a bus have wheels? Do the Yankees play baseball in the Bronx? I sip my whiskey, with sudden judiciousness.

"I would sure think about it," I answer. "I'd have to consider practice. I'd have to figure out the money. But I'd sure think about it."

"We'll see how things turn out, then. Those guys'll owe me something. They'll want me to go out smiling. Party loyalty. All that shit. I should have the swag to look after a few people."

"I appreciate that."

Raymond gives himself another.

"How are things going with my favorite unsolved murder case?"

"Badly," I say. "In general. We know a little more about what seems to have happened. That is, if you can believe the pathologist. Did Mac tell you about Molto?"

"I heard," he says, "I heard. What is this crap?"

"Looks like Dubinsky had it right: Nico's got Tommy out there shadowing our investigation."

"Shadowing," asks Raymond, "or subverting?"

"Probably a little of both. I'd guess, for the most part, Molto's just picking up information. You know, calling up old buddies in the department, getting them to bootleg reports. Maybe they've slowed some of the lab work down, but how would you prove it? I'm still not positive what the hell they're up to. Maybe they really think I'm a clown, and they're trying to solve the murder on their own. You know: come up with the whopper before Election Day."

"Nah," says Raymond, "that's just what they'll say. I blast them between the eyes for fucking around with our investigation and they come back with Molto, acting head of my Homicide Section, saying he was worried we would screw things up. Nah," Raymond says again, "I'll tell you why Nico has Tommy out there digging up information. It's surveillance. Very clever. He watches how we're doing and knows exactly how hard he can hit the issue, with very little risk. Every time he sees us stumble, he can turn the knob a little higher on his volume control."

We talk a moment about Kumagai. We both agree it is unlikely that he changed results. He was just holding back. We could have his assistant assigned to go over his work, but it does not seem to make much difference now. When this poll hits tomorrow, we'll be done commanding loyalty in the police department. Any cop who ever called Nico by his first name will be feeding him information, investing in the future.

"So where does this path stuff leave us?" Raymond wants to know. "Who's our bad guy?"

"Maybe it's a boyfriend, maybe it's a guy she picked up. Seems like it's somebody who knew enough about her to realize what to make it look like, but that could be coincidence. Who knows?" I stare at the moon of light on the surface of my whiskey. "Can I ask a question?"

"I guess." It is the natural moment for me to find out what the hell Raymond was doing with the B file in his desk drawer. No doubt that is what he expects. But there is something else I've wanted to put to him. This is bushwhacking, two drinks along, and enjoying the nicest moment that I've had with Raymond Horgan since the last case we tried together, one of the Night Saints conspiracies, years ago. And I know it is unfair to use the investigator's pose to explore my own obsessions. I know all of that, but I ask anyway.

"Were you fucking Carolyn?"

Raymond laughs, a big beefy laugh, so that all of him shakes, making it seem that he's feeling more whiskey than he is. I recognize a practiced barroom gesture, a way to stall when you're getting loaded and you need time to think: the wrong bimbo who wants to go home with you, an assistant ward committeeman whose name you can't recall, a reporter joshing but trying to get a little too close to the bone. If there was any ice in his glass he'd chew the cubes now, so that there'd be something in his mouth.

"Listen," he says, "I gotta tell you something about your technique as an interrogator, Rusty. You beat around the bush too much. You have to learn to be direct."

We laugh. But I say nothing. If he wants off the hook, he'll have to wriggle.

"Let's say that the decedent and I were both single and both adults," he says finally, looking down into his cup. "That isn't any kind of problem, is it?"

"Not if it doesn't give you any better idea who killed her."

"No," he says, "it wasn't that kind of thing. Who knew that dame's secrets? Frankly, it was short and sweet between us. It's been history, I'd say, four months."

There's a lot of chess here, many poses. But if Carolyn caught Raymond at the quick, he doesn't show it. He seems to have been let down easy. Better than I can say. I look again into my drink. The B file, some of her son's comments, all were hints, but the truth is that I'd guessed at Carolyn's relationship with Raymond a long time ago, just watching the telltale signs, how often she trotted down to the office, the hours the two of them left. Of course, by then I was familiar with the local customs. I'd made my own journey to Carolyn's quaint county—and an abrupt departure. I had watched their doings with my own burning mix of tourist nostalgia, and a yearning far harsher. Now I wonder why I risked the offense of even bothering to hear it all confirmed.

"You knew some of her secrets," I say. "You met the kid."

"That's true. You've talked to him?"

"Last week."

"And he blew Mommy's cover?"

I say yes. I know how much a man in Raymond's shoes wants to believe he was inscrutable.

"An unhappy kid," Raymond observes.

"You know, he told me that she wanted to be P.A."

"I heard that from her. I told her she had to work the vineyards a little. Either you got to have professional standing or political connections. You can't just walk into it." Raymond's tone is casual, but he gives me a penetrating look: I'm not as dumb as you think, he is saying, I can see the forest for the trees. A dozen years of power and flattery have not dulled him that much. I feel, with pleasure, a gust of pride and respect again for Raymond. Good for you, I think.

So that's the way it worked. Four months ago they ended, Raymond said. Well, the arithmetic fits: Raymond announced and Carolyn went her own way. She had figured, like everybody else, that Raymond wasn't running, that he could hand the mantle to anyone he chose. Maybe he could be persuaded to make it a woman—depart with one final gesture in the direction of progress. The only puzzle is why Carolyn's train to glory had stopped first with me. Why tarry with the local when you're ready to hop the express. Unless it was all a little less calculating than it now seems.

"She was one tough cookie, that one," Horgan says. "A good kid, you know. But tough. Tough."

"Yeah," I say, "good and tough and dead."

Raymond stands.

"Can I ask one more?" I ask.

"Now you want to get personal, huh!" Raymond smiles, all Irish charm and teeth. "Let me guess: What the fuck was I doing with that file?"

"Close," I say. "But I understand why you didn't want it floating around. Why'd you give it to her in the first place?"

"Shit," he says, "she asked. You wanna be cynical? She asked *and* I was sleeping with her. I guess she heard about it from Linda Perez." One of the paralegals who read the crank mail. "You know Carolyn. Hot case. I suppose she thought it would be good for her. I considered it bullshit all along. What's the guy's name?"

"Noel?"

"Noel, right. He rainmade this guy." Swindled. Kept the money. "That's my take. Don't you think?"

"I don't know."

"She looked at it, went out, and shoveled through the records in the 32nd District. There was nothing there. That's what she told me."

"I would like to have heard about the case," I say, with the lightning tongue of a quick drunk.

Raymond nods. He drinks more of his whiskey.

"You know how it is, Rusty. You do one dumb thing, you do another dumb thing. She didn't want me to talk about it. Somebody asks why I gave her the case and pretty soon everyone knows she's balling the boss. The boss didn't mind keeping that one to himself, either. You understand. Who'd it hurt?"

"Me," I say, as I have meant to do for many years.

He nods at that one, too.

"I'm sorry, Rusty. I really am. Shit, I'm the sorriest son of a bitch in town." He goes to a sideboard and looks at a picture of his kids. There are five of them. Then he goes to put on his coat. His arms and hands move unevenly; he has a hard time smoothing down the collar. "You know, if I really do lose this fucking election, I'm just gonna quit. Let Nico run the show, he wants to so bad." He stops. "Or maybe you. You wanna do this job for a little while?"

Thanks, Raymond, I think. Thanks a lot. In the end, maybe Carolyn had the right approach.

But I cannot help myself. I get up, too. I turn down Raymond's collar. I shut off the lights and lock his office and point him down the hall in the right direction. I make sure that he will take a cab. The last thing I say to him is "Your shoes are too big to fill." And, of course, old habits being what they are, when the words come out of me, I mean them.

12

Somehow the dizzy, mad hunger I felt for Carolyn showed itself in a revived addiction to rock music.

"This had nothing to do with Carolyn's tastes," I explained to Robinson. Even in the madhouse of the P.A.'s office, she kept a symphonic station on in her office. And it wasn't some kind of adolescent nostalgia. I did not crave the vintage sixties soul and rock, which had sound-tracked my late teens and early twenties. This was New Wave junk: screechy, whiny music with perverse lyrics and rhythms mindless as rain. I began driving to work, telling Barbara I was going through my annual phobic reaction to the bus. The car, of course, made my evening escapes to Carolyn's apartment easier; but those, in any event, could have been arranged. What I wanted was the chance to drive for fifty minutes with the windows cranked tight while Rock Radio, WNOF, screamed from the wagon's speakers, the volume so high that the windshield rattled when the bass line became prominent on certain songs.

"I was messed up, all strung out." When I walked down the street after parking the car, I was half-tumescent because I was starting a day which was, I felt, a tantalizing sweet crawl toward my secret plunder of Carolyn. I sweated all day, my pulse raced. And every hour or so, in the midst of a phone call or a conference, I was visited by visions, so palpable and immediate, of Carolyn in passionate repose, that I would become lost in space and time.

Carolyn, for her part, was chilling in her command. The weekend after our initial night together, I spent hours—dazed, unrooted hours—pondering our next encounter. I had no idea what was to follow. At the door to her apartment, she had kissed my hand and said, simply, See you. For me, there was no thought of resistance. I would take whatever was allowed.

On Monday morning, I appeared at her office door with a file in my hand. My pose, my pace, had already been endlessly planned. Nothing urgent. I leaned against the doorjamb. I smiled, hip and calm. Carolyn was at her desk. The Jupiter Symphony was surging.

About the Nagel case, I say.

The Nagels were another visit to the dark side of suburbia: a husband-and-wife rape-and-sodomy team. She would approach women on the street, assist in the abduction, engage in imaginative uses of a dildo. Carolyn wanted to plead the case out, with the wife taking a lesser charge.

I can live with the plea, I tell her, but I think we need two counts.

Only now does Carolyn look up from her work. Impassive. Her eyes do not quiver. In a mild collegial way she smiles.

Who's got her? I ask, meaning who is her defense lawyer.

Sandy, Carolyn answers, referring to Alejandro Stern, who seems to represent every person of genteel upbringing who is charged with a crime in this state.

Tell Sandy, I say, that she has to plead to an Agg Battery, too. We don't want the judge to think we're trying to tie his hands.

Or the press to think we're pushing probation for female sex violators, says she.

That too, I say. We're equal-opportunity prosecutors.

I smile. She smiles. I linger. I have gotten through this, but my heart is knocking, and I fear that there is something fluttering and insipid in my expression.

Okay, I flap the file against my thigh, I turn.

We should have a drink, she says.

I nod with buttoned-up lips. Gil's? I ask.

How about, she says, the place we ended up on Friday?

Her apartment. My soul expands. She has the barest inkling of a smile, but she has looked back to her work, even before I have departed.

"In reflection, I see myself on that threshold with immense pity. I was so full of hope. So grateful. And I should have known the future from the past."

There was great passion in my love for Carolyn, but seldom joy. From that instant forward, when I realized this would go on, I was like the mandrake in the old poems I read in college, pulled screaming from the earth. I was devastated by my passion. I was shattered. Riven. Decimated. Torn to bits. Every moment was turmoil. What I'd struck upon was old and dark and deep. I had no vision of myself. I was like a blind ghost groping about a castle and moaning for love. The idea of Carolyn, more even than the image, was upon me every moment. I wanted in a way I could not recall—and the desire was insistent, obsessive, and, because of that, somehow debased. Now I think of Pandora, whom as a child I always confused with Peter Pan, opening her box and finding that torrent of miseries unloosed.

"There was something so real in the flesh of another woman," I told the shrink.

After almost twenty years of sleeping with Barbara, I no longer went to bed with only her. I lay down with five thousand other fucks; with the recollection of younger bodies; with the worries for the million things that supported and surrounded our life: the corroding rain gutters, Nat's unwillingness to study mathematics, the way Raymond, over the years, had come to greet my work with an eye to its defects rather than successes, the particular arrogant glint that came into my mother-in-law's eye when she discussed any person outside her immediate family, including me. In our bed, I reached for Barbara through the spectral intervention of all these visitors, all that time.

But Carolyn was pure phenomenon. I was dizzy. I was disoriented. After seventeen years of faithful marriage, of wandering impulse suppressed for the sake of tranquil domestic life, I could not believe that I was here, with fantasy made real. Real. I studied her naked body. The gorgeous large areolas, her long nipples, the sheen of her flesh running from her belly to her thighs. I was lost and high, here in the land beyond restraint, rescued from the diligent, slowly moving circles of my life. Each time I entered her, I felt I divided the world.

"I was with her three or four nights a week. We tended toward a routine. She left the door unlocked for me and the news was on when I arrived." Carolyn was cleaning, drinking, opening her mail. A bottle of white wine, cool and wet like some river-bottom stone, was uncorked on the kitchen table. She never rushed to greet me. Her business, whatever it was, preoccupied her. Usually her comments to me as she traveled between rooms were about the office or local political events. The rumors were thick by then that Raymond would not be running, and Carolyn followed this possibility with great interest. She seemed to gather scuttlebutt from everywhere—the office, the police force, the bar association.

And then, sometime, finally, she would find her way to me. Open her arms. Embrace me. Welcome me. I found her bathing once and made love to her there. I caught her once while she was dressing. But usually we would go through that wandering toward one another, time passing until she was finally ready to lead me to the bedroom, where my hour of worship would begin.

My approach to her was prayerful. Most often, I found myself on my knees. I would unpeel her skirt, her slip, her pants, so that her perfect thighs, that lovely triangle, were exposed as she stood before me; even before I began to push my face in her, that heavy female aroma overpowered the atmosphere. Perfect mad wild moments. On my knees, straining and blind, driving my face inside her, my tongue at work in fevered, silent ululation, while I stretched my hands upward, probing in her garments for her breasts. My passion at those moments was as pure as music.

Then, slowly, Carolyn would take control. She liked it rough, and in time, I would be called upon to slam myself inside her. I stood beside the bed. I dug my hands into her behind and shook her.

"She did not stop speaking."

"Saying what?" Robinson asked.

"You know: Mumbles. Words." 'Good.' 'More.' 'Yes, yes. Oh yes.' 'Oh, hard.' 'Hold on, hold on, hold on, oh, please, baby, yes.'

We were not, I realized later, lovers who fulfilled each other's needs. As time went on, Carolyn's mood with me seemed to become more confrontational. For all her pretense to sophistication, I found that she could border on the gross. She liked to talk dirty. She boasted. She liked to talk about my parts: I'm going to suck your cock, your hard hairy cock. These outbursts would astound me. One time I laughed, but her look revealed such obvious displeasure, almost fury, that I learned to absorb these predatory remarks. I let her have her way. For her, over days, I realized there was a progression. This lovemaking seemed to have for her a destiny, a goal. She was to be given her own dominion. She would roam, take my penis in her mouth, let it go, and slide her hand past my scrotum, probing in that hole. One night she spoke to me. 'Does Barbara do this for you?' Working there. And looking up to ask again, serene, commanding, 'Does Barbara do this for you?' She showed no reluctance, no fear. By now, Carolyn knew there would be no wilting paroxysm of shame from me at the mention of Barbara's name. She knew. She could bring my wife into our bed and make her one more witness to how much I was willing to abandon.

Most nights we ordered out for Chinese food. The same kid always brought it, squint-eyed and looking greedily at Carolyn in her orange silk robe. Then we would lie in bed, passing the cartons back and forth. The TV was on. Always, wherever she was, a TV or a radio was going, a habit, I realized, of her many years alone. In bed, we would gossip. Carolyn was an acute observer of the maelstrom of local politics and its endless crabbed quests for private aggrandizement and power. She viewed it in those terms, but with more excitement than I did and less amusement. She was not as willing as I to disown the quest for personal glory. She viewed it as the natural right of everyone, including her.

While I was seeing Carolyn, Nico was in the initial phases of his campaign. At that point I did not take him seriously. None of us, including Carolyn, gave him any chance to win. Carolyn, however, saw a different potential, which she explained one night not long before our little paradise came to an end. I was telling her my latest analysis of Nico's motives.

He wants a sop, I told Carolyn. He's waiting for Raymond's friends to find something for him. It's not good party politics in Kindle County to begin a primary fight. Look at Horgan. Bolcarro's never let him forget that Raymond ran against him for mayor.

What if Bolcarro wants to get even?

Bolcarro's not the party. Someday he'll be gone. Nico is too much of a sheep to set out on his own.

Carolyn disagreed. She saw, much more clearly than I, how determined Nico was.

Nico thinks Raymond is tired, she said. Or that he can convince him that he should be tired. A lot of people think Raymond shouldn't run again.

Party people? I asked her.

At that point, I had never heard that. Many people had said Raymond wouldn't run, but not that he was unwelcome.

Party people. The mayor's people. Nico hurt him just by announcing. They're saying Raymond should move over.

She reached for another carton, and a breast fetchingly swung free when the sheet fell away.

Does Raymond talk about it? she asked.

Not to me.

If he starts getting the wrong kind of vibes, will he think about it?

I made a face. The truth was that I did not have much idea about what Raymond thought these days. In the time since his divorce, he had grown increasingly insular. Although he had made me his chief deputy, he probably confided in me less.

If he agrees to step aside, said Carolyn, the party would probably let him decide who should be slated. He could bargain for that. They know he's not going to just hand it all to Nico.

That's for sure.

Who would he choose? she asked.

Probably someone from the office. Carry on his traditions.

You? she asked.

Maybe Mac. She'd make a hell of a candidate in her wheelchair.

No way, said Carolyn, elevating moo shu in her chopsticks. Not these days. That chair is not very telegenic. I think he'd pick you. You're the natural.

I shook my head. It was a reflex. Perhaps, at that moment, I even meant it. I was in Carolyn's bed and felt I had already indulged one temptation too many.

Carolyn put the food down. She grasped my arm and looked at me levelly.

Rusty, if you let him know you want it, it'll be you.

I watched her a moment.

You mean you think I should go to Raymond and tell him his

time is up?

You could be tactful, said Carolyn. She was looking at me quite directly.

No way, I said.

Why not?

I'm not gonna bite that hand. If he wants out, he has to make up his own mind. I don't even think if he asked my advice I'd tell him to quit. He's still the strongest candidate around against Della Guardia.

She shook her head.

Without Raymond, Nico doesn't have an issue. You pull the party people and Raymond's people together behind somebody else, that person would walk into the P.A.'s office. It wouldn't be close.

You've really thought about this, I told her.

He needs a push, she said to me.

Push him yourself, I told her. It's not in me.

Carolyn stood up naked from the bed. Standing barefoot, she looked limber and strong. She put on her robe. I realized then she was upset.

Why are you unhappy? I asked. Were you ready to become chief deputy?

She did not answer that.

"The last time I slept with Carolyn she pushed me off her in the midst of our lovemaking and turned away from me."

At first I did not understand what it was she wanted. But she bumped her behind against me until I realized that was what I was being offered, a marble peach.

No, I said.

Try it. She looked over her shoulder. Please.

I came up close behind her.

Just easy, she said. Just a little.

I went in too fast.

Not that much, she said.

She said, Oh.

I pressed in, remained, pumped. She arched, clearly in some pain.

And I found, suddenly, that I was thrilled.

Her head lolled back. Her eyes held tears. Then she opened them and looked back at me directly. Her face was radiant. Does Barbara? she whispered, does Barbara do this for you?

13

In the 32nd District the normal turmoil of a police station is concealed. About seven years ago now, while we were in the midst of our investigation, one of the Night Saints entered the station with a sawed-off in his windbreaker. It was nuzzled against his chest like a baby protected from a chilly breeze, and as a result, he merely had to lower the zipper slightly before placing the muzzle beneath the chin of the unfortunate desk officer, a twenty-eight-year-old guy named Jack Lansing, who had continued writing some report. The young man with the shotgun, who was never identified, is reported to have smiled and then blown off Jack Lansing's face.

Since then, the cops of this station house have dealt with the public from behind six inches of bulletproof glass, carrying on conversations through a radio system which sounds as if the signal must have been bounced first off the moon. There are public areas where the complainants, the victims, the police groupies loiter, but once you pass beyond the four-inch-thick metal door, with its electronic bolt, there is almost sterility. Prisoners are in a block downstairs, and are never permitted, for any purpose, above that level. Upstairs, so much of the usual turbulence has been removed that it feels a little like an insurance agency. The working cops' desks are in an open area that could pass for any other large office, the guys with rank in partitioned areas along the back wall. In one of the larger offices, I find Lionel Kenneally. We have not seen much of each other since the Night Saints cases ended.

"Fucking Savage," he says, "fucking Savage." He puts out his cigarette and claps me on the back.

Lionel Kenneally is everything a sensible person does not like about police. He is tough-talking, opinionated, downright mean, an unabashed racist. I have yet to see the situation in which I'd bet even an hour's wages on his scruples. But I like him, in part because he is a pure form, unalloyed and unapologetic, a coppers' cop, dedicated to the shadowy loyalties and mysteries of life out on the street. He can make out the riffs and scams of the inner city like a dog picking up a scent by lifting his muzzle to the breeze. During the Night Saints investigation, Lionel was the guy I went to when I needed someone found. He never faltered—he'd pull them out of shooting galleries or go into the Grace Street projects at four in the morning, the only hour that a police officer can safely move about there. I saw him at it once or twice, six foot three or thereabouts, pounding on a door so hard you could see it buckle in its frame.

Who that?

Open up, Tyrone. It's your fairy godmother.

We reminisce; he tells me about Maurice Dudley. I have already heard the story, but I do not interrupt. Maurice, a 250-pound brick, a killer, a cur, is deep in Bible studies down at Rudyard. He is going to be ordained. "Harukan"—the Night Saints' leader—is so pissed, they say, he don't even talk to him. Can you imagine?"

"Who said there's no such thing as rehabilitation?" This strikes both of us as unbearably funny. Maybe we're each thinking of the woman on whose arm Maurice, with a kitchen knife, once wrote his name. Or the coppers from this station house who swore, in the inflated lore of cop and courthouse stories, that he had misspelled it.

"Are you passing through or what?" Kenneally asks me finally.

"I'm not really sure," I say. "I'm trying to figure something out."

"On what now? Carolyn?"

I nod.

"What's the story there?" Kenneally asks. "Latest thing I'm hearing from downtown is they're sayin it's not really rape."

I give Lionel two minutes' worth on the state of our evidence.

"So you're figurin what?" he asks. "The guy she's having cocktails with is the one who done her?"

"That seems obvious. But I keep wondering. Didn't we have a

Peeping Tom, maybe ten years ago, who'd watch couples and then go in later and take a piece of the lady himself at gunpoint?"

"Christ," says Kenneally. "You really are lost. You're lookin for a law enforcement type—a cop, a P.A., a private dick—somebody who knew what he wanted to make it look like when he cooled her. That's what I'd figure. She had any boyfriend who was with her that night, and left her alive, you'd have heard from him by now. He'd *want* to help."

"If he doesn't have a wife to explain things to."

Kenneally considers that. I get something like a shrug. I might be right.

"When's the last time you saw her?" I ask.

"Four months or so. She come out here."

"Doing what?"

"Same shit you're doin: investigatin somethin and tryin not to let on what."

I laugh. A coppers' cop. Kenneally gets up. He goes to a pile of transfer cases in the corner.

"She got some rookie to look through all this crap for her, so she didn't chip her nails or run her nylons."

"Let me guess," I say: "booking sheets on cases from nine summers ago."

"Right you are," he says.

"Did she have a name she was looking for?"

Kenneally considers this. "I think she did, and I'll be fucked if I remember. Somethin was wrong with it, too."

"Leon?" I ask.

Lionel snaps his fingers. "La Noo," he says. L-N-U: Last Name Unknown. "That's what was wrong. She was playin in the dark."

"What'd she come up with?"

"Spit."

"You sure?"

"Fuck yes. Not that she'd much notice. She was most of the time tryin to keep track of everybody who was watchin her ass. Which was everybody in the house, as she well knows. She was havin a good time bein back here, let's say."

"Back?"

"She worked the North Branch when she was a P.O. She didn't know what the fuck she was doin then, either. A real social-worker type. I never could figure Horgan hiring her as a P.A."

I had forgotten that. I probably knew it, but I did not remember. Carolyn worked the North Branch as a probation officer. I think about the secretary that Noel's boyfriend mentioned. He didn't say white or black, fat or skinny. But he did say Girl. Would anybody hang "Girl" on Carolyn, even nine years ago?

"You didn't like her much."

"She was a cunt," says Kenneally, to the point. "You know," he says, "out for herself. She was sleepin her way to the top, right from the git-go. Anybody coulda seen that."

I look around a moment. Our conversation seems to have come to an end. I ask one more time if he's sure she did not find anything.

"Not a fuckin thing. You can talk with the kid that helped her if you want."

"If you wouldn't mind, Lionel."

"What the fuck do I care?" He reaches for the intercom and summons a cop named Guerash. "Why you still botherin with this thing?" he asks me, while we wait. "It'll be somebody else's problem pretty soon, don't you think?"

"You mean Delay?"

"I think he's got it in the bag." In the last week, that is all you hear from coppers. They've never pretended to like Raymond.

"You can never tell. Maybe I'll crack this thing and save Raymond's ass."

"God come down from Sinai ain't gonna save him, the way I hear it. Downtown they say Bolcarro's comin out for Nico this afternoon."

I chew on that one. If Bolcarro endorses Nico six days before the election, then Raymond will be no more than a political memory.

Guerash enters. He looks like half the young men on the force, handsome in an old-fashioned way, with an erect bearing and a military order to his person. His shoes are spit-shined and the buttons on his jersey gleam. His hair is cleanly parted.

Kenneally addresses him.

"You remember this lady P.A. was out here—Polhemus?"

"Nice set of lungs," says Guerash.

Kenneally turns to me. "See, this kid's gonna make a copper. Never forgets a bra size."

"She the one that got it over by the riverside?" Guerash asks me.

I tell him she is. Kenneally continues with Guerash.

"Okay, Rusty here is the chief deputy P.A. He wants to know if she took anything when she come out here?"

"Not that I know of," says Guerash.

"What'd she look at?" I ask.

"She had one day where she wanted to see the bookings. She told me there'd be like sixty, seventy people booked on public indecency. We're talking back forever, eight, nine years ago, or something. Anyway, I hauled up the boxes, right here."

"How'd she come up with one day?"

"Beats me. She seemed to know what she was looking for. She just told me look for the day when there were the most arrests. So that's what I did. I mean, it must have took me a week to go through that crap. There were like five hundred arrests for 42's." A 42 is a public-indecency violation.

One day. I think again about the letter. There was nothing in the file I saw that narrowed the time frame like that. Maybe Carolyn gave up before she started, figured she'd just do a sample.

"Did you find what she wanted?"

"I thought so. I called her back and she came out to see it. I left her with the stuff right here. She told me she didn't find nothin."

"Do you remember anything about what you showed her? Anything common about the arrests?"

"All in the Public Forest. All guys. I thought it was probably some demonstration or something. I don't know."

"Jesus," says Kenneally to Guerash in disgust. "For public indecency? This is the faggots, isn't it?" he asks me. "Back when Raymond got some balls for about a day and a half."

"Did she tell you anything about what she was looking for? A name? Anything?"

"She didn't even have a last name. Just a first. I wasn't real clear on whether she knew this guy or what." Guerash pauses. "Why do I think it had something to do with Christmas?"

"Noel? She gave you that name?"

Guerash snaps his fingers. "That's it."

"Not Leon?"

"No way. Noel. She told me she's looking for Noel LNU. I remember that because she wrote it down for me, and the Christmas thing went through my head."

"Can you show me what she saw?"

"Boy, I don't know. I think I put it away."

"Fat fuckin chance of that," says Kenneally. "I fuckin asked you three times. Here, help yourself."

He points us to the transfer cases in the corner.

When Guerash opens the first case he swears. He picks up a clutch of loose sheets lying on the top of the file folders.

"She wasn't real neat, I'll say that. These records were in nice order when I gave them to her." I would ask Guerash if he's sure, but there's no point. It's the kind of thing he would remember, and I can see the orderly ranks of the remaining records. Besides, that would be like Carolyn, to take records that other people have spent years maintaining and treat them like debris.

Guerash out of instinct begins to sort the booking sheets and bond slips, and I help. Kenneally pitches in, too. We stand around his desk, cursing Carolyn. Each booking jacket should contain a police report, an arrest card bearing the defendant's photo and fingerprints, a complaint, and a bond slip, but none of these sixty or seventy files is complete. Papers are missing from each and the sheets inside have been turned back to front, and at angles. The numerical order is gone.

Kenneally keeps saying cunt.

We are about five minutes along before the obvious strikes me—this disorder is not accidental. These papers have been shuffled.

"Who the hell has been at these boxes since Carolyn?" I ask Kenneally.

"Nobody. They been sittin in the corner for four months, waitin for fuckhead here to put em back. Nobody but him and me even know they're here. Right?" he asks Guerash. Guerash agrees.

"Lionel," I ask, "do you know Tommy Molto?"

"Fuck yes, I know Tommy Molto. About half my life. Little fuck was a P.A. out here."

I knew that, if I had thought about it. Molto was notorious for his battles with the North Branch judges.

"Was he out here at the same time Carolyn was with

probation?"

"Probably. Lemme think. Shit, Rusty, I don't keep a duty roster on these guys."

"When was the last time you saw him?"

Lionel ponders. "Three, four years. Maybe I run into him at a dinner or something. You know, he's all right. I see him, I talk. You know me."

"But he hasn't been looking at these records?"

"Hey," says Lionel, "watch my lips. You. Me. Guerash. Her. That's it."

When we are done sorting, Guerash goes through the files twice.

"One's missing, right?" I ask.

"We're missing a number," he says. "Could have been a mistake."

"You book sixty faggots, you don't exactly worry about keeping a perfect count," says Kenneally.

I ask Lionel, "But it could be that the file is gone?"

"That too."

"There would still be a court file, wouldn't there?" I ask. Kenneally looks at Guerash. Guerash looks at me. I write down the number. It should be on microfilm. Lipranzer will love doing this.

When Guerash is gone, I spend one more moment with Kenneally.

"You don't want to say what this is about maybe?" he asks. "I can't, Lionel."

He nods. But I can tell it grates.

"Oh yeah," says Lionel, "those were funny old days around here. Lots of stories." His look lingers casually, just so I know that we both have our secrets.

Outside, there is real heat, 80 degrees. Pushing a record for April. In the car, I turn the radio to the news station. It's a live feed from the mayor's office. I just catch the tail end, but I hear enough of His Honor's blarney to get the drift. The P.A.'s office needs new blood, a new direction. The people want that. The people deserve that.

I am going to have to start looking for work.

14

Tee ball. In the waning light of the spring evening, play commences in the second-grade Fathers/Students League. The sky hangs low across the open field, a meadow of landfill laid over what was once a marsh, while Mrs. Strongmeyer's Stingers idly occupy the diamond, boys and girls sporting windbreakers zipped to the collars and baseball gloves. Dads creep along the baselines calling instructions as the dusk gathers in. At the plate, a behemoth of an eight-year-old named Rocky circles his bat two or three times in the vicinity of the rag ball perched atop the long-necked rubber tee. Then, with an astounding concentration of power, he smashes the ball into outer space. It lands in left center, beyond the perimeter of the Stingers' shaky defense.

"Nathaniel!" I yell, along with many others. "Nat!" Only now he wakes. He reaches the ball a step ahead of an agile sprite named Molly, whose ponytail flows behind her baseball cap. Nat grabs it, whirls, and wings it in a single motion. The ball travels in a tremendous arc back toward the infield and lands with a dead thump between shortstop and third, just as Rocky lopes across the plate. Following the local etiquette, I alone may scold my son, and so I stroll along the foul line, clapping my hands. "Wake up! Wake up out there." For Nat, I hold no fear. He shrugs, throws up his gloved hand, and displays the full range of his gaptoothed jack-o'-lantern smile, his new ragged-edged teeth still looking a little like candles stuck into a cake.

"Dad, I just lost it," he yells, "I really did." The pack of fathers on the side join me in sudden laughter. We all repeat the remark among ourselves. He lost it. Cliff Nudelman pats me on the back. At least the boy has learned the lingo.

Did other men, as boys, dream about their sons? I looked twenty years ahead with passion and with hope. As I always saw him, my son was a gentle, obedient soul. He was good; he was full of virtue and skill.

Nat is not like that. He is not a bad boy. That's a song around our house. Barbara and I have been telling each other that since he was two. Nat is not, we say, actually, we say, a bad boy. And I believe that. Fervently. And with a heart engorged with love. He is sensitive. He is kind. And he is wild and distracted. He has been on his own schedule since the time of his birth. When I read to him, he flips the pages in my hand to see what lies just ahead. He does not listen, or at least does not seem to care to. In school, he has always been a problem.

He is saved by his insouciant charm and his physical gifts. My son is beautiful. I am talking about more than the usual child-beauty, the soft features, the floral glow of being new. This boy has dark, acute eyes, a prepossessing look. These fine, regular features do not come from me. I am larger and squat, I have a bulky nose; a kind of Neanderthal ridge over the eyes. Barbara's people are all smaller and good-looking, and it is to them we routinely give the credit. Privately, however, I have often thought at moments, with discomfort, about my father and his piercing, somber, Slavic handsomeness. Perhaps because I suspect that source, I pray all the time, at my own inner altar, that this blessing should not lead Nat astray, into arrogance, or even cruelty—traits the beautiful people I have encountered have sometimes seemed to regard in themselves as natural afflictions, or worse, a sign of right.

With the end of the ball game, we disperse in pairs toward the herd of station wagons corraled in the gravel parking lot. In May, when the time changes and the weather mellows, the team will stay after the games to picnic. Sometimes a pizza delivery will be arranged. The fathers will rotate the weekly responsibility of bringing beer. After dinner, the boys and girls will renew their baseball game, and the dads will recline in the grass, talking casually about our lives. I look forward to these outings. Amid this group of men I do not know well, there seems a gentle compact, something like the way worshippers must feel about one another as they leave church. Fathers with their kids, beyond the weekly preoccupations of professional life, or even the pleasures and responsibilities of marriage. Fathers mildly lit on Friday nights, at ease with these immeasurable obligations.

In this cooler, darker season, I have promised Barbara that we will meet for a quick dinner at a local pancake house. She is waiting on the red vinyl bench when we arrive, and even while she is kissing Nat and receiving a report on the Stingers' near-triumph, she gazes beyond him to greet me with a look of cold reproof. We are in the midst of a dismal period. Barbara's fury with me for my role in the investigation of Carolyn's murder has not abated, and tonight I perceive at once that there is some new edge to her displeasure. My first thought is that we must be very late, but when I check the restaurant clock I find we are even a minute early. I can only guess at what I have done to provoke her.

For Barbara, though, it has become so easy over the years to disappear into the black forests of her moods. The elements of the outside world that might have once detained her by now have been relegated to the past. Six years of teaching in the North End struck at her faith in social reform. When Nat was born, she gave up being other-seeking. Suburban life, with its tight boundaries and peculiar values, has quieted her and exaggerated her willingness to be alone. Her father's death, three years ago, was taken as an act of desertion, part of his lifelong pattern of ignoring Barbara's and her mother's needs, and whetted her sense of deprivation. And our soulless moments of marital disconnection have robbed her of the outright gaiety that once counterpointed these darker spells. During these periods, her disappointments with virtually everyone are often worn so openly that at instants I believe the taste would be bitter if I were to grasp her hand and lick her skin.

And then the weather breaks. In the past it always has. Although this disruption, caused by my infidelity, is naturally the most prolonged one of our married life, I still maintain some expectation of improvement. Even now Barbara does not speak of lawyers and divorce, as she did in late November. She is here. Set out so plainly, this fact inspires some calm. I am like a shipwrecked survivor holding fast to the debris, awaiting the arrival of the scheduled liner. Sooner or later, I believe, I will see a woman of good humor, of blazing intelligence, full of quirky insight and sly wit, who is keenly interested in me. That is the person I still think of as my wife.

Now that same woman wears a look of diamond hardness as we wait in line to be seated. Nat has slipped away and gazes adoringly into the candy counter. His baseball pants have drooped almost to his shoe tops, and he stands with one knee and both hands against the glass case, staring with fixed appreciation at the forbidden rows of sugared gum and chocolate bars. He jiggles a bit, of course—the object in motion. As ever, Barbara and I both watch him.

"So?" she suddenly asks me. This is a challenge. I am supposed to entertain her.

" 'So' what?"

"So how's work? The big investigation still going gangbusters?"

"No leads," I tell her, "and no results. It's mass confusion. Frankly, the whole place is sagging. It's like they let the air out of a balloon. You know—now that Bolcarro has come out for Delay."

With the mention of this event, Barbara winces, then once more turns an acid eye on me. At last, I recognize my latest outrage. Yesterday I came home very late and stayed downstairs, thinking she was asleep. Barbara descended in her nightgown. From the staircase she asked what I was doing. When I told her I was working on my résumé, she turned directly and went back up.

"Raymond didn't mention making you a judge today?" she asks.

I wince myself, lanced with regret at the foolish vanity that led me to mention this prospect. My chances now are dim. Bolcarro showed two days ago how concerned he is about making Raymond Horgan happy.

"What do you want me to do, Barbara?"

"I don't want you to do anything, Rusty. I've stopped wanting you to do anything. Isn't that what you prefer?"

"Barbara, he did a good job."

"And what did he do for you? You're thirty-nine years old. You have a family. And now you're looking forward to unemployment compensation. He let you carry his bags and solve his problems, and when he should have quit, he took you with him down the drain."

"We did good things."

"He used you. People have always used you. And you don't just let them do it. You like it. You actually like it. You'd rather be abused than pay attention to the people who have tried to care about you."

"Is that supposed to mean you?"

"Me. Your mother. Nat. It's a lifelong pattern. It's hopeless."

Not Nat, I nearly answer, but a sense of diplomacy or self-preservation intervenes. The restaurant hostess, a tiny younger woman with the trimmed-up figure of the health-club set, leads us to our table. Barbara negotiates his meal with Nat. French fries yes, but milk, not Coke. And he must eat some salad. Nat whines and flops around. I cuff him gently and recommend sitting up straight. Barbara remains aloof behind the barrier of her menu.

Was she happier when I met her? That must have been the case, although I have no clear recollection. She tutored me when I connived—insanely—to beat the university science require-ment by taking calculus. She never got the chance to collect her fee. She fell for me; I fell for her. I loved her ferocious intellect, her teen-queen beauty, her suburban clothes, the fact that she was a doctor's daughter, and thus, I thought, someone 'normal.' I even loved the rocky currents of her personality, her ability to express so many things which, to me, remained remote. Most of all, I loved her omnivorous passion for me. No one in my life had been so openly desirous of my company, so alight with manifest appreciation of every angle of my being. I met half a dozen men who coveted Barbara. She wanted only me, pursued me, in fact, with an ardor that I at first found embarrassing. I supposed it was the spirit of the era that made her want to soothe this awkward boy, dark and full of secret woe, whom she knew her parents would regard as less than she deserved.

Like me, like Nat, she was an only child, and she felt oppressed by her upbringing. Her parents' attentions had been suffocating and, she felt, in some ways false. She claimed to have been directed, used at all times as an instrument of their wishes, not her own. She told me often that I was the only person she had met who was like her—not just lonely, but always, previously, alone. Is it the sad reciprocity of love that you always want what you think you are giving? Barbara hoped I would be like some fairy-tale prince, a toad she had transformed with her caresses, who could enter the gloomy woods where she was held captive and lead her away from the encircling demons. Over the years I have so often failed in that assignment.

The atomized life of the restaurant spins on about us. At separate tables, couples talk; the late-shift workers dine alone; the waitresses pour coffee. And here sits Rusty Sabich, thirty-nine years old, full of lifelong burdens and workaday fatigue. I tell my son to drink his milk. I nibble at my burger. Three feet away is the woman whom I have said I've loved for nearly twenty years, making her best efforts to ignore me. I understand that at moments she feels disappointed. I understand at times she is bereft. I understand. I understand. That is my gift. But I have no ability to do anything about it. It is not simply the routines of adult life which sap my strength. In me, some human commodity is lacking. And we can only be who we can be. I have my own history; memories; the unsolved maze of my own self, where I am so often lost. I hear Barbara's inner clamor; I understand her need. But I can answer only with stillness and lament. Too much of me—too much!—must be preserved for the monumental task of being Rusty.

15

Election Day the weather is bright. Last night, when I sat in Raymond's office, with Mike Duke and Larren and Horgan, they thought that good weather would help. Now that the party belongs to Della Guardia, Raymond needs the voters who are inspired by their candidate rather than the precinct captain's wishes. The last week has been an odd lesson. Every time there's a negative development, you say it's hopeless. Then you look ahead. In Raymond's office last night, they were still talking about winning. The last poll, sponsored again by the paper and Channel 3, was taken the day of Bolcarro's endorsement and showed Raymond only five points back. Duke said that he believes things have improved since then, that Raymond seems to have gained some of his old momentum by being the underdog. We sat there, four grown men, acting as if it could be true.

At work, as ever, Election Day brings a loose feeling, all at ends. The employees of the prosecuting attorney's office, once a group of wardheelers and hacks, have been discouraged throughout Raymond's tenure from active political involvement. Gone are the days of deputies selling tickets in the courtrooms to the P.A.'s campaign outings; in twelve years, Raymond Horgan has never solicited a dime in donations, or even a minute of campaign help, from the members of his staff. Nonetheless, many of the administrative employees who came on before Raymond was elected have continuing political obligations to the party sponsors who secured employment for them. As part of the uneasy compact struck a decade ago with Bolcarro, Raymond agreed to give most of the P.A.'s staff Election Day off.

That way the party types can do the party thing: knock on doors, distribute leaflets, drive the elderly, watch the polls. This year they will be doing that for Nico Della Guardia.

For the rest of us, there are no established obligations. I am in the office most of the day, first mate at the helm of this sinking ship. A few others are around, mostly lawyers working on briefs or trials, or clearing up their desks. About two dozen younger deputies have been delegated to work with the U.S. Attorney's office on a vote-fraud patrol. This generally involves responding to junk complaints: a voting machine won't work; someone's got a gun in the polling place; an election judge is wearing a campaign button, or overcounseling elderly voters. I receive occasional updates by phone and answer press calls in which I dutifully report that there is no sign of tampering with the democratic process.

Around 4:30, I get a call from Lipranzer. Somebody's propped up a TV set in the hallway, right outside my door, but there is nothing to report. The polls won't close for another hour and a half. The early news is just happy-talk stuff about the heavy turnout.

"He lost," Lip tells me. "My guy at Channel 3 saw their exit polls. He says Nico's gonna win by eight, ten points, if the pattern holds."

Again my heart plunges, my gut constricts. Funny, but this time I really believe it. I look out the window toward the columns of the courthouse, the flat tarred roofs of the other downtown buildings, the rippled black waters of the river, which turns, like an elbow, two blocks away. My office has been on the same side of this building for almost seven years now, yet the sight does not quite seem familiar.

"All right," I finally announce solemnly. "What else?"

"Nothing," Lip says. "Just thought I'd let you know." He waits. "We still workin on Polhemus?"

"You have something better to do?"

"No," he says, "no. They come down here today to get all my reports. For Morano." The police chief. "He wants to look em over."

"So?"

"Struck me strange. You know. His mother-in-law got stuck up at gunpoint three years ago, I don't think he looked at the reports."

"You'd understand that," I say, "if you had a mother-in-law." Lip takes my humor as intended: an offering, an apology for my impatience a moment before. "They're just trying to make sure Nico's briefed. Which is a joke," I say. "Molto's probably been getting copies of the police reports from the steno pool."

"Probably. I don't know. Somethin didn't sit right. Schmidt come in here himself. Real serious. You know. Like someone shot the President."

"They just want to look good."

"I guess. I'm goin over to the North Branch courthouse to finish up on those court files," Lip says, referring to the records we have been looking for since my visit to the 32nd District. "They promised they'd have the microfilm from the warehouse before five. I want to get there before they send it back. Where are you tonight in case I come up with somethin?"

I tell him I'll be around Raymond's party, somewhere in the hotel. It's beside the point by now to rush back with investigative results, but Lip says he'll be stopping in anyway, more or less to pay his respects.

"The Irish," Lip says, "always run a real fine wake."

Lipranzer's estimate proves accurate. The band plays loud. The young girls who are always here are still full of that soft glow of eventfulness, with banners across their chests and campaign boaters balanced neatly on their hairdos. HORGAN! everything says in limegreen Gaelic script. In the front, at either side of the unoccupied speakers' platform, two ten-foot enlargements of The Picture stand. I drift around the ballroom, spearing meatballs and feeling bad.

Around 7:30, I go up to Raymond's suite on the fifth floor. Various people from the campaign are moving through the rooms. There are three trays of cold cuts and some liquor bottles on one of the dressers, but I decline the invitation to consume. There must be ten phones in these three rooms, all of them ringing.

All three local TV stations have projected Della Guardia the winner by now. Larren—Judge Lyttle—comes by with a tumbler of bourbon in his hand, grumbling about the exit polls.

"First time," he says, "I've seen a body pronounced dead before it hit the floor."

Raymond, however, is sanguine. He is seated in one of the interior bedrooms, watching television and talking on the phone. When he sees me he puts the phone down and comes to hug me. "Rožat," he says, my given name. I know that this gesture has probably been repeated with a dozen other people this evening, but I find myself deeply grateful and stirred to be included in the grieving family.

I sit by Raymond on the footstool of the easy chair he is occupying. An open bottle of Jack Daniel's is on the candle table at the chair side, as well as a half-eaten sandwich. Raymond goes on taking phone calls, conferring with Larren and Mike and Joe Reilly. I do not move. I recall the nights I used to sit beside my father while he watched a ball game on TV or listened to the radio. I always asked his permission before taking a place next to him on the divan. They were the warmest moments that we had. As I became older, my father would drink his beer and occasionally pass the bottle to me. At moments he would even make a remark aloud about the game.

Eventually the conversation begins to turn to the protocol of concession. Does Raymond communicate with Della Guardia first, or does he go downstairs to address the faithful? Della Guardia, they decide. Mike says Raymond should call him. Joe says send a telegram.

"Screw that," Raymond says, "the man's across the street. I'm going over there to shake his hand." He asks Larren to make arrangements. He'll see Nico, make his speech, then come back up here to do one-on-one interviews with print and media reporters. No point in spite with them. He tells Mac she should start scheduling those meetings about 9:30. He'll go live at 10:00 with Rosenberg. I have not noticed Mac until now, and when she turns her chair around she says one word to me: "Sad."

Raymond asks to see me alone. We go into a dressing room, between the two bedrooms in the suite, nothing more than a large closet with a lavatory.

"How are you?" I ask.

"There've been things that hurt worse. Tomorrow will be bad. The day after. We'll survive. Listen," Raymond says. "About what I mentioned the other night: when I see Nico, I'm going to offer to resign. I don't want any lame-duck crap. I don't want to appear to be playing around with the office. I'd like to make a clean break. If Nico wants to run in the general election as an incumbent, let him. I'll tell him he's free to assume office, if the county executive approves." This is humor. Bolcarro is the county executive. Party chairman. Mayor. The guy has more titles than the leader of a banana republic.

I tell Raymond he's made a wise decision. We look at each other.

"I feel like I should apologize to you, Rusty," Raymond says. "If there was any deputy I would have wanted to take over, you know it would be you. I should have tried to make that happen, instead of running. The guys just pushed me so damn hard to give it one more shot."

I wave my hand, I shake my head. I prohibit his apology. Larren sticks his head in.

"I was just telling Rusty," Raymond tells him, "I never should have run again, I should have given him the shot. New face. Career prosecutor. Apolitical. Really could have revved things up. Wouldn't you say?"

"Shit," says the judge, "pretty soon you'll have me believing it."

We all laugh.

Larren reports on his conversation with Della Guardia's people. He talked to Tommy Molto, who has emerged tonight as the primary aide-de-camp. They'd rather not have a face-to-face this evening. Instead, Molto and Nico want to see Raymond in the morning.

"Ten o'clock," says Larren. "He told me, didn't ask. And says, Please make sure it's with Raymond alone. How do you like that? Bossy little shit." Larren takes a private moment with his discontent. "I said you'd call Nico to make a formal concession. When you're ready."

Raymond takes Larren's bourbon from him and has a belt.

"I am ready," he says.

Loyalty goes only so far. I do not want to listen. I head back to the ballroom.

Near the bar, I run into George Mason, an old friend of Raymond's. He is already drunk. We both are being jostled.

"Pretty good crowd," he tells me.

Only near the bar, I think. But I save the thought.

"He had a good run," George says. "He did a good job. You guys should all be proud."

"We are," I say. "I am."

"So what's with you? Private practice?"

"For a while, I guess."

"Gonna do criminal stuff?"

How many times have I had this conversation tonight? I tell George probably, I'll see, who can tell. I'm going to go on a vacation, that's for sure. George gives me his card and tells me to call. He may know some people I might want to talk to.

Horgan arrives in the ballroom twenty minutes later. The assholes from TV shove their way to the front, hold up their cameras and lights and boom mikes so that you cannot see much. Raymond is smiling and waving. Two of his daughters are with him on the platform. The band is playing an Irish jig. Raymond has said "Thank you" for the third time, about halfway along to quieting the crowd, when somebody grabs my arm. Lipranzer. He looks harried from having had to push his way through to reach me. There is too much noise in here to speak: stamping, hooting, whistling. Some folks in the back have even started to dance. Lipranzer motions me outside and I follow him beneath an exit sign. We end up, unexpectedly, in an alley outside the hotel, and Lip walks down toward a street lamp. When I see him now, I can tell that something's wrong. He looks almost caved-in, compressed by some kind of worry. The sweat shines near his temple. From here, I can hear Raymond's voice inside but not what he's saying.

"This is too strange," Lip says. "Something's fucked-up over in the Hall. It's way wrong."

"Why?"

"I don't know," he says. "But I'm gettin vibes like I haven't had in years. I got a message I'm supposed to be in Morano's office, 8:00 tomorrow morning to be interviewed. By Molto. That's the message. Not talk. Not discuss. Interview. Like they're after me. And here's another one. When I come back in tonight they tell me that Schmidt took all the receipts for the evidence I've inventoried on Polhemus. Any questions, see him."

"Sounds to me like you're off this case."

"Sure," he says. "Fine. But figure this in. I'm out in the North

Branch before 5:00. All of this hits by 6:00, 6:30. And look at what I picked up out there."

He reaches inside his windbreaker to his shirt pocket. He has four or five sheets of foolscap, xeroxes, I see, of court documents. The case number I recognize: it matches the complaint number missing from the 32nd District. The first sheet is a copy of the case jacket. *People versus Leon Wells*. A public-indecency complaint. Dismissed by court order a day in July nine years ago.

"Bingo," I say out loud.

"This page," Lip tells me. It is the bond order. In our state, a defendant is permitted to satisfy bail in minor cases merely with his signature on a promissory note, promising to pay a sum—by law less than $5,000—in the event of his default. The only conditions are that he refrain from other crimes and report once weekly by phone to a member of the court's probation department. Leon's assigned probation officer according to his bond slip was Carolyn Polhemus. Her name and telephone number are right there.

"Wait. Here's the best." He pulls the last sheet out. It is a copy of the court half-sheet, a form dismissing the case. Motion to Dismiss Without Prejudice, it is captioned. The attorney presenting the motion is the prosecutor. "Raymond Horgan, Kindle County Prosecuting Attorney, By" is printed at the bottom of the form. The deputy handling the case is supposed to sign the blank. I cannot read the signature at first. Then I get it.

"Molto?"

Lipranzer and I stand a moment in the street lamps, looking at the papers again. Neither one of us says much. From inside there's an enormous roar; then you can hear the band striking up again, "When Irish Eyes Are Smiling." Raymond, I take it, has admitted defeat.

I try to pacify Lipranzer. Hang tight, I tell him. We're not sure of anything.

"You take this." He gives me the copies from the court file.

I move back toward the ballroom. Lip heads off alone, past the dumpsters and debris, into the darkness of the alley.

16

"So we ended," I told Robinson, "and we ended badly. One week she saw me less. The next week not at all. No lunches, no calls, no visits to my office. No 'drinks,' as we so quaintly put it. She was gone."

I knew she valued independence. And at first I tried to stanch my panic by telling myself it was only that: a show of freedom. Best not to resist. But each day the silence worked on me—and my pathetic longing. I knew she was only one floor down. I wanted nothing so much as simply to be in the same room. I went three days running to Morton's Third Floor, where I knew she liked to go for lunch. On the third day, she appeared—with Raymond. I thought nothing of that. I was blind then. I did not imagine rivals. I sat for half an hour, by myself, shifting lettuce leaves across my salad bowl and gazing at a table two hundred feet away. Her coloring! Her hair! When the feel of her skin came over me, I sat alone in a public dining room and groaned.

By the third week, I had passed the edge. I did not have to gather strength; I merely let myself go to impulse. I walked directly to her office, eleven o'clock one morning. I did not bring a file, a memo, any item for excuse.

She was not in.

I stood there on her threshold with my eyes closed, burning in humiliation and sadness, feeling I would die from being thwarted.

While I stood there, in that pose, she returned.

Rusty, she said brightly. A chipper greeting. She pushed past me. I watched her bend to pull a file from her drawer. A parched arrow of sensation ran through me, at the way her tweed skirt pulled across her bottom, the smoothness of her calves flexing in her hose. She was busy. She stood over her desk, reading the notations on the jacket, tapping a pencil on a pad.

I'd like to see you again, I said.

She looked up. Her face was solemn. She stepped around her desk and reached past me with one hand to close the door.

She spoke immediately.

I don't think that's a very good idea. Not now. It's not right for me now, Rusty. Then she opened up the door.

She went back behind her desk. She worked. She turned to flip on the radio. She did not glance toward the place where I remained another moment.

I do not think I believed at any time that Carolyn Polhemus loved me. I thought only that I pleased her. My passion, my obsession flattered and enlarged her. And so I did not suffer rejection; I was not ravaged by grief. When it finally occurred to me that I might have a successor, I did not have fantasies of his destruction. I would have agreed to share. I was devastated by denial, by longing. I wanted, simply, what it was I'd had. I craved Carolyn and my release in her in a way that did not end.

For me it never ended. There was nothing to make it end. Her willingness had always been only secondary, convenient. I wanted my passion, in its great exultant moments, the burning achievement of my worship, of my thrall. To be without it was to be in some way dead. I longed. I longed! I sat up nights in my rocking chair, imagining Carolyn, overcome by pity for myself.

In those weeks, my life seemed to have exploded. My sense of proportion left me; my judgment took on the grotesque exaggerations of a cruel cartoon. A fourteen-year-old girl was abducted, stored like merchandise in the defendant's trunk, sodomized in one manner or another every hour or two for three days, and then was beaten by him, blinded (so she could make no identification), and left for dead. I read reports about this case, attended meetings where the evidence was discussed. To myself I thought, I hurt for Carolyn.

At home I made my absurd confession to Barbara, weeping at the dinner table, crying in my highball. Do I have the guts to say it? I wanted her sympathy. That mad egoistic instant naturally went to make my suffering worse. Barbara would not endure the sight of me in any visible pain. Now there was no place left. At

work, I did nothing. I watched the hallways for some glimpse of
Carolyn passing by. At home, my wife was now my warden,
daring me, with the threat of the imminent end of family life, to
wear any sign of any neediness. I took to walks. December
turned to January. The temperature sunk near zero and stayed
that way for weeks. I trudged hours through our little town, with
my scarf across my face, the fur trimming of my parka burning
when it touched the exposed portion of my forehead and my
cheeks. My own tundra. My Siberia. When would it end? I wanted
simply to have—or if not to have, to find some peace.

Carolyn avoided me. She was as artful at that as at so many
other things. She sent me memos, left Eugenia phone messages.
She did not go to meetings I was scheduled to attend. I'm sure I
drove her to it, that in the moments when we caught sight of
each other, she could see my pathetic, hungering expression.

In March, I called her from home. It happened a few times. She
had drafted an indictment in a recidivist case, complex charges
with allegations going back to the 1960s. I told myself it would be
easier to discuss involved legal problems without the interruptions of the office. I waited until Nat was asleep and Barbara was
stowed in the closed womb of her study, from where I knew she
could never hear me calling downstairs. Then I paged to
Carolyn's listing in the little mimeographed directory Mac put
out, containing all the deputies' home phones. I hardly needed to
look to recall the number, but I suppose that in those moments
of compulsion I took some strange satisfaction from seeing her
name in print. It prolonged, in a way, the communication; it
meant my fantasy was real. As soon as I heard Carolyn's voice, I
knew how false my excuses had been. I could not bring myself to
utter a sound. "Hello? Hello?" I melted when I heard her speak in
a tone without reproach. Who was it she was awaiting now?

Each time I did it, I was sure that pride would bear my saying a
word or two. I intricately plotted the conversations beforehand.
Humorous cracks to dislodge her from indifference or chagrin.
Sincere declarations for the instant when I was given half a
chance. I could not make any of it take place. She answered, and
I waited in a fiery pit of shame. Tears came to my eyes. My heart
felt squeezed. "Hello? Hello?" I was relieved when she slammed
down the phone, when I quickly tucked the office directory into
the hallway bureau.

She knew, of course, that it was me. There was probably, something forlorn and beseeching in my breathing. One Friday night, late in March, I sat in Gil's, finishing a drink I had started with Lipranzer before he headed home. I saw her staring at me in the long beveled mirror behind the bar. Her face was there above the whiskey bottles; her hair was newly done, shining and stiff beneath the spray. The anger in her look was cruel.

Pretense was so much easier. I moved my glance from hers and told the bartender to give her an Old-Fashioned. She said no, but he did not hear her, and she waited until he brought the drink. She was standing. I was sitting. The burly Friday-evening tumult of Gil's went on around us. The juke was screaming and the laughter was wild. The atmosphere had the beefy smell of Fridays, the musk of sexuality unlimbering from the week's restraint. I finished my beer, and finally, thank God, found the strength to speak.

I'm like a kid, I told her. I was talking without looking her way. I'm so uncomfortable right now, just sitting here, I want to walk away. And most of the time, the only thing I think I want in life is to talk to you.

I looked up to see how she was taking this and found her expression largely abstracted.

That's what I've been doing for months now, walking past you. That's not cool, is it?

It's safe, she said.

It's not cool, I repeated. But I'm inexperienced. I mean, I want to have this war-weary, so-what thing about it all, but I'm not making it, Carolyn. I got engaged when I was twenty-two years old. And right before the wedding I did my time in the Reserves, and I got drunk and screwed some woman in a station wagon behind a bar. That's it, I said, that's the history of my infidelities, my life of wild amours. I'm dying, I said. Right this minute. Sitting on this fucking bar stool, I am just about dead. You like that? I'm shaking. My heart is hammering. In a minute, I'll need air. That's not very cool, is it?

And what do you want from me, Rusty? It was her turn now, looking dead into the mirror.

Something, I said.

Advice?

If that's all I can get.

She put her drink down on the bar. She put her hand down on my shoulder. She looked straight at me for the first time.

Grow up, she said, and walked away.

"And for a minute then," I said to Robinson, "I felt the most desperate wish that she were dead."

17

Around the office, Tommy Molto was nicknamed the Mad Monk. He is a former seminarian; five foot six inches if he is lucky, forty or fifty pounds overweight, badly pockmarked, nails bitten to the quick. A driven personality. The kind to stay up all night working on a brief, to go three months without taking off a weekend. A capable attorney, but he is burdened by a zealot's poverty of judgment. As a prosecutor, he always seemed to me to be trying to make facts rather than to understand them. He burns at too high a temperature to be worth much before a jury, but he made a good assistant to Nico—he has qualities of discipline that Della Guardia lacks. He and Delay go all the way back to grade school at St. Joe's. Dago society. Molto's one of the guys who were included before they were old enough to worry about who was cool. Tommy's personal life is a cipher. He is single and I've never seen him with a woman, which inspires the usual conjecture, but if I were to guess, I'd imagine he's still celibate. That singular intensity seems to have a subterranean source.

Tommy, as usual, is whispering to Nico hotly when I come through the reception room. There's been a lot of rubbernecking in the office, file clerks and secretaries rushing to the reception-ist's window to see what the new boss looks like. As if they could have forgotten in nine months. The TV crews followed Nico up here and did their takes of Nico and Tommy sitting in hard wooden chairs, waiting to meet with Horgan, but that is over now. The reporters have dispersed, and the two of them actually look somewhat forlorn when I come by. Nico does not even have his flower. I cannot resist giving it to Molto.

"Tommy Molto," I say. "We once had a guy of that name who

worked here, but we think he might be dead. Keep those calls and letters coming, Tom."

This joshing, which I intend in all good humor, seems not merely to fall flat but to inspire a look of horror. Molto's heavy brows knit and he actually appears to recoil when I offer my hand. I try to ease the moment by turning to Delay. He takes my hand, although he, too, seems somewhat reluctant to accept my congratulations.

"I will never say you did not tell me so," I admit.

Nico does not smile. In fact, he looks the other way. He is extremely ill at ease. I do not know if the campaign has left a wake of bitterness or if Delay, like so many of us, is simply scared to death now that he finally has what he so long wanted.

One thing I am certain of after this encounter: Nico will not be bidding to retain my services. I go so far as to call the file room and ask them to begin putting together some boxes. Late in the morning, I call Lipranzer's number at McGrath Hall. His phone, which is never answered when he's out, is picked up by someone whose voice I do not recognize.

"34068."

"Dan Lipranzer?"

"Not in. Who is this, please?"

"When do you expect him?"

"Who is this?"

"No message," I say, before hanging up.

I knock on the adjoining door to see what Mac makes of all this. She's gone. When I ask Eugenia where, she tells me that Mac is in Raymond's office, meeting, as she puts it, "with Mr. Della Guardia." She has been there almost an hour. I stand next to Eugenia's desk, battling my own bitterness. All in all, this has not worked out. Nico is now Mr. Della Guardia. Mac is on his staff, until she takes the bench. Raymond is going to get rich. Tommy Molto has my job. And I'll be lucky if next month I can pay the mortgage.

I'm still standing by Eugenia, when the phone rings.

"Mr. Horgan wants to see you," she says.

In the face of all the stern rebukes I have given to myself while I was marching down the hallway, the juvenile rush of sensation I feel when I see Nico in the P.A.'s chair astonishes me. I am immobilized by anger, jealousy, and revulsion. Nico has assumed a perfect proprietary air. He has removed his suit coat and his face is gravely composed, an expression which I know Nico well enough to realize is completely affected. Tommy Molto is sitting beside him, his chair somehow dropped a few inches back into the room. It strikes me that Tommy has already mastered the art of being a toady.

Raymond motions for me to sit. He says that this is really Nico's meeting now, so he offered him the chair. Raymond himself is standing up beside his sofa. Mac has her chair wheeled up to the window and is looking out. She still has not greeted me, and I realize now, from her demeanor, that Mac wants to be nowhere near this scene. The old saw: harder for her than for me.

"We've made some decisions here," Raymond says. He turns to Della Guardia. Silence. Delay, in his first assignment as P.A., is wordstruck. "Well, perhaps I should explain this first part," Raymond says. He is extremely grim. I know his forced expression well enough to realize that he is angry and laboring to remain composed. You can tell, just from the atmosphere, that there were bruises raised during the preceding meeting.

"I spoke last night with the mayor and told him that I had no desire to remain in office in light of the voters' preferences. He suggested to me that as long as I felt that way that I ought to talk it over with Nico to see if he wants to come on early. He does—and so that's what's going to happen. With the County Board's concurrence, I'll be leaving Friday."

I can't help myself. "Friday!"

"It's a little faster than I would have thought myself, but there are certain factors—" Raymond stops. Something is precarious in his manner. He is struggling. Horgan straightens the papers on the coffee table. He drifts to the sideboard and looks for something else. He is having a miserable time. I decide to make it easy for everybody.

"I'll be taking off then, too," I say. Nico starts to speak and I interrupt. "You'll be better off with a fresh start, Delay."

"That's not what I was going to say." He stands. "I want you to know why Raymond is leaving so soon. There's going to be a criminal investigation of his staff. We have information—some of it came to us during the campaign, but we didn't want to get into that kind of gutter stuff. But we have information and we think there's a serious problem."

I am confused by Nico's apparent anger. I wonder if he is talking about the B file. Perhaps there's a reason for Molto's connection to that case.

"Here, let me butt in," Raymond says. "Rusty, I think the best way to deal with this is to be direct. Nico and Tom have raised some questions with me about the Polhemus investigation. They're not confident in the way you've handled it. And I've agreed now to step aside. They can examine that question in any way they think is best. That's a matter for their professional judgment. But Mac suggested—well, we all agreed to make you aware of the situation."

I wait. The sense of alarm spreads through me before the instant of comprehension.

"I am under criminal investigation?" I laugh out loud.

From across the room Mac finally speaks. " 'Tain't funny, McGee," she says. There is no humor in her voice.

"This," I say, "is a crock. What did I supposedly do?"

"Rusty," Raymond says, "we do not need that kind of discussion now. Nico and Tom think that there are some things you should have spoken up about. That's all."

"That is not all," Molto says suddenly. His look is piercing. "I think you've been engaged in misdirection, hide the ball, ring around the rosy for almost a month now. You've been covering your ass."

"I think you're sick," I tell Tommy Molto.

Mac has wheeled her chair about.

"We don't need this," she says. "This discussion should take place somewhere else, with somebody else."

"The hell with that," I say. "I want to know what this is about."

"It's about," says Molto, "the fact that you were in Carolyn's apartment the night she was killed."

My heart beats so hard that my vision shifts, lumps. I was waiting for someone to chastise me because I had an affair with the decedent. This is incomprehensible. And I say so. Ludicrous. Bullshit.

"What was that? A Tuesday night? Barbara's at the U. and I was babysitting."

"Rusty," says Raymond, "my advice to you is to shut your fucking mouth."

Molto is on his feet. He is approaching me, stalking. He is enraged.

"We've got the print results. The ones you never could remember to ask for. And they're your prints on the glass. Yours. Rozat K. Sabich. Right on that glass on the bar. Five feet from where the woman was found dead. Maybe you didn't remember at first that all county employees get printed."

I stand. "This is absurd."

"And the MUDs you told Lipranzer not to get? The ones from your house? We had the phone company pull them this morning. They're on the way down here right now. You were calling her all month. There's a call from your house to hers that *night*."

"I think I've had enough of this," I say. "If I can be excused."

I have gotten as far as Loretta's little office outside Raymond's when Molto calls out behind me. He follows me into the anteroom. I can hear Della Guardia yelling Molto's name.

"I want you to know one thing, Sabich." He points his finger at me. "I know."

"Sure you do," I say.

"We're going to have a warrant for your butt the first day we're here. You better get yourself a lawyer, man, a damn good one."

"For your bullshit theory of an obstruction case?"

Molto's eyes are burning.

"Don't pretend that you don't get it. I know. You killed her. You're the guy."

Rage; as if my blood had quickened; as if my veins were filled only with that black poison. How old and familiar, how close to my being it seems. I come near Tommy Molto. I whisper, "Yeah, you're right," before I walk away.

SUMMER

IN THE SUPERIOR COURT OF KINDLE COUNTY

)	
)	
PEOPLE)	————————————————
vs.)	VIOLATION:
ROŽAT K. SABICH)	Section 76610 R.S.S.
)	
)	

THE KINDLE COUNTY GRAND JURY, JUNE SESSION, charges as follows:

On or about April 1 of this year, within the venue of Kindle County,

ROŽAT K. SABICH

defendant herein, did commit murder in the first degree in that he did knowingly, intentionally, and with malice aforethought trespass with force and arms upon the person of Carolyn Polhemus, thereby taking the life of the aforementioned Carolyn Polhemus;

In violation of Section 76610 of the Revised State Statutes.

A TRUE BILL:

————————————————————/s
Joseph Doherty, Foreperson
Kindle County Grand Jury
June Session

————————————————————/s
Nico Della Guardia
Kindle County Prosecuting Attorney

Done this Twenty—third day of June

[SEAL]

18

"The documents and reports are in the front. The witness statements are in the back," says Jamie Kemp as he sets a heavy cardboard box on the faultless finish of the walnut meeting table. We are in the small conference room in the offices of his employer, Alejandro Stern, my attorney. Kemp is sweating. He walked two blocks in the July sun from the County Building with these papers. His navy tie has been pulled away from his collar and some of his fancy blond Prince Valiant hairdo, an affectation left over from his younger days, is matted to his temples.

"I'm going to check my phone messages," Kemp says, "then I'll be back to look at this stuff with you. And remember—" Kemp points. "Don't panic. Defense lawyers have a name for what you're feeling. They call it clong."

"What's clong?"

"Clong is the rush of shit to your heart when you see the state's evidence." Kemp smiles. I am glad he thinks I can still take a joke. "It is not fatal."

It is July 14, three weeks since my indictment for murdering Carolyn Polhemus. Later this afternoon I will appear before Chief Superior Court Judge Edgar Mumphrey for my arraignment. Under State statutes governing discovery in criminal cases, the prosecution is required, prior to arraignment, to make available to the defense all physical evidence they intend to introduce, and a list of witnesses, including copies of their statements. Thus, this box. I stare at the familiar label applied to the cardboard: PEOPLE V. ROŽAT K. SABICH. I am full of that feeling again: This hasn't happened. Alone in this comfortable room, with its dark wainscoting and rows of crimson-jacketed law books, I wait for this now familiar adhesion of dread and longing to pass.

There is another copy of the indictment in the front of the box. I always focus on the same words. Trespass with force and arms. Trespass *vi et armis*, a term of the common law. With these same words for centuries persons in the English-speaking countries were accused of acts of violence. The phrase is archaic, long abandoned in most jurisdictions, but it is part of the text of our state statute, and reading it here always leaves me with the sense of a bizarre heritage. I have made league with the all-stars of crime, John Dillinger, Bluebeard, Jack the Ripper, and the million lesser lights, the half-mad, the abused, the idly evil, and the many who surrendered to a moment's terrible temptation, to an instant when they found themselves well acquainted with our wilder elements, our darker side.

After two months of daily press leaks, of rumor, innuendo, cruel gossip, I said resolutely that it would be a relief if an indictment finally came down. I was wrong. The day before, Delay sent Stern what is called the defendant's "courtesy copy." I first read the charges about forty feet from here, down the hall in Sandy's tasteful cream-colored office, and my heart and all my other organs were at once all stalled and so full of pain that I was certain that something in those regions must have burst. I could feel the blood gone from my face and I knew that my panic was visible. I tried to sound composed, not to show courage but because I suddenly realized it was simply the only alternative.

Sandy was sitting beside me on the sofa, and to him I mentioned Kafka.

'Does it sound horrible and trite to say that I can't believe this?' I asked. 'That I am full of incomprehension and rage?'

'Of course you cannot,' said Sandy, 'of course not. I, who have practiced at the criminal bar for thirty years in this city, am not able to believe it, and by now I thought I had seen everything. *Everything*! And I do not say that loosely. I had a client, Rusty, I cannot use a name, of course, who once placed $25 million in gold bullion in exactly the place that you are sitting. Just the ingots, two feet high. And I, who have seen such things, I sit at home at night and think to myself, Truly, this is remarkable and frightening.'

From Sandy these words had a kind of reach, the span of

authentic wisdom. There is, with his soft Spanish accent, an
elegance to the sound of even his ordinary speech. His dignity is
soothing. Over time, I have found that I hover, like a lover, on
every courtly gesture.

'Rusty,' Sandy said to me, touching the page I held in my hand,
'you make no mention of the only thing'—he searched for a
word—'which is encouraging.'

'What's that?'

'No notice. No Section 5 notice.'

'Ah,' I said, and a shiver passed through me. In our state the
prosecution must give notice at the time of indictment if it is
seeking the death penalty. With all my finely calibrated
calculations of Delay's intentions over the months, some zealous
internal defense had prevented my mind from even lighting on
that possibility. My look, I believe, revealed some of my
embarrassment, even humiliation, that I was already so detached
from routine professional perspectives. 'I assumed,' I said
weakly.

'Ah well.' Sandy smiled gently. 'We have these habits,' he said.

At Sandy's advice, we were not in town when the indictment was
returned. Barbara and Nat and I went to a cabin owned by
friends of her parents, up near Skageon. At night, you could hear
the rushing of Crown Falls, a mile away, and the trout fishing
proved better than at any time I can recall.

But, of course, the calamity four hundred miles south was
never out of mind. The day after, George Leonard from the *Trib*
somehow got the number of the cabin and asked me for a
comment, I referred him to Stern. Later, I came in to hear
Barbara in conference with her mother. After she put down the
phone I asked, somehow feeling that I should:

"It's all over?"

"Everywhere. TV. Both papers. Front page. Pictures. Your old
officemate Delay handed out every scummy detail."

This proved to be an understatement. My case is the stuff of
supermarket tabloids: CHIEF PROSECUTOR CHARGED WITH
MURDER—HAD AFFAIR WITH VICTIM. Sex, politics, and violence mix
in Kindle County. Not only was the local press full of this for
days, but the national media, too. Out of curiosity, I began to

read these accounts myself. The library in Nearing has an excellent periodical section, and I have little to do now during the days. On Stern's advice I refused to resign as a deputy P.A. and was placed on an indefinite administrative leave, with pay. As a result I have spent more time in the library than I would have expected. I join the old men and the bag ladies in enjoying the silence and the air conditioning as I inspect these national reports of my misconduct. *The New York Times* was, as usual, dryly factual, referring to everyone as Mr. and laying out the entire antic circumstance. It was, surprisingly, the national news magazines, *Time* and *Newsweek*, that did their best to make it all seem lurid. Each article was accompanied by the same photo, taken by some asshole I saw lurking in the bushes for a couple of days. Stern finally advised me to walk outside and let him take his picture, on the condition that he promise to beat it. That worked. The Minicam units which, according to the neighbors, were camped before the house for a week, while we were hiding out near Skageon, are yet to return.

That makes little practical difference. After twelve years in which I sometimes prosecuted the biggest cases in town, the papers and TV stations had enough footage of me on file to put my face everywhere. I cannot walk around Nearing without enduring endless staring. There is now a permanent hesitation in everybody's manner, a few portions of a second lost before a greeting. The comments of solace that are made, which are few, are ludicrous and inept—my cleaner telling me, "Tough break," or the teenage gas-station attendant asking if that's really me he's been reading about in the paper. Another thing I like about the library is that no one is allowed to talk.

And how do I feel, so instantly struck low, brought down from my station as model citizen and become a pariah instead? To say that there are no words is inaccurate. There are words, but they would be so many. My spirits keel about wildly. The anxiety is corrosive and I spend much time in a tumult of anger and disbelief. For the most part there is a numbness—a sense of idle refuge. Even in my concern for Nat, and how all of this will warp his future, the dawning thought is that it has happened, ultimately, just to me. I alone am the foremost victim. And to some extent, I can endure that. I acquired more of my father's fatalism than I expected; a side of me has always been without faith in reason or in order. Life is simply experience; for reasons not readily discerned, we attempt to go on. At instants I am amazed that I am here. I have taken to watching my shoes as I cross the pavement, for the fact that I am moving, that I am going anywhere, doing anything, strikes me, at odd moments, as amazing. That in the midst of this misfortune life continues seems bizarre.

And mostly I am like this, floating and remote. Of course, a great deal of the time is also spent wondering why this has occurred. But I find that at some point along the way my ability to assay ceases. My speculation seems to lead to a dark and frightening periphery, the edge of a black vortex of paranoia and rage from which, thus far, I have instantly withdrawn. I know that on some levels I cannot take much more, and I simply do not. I worry instead about when it will be over, and what the result will be. I want, with a desperation whose size cannot be encompassed by metaphor, I want all of this never to have taken place; I want things to be as they were before, before I allowed my life to be ransacked by Carolyn, and everything that followed. And then there is my consuming anxiety for Nat: What will happen to him? How can he be sheltered? How can I protect him from shame? How can I have brought him to the brink of being, for all purposes, half an orphan? These are in some ways my worst moments: this raging, lashing frustration, this sense of incompetence, these tears. And then, once or twice, in the last weeks, an extraordinary feeling, lighter than air, more soothing than a breeze, a hope that seems to settle in without accounting, and which leaves me with the sense that I have mounted some high rampart and have the courage simply to look ahead.

The case against me, as I assess it from the contents of the cardboard box, is straightforward. Nico has listed about a dozen witnesses of substance, more than half of them related to the physical and scientific evidence he plans to introduce. Lipranzer will be called, apparently to say I instructed him not to subpoena my home phone tolls. Mrs. Krapotnik has identified me as someone she saw in Carolyn's building, although she is not positive I am the stranger she observed on the night of the murder. Also listed is a maid from Nearing whose somewhat

cryptic statement suggests that she saw me on the Nearing—
City bus one night close to the time Carolyn was killed. Raymond
Horgan is named; Tommy Molto; Eugenia, my secretary; Robinson, the psychiatrist I saw, on a few occasions; and a number of
scientific experts, including Painless Kumagai.

Nonetheless, this is clearly a circumstantial case. No one will
say they saw me kill Carolyn Polhemus. No one will testify to my
confession (if you do not consider Molto, whose file memorandum pretends to treat my last remark to him that Wednesday in
April as if it was not rendered in a get-screwed tone). The heart
of this case is the physical evidence: the glass with two of my
fingerprints, identified from the knowns I gave a dozen years ago
when I became a deputy P.A.; the telephone MUD records
showing a call from my house to Carolyn's about an hour and a
half before her murder; the vaginal smear, revealing the
presence within Carolyn's genitalia of spermatozoa of my blood
type, thwarted in their urgent blind migration by a contraceptive
compound whose presence implies a consensual sex act; and
finally, the malt-colored Zorak V fibers found on Carolyn's
clothing, and her corpse, and strewn about the living area, which
match samples taken from the carpeting in my home.

These last two pieces of evidence were developed as the
result of a visit to my house by three state troopers, which took
place a day or two after the Black Wednesday meeting, as
Barbara and I now refer to it, in Raymond's office. The doorbell
rang and there was Tom Nyslenski, who has served subpoenas
for the P.A.'s office for at least six years. I was still sufficiently
unfocused that my initial reaction was to be mildly pleased to
see him.

I don't like to be here, he said. He then handed me two grand-
jury subpoenas, one to produce physical evidence—a blood
specimen—and one to testify. He also had a search warrant,
narrowly drawn, which authorized the troopers to take samples
of the carpeting throughout my home, as well as every piece of
exterior clothing I owned. Barbara and I sat there in our living
room as three men in brown uniforms walked from room to room
with plastic bags and scissors. They spent an hour in my closet,
cutting tiny swatches from the seams. Nico and Molto had been
clever enough not to search for the murder weapon, too. A law
enforcement professional would know better than to keep the

thing around. And if the troopers searched for it, the prosecutors would have to admit in court that it could not be found.

Is the stuff in here called Zorak V? I asked Barbara quietly while the troopers were upstairs.

I don't know what it is, Rusty. Barbara, as usual, seemed to be placing a premium on maintaining her composure. She had a little pursed-up expression, peeved but no worse. As if they were fourteen-year-olds setting off firecrackers too late at night.

Is it synthetic? I asked.

Do you think we could afford wool? she replied.

I called Stern, who had me make an inventory of what they took. The next day I voluntarily provided a blood sample downtown. But I never testified. Stern and I had our one serious dispute about that. Sandy repeated the accepted wisdom that an investigation target accomplishes nothing by pre-trial statements except to prepare the prosecutor for the defense. In his own gentle way, Stern reminded me of the damage I had already done with my outburst in Raymond's office. But in late April, unindicted, and convinced I never would be charged, my goal was to prevent this mad episode from damaging my reputation. If I took five and refused to testify, as I had the right to do, it would probably never reach the papers, but every lawyer in the P.A.'s office would know, and through them half the others on the street. Sandy prevailed when the results of the blood test came back and identified me as a secreter—that is, someone who produced A-type antibodies, just like the man who had last been with Carolyn. The chances of this being a coincidence were about one in ten, I realized then that my last opportunity for quick exoneration had passed. Tommy Molto refused to accept any substitute for my assertion of the privilege and so one bleak afternoon in May, I, like so many others I had often ridiculed, snuck into the grand-jury room, a little windowless chamber that looks something like a small theater, and repeated in response to thirty-six different questions, 'On the advice of my attorney, I will decline to answer because it may tend to incriminate me.'

"So," says Sandy Stern. "How do you enjoy seeing the world from the other side?" Engrossed in mysteries of the cardboard box, I did not notice him enter the conference room. He stands, with one hand on the door handle, a short, roundish man, in a flawless suit. There are just a few stray hairs that cross his shining pale scalp, emanating from what was once a widow's peak. Tucked between the fingers is a cigar. This is a habit which Stern indulges only in the office. It would be uncivil in a public place and Clara, his wife, forbids it at home.

"I didn't expect you back so soon," I tell him.

"Judge Magnuson's calendar is dreadful. Naturally, the sentencing will be called last." He is referring to another case on which he has been engaged. Apparently he has spent a good deal of time waiting in court and the matter is not yet concluded. "Rusty, would you mind terribly if Jamie appears with you at the arraignment?" He begins to explain at length, but I interrupt.

"No problem."

"You're very kind. Perhaps then we can take a few moments with what your friend Della Guardia has sent over. What is it you call him?"

"Delay."

Sandy's consternation is apparent. He cannot figure out the reason for the nickname and he is too gentlemanly to ask me to reveal even the most trivial confidence of the P.A.'s office, with which he is so often a contestant. He removes his coat and calls for coffee. His secretary brings it and a large crystal ashtray for his cigar.

"So," he says. "Do we now understand Della Guardia's case?"

"I think I do."

"Fine, then. Let me hear it. Thirty-second summation, if you please, of Nico's opening statement."

When I retained Sandy, within three or four hours of that bizarre meeting in Raymond's office, we spent thirty minutes together. He told me what it would cost—a $25,000 retainer, against a fee to be billed at $150 an hour for time out of court and $300 an hour in, the balance, strictly as a courtesy to me, to be returned if there was no indictment; he told me not to talk to anyone about the charges and, in particular, to make no more outraged speeches to prosecutors; he told me to avoid reporters and not to quit my job; he told me this was frightening, reminiscent of the scenes of his childhood in Latin America; he told me that he was confident that with my extraordinary background this entire matter would be favorably resolved. But

Sandy Stern, with whom I have done business for better than a decade, against whom I have tried half a dozen cases, and who on matters of gravity, or of little consequence, has always known that he could accept my word—Sandy Stern has never asked me if I did it. He has inquired from time to time about details. He asked me once, quite unceremoniously, whether I'd had 'a physical relationship' with Carolyn, and I told him, without flinching, yes. But Stern has remained far clear of ever putting the ultimate question. In that he is like everybody else. Even Barbara, who evinces by various proclamations a belief in my innocence, has never asked me directly. People tell you it's tough. They cling or, more often, seem visibly repulsed. But nobody has sufficient sand to come out with the only question you know they have in mind.

From Sandy this indirection seems more of his classical manner, the formal presence that lies over him like brocaded drapes. But I know it serves for more. Perhaps he does not ask because he is not certain of the verity of the answer he may get. It is a given of the criminal justice system, an axiom as certain as the laws of gravity, that defendants rarely tell the truth. Cops and prosecutors, defense lawyers and judges—everybody knows they lie. They lie solemnly; with sweaty palms and shifty eyes; or, more often, with a look of schoolboy innocence and an incensed disbelief when their credulity is assailed. They lie to protect themselves; they lie to protect their friends. They lie for the fun of it, or because that is the way they have always been. They lie about big details and small ones, about who started it, who thought of it, who did it, and who was sorry. But they lie. It is the defendant's credo. Lie to the cops. Lie to your lawyer. Lie to the jury that tries your case. If convicted, lie to your probation officer. Lie to your bunkmate in the pen. Trumpet your innocence. Leave the dirty bastards out there with a grain of doubt. Something can always change.

Thus it would be an act contrary to his professional acumen were Sandy Stern to commit himself to an unreserved faith in everything I say. Instead, he does not ask. This procedure has one further virtue. If I were to meet any new evidence by frontally contradicting what I had told Sandy in the past, legal ethics might require him to withhold me from the witness stand, where I almost certainly intend to go. Better to see everything the prosecution has, to be certain that my recollection, as the lawyers put it, has been fully "refreshed," before Sandy inquires about my version. Caught in a system where the client is inclined to lie and the lawyer who seeks his client's confidence may not help him do that, Stern works in the small open spaces which remain. Most of all, he desires to make an intelligent presentation. He does not wish to be misled, or to have his options curbed by rash declarations that prove to be untrue. As the trial approaches, he will need to know more. He may ask the question then; and I certainly will tell him the answer. For the time being, Stern has found, as usual, the most artful and indefinite means by which to probe.

"Della Guardia's theory is something like this," I say. "Sabich is obsessed with Polhemus. He's calling her house. Can't let go. He has to see her. One night, knowing that his wife will be going out and that he can get to Carolyn on the sneak, he calls up, begs to see her, and Polhemus finally agrees. She rolls around with him for auld lang syne, but then something goes wrong. Maybe Sabich is jealous of another relationship. Maybe Carolyn says that this was merely the grand finale. Whatever it is, Sabich wants more than she will give. He blows a gasket. He gives her what-for with some heavy instrument. And decides to make it look like rape. Sabich is a prosecutor. He knows that this way there will be dozens of other suspects. So he ties her up, opens the latches to make it look like somebody slipped in, and then— this is the diabolical part—pulls her diaphragm out of her, so there won't be any evidence of consent. Like all bad guys, of course, he makes a few mistakes. He forgets the drink he had when he came in, the glass he left on the bar. And he does not think—maybe even realize—that the forensic chemist will be able to i.d. the spermicide. But we know he did evil to this woman, because he never revealed—he lied—about his presence on the night of the murder, which is established by all the physical evidence."

This exposition is eerily comforting to me. The heartless hip analysis of crime is so much a part of my life and my mentation that I cannot make myself sound ruffled or even feel a fragment of concern. The world of crime has its argot, as ruthless as the jazzman's is sweet, and speaking it again I feel I am back among the living, among those who see evil as a familiar if odious phenomenon with which they have to deal, like the scientist studying diseases through his microscope.

I go on.

"That's Nico's theory, something like that. He has to straddle a little bit on the question of premeditation. He might argue that Sabich had it in mind to do her in from minute one, that he chose this night so he had an alibi, in case she refused to build the old fire anew. Maybe Sabich was on a different trip: You can't live if you won't be mine. That'll depend on evidentiary nuances. Probably Nico will give an opening that won't lock him in. But he'll be close to this. How does it sound?"

Sandy looks over his cigar. They are Cuban, he told me a few weeks ago. A former client gets them, he does not ask how. The wrapper, deep brown, burns so cleanly that you can see the leaf veins etched within the ash.

"Plausible," he says at last. "Evidence of motive is not strong here. And it is usually critical in a circumstantial case. Nothing ties you to any instrument of violence. The state is further disadvantaged because you were, in essence, a political opponent of Della Guardia—never mind that you did not consider yourself a political employee, a jury will not believe that, and for our purposes should not be told that. There is additional evidence of bad feeling between you and the prosecuting attorney inasmuch as you personally fired him from his post. The importance of these matters, however, could be greatly reduced if the prosecuting attorney himself did not try the case."

"Forget that," I say. "Nico would never move out of the spotlight."

Stern seems to smile as he draws on the cigar.

"I quite agree. So we will have those advantages. And these factors, which would raise questions in the mind of any reasonable person, will take on large importance in a circumstantial case, from which you and I both know juries are disinclined. Nevertheless, Rusty, we must be honest enough to tell ourselves that the evidence overall is very damaging."

Sandy does not pause long, but the words, even though I probably would have said as much myself, feel like something driven against my heart. The evidence is very damaging.

"We must probe. It is difficult, of course, and I am sure painful, but now is the time that you must put your fine mind to work on this case, Rusty. You must tell me every flaw, every defect. We must look scrupulously at each piece of evidence, each witness, again and again. Let us not say that any of this hard work will be done tomorrow. Best to begin right now, today. The more deficiencies we find in this circumstantial case, the better our chances, the more Nico must explain, and explain with difficulty. Do not be afraid to be technical. Every point for which Della Guardia cannot account increases your opportunities for acquittal."

Although I have hardened myself, one word catches me like a blow. Opportunities, I think.

*   *   *

Sandy summons Jamie Kemp to take part in our discussion, as it is bound to suggest various motions for discovery that we will soon be called upon to file. To hold down my expenses, Stern has agreed to allow me to assist in research and investigation, but I must act under his direction. With Kemp, I share the work of the junior lawyer, and I have enjoyed this collaboration more than I had counted on. Kemp has been Stern's associate about a year now. As I get the story, quite some time ago Jamie was a guitarist in a medium-popular rock-and-roll band. They say he went through the whole shot, records and groupies and road shows, and when things went downhill he decamped for Yale Law School. I dealt with him in the P.A.'s office on two or three occasions without incident, but he had a reputation there for being preppie and stuck-up, impressed by his own blond good looks and a lifetime of good fortune. I like him, though he sometimes cannot suppress a little of that Waspy amusement with a world by which, he is convinced, he will never quite be touched.

"First," says Stern, "we must file a notice of alibi." This is a declaration, no questions. We will formally notify the prosecution of our intention to stand by my statement in Raymond's office that I was at home the night Carolyn was murdered. This position deprives me of what, in theory, is probably the best defense—conceding that I saw Carolyn that night for an unrelated reason. That posture would dampen the force of the physical evidence and focus instead on the lack of any proof tying me to the murder. For weeks, I have been expecting some artful effort by Stern to discourage the alibi, and I find myself relieved. Whatever Sandy thinks of what I said, he apparently recognizes that to reverse field now would be too difficult. We would have to conceive an innocent explanation for my eruption on Black Wednesday—why I went out of my way to lie, in outraged tones, to my boss, my friend, and the two top lawyers from the new administration.

Stern pulls the box to him and begins sorting through the documents. He starts from the front, the physical evidence.

"Let us go to the heart of the matter," says Stern. "The glass." Kemp goes out to make copies of the fingerprint report, and the three of us read. The computer people made their findings the day before the election. By then Bolcarro was playing ball with Nico, and so Morano, the police chief, surely was as well. This report must have gone straight to the top and right out to Nico. So Delay probably told the truth himself when he claimed that Wednesday in Horgan's office that he had acquired significant evidence against me during the campaign and chose not to publicize it. Too much of a last-minute mess, I would suppose.

As for the report, it says, in brief, that my right thumb and middle finger have been identified. The other latent present remains unknown. It is not mine; it is not Carolyn's. In all likelihood it belongs to one of the initial onlookers at the scene: the street cops who responded to the call, who always seem to run around touching everything before the homicide dicks arrive; the building manager, who found the body; the paramedics; maybe even a reporter. Nonetheless, it will be one of the difficult stray details for Della Guardia to cope with.

"I would like to look at that glass," I say. "It might help me figure some things out."

Stern points at Kemp and tells him to list a motion for production of physical evidence.

"Also," I say, "we want them to produce all the fingerprint reports. They dusted everything in the apartment."

This one Stern assigns to me. He hands me a pad:

"Motion for production of all scientific examinations: all underlying reports, spectographs, charts, chemical analyses, et cetera, et cetera, you know it better than I do."

I make the note. Stern has a question.

"You had drinks in Carolyn's apartment, of course, when you were there in the past?"

"Sure," I say. "And she wasn't much of a housekeeper. But I think she'd wash a glass once in six months."

"Yes," Stern says simply.

We are both grim.

Kemp has another idea.

"I'd like to get a complete inventory of everything in that apartment. Every physical object. Where's the contraceptive jelly or whatever it is that this chemist is saying he finds present? Wouldn't that have been in her medicine cabinet?" He looks to me for confirmation, but I shake my head.

"I don't even remember discussing birth control with Carolyn. I may be male chauvinist of the year, but I never asked her what she was doing."

Stern is ruminating, temporizing in the air with his cigar.

"Caution here," he says. "These are productive thoughts, but we do not want to lead Della Guardia to evidence he has not thought to obtain. Our requests, whatever they are, must be unobtrusive. Remember that everything that the prosecution discovers which favors the defense must be turned over to us. Anything we discuss which might be useful to them will be better left forgotten." Sandy gives me a sidewise look, quite amused. He enjoys being so candid with a former opponent. Perhaps he is thinking of some specific piece of evidence he kept from me in the past. "Best we conduct this search ourselves without disclosing our intentions." He points at Kemp; it is his turn. "Another motion, then: for an inventory of all items seized from the apartment of the decedent and for an opportunity to conduct a view and inspection of our own. The apartment remains under seal?" he asks me.

"I presume."

"Also," says Stern, "your mention of Carolyn's personal habits leads to this thought. We should subpoena her doctors. No privileges survive her death. Who knows what we might discover? Drugs?"

"Rope burns in the past," says Kemp.

We all laugh, a grisly moment.

Sandy, decorous as ever, asks if the name of one of Carolyn's doctors is "known to me." It is not, but all county employees are

covered by Blue Cross. A subpoena to them, I suggest, is bound
to uncover a good deal of information, including doctors' names.
Stern is pleased by my contribution.

The next group of documents we look at are the phone
records from Carolyn's home number and my own, an inch-thick
bundle of xeroxed pages with an endless train of 14-digit
numbers. I hand the sheets one by one to Stern. From my phone,
there are one-minute calls to Carolyn's recorded on March 5, 10,
and 20. When I get to April 1, I spend a long tlme looking. I just
lay my finger on the number that is recorded there at 7:32 p.m. A
two-minute call.

"Carolyn's," I tell him.

"Ah," says Stern. "There must be a commonsense explanation
for all of this." Observing Stern work is like tracking smoke,
watching a shadow lengthen. Is it the accent that allows him to
lay that perfect subtle stress on the word "must"? I know my
assignment.

He smokes.

"You do what at home, when you babysit?" he asks.

"Work. Read memos, indictments, prosecution packages,
briefs."

"Must you confer with other deputy prosecuting attorneys!"

"Occasionally."

"Of course," says Stern. "Now and then, there is the need to
ask a brief question, schedule an appointment. No doubt in all
these months of records"—Stern taps them—"there are a
number of such calls to deputy prosecuting attorneys other than
Carolyn."

I nod with each suggestion.

"There are a lot of possibilities," I say. "I think Carolyn was
working on a big indictment that month. I'll look over some
things."

"Good," says Stern. He looks back to my MUD sheets for the
murder night. His lips are rumpled, his look disturbed.

"No further calls after 7:32," he says finally, and points.

In other words, no proof that I was home, where I say I was.

"Bad," I say.

"Bad," Stern finally says aloud. "Perhaps someone called you
that evening?"

I shake my head. None that I remember. But I know my lines

now.

"I'll think about it," I say. I take back the MUD sheet for April 1, studying it a moment.

"Can those things be dummied up?" asks Kemp. "The MUDs?" I nod.

"I was thinking about that," I say. "The P.A. gets a bunch of xeroxes of the phone company's printouts. If a deputy, or somebody else, wanted to do a job on a defendant, he could make a great cut-and-paste and nobody would know the difference." I nod again and look at Kemp. "These things could be faked."

"And should we pursue that possibility?" asks Stern. Is there some hint of rebuke in his voice? He is studying a thread pulled on his shirt-sleeve, but when his eyes light on mine for the briefest instant, they are penetrating as lasers.

"We might think about that," I say at last.

"Mmm hmm," says Stern to himself. He is quite solemn. He points at Kemp to make a note. "I do not believe we should explore this before the conclusion of the state's evidence. I would not want to see them introduce the fact that we made efforts to challenge the accuracy of these records and failed." He directs this remark to Kemp, but it is clear to me who is meant to catch its import.

Stern reaches resolutely for another file. He checks his watch, a slim golden Swiss piece. The arraignment is in forty-five minutes. Sandy himself is due back in court sooner. He suggests we talk about the witnesses. I summarize what I have read thus far. I mention that Molto and Della Guardia provided no statements from two of the listed witnesses: my secretary, Eugenia, and Raymond. Sandy absently tells Kemp to list another motion for production. He has put his glasses back on, tortoiseshell half-frames, and continues studying the witness list.

"The secretary," he says, "does not trouble me, for reasons I will explain. Horgan, candidly, does."

I start when Sandy says this.

"Certain witnesses," Sandy explains, "Della Guardia must bring to the stand, whatever their disadvantages to him. You know this, of course, Rusty, far better than I. Detective Lipranzer is an example. He was quite candid in his interview with Molto the day after the election and acknowledged that you asked him not to order your home telephone records. That is sufficiently helpful to the prosecution that Lipranzer will be called, notwithstanding the many fine things he will say about you personally. Horgan, on the other hand, is not a witness whom I would think a good prosecutor would ordinarily be eager to see. He will be known to all the jurors, and his credibility is such that it would seem quite risky to call him unless—" Sandy waits. He picks up his cigar again.

"Unless what?" I ask. "Unless he is going to be hostile to the defense? I don't believe Raymond Horgan will put the bricks to me. Not after twelve years. Besides, what can he say?"

"It is a matter of tone, not so much as content. I take it that he is going to testify to your statement in his office on the day after the election. One would think that Nico would be better off putting on Ms. MacDougall, if he had to accept an unfriendly witness. She at least has not been a local personality for more than a decade. On the other hand, if it appears that Horgan, Della Guardia's political opponent, and your friend and employer for a dozen years, is sympathetic to the prosecution—that could be extremely damaging. That is the kind of courtroom nuance on which you and I both know close cases often turn."

I look at him squarely. "I don't believe that."

"I understand," he says. "And you are probably correct. Probably there is something we have missed that will seem obvious when we know Horgan's prospective testimony. Nonetheless—" Sandy thinks. "Raymond would meet with you?"

"I can't imagine why not."

"I will call him and see. Where is he now?" Kemp remembers the law firm. About six names. The League of Nations. Every ethnic group is mentioned. O'Grady, Steinberg, Marconi, Slibovich, Jackson, and Jones. Something like that. "We should plan a meeting for Horgan, you, and me as soon as possible."

Strangely, this is the first thing Sandy has said that is both entirely unexpected, and whose effect I cannot seem to shake. It is true that I have not heard from Raymond since that day in April that I walked out of his office, but he has had his own concerns: new job, new office. More particularly, he is an experienced criminal defense lawyer and knows how circumscribed our talks would necessarily have to be. His silence I had taken as a professional accommodation. Until now. I wonder if this is not simply some malicious effort by the prosecutors to unsettle me. That would be like Molto.

"Why does he need Raymond to testify, if he intends to call Molto?" I ask.

Principally, says Stern, because Molto is, in all likelihood, not going to testify. Della Guardia has referred a number of times to Tommy trying the case. A lawyer is prohibited from being a witness and advocate in the same proceeding. Nonetheless, Sandy reminds Jamie that we ought to file a motion to disqualify Molto, since he is on the witness list. If nothing else, this will promote consternation in the P.A.'s office. And it will force Nico to forswear any use of my statement to Molto. Like me, Sandy considers it unlikely that Nico would really want to offer this in the prosecution's case. As Della Guardia's best friend and chief assistant, Molto would be too easy to impeach. But on the other hand, the statement could be used effectively in cross-examining me. It is best, therefore, to file the motion and force Nico's hand.

Sandy moves ahead. "This I do not understand," he says. He holds aloft the statement of the maid who says she saw me on a bus into the city from Nearing on a night near the time Carolyn was murdered. "What is Della Guardia up to?"

"We only have one car," I explain. "I'm sure Molto checked the registrations. Barbara took it that night. So I had to have another way to get to Carolyn. I bet they had a trooper standing out at the bus station in Nearing for a week, looking for someone who could make my picture."

"This interests me," Stern says. "They apparently accept that Barbara indeed left you at home that night. I understand why they would concede that she took the car. There have been too many unfortunate episodes with women around the university for anyone to believe she would be using public transportation at night. But why agree she left at all? No prosecutor would want to argue that the defendant rode a bus to a murder. It does not sound authentic. They must have found nothing with the taxi companies and rent-a-car. I take it that they are looking at records of some kind which confirm Barbara's absence."

"Probably the log-in sheet at the U.," I say. Nat and I have gone to watch his mother work on the computer on occasion. "It'll show she used the machine. She signs in when she gets there."

"Ah," says Stern.

"What time would that be?" Jamie asks. "Not late, right? She'll know you were home at the time of the murder—or at least that she left you there, won't she?"

"Absolutely. Her computer time's at eight. She leaves for the U. seven-thirty, twenty-to the latest."

"And Nat?" asks Sandy. "When is he in bed?"

"Around then. Most of the time, Barbara gets him down before she goes."

Kemp asks, "Does Nat get up a lot or does he sleep soundly?"

"Like a coma," I say. "But I'd never leave him alone in the house."

Stern makes a sound. That is not the kind of thing we will be able to prove.

"Nonetheless," says Stern, "these facts are helpful. We are entitled to whatever records they have. That is *Brady* material"— evidence favorable to the defense. "We must make another motion. Fiery and outraged. A good assignment for you, Rusty." He smiles, kindly.

I make the note. I tell Sandy, there is only one more witness I want to talk about. I point to Robinson's name.

"He's a shrink," I say. "I saw him a few times." Molto, I'm sure, is behind the ugly gesture of naming my former psychiatrist as a potential witness. Tommy is pulling my chain. I used to do things like that to defendants. Make sure they knew I'd been all over their lives. Last month Molto subpoenaed my bank account in Nearing. The president, an old friend of Barbara's deceased father, Dr. Bernstein, will not look at me now when I come in. From my checks, no doubt, Molto got Robinson's name.

I am surprised by Stern's reaction to my disclosure.

"Yes, Dr. Robinson," Sandy says. "He called me right after the return of the indictment. I neglected to mention that." He was too decorous is what Stern means. "He had seen my name in the paper as your lawyer. He merely wanted me to know he had been identified and that the police had attempted an interview. He was reluctant to trouble you with this information. At any rate, he told me he refused to make any statement on the grounds of privilege. I reaffirmed that and said we would not waive."

"We can waive. I don't care," I say. I don't either. It seems like a minor intrusion, compared to what has taken place in the last few months.

"Your attorney is ordering you to care. Della Guardia and Molto are no doubt hoping we will make a waiver, in the belief that this doctor will testify to your general mental health and the unlikeliness of criminal behavior."

"I bet he will."

"I see I did not make my point," says Stern. "I commented before. Evidence of motive here is weak. You summarized Della Guardia's theory very ably, I think. Sabich is obsessed, you said. Sabich is unwilling to let go. Tell me, Rusty. You have looked over Della Guardia's case. Where is the proof here of any prior amorous relationship between the defendant and the decedent? A few telephone calls that can be accounted for by business needs? There is no diary here. No note that came with flowers. No lovers' correspondence. That, I take it, is what your secretary will be called for, to add what she can, which I assume is not very much."

"Very little," I say. Sandy is right. I did not see this hole. As a prosecutor, I would never have missed it. But it is harder when you have all the facts. Still, I battle back a lightheaded sensation of hope. I cannot believe that Nico could be weak on this essential. I point at the MUD sheets. "There are calls to my home from Carolyn's in late October, last year."

"Yes? And who is to say they are not from Ms. Polhemus to you? You had been lawyers on an important case that was tried the month preceding. No doubt there were continuing developments. Bond questions. As I recall, there was a substantial dispute surrounding custody of the boy. What was his name?"

"Wendell McGaffen."

"Yes Wendell. These are matters to which the chief deputy might have difficulty giving attention in the office."

"And why did I tell Lipranzer not to get my home phone tolls?"

"More difficult." Sandy nods. "But I take it for granted that a person of innocent state of mind would rule himself out as a suspect and prevent a busy detective from wasting his time." The way he puts things. I take it for granted. Like sleight of hand.

"Mrs. Krapotnik?" I ask, alluding to her expected testimony that I was seen around Carolyn's apartment.

"You were on trial together. Matters needed to be discussed. Certainly, if you want to get away from the Kindle County P.A.'s office, a *most* dreary environment, you are not going to go out to Nearing, where you live. No one denies you were in the apartment on occasion. We agree. Your fingerprints are on the glass." Sandy's smile is Latin, complex. His defense is taking shape, and he is quite persuasive. "No," Sandy says. "Della Guardia cannot call you, of course, or, presumably, your wife. And so he faces difficulties. Tongues no doubt have wagged, Rusty. I am sure half the attorneys in Kindle County now believe that they suspected your affair. But gossip will not be admitted. The prosecution has no witnesses. And thus no proof of motive. I would be more hopeful," Sandy says, "were it not for the problem of your testimony." His eyes, large and dark, deep and serious, briefly cross my own. The problem of my testimony. The problem, he means, of telling the truth. "But these are questions for the future. Our job, after all, is merely to raise a doubt. And it may be that when Della Guardia concludes his case the jury will be led to wonder if you are not the victim of a miserable coincidence."

"Or if I was set up."

Sandy is a reasonable man and judicious. He again acquires his grave look in response to my proposal. He would obviously prefer that there be no illusions between client and counsel. He glances at his watch. It is getting close to show time. I touch his wrist.

"What would you say if I told you that Carolyn seems to have had something to do with a case on which a deputy P.A. was bribed? And the P.A. on the case was Tommy Molto?"

Sandy takes a very long time with this, his look tightly drawn. "Please explain."

I tell him in a few moments about the B file. These are, I explain, grand-jury secrets. Until now, I have preferred to keep them to myself.

"And your investigation led where?"

"Nowhere. It stopped the day I left."

"We must find some way to continue. I would suggest an investigator ordinarily. Perhaps you have some other idea." Sandy puts out his cigar. He grinds the stub down carefully and looks at it an instant reverentially. He sighs, before he stands to put on his coat. "To attack the prosecutor, Rusty, is a tactic that is almost always pleasing to the client, and seldom convincing to a jury. These matters I mentioned before—your political opposition to Della Guardia, your firing of him—are items that will tarnish him, diminish his credibility. They will help us explain the prosecutor's zeal to accuse on insufficient evidence. But before we venture down the road to actual accusation, we must consider the matter very carefully. Successes by suggesting sinister motives in the state are, as you well know, quite rare."

"I understand," I say. "I wanted you to know," I tell him.

"Of course. And I appreciate that."

"It's just," I tell him, "that's the way I feel. That it isn't a coincidence it lays out this way. I mean," and now, on sudden impulse, I finally bring myself to say what vestigial pride has so long prevented: "Sandy, I'm innocent."

Stern reaches over and, as only he could do, pats me on the hand. He has a look of deep, if practiced, sadness. And as I meet this brown-eyed spaniel expression I realize that Alelandro Stern, one of this town's finest defense lawyers, has heard these ardent proclamations of innocence too many times before.

19

At ten minutes to two Jamie and I meet Barbara at the corner of Grand and Filer and advance with her to the courthouse. The press horde is waiting for us on the steps beneath the columns. I know a back entrance through the heating and cooling plant, but I figure I can use that trick only once, and I have had the dismal thought that there may come another day when I am particularly eager to avoid this clawing mass, with their halogen lights, their boom mikes, their shoving and their shouting. For the moment, I am content to push my way through, saying, No comment.

Stanley Rosenberg from Channel 5, splendidly handsome except for particularly prominent front teeth, is the first to reach us. He has left his camera person and sound crew behind and approaches me alone, walking beside us, We address each other by first names.

"Any chance you'll do something on camera?"

"None," I answer.

Kemp already is trying to intervene, but I hold him off as we continue walking.

"If you change your mind, will you promise to call me first?"

"Not now," Jamie says, and lays his hand on Stanley's sleeve. Stanley to his credit maintains his good humor. He introduces himself and makes his pitch to Kemp instead. Right before the trial, Rosenberg says, a broadcast interview with Rusty would be good for everybody. Stern will never let me make statements to anyone, but Kemp, as we approach the steps and the waiting crowd of cameras, lights, and microphones, says merely, "We'll think about it." Stanley remains behind as we start up, Kemp and I flanking Barbara, more or less boosting her by the elbows as we shove our way through.

"What do you think about the fact that Raymond Horgan is going to testify against you?" Stanley shouts as we are parting.

I pivot quickly. Stanley's bad teeth are fully revealed. He knew he'd get me with that one. Where does that come from, I wonder. Stanley may have made assumptions upon reading the court file where Nico's witness list was filed. But Rosenberg has long-term connections to Raymond, and instinct tells me that he would not use Horgan's name loosely.

The cameras are barred by judicial order inside the courthouse, and as we swing through the brass revolving doors, it is only the print and radio reporters who follow us in a pack, thrusting out their tape recorders and shouting questions to which none of us respond. As we hurry down the corridor toward the elevators, I reach for Barbara's hand, which is around my arm.

"How are you doing?" I ask.

Her look is strained, but she tells me she is fine. Stanley Rosenberg is not as good-looking as he appears on TV, she adds. None of them is, I tell her.

My arraignment is before the Honorable Edgar Mumphrey, chief judge of the Kindle County Superior Court. Ed Mumphrey was leaving the P.A.'s office just about the time that I began. He was regarded with a kind of awe even then, for one reason: he is very rich. His father opened a chain of movie theaters in this town, which he eventually parlayed into hotels and radio stations. Ed naturally has labored to appear immune to his fortune's influence. He was a deputy for almost a decade; then he entered private practice, where he remained for only a year or two before the call came to the bench. He has proved a straight, capable judge, short just enough candlepower to keep him from being regarded as brilliant. He became chief judge last year, an assignment which is primarily administrative, although he hears all arraignments, and negotiates and takes guilty pleas when they are offered in the early stages of proceedings.

I take a seat in Judge Mumphrey's dark, rococo courtroom, in the front row. Barbara is beside me in a fine blue suit. For reasons that baffle me, she has also chosen to wear a hat, from which descends a coarse black mesh, presumably intended to suggest a veil. I think of telling her that the funeral is not yet, but Barbara has never shared the blacker side of my sense of humor. Beside me, sketching madly, are three artists from the local TV stations drawing my profile. Behind them are the reporters and the court buffs, all awaiting my reactions upon first being called a murderer in public.

At two o'clock Nico enters from the cloakroom, with Molto close behind. Delay is without restraint and goes on answering the questions of reporters who followed him into the little side anteroom. He talks to them through the open door. The prosecuting attorney, I think to myself. The fucking P.A. Barbara has taken my hand, and with Nico's appearance she grips it a little tighter.

When I first met Nico, a dozen years ago, I recognized him instantly as a smart-ass ethnic kid, familiar to me from high school and the streets, the kind who, over the years, I had selfconsciously chosen not to be: savvier than he was smart, boastful, always talking. But with few others to look to, I formed with Nico the sort of fast association of fresh recruits. We went to lunch together. We helped each other with briefs. After our first few years, we drifted, a result of our native differences. Having clerked for the Chief Justice of the State Supreme Court, I was perceived as lawyerly. Nico, like dozens of deputy P.A.'s for decades past, arrived in the office with his political network already thick. I would listen to him on the telephone. He had been a precinct captain in the organization of his cousin, Emilio Tonnetti, a county commissioner who had secured Nico's position, one of the last political hirings Raymond agreed to. Nico knew half the hacks and functionaries in the County Building, and he never stopped buying tickets to the political golf outings and dinners, and making the rounds.

In truth, he proved a better lawyer than was expected. He can write, although he hates to spend time in the library; and he is effective before a jury. His courtroom persona, as I have observed it over the years, is typical of many prosecutors: humorless, relentless, blandly mean. He has a unique intensity which I always illustrate by telling what is known as the Climax story. I told it last week to Sandy and Kemp, when they asked about the last case I tried with Della Guardia.

That was almost eight years ago, right after we had been assigned to the felony courts. We were both hungry for jury work, and therefore we agreed to try a dead-bang loser of a rape case on reassignment from somebody smarter.

'Delay had the complaining witness, Lucille Fallon, on the witness stand,' I told Sandy and Kemp. Lucille, a dark-skinned lady, had been in a bar at four in the afternoon, when she met the defendant. Her husband, on unemployment, was home with the four kids. Lucille got to talking with the defendant, Freddy Mack, and agreed to accept a ride home. Freddy was a four-time loser, with a prior rape and an assault—which the jury of course never heard anything about—and he got a little overeager and took a straight edge from his pocket, thereby helping himself to what by all appearances was already going to come his way. Hal Lerner had the defendant, and he knocked every black out of the box, so there were a dozen middle-aged white people looking over this Negro lady who'd gotten a little rougher treatment than she wanted when she went out to wander.

Nico and I had spent hours attempting to prepare Lucille for her testimony, with no visible result. She looked terrible, a frumpy fat lady in a tight dress, rambling on about this awful thing that happened to her. Her husband was in the front row and she laid it on thick, making up an entirely new version of events right in the courtroom. Now she had met Freddy as he was emerging from the tavern and asked her for directions. She was already heading for devastation on cross when Nico finally began to elicit testimony about The Act.

And what did Mr. Mack do then, Mrs. Fallon?

He done it.

What was that, ma'am?

What he been sayin he do.

Did he have intercourse with you, Mrs. Fallon?

Yes, sir, he done.

Did he place his sex organ inside yours?

Uh huh.

And where was the razor?

Right here. Right here on my throat. Pressin right there, I

thought every time I breathe he goin to slice me open.

All right, ma'am. Nico was about to move on, when I, seated at counsel table, handed him a note. That's right, said Nico, I forgot. Did he have a climax, ma'am?

Sir?

Did he have a climax?

No, sir. He be drivin a Ford Fairlane.

Delay never smiled. Judge Farragut was laughing so hard that he hid under the bench, and one of the jurors, literally, rolled out of his seat. Nico never even quivered. 'And after they came back NG,' I told Jamie and Sandy, 'he swore he would never try a case with me again. He said that because I had not managed to keep a straight face, I gave the jury the feeling it wasn't a serious case.'

Nico is looking happy enough today. The radiance of power hangs around him. He is wearing his carnation again, and he could not possibly carry himself more erect. He looks trim and well turned out in a new dark suit. There is an attractive vitality to him, as he moves back and forth, trading shots with the reporters, mixing answers to serious questions with personal remarks. One thing is for sure, I think, the son of a bitch is enjoying himself at my expense. His is this season's media hero, the man who solved the murder of the year. You cannot pick up a local paper without seeing his face. Twice last week I saw columns suggesting that Nico might try out for the mayoral race, two years down the line. Nico responded by pledging his fealty to Bolcarro, but you wonder where those columns came from.

Nonetheless, Stern has insisted that Nico has endeavored to handle the case fairly. He has talked to the press far more than either of us believes is appropriate, but not all of the leaks have come from him, or even Tommy Molto. The police department is beyond its meager capacities for restraint with a case like this. Nico has been candid with Stern about the progress of the investigation; he shared the physical evidence as it developed, and he gave me notice of the indictment. He agreed that I was not a flight risk, and will consent to entry of a signature bond. Most important, perhaps, he has thus far done me the favor of not adding an additional charge of obstruction of justice.

It was Stern, during one of our early conferences, who first pointed out the jeopardy I was in were I to be indicted for willfully concealing facts material to the investigation.

'A jury, Rusty, is very likely to believe you were in that apartment that night, and that at the very least you should have spoken up about it and certainly not lied in your meeting with Horgan and Molto and Della Guardia and MacDougall. Your conversation with Detective Lipranzer concerning the MUD sheets from your home is also very damaging.'

Stern was matter-of-fact about all this. His cigar was stuck in the corner of his mouth as he spoke. Did his eye flicker up for just an instant? He is the most subtle man I've met. Somehow I knew why the topic had been raised. Should he go to Nico with that deal? That was what he was asking. I could not get more than three years for obstruction of justice. I would be out in eighteen months. I would have my son again before he's grown. In five years I could probably regain my license to practice law.

I have not lost my power to reason. But I cannot overcome the emotional inertia. I want back the life I had. No less. I want this not to be. I do not want to be marked as long as I live. To plead would be the same as conceding to an unneeded amputation. Worse.

No plea, I told Sandy.

No, of course not. Of course. He looked at me with disbelief. He had not raised the subject.

In the weeks that followed, we assumed that Della Guardia would include this surer count in the indictment. In moments of weird buoyancy, particularly in the last weeks, when it became clear that charges were being readied, I fantasized that the indictment might be for obstruction alone. Instead, the indictment charged only murder. There are tactical reasons that a prosecutor might make that choice. An obstruction count would offer a tempting—and to a prosecutor, unsatisfying—compromise for a jury inclined to find me guilty but uneasy with the circumstantial nature of Nico's case. But on the day the indictment was returned, Sandy gave me what I found a surprising account of Nico's decision.

'I have spent a good deal of time, of course, speaking with Nico lately,' Sandy told me. 'He speaks of you and Barbara with some feeling. He has told me on two or three occasions stories of your early days together in the office. Briefs he says you wrote for him. Evenings that he enjoyed with the two of you while he was married. I must say, Rusty, that he seems sincere. Molto is a zealot. He hates every person he prosecutes. But about Nico I am not so sure. I believe, Rusty, that he has been deeply affected by this case and that he made this choice as a matter of fairness. He has decided that it would be irresponsible to put an end to your professional life simply because you were indiscreet, for whatever reason, and to whatever degree. If you are guilty of this murder, then you must be punished, he thinks. Otherwise, he is content to let you go. And I for one applaud him for that. I believe,' said the lawyer whom I have thus far paid $25,000 to defend me, 'that is the correct approach.'

"Criminal Case 86–1246," calls out Alvin, Judge Mumphrey's handsome black docket clerk. My stomach sinks and I head up toward the podium. Jamie is behind me. Judge Mumphrey, who entered only a moment ago, is getting settled on the bench. The cynics sometimes explain Ed's ascension to chief judge as a function of his good looks. He was an elected judiciary's concession to the media age, someone whom voters would think of with comfort when they faced the judge's retention ballot. Ed's appearance is wonderfully judicial, with fine silver hair drawn straight back from the brow and features regular and yet sharp enough to be stern. He is asked a couple times each year to pose for one of the bar journals in some piece of advertising.

Della Guardia ends up standing beside me. Molto is a few feet behind. As good as Nico looks, Tommy is a disheveled mess. His vest, absurd by itself in July, has ridden up on his substantial belly and his shirt-sleeves stick too far out of his jacket. His hair has not been combed. Now that I've seen Molto, the impulse to call him a twerp, which I thought I would have to stifle, has passed. Instead, I seek to look Nico in the eye. He nods.

"Rusty," he says simply.

"Delay," I answer. When I look down toward his waist, I see that he has covertly offered his hand.

I do not have a chance to test the full extent of my charity. Kemp has caught hold of my coat sleeve and jerks it violently to pull me aside. He comes to stand between Della Guardia and me. We both know that I do not have to be told not to talk to the prosecutors.

Judge Mumphrey from the walnut bench looks down and

smiles at me circumspectly before he speaks. I appreciate the recognition.

"This is Criminal Case 86–1246. Let me ask counsel to identify themselves for the record."

"Your Honor, I am Nico Della Guardia, on behalf of the people of the state. With me is Chief Deputy District Attorney Thomas Molto."

Funny, the things that get you. I cannot suppress the briefest sound when I hear my title with Molto's name. Kemp jerks my sleeve again.

"Quentin Kemp, Your Honor, of Alejandro Stern, P.C., on behalf of the defendant, Rožat K. Sabich. I would request leave, Your Honor, to file our appearance."

Jamie's motion is allowed, and the court records now officially indicate that Stern and Co. are my lawyers. Jamie then moves on.

"Your Honor, the defendant is present in court. We would acknowledge receipt of Indictment 86–1246 and waive formal reading. In behalf of Mr. Sabich, Your Honor, we would ask the court to enter a plea of not guilty to the charge."

"Plea of not guilty to the indictment," repeats Judge Mumphrey, making a note on the court record. Bail is set by agreement as a $50,000 signature bond. "Is there a request from either party for a pre-trial conference?" This is the plea-bargaining session, usually an automatic, since it helps both sides buy time. Delay starts to speak, but Kemp interrupts.

"Your Honor, such a meeting would be an unnecessary waste of the court's time." He looks down at his legal pad for the words that Sandy wrote. When Kemp gets outside, he will read the same speech again live for the TV Minicam teams. "The charges in this case are very grave, and they are entirely false. The reputation of one of the city's finest public servants and attorneys has been impugned and, perhaps, destroyed with no basis in fact. In the truest sense of the words, justice in this case must be swift, and we ask the court therefore to set an immediate trial date."

The rhetoric is splendid, but tactics of course govern this demand. Sandy has emphasized to me that a quick disposition will avoid interminable strain on my shattered emotions. But disordered though I may be, I recognize the fundamental rationale. Time is with the prosecutor in this case. Delay's principal evidence will not deteriorate. My fingerprints will not lose their memory. The MUD records will not die. With time the P.A.'s case can only become stronger. A witness from the scene might appear. There may be some account of what happened to the murder weapon.

Kemp's request is a significant departure from form, since most defendants view delay as a second-best alternative to acquittal. Our demand seems to catch Nico and Molto short. Again, Della Guardia starts to speak, but Judge Mumphrey interrupts. For whatever reason, he has heard enough.

"The defendant has waived pre-trial conference. The matter will therefore be set over immediately for trial. Mr. Clerk," he says, "please draw a name." About five years ago, after a scandal in the clerk's office, the last chief judge, Foley, solicited suggestions on a method to ensure that the selection of a trial judge for a lawsuit was completely random. I came up with the idea that the draw be made in court, in front of everybody. The proposal—put forth of course in Horgan's name—was immediately adopted, and I believe was the touchstone for Raymond's belief that I had executive ability. Now wooden plaques, each bearing the name of a judge, are spun inside a closed cage, borrowed from a bingo game. Alvin, the clerk, rolls the bones, as they are known. He pulls the first into the opening.

"Judge Lyttle," he says. Larren Lyttle. Raymond's old partner, the defense lawyer's dream. I am lightheaded. Kemp reaches back and with no other movement squeezes my hand. Molto actually groans. I am pleased to see that up on the bench Judge Mumphrey for an instant seems to smile.

"The case will be set down to Judge Lyttle's docket for motions and trial. Defendant's motions to be filed in fourteen days, the prosecuting attorney to respond according to Judge Lyttle's order." Judge Mumphrey picks up his gavel. He is about to move on, but looks down at Nico for a moment. "Mr. Della Guardia, I should have interrupted Mr. Kemp, but I suppose this case is likely to inspire many speeches by the time that it concludes. I do not mean to endorse what he said. But he is correct when he observes that these are very serious charges. Against a lawyer who I think we all know has served this court with distinction for many years. Let me say to you, sir, simply that I, like all other citizens of this county, hope that in this case that justice will be done—and has been done." Ed Mumphrey nods again to me, and the next case is called.

Della Guardia leaves as he came, through the cloakroom exit. Kemp is straining to maintain a straight face. Jamie puts his pad in his briefcase and watches Nico go.

"He walks pretty well, doesn't he," asks Jamie, "with all that sticking out his behind?"

20

"I take it," Barbara says, "that you're very pleased about Larren."
We are on the highway now, finally free of the downtown traffic.
Barbara is behind the wheel. We have learned in recent weeks
that my distraction is such that the world is not safe when I
drive. There is a primitive relief with the cameras and the clamor
behind us. The press pack followed us from the courthouse,
down the street, snapping pictures, the huge video cameras
lurching toward us like some monster's eyes. We walked slowly.
Try, Stern urged us earlier, to look relaxed. We left Kemp at a
corner two blocks on. If every day goes like this one, he said,
Nico won't get past opening statement. Jamie by nature is a
cheerful soul, but somehow his bonhomie conjured a shadow.
Every day will not be like this one. Grimmer moments are ahead.
I shook his hand and told him he was a pro. Barbara kissed him
on the cheek.

"Larren is a good draw," I say, "the best probably." I hesitate
only because of Raymond. Neither he nor Judge Lyttle would
ever communicate outside of court about the case, but the
presence of the judge's best friend as a witness is bound to have
some impact, one way or the other, depending on the balance of
Raymond's sympathies. I touch Barbara's hand, on the wheel. "I
appreciate your being there."

"I don't mind," she says. "Really. It was very interesting," she
adds, sincere as ever in her curiosity, "if you don't consider the
circumstances."

Mine is what the lawyers call a 'high-profile case'—the press
attention will continue to be intense. In that situation, communication with the eventual jurors begins long before they come to

court for jury service. Nico has been winning the press battles so far. I have to do what I can to project a positive image. Since I am charged, in essence, with murder and adultery, it is important that the public believe that my wife has not lost faith in me. Barbara's attendance at every event the media will cover is critical. Stern insisted that she come downtown so that he could explain this to her face to face. Given her distaste for public occasions, her narrow suspicions of outsiders, I expected her to regard this as a taxing assignment. But she has not resisted. Her support in the last two months has been unfailing. While she continues to view me as the victim of my own follies—this time for having ever been enamored of public life and cutthroat politics—she recognizes that things have passed well beyond the stage where I am being served right. She regularly expresses confidence in my vindication and, without a word from me, presented me with a $50,000 cashier's check to cover Sandy's retainer and the later fees, which was drawn from a trust which her father left exclusively in her control. She has listened with fast attention to hours of table conversation in which I lambaste Nico and Molto or describe the intricacies of little strategies that Stern has devised. In the evenings, when I am apt to recede to a withdrawn vacancy, she will come to stroke my hand. She has taken on some of my suffering. Although she evinces bravery, I know that there are moments, alone, when she has cried.

Not only the stress of these extraordinary events, but the radical alteration of my schedule has added a new tempo to our relations. I journey to the library; draft notes for my defense; root pointlessly in the garden. But we are alone together now, much of the time. With the summer, Barbara has few responsibilities at the U. and we linger over breakfast after I drop Nat off for camp. At lunch, I go out and pick greens for our salad. And a new sexual languor has moved softly into our relationship. 'I was thinking we should do it,' she announced one afternoon from the sofa, where she was reclining with obscure reading material and Belgian chocolates. Thus, an afternoon encounter has become part of our new routine. It is easiest for her to come crouched over me, hunkered down. The birds sing outside the windows; the daylight seeps beyond the edges of the bedroom blinds. Barbara rolls around with my pin driven deep inside her, that muscular vortex at work, her eyes closed but rolling, her face otherwise serene as her hue increases and she works toward the point of release.

Barbara is an imaginative, athletic lover; it was not sensual deprivation which drove me to Carolyn. I cannot complain about hang-ups or fetishes or what Barbara will not do. Even in the worst of our times, even amid the upheaval that followed my idiotic confessions last winter, sex was not abandoned. We are of the revolutionary generation. We spoke openly of sexuality. When we were young we tended it like a magic lantern, and we continue to find its place. We have become expert in the physiognomy of pleasure, the nodes to press, the points to massage. Barbara, a woman of the eighties, would find it a further insult to do without.

For the time being, the clinical aspect which inhabited our relations for months is gone. But even now I find something desperate and sad in Barbara's loving. There are distances yet left to cross. I lie in bed in the sweet afternoons while Barbara dozes, the midday suburban quiet soothing and beguiling after years of downtown racket, and consider the mystery to me that is my wife.

Even at the zenith of my passion for Carolyn, I gave no thought to leaving. If my marriage to Barbara at times has been equivocal, our family life has not. We both dote relentlessly on Nat. I grew up knowing that other families lived differently from mine. They spoke across the dinner table; they went together to the movies and soda fountains. I saw them running, playing ball in the open fields of the Public Forest. I yearned. They shared a life. Our existence as a family, as parents and child, is the single aspiration of my childhood that I feel I have fulfilled, the only wound of that time I have healed.

And yet to pretend that Nathaniel is our sole salvation is too cynical. Pessimistic. False. Even in the grimmest period, we both respond to the inner commandments that find some value here. My wife is an attractive woman—extremely so. She minds the mirror carefully, assuming certain predetermined angles to be sure she remains intact: her bustline still peaked; the waist, notwithstanding pregnancy, still girlish; her dark, precise features not yet losing fineness in any gathering of adipose, or slackening from beneath the jaw. She could certainly find suitors; she chooses not to. She is an able woman. And on her father's death, $100,000 was placed in trust for her, so that it is not need which keeps her from departing. For better or for worse, there must be truth in the bitter words that she will sometimes hurl at me in the heat of quarrels: that I am the only one, the one person, save Nat, whom she has ever loved.

In the clement periods, as now, Barbara's devotion is apt to be extreme. She is eager to have me absorb her attentions. I become her ambassador to the outside world, bringing back to Nearing observations and stories. When I am on trial, I will frequently arrive home at 11 p.m. or midnight to find Barbara waiting in her housecoat, my dinner warm. We sit together and she listens with her intense, abstracted curiosity to what has taken place that day, much like a thirties child before the radio. The dishes clank; I speak with my mouth full, and Barbara laughs and marvels about the witnesses, the cops, the lawyers whom she sees only through me.

And for me? What is there? Certainly I value loyalty and commitment, kindness and attention, when they are shown. Her instants of selfless love, so focused upon me, are balm for my abraded ego. But it would be phony and hollow if I were to claim that there are not also moments when I despise her. The injured son of an angry man, I cannot fully master my vulnerabilities to her blackish moods. In her fits of lacerating sarcasm, I feel my hands twitch with the impulse toward strangulation. In response to these periods, I have taught myself to manifest an indifference, which, over time, has begun to become real. We stumble into a sickening cycle, a tug of war in which we are each maneuvering for position by forever stepping back.

But those times are far off now, and almost forgiven. We wait instead on the brink of discovery. What is it that holds me? Some yearning. In the languid afternoons, I seem almost to seize it, even while the doors and windows of my soul are thrown open to a fundamental gratitude. We have never been without momentary eruptions; Barbara is incapable of long-term serenity. But we have also made our trips to the brightest spots and highest places; with Barbara Bernstein I certainly have known the finest moments of my life. The first years were innocent, spirited, full of that clamorous passion and a sense of mystery that exceeds what can be described: I *long* at times, in transported recollection I pine, I perish with a groping sensation—I am like some misbegotten thing left at the end of science-fiction adventures which reels about with stumps outstretched, beckoning toward the creatures of which it was once one: Let me in again! Unwork time.

When I was in the law school at the U., Barbara was teaching. We lived in a two-and-a-half-room apartment, ancient, vermin-ridden, in scandalous disrepair. The radiators shot out streams of boiling water in the middle of the winter; the mice and roaches claimed as their own domain any cabinet space below the level of the sink. Only because it was considered student quarters did this home escape categorization as what was then called slum housing. Our landlords were two Greeks, a husband and a wife, one sicker than the other. They lived a floor above and across the courtyard. We could hear his emphysemic eruptions in any season. Her problem was arthritis and degenerative diseases of the heart. I dreaded bringing up the rent each month, because of the odor of decay, a dense, foreign, rotting smell, something like cabbage, that came into the air as soon as their door opened. But it was all that we could afford. With my tuition deducted from a starting teacher's salary, we approached the bureaucratic standards for recognized poverty.

We had a standing joke, that we were so poor that the only form of entertainment we could afford was fucking. This humor was more in the nature of shared embarrassment, for we knew that we verged on the excessive. Those were sensuous years. The end of the week was something I would drag myself toward. We made our own kind of Sabbath: dinner alone, a bottle of wine, and then lovely, long, ambling amours. We could start anywhere around the apartment, and move, in growing deshabille, across the rug and toward the bedroom. This would sometimes go on for more than an hour, me aching and priapic, and my dark little beauty, her breasts tipped in ecstasy, as we lolled and meandered over one another. And it was one night like this, as I led Barbara toward the final steps into the bedroom, that I saw our blind was open and, above, our two elderly neighbors, their faces toward the window, were watching. There was something so starstruck and innocent about their expressions that in recollection they appear to me like startled animals: does, rabbits: a look of uncomprehending, roundeyed wonder. I never suspected them of having spied for long, a feeling which in no

way eased my shame. I stood there with my erect member at
that instant in Barbara's palm, which was wet with almond oil.
Barbara saw them, too, I know. Because as I drew back and
started toward the blind she stopped me. She touched my hand;
and then she took hold of me again. "Don't look," she said, "don't
look," she murmured, her breath sweet and warm on my face.
"They're almost gone."

21

One week after my arraignment, Sandy and I stand together in the reception area of the law firm in which Raymond Horgan has been a partner since May. A very classy affair. The floor is parquet, covered by one of the largest Persian rugs I have ever seen, rose hues on a vibrant navy field. Lots of expensive-looking abstract art is on the walls, and glass-and-chrome end tables are set at each corner of the room, with copies of *Forbes* and *The Wall Street Journal* laid out in ranks. A sweet blonde who probably gets an extra couple grand a year for being so good-looking is behind a fancy rosewood desk, taking names.

Sandy has hold of my lapel in the lightest way, instructing me in a murmur. The young lawyers who hustle by in their shirt-sleeves probably cannot even see his lips move. I am not to hold a discussion, Sandy says. He will ask the questions. My presence is intended, as he puts it, merely as a stimulant. Above all, he says, I am to remain collected, whatever the climate of our reception.

"Do you know something?" I ask.

"One hears things," Sandy says. "Speculation is pointless when we will so soon know answers firsthand." Sandy, in fact, hears many things. A good defense lawyer has an intricate network. Clients bring information. Reporters. Sometimes there are cops who are friends. Not to mention other defense lawyers. When I was a prosecutor, the defense bar seemed to be a kind of tribe, always on their tom-toms whenever there was any piece of news that they could properly communicate. Sandy has told me that Della Guardia subpoenaed Horgan to the grand jury right after Nico took office and that Raymond tried to resist on grounds of executive privilege. Sandy knows this, he has said, from an excellent source. Given this skirmishing, I would expect continuing hostility between Raymond and Nico, but Sandy's reaction when he saw Raymond's name on the witness list implies other knowledge. Sandy, of course, would never betray the confidence of whoever it is who gave him a notion of Raymond's intentions.

Horgan's secretary comes out to retrieve us, and halfway to his office, Raymond himself is there. He is in his shirt-sleeves, without his coat.

"Sandy. Rusty." He claps me once briefly on the shoulder as he shakes my hand. He has put on more weight, and his gut is straining against the lower buttons on his shirt. "Have you fellas ever been up here?"

Raymond takes us on a tour. With the incentives of the tax code, the law firms and corporations have become the new Versailles. Raymond tells us about the artwork, names I know he has learned only from magazines. Stella. Johns. Rauschenberg. "I especially like this piece," he says. Squiggles and squares. In a conference room, there is a thirty-foot table milled from a single piece of green malachite.

Sandy asks about Raymond's practice. Mostly federal work so far, Raymond says, which he thinks is a good thing. He has a grand jury going great guns in Cleveland. His client sold parachutes to the Defense Department; they contain defective rope. "A purely inadvertent oversight," Raymond tells us, with a knavish smile. "One hundred ten thousand pieces."

Finally, we arrive at Raymond's office. They have given him a corner and he has the fancy views, west and south. The Wall of Respect has been reinstalled here with a few additions. A panoramic shot of the dais at Raymond's last inauguration is at the center now. With forty others, I am there, way off on the right.

I had not noticed a young man until Raymond introduces him. Peter something. An associate. Peter has a pad and pen. Peter is the prover. He will cover Raymond in the event there is later controversy about what he said.

"So what can I do you for?" Raymond asks, after he has called out for coffee.

"First," says Sandy, "Rusty and I both want to thank you for taking the time to meet. You are very gracious."

Raymond waves this off. "What can I say?" A non sequitur of sorts. I think he means to suggest he wants to help without saying that.

"I think it best, I am sure you understand," says Stern, "that Rusty not take part in our conversation. I hope you do not mind if he simply listens." As he says this, Sandy glances toward Peter, who has raised his pad and is already relentlessly making notes.

"Sure, it's your ball game." Raymond starts fussing on his desk, brushing at dust neither I—nor he—can see. "I'm surprised you wanted him to come. But that's up to you guys."

Sandy flexes his brow characteristically, one of those Latin gestures reflecting something too delicate or imprecise to say.

"So what do you want me to tell you?" Raymond again asks.

"We find your name on Della Guardia's witness list. That, of course, motivates our visit."

"Sure," says Raymond, and throws up his hands. "You know how it is, Alejandro. The guy sends you a party invitation, you gotta go to the ball." I have seen this bluff, hearty manner from Raymond a thousand times before. He gestures too much; his broad features are always tending toward a smile. His eyes seldom meet those of the person to whom he is speaking. This was how he negotiated with defense lawyers. I'm a great guy, but I just can't help. When his visitors left, Raymond would often call them names.

"So you will be appearing by subpoena?"

"You bet."

"I see. We received no statement. Do I take it that you have not spoken to the prosecutors?"

"No, I've talked to them a little bit. You know, I talk to you, I talk to them. We had some troubles at first. Mike Duke had to work some things out. I've sat down with Tom Molto a few times now. Shit, more than a few times. But you know, it's one on one. I haven't signed a statement or anything like that." A bad sign. Very bad. Panic and anger both are rising in me, but I try to stave them off. Raymond is getting star-witness treatment. No formal statements to minimize the inconsistencies that would endanger him on cross-examination. Multiple sessions with the prosecutor, because he is so important to the case.

"You mention troubles," says Sandy. "There is no question of immunity, I take it?"

"Shit no. Nothing like that. It's just that some of these guys around here, my new partners— This whole thing makes them nervous. It could be a little embarrassing for me, too." He laughs. "That's a hell of a way to start out. I'm here three days and I get a grand-jury subpoena. I bet Solly Weiss loved that," he says, referring to the firms managing partner.

Sandy is silent. He has his hat and briefcase positioned decorously in the center of his lap. He studies Horgan, without apology, searching him. The man is volunteering nothing. Stern becomes like this at moments, suddenly abandons all his comfortable civility and seems to sink beneath the surface of things.

"And what have you told them?" Sandy finally asks quietly. He is very still.

"My partners?"

"Certainly not. I was wondering what we might expect in terms of your testimony. You've been on this side of things before." Sandy subsides into his more familiar tone, gentle and indirect. When he asked what Raymond told them, a second ago, it was like a flash of light suddenly reflected. His mettle was at once obvious and fully summoned.

"Well, you know, I don't want to get into a word-for-word." He nods in the direction of the young man taking notes.

"Of course not," Sandy says. "Topics. Areas. Whatever you feel you can comfortably tell. It is very difficult from the outside even to guess sometimes what a witness might be called to discuss. You know this yourself, so well."

Sandy is probing for something that I do not completely understand. We could get up now and leave if we were merely here to accomplish the previously announced purpose of our visit. We know where Raymond Horgan stands. He is not a friend.

"I'm going to testify about Rusty's conduct of the investigation. How he told me he'd be interested in handling it. And a later conversation we had, about aspects of my personal life—"

"Just a second." I can take no more. "How *I* was interested in handling the investigation? Raymond, you asked me to take the case."

"There was a conversation between us."

From the corner of my eye, I note Stern raising a hand, but I fix on Horgan.

"Raymond, you *asked* me. You told me that you were busy with the campaign, it had to be in the best hands, you couldn't worry about somebody else lousing this up."

"That's possible."

"That's what happened."

I look to Stern, seeking support. He is sitting back in his chair, staring at me. He is simply furious.

"I'm sorry," I say quietly.

Raymond goes on, oblivious to my exchange with my lawyer.

"I don't remember that, Rusty. Maybe that's what happened— as you said, I was busy with the campaign. But the way I remember it, we had a conversation, a day, two days before the funeral, and at the end of that conversation we had agreed that you'd be handling the case, and the idea that you handle it, it's my feeling that that was more your idea than mine; I was receptive, I admit that, but I remember some surprise about the way things ended up."

"Raymond— What are you trying to do to me, Raymond?" I look at Sandy, who has his eyes closed. "Can't I just ask him that?"

But I have finally pushed things beyond the crest; Raymond is traveling full speed downhill on his own momentum. He leans as far as he can across his desk.

"What am I trying to do to you?" He repeats the question twice, growing flushed. "What were *you* trying to do to *me*, Rusty? What the hell are your fingerprints doing all over that goddamn glass? What's all this bullshit of sitting in my office asking about who I'm fucking, and never then, when it would have been friendly, or two weeks before, when I assigned you to that investigation—which, as I remember, I bawled you out a couple times for not pushing—" He turns abruptly to Sandy and points. "That's something else I'm going to testify to," he tells Sandy, then looks back at me. "—Never, two weeks before, when it was the professional thing to have done, *never* at any time do you tell me you were dicking the same gal. I've spent a whole long time on that conversation, Rusty, asking myself what the hell you were doing there? What *were* you doing?"

This scene is more than Peter the associate can handle. He has stopped writing entirely and is just watching us. Stern points at Peter.

"Under the circumstances, I am advising my client to make no response. Clearly he would like to."

"So that's what I'm going to testify to," Raymond tells Sandy. He stands up and ticks the points off on his fingers. "That he wanted the case. That I had to chew his ass repeatedly to move it. That he was more interested in finding out who else was fucking Carolyn than who had murdered her. And that when push finally came to shove, he sat in my office and gave us all a bunch of happy horseshit that he'd been nowhere near Carolyn's apartment that night. That's what I'll testify to. And I'll be goddamned pleased to do it."

"Very well, Raymond," says Sandy. He picks up his hat, a gray felt homburg, off the chair on which he laid it in the midst of his efforts to quiet me.

I stare directly at Horgan. He looks back.

"Nico Della Guardia was honest about the fact that he was out to screw me," Horgan says.

Sandy steps between us. He hauls me to my feet, both hands on my arm.

"Enough," he declares.

"Son of a bitch," I say as we are moving briskly ahead of Peter, on our way out. "Son of a bitch."

"We know where we stand," Stern says quietly. As we enter the reception area, he tells me in the barest sibilance to please hush. This enforced silence sits in my mouth like a bit. As the elevator sinks, I find myself with a bursting desperation to speak, and I grab Sandy's arm as we reach the ground floor.

"What is it with him?"

"He is a very angry man." Stern walks determinedly through the marble lobby.

"I see that. Has Nico convinced him that I'm guilty?"

"Probably. Certainly he thinks you could have been a good deal more cautious, particularly on his behalf."

"I wasn't a faithful servant?"

Sandy makes another of his Latin movements: hands, eyes, brow. He has other matters on his mind. As he walks, he cocks a grave eye in my direction.

"I had no idea that Horgan had an affair with Carolyn. Or that you had conversed with him on that subject."

"I didn't remember the conversation."

"No doubt," says Stern in a tone which implies that he doubts me a good deal. "Well, I think Della Guardia will be able to use that to his advantage. When was it that this relationship took place between Raymond and Carolyn?"

"Right after she stopped seeing me."

Sandy stops. He makes no effort to mask his pain. He talks to himself an instant in his native tongue.

"Well, Nico is certainly coming closer to a motive."

"But he's still some distance," I say hopefully. He still cannot prove the principal relationship between Carolyn and me.

"Some," Sandy tells me. There is a deliberate flatness in his expression. He is clearly quite put out with me, both for my performance upstairs and for keeping so significant a detail from him. We will have to speak at length, he says. Right now he has a court call. He puts his homburg on and ventures into the blazing heat without glancing back at me.

In the lobby I feel instantly bereft. So many emotions are surging that there is a kind of dizziness. Most of all, there is caustic shame for my own stupidity. After all these years, I still failed to recognize how these events would impact on Raymond Horgan, although now the trajectory of his emotions seems as predictable as a hyperbolic curve. Raymond Horgan is a public man. He has lived to make a reputation. He said he was not a pol, but he has a pol's affliction: he thrives on acclamation, he yearns for the good opinion of everyone. He does not care about my guilt or innocence. He is devastated by his own disgrace. His own chief deputy indicted for murder. The investigation, which he let me run, sabotaged right before his face. And he will have to sit upon the witness stand and broadcast his own indiscretions. There will be tavern jokes for years about being a deputy P.A. *under* Raymond Horgan. Between his conduct and mine, the office will sound more active than a Roman bath. Worst of all is the fact that the murder took Raymond from the life he really loved; it changed the course of the election; it sent him here to his glass-and-steel cage. What infuriates Raymond, inspires his rage, is not really that I committed this crime. It is that he believes he was intended to be another victim. He said as much when he finally let things loose. I screwed him. I killed Carolyn to bring him down. And I succeeded. Horgan thinks he has the whole thing figured out. And he has clearly planned his vengeance.

I finally leave the building. The heat is intense; the sun is blinding. I feel instantly unsteady on my feet. Compulsively, I try to calculate the one thousand subtle impacts on the trial of Raymond's testimony and his evident hostility to me, but that soon gives way. Ideas come and go erratically. I see my father's face. I cannot make things connect. After all these weeks, after all of this, I feel that I am finally going to go to pieces, and I find, stunningly, that as I turn about in the street, I am praying, a habit of my childhood, when I would try to cover my bets with a God in whom I knew I did not much believe.

And now, dear God, I think, dear God in whom I do not believe, I pray to you to stop this, for I am deathly frightened. Dear God, I smell my fear, with an odor as distinct as ozone on the air after a lightning flash. I feel fear so palpably it has a color, an oozing fiery red, and I feel it pitifully in my bones, which ache. My pain is so extreme that I can barely move down this hot avenue, and for a moment cannot, as my backbone bows with fear, as if a smelted rod, red-hot and livid, had been laid there. Dear God, dear God, I am in agony and fear, and whatever I may have done to make you bring this down upon me, release me, please, I pray, release me. Dear God in whom I do not believe, dear God, let me go free.

22

In the United States, the prosecution in a criminal case may not appeal the outcome. This is a constitutional principle, declared by the U.S. Supreme Court. An American prosecutor, alone among all the advocates who stand before the bench—among the sophisticates and hacks, the collection lawyers in their rayon suits, the bankruptcy moguls, the divorce-court screamers, the gold-chained dope lawyers or the smooth likes of Sandy Stern, the big-firm "litigators" who perform even routine courtroom tasks in pairs—the prosecutor alone is without right to seek review of a judge's trial rulings. Whatever the majesty of his office, the power of the policemen he commands, the bias in his favor jurors always bring to court, a prosecutor is often under a continuing duty to endure in silence various forms of judicial abuse.

Nowhere, while I was a P.A., was that obligation more regularly or onerously borne than in the courtroom of Judge Larren Lyttle. He is sly and learned and indisposed by the experience of a lifetime to the state's point of view. The habits of twenty years as a defense lawyer, in which he regularly manhandled and belittled prosecutors and police, have never left him on the bench. And beyond that, he has a black man's authentic education in the countless ways that prosecutorial discretion can be used to arrogantly excuse unreasoning caprice. The random and complete injustices which he witnessed on the streets have become a kind of emotional encyclopedia for him, informing each decision that is made almost reflexively against the state. After two or three years, Raymond gave up coming to court to argue. The two of them would bellow at each other as they must have done in their old law office. Then Larren would bang his gavel, more adamant than ever, and declare a recess so that he and Raymond could make up back in chambers and plan to have a drink.

Judge Lyttle is on the bench, receiving status reports on other cases, when Stern and I arrive. It is always as if there is a spotlight. He is the only person you see—handsome, mercurial, extraordinarily prepossessing. Judge Lyttle is a big human being, six foot four or five and broad across. His first fame came as a football and basketball hero at the U., where he went on scholarship. He has a full head of medium-length African hair, most of it gone gray, a big face, enormous hands, a princely style of oratory, with a large voice, full across all the male ranges. His intelligence, which is mighty, is also somehow transmitted by his presence. Some say Larren sees his future on the federal bench; others guess that his real goal is to succeed Albright Williamson as the congressman from the district north of the river, whenever it is that Williamson ceases defying age and his cardiologist's predictions. Whatever his inclinations, Larren is someone whose prospects and personal powers make him in these parts a man of capital importance.

We were summoned here yesterday morning by a phone call from the judge's docket clerk. With the filing of the defendant's pre-trial motions two days ago, His Honor desires to hold a status hearing on my case. I suspect that he is going to rule on some of our requests, and perhaps discuss a trial date.

Sandy and I wait in silence. Kemp has stayed behind. The three of us spent yesterday together and I told them everything I knew about each witness Nico has listed for the case. Stern's questions remained precise and limited. He still did not ask me if I screwed Carolyn that night, or was there for any other reason, or whether, notwithstanding my prior proclamations, I own any instrument that might conform to the crack atop her head.

I spend these moments, familiar downtime in a courtroom lawyer's life, looking about. The reporters are all here again, although the sketchers have stayed home. Judge Lyttle, politic in the ways a judge can be, treats reporters well. There is a table set aside for them against the western wall and he always gives the press room a call before issuing any decision of import. The courtroom where the course of the rest of my life will be determined is a jewel. The jury box is set off by a walnut rail and descending baubles, round spheres of beautifully grained wood. The witness stand is similarly constructed and abuts the judge's bench, which is well elevated and covered by a walnut canopy supported by two red marble pillars. The docket clerk, the bailiff, and the court reporter (whose job is to write down every word spoken in open court) are in a well before the bench. A few feet in front of them, two tables have been placed, finely hewn, again in darker walnut, with carefully turned legs. These tables for the lawyers on trial sit perpendicular to the bench. The prosecution, by tradition, will sit nearer the jury.

When all the other business is finished, our case is called. Some of the reporters creep up to the defense table to better hear the proceedings, and the assembly of lawyers—and me—convene before the bench. Stern, Molto, and Nico state their names. Sandy notes my presence. Tommy shoots me a little grin. I bet he's heard about our meeting with Raymond last week.

"Gentlemen," Judge Lyttle begins, "I asked you here because I thought we could do a little work to move this case along. I have some motions from the defendant and I'm prepared to rule on them, unless the prosecutors are particularly anxious to make a response."

Tommy speaks in Nico's ear.

"Only to the motion to disqualify Mr. Molto," Nico says.

Naturally, I think. An entire office working for him, and he's still gun-shy about putting things on paper.

Larren says that he will leave the motion to disqualify to the end, although he has some thoughts about it.

"Now the first motion," Larren says, with the stack of paper right before him, "is a motion to set an immediate trial date. And I've thought about this, and as the prosecutors know, the *Rodriguez* case pled earlier this morning, so I will be free for twelve trial days beginning three weeks from today." Larren looks to his calendar. "August 18. Mr. Stern, can you be here?"

This is an extraordinary development. We had expected nothing sooner than the fall. Sandy will have to set everything else aside—but he barely hesitates.

"With pleasure, Your Honor."

"And the prosecution?"

Nico at once begins to back and fill. He has a vacation planned.

So does Mr. Molto. There is still evidence to be developed. With that, Vesuvius erupts.

"No, no," says Judge Lyttle, "I will hear none of that. No, sir, Mr. Delay Guardia." He pronounces Nico's name that way, as if he is trying to incorporate the nickname. With Larren, you can never tell. "These charges here— These charges are the most serious crime— What else could you do to Mr. Sabich? A prosecutor his entire professional life, and you bring charges like this. We all know why Mr. Stern wants a quick trial. There're no secrets here. We've all been tryin cases for a good part of our lives. Mr. Stern has looked at the evidence you have provided by way of discovery, Mr. Delay Guardia, and he doesn't think you have much of a case. He may not be right. I wouldn't know about that. But if you come into this courtroom chargin a man with a crime, you better be ready to prove it. Right now. Don't be tellin me about what's going to develop. You can't leave this hangin over Mr. Sabich like that old sword of Damocles. No, sir," Larren says again. "We're gonna have a trial three weeks from today."

My blood is ice. Without excusing myself, I take a seat at the head of the defense table. Stern glances back momentarily and seems to smile.

"Now, what else have we got?" says Larren. Just for an instant, as he looks about, there is a private smile. He can never quite hide his satisfaction with himself for trashing a prosecutor. He passes quickly on our motions for production. Every one is granted, as they should be. Tommy complains a little bit about the motion to produce the glass. He reminds the court that the prosecution has the burden of proving a chain of custody—that is, that the glass was never out of the state's hands—an impossibility if the glass is turned over to the defense.

"Well, what is it that the defense wants to do with this glass?"

I stand immediately. "I want to take a look at it, Your Honor."

Sandy gives me a corrosive glance. With his hand on my forearm, he puts me back down in my seat. I will have to learn: it is not my place to speak.

"Fine," says Larren, "Mr. Sabich wants to look at the glass. That's all. He's got that right. The prosecution has got to show him the evidence. You know, I've looked over the discovery and I understand why Mr. Sabich might want to look very carefully at that glass. So that motion will be allowed." Larren points at me. It is the first real notice he has taken of my presence. "And by the way now, Mr. Sabich, you of course will be heard through counsel, but if it's your desire to speak yourself, you have that right. At any time. When we have our conferences in chambers or during the proceedings, you have every right to attend. I want you to know that. We all know Mr. Sabich is a fine trial lawyer, one of the finest trial lawyers we have in these parts, and I'm sure he'll be curious about what we're doin from time to time."

I look at Sandy, who nods, before I answer. I thank the court. I tell him I will listen. My lawyer will speak.

"Very well," the judge says. But his eyes hold the light of a warmth that I have never seen from him in court. I am a defendant now, in his special custody. Like a chieftain or a Mafia don, he owes me some protection while I am in his domain, "Next we have this motion to get into the apartment."

Molto and Nico confer.

"No objection," Nico says, "so long as a police officer is present."

To that, Sandy instantly objects. A few moments of typical courtroom skirmishing follow. Everybody knows what's going on. The prosecutors want to figure out what we are looking for. On the other hand, they have a valid point. Any disturbance of the contents of Carolyn's apartment will hinder their ability to make further use of the scene for evidentiary purposes.

"Well, you have pictures by now," Larren says. "Every time I have one of these cases, I wonder if the prosecutors haven't formed some kind of alliance with Kodak." The reporters all laugh and Larren himself smiles. He is like that. He loves to entertain. He directs his gavel at Della Guardia. "You can have a trooper by the door so you can be sure that no members of the defense remove anything, but I'm not gonna let you snoop on what they're lookin at. The prosecution's had four months to look all over that apartment," Larren says, including in his count the month when I was head of the investigative team. "I think the defense is entitled to a few minutes in peace. Mr. Stern, you draft an appropriate order and I'll sign it. And let's be sure that you give notice in advance to Ms. Polhemus's administrator or executor or whoever represents her estate, so they know what the court intends to allow.

"Now, let's talk about this motion to disqualify Mr. Molto." This is our request to prevent Tommy Molto from acting as one of the trial lawyers on the case, because Nico has said Molto may be a witness.

Nico starts right in. To disqualify one of the prosecutors with three weeks to trial would be an onerous burden. Impossible. The state could never be ready. I do not know if Nico is looking for more time, or trying to defeat the motion. He is probably not sure himself.

"Well, look now, Mr. Della Guardia, I'm not the person who told you to put Mr. Molto on your witness list," Judge Lyttle says. "I cannot imagine how you thought you were going to proceed with a prosecutor who might be a witness. A lawyer may not be an advocate and a witness in the same proceeding. We've been doin business in our courts the same way for about four hundred years now. And I do not intend to change it for this trial, no matter how important it is to any of the participants, no matter how many reporters show up from *Time* or *Newsweek* or anyplace else." Judge Lyttle pauses and squints toward the reporters' gallery, as if he only now had noticed them there.

"But let me say this—" Larren stands up, and wanders behind the bench. Five feet off the ground to start with, he speaks from an enormous height. "Now, I take it, Mr. Delay Guardia, that the statement you are speaking of is the one where Mr. Sabich responds to Mr. Molto's accusation of murder by saying, 'You're right.' "

" 'Yeah, you're right,' " says Nico.

Larren accepts the correction, bowing his large head.

"All right. Now, the state has not offered the statement yet. However, you've indicated your intentions and Mr. Stern has made his motion for that reason. But this is what occurs to me. I really am not sure that statement will come into evidence. Mr. Stern hasn't made any objection yet. He would rather see Mr. Molto disqualified first. But I imagine, Mr. Delay Guardia, that when we get there Mr. Stern is gonna say that this statement is not relevant." This is one of Larren's favorite means of assisting the defense. He predicts objections he is likely to hear. Some of them—like this one—are clearly—going to come. Others never would have occurred to defense counsel. In either event, when formally made, the objections foretold inevitably succeed.

"Your Honor," says Nico, "the man admitted the crime."

"Oh, Mr. Delay Guardia," says Judge Lyttle. "Really! You see, that is my point. You tell a man he's engaged in wrongdoing and he says, 'Yeah, you're right.' Everyone recognizes that's facetious. We all are familiar with that. Now, in my neighborhood, had Mr. Sabich come from those parts, he would have said, 'Yo' momma.'"

There is broad laughter in the courtroom. Larren has scored again. He sits on the bench, laughing himself.

"But you know, in Mr. Sabich's part of town, I would think people say, 'Yeah, you're right,' and what they mean is 'You are wrong.'" Pausing. "To be polite."

More laughter.

"Your Honor," Nico says, "isn't that a question for the jury?"

"On the contrary, Mr. Delay Guardia, that is initially a question for the court. I have to be convinced this evidence is relevant. That it makes the proposition for which it is offered more probable. Now, I am not ruling yet, but, sir, unless you are a good deal more persuasive than you have been so far, I expect that you will find me ruling that this evidence is not relevant. And you might want to keep that in mind in addressing Mr. Stern's motion, because if you're not going to be offering that evidence, or relying on it in cross-examination of the defendant, why then, I'd have to deny the defendant's motion."

Larren smiles. Nico, of course, is screwed. The judge has as much as told him that the statement will not be admitted. Nico's choice is to lose Molto and make a futile effort to introduce the evidence, or to keep Tommy and abandon the proof. It is really no choice at all for him—better to take half a loaf. My statement to Molto has just disappeared from this case.

Molto approaches the podium. "Judge—" he says, and gets no further. Larren interrupts. His face drains of all good humor.

"Now, Mr. Molto, I will not listen to you address the admissibility of your own testimony. Maybe you can convince me that that time-honored rule prohibiting a lawyer from bein a witness in a case he tries shouldn't be applied here, but until you do, I will not hear further from you, sir."

Larren closes business quickly. He says he will see us for trial on August 18. With one more glance toward the reporters, he leaves the bench.

Molto is still standing there, his look of disgruntlement plain.

Tommy's always had a bad habit for a trial lawyer of allowing his
dissatisfaction to be evident. But Judge Lyttle and he have been
going at each other now for many years. I may not have recalled
Carolyn's service in the North Branch, but I could never have
forgotten Larren and Molto. Their disputes were notorious.
Exiled by Bolcarro to that judicial Siberia, Judge Lyttle applied
his own rough justice. The cops were guilty of harassment,
unless proven otherwise. Molto, beleaguered and bitterly unhappy, used to claim that the pimps and junkies and sneak thieves,
some of whom made daily appearances in Larren's courtroom,
would rise to applaud him when he assumed the bench for the
morning call. The police despised Judge Lyttle. They invented
racial epithets that showed the same imagination which put
humankind upon the moon. Larren had been downtown for
years by the time I finished the Night Saints investigation and
Lionel Kenneally was still complaining whenever he heard
Larren's name. There was one story Kenneally must have told
me ten times about a battery case, brought by a cop who claimed
that the defendant had resisted arrest. The cop, named Manos,
said he and the defendant had gotten into a tussle shortly after
the defendant called the cop a name.

What name? Larren asked him.

Here in court, said Manos, I'd rather not say, Judge.

Why, Officer, are you afraid you might offend those present?
Larren gestured toward the forward benches, where the
defendants on the morning call were seated, an assemblage of
hookers, pickpockets, and junkie thieves. Speak freely, Judge
Lyttle said.

He called me motherfucker, Your Honor.

From the benches there were whistles, catcalls, lots of
joviality. Larren gaveled silence, but he was laughing, too.

Why, Officer, said Larren again, still smiling, didn't you know
that is a term of endearment in our community?

The folks on the benches went wild: black-power salutes and a
frenzy of stroking palms. Manos took all of this in silence. A
minute later, when Molto rested, Larren directed a verdict for
defense.

'And the great part,' Kenneally told me, 'is that Manos comes
up to the bench then, stands there with his hat in his hand, and
says to Lyttle, sweet as a school kid, "Thank you, motherfucker,"

before he walks away.'

I have heard this story from two other people. They agree on the final exchange. But both of them swear the last remark came from the bench.

23

Every week, usually on Wednesday night, the phone rings. Even before he starts I know who it is. I can hear him pulling on his goddamn cigarette. I am not supposed to talk to him. He is not supposed to talk to me. We both have our orders. He does not say his name.

How you doin? he asks.

Hanging in.

You guys okay?

Getting by.

This is a tough thing.

Tell me about it.

He laughs. No. I guess I don't gotta tell you. Well, you need anything? Anything I can do?

Not much. You're good to call.

Yeah, I am, but I figure you'll be runnin the joint again soon. I'm coverin my bets.

I know you are. What about you? How you doing?

Good. Survivin.

Schmidt still on your case? I ask, referring to his boss.

Hey, always. That's the guy. Screw him, I figure.

How tough are they making it on you?

These cupcakes? Come on.

But I know Lip is having a hard time. Mac, who has also called on a couple of occasions, told me they pulled him back into McGrath Hall, took him off the Special Command in the P.A.'s office. Schmidt has got him chained to a desk, signing off on other dicks' reports. That is bound to drive him crazy. But Lip always was doing a high-wire act with the department. He had to keep dazzling the crowds to hold off his detractors. Plenty of people were waiting to see him fall. Now he has. Cops will always figure that Lipranzer knew and let me hide it. That's just the way they think.

I'll call next week, he always promises at the end of every conversation.

And he does, faithfully. Our talks do not seem to vary more than a line or two. About a month along, when it was becoming clear to everyone that this was serious, he offered money. I understand these kinda things can be expensive, he said. You know a bohunk's always got some dough salted away.

I told him Barbara had come through in the pinch. He made a remark about marrying a Jewish girl.

This week, when the phone rings, I have been waiting.

"How you doin?" he asks.

"Hanging in," I say.

Barbara picks it up, just in time to hear that exchange.

"It's for me, Barb," I say.

Unaware of our arrangement, she says simply, "Hi, Lip," and puts the phone back down.

"So what's goin on?"

"We're going to trial now," I say. "Three weeks. Less."

"Yeah, I know. I seen the papers." We both hang on that for a while. There is nothing Dan Lipranzer can do about his testimony. It is going to break my back, both of us know it, and there is no choice. He answered Molto's question the day after the election, before Lip could guess the score; and I tend to think that the answers would have been the same, even if Lip knew the consequences. What happened happened. That's the way he would explain it to himself.

"So you gettin ready?" he asks.

"We're working real hard. Stern's amazing. He really is. He's the best by a time and a half."

"That's what they say." When he pauses, I recognize the click of his lighter. "Well, okay. Anything you need?"

"There is," I say. If he hadn't asked, I wasn't going to say anything. That's the deal I made with myself.

"Shoot," he tells me.

"I've got to find this guy Leon. Leon Wells. You know, the guy who's supposed to have paid off the P.A. in the North Branch?

The defendant in the court file you dug up, the one with Carolyn and Molto? Stern hired some skip tracer and he came back with a complete zip. As far as he can tell, no such guy even exists. I don't know any other way to go. I can't have a heart-to-heart with Tommy Molto."

This private investigator was named Ned Berman. Sandy said that he was good, but he seemed to have no idea what he was doing. I gave him copies of the pages of the court file. Three days later he was back saying he could not help. The North Branch, man, in those days, he said, it was a real zoo. I wish you luck. I really do. You couldn't tell out there who was doing what to who.

Lipranzer takes some time with this request, more than I expected. But I know the problem. If the department finds out he helped in the preparation of my defense, they will can him. Insubordination. Disloyalty. Fifteen years plus, and his pension, in the dumper.

"I wouldn't ask, you know I wouldn't. But I think it might really matter."

"How?" he asks. "You thinkin Tommy's kinky on this? Set you up to keep you from lookin?" I can tell that even though he is trying not make judgments, Lipranzer regards that notion as farfetched.

"I don't know what to say. You want to hear me say I think it's possible? I do. And whether he's sandbagging me or not, if we could get that kind of stuff out, it would look real bad for him. Something like that can really catch a jury's attention."

He is silent again.

"After I testify," he says. "You know, those guys have got their eye on me. And I don't want anybody askin me any questions where I got to give the wrong answer under oath. A lot of people would like to see that. When I get off the stand, they'll ease up. I'll work on it then. Hard. Okay?"

It is not okay. It is likely to be too late. But I've asked for much too much already.

"That's great. You're a pal. I mean that."

"I figure you'll be runnin the joint again soon," he says. He says, "I'm just coverin my bets."

Tee ball, again. The summer league. In this circuit, mercifully, there are no standings, for the Stingers are only marginally improved. In the heavy air of the August evenings, the fly balls still seem to mystify our players. They fall with the unhindered downward velocity of rain. The girls respond better to tutoring. They throw and bat with increasing skill. But the boys for the most part seem unreachable. There is no telling them about the merit of a measured swing, Each eight-year-old male comes to the plate with dreams of violent magic in his bat. He envisions home runs and wicked liners. For the boys, there is no point in the repetitive instructions to keep the ball on the ground.

Nat, surprisingly, is something of an exception. This summer he is changing, beginning to acquire some worldly focus. He seems newly aware of his powers, and of the fact that people regard the manner in which you do things as a sign of character. When he takes his turn at bat and hits, I watch the way his eyes lift as he comes around first base before he sprints for second. It is not enough to say that he is merely imitating the players on TV, because what is significant is that he noticed in the first place. He is starting to care about style. Barbara says he seems more particular about his clothes. I would be more delighted by all of this were I not wary about the motives for this sudden maturation. He has not reached and developed so much as he has been plucked by the heels from his dreaminess. Nathaniel has turned his attention to the world, I suspect, because he knows that it has caused so much trouble for his father.

After the game, we head home alone. No one has been so heartless as to suggest we skip the picnic, but it is for the best. We attended once after the indictment, and the time passed so fitfully, with such sudden ponderous silences arising at the mention of the most ordinary topics—work to which I do not go; TV detective shows that turn on predicaments like mine—that I knew we could not return. These men are generous enough to accept my presence among themselves. The risk I pose is for the kids. We all must think about the months ahead, the impossibility there would be of explaining where I'd gone—and what I did. It is unfair to hobble these splendid evenings with the omen of evil. Instead, Nat and I depart with a friendly wave. I carry the bat, the glove. He goes along stomping out dandelions.

From Nathaniel, there are no words of complaint. I am pathetically touched by this, by my son's loyalty. God only knows what mayhem his friends are wreaking on him. No grownup can fully imagine the smirking wisecracks, the casual viciousness he bears. And yet he refuses to desert me, the vessel from which this pain has poured. He does not dote. But he is with me. He pulls me to my feet from the sofa to work with him on the slider; he accompanies me at night when I venture out to get the paper and a gallon of milk. He walks beside me through the small woods between our subdivision and the Nearing village green. He shows no fear.

"Are you scared?" I ask suddenly tonight as we are walking.

"You mean scared you won't get off?" The trial looms so near, so large, that even my eight-year-old knows at once what I must mean.

"Yes."

"Naw."

"Why not?"

"I'm not, that's all. It's just a bunch of junk, right?" He squints up at me, from beneath the bill of his cockeyed baseball cap.

"In a manner of speaking."

"They'll have this trial, and you'll tell what really happened, and that'll be the end of it. That's what Mom says."

Oh, bursting, bursting heart: that's what his mom says. I put my arm around my son, more amazed than ever by his faith in her. I cannot imagine the lengthy therapeutic sessions between mother and child in which she has pitched him up to this level of support. It is a miracle which Barbara alone could have achieved. As a family, we are bound together by this symmetry: in the world, I love Nat most, and he adores his mother. Even at this scrappy age, full of the furious energy of a person of eight, he softens for her as no one else. She alone is allowed to hold him at length; and they enjoy a special sympathy, communion, a dependence that goes deeper even than the unsounded depths of mother and child. He is more like her than me, high-strung and full of her driving intelligence, those dark and private moods. She equals his devotion. He is never out of her imagination. I believe her when she says she could never wrest from herself the same emotion for another child.

Neither of them parts from the other comfortably. Last summer Barbara spent four days in Detroit, visiting a college friend, Yetta Graver, who she discovered is now a professor of mathematics. Barbara called twice a day. And Nat was like a running sore, crabby, miserable. The only way I could quiet him for bed was by imagining for him precisely what his mother and Yetta were doing at that moment.

They are in a quiet restaurant, I would tell him. Each of them is eating fish. It is broiled with very little butter. They each have had a glass of wine. At dessert they will break down and eat something they find too tempting.

Pie? asked Nat.

Pie, I said.

My son, the one I always dreamed of, fell asleep thinking of his mother eating sweets.

24

"Hi," Marty Polhemus says.

"Hi," I answer. As I came off the landing and caught my first glimpse of the figure and the long hair, I thought it was Kemp, who I'm supposed to meet here. Instead, I find this boy, who I have not even thought about for months. We stand alone in the hallway outside Carolyn's apartment looking at one another. Marty extends his hand and shakes mine firmly. He has no obvious reluctance, almost as if he is pleased to see me. "I didn't expect to see you," I finally say, casting about for some way to ask why he is here.

From his shirt pocket, he pulls a copy of Judge Lyttle's order allowing us to inspect the premises. "I got this," says Marty.

"Oh, I get it now," I say out loud. "That was only a formality." The judge ordered us to notify the lawyer for the estate, a former P.A. named Jack Buckley. Jack apparently sent the notice on to the boy. "The idea was just to let you object if you mind us going in and looking at some of Carolyn's things. You didn't have to be here."

"That's okay." This boy sort of shucks and bows as he talks. Back and forth. He shows no sign of leaving.

I try to make conversation, ask what he is up to. "Last time we talked you were planning to flunk out and go back home."

"I did," he says, without ceremony. "Actually, I got like suspended, I flunked physics. And I made a D in English. I was pretty sure I was going to flunk that, too. I went home six weeks ago. I just drove back here yesterday to get together all my junk."

I apologize and explain that from his presence I had assumed that things had worked out.

"Well, they did. Work out. I mean, so far as I'm concerned."

"How'd your father take it?"

He shrugs.

"He wasn't real happy. About the D especially. That like hurt his feelings. But he said I had a tough year. I'll work for a while and go back." Marty looks around at nothing in particular. "So anyway, when I got that thing, I thought I'd like to come by and see what it was all about."

The psychologists have a term, 'inappropriate.' That is this kid. Just sort of shooting the breeze outside the apartment where his mother was killed with the guy who everybody thinks did it. For a second, I wonder if he even knows what's going on. But the caption was right on the notice: PEOPLE VERSUS SABICH. And he could not have missed the buildup to the indictment in the papers. He has not been gone that long.

I do not get a chance to probe further, because Kemp comes along then. I can hear him on the stairs. He is arguing, and when he turns the corner off the landing I see with whom—Tom Glendenning, a big cop I never much liked. Glendenning is a white man's white man. Lots of ethnic and racial cracks. Not kidding around either. His whole sensibility revolves around the fact that he was born white and is now a cop. He treats everybody else like they're intruders. No doubt he'll be just as happy to view me that way. The more there are, the better Tom feels. Kemp is explaining that Glendenning may not enter while we view the apartment, and Glendenning is saying that's not what he understands from Molto. Finally, they agree that Glendenning will go downstairs and use the phone. While he's gone I introduce Kemp to Marty Polhemus.

"You're right," Glendenning says when he comes back. "That judge entered such an order." The way he says "that," you know what he's thinking.

Kemp rolls his eyes. He is a good lawyer but still awfully Ivy League. He will not hesitate to let people know when he regards them as fools.

A large phosphorescent-orange notice with an adhesive backing has been applied to the door of Carolyn's apartment. It states that this is a crime scene, sealed by order of the Superior Court of Kindle County, and that entry is forbidden. The notice overlaps the threshold so that the door cannot be opened. The locks have been filled with plastic blocks. Glendenning cuts the notice with a razor, but it takes him some time to clear the locks. When he finishes, he produces Carolyn's key ring from his pocket. It has a large red-and-white evidence tag on it. There is a door handle lock, and a dead bolt. As I told Lipranzer a long time ago, Carolyn did not fool around.

With the keys in the lower lock, Glendenning turns and, without a word, frisks Kemp and me, then Marty. This will prevent us from planting anything. I show him a pad of paper I have in my hand. He asks for our wallets. Kemp starts to object, but I motion him to be quiet. Again, without a word, Glendenning does the same to Marty, who already has his wallet in his hand.

"Jeez," says Marty. "Look at all this stuff. What am I ever going to do with it?" He just wanders in ahead of Kemp and me. I pass a look with Jamie. Neither of us knows if we have the authority to keep him out, or if there is any reason to bother. Glendenning calls in after him.

"Hey there. Don't touch anything. Nothing. Just them can touch. All right?" Marty seems to nod. He drifts through the living room toward the windows, apparently to check the view.

The air in here is stale and heavy, used up and burned out by the summer heat. Something somewhere in here may be rotting; there is a faint smell. Although the temperature outside is moderate today, the apartment, with the windows sealed, never cooled after last week's intense heat. It must be close to 85 degrees.

I never believed in ghosts, but it is unsettling to be back. I feel a little curl of strange sensation working its way down from the bottom of my spine. The apartment seems oddly settled, especially since everything has been left largely as it was found. The table and mauve seating piece are still overturned. On the light oak floor, just off the kitchen, an outline of Carolyn's body has been chalked. But everything else seems to have acquired some added density. Beside the sofa, on another glass table, a little inlaid box remains which I had purchased for Carolyn. She had admired it at Morton's the day I walked over there with her during the McGaffen trial. One of the red dragons on her Chinese screen assesses me with its fiery eye. God, I think. God, did I ever get myself in trouble.

Kemp motions to me. He is going to start looking about. He

hands me a pair of plastic gloves, loose ones like Baggies with fingers. There's no real need for this, but Stern insisted. Better not to be fighting about fingerprints Tommy Molto claims they discovered long before.

I stop a minute by the bar. It's on the wall directly by the kitchen. I thought I could see what I'm looking for from the police photographs of the scene, but I want to be certain. I stand three feet from the glassware and count the tumblers lined up on a towel. It is on one of the glasses of this set that my prints have been identified. There are twelve of them here. I count them twice to be sure.

Jamie comes beside me. He whispers, "Where in the hell do we look?"

He wants to see whether there are accessories on hand used by Carolyn for birth control.

"There's a john over that way," I say quietly. "Medicine cabinet and vanity."

I tell him I will check the bedroom. I look first inside her closet. Her smell is on everything; I recognize the clothes I saw her wear. These sights stir mild sensation, buffeting against something that wants this all suppressed. I don't know if it is an impulse to be clinical or the sense—which I always previously seemed to check at the door here—of what is properly forbidden. I move on to her drawers.

Her bedside table, a chubby-looking piece with clubbed Queen Anne feet, holds the telephone. This is as likely a spot as any, but when I open the single drawer I see nothing but her panty hose. I push them around and find a phone directory, a skinny volume covered in light brown calf's leather. The coppers always miss something. I can't resist. I check under S. Nothing. Then I think of R. Yes. At least I made the book. My work and home numbers are listed. I graze a minute. Horgan is here. Molto is not listed by name, but there is somebody called TM, which is probably him. I realize I should see about her doctors. D is it. I write the names down and put the paper in my pocket. Outside I hear a stirring. For some reason my first thought is that it is Glendenning, who has decided to ignore the dark-skinned judge and snoop. I flip the pages on the book to protect what I have found, but when the figure passes by the door, it is only Marty wandering. He looks in and waves. The page I turned is L. "Larren," it says right at the top. There are three numbers listed. Well, I think. That must have been a cozy group out in the North Branch. Everybody's here. Then I think again. Not quite. I check N and D, even G. Nico never made it. I tuck the book back in under the panty hose.

Marty is lurking at the bedroom door.

"Pretty strange, huh?"

That it is. I nod sadly. He tells me that he is going to wait outside. I try to let him know that he is free to leave, but the kid is dense and doesn't get the hint.

When I find Kemp, he is going through the living room.

"There's nothing here," he tells me. "No foam, no cream. I don't even find a case for a diaphragm. Am I missing something? Do women hide that stuff?"

"Not that I know of. Barbara keeps hers in the top drawer of the dresser. I wouldn't have any ideas about anyone else."

"Well, if the chemist says contraceptive cream is present, and it's not seized from the apartment," Kemp says, "you tell me where it's at."

"I guess I took it," I say, "when I grabbed the diaphragm." With both Kemp and Stern, I have fallen into this habit, speculating in the first person on what Nico will say I did. Jamie, especially, finds it amusing.

"Why would you do that?"

I consider for a moment. "Maybe it would hide the fact that I took the diaphragm."

"That doesn't make sense. It's supposed to be rape. What difference does it make what the hell she did when she *wanted* to have sex?"

"I guess I wasn't thinking clearly. If I had been, I wouldn't have left the glass on the bar."

Kemp smiles. He likes the byplay, fast words.

"This helps," he says. "There's no way around it. I want to get hold of Berman," he says, referring to the P.I. "He should search himself, so he can testify about it. He'll be available in about an hour. Wait until Glendenning hears he has to wait. He'll blow a gut."

The four of us meet outside the apartment and watch Glendenning lock the door. He pats each one of us down again. Glendenning, as Kemp predicted, refuses to wait for Berman.

Kemp tells him that he has to, the court order gives us access for the day.

"I don't take orders from any rock 'n' roll defense lawyer," says Glendenning. Even when I was on his side, I thought this guy was all charm.

"Well, let's go see the judge, then," Kemp says. Jamie got Glendenning's number quick. The copper looks to the ceiling like this is the most ridiculous thing he's ever heard, but by now he's trapped. He and Kemp pound down the stairway, exchanging words. I am left with Marty Polhemus.

"Nice guy, huh?" I ask Marty.

He asks me, in all seriousness, "Which one?"

"I was talking about the policeman."

"He seemed all right. He said that what's-his-name, Mr. Kemp, used to be in the Galactics." When I confirm that, the boy predictably says "Wow." Then he goes silent. He still seems to be waiting for something.

"I talked to them, you know. The cops."

"Did you?" I am thinking about the glassware by the bar.

"They asked me about you, you know? About when you came out to see me."

"Well, that's their job."

"Yeah, they wanted to know if you like said anything about your relationship with her, I mean with Carolyn. You know?"

I have to exert control to avoid a reflex to pivot. I had forgotten. I had forgotten that I told this goddamned kid. That is Nico's evidence, that is how he's going to prove up the affair. A thick bilious feeling cuts deep in my throat.

"They asked me a couple of times, you know. I said—I mean, I thought we had a real talk, you know?"

"Sure," I say.

"And I told them that you didn't say anything about that."

I look at the boy.

"Okay?" he asks.

I am, of course, supposed to remind him to tell the truth.

"Sure," I say again.

"I don't think you're the guy who killed her."

"I appreciate that."

"It's like karma," he says. "It isn't right."

I smile. I lift my hand to direct him to the landing, and just like that it hits me. It's like running into a wall, the recognition and the panic. I am so frightened that my legs begin to give out, actually buckle, and I reach for the railing. You fool, I think, you fool. He's wired. He is wearing a tape recorder. Nico and Molto wired him up. That is what he's doing here, that's why he does not seem right. He isn't. He follows us into the apartment and watches everything we do, then gets me out here to suborn him. And I've just convicted myself. I'm gone. I feel that I am going to faint. I falter again, but this time I turn backward.

Marty extends his hand. "What is it?"

When I look at him I know I'm crazy. Absurd. He is dressed for the season, a tight T-shirt and shorts. Not even a belt. Nobody can hide equipment under that. I watched Glendenning frisk him. And it's not there in his eyes either. All I see is this spaced-out kid, kindly, timid, terribly lost.

I have suddenly sweated through my shirt. I am wrung out now and weak. My pulse is beating far up in my arms.

"I'm okay," I tell him, but Marty takes my elbow anyway as we start down the stairs. "It's the place," I say. "It does bad things to me."

25

Three a.m. When I awake my heart is racing and cool traces of sweat are abrading my neck, so that in the idiocy of sleep I am trying to loosen my collar. I grope; then lie back. My breath is short, and my heartbeat thunders intermittently in the ear against the pillow. My dream is still clear to me: my mother's face in agony; that worn cadaverous image as she neared the end, and worse, her look of lost, unspeaking terror.

When my mother became sick, and quickly died, she was in the most peaceful period of her adult life. She and my father were no longer living together, although they still worked side by side each day in the bakery. He had moved in with a widow, Mrs. Bova, whose urgent bearing when she came into the shop I can remember even from the years before her husband died. For my mother, whose life with my father had been a dominion of fear, this arrangement became a kind of liberation. Her interest in the world outside her suddenly increased. She became one of the first of the regular callers on those listener-participation talk shows. Tell us what you think about interracial dating, legalizing marijuana, who killed Kennedy. She stacked the dining-room table with old newspapers and magazines, pads and index cards on which she made notations to herself, preparing for tomorrow's programs. My mother, who was phobic about venturing beyond our apartment building or the shop, who had to begin her preparations early in the morning if she was going to depart her home sometime that afternoon, who from the time I was eight sent me to the market so that she could avoid leaving the house—my mother became a local personality of sorts for her outspoken views about various worldly controversies. I could not reconcile this development with the accommodations I had made long before with myself to accept her wildly verging eccentricities, or the narrow margins of her former life.

She had been twenty-eight, four years my father's senior, when they were married, the sixth daughter of a Jewish union organizer and a lass from Cork. My father wed, I'm sure, for her savings, which allowed him to open up the shop. Nor was there ever any sign that my mother had married for love. She was an old maid and, I would guess, far too peculiar to gather other suitors. Her behavior, as I witnessed it, was apt to be excessive and ungovernable, with manic tours from pinnacles of rosy hilarity to hours of brooding looks. Sometimes she became frantic. She was forever running to ransack her crowded dresser drawers, rummaging in her sewing box as she made high-pitched excited noises. Because she seldom left home, her sisters made it a habit to look after her. This was a brave endeavor. When my aunts visited, my father would assail them in loud conversation with himself as busybodies, and he was not above actual threats of violence if they came when he was drunk. The two who ventured most often, my Aunts Flo and Sarah, were both bold, determined women, their father's daughters, and they were apt to control my father with stern looks and fearless demeanor, not much different than if they were confronting some barking cur. They were undeterred in their unannounced mission to protect the meek—Rosie (my mother) and, especially, me. For me these sisters were a hovering presence throughout my childhood. They brought me candies; they took me for haircuts and bought my clothes. They supervised my upbringing in such routine fashion that I was in my twenties before I recognized their intentions—or their kindness. And somehow, without ever realizing it had happened, I grew to know there were two worlds, my mother's and the other one dwelled in by her sisters, the one to which I eventually recognized I, as well, belonged. It was a fixed star of my youth to think that my mother was not, as I put it to myself, regular; to know that my adoration of her was a purely private matter, unintelligible to others and beyond my power to explain.

Do I really care what she would think now? I suppose. What child would not? I am almost glad she did not live to witness this. In her last few months she was with us. We were still living in the

city in a one-bedroom apartment, but Barbara refused to see my
mother anywhere else. She slept on a daybed in the living room
from which she seldom rose. Barbara, most of the time, sat on a
hard wooden chair drawn close. Near the end, my mother spoke
constantly to Barbara. Her head was laid on her pillow, her face
sadly reduced by disease, her eyes narrowly focused, their light
growing weak. Barbara held her hand. They murmured. I could
not make out the words—but the sound was constant, like a
running tap. Barbara Bernstein, daughter of a sleek suburban
matron, and my mother, of roaming mind and indelibly sweet
disposition, voyaged to one another, crossed the straits of
loneliness, while I, as ever, was too full of private grief to make
my own approach. I watched them from the door: for Barbara,
the mother who made no demands; for Rosie, a child who would
not disregard her. When I took Barbara's place, my mother held
my hand. I had the decency to tell her often that I loved her; she
smiled weakly, but seldom spoke. Near the end, it was Barbara
who gave her the shots of Demerol. A few of the syringes are still
downstairs in a box of odd keepsakes of my mother that Barbara
maintains: antique bobbins and index cards; the gold-tipped
Parker pen she used to make notes for her radio appearances.

I walk through the dark to find my slippers, slide my robe from
the closet. In the living room, I sit, feet up, huddled in a rocking
chair. Lately I have been thinking of taking up cigarettes again. I
feel no cravings, but it would give me something to do in these
abject hours in the dead of night when I am now so often awake.

A game I play with myself is called What Is the Worst Part? So
many things seem trivial. I do not care much now about the way
the women gape at me when I walk around in the village center. I
do not worry about my reputation, or the fact that for the rest of
my life, even if charges are dropped tomorrow, many people will
cringe reflexively whenever they hear my name. I do not worry
about how hard it will be for me to find work as an attorney if I
am acquitted. But the steady emotional erosion, the sleeplessness, the manic anxiety I cannot pretend about or minimize.
What is worst are these midnight wakings and the instants
before I can gather myself, when I am sure that the terror is
never going to end. It is like groping for the switch plate in the
dark, but I am never certain—and here the terror is the worst—I
am never sure that I will find it. As the search becomes more and

more prolonged, the little bit of sense that holds forth in me erodes, gives way, bubbles off like a tablet dropped into water, and the wild blackness of some limitless and everlasting panic begins to swallow me.

That is what is worst; that and my worries about Nathaniel. On Sunday, we will put him on a train for Camp Okawaka near Skageon, where he is scheduled to remain for the three weeks the trial is projected to last. Recalling this, I quietly tread the stairs and stand in the dark hall outside his door. I listen until I can catch the rhythm of his breath, and then force my own breathing down to that same measure. As I watch Nat sleep, the weirdness of science overcomes me: I think of atoms and molecules, skin and veins, muscle and bones. I try to comprehend my son for an instant as a compilation of parts. But that fails. We cannot ever enlarge the realm of our final understanding. I know Nathaniel as the hot mass of my feelings for him; I behold him as something no smaller or more finite or reducible than my passions. He will not piece or parse. He is my boy, gentle and beautiful in sleep, and I am grateful, grateful so that my heart is sore and breaking, that in this rough life I have felt such tenderness.

If I am convicted, they will take me away from him. Even Larren Lyttle will send me to prison for many years, and the thought of missing the remainder of his young life shatters me, breaks me into pieces. Oddly, I feel little conscious fear of prison itself. I dread the exile and the separation. The thought of confinement can make me ill at ease. But the actual physical horrors I am sure to suffer are seldom in my mind, even when I pierce myself with the thought of the extreme consequences I may face.

And yet I know. I have spent days at Rudyard, the state pen, where every murderer is sent. I have been there usually to interview a witness, but the sights are chilling. The bars are heavy iron slats, painted flat black, two inches deep, one-half inch wide, and behind them are all these bastards who now— now it strikes you—are so much the same. The black guys chattering their manic raging stuff. The white guys in their rolled-up stocking caps. The Latinos who look out with pointy-eyed rage. They are collectively every man you have avoided in a hallway or a bus station, every kid you picked out in high school as destined to be a bum. They are the ones who always wore their deficits like scars, headed here almost as certainly as a skyward-shot arrow plunging back to earth.

About this group it is no longer possible to harbor any kind of sentiment. I have heard every horror story. And I know that these grisly anecdotes are some of the unseen ink that blackens my dreams. For me this will not be far from torture. I know about the nighttime shivs, about the showers where blow jobs are given in the open. I know about Marcus Wheatley, one of the guys I tried to get to talk in Night Saints, who hosed somebody on a dope deal down there, and was laid on his back in the weight room, told to put up his hands, and then given a barbell with 250 pounds on each end, which asphyxiated him, even while it acted half like a guillotine. I know about the demographics of that neighborhood, 16 percent murderers, and more than half the inmates there for some form of violent crime. I know about the gray food. The four men in a cell. The odor of excrement that is overpowering on certain tiers. I know that every month there are areas where the gang control becomes so complete that the guards refuse to walk through for days. I know about the guards themselves and the eight of them who were convicted in the federal court for a New Year's party they threw in which they used shotguns to line up twelve black prisoners whom they took turns beating with flagstones and bricks.

I know about what happens to men like me there, because I know what happened to some I helped to send. I know about Marcy Lupino, who, whenever my thoughts loiter here, is the person most likely to come to mind. Marcello was a regular type, your basic hustling American, a C.P.A. who early in his career did a little work setting odds for some of the boys from his old neighborhood. Eventually Marcy's accounting practice prospered and he determined that he no longer required outside employment, at which time John Conte, one of the Boys, informed him that his was not the kind of job that he was free to quit. And that's the way it went. Marcy Lupino, respected C.P.A., PTA president, and member of the board of directors of two banks, a guy who wouldn't monkey with the books of his biggest client, left his office every afternoon at 3:30 p.m. sharp to set the spread on ball games, to tote the odds for tomorrow's ponies. All well and good, until one day when a federal snitch gave away a

wire room. The IRS came through the door and found Marcy
Lupino among half a dozen other people and three million
dollars in betting slips. The feds wanted him to talk in the worst
way. But Marcy was very good at arithmetic. Two years on a
gambling beef, mail fraud, wire fraud, racketeering charges,
whatever the feds could put to him, was not worth ten minutes
of what John Conte and the Boys would do. They would cut out
his testicles and feed them to him, make him chew. And this,
Marcy Lupino knew, was not a figure of speech.

So Mike Townsend from the Organized Crime Strike Force
called me. He wanted to provide Marcy with incentives. We
charged Marcy stateside, and when he was convicted he went to
Rudyard instead of the federal overnight camp he had been
counting on, a place with a salad bar and tennis courts, a place
where he would teach bookkeeping to inmates working on
college degrees and copulate with Mrs. Lupino every ninety days
as part of the furlough program. Instead, we sent him off in
manacles, chained to a man who had put out his infant
daughter's eyes with his keys.

Six months later Townsend called and we took a trip north to
see if Lupino had responded. We found him in a field with a hoe.
He was scraping at the ground. We reintroduced ourselves,
hardly a necessity. Marcy Lupino took his hoe, propped it under
his arm, and leaned on it as he wept. He cried like I have never
seen a man cry; he shook from head to toe, his face turned
purple, and the water poured from his eyes, truly, as from a
faucet. A little fat bald-headed forty-eight-year-old man, crying
as hard as he could. But he would not talk. He said one thing to
us: 'I got no teet.' Nothing else.

As we were walking back, the guard explained.

Big buck nigger, Drover, wanted Lupino as his babe. He's the
kind, man, nobody says no, not even the Italians in this joint. He
gets himself into Lupino's cell one night, takes out his dingus,
and tells Lupino to suck. Lupino won't, so Drover takes Lupino's
face and bangs it on the bunk rail until there is not a whole tooth
left in Lupino's head; some aching roots, some pieces, but not
one tooth.

Warden's got a rule, the guard says. You get bandages for your
wounds, we'll sew you up, but no special treatment unless you
talk. Fuckin Lupino ain't getting his false teeth until he tells who

did the tap dance on him. And fuckin Lupino, he ain't tellin, he knows what's good for him, nobody here is that dumb. No, the guard says, he ain't tellin. And ol' Drover, he is laughin, he says he done a real good job, and that his big Johnson goes in there now, smooth as silk; he says he been in many pussies that don't feel that good. The guard, a fine humanitarian, leaned on his shotgun and laughed. Crime, he reported to Townsend and me, sure don't pay.

Run, I think now as I sit in the dark contemplating Marcy Lupino. Run. The thought always comes that suddenly: run. As a prosecutor, I could never understand why they stayed around to let it fall, to face trial, sentencing, prison. But they remained for the most part, as I have. There is $1600 in my checking account and I have no other money in the world. If I looted Barbara's trust, I would have enough to go, but then I would probably lose the only real motive I have for freedom—the chance to see Nat. And even if I could spend summers with him in Rio or Uruguay or wherever it is that they do not extradite for murder, the powers of even a desperate fancy are too meager to imagine how I would survive without a language I know or a skill those cultures would recognize. I could simply disappear to the center of Cleveland or Detroit, become somebody different, and never see my son again. But the fact is that none of these are visions of what I recognize as life. Even in these lightless hours, I want the same things I wanted when I got off the bus at night in the village green in Nearing. We are so simple sometimes, and fortified so strangely. I sit here in the dark with my heels drawn against me, and as I shiver, I imagine the odor of the smoke of cigarettes.

26

"People versus Rozat K. Sabich!" calls Ernestine, Judge Lyttle's docket clerk, into the crowded courtroom. She is a stern-looking black woman, six feet tall. "For trial!" she cries.

Not much is like the first day of a murder trial. Sunup on the morning of battle; Christians against lions back in Rome. Blood is on the air. Spectators have crammed themselves into every linear inch available along the public benches. There are four full rows of press, five sketch artists at the head. The judge's staff—his secretary and law clerks, who are not ordinarily present—are in folding chairs against the rear wall of the courtroom, next to his chambers door. Bailiffs, armed for this solemn occasion, are positioned at the forward corners of the bench beside the marble pillars. The atmosphere is busy and intense, full of a racing murmur. No one here is bored.

Judge Lyttle enters and the room comes to its feet. Ernestine makes her announcements. "Oyez, oyez. The Superior Court for the County of Kindle is now in session, the Honorable Larren L. Lyttle, Judge Presiding. Draw near and give your attention and you shall be heard. God save the United States and this Honorable Court." Ernestine bangs her gavel. When everyone is seated, she calls my case for trial.

The lawyers and I move to the podium. Stern and Kemp; Molto and Nico; Glendenning has appeared and will be the case investigator, sitting with the prosecutors. I stand behind the lawyers. Judge Lyttle looms above, his hair newly cut and smoothly groomed. It is August 18, a few days short of two months since I was indicted.

"Are we ready to call for a jury?" Larren asks.

"Judge," says Kemp, "we have a few matters that we can address while you are bringing up the prospective jurors." Kemp's role on this case will be Law Man. Stern has put him in charge of research and Jamie will address the judge with regard to points of law, outside the jury's presence. When they are in the box, he will not say a word.

From the courtroom phone, Ernestine calls the clerk's reception room and asks for a venire, citizens summoned for jury duty who will be questioned by the judge and lawyers to determine if they should serve in this case.

"Judge," Kemp says again, "we have received all the production you ordered from the prosecution. With one exception. We have still not been given an opportunity to see that glass."

Stern has instructed Jamie to raise this for reasons besides our curiosity about the glass. He wants Judge Lyttle to know that the prosecutors are conforming to the judge's dim expectations. It works. Larren is upset.

"What about this, Mr. Delay Guardia?" Nico clearly does not know. He looks for Molto.

"Judge," says Tommy, "we'll take care of it after court."

"All right," says Larren. "That will be done today."

"Also," Kemp says, "you have not ruled on our motion to disqualify Mr. Molto."

"That is correct. I have been waiting for the prosecutor's response. Mr. Delay Guardia?"

Tommy and Nico exchange glances and nod to one another. They will proceed according to their prior agreement, whatever that is.

"Your Honor, the state will not call Mr. Molto. So we suggest that the motion is moot."

Stern steps forward and asks to be heard.

"Do I understand then, Your Honor, that Mr. Molto will not be called under any circumstances—that his testimony is forsworn throughout the case and at all stages?"

"That's right," Larren agrees. "I'd like us all to be clear at the start, Mr. Delay Guardia. I don't want to be hearin later about you didn't expect this or you didn't expect that. Mr. Molto is not testifying at this trial. Correct?"

"Correct," Nico says.

"Very well. I will deny the defendant's motion on the

representation of the prosecutors that Mr. Molto will not be
called as a witness at this trial."

Ernestine whispers to him. The prospective jurors are in the
corridor.

So in they come, seventy-five people, twelve of whom will
soon be in charge of deciding what happens to my life. Nothing
special, just folks. You could skip the summonses and the
questionnaires and grab the first seventy-five people who
walked by on the street. Ernestine calls sixteen to sit in the jury
box, and directs the remainder to the first four rows on the
prosecution side, from which the bailiffs have dismissed the
spectators amid great grumbling, sending them to form a waiting
line out in the hall.

Larren starts by telling the venire what the case is about. He
has probably seen a thousand juries chosen during his career.
His rapport is instantaneous: this big, good-looking black man,
kind of funny, kind of smart. The white people take to him too,
thinking, probably, they all should be like this. Nowhere in a trial
is Larren's advantage to the defense likely to be greater than at
this juncture. He is skilled in addressing juries, canny in divining
hidden motivations, and committed to the foundation of his soul
to the fundamental notions. The defendant is presumed innocent. Innocent. As you sit here you have gotta be thinking Mr.
Sabich didn't do it.

"I'm sorry, sir. In the first row, what is your name?"

"Mahalovich."

"Mr. Mahalovich. Did Mr. Sabich commit the crime that he is
charged with?"

Mahalovich, a stout middle-aged man who has his paper
folded in his lap, shrugs.

"I wouldn't know, Judge."

"Mr. Mahalovich, you are excused. Ladies and gentlemen, let
me tell you again what you are to presume. Mr. Sabich is
innocent. I am the judge. I am tellin you that. Presume he is
innocent. When you sit there, I want you to look over and say to
yourself, There sits an innocent man."

He goes through similar exercises, expounding upon the
state's burden to prove guilt beyond a reasonable doubt and the
defendant's right to remain silent. Talking to a thin, gray-haired
lady in a shirtwaist dress, who is seated in the chair beside the

one Mahalovich once occupied:

"Now don't you think, ma'am, that an innocent person oughta get up there and tell you it's not so?"

The lady is torn. She saw what happened to Mahalovich. But you don't lie to a judge. She touches her dress at the collar before she speaks.

"I would think so," she says.

"Of course you would. And you have to presume that Mr. Sabich thinks the same thing, since we're presumin that he's innocent. But he doesn't have to do that. Because the Constitution of the United States says he doesn't have to. And what that means is that if you sit as jurors on this case, you have promised to put that thought out of your mind. Because Mr. Sabich and his lawyer, Mr. Stern, may decide to rely on that constitutional right. The folks who wrote the Constitution said, God bless you, sir, God bless you, Mr. Sabich, you don't have to explain. The state's got to prove you guilty. You don't have to say a thing if you don't want. And Mr. Sabich can't really receive that blessing if any of you have it in your mind that he should explain anyway."

As a prosecutor, I used to find this part of Larren's routine unbearable, and Nico and Molto both look pale and upset. No matter how many times you tell yourself that the judge is right, you can't believe that anybody ever thought it was going to be explained so emphatically. Nico looks particularly drawn. He listens with an alert, humorless expression. He has lost weight and there is a new darkening in the sallow skin beneath his eyes. To get a case of this stature prepared in three weeks is a terrible burden, and he has an office to run as well. Moreover, it must have occurred to him often how much he has put on the line. He has taken klieg lights and run them across the sky telling the near world to watch Nico Della Guardia. If he loses, he will never have the same credibility in office. His silent campaign to be earmarked as Bolcarro's successor will be finished not long after its start. His career, much more than mine, hangs in the balance. I have lately come to realize that my career, after this indictment and the hoopla of this trial, is probably over in any event.

Next, Larren takes up the subject of publicity. He questions jurors about what they have read. For those who are being coy he points out the article announcing the start of the trial on the front page of today's *Trib*. Jurors always lie about this. People who want to get out of jury service usually find a way. The ones who come to the courthouse are, for the most part, eager to serve and less willing to confess to obvious disqualifications. But Larren slowly wins the truth from them. Nearly everybody here has heard something about this case, and over about twenty minutes Judge Lyttle tells them that is worthless information. "Nobody knows anything about this case," he says, "because there has not been a word of evidence heard." He excuses six people who admit that they will not be able to put the publicity out of their minds. It is unsettling to consider what the others, subjected to Nico's media splash, must think about the case. It's hard to believe that anyone can really fully put aside those preconceptions.

Late in the morning, questioning about the jurors' backgrounds begins—this process is called *voir dire*, truth-telling, and it continues throughout the afternoon and into the second morning. Larren asks everything he can think of and the lawyers add more. Judge Lyttle will not allow questioning directed to the issues of the case, but the attorneys are permitted to roam freely into personal details, limited largely only by their own reluctance to give offense. What TV shows do you watch, what newspapers do you read? Do you belong to any organizations? Do your children work outside the home? In your house, are you or your spouse in charge of the monthly bookkeeping? This is the subtle psychological game of figuring out who is predisposed to favor your side. Consultants now earn hundreds of thousands of dollars making such predictions for lawyers, but an attorney like Stern knows most of this by instinct and experience.

To pick a jury effectively you must know the case you want to try. Stern has not said anything to me, but it is becoming clearer that he has a strong notion not to offer evidence for the defense. He thinks he can whittle away at Nico's proof. Perhaps my actions in the past, when I have been beyond control in spite of his instructions, have convinced him I would be a poor witness in my own behalf. No doubt the decision to testify or not will be mine in the end. But I suspect that Stern is simply trying to move things to the point that I am convinced we can win without my testimony, before he forces my hand. In any event, he has spent little time talking to me about the defense case. Mac and a few of the judges have agreed to appear as character witnesses. Stern also has asked me about neighbors who would be willing to offer that kind of testimony. Clearly, though, he wants to try a reasonable-doubt case. At the end, if all goes as he hopes, no one will know what happened. The state will have failed to meet its burden of proof and I should be acquitted. With that goal, we need jurors bright enough to appreciate the legal standard and strong enough to forthrightly apply it—people who will not convict merely because they are suspicious. For that reason Sandy has told me that he thinks younger jurors will be better overall than old. In addition, they may be more in tune with some of the nuances of male and female relations that so strongly flavor the case. He wants, in other words, people who might believe that co-workers adjourn to a woman's apartment for reasons other than sexual intercourse. On the other hand, he has said, older people will have more immediate respect for my past attainments, my position, and my reputation.

Whatever the plans, you usually go in the end on gut impressions. Certain jurors just seem to be people you think you like, folks you can talk to. On the second morning, as we begin making our choices, Stern and Kemp and I have few disagreements. We huddle together at the counsel table, directing our decisions to prospective jurors taken up in groups of four. Barbara is invited by Sandy to come up from the nearest spectator bench to join in our consultation. She places her hand lightly, on my shoulder, but offers no comment. Standing close to me as we confer, dressed in a dark blue silk suit and, again, a matching hat, she conveys an impression of somber dignity, of grieving well restrained. Overall, the effect is a little like the Kennedy widows. She is playing her small part well. Last night, after the *voir dire* started, Sandy explained to Barbara that he would be calling on her in this fashion. At home, she expressed appreciation for Sandy's courtesy and I explained to her that courtesy was not his prime intent. Stern again wants all the jurors to see at the outset that my wife is still on my side and that we, in this modern age, defer to the opinions of women.

The defense gets to excuse ten jurors without explanation so-called peremptories. The prosecution gets six. Nico's plan seems to be pretty much the inverse of ours, although with fewer challenges he does not have the same opportunity to shape the panel. In general, he seems to be looking for his voters, older ethnic types, generally Roman Catholics. For that reason, without having planned to do it earlier, we strike all the Italians.

I am more comfortable with the group that we end up with than was often the case when I was a prosecutor. There is a preponderance of younger people, many of them single. A female drugstore manager in her late twenties. A young woman who is an accountant with a brokerage house. A twenty-six-year-old man is an assembly-line foreman, and another fellow about his age runs restaurant services at a local hotel and fiddles part-time with computers. There is a young black woman who does auditing at a local insurance company. Among the twelve, we have a divorced female schoolteacher, a secretary for a local rail line, a man who retired last year from running a high school music program, and an auto mechanic; also a Burger King management trainee, a retired nurse's aide, and a cosmetics saleswoman from Morton's. Nine whites, three blacks. Seven women, five men. Larren also seats four alternates, who will hear the evidence but not take part in deliberations unless one of the twelve regulars falls ill or is otherwise excused.

With the jury chosen, early in the second afternoon we are ready to start my trial.

* * *

At ten minutes to two we arrive again at the courthouse for opening statements. The atmosphere is now the same as yesterday morning. The lull of jury selection is past and the blood urge is on the air. The adrenalized excitement of beginning becomes a kind of painful irritant that I feel seeping into my bones. Kemp calls me into the hallway outside the courtroom, and we walk some distance to get away from the gaggle of unhappy onlookers for whom the bailiffs have not been able to find seats. Out here you can never be certain who is listening. The best journalists would not report something they overheard, but you can never tell who is talking to the prosecutors.

"I want to say something," Jamie tells me. He has chopped a good two inches off the curled edges of his pageboy, and he is turned out in a distinguished blue pinstriped suit purchased from J. Press in New Haven. He is handsome enough to have chosen Hollywood instead of law. From comments, I have come to realize that he made enough money playing his guitar to be quite comfortable without working. Instead, he is in the office, reading cases, writing memos, conferring with Stern and me until eleven and twelve o'clock at night.

"I like you," Jamie says.

"I like you, too," I answer.

"And I really hope you beat this thing. I've never told a client this before. But I think you will."

There are no more than a year or two's worth of clients in Jamie's life and so the comment is not worth that much as a prediction, but I am touched by his good feeling. I put a hand on his shoulder and I thank him. He did not tell me, of course, that I am innocent. He knows better than to be convinced of that; the evidence is against me. Probably if you shook him awake in the middle of the night and put the question, he would tell you he does not know.

Stern appears now. He is almost jaunty. His flesh is invigorated by the high excitement; the broadcloth of his shirt is so white and free of creases that it appears almost holy as it meets his full cheeks. He is about to give the opening statement in the most noted case of his career. Suddenly I am full of envy. I have not thought in all the months about how much fun it would be to try this case, an understandable omission. But those old inclinations suddenly surge forth amid this supercharged air. The big Night Saints case, a twenty-three-defendant conspiracy which I tried with Raymond, had a fraction of this attention, but it was still like taking hold of a live wire, a drumming excitement that did not stop, even in sleep, for seven weeks. Like motorcycling or mountain climbing: you know that you have been here. I am sad suddenly, briefly despairing over my lost trade.

"So?" Sandy asks me.

"I told him I thought that he would win," says Kemp.

Stern speaks Spanish; his eyebrows shoot up toward the hairless crest of his scalp.

"Never out loud," he says. "Never." Then he takes my hand and faces me with his deepest look. "Rusty, we will do our best."

"I know," I say.

Coming back into the courtroom, Barbara, who has gone back and forth from the U. over lunch, emerges from the crowd to hug me. It is half an embrace, one arm firmly around my waist. She kisses my cheek, then wipes away the lipstick with her hand. She talked to Nat.

"He wants you to know he loves you," she says. "I do too." She says this in a cute way, so that the tone, in spite of her good intentions, is still somewhat equivocal. Nonetheless, she has done her best. It is the right time and the right place for maximum performance.

The jury files in from the waiting room, where they will eventually deliberate. It is located right behind the jury box. The divorced schoolteacher actually smiles at me as she takes her seat.

Larren explains the function of opening statements: a prediction of the evidence. A forecast. "It is not an argument," he says. "The lawyers will not set forth the inferences which they think arise from the proof. They will simply tell you in an unvarnished fashion what the actual evidence will be." Larren says this no doubt as a warning to Delay. In a circumstantial case, a prosecutor needs some way at the outset to make a jury see how it all fits together. But Nico will have to do this carefully. However Della Guardia feels about Larren, the jury is in love with the judge already. His charm is like a floral scent he emits into the air. Nico will gain nothing from being upbraided.

Larren says, "Mr. Delay Guardia," and Nico stands. Trim, erect, bristling with anticipation. A person at the very top.

"May it please the court," he says, the traditional beginning.

Right from the start, he is surprisingly bad. I know immediately what has happened. The time constraints and the burden of running the office have impinged severely on his preparation. He has never gone over this before. Some of it is being improvised, perhaps in response to Larren's warning right before he began. Nico cannot shake his drawn, nervous look, and he cannot find a rhythm. He keeps hesitating in spots.

Even with Nico's inadequate preparation, much of this is difficult for me to hear. Nico may lack his usual style and organization, but he is still hitting the high spots. The counterpoint of the physical evidence against what I said and did not say to Horgan and Lipranzer is, as I always feared, particularly effective. On the other hand, Delay misses points of emphasis. He tells the jury too little about things he should be the one to disclose. A smart prosecutor usually seeks to defuse defense evidence by mentioning it first, demonstrating from his own mouth that his case can stand the defense's strongest blows. But Nico does not adequately detail my background—he fails to say that I was second-in-command of the office—and, in describing my relationship with Carolyn, he omits any mention of the *McGaffen* trial. When Stern gets up, in his own quiet way he will make these abbreviations appear to be concealment.

In the area of my relations with Carolyn, Nico makes the only deviation from what we had predicted. Nico's problem is deeper than I, or even Stern, had understood. Delay does not simply lack proof of my relationship with Carolyn. He has not even correctly guessed what occurred.

"The evidence," he tells the jury, "will show that Mr. Sabich and Ms. Polhemus had a personal relationship that had gone on for many months, at least seven or eight months before the murder. Mr. Sabich was in Ms. Polhemus's apartment. She called him on the phone. He called her. It was, as I say, a personal relationship." He pauses. "An intimate relationship.

"But all was not well in this relationship. Mr. Sabich was, apparently, very unhappy. Mr. Sabich was, it seems, intensely jealous."

Larren on the bench has swung about and now is glaring. Nico is doing what the judge warned him about, arguing rather than simply describing his witnesses and exhibits. In his agitation, the judge glances now and then in Sandy's direction, a signal for Sandy to object, but Stern is quiet. Interruptions are discourteous, and Sandy is himself in court. More important, Nico is at the point in his oration where he is saying things that Stern knows he may not prove.

"Mr. Sabich was jealous. He was jealous because Ms. Polhemus was seeing not only him. Ms. Polhemus had formed a new relationship, a relationship that apparently infuriated Mr. Sabich." Another weighty caesura. "A relationship with the prosecuting attorney, Raymond Horgan."

This detail has never before found public life. Nico undoubtedly cabined it to protect his new alliance with Raymond; but he cannot help himself, he is still Nico, and he actually turns to the press rows as he lets this news into the world. There is an audible stirring in the courtroom, and Larren, with the mention of his former partner, finally loses his cool.

"Mr. Delay Guardia!" he thunders, "you were warned, sir. Your remarks are not to be in the nature of a closing argument. You will confine yourself to a *sterile* recitation of the facts or your opening will be over. Do I make myself clear?"

Nico faces the bench. He actually looks surprised. His prominent Adam's apple bobs as he swallows.

"Certainly," he says.

Jealousy, I write on my notepad, and pass it to Kemp. Given the choice between no motive and a motive he cannot quite prove, Nico has chosen the latter. It may even be the smarter gamble. But at the end, he will be working hard to stretch the facts.

Stern moves to the podium as soon as Nico is through. The judge offers a recess, but Sandy smiles gently and says he is prepared to go on right now, if the court please. Sandy is unwilling to let Nico's remarks accumulate force on reflection.

He steps around the podium and rests one elbow on it. He wears a brown suit, tailor-made, that conforms subtly to his full shape. His heavy face is still with portent.

"How are we to answer this," he asks, "Rusty Sabich and I? What can we say when Mr. Della Guardia tells you about two fingerprints but not another? What can we say when the evidence will show you gaps and suppositions, gossip and cruel innuendo? What can we say when a distinguished public servant is put on trial on the basis of circumstantial evidence which, as you will be able to determine, does not approach that precious standard of reasonable doubt?

"Reasonable doubt." He turns, he steps, he comes two feet closer to the jury. "The prosecution must prove guilt beyond a reasonable doubt." He harks back to everything they heard over the last two days from Judge Lyttle. At the outset, Stern has locked arms before the jurors with that mighty and learned jurist, a particularly effective device in light of Larren's first putdown of Delay. Sandy uses the term 'circumstantial evidence' repeatedly. He mentions the words 'rumors' and 'gossip.' Then he talks about me.

"And who is Rusty Sabich? Not simply, as Mr. Della Guardia

told you, a top deputy in the prosecuting attorney's office. *The* top deputy. Among a handful of the finest trial lawyers in this county, this state. The evidence will show you that. A top graduate of the University Law School. A member of the *Law Review*. Clerk to the Chief Justice of the State Supreme Court. He gave his career, his life to public service. To stopping and preventing and punishing criminal behavior, not"—Stern glances contemptuously toward the prosecutors—"to committing it. Listen, ladies and gentlemen, to the names of some of the persons whom the evidence will show you Rusty Sabich brought to justice. Listen, because these are persons whose wrongdoing was so well known that even you who are not regularly in this courthouse will recognize these names, and, I am sure, will once again be grateful for Rusty Sabich's work." He spends five minutes talking about the Night Saints and other cases, longer than he should, but Della Guardia is hard put to object after Sandy endured his opening without complaint.

"He is the son of an immigrant, a Yugoslavian freedom fighter who was persecuted by the Nazis. His father came here in 1946 to a land of freedom, where there would be no more atrocities. What would Ivan Sabich think today?"

I would squirm were I not under the sternest orders to show nothing. I sit with my hands folded and look ahead. At all moments, I am to appear resolute. Lamentably, Stern did not give me a preview of this portion. Even if I testify, I will not testify to this—not that the prosecutors would be likely to disprove it.

Stern's manner is somehow commanding. The accent lends an intrigue to his speech, and his considered formality gives him substance. He makes no predictions of what the defense will show. He steers clear of promising my testimony. Instead, he focuses on deficiencies. No evidence, not a scintilla of direct evidence that Rusty Sabich handled any murder weapon. No sign that Rusty Sabich took part in any violence.

"And what is the cornerstone of this circumstantial case? Mr. Della Guardia told you many things about the relationship of Mr. Sabich and Ms. Polhemus. He did not tell you, as the evidence will show, that they were co-workers, that they worked as trial lawyers, not as lovers, on a case of tremendous importance. He did not mention that. He left that for me to tell you. All right, then, I have, and the evidence will show that to you, too. You should mind closely what the evidence shows you, and does not show you, about the relationship of Rusty Sabich and Carolyn Polhemus. Mind that closely in this circumstantial case where Mr. Della Guardia seeks to prove guilt beyond a reasonable doubt. I tell you flatly, flatly, that the evidence will not show you what Mr. Della Guardia has said it would. It will not. You see this case will not involve facts, but rather supposition upon supposition, guess upon guess—"

"Mr. Stern," says Larren mildly. "You seem to be falling into the same trap as Mr. Della Guardia."

Sandy turns; he actually bows in an abbreviated way.

"I am so sorry, Your Honor," he says. "He seems to have inspired me."

A laugh, a small one, from everyone. The judge. A number of members of the jury. A small laugh at Delay's expense.

Sandy turns back to the jury, and remarks as if he were speaking to himself: "I must keep myself from getting carried away by this case." Then he plants his last seed. No commitments, just a few words.

"Well, one cannot help asking why. As you listen to the evidence, ask why. Not why Carolyn Polhemus was murdered. That regrettably is something no one will be learning from this proof. But why Rusty Sabich sits here falsely accused. Why offer a circumstantial case, a case that is supposed to show guilt beyond a reasonable doubt and does not?"

Sandy stops. He tilts his head. Perhaps he knows the answer; perhaps he does not. He speaks softly.

"Why?" is the last thing that he says.

27

They cannot find the glass.

Nico admits this as soon as Stern and Kemp and I arrive on the third morning of trial. The first witnesses will be called today.

"How in the world?" asks Stern.

"I apologize," says Nico. "Tommy tells me he forgot about it at first. He really did. Now they're looking high and low. It'll turn up. But I have a problem." Della Guardia and Stern stroll away, conferring. Molto watches them with obvious concern. He seems reluctant to leave his place at the prosecution table, like a whipped dog. Really, Tommy does not look well. It is too early in the trial to be as exhausted as he appears. He has a yellow cast to his skin, and his suit, the same as yesterday's, does not seem to have had any time to rest. I would not be surprised if Molto never made it home last night.

"How can they lose a piece of evidence like that?" Kemp asks me.

"Happens all the time," I answer. The Police Evidence Center, over in McGrath Hall, has more unclaimed items than a pawnshop. Tags get knocked off; numbers are reversed. I started many cases with evidence misplaced. Unfortunately, Nico is right: the glass will turn up.

Stern and Della Guardia have agreed to advise the judge of this development, before he takes the bench. We will all go back to chambers. This will save Nico from a public whipping. Stern's concession on points like this, minor courtesies, is the kind of thing that has made him popular around the P.A.'s office. Other lawyers would demand to be on the record so that Nico could take a hiding before the press.

We all wait a moment in the judge's outer office, while his secretary, Corrine, keeps an eye on the phone light to see when the judge completes the call he is presently taking. Corrine is stately and large-chested, and the courthouse wags regularly speculated on the nature of her relationship with Larren, until last fall, when she married a probation officer named Perkins. Larren has always been a ladies' man of some renown. He divorced about ten years ago, and over time I've heard a lot of tales about him drinking Jack Daniel's in the pretty-people night spots down on Bayou Boulevard, that pickup strip which certain sages refer to as the Street of Dreams.

"He says come right in," Corrine tells us, putting down the phone after a brief conversation with the judge to announce our group. Kemp and Nico and Molto precede us. Stern wants a moment with me to confer.

When we enter, Nico has already begun telling the judge the problem. He and Kemp are in armchairs before the judge's desk. Molto sits a distance away on the sofa. The chambers, the judge's inner sanctum, has a distinguished bearing. One wall is solid with the gold-toned spines of the state law reports, and Larren also has his own Wall of Respect. There is a large picture of the judge and Raymond, among a number of photos of the judge with politicians, mostly black.

"Your Honor," Nico is saying, "I learned the first time last night from Tommy—"

"Well, I thought Tommy indicated yesterday that you had the glass and he simply had overlooked this matter. Tommy, I'll tell you something right now." The judge is on his feet behind his desk, looking rather regal in a purple-toned shirt with white collar and cuffs. He has been roaming in his books and papers as he listens, but now he turns about and points a stout finger at Molto. "If I have the same kind of bullshit from you in this case I've had in the past, I'll throw you in the lockup. I really will. Don't be tellin me one thing and meanin something else. And I want to say this right in front of the prosecuting attorney. Nico, you know we've always gotten along. But there's a history here." The judge tips his large head in Molto's direction.

"Judge, I understand. I really do. That's why I was concerned as soon as I learned of the problem. I really do believe that it's an oversight."

Larren glances balefully at Della Guardia from the corner of his eye. Nico does not even flinch. He is doing a pretty good job. He has both hands in his lap and is making his best effort to appear the suppliant. This is not an attitude that comes to him naturally, and his readiness to humble himself before the judge is actually quite winning. There must have been hell to pay last night between Molto and him. That's why Tommy looks so bad.

Larren, however, is not about to let the subject go. As usual he has caught all the implications quickly. For better than a month the prosecutors have been promising to produce a glass they knew they could not find.

"Isn't this somethin?" the judge asks. He looks, for support, to Stern. "You know, Nico, I don't issue these orders just for the hell of it. You do with your evidence as you like, but really— Who had this glass last?"

"There's some disagreement, Judge, but we believe it was the police."

"Naturally," says Larren. He looks off toward the distance in disgust. "Well, you see what we have here. You have defied an order of the court. The defense has not had an opportunity to prepare. And you have given an opening statement, Nico, in which you must have referred to this evidence half a dozen times. Well, that's your problem now. When you find the glass, assuming you find it, then we'll determine whether or not it comes into evidence. Let's go try this case."

Nico's difficulties, however, are more complex than one angry judge. The state case has been prepared with the witnesses expected in an established sequence, referred to as an order of proof. The first person to testify is supposed to describe the crime scene, and accordingly, he will mention the glass.

"Not in my courtroom," says Larren. "No, sir. We're not gonna be talkin anymore about evidence that nobody can find."

Stern finally speaks up. He announces that we have no objection to Delay proceeding as he had planned.

"Your Honor, if the prosecution fails to find the glass, we will object to any further evidence regarding it." He means, of course, the fingerprints. "But for the time being, there is no purpose to delay, if Your Honor will permit it."

Larren shrugs. It's Sandy's lawsuit. This is the subject Sandy and I discussed in the judge's outer office. If we object, we can

make Nico take witnesses out of the order he had planned, but
Sandy thinks the advantage is greater if Nico's first witness has
to explain that a piece of evidence is missing. Better that they
look like Keystone Kops was how Stern put it. The disorganiza-
tion will make a poor impression on the jury. Besides, there is
little damage to me in the bare fact that a glass was found. And
as I pointed out to Kemp, the police-evidence custodians will
eventually locate the glass; they always do.

"I would think you should give Mr. Stern an order of proof so
that he has notice of when we're coming to this area again."

Molto speaks up. "We have one, Judge. We'll give it to them
right now." Tommy fiddles in the sloppy heap of papers on his
lap, and eventually passes a sheet to Kemp.

"And let's put this on the record," Larren says. Nico's
punishment. He must explain this screw-up in public after all.

While the lawyers are before the bench, repeating our
chambers conference in the presence of the court reporter, I
examine the order of proof. I am eager to know when Lipranzer
will be testifying. The sooner he does, the sooner the search for
Leon can resume. I have tried to get Sandy's P.I. to look further,
but he claims there is nothing to do. The list, however, provides
no good news. Lip is scheduled toward the latter part of the case.
Leon and I will have to wait.

Even in my disappointment, I recognize that Tommy and Nico
have constructed their case with care. They will begin with the
murder scene and the collection of the physical evidence, and
will then start a slowly accelerating demonstration of why I am
the murderer. First will come their proof, equivocal as that is, of
my relationship with Carolyn; then my questionable handling of
the investigation; near the end they will offer the various bits of
evidence that put me at the murder scene: the fingerprints, the
fibers, the phone records, the Nearing maid, the blood test
results. Painless Kumagai will testify last and, I suppose, offer an
expert opinion on how it was done.

Up on the bench Larren is still chewing Nico out, for the
record.

"And the prosecutors will immediately advise the defense
when the evidence is located. Is that correct?"

Nico promises.

With that matter settled, the jury is brought in, and Nico

announces the name of the prosecution's first witness, Detective Harold Greer. He enters from the corridor and stands before Larren to be sworn.

As soon as Greer is up there, it is obvious to all of us why Nico wanted to maintain the predetermined order of proof. Juries for obvious reasons tend to remember the first witness, and Greer is impressive, a huge, well-spoken black man, calm and orderly in his presentation of himself. With or without the glass, he is the image of competence. The department is full of officers like Greer, men and women with the IQ's of college professors who became cops because it was, within their horizons, the best thing available.

Molto is doing the questioning. He looks rumpled but his direct examination is well prepared.

"And where was the body?"

Greer was the third officer on the scene. Carolyn was discovered about 9:30 a.m. She missed an eight o'clock meeting and a nine o'clock court call. Her secretary called the super directly. All he did, he told me months ago, was push the door open and look around. He could see then he needed the cops. The beat guys called for Greer.

Greer describes what he observed and the way the evidence techs did their work under his direction. Greer identifies a sealed plastic packet that contains the fibers that were lifted from Carolyn's body, and a larger packet that contains her skirt, from which more of the Zorak V fibers were obtained. Molto and he smooth over the glass. Greer describes finding it on the bar, watching the evidence techs seal the Baggie.

"And where is the glass at present?"

"We've had a little trouble locating it. It should turn up in the police evidence room."

Next Molto raises the specter of the removed diaphragm. Greer says that in a thorough search of the apartment he found no contraceptive device. Then, with all the little bits of evidence which the police discovered inventoried before the jury, Molto moves to his climax.

"Based on your experience in nine years as a homicide detective, and the appearance of the scene, did you have any opinion as to what had taken place?" Molto asks.

Stern makes his first objection before the jury.

"Your Honor," Stern scolds, "this is speculative. This cannot be regarded as an expert opinion. Mr. Molto is asking about a hunch."

Larren strokes his cheeks with his big hand, but shakes his head. "Overruled."

Molto repeats the question.

"Based on the position of the body," Greer responds, "the way it was tied, the signs of disturbance, the open window over the fire escape, on first looking at the scene I was of the opinion that Ms. Polhemus had been murdered in the course of, or as the result of, a sexual assault."

"A rape!" asks Molto, a leading question, not usually permitted on direct examination but harmless under the circumstances.

"Yes," says Greer.

"And were police photographers at the scene?"

"They were."

"What, if anything, did they do?"

"I asked them to take a number of photos of the scene. And they did that."

"In your presence?"

From the evidence cart the prosecutors wheeled into court this morning, Molto takes the collection of photos I looked at four months ago in my office. He shows each to Sandy before he presents them to Greer. Molto has set his examination up cleverly. Usually a judge will limit the prosecution's use of photos in a murder case. It is grisly and prejudicial. But by emphasizing the appearances, which the prosecution of course will argue were staged, Tommy has deprived us of the usual grounds for objections. We sit, attempting to appear implacable, while Greer describes each of the gruesome photos and identifies them as having accurately reflected the scene. When Molto offers them, Sandy approaches the bench and asks the judge to look them over himself.

"We can do with just two of the body," Larren says. He removes another two, but he allows Molto to pass the ones admitted among the jurors at the end of Greer's examination. I do not dare to look up often, but I can sense from the stillness in the box that the blood and Carolyn's contorted corpse have had the effect the prosecutors hoped. The schoolteacher will not be smiling at me again for quite a while.

"Cross-examination," says the judge.

"Just a few matters," says Sandy. He smiles a bit at Greer. We will not be challenging this witness. "You mentioned a glass, Detective. Where is that?" Stern starts to look among the exhibits Greer identified.

"It's not here."

"I am sorry. I thought you testified about it."

"I did."

"Oh." Sandy appears flustered. "But you do not have it?"

"No, sir."

"When was the last time you saw it?"

"At the scene."

"You have not seen it since?"

"No, sir."

"Have you tried to find it?"

Greer smiles, probably the first time since he took the stand. "Yes, sir."

"I see from your expression you have put some effort into this?"

"Yes, sir."

"And the glass still cannot be found?"

"No, sir."

"And who would have handled it last?"

"I don't know. Mr. Molto over there has got the evidence receipts."

"Oh." Sandy turns in Tommy's direction. Molto appears faintly amused. It is Sandy's playacting that he finds humorous, but the jury of course does not realize that is the source of this slight grin. To them Tommy must appear somewhat arrogant. "Mr. Molto has them?"

"Yes, sir."

"Ordinarily he would have the evidence, too?"

"Yes, sir. The prosecutor gets the evidence and the original tags."

"So Mr. Molto has the tag but not the glass?"

"That's right."

Sandy turns again to Molto. While looking at him, Stern says, "Thank you, Detective." He appears to ruminate before he again faces the witness.

Stern spends a few minutes on the details of the collection of various pieces of evidence. When he reaches the diaphragm he pauses with some apparent emphasis.

"A contraceptive device was not the only item you failed to find, is that right, Detective?"

Greer's face narrows. He did not find the Hope Diamond or Aunt Tillie's missing lace hankie. The question can't be answered.

"Well, Detective, you and the officers under your command made a very thorough search of the apartment, did you not?"

"We certainly did."

"And yet, sir, you failed to find not merely a diaphragm but also any cream or jelly or other substance that could be expected to be utilized with it—is that not correct?"

Greer hesitates. He had not thought of this before.

"That's correct," he says at last.

Nico turns immediately to Tommy. They are seated fifteen feet in front of me, facing the jury. I've never had the chance before to watch my opponents. From the prosecutor's table you focus on the jurors. Nico is whispering. It seems to be something like, Where the hell is the stuff? A couple of the jury members respond alertly to this part of the examination.

Stern is about to sit down when I ask him to bring the photos over. Sandy casts me a black look. This is proof that Stern would just as soon be forgotten. I motion to him again, however, and he hands me the stack. I finally find the picture of the bar and make my point to Stern. He bows briefly to me before returning to the witness.

"You identified this photograph, Detective Greer, State Exhibit 6—G?"

"Yes, sir."

"It reflects the bar where you found this glass?"

"It does."

"Tell me, sir—this would be easier if we had the glass, but is your recollection of it good?"

"I think so. It's like the ones in the picture."

"Just so. The glass you seized was one of this set of barware laid out here on this towel?" Sandy has turned the photograph around so both Greer and the jurors can see the portion of the picture Stern means to indicate.

"Right."

"Count the glasses, would you?"

Greer lays his finger on the photo and does it slowly. "Twelve," he says.

"Twelve," Stern repeats. "So the missing glass would make thirteen?"

Greer knows this is peculiar. He waggles his head. "I guess so."

"An odd set?"

Molto objects, but Greer answers, "Very," before Larren can rule.

"Really," Sandy says to me when we break for lunch, "I appreciate your thoughts, Rusty, but you must share them with us before the last moment. This detail may be significant."

I look at Stern as we are heading out of court.

"I just noticed," I tell him.

The prosecutors have a dismal afternoon. I never tried a case as a deputy P.A. that did not have a low spot, a trough, a place where my evidence was weak. I used to talk about walking through the Valley of Death. For Nico, as we've long known, the valley is trying to prove what went on between Carolyn and me. His hope, quite clearly, is to get just enough evidence before the jury that they can make a comfortable guess. The overall plan Molto and he seemingly made was to start strong with Greer, stagger through this portion, and then dash for home, with the physical evidence providing a note of rising credibility. A reasonable strategy. But all the lawyers come to court after lunch knowing that these hours will belong to the defense.

The state's next witness is Eugenia Martinez, my former secretary. She clearly sees this as her moment. She comes to the stand in a broad slouch hat and dangling earrings. Nico presents her testimony, which is succinct. Eugenia testifies that she has been employed in the P.A.'s office fifteen years. For two of those fifteen years, ending last April, she worked for me. One day last September or October, in answering the phone, Eugenia picked up the wrong line. She heard just a few words of conversation, but she recognized the voices as those of Ms. Polhemus and me. I was talking about meeting Ms. Polhemus at her home.

"And how did they sound to you?" asks Nico.

"Object to 'sound,'" says Stern. "It calls for a characteriza-tion."

"Sustained."

Nico faces Larren. "Judge, she can testify to what she heard."

"What she heard, but no opinions." From the bench, Larren addresses Eugenia. "Ms. Martinez, you cannot tell us what you thought when you heard the conversation. Just the words and the intonation."

"What was the intonation?" Nico asks, back close to where he wanted to be.

Eugenia, however, is not ready for the question.

"Nice-like," she finally answers.

Stern objects, but the response is too innocuous to merit exclusion. Larren flips a hand and says that the answer may stand.

Nico is having a difficult time with something important. Again, I am struck by how difficult it has been for him to prepare.

"Did they sound intimate?" he asks.

"Objection!" Stern shoots to his feet. The question is leading and unfairly suggestive.

Larren again takes off on Nico before the jury. The question was clearly improper, Larren says. It is stricken and the jurors are ordered to disregard it. But there is method to Nico's breach. He was trying to find some way to signal Eugenia.

He asks, "Could you further describe the tone of the remarks you heard?"

Stern objects again with force. The question has been previously asked and answered.

Larren peers down. "Mr. Delay Guardia, I suggest that you move on."

Suddenly help comes to Nico from an unexpected source. "He say 'my angel,'" Eugenia volunteers.

Nico faces her, stunned.

"That's what he say. Okay? He say he be comin at eight o'clock and call her 'my angel.'"

For the first time since the trial began my composure fails before the jury. I let out a sound. My look, I'm certain, is inflamed. Kemp lays a hand on mine.

"My angel!" I whisper. "For Chrissake."

Over his shoulder, Stern looks at me severely.

Suddenly ahead of where he expected to be, Nico sits down. "Cross-examination."

Sandy advances on Eugenia. He speaks as soon as he reaches his feet, not waiting to arrive at the podium. He has maintained the same scolding expression which only seconds ago he turned on me.

"For whom do you work now in the prosecuting attorney's office, Ms. Martinez?"

"Work?"

"Whose typing do you do? Whose phones do you answer?"

"Mr. Molto."

"This gentleman? The prosecutor at the table?" Eugenia says yes. "When Mr. Sabich was forced to take leave because of this investigation, Mr. Molto advanced to Mr. Sabich's position, is that right?"

"Yes, sir."

"And that position is one of considerable authority and influence in the P.A.'s office, is that right?"

"Number-two man," answers Eugenia.

"And Mr. Molto was in charge of the investigation that brought him Mr. Sabich's job?"

"Objection!"

"Your Honor," Sandy says to the judge, "I am entitled to develop bias. The woman is testifying before her employer. Her perception of his motives is important."

Larren smiles. Stern is developing more than that, but his excuse will pass. The objection is overruled.

The court reporter rereads the question and Eugenia answers yes. Sandy, in his opening, touched only lightly on the election and the change of administration. This is his first attempt to develop rivalry for power as a theme. It will answer, in part, his question to the jury in his opening statement about why the prosecutors might move ahead on an insufficient case. It had never struck me that he might do that by picking on Molto rather than Della Guardia.

"Now, in the course of investigating Mr. Sabich, did Mr. Molto ask you to speak to a police officer about what you remembered of Mr. Sabich's relationship with Ms. Polhemus?"

"Sir?"

"Didn't you speak in May to Officer Glendenning?" Tom is in and out of court, but right now he is here and Sandy points at him, seated in uniform at the prosecutor's table.

"Yes, sir."

"And you knew that the investigation was a very important one, particularly to your boss, Mr. Molto, did you not?"

"Seemed like."

"And yet, madam, when you were asked about Mr. Sabich's relationship with Ms. Polhemus, you never told Officer Glendenning that you heard Mr. Sabich call Ms. Polhemus 'my angel,' did you?" Sandy says it with a special cold emphasis. He appears furious with the perjury. He has Glendenning's report in his hand.

Eugenia suddenly recognizes that she is trapped. She gets a slow, unwilling look and sags a little. She probably had no idea that the defense would know what she said before.

"No, sir," she says.

"You didn't tell Officer Glendenning that you recalled Mr. Sabich using any term of endearment, did you, madam?"

"No, sir." She is brooding; I have seen this look a hundred times. Her eyes close; her shoulders draw around her. This is when Eugenia is at her meanest. "I never said anythin like that."

"Not to Mr. Glendenning?"

"No time."

Sandy, before I do, recognizes where Eugenia is going. She has thought of a way out. He walks a few steps toward her.

"Didn't you testify five minutes ago, madam, that Mr. Sabich called Ms. Polhemus 'my angel'?"

Eugenia draws herself up in the witness stand, fierce and proud.

"No way," she says loudly. Three or four of the jurors look away. One of them, the man who is learning about hamburgers, laughs out loud, just one little hiccup.

Sandy studies Eugenia. "I see," he finally says. "Well, tell me, Ms. Martinez, when you answer Mr. Molto's phone these days do you listen in on *his* conversations?"

Her thick eyes go sidelong with contempt. "Nope," she says.

"You would not listen a moment longer than you had to in order to recognize that someone is on the line, is that not correct?"

This, of course, is Eugenia's problem. She probably heard a good deal more pass on the telephone between Carolyn and me than she has disclosed. But even with the P.A. and his chief deputy prosecuting the case, she cannot admit to eavesdropping. The winds of fortune change too quickly, and Eugenia, a bureaucratic animal, knows that such an admission would eventually be the long-awaited dynamite to dislodge her from her sinecure in civil service concrete.

"What you heard, you heard in an instant?"

"That's all."

"No more?"

"No, sir."

"And you tell us it was 'nice-like'? Were those not your words?"

"What I say, yes, sir."

Stern comes and stands beside Eugenia. She weighs about two hundred pounds. She is broad-featured and surly, and even dressed in her finest, as she is today, she still does not look very good. Her dress is much too loud and is stretched tight over her bulk.

"You base this answer," he asks, "on your experience in such things?"

Sandy is poker-faced, but a couple of the jurors get it. They look down as they smile. Eugenia certainly gets it. Killers' eyes do not grow colder.

Stern does not ask for an answer.

"And this conversation about meeting at Ms. Polhemus's apartment took place last September, you say?"

"Yes, sir."

"Do you remember that Mr. Sabich and Ms. Polhemus tried a case together as co-prosecutors last September?"

Eugenia stops. "Uh-uh," she says.

"You do not remember the *McGaffen* case? A child, a little boy, had been hideously tortured by his mother? His head put in a vise? His anus burned with cigarettes? You do not remember Mr. Sabich securing the conviction of this—" Stern makes it look as if he is searching for a word, before he ends with "woman?"

"Oh, that one," she says. "I recall."

"The *McGaffen* case, I take it, was not recalled in your discussions with Mr. Molto?"

"Objection."

Larren ponders.

"I will withdraw it," says Stern. He's made his point to the jury. Prosecutor Molto seems to be taking it in the shorts so far today. He has the tag for the missing glass. He has inspired Eugenia's perjury.

"Ms. Martinez, do you remember how warm it was in Kindle County last year around Labor Day?"

Her brows close. She has taken enough of a beating that she is trying to cooperate.

"Past 100 two days."

"Correct," Stern says, improperly. "Is the P.A.'s office air-conditioned?"

Eugenia snorts. "Only if you believe what they say."

Laughter throughout the courtroom. The judge, the jury, the spectators. Even Stern finally smiles.

"I take it you try to leave as soon as the day ends when the heat is like that?"

"You got that right."

"But the prosecutors, when they are in the midst of a trial, do not leave at the end of the day, do they?"

She looks at Sandy suspiciously.

"Isn't it commonplace, in your experience, for the deputy P.A.'s to prepare for the next day of trial in the evenings?" Stern asks.

"Oh yes."

"Now, madam, would you not prefer to work in air conditioning rather than the P.A.'s office on a very warm evening?"

"Objection," Nico says. It's largely pointless.

"I'll let it stand."

"Sure would."

"You don't know of your own knowledge that Ms. Polhemus's apartment was air-conditioned, I take it?"

"No, sir."

"But you do know that the riverfront is much closer to the P.A.'s office than Mr. Sabich's home in Nearing?"

"Yes, sir."

Whatever the jury makes of Eugenia, it is probably favorable compared to their opinions of Mrs. Krapotnik, who is called next. Her few minutes on the witness stand achieve the level of pure burlesque. Mrs. Krapotnik is a widow. She does not say what Mr. Krapotnik died from, but it is hard to believe that Mrs. Krapotnik was not partly the cause. She is heavy-bosomed and garishly made up. Her hair is reddish, teased out so that it stands like a shrub, and her jewelry is thick. A difficult human being. She refuses to answer questions and narrates, free-flow. Mrs, Krapotnik explains as she is going along that the late Mr. Krapotnik was an entrepreneur of sorts. He bought their loft building on the riverfront when, as Mrs. K. puts it, "the neighborhood was still a mess, with trucks and junk, whatever." She nods to the jury when she says this, confident that they know what she means. Mr. Krapotnik directed the refurbishment of the property himself.

"He was a visionary. Do you know what I'm saying? He saw things. That place—you know what was in there? Tires, I'm not kidding, Mr. Dioguardi. Tires. Really, you could not believe the smell. I am not squeamish and it is embarrassing to say it, but one time he took me in there, I swear to God I thought I would retch."

"Madam," Nico says, not for the first time.

"He was a plumber. Who thought he knew real estate? Yes, Mr. Dioguardi?" She squints. "Is that your name? Dioguardi?"

"Della Guardia," says Nico, and casts his face despairingly toward Molto, seeking help.

By and by Mrs. Krapotnik reaches Carolyn. She was their tenant originally when she moved in almost a decade ago. During the conversion craze, the building went condo and Carolyn bought. Listening to Mrs. Krapotnik, I write Kemp a note. "Where does a probation officer going to law school at night get the money to rent on the waterfront?" Kemp nods. He has thought of the same thing. For almost a decade, Carolyn lived on the second floor and Mrs. Krapotnik the first. Carolyn sent flowers, not really the right thing, when Mr. Krapotnik died.

Nico is eager to get Mrs. Krapotnik out of there. The lady is beyond control. He does not bother asking about the night Carolyn was murdered. Any identification Mrs. Krapotnik made at this point would be sorely impeached by her prior failures.

Instead, Nico simply asks, "Do you see in the courtroom, Mrs. Krapotnik, anyone you have seen in the vicinity of Ms. Polhemus's apartment?"

"Well, I know I seen that one," she says. She throws both hands and her bangle bracelets in the direction of the judge.

Larren covers his face with both hands. Nico pinches the bridge of his nose. The laughter in the spectator sections is suppressed, but seems after an instant to grow. Mrs. Krapotnik, recognizing that she has blown it, looks about desperately. She points at Tommy Molto, seated at the prosecutor's table.

"Him too," she says.

Molto makes matters worse by turning to see if there is anyone behind him.

By now the jurors are laughing.

Nico retreats to the evidence cart and brings Mrs. Krapotnik the photo spread from which she has previously identified a snap of me. She looks at the spread, glances up in my direction, and shrugs. Who knows?

"Do you recall previously identifying photograph number 4?" Nico asks.

This time she says it out loud: "Who knows?" When Nico closes his eyes in frustration, she adds, "Oh, all right. I said it was him."

Nico heads for his seat.

"Cross-examination."

"One question," says Stern. "Mrs. Krapotnik, I take it your building is air-conditioned?"

"Air condition?" She turns to the judge. "What's his business if we got air condition?"

Larren stands to his full height and places his hands on the far side of the bench, so he is canted over Mrs. Krapotnik, five or six feet above her head.

"Mrs. Krapotnik," he says quietly, "that question can be answered yes or no. If you say anything else I will hold you in contempt."

"Yes," says Mrs. Krapotnik.

"Nothing further," says Stern. "Your Honor, the record will reflect that there was no identification of Mr. Sabich?"

"The record will reflect," says Judge Lyttle, shaking his head, "that Mr. Sabich was one of the few persons in the courtroom Mrs. Krapotnik missed."

Larren leaves the bench, with the laughter still ringing.

Afterward the reporters crowd around Stern. They want a

comment from him on the first day's testimony, but he will make none.

Kemp is packing back into Sandy's large trial case the documents—duplicates of statements and exhibits—that we withdrew during the day and which now litter the table. I am helping, but Stern takes my elbow and steers me toward the corridor.

"No gloating," he says. "We have a long night's work. Tomorrow they will be calling Raymond Horgan."

How familiar it all seems. I come home at night with the same laborer's weariness that has always followed a day in court. My bones feel hollowed out by the high-voltage impulse of the day; my muscles have a neuralgic tenderness from the adrenalized superheating. My pores, it seems, do not close down rapidly, and the low-tone body sweat of high excitement continues through the evening. I return home with my shirt encasing me like a package wrapper.

Sitting in court, I actually forget at certain moments who is on trial. The performance aspect is of course not present, but the premium on close attention is large. And once we get back to the office, I can be a lawyer again, attacking the books, making notes and memos. I was never short on intensity. When the bus pulls into Nearing shortly before 1 a.m. and I walk down the lighted and silent streets of this gentle town, the feelings are all known and, because they are known, safe. I am in a harbor. My anxiety is stanched; I am at peace. As I have for years, I stop by the door, in a rocking chair, and remove my shoes, so that when I go upstairs I will not disturb Barbara, who by now must be asleep. The house is dark, I absorb the silence and, finally alone, reflect on the events of the day. And in this moment, stimulated perhaps by all the talk of her, or simply by the momentary feeling that I have at last receded to the better past, or even by an unconscious recollection of other stealthy re-entries to my home, I am startled as Carolyn rises before me, rises as she rose for me that month or so when I thought I had found Nirvana, naked to the waist, her breasts high and spectacularly round, the nipples red, erect, and thick, her hair full of static from our bedroom romping, her sensuous mouth parted to offer some clever,

salacious, stimulating remark. And again I am made almost
without the power of movement by my own desire, so fierce, so
hungry, so wanton. I do not care that it is mad, or hopeless: I
whisper her name in the dark. Full of shame and longing, I am
like a piece of crystal trembling near the breaking pitch.
"Carolyn." Hopeless. Mad. And I cannot believe my own
conviction, which is not really an idea but instead that deep
imbedded thing, that rope of emotion which is a wish that I could
do it all again. Again. Again.

And then the ghost recedes. She folds into the air. I sit still,
spine stiffened in my chair. I am breathing quickly. It will be
hours now, I know, before I can sleep, I grope in the hall cabinet
for something to drink. I should make my mind work over the
meaning of this nighttime visitation. But I cannot. I have the
sensation, as determined as the longing of only moments before,
that it is all past. I sit in the rocking chair in my living room. For
some strange reason, I feel better with my briefcase, and I place
it in my lap.

But its protection is incomplete. The wake of this intrusion
leaves the currents of my emotions roily and disturbed. In the
dark I sit, and I can feel the force of the large personages of my
life circling about me like the multiple moons of some far planet,
each one exerting its own deep tidal impulses upon me. Barbara.
Nat. Both my parents. Oh, this cataclysm of love and attachment.
And shame. I feel the rocking sway of all of it, and a moving
sickness of regret. Desperately, desperately I promise
everyone—all of them; myself; the God in whom I do not
believe—that if I survive this I will do better. Better than I have.
An urgent compact, as sincere and grave as any deathbed wish.

I drink my drink. I sit here in the dark and wait for peace.

28

The first thing I notice as Raymond Horgan comes into the courtroom is that he has on the same suit he wore to bury Carolyn, a subtle blue serge. The added weight does not detract from his public bearing. You would describe him now as burly, and still, in the rolling way he walks, a person of stature. He and Larren exchange the same sage grin while Raymond is sworn. Seated, Horgan looks outward to assess the crowd in a composed professional manner. He nods to Stern first, then his glance crosses mine and he acknowledges me. I do not move. I do not allow an eyelash to flutter. At this moment I wish with all my heart that I may be acquitted, not for the general sake of freedom, but so that I can see the look on Raymond Horgan the first time he has to face me on the street.

Here in the courtroom, awaiting Raymond's entry, there was more of that epic atmosphere, the extra amperage of a special moment—four hundred people on edge, an urgent undertone in the courtroom murmur. Today, I notice, the press gallery is larger by a row and a half, and the journalistic first-string is on hand—the anchor people and columnists. I have been surprised during the trial by the extent to which the reporters have been willing to honor Stern's injunctions to keep wide berth of me. Now that they have their file footage of me entering the courthouse, which they can show with each night's story on TV, Barbara and I are able to come and go in relative peace. Now and then someone—usually a journalist whom I have known for years—will stop me with a question in the hallway. I refer all these matters to Stern. Last week I also encountered a freelance journalist from New York who says he is considering writing a book about the case. He believes it will make good reading. I declined his invitation to buy me dinner.

I would be oblivious to the press were it not for the morning papers. I have stopped watching the accounts on TV. The summaries seem so inept that they make me furious, even when the errors favor me. But I cannot avoid the headlines, which I see on the paper-dispensing machines as we drive into the city. The two dailies seem to have sworn a feud to see which can take the lead in trashy tabloid coverage of the case. Nico's revelation in opening of Raymond's amours with Carolyn produced tasteless headlines for two days. P.A. SEX the *Herald* blared, with all kinds of kickers and subheads. It is impossible that the jury does not view these headlines, too. They pledged during *voir dire* not to read the papers, but that is a promise few trial lawyers trust.

In the jury box, at the moment, there is a considerable stirring. The jurors seem far more excited to see Raymond than was the case, for example, when they first glimpsed Nico during the *voir dire*. Then I noticed only a few of the prospective jury members leaning over to one another and nodding in Delay's direction. Horgan brings a greater aura to the courtroom. He has been well known for most of everybody's adult life. He is a celebrity; Della Guardia is a replacement. Perhaps the suggestion of fleshy intrigue Nico floated in opening also contributes to the high interest. It is clear, however, that as Stern weeks ago predicted, we have reached a critical juncture in this trial. Each juror has revolved his chair to face the witness stand. As Molto comes to the podium to begin the direct examination, the large courtroom is quiet.

"State your name, please."

"Raymond Patrick Horgan," he answers. "The third." With that he grins very briefly up at Larren. A private joke. I never knew that Raymond was a third. Amazing, sometimes, what comes out under oath.

Molto again has readied himself with care for the examination. Raymond clearly knows what is coming, as he should, and he and Tommy develop a nice rhythm at once. Horgan's hands are folded. In his blue suit and finest public manner, he looks serene. All his beguiling charm is present; his candor. His gruff baritone is reduced one marking on the volume register in an effort at understatement.

Tommy is taking his time. They are going to get everything they can from Horgan, recover quickly from yesterday's debacle in the war of impressions. They cover Raymond's background. Born right here. High school on the East End at St. Viator's. Two years' college, then his dad died. He became a cop. Seven years on the force, was already a sergeant when he graduated from night law school. I am afraid for a moment that Molto is going to bring out the fact that Raymond practiced law with Larren, but that is elided. Horgan simply says it was a three-man partnership, doing primarily criminal work. After sixteen years in practice, politics.

"Some elections I won," says Raymond, "some I lost." With that he turns to smile fondly at Nico at the prosecutor's table. Delay rears his half-bald head from taking notes and beams back. My God, how they look at each other! The fastest friends. The jurors seem delighted by this alliance, forged on well-known past adversity. The smiling schoolteacher watches the unspoken exchange between the two with apparent delight. I feel my soul sinking. This will be a very hard day.

"And do you know the defendant, Rozat Sabich?"

"I know Rusty," Raymond says.

"Do you see him here in court?"

"I do."

"Would you point to him and describe what he is wearing."

"Next to Mr. Stern. Second at the defense table, in a blue chalk-stripe suit."

This is a formality to establish that the Sabich spoken of is me. Yesterday with Eugenia, Sandy rose and agreed—"stipulated" is the term—to the identification so that we did not have to go through this exercise in finger-pointing. But now Stern quietly says to me, "Stand." I do. I rise slowly and face Raymond Horgan. I do not smile or grimace, but I am sure my abject fury is plain. Certainly Raymond's affability fades somewhat, even while his hand is in the air.

"That's him," says Raymond quietly.

Molto breezes through the history of my association with Raymond. Sandy will bring it out in detail anyway. Then he asks Raymond about Carolyn. Here Horgan becomes instantly somber. He lets his eyes fall to the rail of the witness box and says,

"Yes, I knew her, too."

"What was the nature of your relationship?"

"I met her first as a probation officer. For eight years she was employed as a deputy prosecuting attorney in our office, and for a very brief time at the end of last year we had a personal relationship as well."

Nice, succinct. They move to the murder, Molto never mentions the election, but it emerges in Raymond's answers by reference.

"And is there any practice in the P.A.'s office in supervising police investigations?"

"Certainly in a major case—and this was a very major case in my mind—there was a practice to assign a deputy P.A. to guide and assist the police."

"Who made the assignment in this case?"

"Well, to short-circuit things a little bit, I would say that Mr. Sabich and I decided that he should have that role in this case."

Tommy for the first time pauses. Raymond, it seems, may have backed down a little as a result of his meeting with Stern and me. Molto did not expect that. He asks again:

"How did Mr. Sabich get that assignment?"

"I don't really remember whether I suggested it or he did. Like everybody else, I was confused and upset at that time. He got the case. But he was glad to have it. I remember that. He was not reluctant at all, and promised to pursue it vigorously."

"Did he?"

"Not to my way of thinking." This is objectionable as a conclusion but Stern does not want to interrupt. One of his thick fingers has been laid from his chin to his nose and he watches intently, not even bothering to take notes. At many times his concentration in court is trance-like. He shows very little, just absorbs. I have the same sense that I did when we were in Horgan's office that Sandy's calculations are not about facts or strategy but character. He is trying to figure Horgan out.

Raymond registers his complaints with my handling of the case, including having to urge me to speed up the fingerprint and fiber reports. The impression comes through clearly that I was dogging it. Then he describes the conversation in his office that night we both first realized he was going to lose.

"He asked me if I had been intimate with Carolyn."

"And what did you tell him?"

"The truth," says Raymond, quite simply. No big deal. "We'd been on for three months, then off."

"And when you told him this, did Mr. Sabich express surprise in any way?"

"None at all."

I get it. They're going to reason backward. I asked, but I knew anyway. What is their theory? That I was outraged when I found out? Or that I gave in to the weight of accumulated grievances? Neither one makes complete sense, when you suppose, as Nico has, that my relationship with Carolyn was ongoing. Not having the right facts always hurts. I can feel many of the jurors watching me now, trying to read in me the truth of the prosecutors' surmise.

"And at any time in this conversation or at any time earlier, did Mr. Sabich inform you that he himself had a personal relationship with Ms. Polhemus?"

Sandy is instantly back to life, on his feet.

"Objection. Your Honor, there is simply no proof of record of any personal relationship between Mr. Sabich and Ms. Polhemus." A good tactic, if for no other reason than to break the rhythm now and draw the jury back to yesterday. But this obstacle we are throwing up still presents a painful straddle for me. We cannot continue to make an issue of this failure of proof if I am going to get on the witness stand and tell the jury that everything Stern contested for two weeks is true, that Carolyn and I indeed had a warm romance. This is one of the many delicate means that Stern is employing seemingly to discourage my testimony.

"We-e-e-ll," drawls Larren. He turns around in his chair. "I would say *almost* no proof." A nice comment for the defense. "I'm gonna let the question stand, but I want to give the jury a limiting instruction." He faces them. "Ladies and gentlemen, Mr. Molto is asking a question based on an assumption. It's up to you to decide, based on the evidence you hear in court, whether that assumption is true. Just because he says this doesn't make it so. Mr. Stern says there is not sufficient evidence to warrant that assumption, and at the end of the case that will be one of the things for you to determine. Proceed, Mr. Molto."

Molto repeats the question.

"Certainly not," says Raymond. The Gaelic humor has now left his face.

"Is that something you would have wanted to know?"

"Objection."

"Rephrase it, Mr. Molto. Is it something that the witness would have expected Mr. Sabich to tell him, based on the witness's understanding of his office's practices?" It is rare for Larren to be so helpful to the prosecutors. I can see that Raymond is having the impact I long feared.

When the question is put as the judge suggested, Raymond buries me.

"I certainly did expect that. I never would have allowed him to handle that investigation. It raises more questions than it answers. The public should know that things are being done for professional, not personal, reasons," he adds, a gratuitous shot. Stern, in front of me, frowns.

Molto then takes Raymond to the end. The meeting in his office. Horgan faithfully recounts my outbursts in spite of Mac's and his warnings.

"Describe Mr. Sabich's appearance as he left the meeting."

"He looked quite excited, I would say. Very upset. He seemed to have completely lost his composure."

Molto looks at Nico, then says he has nothing further on direct.

Larren takes a recess before cross. In the john, as I come out of a stall, I find Della Guardia two sinks down. His hair is too thin now to comb; instead, he tries to tickle it into place with his fingertips. His eyes flick a little bit when he notices me in the mirror.

"Not a bad witness, huh?" he asks. His intent is hard to divine. I don't know if this is a casual aside or gloating. I keep getting the feeling that Nico is out of place emotionally. He is not oriented in this case—like offering me his hand on the day of the arraignment. He has never been the kind of person to make a frontal approach to unpleasantness, especially once someone has reached him. I remember when he divorced Diana; even though she had been running around, he took her back into the apartment for a few weeks when she was thrown out by the other guy. Nico reads something in my hesitation. "I mean, you have to admit, he is not a bad witness."

I dry my hands. I realize now what it is. Nico still wants me to like him. God, human beings are strange. And maybe Nico even has his redeeming side. Horgan at this moment would be cold as a saber's edge. It seems pointless at this little minute to resist him. I smile a bit. I use his nickname.

"Better than Mrs. Krapotnik, Delay."

"Now, Mr. Horgan, you mentioned that you had a personal relationship with Ms. Polhemus? Is that correct?"

"It is."

"And you also told us that you believe Mr. Sabich should have informed you that he had had such a relationship as well?"

"At a later time," says Raymond carefully. He wants to rule out jealousy on his part. "I felt when the investigation began he had a professional obligation to tell me."

"Have you any personal knowledge, Mr. Horgan, that there was ever such a relationship between Mr. Sabich and Ms. Polhemus?"

"That's the point," says Horgan. "He never told me."

Sandy does not take getting stuck cheerfully. He looks at length toward Horgan. He wants the jury to notice that Raymond Horgan is taking shots.

"Please answer the question I asked you. Do you remember it?"

"I do."

"But you chose not to answer it?"

Raymond's mouth moves without words. "I apologize, Mr. Stern. I have no personal knowledge of such a relationship."

"Thank you." Sandy strolls. "But assuming there was something to reveal, you believe an honest official would make such disclosures to someone in a responsible position?"

"I do."

"I see," says Stern. He takes a moment to face Raymond. Sandy is short and soft, but in the courtroom he emits tremendous power. He is clearly equal to Raymond Horgan, who, too, is looking very firm. He sits there with his reddened Irish bulk, his hands folded, waiting for Sandy to take him on. Assuming that he comes out of this intact, Raymond's combination of prominence and skill is likely to make him the leading defense attorney in this city. His nearest rival will be the man who is examining him now. In the years ahead there are no doubt going to be a number of multiple-defendant cases in which they will sit together as co-counsel. In a very real sense, preservation of his relationship with Raymond is of far more practical importance for Stern than anything that happens to me. The rule of life in the defense bar ordinarily is to go along and get along. The state is the only professional enemy these guys want to have.

Recognizing all of that, I have put my hostility aside and told Sandy that he has my blessings to treat Raymond gently. As Stern has pointed out before, Raymond's credibility, born of years in the public light, will make him hard to successfully assail, in any event. But it is clear from Stern's demeanor that he will be neither courtly nor accommodating to Raymond. Perhaps Stern believes the direct was too damaging to simply absorb. But I am surprised that Sandy has begun any attack this abruptly. There are some favorable things Raymond will have to concede—compliments on my performance in the office in the past, for example. The traditional wisdom is that you take what a witness will give before you slap him.

"And you applied these standards for disclosure to yourself as well?"

"I tried."

"Certainly you would give all appropriate information to someone on your staff doing a job for you?"

"Again, Mr. Stern, I'd try."

"And certainly the case concerning Ms. Polhemus's death was a very important case in your office?"

"Given its political significance, I would call it critical." Raymond looks in my direction as he says this. His eyes are hard as ball bearings.

"But even though you yourself saw this as a critical case, you did not give Mr. Sabich all the information at your disposal about the matter, or about Ms. Polhemus, did you?"

"I tried."

"Did you? Was it not very important to know everything Ms. Polhemus was working on, so that any person who might have a motive to do her harm could be identified?"

Raymond suddenly sees where this is going. He sits back in his chair. But he still tries to fight.

"That wasn't the only thing that was important."

Bad mistake. Lawyers really are lousy witnesses. Raymond is going to deny that Carolyn's docket was an important source of leads. Sandy embarrasses him badly in the next few moments. People in law enforcement often fear reprisals from those they prosecute? Such reprisals all too frequently occur? Law enforcement would be impossible if prosecutors and police could be assaulted, maimed, murdered by those they investigate? Certainly when Ms. Polhemus was killed it was a thought, indeed it was speculated in the press, was it not, that a former defendant might have been her attacker? Raymond sees he's lost after a few questions, and answers simply yes.

"So all of Ms. Polhemus's cases were important? It was important to know whom she was investigating, what she was looking into?"

"Yes."

"And in spite of knowing that, Mr. Horgan, you personally removed a file from Ms. Polhemus's drawer after the investigation of her murder began, didn't you?"

"Yes."

"A very sensitive matter, was it not?"

Larren has observed the cross, lying back in his chair. For the most part he has appeared faintly amused by this contest between two well-known professionals. Now he interrupts.

"What's the relevance of this, Counsel?"

Sandy for a moment is wordstruck.

"Your Honor, I think that the relevance of this is clear."

"Not to me."

"The witness has testified on direct examination that Mr. Sabich did not bring to his attention information that Mr. Horgan regarded as pertinent. The defendant is entitled to explore Mr. Horgan's standards in this regard."

"Mr. Horgan was the prosecuting attorney, Mr. Stern. You're mixing apples and oranges," says the judge.

Relief comes from an unexpected source. Della Guardia is on his feet.

"We have no objection to this line of questioning, Judge."

Larren lets his glance linger in Nico's direction. Molto immediately grabs Delay's forearm. I assume that Nico wants the discussion about professional standards to continue in the belief that it will further educate the jury about the extent of my deviation. But he is well out of place here. For one thing, Horgan is not his witness. And I take it from the heated way that Molto speaks to him as Delay resumes his seat that Nico does not recognize the drift of Sandy's questioning. I wonder if he even knows about the B file or has just forgotten. I make a note which I will give to Stern at the break: Who did Horgan tell *re* B file? Molto? Nico? Neither?

With new daylight, Sandy quickly proceeds.

"As I said, this was a very sensitive matter, was it not?"

"Yes."

"It involved allegations—"

Larren again injects himself, more faithful than a Labrador. "We don't need the details of the internal workings of the prosecuting attorney's office or of its investigations, many of which, I remind you, Mr. Stern, are protected by rules of grand-jury secrecy. This was a sensitive case. Let us move on."

"Of course, Your Honor, I had no interest in disclosing any secrets."

"Of course not," says Larren. He smiles with apparent disbelief and turns toward his water carafe, which, it so happens, is in the direction of the jury. "Proceed."

"And, in fact, this case was so sensitive, Mr. Horgan, that you assigned it to Ms. Polhemus without informing any other person in your office that you had done so. Yes?"

"Yes."

Sandy quickly lists everyone in the office who was not told: Mac. The Special Investigations Chief, Mike Dolan. Three or four more names. He ends with me. Raymond acknowledges each.

"And you gave the file to Mr. Sabich only when he personally informed you that a file appeared to be missing from Ms. Polhemus's office, is that not true?"

"True."

Sandy takes a little tour around the courtroom to let all of this sink in. Raymond has been tarnished. The jury is paying close attention.

"Now, Ms. Polhemus was an ambitious woman, was she not?"

"I suppose it depends on what you mean by ambitious."

"She enjoyed being in the public eye, she wanted to progress in your office, did she not?"

"All true."

"She wanted to handle this case?"

"As I recall."

"Now, Mr. Horgan, you assigned this case to Ms. Polhemus, this highly sensitive matter to her, this case that only you and she knew about, this case she was eager to handle while you two were personally involved, correct?"

Raymond begins to roll again in his seat. He knows that Stern will spare him nothing now. He has hunkered down a little, so that to my eye it looks as if he is trying to duck.

"I really don't recall exactly when I made that assignment."

"Let me remind you, then." Sandy gets the file jacket, shows Raymond the docketing date, reminds him of his direct testimony about when he and Carolyn were dating. "So," he concludes, "you assigned this very sensitive case to Ms. Polhemus while you were personally involved with her?"

"That appears to be when it happened."

Stern stands still and looks at Horgan.

"The answer to the question," says Raymond, "is yes."

"Your failure to inform anyone of this assignment contradicted established procedure in your office, did it not?"

"I was the prosecuting attorney. I decided when there would be exceptions to the rules." He has picked up Larren's hint.

"And you made an exception for Ms. Polhemus?"

"Yes."

"With whom you were— Strike that. Ordinarily such a case would have been assigned to a lawyer with more experience in such matters, would it not?"

"That's a consideration ordinarily."

"But that wasn't a consideration here?"

"No."

"And this remained your secret with Ms. Polhemus, did it not, even after your relationship with her ended?"

"True," says Raymond. He smiles for the first time in a while. "There was no change in my conduct."

"Because you were embarrassed?"

"It didn't occur to me."

"And when Mr. Sabich was trying to assemble all the information in the office about Ms. Polhemus's cases, it did not

occur to you that you had gone to her office and put the file in
your drawer?"

"I suppose it didn't."

"You were not attempting to conceal anything, were you, Mr.
Horgan?"

"I was not."

"There was an election campaign taking place, was there
not?"

"Yes."

"A tough campaign?"

"Brutal."

"A campaign in which, as it turned out, you were losing?"

"Yes."

"A campaign in which your opponent, Mr. Della Guardia, had
been a deputy in your very office and had many friends there?"

"That's true."

"And you were not concerned, Mr. Horgan, in the midst of this
brutal campaign about word leaking out, through one of Mr.
Della Guardia's friends, that you had given choice assignments
to an assistant with whom you were sleeping?"

"Maybe it crossed my mind. Who knows, Mr. Stern? It was not
an ideal situation."

"Far from it," says Stern. "I ask you again, sir, were you not
trying to hide the fact that you had had an affair with a member
of your staff?"

"It wasn't something I ordinarily talked about, if that's what
you mean."

"No indeed. It could be viewed as unprofessional."

"It could be, but it wasn't. We were both adults."

"I see. You had confidence in your judgment, notwithstanding
this affair?"

"Very much so."

Stern has gradually approached Horgan. Now he takes the last
few steps and reaches out to touch the rail of the witness stand,
so that he stands only a few feet from Raymond.

"And yet, sir, you come to this courtroom where the life of a
man who served you faithfully for a dozen years now hangs in
the balance, and you tell us that you would have none of the
same confidence in him?"

Horgan's look locks with Stern's. From where I am, I cannot

quite see Raymond's expression. He finally faces about and when he does he has his tongue tucked into his cheek. He is looking now in Della Guardia's direction, somewhat sheepishly. I am not sure if he is seeking help or casting apologies.

"I wish he had said something, that's all. It would have looked better for him. It would have looked better for me."

One of the jurors says, "Hmm." I hear the sound, but do not see whom it came from. Others are looking toward the floor. It is hard to figure why this seems to have such impact. Nothing has changed the fingerprints, or the fibers, or the records from my phone. But it has been a splendid moment for the defense. Molto and Nico have brought Raymond Horgan to this courtroom as the model of propriety, the arbiter of standards. Now it turns out that things have been overblown. Just as he did in representing Colleen McGaffen, Sandy Stern has found the message to this jury that he wishes to send but never speak aloud. So what? he is saying. Suppose it is true that Sabich and the decedent had been intimate. Suppose that he chose, wisely or not, to keep that to himself. It is still no different from what Horgan did. If I was too embarrassed to confess aspects of my past conduct, everyone should understand. The knot between what I did not say and what I did has been untied; the juncture has been severed between murder and deceit.

Sandy walks away. He lets Horgan sit. Raymond sighs a couple of times and removes his handkerchief. As Stern paces by our table, he places his hand on my shoulder and I cover it with mine. A spontaneous gesture, but it seems to go down well with one or two jurors who notice.

"Let us turn to another subject, Mr. Horgan. How did you meet Mr. Sabich?"

Sandy is still strolling, headed back now toward the witness, and below the table I motion to him, no. I forgot to tell him not to ask that question.

"Perhaps we should not loiter with ancient history," says Sandy casually. "I shall withdraw that question, if the court please. As a matter of fact, Your Honor, if this would be a convenient point, perhaps we could all do with some lunch."

"Very well," says Larren. He seems particularly sober after Raymond's performance. Before he leaves the bench, Judge Lyttle glances back at Horgan, who has still not moved.

29

"So what did you think of this morning? Hmm?" asks Stern. He reaches for the relish tray. "You must try the corn willie, Rusty. Such a simple dish, but really very well prepared."

Stern has worked through lunch each day preceding, but you can tell that it is not his chosen routine. A civilized life includes a meal at noontime, he would say, and today, Horgan or not, he takes me to his dining club for lunch. It is on the forty-sixth floor of Morgan Towers, one of the tallest buildings in town. From here you can see the river bend and sway, the serried ranks of the city skyline, which these days looks mostly like so many shoe boxes end on end. If you had a telescope you could probably make out my home in Nearing.

I would have expected to become closer to Sandy. I am fond of him, and my respect for his professional abilities, never slight, has grown progressively. But I would not say that we have become friends. Perhaps it is because I am a client, charged with murder no less. But Stern's view of human capacity is itself large enough that I doubt any one act, no matter how heinous, would disqualify someone from his affections. The problem, if there is a problem, is the man and his inner restraints. He draws his lines in his professional life and I doubt anyone passes. He has been married thirty years. I have met Clara once or twice. Their three children are now spread all around the country; the youngest, a daughter, will finish at Columbia Law School next year. But as I think about it, I do not know many other people who claim to be close to Stern. He is a pleasant companion on any social occasion, and he is a polished raconteur. I remember that a friend of Barbara's father told me years ago that Stern tells marvelous stories in Yiddish, a skill I, of course, cannot confirm. But there are sharp limits on Sandy Stern's sense of intimacy. I know very little of what he really thinks, particularly about me.

"I have two comments about this morning," I say, as I help myself to corn. "I thought it went very well, and I enjoyed it a great deal. The cross has been brilliant."

"Oh well," says Stern. Sandy, despite his fine manners, is a considerable egotist, like every other noted trial lawyer. He shakes his head, but then takes a moment to savor my praise. A number of the reporters and courtroom observers whispered their compliments as we were on the way over here. Stern, only halfway through the cross, still wears the light air of triumph. "He did it to himself, really. I do not think I recognized before the start of this case how vain a person Raymond is. Even so, I do not know how far it takes us."

"You embarrassed him very badly."

"Apparently. He is bound to remind me of it someday. But that is not our problem now."

"I was surprised Larren was so protective of Raymond. If I had to guess, I would have bet that he'd have bent over backward to appear neutral."

"Larren has never been afraid of being regarded as a man with his own affinities." Sandy sits back as a waiter sets down his plate. "Well," says Stern, "I only hope we do as well at the next critical juncture. I am not as optimistic."

I do not understand what he is talking about.

"There are two pivotal cross-examinations in this trial, Rusty," he says. "We are only in the midst of the first."

"What's the other—Lipranzer?"

"No." Stern frowns a bit, unhappy, apparently, merely with the prospect of Lip's testimony, "Detective Lipranzer for us will be primarily a holding action. In that case, we will be hoping, merely, to ease the sting. No, I was thinking of Dr. Kumagai."

"Kumagai?"

"Oh yes." Sandy nods to himself. "You see, of course, that the physical evidence is the center of the prosecutors' case. But in order to fully utilize that evidence, Nico must call a scientific expert. Della Guardia cannot stand before the jury at the end of the case and offer only conjecture on how this act took place. His theories must be buttressed by a scientist's opinions. So he will

call Kumagai." Sandy samples his lunch with obvious appreciation. "Forgive me for being didactic. I am unaccustomed to
counseling trial lawyers. At any rate, Kumagai's testimony
becomes critical. If he performs well, he will solidify the
prosecution case. But his testimony also offers an opportunity
for us. It is really the only chance we will have to blunt the edge
somewhat on the physical evidence—the fingerprints, the fibers,
all of these items that are normally unassailable. If we make
Kumagai look dubious, the physical evidence, all of it, suffers as
well."

"And how do you do that?"

"Ah," says Stern, somewhat wistfully, "you ask all the difficult
questions. We must turn our attention to that shortly." He taps
his bread knife and casts his eyes toward the skyline, not really
focused on it. "Kumagai is not a pleasant individual. A jury will
not warm to him. Something will suggest itself. In the meantime,"
Stern says, looking back to me abruptly, "what was this blunder I
almost made? Something awful would have been disclosed when
I asked how you and Horgan met?"

"I didn't think you wanted the jury to hear about how the
Yugoslavian freedom fighter went to federal prison."

"Your father? Oh dear. Rusty, I must apologize to you for that
improvisation the other day. It came to me as I was there. You
understand these things, I am sure."

I tell Sandy that I understand.

"Your father went to jail? How did that happen? Horgan
represented him?"

"Steve Mulcahy. Raymond just covered a couple of the court
calls. That was how we met. He was very nice to me. I was quite
upset."

"Mulcahy was the other partner?" In those days it was
Mulcahy, Lyttle & Horgan. "He has been dead many years. We
are talking about some time ago, I take it."

"I was still in law school. Mulcahy was my professor. When my
father got the first summons, I went to him, I was terribly
embarrassed. I thought character and fitness might keep me
out."

"Of the bar? My Lord! What was the crime?"

"Taxes," I say. I take the first bite of my lunch. "My father
didn't file for twenty-five years."

"Twenty-five years! Oh my. How is your fish?"

"Good. Would you care for a little?"

"If you don't mind. Thank you. You are much too kind. They really do this very well here."

Sandy chats on. He is serene and comfortable amid the silverplate table settings and the waiters in pastel cutaway coats. His retreat. In forty-five minutes he will resume cross-examining one of the most prominent lawyers in the city. But like all virtuosos he has a well-deserved faith in his instincts. He has worked hard. The rest is inspiration.

When the meal is near its end, I show Sandy the notes I made this morning. "Oh yes," he tells me. "Very good." Some matters he is determined not even to respond to. "You are falsely accused and he says you seem to lack composure? Really, this is too silly to repeat."

At another table, he sees a friend, an older red-haired man. Sandy departs for a second to greet him. I review the pad I have brought along from the courthouse, but most of it has been covered in our discussion. Instead, I look out toward the city and, as usual, think about my father with despair. I had been wildly angry with him throughout that episode, both because of my own discomfiture and because I felt he had no right to seek attention after ignoring my mother's illness, then in its initial stages. But as I watched my father in Mulcahy's outer office, a worm of pain began to eat at my heart. In his distraction, my father, usually rigid about his personal hygiene, had failed to shave. His beard grew quickly and his cheeks were whitish with the stubble. He held the felt brim of his hat in his fingers and turned it in his hands. He had a tie on, which he seldom wore; the knot was a kind of crumbled mess pulled off to the side, and his shirt was soiled around the collar. He did not seem to fill his chair, or even his clothing. He looked at his feet on the floor. He appeared much older than he was. And terribly afraid.

I do not believe I had ever seen my father visibly frightened before that. His almost invariable mien was of a rough-tempered, sullen indifference. I did not wonder what produced the change. My father seldom spoke to me about his history. Virtually everything I knew came from his relatives. The shooting of his parents; my father's flight; the camps of one side or the other where my father passed the last years of his youth. They ate a horse, my cousin Ilya told me once when I was nine or ten. The story inspired nightmares for most of a week. An old nag had died. It keeled over in the night and froze. It lay in the snow for three days, and then some guard allowed it to be dragged beyond the barbed-wire fence of the compound. The inmates attacked it; they pulled off the hide with their bare hands and grabbed at the flesh. Some meant only to take something to cook, but others in their panic began to eat it there. My father had seen that. He came to America. He had survived. And now in a lawyer's office, almost three decades later, he could foresee a repetition. I was twenty-five years old, and I understood more of my father's life then, and how his deprivations, in that odd heredity of material effects, had become my own—I recognized more of that in a moment than in all the time before. And I was overcome by grief.

Mulcahy pled my father guilty. The assistant U.S. attorney promised not to recommend more than a year in jail, and old Judge Hartley, a soft touch, gave him only ninety days. I saw him just once while he was in. I had no stomach for it, and my mother by then was nearing the end.

When I asked how he was, he looked around, as if he were only now seeing the place for the first time. He was chewing on a toothpick.

I been in worse, he told me. He had regained all his old harshness, and I found it more upsetting than his fear. Iron-headed, ignorant, he embraced his deepest misfortunes with a kind of pride. The things for which not only he, but I, eventually, had come to suffer he claimed as badges of achievement. He had played in the Olympics of confinement. He could survive a local jail. He had no gratitude to me; no apologies for my shame, or for his stupidity. No knowledge of his real prison. It was late in his life; he died not quite three years later. But the truth is that for everything that went before, it was not until that moment that I finally gave him up.

The afternoon's cross begins where I thought the morning's might, in those areas where Horgan is our witness. Stern starts with the calls in March from my phone to Carolyn's. Horgan promptly recollects the recidivist rapist indictment she was trying to draw together that month, and he acknowledges that one of the chief deputy's primary functions is to assist in the drafting of charges, especially in complex cases. Raymond does not resist Stern's suggestion that Carolyn's trial schedule and my crowded daytime calendar could easily have led to those consultations taking place by phone at night, or, at least, to calls aimed at scheduling meetings about the proposed indictment.

From the calls, Stern moves on to the conversation in Raymond's office the Wednesday after the election. By offering my statement that I was at home the night Carolyn was murdered, the prosecution has, in essence, put in evidence of my defense and Stern elaborates upon it.

Sandy emphasizes that my statement was voluntary. Ms. MacDougall encouraged Mr. Sabich not to speak? You, Mr. Horgan, asked him not to speak? You, sir, in the strongest terms? You told him to keep his mouth shut? Yet he spoke, and he was clearly quite provoked, was he not? Nothing calculated in his manner? His remarks appeared spontaneous? Stern develops at length a prosecutor's learning about the hazards to an investigation subject of talking. The implication, carefully teased out, is that any person of my background who'd had time to contemplate the prospect of confrontation would have known better than to speak up, especially in this fashion. A man who had been at the scene, Stern is suggesting, who had done what the prosecutors say I did, and who was in charge of the investigation, would know better than to choose a lie so easily exposed. Only a person who truly had not been there and who was ignorant of the real circumstances could be provoked by fresh insult to burst out with this truthful response, which chance has bizarrely undermined. Watching Stern do the cross, I foresee his closing argument, and perceive clearly the reasons for keeping me off the stand. Rusty Sabich made his spontaneous explanation the day he was first confronted. What else is there really that he can add now, so long after the fact?

With my version before the jury, Stern goes about building my credibility. He takes Raymond on an extensive tour of my achievements as a deputy P.A. He begins, in fact, with *Law Review* and goes through the succeeding years. When Molto finally objects that this is unnecessary, Sandy explains that Horgan has questioned my judgment in the direction of the

Polhemus investigation. It is appropriate that the jury know the full extent of my professional background, so that they are able to recognize that what has been portrayed as unwillingness or insubordination may merely be a disagreement between two veteran prosecuting attorneys. The logic of this position is largely unassailable and Larren directs Molto to resume his seat. The canonization of St. Rožat goes on.

"And so, nearly two years ago now," Sandy eventually asks, "when Mr. Sennett, then your chief deputy, moved to San Diego, you turned to Mr. Sabich to fill that spot?"

"I did."

"And is it fair to say that the chief deputy is the person in the office in whose judgment you place the greatest confidence?"

"You could say that. I regarded him as the best lawyer for the job."

"All right. You had 120 other deputies?"

"About that."

"Including Mr. Della Guardia and Mr. Molto?"

"Yes."

"And you chose Mr. Sabich?"

"I did."

Nico looks up, irked, but neither he nor Molto objects. Sandy works like a jeweler, tapping, tapping at his themes of past resentments. Two of the jurors seem to nod.

"And you did not think Mr. Sabich would commit a crime, you had absolute and complete confidence in his judgment and integrity, based on working closely with him for more than a decade?"

The question is compound, and argumentative, but also obvious. "Let it stand," says Larren when Molto objects. Raymond weighs the answer.

"That's fair," he finally says. This small concession seems to have had a substantial effect in the jury box. I see now why Stern attacked Raymond at the outset. He had a point to make. Not with the jury—but with Raymond Horgan. Matters are not as clear to Raymond as they were when he walked into the courtroom.

"Just so. And it was not necessary for him to check with you on all matters to be sure that he was proceeding in exactly the manner you wished?" Stern asks. I take it that he is trying to minimize the significance of my delay in pursuing the fingerprint report.

"I always gave the people who worked for me some leeway."

"Well, is it not true, Mr. Horgan, that in conducting the investigation of Ms. Polhemus's murder, Mr. Sabich knew that you had trusted his judgment on many occasions in the past, including on many substantial matters?"

"I don't know what he knew, but I had obviously approved of his judgment in the past on a lot of things."

"For example," says Sandy, without any indication of what is coming, "you gave Mr. Sabich the authority to decide where and when to fire Mr Della Guardia."

Nico, understandably, erupts. Larren is disturbed. He calls immediately for a conference with the lawyers outside the jury's presence. Some judges hold these meetings, known as sidebars, in the courtroom at the side of the bench away from the jury. Larren's practice—designed to keep the jury from overhearing the lawyers' arguments—is to leave the courtroom entirely and stand in the small anteroom outside his chambers.

Della Guardia, Molto, Kemp, Stern, the court reporter, and I all follow the judge out the back door to the courtroom behind his bench. It is clear even before everyone has assembled that the judge is put out with Stern. He regards the last question as a cheap shot.

"Now what are we going to do here?" he demands of Sandy. "Relive ancient history day by day? We are not gonna turn this lawsuit into a contest over personalities."

Molto and Nico are both talking. Any past antagonism between the prosecutor and the defendant is irrelevant, they say. Judge Lyttle is clearly inclined to agree.

"Your Honor," says Stern, "we do not accuse Mr. Della Guardia personally of bad faith. But we believe this is a circumstance indicating how and why he might be misled." Without saying it, Stern is focusing again on Molto. He has been careful to pick on him, and not Nico, from the start. Della Guardia is a popular person in this town right now, and known to the jurors. Molto is a cipher. Perhaps Sandy also means to take advantage somehow of the unequivocal promise made at the start that Molto would not testify.

"Why Mr. Della Guardia might be misled, Mr. Stern, is

irrelevant. What the prosecutor thinks of his case is no matter to this jury. Lord knows, you don't want to start gettin into that."

"Your Honor," says Stern solemnly, "it is the theory of the defense that Mr. Sabich has been framed in this case."

From this huddled group, I take a step backward myself. I am stunned. Stern had so thoroughly rejected this tactic weeks ago that I had given it no further thought. And things seemed to be going so well without it. Was Horgan's direct that devastating? I no longer understand my own lawyer's theory of defense. Just a moment ago, I thought he was working up one of his delicate unspoken messages to the jury: Molto wanted Sabich's job. He pressed too hard to make a case in order to obtain it, and Della Guardia failed to recognize this because he, even unconsciously, was nursing a grudge of his own. That was vintage Sandy Stern, an artful assessment of human frailty, quietly communicated, designed to diminish the prosecutors' credibility and to demons-trate how this grotesque error—accusing me—came to be made. That is the kind of believable undercurrent juries eagerly receive. But this is a blunderbuss technique, one which, I had come to agree with Stern, was not worth the risk. Certainly I was not prepared for this change of direction without consultation. And on the record. These corridor conferences are available to the public. The reporters at the break will crowd around the court reporter and beg her to read her notes. I can see the headline: SABICH FRAMED, LAWYER SAYS. Lord knows what the jurors will think, if any of them fail to miss the unavoidable. Improvising, Sandy has raised the stakes.

In the meantime, Nico walks up and down the corridor snorting. "I don't believe it," he says two or three times.

Larren looks to Molto for a response.

"Ridiculous," Molto says.

"Your denial is noted for the record. I mean your response on the point of evidence. If Mr. Stern is truly going to endeavor to prove that the case against Mr. Sabich has been manufactured, then I suppose this history of antagonism is relevant for those purposes."

That of course is one reason why Stern may have gone down the road now, to get normally inadmissible proof before the jury.

"I must say," the judge says, "Mr. Stern, that you are playing with fire. I don't know where this is gonna lead us. But I'll tell you two things. You had better be prepared for the prosecution's response. Because the prosecutor will be entitled to quite a bit of latitude in answering. And secondly, proof of this charge better be forthcoming or I'll strike all the cross-examination on this theme and I'll do that in the jury's presence." Larren from his considerable height looks down at Stern directly. At this juncture, most defense lawyers, caught running out of bounds, back off and withdraw the question.

Stern says simply, "I understand. Your Honor, I think, will see exactly how this will develop. We will offer evidence addressed to the issue."

"Very well."

We return to the courtroom.

"What the hell is he doing?" I ask Kemp as we sit down again at the defense table. Jamie shakes his head. Sandy has not conferred with him either about this.

Stern quickly leaves the subject of Nico's firing and moves on to smaller matters. He makes a few more minor points at random and then comes back to the counsel table to confer.

"Almost done," he whispers to Kemp and me. "I have one further area. Anything more?"

I ask what he was doing out in the hallway and he places his hand on my shoulder. He says he will discuss it later. Kemp tells Sandy he has nothing else and Stern once more addresses the witness.

"Just a few more questions, Mr. Horgan. You have been most patient. We spoke earlier about a file you assigned Ms. Polhemus, a very sensitive case. Do you recall that part of the examination?"

"I believe I'll remember it for quite some time," says Raymond. He smiles, though.

"Did you know, Mr. Horgan, that Mr. Molto was involved in the case described there?"

Nico is on his feet first, bellowing in outrage. Larren for the first time before the jury shows anger with Stern.

"Sir, I have warned you about this area of inquiry."

"Your Honor, it is relevant to the defense position I set forth earlier at sidebar." He means the frame-up theory. Stern is being elliptical in order to keep the content of the hallway conference from the jury, who were not supposed to hear that conversation.

"I must tell the court that we have every intention of continuing to investigate this file with the jury, and to offer evidence about it when it is our turn. Indeed, this is the proof I alluded to." Stern is saying that we are going to put in proof about the B file to support the charge that the case is manufactured. Again, I am astounded by his position. The judge sits back; he rests his hands atop his head and puffs out his cheeks to blow off steam.

"For the time being, we have heard enough," he says.

"Two questions more," says Sandy with magisterial authority, and turns back to Horgan without waiting for the judge to tell him he may not.

"Did Mr. Molto ever ask you about that file?"

"As I recall, yes. After I resigned as P.A. he went over everything Rusty—Mr. Sabich—had done on the Polhemus case."

"And Mr. Molto had that file then?"

"He did."

"And do you know what investigation, if any, he conducted of the allegations contained there?"

"I do not."

"I'll answer that," says Nico suddenly. He is standing. He has quite clearly lost his temper. His color is up and his eyes are wide. "He took no action. He wasn't going to chase Rusty Sabich's red herrings." This speech before the jury would ordinarily be grossly improper. But it is precisely the kind of riposte that Larren's warning in the hallway seemed to invite, and Della Guardia has taken full advantage of the opportunity. No doubt he and Tommy discussed this on the way back in from the corridor and decided that Nico would attempt to make a spirited defense of Molto in the jury's presence. Stern ventures no objection. Instead, he slowly turns to face Molto.

"Mr. Della Guardia," he says, "perhaps we will all learn something about red herrings." He pauses. "And scapegoats."

Those are the last words from Stern on Raymond's cross.

Larren recesses for the week. On Fridays he hears motions in other cases. I wait for some explanation from Stern of his new tactics, but he goes on picking up papers from the defense table. Raymond stops by to shake Sandy's hand on his way from the courtroom. He wanders wide of me.

Finally Stern comes to see me. He wipes his face with his

handkerchief. He appears relaxed. Leaving aside the last bit, the cross-examination of Horgan went exceptionally well.

I am too concerned, however, to congratulate him.

"What is this?" I ask. "I thought you told me we weren't going down the road to accusation."

"Clearly, Rusty, I changed my mind."

"Why?"

Stern gives me his Latin smile: the world is full of mystery. "Instinct," he replies.

"And what evidence are we going to offer?"

"Now you remind me," he says. He is quite a bit shorter than I am and he cannot comfortably swing his arm around my shoulder. Instead, he uses another confidential gesture and touches my lapel. "For the time being, I will have to leave that concern to you," he says, and turns away.

30

Tonight I say that I am bushed and leave Stern and Kemp early, but there is an appointment that I want to keep. I called after court, and good to his word, Lionel Kenneally is here, in a neighborhood tavern called Six Brothers. The cabbie gives me a peculiar look when he drops me. It is not that there are no white people around here. There are a few stoical families holding on against the Ricans and the blacks, but they do not wear chalk-striped suits and carry briefcases. Instead, their shingle-sided bungalows are tucked in among the warehouses and factories which cover most of every block. There is a sausage plant across the street, and the air is heavy with the scent of spices and garlic. The tavern is like so many others out this way: just a joint with Formica tables, a vinyl floor, lights over the mirrors. Above the bar, there is a neon Hamm's sign which casts weird shadows from the reflective spangles of the continuous waterfall.

Kenneally does not even wait for me. Instead, he starts to move when I enter and I follow him back to a smaller room with four tables where he says we won't be bothered.

"So what the fuck is this about?" He is smiling but his tone is not altogether friendly. I've got the frigging watch commander out with an indictee, an enemy of the state, an accused homicidal felon. It is no place for a ranking police officer to be seen.

"I appreciate your coming, Lionel."

He waves that off. He wants me to get down to business. A woman pokes her head in. I decline to drink at first, then think better of it and order a Scotch-rocks. Lionel already has a whiskey in his hand.

"I need to ask you some questions I should have asked when I came out to see you in the district in April."

"About?"

"About what the hell was going on out in the North Branch eight or nine years ago."

"Meaning?" His look is close: he does not want to get led astray.

"Meaning, was somebody taking money?"

Kenneally bolts his drink. He's thinking.

"You know you're hot fucking stuff, don't you?" he asks.

"I see the papers."

He looks at me. "You going down on this thing?"

I tell him the truth.

"I don't think so. Stern is a magician. He's got three of the jurors thinking about inviting him for dinner, you can tell from the looks on their faces. He cut a good piece out of Horgan today."

"They say downtown that Nico doesn't have the horses. They say he went too soon, Molto forced his hand. They say if he had any brains he would've got you in a room with a tape recorder and somebody you trust instead of lettin Mac make him tell you what he had." I recognize now that what I thought might be a glaze of alcohol is anger. Lionel Kenneally is pissed. He's heard enough about this case to figure that he did something he doesn't do frequently: made an error in judgment. "Myself, I figure you might be goin down anyway. Sure as fuck, you didn't tell me you were in there handlin her glassware when you was out here before."

"You want me to tell you I didn't kill her?"

"Fuckin-A right I do."

"I didn't kill her."

Kenneally stares, a fierce, immobile look. I know my delivery was too measured to provide him with any assurance.

"You are one fuckin strange son of a bitch," he says.

The barmaid, wearing one of those old ruffled tops to show the beginning of her cleavage, comes in with my drink. She also puts another tumbler of whiskey in front of Lionel K.

"You know," I tell Kenneally as I sip, "that is something I never understood about myself. I mean, my old lady was as weird as those women downtown carrying around shopping bags, and my old man had spent most of World War II eating dead horses and stuff such as that, which does some work on your cerebrum, believe me. Everything in my whole life was weird. And until this happened, I really thought I was Joe College. That's who I wanted to be and that's what I thought I was. Really, I thought I was fucking Beaver Cleaver, or whoever the boy next door is these days. I really did. And about the only thing I've gotten out of this experience to date is hearing you tell me I am one strange son of a bitch and listening to that little harp string that sounds in my chest when somebody, even if he's half-crocked, has said something that is really right. So I thank you." I tap his glass with mine.

I am not sure that Lionel particularly enjoyed this routine. He watches me for a minute.

"What'd you come here for, Rusty?"

"I already told you. Just answer that one question."

Kenneally sighs. "Ain't you a fuckin pip. One question, all right? And what's said here stays here. It's me and you. I ain't listenin to any fuckin sob stories about your constitutional rights or that shit. Nobody's fuckin callin me to to testify against the P.A. That happens, world's gonna think you confessed right here tonight."

"I have the ground rules."

"Your short answer is, I don't exactly know. Maybe I heard some things, all right? But that wasn't my show. Things out this way were a little loose. You know what I'm sayin? Remember, we're talkin before Felske stepped in shit." Felske was a bail bondsman who used to take care of certain cops for referring him business. When the bail law was reformed, permitting personal-recognizance bonds and obviating the need for outside sureties, Felske and his coppers maintained their income by selling the coppers' assistance on occasion. Sometimes the cops would talk a witness into not showing up. Sometimes the cops would forget things when they testified. Felske, however, made such a proposition one day to a man with an electronic lapel pin. The copper involved, named Grubb, flipped for the FBI and took down Felske and three other officers. That was five years ago. "Back then, this was a wide-open place."

"Was Tommy Molto one of the people you heard things about?"

"I thought you said one question."

"It had subparts."

Kenneally doesn't smile. He looks down in his drink.

"In this job, you learn you better not say never." Kenneally laughs. "Lookit you. Right?" He laughs again. He is still angry with himself. All of this is against his better judgment. "But Molto," he says. "Never. He's from the fuckin seminary. He'd bring his rosary to court. No chance this guy would take."

"Was Carolyn involved with whatever was going on?"

He shakes his head. He is not saying no. He is refusing to answer.

"Look. I don't owe you, Rusty. Okay? I thought you done your job like a Professional guy. You come out here before people in the suburbs even knew from gangs, and you worked hard. I give you credit. What else you done, you done. But you come into the projects with me in the middle of the night. You got your fuckin hands dirty. But don't push, all right. There guys I owe. You ain't one."

Cop loyalty. He won't even drop a dime on a dead lady. Kenneally drinks his drink and looks out the door.

"Did Carolyn have anything going with Molto? You know, a personal thing?"

"Jesus. What's your hang-up with Molto? Guy's strange like everybody else."

"Let's just say he's my best alternative."

"What the fuck does that mean?"

I wave the question off.

"Well, I don't see that guy even catchin a whiff of Polhemus. You seen him. Buddy Hackett, right? They were friends, that's all. Buddies. Sometimes she'd smooth shit out for him." Kenneally takes another drink. "It wasn't him she was bangin."

"Who?"

"No chance," he says. "You got enough."

"Lionel." I really don't want to beg. He will not look at me. "This isn't gossip, for Chrissake. This is my goddamned life."

"The nigger."

"What?"

"She was sleepin with the nigger."

I don't get it at first. Then I do.

"Larren?"

"You been out at the North Branch. You remember how it was. It was like everybody used to work in one room. Three doors, and all of em let you into one office. P.O. P.A. Nick Costello was signin in the coppers who come out to testify. He had a desk there. Judge's chambers used to open up there, too. He'd get off the bench noontime, she'd go sashaying in. They weren't makin no secret of it."

"Fuck," says Kenneally, "I halfway told you last time you was out here. Don't you remember? I told you how she fucked her way to the top, I couldn't figure Horgan hiring her. That's who got her in. Your old buddy there, Judge Motherfucker. He and Horgan got some kinda tie-in."

"They were law partners," I say. "Years ago."

"Figures," says Lionel. He shakes his head in disgust.

"And you won't tell me whether Carolyn was dirty?"

He raises a finger. "I'm gonna leave," he says. He's quiet for a while. "Sometimes she'd smooth things out, like I say. Molto and the judge, they didn't get along so well. Maybe you heard them stories."

"A number."

"You know, she was everybody's pal back then. The P.O. Sometimes she'd get the judge to lay off. Sometimes she'd get Molto to take two steps back. She was kinda the referee. Maybe you're right. Maybe Molto was really carryin a big fuckin torch for her. Maybe that's why he had sand in his ointment whenever he had to go before the judge. Who knows? Go figure people," he says.

I can tell that I've had everything now that I'm going to get. This last little bit was strictly for charity.

I pick up my briefcase and leave money for the drinks.

"You're a good sod, Kenneally."

"I'm a fuckin fool, is what I am. Halfa downtown's gonna be talkin about this tomorrow. Whatta I tell em we said?"

"I don't give a shit. Say what you want. Tell them the truth. Molto knows what I'm looking for by now. Maybe that's why I'm in this soup to begin with."

"You don't believe that."

"I don't know," I tell him. "Something's not right."

31

We spend the weekend at work, both days. My assignment is to prepare for the end of the state's case, when the defense, as a matter of routine, makes a motion for a directed verdict of acquittal—a request that the judge terminate the trial, declaring that there is not enough evidence for a reasonable jury to convict. This is usually futile. In ruling on the motion, the judge is required to evaluate the evidence in the light most favorable to the state, meaning, for example, that for the purposes of this decision Judge Lyttle will have to accept Eugenia's testimony, right down to her angels. However, a directed-verdict ruling is unreviewable; the state may not appeal. As a result some judges—Larren quite notoriously—use this as a device for imposing the result they favor. Thus, while our prospects are dim, Stern wants to make as strong a presentation as possible. My assignment is to find cases which in some fashion condemn the absence of proof of motive in a circumstantial case. I pass hours in the library.

Sunday morning we meet to talk strategy. Sandy still does not want to speak in detail about the defense case. He makes no mention of my testimony or that of other witnesses. Instead, we analyze the remainder of the state's proof. Lipranzer is supposed to testify Monday. The state's case will now begin to gather speed. Their physical evidence will be coming in: the fibers, the phone records, the fingerprints (assuming they can find the glass); the maid who thinks she saw me on the bus; and Kumagai.

Stern again emphasizes the point he made to me the other day at lunch: our need to raise doubt in some way about Kumagai. If we cannot, the prosecutors will reach the end of their case having built up tremendous momentum; that, in turn, may force Sandy to change his strategy for our presentation. This is one reason Stern is unwilling to arrive at any final opinions about what we should do. Together Kemp and Stern and I puzzle out ways to attack Kumagai. Stern has examined Painless a number of times and he shares the common opinion that Kumagai is an unpleasant hack. The jury will not be eager to believe him. There are old stories about Painless which I share; finally, I mention that his police department personnel file, where complaints about Kumagai's past performance might be jacketed, would be a good source for us to examine.

"Excellent," says Stern. "How wonderful to have a prosecutor on our side." He directs Jamie to draft at once a trial subpoena for the file, and another for records of the Pathology Lab, so we can see what else Painless was up to in April. We have not issued most of our subpoenas, inasmuch as many of the deputy sheriffs who serve them tend to alert the prosecutors, giving the P.A.'s an opportunity to combat the evidence gathered or, even worse, to utilize it themselves if it is helpful to the state. But now that the prosecution case is almost complete, we should proceed. Jamie forages through his old notes to be sure we do not miss any of the items we have said we wanted to acquire. He drafts subpoenas for each of Carolyn's doctors, identified from her little phone book, which I found in her apartment.

"And you wanted to subpoena the phone company," Kemp says to me, "so we can look at their backup data on the MUDs from your house."

"Don't bother with that," I say quickly. I do not look up, but I can feel the weight of Kemp's startled glance upon me. Stern, however, goes on, without dropping a beat.

"Perhaps if it is not productive to raise questions," says Sandy, "we should consider stipulations." A stipulation is a statement agreed to by the prosecution and defense which recites what a witness would say, so that he need not be called. As Stern thinks aloud about that possibility, he becomes more convinced it is the right way to proceed. We will agree to the testimony not only of the phone company representatives but also the Hair and Fiber experts and the forensic chemist. By doing that, we will shorten the time in which this damaging evidence is actually before the jury. Della Guardia may not accept the proposal, but he is likely to. For the prosecutor, there is always a blessing in not having to come forward with your proof.

With these decisions made, Kemp and I return to the library, a central conference room in Stern's suite where the statute books and law reporters are shelved floor to ceiling in dark oak cases on each of the four walls. I work at one table, Kemp at another. I become aware after a few minutes that Jamie is watching me, but I still do not look up.

"I don't get it," he finally says out loud, giving me no choice. "You said there was something wrong with those phone records."

"Jamie, cut me a break, I've thought about it since."

"You said we should look into whether or not they'd been doctored."

The intensity in his eyes is not really anger. There is something vulnerable. As he seldom does, Quentin Kemp, in his cowboy boots and tweed sportcoat, looks undefended and young. He thinks of himself as much too hip to be capable of being misled.

"Jamie, it's something I said. Okay? Under the circumstances. You understand."

But I can see that he does not understand at all. It bothers me, the look in his eye, his knowing that now he can't believe me. I fold my pad and put on my coat. Sandy is still in his office when I tell him I am leaving for the night. He is studying the reams of scientific evidence that Nico produced in response to our motions. Spectrographs. Print charts. The full report of Carolyn's autopsy. He is dressed in casual clothes, a handsome sweater and slacks, and he seems relaxed under the green glass shade of an auditor's lamp, smoking his precious cigar.

*   *   *

Lipranzer is on the stand on Monday morning, Nico takes care to keep him away from me. The prosecution team walks down the corridor with Lip, just as Ernestine is calling court to session. Lipranzer is wearing a suit, something he hates to do, but he still looks more like a convict than a policeman. It is an awful double-knit thing with a kind of carpetbag pattern. His duckass hairdo is particularly slick. I end up holding the door as Lip enters the courtroom, and in spite of the presence of Nico in front of him and Glendenning behind, Lipranzer gives me both a wave and a wink. I am fortified just to see him again.

Nico handles Lip well. It is his best examination of the trial so far. He is matter-of-fact and gets what he has to quickly. He knows that Lip is not friendly. He will tell the truth, but—so different from Horgan—is awaiting any opportunity to bite Nico's heels. Delay is careful not to give him the chance. If he is professional, he knows he can count on Lip to act the same way. They are both suppressed and brief.

"Did Mr. Sabich ever tell you that he had a personal relationship with Carolyn Polhemus?"

"Objection."

"On the same basis as with Mr. Horgan, Mr. Stern?" the judge asks.

"Indeed."

"The objection will be overruled. Ladies and gentlemen, I'm sure you remember what I told you last week about questions based on assumptions. Because Mr. Della Guardia is sayin it, doesn't make it so. You may proceed."

I have wondered how Lip will answer the question. But he says simply, No. Nico did not ask whether I suggested that such a relationship might exist, or whether it was clearly understood by both of us, a question Della Guardia in fact cannot properly put. He asked if I told him, and Lipranzer has responded correctly. Hedged in by the formalities of the rules of evidence, our truthfinding system cuts off the corners on half of what is commonly known.

In a clipped, almost British way, Nico elicits the fact that I told Lip not to collect the MUD records from my home. And he also brings out from Lipranzer the occasions on which he had to remind me to request computer analysis of the fingerprints found on the glass and elsewhere in Carolyn's apartment. It all emerges between the two of them with a strange undercurrent. I am sure the jury knows something is not right here. And Nico is smart enough at the end to let them know what it is. When he has got what he needs from Lipranzer, he sets up the cross, by showing bias. He asks about the cases that Lip and I have worked together.

"Would it be fair to say that by now the two of you have formed a kind of prosecutorial or investigative team?"

"Yes, sir."

"And as a result of working as a team, have you formed a personal friendship?"

"Definitely."

"A close friendship?"

Lip's eyes skate toward me for a moment.

"I suppose so."

"You trust him?"

"I do."

"And he knows that?"

Stern objects: Lip can't answer about what I know, and the prosecutor is leading. The witness has already characterized the relationship. Larren sustains the objection on all grounds.

"Well, let me put the question like this: Were you assigned to the case initially?"

"No, sir."

"Who was assigned?"

"Harold Greer, a detective from the 18th District, where the crime occurred."

"Is he a competent investigator?"

"In my book?"

Nico is careful here, in order both to avoid objections and to keep Lip from zinging him.

"Has Mr. Sabich ever expressed to you any reservations about Harold Greer's abilities?"

"No, sir. Everybody I know thinks of Harold Greer as a topgrade cop."

"Thank you." Nico smiles, savoring the bonus. "And who, to your knowledge, decided to make this a Special Command matter and bring you in on this case, Detective Lipranzer?"

"Mr. Sabich requested my assignment, if that's what you're askin. He had Mr. Horgan's say-so."

"To your knowledge, Detective Lipranzer, does the defendant have a closer personal relationship with anyone on the police force?"

Lip shrugs. "Not that he's mentioned."

Nico struts a little.

"So it's fair to say, Detective, is it not, that you are the person on the city police force least likely to suspect Mr. Sabich of murder?"

The question is objectionable. Stern starts to move, then ceases, with his hands poised on the arms of his chair. This time I am keeping pace with him. He has seen Lip hesitate and knows that Nico, by improvising, has made his first error. He has given Lipranzer an opening and is going to take a blow.

"I would never believe that," Lip says simply. He leans on 'never.' Just right. That will sit well with the jury. He's not going out of his way to hose Nico. But he's taken the opportunity to make his feelings known.

Sandy rises to cross. We talked last night about not crossing Lip at all. Stern did not want to emphasize Nico's favorable points. But apparently the direct went even better for the state than Stern anticipated. Nico's direct has opened the door to a kind of catalogue of the successes Lip and I have scored together as a way of explaining why I would choose him for this case. Stern runs through them one by one.

"And as a matter of fact," says Stern, when he is at the end of that, "even in the midst of this murder investigation you and Mr. Sabich were inquiring about yet another matter, weren't you?"

Lip is puzzled.

"Wasn't there a file, which had been stored in Mr. Horgan's drawer—"

Sandy does not get any further before Nico is on his feet yelling. Larren picks up his gavel and points it at Stern.

"Mr. Stern. I have told you on too many occasions that I do not wanna be hearin any more about that file during the prosecutor's case. You went much too far while Mr. Horgan was testifying and I'm not gonna abide any reoccurrence."

"Your Honor, this evidence is critical to our defense. We intend to continue exploring the matter of this file when it is our turn to present evidence."

"Well, if this is critical to your defense, then we can talk about calling Detective Lipranzer back at that time. But I advise you, sir, to move on to another area of inquiry, because I have not heard near enough to let you go chasin that hare all over the courtroom at this time. Am I clear?" Judge Lyttle peers over the bench with an impressive concentration of his features.

Stern does his little cut-rate bow, inclining his head and

shoulders. I find myself disconcerted by Sandy's lapse of judgment. He has taken a beating in the presence of the jury, a setback which was entirely predictable, and I still do not understand what he is trying to accomplish. He's already cast his shadow over Molto with that file. Why does he harp on it? The jury is bound to be disappointed, particularly when he keeps promising to produce evidence that we do not have in hand. We cannot offer the letter I found in the B file, because it is hearsay. I do not understand Stern's bluff, and he is cavalier whenever I steer him toward the subject. He treats it as if it is just another courtroom effect.

Stern, in the meantime, has come back to the defense table.

"Now, Detective Lipranzer, Mr. Della Guardia asked you some questions about the telephone records," Sandy holds up the documents. "As I understand your testimony, it was you who raised the matter of his home number with Mr. Sabich, is that right?"

"Yes, sir."

"He did not bring it up?"

"No."

"He did not ask you in advance not to obtain the records from his home? Am I right?"

"Absolutely correct."

"In point of fact, he informed you at the start that you might find calls from Ms. Polhemus to one of his phones?"

"In his office, right."

"He didn't ask you or tell you not to seek any records for that reason, did he?"

"No, sir."

There is a ringing emphasis to all of Lip's answers. Stern is putting on a demonstration now, showing what a cross-examiner can do with a friendly witness. But it is all too clear. There is no resistance. Lip is more or less allowing Stern to testify. He quickly endorses Stern's proposal that it was Lipranzer's own idea not to obtain my home records. He considered them irrelevant; I simply acquiesced in the suggestion, saying, as people often do, that a subpoena was best avoided since it might upset my wife. Sandy returns to counsel table for a document. He numbers it, and hands it to Lip for identification. It is the original subpoena *duces tecum* to the phone company.

"Now, what prosecutor issued that subpoena?"

"Rusty. Mr. Sabich."

"His name appears as the authorizing signatory on the face, does it not?"

"Yes."

"And by its terms does that subpoena require production of these very records?"

"According to what it says?"

"That's my question."

"The answer is yes. The subpoena would cover these records."

"Does it contain any exemption for Mr. Sabich's home?"

"No."

"And any time you or anyone else wanted to examine the records of Mr. Sabich's home, this subpoena would require the production of those records?"

"Yes."

"As a matter of fact—please do not answer if this is beyond your knowledge—when Mr. Molto and Mr. Della Guardia decided that they wanted those records, they relied on the authority of this subpoena to obtain them, did they not?"

"I think that's right."

"And so Mr. Sabich stands on trial here on the basis of evidence that he himself subpoenaed, correct?"

The courtroom ruffles. Nico objects. "The question is argumentative."

Larren shakes his head benignly.

"Mr. Della Guardia, you're tryin to show here that Mr. Sabich hindered the gathering of evidence, as a way to prove guilty knowledge. And the prosecution is entitled to do that, but the defense is entitled to show that the evidence that is being presented was actually gathered through his efforts. I don't know how else they meet your proof. Overruled."

"I repeat," says Stern, standing before Lipranzer, "Mr. Sabich is being tried here with evidence he himself subpoenaed."

"Right," says Lip. Eager as a recruit, he adds, "Just like the fingerprints."

"Just so," says Sandy. He proceeds to the fingerprints. It was Sabich who personally visited McGrath Hall, met with Lou Balistrieri, demanded that the prints be processed. True, Sabich was busy, running the entire P.A.'s office while Horgan campaigned, but again it was his own efforts that produced the evidence now being used in an attempt to convict him.

"Did he obstruct you?" Sandy asks at the end.

Lip sits straight up in his chair. "No."

"Did he impede you?"

"Not in my book."

"Indeed, Detective, I believe you told Mr. Della Guardia that even if you had known of this evidence, your respect and affection for Rusty Sabich after many years' association is such that you would never have suspected, let alone believed, that he had committed this murder. Is that right?"

The way Lip hesitates, I fear for a moment that Stern has gone too far. But then I see that Lip is merely making his own ungainly effort at dramatic effect.

"Never," he repeats, and Stern sits down. As he does, he smiles furtively at me, a gesture meant largely for the jury. Nonetheless, for the first time I have the feeling that the jurors are not satisfied by Stern's performance. It is unconvincing. This tour de force still does not explain why I did not volunteer to Lip the information about the calls from my phone, especially the one on the night of the murder. Stern's cross does not offer any reason why I could not work with Harold Greer, whose appearance is surely far more impressive to the jury than Lipranzer's. It does not show what alternatives I had to going to Lou Balistrieri when Lipranzer—not to mention Horgan—was nagging me to do that. And this last exchange, while touching in its awkwardness, is simply baloney. No one could fail to be discomfited by the discovery of the phone records and the prints. The doubtful nature of the cross is emphasized by Lip's obedient response to Stern's guidance. It is all too clear: Lipranzer is a friend, willing to be misled. The jury will not fail to perceive this. It is as I always feared. The rule of equal and opposite reactions applies in the courtroom as well. Due in large part to his visible reluctance, Dan Lipranzer has been the most damaging witness against me to date.

The afternoon continues the downward movement. The stipulations are prepared and read. Coming on the heels of Lipranzer's testimony, the revelation of the actual content of the telephone records is crushing. Nico reads the stip himself. He has finally caught the measure of this jury. They are a bright bunch and want the facts delivered without varnish. Nico assumes a flat, understated tone and looks up just a little when he finishes reading so that he can watch the evidence drive home. The jurors are attentive to him and I feel the weight of their calculations. I discover that, as a defendant, you experience the lows in the courtroom far more acutely than as an advocate. My afternoon settles into a feeling of weakness, suppression with a coefficient of palpable nausea.

The stipulation about the carpet fibers is lengthy, but it has a similar impact. By agreeing to forgo the testimony, Nico, in theory, lost the drama of a live presentation. But the technical witnesses tend to be dry and overly involved. The written summaries are direct enough to have some bite. There is no chance this way that Stern can engage in any of his masterful misdirection or minimization. The facts, as they are, emerge with painful salience. The one favorable aspect—that none of my clothing matched any of the fibers found—is too easily explained. The clothes I wore that night were discarded—with the murder weapon. Or simply did not shed. These conclusions, inevitable and arithmetically direct, seem to thicken the air of the courtroom. I can sense them taking place in every quarter. And with them a kind of hush or calm inhabits the place, a dawning resolution. It is more than the mid-afternoon lull. Instead, it seems that all of the observers, including the jurors, have perceived a change in direction, a swing of momentum more in line with original expectations. It has taken the prosecutors longer than it should have, but they are assuming control of the trial, proving their case.

As usual, it is Molto, heedless and overeager, who begins to drag me back from the abyss. When the last stipulation is read, he asks for a corridor conference.

"What is it?" asks Larren when we are all assembled.

"Judge," he says, "we are ready to proceed with the fingerprint expert. There is just one small difficulty."

Kemp eyes me with wicked glee. The difficulty, so called, is obvious to both of us: They have not found the glass. Jamie's smile is welcome. It is the first sign of any renewed warmth between us in better than a day, and it comes at the right moment, for the members of the defense have each been wordless and grim all afternoon. During the 3:30 recess, I encountered Stern in the john and we did not say a thing aloud. He gave me one of his Judeo-Latin shrugs. His eyes were listless. We knew this was coming, he seemed to say. Our time on the high wire has ended.

Now, in the small anteroom to his chambers, Judge Lyttle fulminates. Molto still cannot do anything right in Larren's eyes.

"Are you telling me that you have completed your search and this object absolutely cannot be found?"

"Judge—" he starts to say.

"Because that's one set of facts. And I'll have to rule on that basis. But if you're tellin me that you think the thing is gonna turn up but it's convenient right now for you to go ahead without it, then that's quite another. We aren't gonna be talkin about proceeding now and discovering the evidence later. Am I understood?"

Nico catches Tommy's arm. He tells the judge they would like to take one more night.

"That's fine, then," Larren says. "Do I take it that you're moving for an adjournment for the day?"

Nico crisply says, "Yes." It is clear that the day's success has fortified him. He can tolerate adversity without distress. His old confidence seems to possess him again.

"Your Honor," says Stern. "I hope the court has not decided to let the prosecution proceed with the fingerprint evidence in the absence of the glass. Certainly, if Your Honor please, we would ask to be heard on that question."

"I quite understand," says Larren. "You may want to do some research on this issue, Mr. Stern. And I'll be happy to hear you. And I can tell you right now, I'm not eager to let anybody get up on the witness stand in my courtroom and give his opinions about what he says was once observed on some physical object that nobody can even find anymore." He casts a rough-tempered glance toward Molto. "So you look in the books tonight and I'll listen to you. And, Mr. Della Guardia, if I were you, I'd roll up my shirt-sleeves and get over to that evidence room myself."

"Yes, Your Honor," says Nico dutifully.

Stern gives me a meaningful look from beneath his extended brow as we head into the courtroom. He seems to be inquiring. It is almost as if he thinks that I can account for the glass's absence. Perhaps it is merely a sense of promise that gives Sandy this expression. If Larren were to keep the prosecutors from presenting the fingerprint evidence, the case against me would certainly fail. Stern is not sure whether or not he should be hopeful. Nor am I.

"Would he really think about keeping out that proof?" I ask Stern as we stand behind counsel table. We are waiting for the jury to return to the courtroom, so that the judge can tell them they are being dismissed for the day.

"It strikes me as a serious question of evidence. Is it not? We must study tonight." More time for Kemp and me in the library. I nod, accepting Stern's unspoken instruction.

* * *

About 9:30 that night, Kemp comes back to Stern's small library to tell me that I have a call. He remains behind to inspect the series of cases I have copied from the reports of the state supreme and appellate courts, while I go to the receptionist's desk, where Jamie has picked up the phone. A line is blinking, on hold. I assume it is Barbara. She usually calls about now, hoping to review the day's evidence for a few moments; and every evening I go through an arabesque of diffidence and contained response.

The truth is that I have done my best to avoid Barbara since the days immediately before the trial. I have suggested she go to sleep each night before I return; I have eaten dinner with Stern and Kemp, enjoining her even from leaving me a meal. I cannot stand to have her abstracted curiosity turned on this evidence like some high-powered light. I do not want those late-night scenes where we chew over the events of my trial as we did those malefactors I accused. It would make me unbearably ill at ease to hear Barbara engage in close analysis of the tactical decisions undertaken in this trial for my life. Most of all, I do not wish to get drawn into discussions of my discomfort. With the evidence being trotted out each day before us, I know the conclusions she might reach, and in my present state I could not abide that confrontation—to allay suspicions or confirm them.

But when I pick up the phone, it is not Barbara's voice I hear.

"How'd I do?" Lip says. "I thought they were goin to give you a medal or somethin with all these terrific things you and I done."

"You were great," I tell him. There is no point in the truth.

"Fuckin Delay, I'll tell you," he says. "Schmidt come to see me this mornin before I got on. He says a little birdie wanted to make sure that I got the message that if I fucked around on the stand, I'd be walkin beats in the North End by myself in the middle of the night. Nice subtle stuff with this guy."

I make a sound, general agreement. I have sent a few such messages myself from time to time—to coppers who have a peculiar friendship with defense counsel; who know the defendant from the 'hood. It's part of the job.

"I thought maybe we could get together tonight," Lip says. "Talk about that thing I said I'd help you with." He means finding Leon. "How about I drive you home? You be there a while?"

"Another two hours probably."

"That's good for me. They got me workin 4:00 to midnight. I'll take my coffee early. Corner Grand and Kindle at 11:30? I'll be drivin the unmarked Aries."

We work it like a spy movie. I am in the lobby until the car hoves into sight and Lip is barely at the curb five seconds before he is moving. Now that he is off the witness stand, the pressure on him has lessened, but there are many people who would tell him that the better part of wisdom right now lies in staying away from me. He pulls around the corner so quickly that the rear end gives way a little bit on the pavement, which is slick from a light rain.

I compliment him again on his testimony. "It was good," I say, "because you played it straight."

"I'm tryin," he says, and reaches for his radio, which is putting out a tremendous ruckus. "This is great," says Lip, of the radio. "We're workin on a dope bust with the G-men to make up for that fiasco in April and these guys can't get on the air together often enough to make sure nobody gets turfed. They better hope their subject don't have a scanner, because he couldn't miss this posse comin."

I ask about what is going down.

"It's cute," says Lip. "They got a nice-lookin little female agent in a mink coat that got seized last time the Strike Force went in on Muds Corvino's bolita game. She's makin out to be some dopecrazed suburbanite and she's gonna buy ten keys of coke from somebody in Nearing."

"Probably one of my neighbors," I say. "There's a guy down the block named Cliff Nudelman whose nose is redder than Rudolph's."

We are quiet, listening to the radio traffic. Cops and robbers. I feel a vague melancholy when I admit to myself that I miss it. There is lots of static because of the rain. Thunder and lightning must not be far off. I am reluctant to mention Leon first, but I finally ask how Lip is doing.

"I haven't started," he says. "I will. First thing. Only I haven't got a fuckin idea where I oughta look. That's what I wanted to hear. You got some suggestions?"

"I don't know, Lip. It shouldn't be that hard to find a faggot named Leon. Go interview waiters. Or interior decorators."

"Probably moved to San Francisco, you know. Or died of AIDS or some crap." I refuse to respond to Lip's suggestion that his efforts will be futile. We are quiet a moment; the radio barks. "Can I ask a question?" he says after a while. "Is this really so important?"

"To me?"

"Yeah."

"Damn right."

"Can I ask why? I mean, you really think this jamoche's gonna give you somethin?"

I tell him what I told him before. "I *want* to find something, Lip. That's the most honest way I can put it."

"On Molto?"

"On Molto. Right. That's the way I've got it figured. As much as I can figure at all." We are down near the bus terminal, a bleak place at any hour, but especially at midnight with rain. I look out toward it, a sad hulk in the dark. Lip's dwindling faith in me hangs in here with a misty sadness of its own. More even than the risks, that is what bothers him. From his own perspective he's figured it out. I want to use this thing with Molto as a diversion—as Nico put it, a red herring. Lip's reluctance is obvious to both of us, and it is a dismal sign of where I am that I must lever him with our friendship to make him do what I know he would resist for almost anyone else. "Let's run a sheet at least. Berman, Sandy's P.I., says he couldn't even get a rap sheet out of the department."

"I told you, man, they closed down tight on this thing. They're gonna be in Kenneally's shit in a big way for givin you the time of day."

I take a moment.

"How did you hear about that?"

"Watch commander don't get anywhere that people don't notice." The rain beads on the window. The air is close. I understand the spy stuff on the street corner now. "What'd he tell you?" Lip asks.

"Not much. He told me that Carolyn and Larren used to be an item a long time ago. What do you think of that?"

"I think she got around," says Lipranzer, "same thing I always thought."

"He said that Larren clouted her into the P.A.'s office through Raymond."

"That fits," says Lip.

"That's what I thought."

"He tell you anythin else?"

"More ancient history. You know: the North Branch used to be a dirty old place, but he thinks Molto was clean."

"And you believe him? About Molto?"

"I don't want to."

"I wouldn't take that guy's advice on clean or dirty, I'll tell you that. God only knows where he's comin from."

"What is it with you and Lionel?"

"Not my kinda cop," says Lipranzer simply. We have crossed the Nearing bridge by now and have entered the sudden dark of the suburban neighborhoods, out of the garishness of the highway's yellow sulfur lights. "I worked out his way when I started, you know."

"I didn't know that."

"Yeah," he says. "I seen him in action. Not my kinda cop." I decide I won't ask.

Lip looks out the windshield. The shadows of the wipers move across his face.

"We're talkin twelve, fourteen years ago now," he says at last. "Things were different. I'm the first to admit that. Okay? Everybody's on the pad back then. All right? Everybody." Lip looks straight at me and I know what he means. I find it unsettling. "The pimps, the barkeeps, they just put up the dough. You didn't even talk about it" It was there. So I'm not castin stones, okay?

"But one night, I'm comin out of a place—two, three in the mornin—squad comes runnin down the street full speed and stops dead. First I think it's me he wants. So I come a little closer. But he don't even see me. It's Kenneally. You know, he's a sergeant by then, so he's ridin alone, beat supervisor. And he's lookin across the street. Right in a doorway. There's a hooker, okay? Black gal. You know, she's got the skirt on up to her chin, and leopard top or some such shit. Anyway, I hear him whistle. You know? Like for a dog or horse. Big loud number like that. And he pulls the black-and-white into the alley. Gets out and looks down the street toward this pro, and he's pointin like this." Lip shoots an index finger down toward his groin. "Big smile. And this lady, she waits and she waits. And he keeps pointin and smilin. He says somethin I don't quite hear. Don't say no. Somethin like that. Anyway, she goes slow down the street like, Oh, man, don't tell me, draggin her purse like she's got maybe an anvil inside. And Kenneally's got his big smile. Sits down right there in the squad. All I see is his legs stickin out the door, his shorts down around his ankles, and this lady on her knees while she's workin. Fucker didn't even take off his hat."

Lip swings into my driveway. He takes the car out of gear and lights a cigarette. "He ain't my kinda cop," he says again.

32

The trial's first pitched battle over an issue of law occurs the next day and occupies the entire morning. Nico describes a six-hour item-by-item search of the police evidence room. They cannot find the glass. Both sides have prepared written memoranda addressed to whether testimony about the finger-prints on the glass may nonetheless be received. Kemp wrote our brief sometime after midnight. Molto must have started later than that, since Nico said they were in the warrens of the evidence room past one o'clock. Each man wears the hazy red-eyed look of a lawyer on trial. Larren retires to his chambers to read both briefs, then returns to hear oral argument. At the start, it is supposed to be only Nico and Stern addressing the court, but each turns so often to his second that before long all four lawyers are talking, with the judge interrupting, posing hypothetical questions and, on occasion, thinking out loud. Stern makes his points with greater vehemence than at any time during the trial. Perhaps he senses an opportunity for triumph; perhaps desperation is gathering after yesterday's sobering events. He keeps emphasizing the fundamental unfairness of forcing the defendant to confront scientific testimony whose basis we have had no chance to assess. Nico, then Molto, repeatedly state that the so-called chain of custody has gone uncontested. Whether the glass can be found or not, the testimony of Greer, Lipranzer, and Dickerman, the lab supervisor, will establish, taken together, that the prints were identified from lifts obtained from the glass the day after the murder.

The back-and-forth between the lawyers is endless, and I find my spirits in a sickening spiral, escalating, then instantly descending from elation to bitter lament. It is clear that the judge is undecided. This is one of those issues, of which there are so many during a trial, where a judge is within legal boundaries no matter what he does. The authorities support a ruling for either side. The way Larren gives it to Nico and Tommy about the carelessness of the police makes me certain, at moments, that the evidence is going to be excluded. But the prosecutors are frank about the devastation that this would bring to their case, and without saying it aloud, they hint at the impropriety of disposing of a celebrated prosecution as the result of police negligence. In the end, this thought appears persuasive and Larren rules against the defense.

"I'm gonna admit this testimony," the judge says, shortly after the court clock has reached noon. Then he explains the basis of his ruling for the record, so that the court of appeals can assess his judgment, if it ever comes to that.

"I must say that I'm pretty reluctant to do so, but I am influenced by its obvious importance to the case. Naturally, that same fact, given the overall tone of some of the things that have occurred here"—the judge looks toward Molto—"leads me to understand the defense's skepticism. They are right that they have not had the opportunity to examine an object of physical evidence. On the other hand, the object itself is not gonna be presented. The absence of this exhibit is attributed to the police evidence room. I want to note for the record that the police evidence room custodians have been guilty for years of this kind of slipshod record keeping and handling of exhibits. This is probably the most dramatic, but certainly not the only example that we all know about. And I must say that it is that knowledge, derived outside the record, that influences me to allow the testimony. The fact of the matter is that the best-intentioned prosecutors—and I by no means am ruling on the intentions of Mr. Della Guardia or of Mr. Molto, who seems to have had the glass last—" Again Larren stares darkly at Tommy. Did Greer really say that? I wonder. "—but the best-intentioned prosecutors cannot seem to control what happens to exhibits once they leave their hands. It could be that there is bad faith here. I will be lookin out for further evidence of that, and if there is that kind of bad faith, then this prosecution is gonna end. Period. But overall, that thought strikes me as so unpalatable that I'm gonna assume it isn't true. So I will admit this proof, over objection, and with my own reservations noted. I am, however, gonna give the jury a strongly worded limiting instruction, which I want to take some time to craft over the lunch hour. We will resume at two o'clock."

The judge leaves the bench, asking the lawyers to remain for a few moments so he can have their thoughts on the instruction he wants to draft. Sandy is philosophical. It is clear now that he believed we were going to win. I explain what has occurred to Barbara, who appears particularly upset by Larren's ruling. "It isn't fair," she tells me. "You haven't even had a chance to look at it."

"I understand," I say. "It's one of those calls a judge gets to make." I'm not trying to be heroic. All along I have tested Larren against my own internal barometer. On this one, I would have ruled the same way.

I go to the john. When I come out, Nico again is at the sink, washing his hands as he feints left and right to see the position of his hairs under the light.

"Well, Rusty," he says. "Are we going to be hearing from you next week?"

Under the state discovery laws, the defense is under no obligation to inform the prosecution of its witnesses. Whether or not the defendant will testify is often the most closely guarded secret of the defense camp. The prosecution should rest tomorrow. Assuming the judge takes a day for arguments on the directed-verdict motion, our case will begin next Monday. If the prosecutors receive no indication of our intentions, they will not know whether to spend the weekend preparing for cross-examination or closing arguments. Most of the time, you end up strung out in both directions.

"I'm sure Stern will tell you, Delay, whenever we make up our minds."

"I have a sawbuck that says you're coming."

Nico is playing games, testing my nerve. He is a lot harder than he was during our encounter here last week. This is the crafty Delay of old.

"Maybe you'll win," I tell him. "You got the cross!"

"Had to," he says. "I couldn't cross Barbara. She's too nice a lady."

Again Nico is probing. He wants to know if Barbara will testify to support my alibi. Perhaps he's trying to see if I flinch at the thought of Molto working over my wife.

"You're just a softie, Delay." I look at myself in the mirror. I've had enough of this conversation. Nico, upbeat with the pleasant current of events the last two days, will not let it go.

"Don't let me down, Rusty. I really want to hear it. You know, sometimes I wonder. I think, How could the guy I knew do a thing like that? I admit it. I wonder sometimes."

"Nico, if I told you what really happened, you wouldn't want to believe it."

"Now, what does that mean?"

I turn away and he takes my elbow.

"Really, what does that mean?" he asks. "This isn't that crap about Tommy framing you, is it? I mean, that's for the papers, Rusty. This is Delay." He touches his shirt. "You can't believe that. That's a bunch of crap. I mean, off the record, all that shit. Me and you. Right here. Old buddies. Nobody repeats anything. You're telling me you believe that crap?"

"Where's the glass?"

"Oh, screw that. The cops lose everything. We both know that."

"He seemed to have primed the pump with Eugenia."

"What? You really think he told her to say 'my angel'? Come on. He heated her up too much. I admit that. And that was stupid. I told him that. I *told* him that. He's compulsive. You know. He was very fond of Carolyn. Very close to her. He considered her one of his closest friends. Big sister kind of thing almost. Looked up to her. He's very committed to this case."

"Did you ever look at that file, Nico?"

"The one from Raymond's drawer?"

"Do some homework. On your own. You may get some surprises. About big sister and little brother."

Nico smiles and shakes his head to show he isn't buying it. But I can tell that I've gotten under his skin now. I enjoy the advantage. I've had Nico's number for years. I dry my hands on one of the paper towels, with my mouth pursed to show that I will say no more.

"So that's it, huh? That's the big secret. Tommy done it. That's what I'm waiting to hear?"

"Go ahead, Delay," I say quietly, while my back is to him. "I'll give you a preview. One question. Right here. Me and you, as you say. Off the record. Just the old buds. Nobody repeats anything to anyone else." I revolve and look at him directly.

"Did you do it?" he asks.

I knew he would. Sooner or later somebody had to put it right to me. I finish drying my hands, and I summon up everything in me that belongs to the truth, every badge of sincerity I own in my manner.

"No, Nico," I say very quietly, and look him dead in the eye, "I did not kill Carolyn."

I can see that I reach him: some kind of enlargement in the pupils; his eyes become darker instantly. Some tone seems to change in his face.

"Very good," he says at last. "You'll be very good." Then he finally smiles. "So this has been kind of a bitch, huh? Falsely accused and all of that?"

"Go fuck yourself, Delay."

"I knew I'd hear that, too."

Both of us come out of the john laughing. When I look up, I see that I have attracted the attention of Stern and Kemp, who are standing a short distance down the corridor conferring with Berman, the private investigator. He is very tall, with a large belly and a loud tie. Stern's look is nettled. Perhaps he is upset to see me with Nico, but it seems that he has been interrupted. He waves his hand, dismissing the other two, and returns to the courtroom. Kemp walks off with Berman a few steps, then comes back to me. We watch Delay follow Sandy inside.

"I won't be here this afternoon," Jamie says. "Something came up."

"Something good?"

"Very good, if it pans out."

"Is this a secret?"

Jamie looks back at the courtroom door.

"Sandy said not to discuss it right now. Don't raise false hopes. He wants to be cautious. You understand."

"Not really," I say.

Berman, some distance away, tells Jamie they have to go. Kemp touches my sleeve.

"If it works out, you'll be delighted. Trust me."

My look, I'm sure, is abject, confused and thwarted by my own attorneys. But I know I cannot object. I myself have taught Jamie Kemp to be frugal with his confidence. I educated him in professional skepticism, in believing that the best judgment waits.

"Something came up with one of the subpoenas," he says. Berman calls again: They told the guy they'd be there at one. Jamie backs away. "Trust me," he says once more before he jogs off down the hall.

"Ladies and gentlemen," Larren reads to the jury. "You are about to hear the testimony of a fingerprint expert, Maurice Dickerman, concerning evidence he claims to have identified on a certain glass. In considering this evidence you must—I say *must*—bear in mind that the defense has had no chance to examine that glass. The testimony is proper, but it is up to you to determine what weight to give it. The defense hasn't had any opportunity to see what scientific explanation there may be for the prosecution's evidence. They have had no opportunity to see whether there was some form of chicanery—I'm not sayin there was, but I'm tellin you that the defense hasn't had the chance to get a scientist of their own to say yea or nay about that. They haven't had a chance to see if there's some mistake. An innocent mistake, but still a mistake. They haven't even had the chance to see if some other scientist would look at the glass and say those were another person's fingerprints.

"And I am instructing you as a matter of law, ladies and gentlemen, that when this case is over and you are deliberating on it, that you are entitled to consider not just this testimony but the failure of the prosecution to make the glass available to the defense. And it is permissible—I'm not tellin you what to do— but it is permissible for that one fact alone to raise a reasonable doubt in your mind which would require Mr. Sabich's acquittal.

"All right. Proceed."

Molto, at the podium, takes a moment to stare up at the judge. By now both men have abandoned pretense. There is an outright hatred between them, and it is visible and intense. In the meantime, the force of Larren's limiting instruction settles over the courtroom. The defense, in this instant, has staged a nine-run rally. The fingerprint evidence has been impeached from the mouth of the judge. Acquittal, he says, is a permissible conclusion. The suggestion that an error has been made, that there has been a mistake, is like a cut to the bone in a criminal trial.

Morrie Dickerman comes to the witness stand. The pure professional. An angular New Yorker with large, dark-framed glasses, Morrie finds fingerprints fascinating. He used to like me because I would sit there and listen to him. Morrie is as good as Painless Kumagai is bad—the kind of grab bag of abilities you encounter in public service. He sits there with his photographs and slides and shows the jury how it is done. He explains how prints are made, a residue of oils left by certain persons, at certain times. Some people don't ever leave prints. Most people will leave prints at some times and not at others. It depends on how much they sweat. But when they leave a print, it is unique. No one fingerprint is like any other. Morrie lays all of this out in his openhanded way, then nails my butt to the barn door in the last five minutes of his testimony with his pictures of the bar, the glass, the lifts, and enlargements from my county employee's file card. All the matching points of comparison have been identified with red arrows. Morrie, as usual, has prepared well.

Stern spends some time on his feet, studying the photographic blowup of one of my fingerprints from the glass before he begins. He turns the picture toward Morrie.

"What time on April first was that fingerprint made, Mr. Dickerman?"

"I would have no idea."

"But you're certain it was made on the first of April?"

"No way to tell that, either."

"I'm sorry?" Stern draws his mouth downward in mock surprise. "Well, certainly you can tell us that it was made around April first?"

"No."

"Well, how long can fingerprints last?"

"Years," says Dickerman.

"I'm sorry?"

"It can be years before the oils break down."

"What is the oldest fingerprint you have taken in all the time you have worked for the police department?"

"In a kidnapping case, I took a fingerprint off the steering wheel of an abandoned car that had to be three and a half years old."

"Three and one half years?" Stern makes a sound. He is a marvel. The man who laid waste to Raymond Horgan now feigns gentle-spirited befuddlement, deference to the expert. He acts as if he is slowly figuring all of this out as he goes, "Then Mr. Sabich could have handled this glass six months earlier when he was at Ms. Polhemus's apartment in connection with the *McGaffen* trial?"

"I can't tell you when Mr. Sabich handled it. I can tell you it has two of his fingerprints. That's all."

"Suppose Mr. Sabich had touched it for some reason—merely had an unnoticed drink of water, or only the interior of the glass had been rinsed after he used it—is it possible that his prints would remain?"

"Yes. And by the way, it is theoretically possible that the entire glass could have been immersed. Usually soap and water will remove the oils, but there are cases in the literature where fingerprints have been identified even after the object was rinsed in soap and water."

"No," says Sandy Stern in wonder.

"I've never seen that," says Dickerman.

"Well, at least we know that no one else handled the glass, because there were no other fingerprints on it."

"No."

Stern goes still, "I'm sorry?"

"There's another latent."

"No," says Stern again. He is laying it on self-consciously. There is an odd theatricality to Sandy. Early in the trial the jury had not seen him enough to know that he was acting. Now in our second week, he is more broad in some gestures, as if to acknowledge the deliberateness of his behavior. I know and you know, he is saying to them. An act of confidence. So they understand that he is not really trying to put anything past them. "You mean there is another fingerprint on the glass?"

"That's what I mean."

"Could it be, sir, that Mr. Sabich touched the glass months before, and someone else handled the glass on April first?"

"It could be," says Dickerman evenly. "It could be anything."

"Well, we know Mr. Sabich was there that night because his

prints are on many other objects in the apartment, are they not?"

"No, sir."

"Well, there must be some things. For example, the window latches were opened. Were there identifiable prints there?"

"Identifiable, sir. But not identified."

"These were the fingerprints of someone, but not Mr. Sabich?"

"Or Ms. Polhemus. We excluded her."

"A third person left those prints?"

"Yes, sir."

"Just as with the glass?"

"True."

Stern goes through the entire list of locations within the apartment from which lifts were taken without discovery of my prints. The coffee table that was upset. The fireplace tools printed with the thought that one might be the murder weapon. The surface of the bar. The cocktail tables. The window. The door. Five or six other places.

"And Mr. Sabich's prints appeared in not one of those places?"

"No, sir."

"Only on this glass that can no longer be found?"

"Yes, sir."

"One place?"

"That's all."

"He would have left prints throughout the apartment had he been there, would he not?"

"He might have. He might not have. Glass is an unusually receptive surface."

Stern, of course, knew the answer.

"But the table," asks Stern, "the windows?"

Dickerman shrugs. He is not here to explain. He is here to identify fingerprints. Stern makes the most of Dickerman's inability and, for the first time since we started, looks directly to the jury, as if for consolation.

"Sir," says Stern, "how many other identifiable prints were there of a third person, not Mr. Sabich, not Ms. Polhemus?"

"Five, I think. One on the latch. One on the window. A couple on the liquor bottles. One on a cocktail table."

"And are any of those made by the same person?"

"I wouldn't know."

Stern, who has still not left the side of the defense table, bends forward a bit to indicate that he does not understand .

"I'm sorry?" he says once more.

"No way to tell. I can tell you whoever it is has not been printed by the county, because we did a computer run. They don't have a criminal record. They haven't worked for the county. But they could be five different people or the same person. It could be the cleaning lady or a neighbor or some boyfriend. I can't tell you.

"I don't understand," says Stern, who understands very well.

"People have ten fingers, Mr. Stern. I don't know that unknown A isn't the index finger, and B is the third finger. Plus left hand and right hand. There's no way to tell without knowns to work from."

"Well, certainly, Mr. Dickerman—" Stern stops. "Which prosecutor supervised your activities after Mr. Sabich?"

"Molto," says Dickerman. You get the feeling at once that Morrie does not care for Tom very much.

"Well, certainly he asked you to compare these five unidentified prints to see if two of them might be from the same finger?"

Very good, I think to myself. Excellent, This is the kind of detail that I always overlooked as a prosecutor. I thought about the defendant, and the defendant of course thought about everybody else.

But when Dickerman answers, "No, sir, he did not," one of the jurors, the part-time computer jock, turns away shaking his head. He looks straight at me, like, Can you believe this? I am astounded that we have come back so far from yesterday. The juror turns to the person beside him, the young woman who runs the drugstore, and they exchange remarks.

"It can be done overnight," says Dickerman.

"Well, I'm sure," says Stern, "that Mr. Molto may remember now." Stern is about to sit down. "Do you know, Mr. Dickerman, why Mr. Molto did not ask you to make that comparison of the other prints?" A good trial lawyer never asks why, unless he knows the answer. Stern does, as I do. Neglect. Too much to do and not enough time to do it. The problem of focus. Any answer will suffice to raise doubts about Molto.

"I assume he didn't care," says Dickerman. He is trying to downplay the significance of the omission, but his answer has an ominous air, as if Molto would not be concerned about the truth.

Stern, who has never moved from the defense table, stands there one second more.

"Just so," he says. "Just so."

Molto approaches the podium and Ms. Maybell Beatrice, who works as a domestic in Nearing, is called. I am relieved to see Tommy up there again. For all of Nico's sloppiness, he now seems to have found his place in the courtroom. Tommy is far less adaptable. In the P.A.'s office there was always a kind of cultural divide, a barrier over which my friendship with Nico was ultimately stranded. Raymond picked an elite corps, young lawyers with law-school credentials he liked and, after an apprenticeship, set them to work on Special Investigations. We prosecuted the guilty and rich for bribery and fraud; we ran long-term grand-jury investigations; we learned to try cases against the likes of Stern, lawyers who argued law to the judges and nuance to the jurors. Molto—and Della Guardia—never rose above the advanced prosecution of street crimes. Tommy's particular mix of pride and passion has been nurtured too long in the homicide courtrooms and branch courts. Those are places where no holds are barred, where defense lawyers use every cheap strategy and device, and prosecutors learn to imitate them. Tommy has become the kind of prosecutor that the P.A.'s office too often breeds: a lawyer who can no longer make out the boundaries between persuasion and deception, who regards the trial of a lawsuit as a series of gimmicks and tricks. I thought at the start that it would be his molten-hot personality that would be a detraction for the state. Instead, the burden he attaches to the prosecution is his inability to escape from his experience. He is brighter than Nico, with a gimlet-eyed cleverness, and he is always prepared, but by now every person in the courtroom suspects that his zeal has no limit. He will do anything to win. Whatever the old rivalry or jealousy surrounding Carolyn, I take it that this trait as well must be a partial source of the antipathy between the judge and him.

And it is the same thing that keeps my curiosity high about Leon and the B file, and whatever shadows lurk in Molto's past. I found Nico's comment about Molto's close relations with Carolyn intriguing. Who knows exactly how she beguiled him? More and more, like everyone else here, I find myself persuaded that there is something sinister in Molto's character. It is too easy for Molto to justify all of his behavior; there is no obvious catch point below which he won't sink. What started out as another of Stern's courtroom illusions seems to have acquired a life of its own. I have wondered, as I have tried to guess at the revelation that Kemp is off chasing, if Molto is not the target. Certainly as Stern has gone on with the old defense lawyer's artifice of placing the prosecutor on trial, Molto has responded poorly. He makes what is perhaps his biggest blunder yet in his direct examination of this Nearing maid.

Ms. Beatrice says that she saw a white man on the eight o'clock bus one Tuesday night in April. She does not know what Tuesday night it was, but it was Tuesday, because she works late on Tuesdays, and it was April, because she remembered it as last month when she first spoke to the police, who were doing random interviews in the bus station in May.

"Now, ma'am," Molto says, "I ask you to look around the courtroom to see if there is anyone you recognize."

She points at me.

Molto sits down.

Stern begins cross. Ms. Beatrice greets him without apprehension. She is an elderly woman, quite stout, with a lively and kindly face. Her gray hair is drawn back in a bun, and she wears round wire-rimmed glasses.

"Ms. Beatrice," says Stern amiably, "I take it that you are the kind of person who gets to the bus station a bit early." Stern knows this, of course, because of the time shown in her police interview.

"Yes, sir. Ms. Youngner run me up each night at quarter to so's I can buy me a paper and a Baby Ruth and get me a seat."

"And the bus on which you go into the city is the same bus that comes out of the city, is that right?"

"Yes, sir."

"It terminates—that is, it ends its run in Nearing and goes back in?"

"It turn round in Nearing, that's right."

"And you are there each night when that bus arrives at a quarter to?"

"Quarter to six. Most every night, yes, sir. 'Cept Tuesday, as I explain."

"And the people coming home from downtown get off the bus and walk past you, is that right, and you have occasion to see their faces?"

"Oh, yes, sir. They looks tired and weary, many a them."

"Now, ma'am—well, I shouldn't ask you this—" Stern looks again at the report of the police interview. "You are not saying you recognize Mr. Sabich as the man you saw on the bus that Tuesday night, are you?" There is nothing to lose with the question. Molto's direct has left the impression that is, in fact, the case. But Ms. Beatrice makes a face. She shakes her head most emphatically.

"No, sir. They is somethin here I like to explain."

"Please do."

"I knowed I seen this gentleman." She nods to me. "I tol' Mr. Molto that many a time. I seen this man when I go to get on the bus. Now I recollect, they was a man on that bus one Tuesday night, cause I works late that night on account of Ms. Youngner don't get home till near 7:30 on Tuesdays. And I recollect he was a white man, cause we don't get many white gentlemens that ride on the bus goin into town that time a night. Now I just can't remember whether 'twould be this man or another man. I know he look real familiar to me, this man do; but I can't say that's cause I seen him in the station or cause I seen him on the bus that night."

"You have some doubt that it was Mr. Sabich you saw that night."

"That's right. Can't say 'twas him. Coulda been him. I just can't say."

"Have you spoken with Mr. Molto about your testimony?"

"Many a time."

"And have you told him all of what you've just told us?"

"Oh, yes, sir."

Sandy turns in Molto's direction with a look of silent and lofty reproof.

After court, Stern tells me to go home. He takes hold of Barbara and draws her toward me.

"Take your pretty wife to dinner. She certainly deserves some reward for her fine support."

I tell Stern that I was hoping we would begin talking about the defense, but Sandy shakes his head.

"Rusty, you must forgive me," he says. As chairman of the Bar Association's Committee on Criminal Procedure, he is responsible for a formal dinner to be given tomorrow night in honor of the retirement of Judge Magnuson, who has sat as a felony judge for three decades. "And I must spend an hour or two with Kemp," he adds offhandedly.

"Would you like to tell me where he has been?"

Stern screws up his face.

"Rusty, please. Indulge me." He again takes Barbara's arm and mine. "We have some information. I will tell you that. It bears on my examination tomorrow of Dr. Kumagai. But it is not worth repeating now. It may be a complete misunderstanding, I do not wish to raise false hopes. You are better off in the dark, rather than having your expectations dashed. Please. Accept my advice on that. You have been working long hours. Take an evening off. Over the weekend, we can discuss a defense, if it comes to that."

" 'If it comes to that'?" I ask. His meaning is elusive. Is he proposing we rest—offer no evidence? Or is this new information so explosive that the trial will come to a halt?

"Please," Sandy says again. He begins leading us out of the courtroom. Barbara now intervenes. She takes my hand.

So we have dinner at Rechtner's, an old-fashioned German place near the courthouse which I have always liked. Barbara seems especially cheerful after the pleasant developments today. She, too, was apparently affected by the dour events of yesterday. She suggests a bottle of wine and, once it is open, questions me about the trial. She enjoys the opportunity to finally have me at close quarters. Clearly, my unavailability has frustrated her. She asks serial questions with her large dark eyes still and intent. She is very concerned about the Hair and Fiber stipulation of yesterday. Why did we choose that, rather than testimony? She requires a full account of everything the lab report revealed. Then she inquires at length about Kumagai and what his testimony is expected to show. My responses, as they have been throughout, are laconic. I answer briefly, telling her to eat her meal, while I try to contain my discomfort. As ever, there is an aspect to Barbara's interest that I find frightening. Is her wonder truly as abstracted as it seems? Is it the procedures and puzzles that attract her, more even than their impact on me? I try to shift the conversation, asking what we hear of Nathaniel, but Barbara realizes she is being put off.

"You know," she says, "you're getting like you were before."

"What does that mean?" A terrible evasion.

"You're like that again—distant."

I am where I am and she complains. Even with the wine, a jolt of galvanic anger rockets through me. My face, I imagine, is like my father's, with that monumental look of something dark and untamed. I wait until it has passed.

"This is not an easy experience, Barbara. I am trying to get through it. Day by day."

"I want to help you, Rusty," she says. "However I can."

I do not answer. Perhaps I should be angry again, but as always happens, in the wake of rage I am left in the lightless caverns of the deepest sadness of my life.

I reach across the table and take both her hands between mine.

"I have not given up," I say. "I want you to know that. It is very hard now. I am just trying to get to the end. But I am not giving up on anything. I want as much left as possible, if I get the chance to start again. All right?"

She looks at me with a directness she seldom has, but she finally nods.

As we are driving home, I ask again about Nat, and Barbara tells me, as she has not before, that she has had a number of calls from the director of his camp. Nathaniel is waking twice a night with screaming nightmares. The director, who originally put this off under the rubric of adjustment, has now decided that the problem is acute. The boy is more than homesick. There is a special anxiety about my fate which has been exaggerated by being away. The director has recommended sending him home.

"How does Nat sound on the phone?"

Barbara has called him twice, during luncheon recesses, the only time he can be reached. I have been with Stern and Kemp on both occasions.

"He sounds fine. He's trying to be brave. But it's one of those things. I think the director is right. He'll be better off home."

I readily agree. I am touched and, with whatever perversity, heartened by the depth of my son's concern. But the fact that Barbara has kept this to herself plays on old strings. I find myself once more on the brink of anger, but I tell myself that I am unreasoning, irrational. The idea, I know, is not to increase my burdens. Yet she has a flawless and undetectable way of keeping things to herself.

As we unlock the door, the phone is ringing. I imagine that it is Kemp or Stern, finally ready to share the big news, whatever it is. Instead, it is Lipranzer, who still does not give his name.

"I think we got somethin," he says. "On that matter." Leon. "Can you talk now?"

"Not really. I just want to be sure you're free tomorrow night. Late. After I'm off."

"After midnight?"

"Right. Thought maybe we could go for a drive. See a guy?"

"You found him?" My heart picks up. Amazing, Lipranzer found Leon.

"Seems like. I'll know tomorrow for sure. You're gonna love this one, too." In the phone, I hear someone speaking nearby. "Look, I gotta go. I just wanted to let you know. Tomorrow night," he says. He laughs, a rare sound from Dan Lipranzer, especially in these times. "You're gonna love it," he says.

33

"Doc—tor Kumagai," says Sandy Stern in a tone which from its first syllable bristles with derision. It is five past two, the beginning of the afternoon session, and these are the first words of a cross-examination which both Kemp and Stern have promised me privately will be the most eventful of the trial.

Tatsuo Kumagai—Ted to his friends—the state's final witness, faces Stern, limp with indifference. His hands are folded. His brown face is placid. To this audience, he presents himself as a man without need of expression. He is an expert, an unaffected observer of facts. He is dressed in a blue pincord suit, and his abundant black hair is folded back neatly in a small pompadour. His direct examination this morning was the first occasion on which I've seen Painless testify and he was somewhat better than I expected. The medical terminology, and his unique speech patterns, caused the court reporter to interrupt a number of times to ask for answers to be repeated or spelled. But he has an undeniable presence. His native arrogance is translated by the witness chair into a developed confidence becoming an expert physician. His qualifications are impressive. He has studied on three continents. He has given papers all over the world. He has testified as a forensic pathologist in homicide cases throughout the United States.

These credentials emerged as part of the lengthy process of qualifying Painless as an expert. Unlike a so-called occurrence witness, who is confined to telling what he saw or heard or did, Painless is charged with considering all of the forensic evidence and rendering an opinion on what occurred. Prior to his appearance, various stipulations were read. The forensic chemist's analysis. The results of blood tests. On the stand, Painless used these facts and his own examination of the body to provide a comprehensive account. On the night of April 1, Ms. Polhemus had had sexual relations, almost certainly consensual in nature. This opinion was based on the presence of a 2 percent concentration of the chemical nonoxynol-9 and various jelly bases, indicating the use of a diaphragm. The man with whom Ms. Polhemus had intercourse was, as I am, a type-A secreter. Soon after she had had sex—the relative time indicated by the depth within the vagina of the primary seminal deposit—Ms. Polhemus was bludgeoned from behind. Her attacker was right-handed, as I am. This can be determined from the angle of the blow to the right side of her head. His height cannot be approximated without knowing her posture at the time of the attack or the length of the murder weapon. The best indication from the cranial wound is that she had reached her feet, if only briefly, when she was struck. The diaphragm was apparently removed at this time, and Ms. Polhemus, already dead, was bound. Without Stern's objection, Painless testified that the presence of the spermicidal compound, coupled with the unlocking of the doors and windows, led him to believe that a rape had been simulated in order to conceal the murderer's identity, and that the murderer was someone familiar with the methods of detection of crime and Ms. Polhemus's routine responsibilities in the P.A.'s office.

When Nico had led Painless through this summary, he asked if his opinion of how the crime occurred had ever been communicated to me.

"Yes, sir, I met Mr. Sabich about April 10 or 11 this year and we discuss this case."

"Tell us what was said."

"Well, Mr. Sabich try to convince me that Ms. Polhemus must have die accidentally as part of some kind of deviant sexual activity, in which she had voluntarily been bound."

"And how did you respond?"

"I say that was ridiculous, and I explain what the evidence show really occur."

"And after you informed Mr. Sabich of your theory of what occurred, did you have any further discussion?"

"Yes. He became quite upset. Angry. He stood up. He threaten me. He say that I better be careful or he gonna prosecute for tamperin with an investigation. There's some more, but basically, that's it."

Both Stern and Kemp on either side of me watched Painless do his stuff with a calm approaching the beatific. Neither one bothered to take notes. I do not yet know what is coming, although that is my choice.

Kumagai made a mistake, Kemp told me when I arrived at their offices this morning. A big one.

How big? I asked.

Enormous, said Kemp. Huge.

I nodded. To myself I thought that if it were somebody other than Painless, I would be more surprised.

Do you want to know what it is? Kemp asked me.

Strangely I found that Stern's assessment was right. It was better not to know details. Simply hearing that there was some outsized error was enough to steer me directly to the peripheries of my deepest rage. I had no desire to enter that region of disorder.

Surprise me, I told Kemp. I'll hear it in court.

Now I wait. Painless sits there, unfluttered, impassive. At lunch, Kemp told me he believed that Kumagai's career could be over tonight.

"Doc—tor Kumagai," Stern begins, "you have testified here as an expert, is that right?"

"Yes, sir."

"You have told us about your papers and your degrees, have you not?"

"I answer questions about that, yes."

"You said you have testified on many prior occasions."

"Hundreds," says Painless. Each answer has a kind of screw-you brittleness. He means to be a smart guy and tough, the better of any cross-examiner.

"Doctor, has your competence ever been called into question, to your knowledge?"

Painless adjusts himself on the stand. The assault has begun.

"No, sir," he says.

"Doctor, is it not true that many deputy prosecuting attorney's over the years have complained about your competence as a forensic pathologist?"

"Not to me."

"No, not to you. But to the chief of police, resulting in at least one memorandum being placed in your personnel file?"

"I don't know about that."

Sandy shows the document first to Nico, then to Kumagai on the stand.

"No, I never seen that," he says at once.

"Do you not have to be notified under police regulations of any addition to your personnel file?"

"Could be, but you ask what I remember. I don't remember that."

"Thank you, Doctor." Sandy removes the document from Kumagai's hands. As Stern is strolling back to our table, he asks, "Do you have any nicknames?"

Kumagai stills. Perhaps he is wishing that he had acknowledged the letter.

"Friend call me Ted."

"Aside from that?"

"Don't use nicknames."

"No, sir, not that you use. But by which you are known?"

"I don't understand question."

"Has anybody ever referred to you as Painless?"

"To me?"

"To anyone, to your knowledge?"

Again Painless takes a moment to shift around in his seat. "Could be," he says finally.

"You do not enjoy that nickname, do you?"

"Don't think about it."

"You acquired that nickname some years ago from the former chief deputy prosecuting attorney Mr. Sennett, in an unflattering context, did you not?"

"If you say."

"Mr. Sennett told you to your face, did he not, that you had bungled an autopsy and that the only person who found working with you painless was the corpse, because it was dead?"

The laughter thunders in the courtroom. Even Larren is chuckling up on the bench. I shift in my seat. Whatever Stern has better be good, because for the first time he has abandoned his innate decorousness. His cross so far verges on the cruel.

"I don't remember that," says Painless coldly when the room has come back to order again. Over the years he has grown adroit in his knowledge of the rules of evidence. Every cop and P.A. in Kindle County knows that story. Stan Sennett would be happy to tell it from the stand. But the judge is not likely to allow such a diversion, called collateral impeachment. Painless has drawn his shoulders around him. He looks out at Stern, waiting for more. He has apparently taken some pleasure in what he regards as his own small triumph.

"Now, Mr. Della Guardia and Mr. Molto are two persons from the P.A.'s office with whom you have worked with less—let us say disagreement, is that right?"

"Sure. They my good friends." On this point, Painless has apparently been well schooled. He will acknowledge his contacts with Tommy and Delay, in order to minimize their importance.

"Did you discuss this investigation with either one of them while it was in progress?"

"I talk to Mr. Molto sometime."

"How often did you speak to him?"

"We stay in touch. We talk now and then."

"Did you talk to him more than five times in the first few weeks of April?"

"Sure," he says, "if you say." Painless is taking no chances. He knows that subpoenas are out. He can't be sure whose MUDs we have obtained.

"And you talked in detail about this investigation?"

"Mr. Molto's a friend. He ask what I'm doin, I tell him. We talk about public information. Nothin from the gran jury." Painless resumes his satisfied smile. These answers, of course, have been the subject of prior discussion with the prosecutors.

"Did you tell Mr. Molto the results of the forensic chemist's analysis prior to conveying them to Mr. Sabich? I am talking specifically about the specimen which showed the spermicidal jelly."

"I understand," says Painless curtly. He looks directly over at Tommy. Molto has his hand over part of his face, and with Kumagai's glance, he straightens up and takes it away.

"I think so," says Kumagai.

He has not quite finished his response when Larren interrupts.

"Just a second," says the judge, "Just *one* second. The record
will reflect that Prosecuting Attorney Molto has just made a
gesture which I recognize to be a signal to the witness in
connection with his last answer. There will be further proceedings with regard to Mr. Molto at a later time. Proceed, Mr. Stern."

Tommy is crimson as he struggles to his feet.

"Your Honor, I am terribly sorry. I don't know what you are
talking about."

Neither do I, and I was watching Molto. But Larren is inflamed.

"This jury is not blind, Mr. Molto. And neither am I. Proceed,"
he says to Stern, but his anger is too great to store away and he
immediately wheels his chair around in Molto's direction and
gestures with the gavel. "I warned you. I told you before. I am
very upset with your conduct during this trial, Mr. Molto. There
will be proceedings."

"Judge," says Tommy despairingly.

"Resume your seat, sir. Mr. Stern, proceed."

Stern comes over to the table. I explain what I saw. He, too,
observed nothing. But Stern does not let the incident pass. In a
mincing tone he asks, "It is fair to say, Dr. Kumagai, that you and
Mr. Molto have always had good communication, is it not?"

The question evokes a few snickers, especially from the
reporters' section. Kumagai blinks with disdain and fails to
answer.

"Dr. Kumagai," asks Stern, "it is your ambition, is it not, sir, to
become coroner of Kindle County?"

"I like to be coroner," says Painless with disarmingly little
hesitation. "Dr. Russell doin a good job now. Couple years he
retire, maybe I put in for the job."

"And the P.A.'s recommendation would help you obtain that
position, would it not?"

"Who knows?" Painless smiles. "Can't hurt."

Grudgingly, I must admire Delay. Kumagai is his witness and
he has obviously counseled him to play it straight about
whatever was going on during the election campaign. Nico quite
clearly wants to have some prosecutorial candor to troop before
the jury to make up for some of Molto's gaffes. And his judgment
strikes me as correct. If it were not for the incident with the
judge a moment ago, it would all sit pretty well.

"By April, had you and Mr. Molto ever discussed the

possibility of you becoming coroner, Dr. Kumagai?"

"I say. Mr. Molto and me friends. I talk about what I wanna do, he talk about what he wanna do. Talk all the time. April. May. June."

"And in April you also spoke about this investigation a number of times before you received the forensic chemist's report?"

"I'd say so."

"Now, that report, sir, concerned the semen specimen which you had taken from Ms. Polhemus during the autopsy, is that right?

"Right."

"And it is that specimen which has been identified as being of Mr. Sabich's blood type and as containing chemicals consistent with the use by Ms. Polhemus of a birth-control device—a diaphragm. Am I correct?"

"You are correct."

"And the presence in that specimen of this birth-control chemical, the spermicide, is critical to your opinion, is it not?"

"All facts important, Mr. Stern."

"But that fact is particularly important, because you, sir, want us to believe that this tragic incident merely had the appearance of a rape, do you not?"

"Don't want you to believe nothin. I give you my opinion."

"But it is your opinion—to get down to brass tacks, as they say—that Mr. Sabich tried to make this look like a rape, correct?"

"If you say so."

"Well, is that not what you are trying to suggest? You and Mr. Molto, and Mr. Della Guardia? Let us be plain with these people." Sandy points to the jury. "Your opinion is that this was a staged rape. And that the way it was done suggests some knowledge of investigative techniques and of Ms. Polhemus's regular duties in the P.A.'s office, correct?"

"That's what I say on direct."

"And all of that points at Mr. Sabich, does it not?"

"If you say so," Painless says eventually, with a smile. You can see his reluctance to believe that Stern is inept enough to implicate his own client. But Sandy keeps forcing the issue, saying more than Kumagai would risk on his own, and Painless takes his characteristic pleasure in someone else's misfortune.

"And all of those deductions depend in the end on the

presence of spermicidal jelly in the specimen you sent to the forensic chemist, do they not?"

"More or less."

"Much more than less, is it not?"

"I would say."

"So this specimen, and the presence of the spermicide, is critical to your expert opinion?" says Stern, arriving at the point where he was a moment ago. This time Painless concedes. He shrugs his shoulders and says all right.

"Now, does your expert opinion, Dr. Kumagai, take any account of the fact that no spermicidal jelly was found in Ms. Polhemus's apartment? Are you familiar with that testimony that was given here by Detective Greer?"

"My opinion on scientific evidence. I don't read the transcript."

"But are you familiar with that testimony?"

"I heard about it."

"And are you not concerned, as an expert, that your opinion depends on the presence of a substance not found in the victim s belongings?"

"Am I concerned?"

"That is my question."

"Not concerned. I got an opinion on scientific evidence."

Stern gives Painless the long look.

"Spermicide came from somewhere, Mr. Stern. I don't know where lady hides this stuff. It's in the specimen. Test says what it says."

"Just so," says Sandy Stern.

"You stipulated," says Kumagai.

"That the spermicide was in the specimen you sent. Yes, sir, we did agree to that." Sandy walks around the courtroom. I still cannot guess what it is that Kumagai missed. Until Painless mentioned the stipulation I was ready to bet that the spermicide was misidentified.

"Now, sir," says Stern, "your initial impressions at the time of the autopsy took no account of the presence of a spermicide, did they?"

"Can't remember now."

"Well, think back, please. Was it not your original theory that the person who had last had intercourse with Ms. Polhemus was sterile?"

"Don't recall."

"Really? You told Detective Lipranzer that Ms. Polhemus's attacker seemed to have a condition in which he produced dead spermatozoa, did you not? Detective Lipranzer has already testified once before the jury, I am sure it would be no problem for him to return. Please reflect, Dr. Kumagai, is that not what you said?"

"Maybe. Very preliminary."

"All right, it was your very preliminary opinion. But it was your opinion then?"

"I guess."

"Now, do you recall the physical findings that led you to that opinion?"

"No, sir."

"As a matter of fact, Doctor, I am sure it is difficult for you to recall, unaided, any autopsy within days of when it took place, is that right?"

"Sometime."

"How many autopsies do you do in a week, Dr. Kumagai?"

"One, two. Sometime ten. Depends."

"Do you remember how many you performed in the thirty days surrounding Carolyn Polhemus's death?"

"No, sir."

"Would you be surprised to know that it was eighteen?"

"Sound right."

"And with that number, it is obvious, is it not, that the specifics of any one examination may slip your mind?"

"True."

"But when you spoke to Lipranzer the details were fresher. Were they not?"

"Probably."

"And you told him then that you believed the attacker was sterile?"

"I say, I somewhat remember that."

"Well, let us review for a moment those findings you presently recall that might have led to that preliminary opinion."

Sandy runs through it quickly. The rigor mortis, blood coagulation, and digestive enzymes established the time of death. The primary deposit of male fluids in the rear of the vagina, away from the vulva, indicated that Carolyn had spent little time on her feet after sex, meaning that intercourse had occurred near the time of her attack. And there was an absence in the fallopian tubes of any live spermatozoa, which one would expect to find ten to twelve hours after intercourse, assuming no contraception had been used.

"And to explain those phenomena, particularly the dead spermatozoa, you theorized that the attacker was sterile. It did not occur to you at first, Doctor, that a spermicide had been used, did it?"

"Apparently not."

"As you look back, you must think you were a fool to have missed something so obvious as the use of a contraceptive spermicide?"

"Make mistakes," allows Painless with a flip of his hand.

"You do?" asks Stern. He eyes the state's expert. "How often?"

Kumagai does not answer that. He recognizes his miscue.

"Mr. Stern, I find no birth-control device. No diaphragm. Apparently, I assume no birth control used."

"But certainly, Dr. Kumagai, an expert of your stature could not have been so easily misled?"

Kumagai smiles. He knows he is being taunted.

"Any single fact important," he says. "Kind of thing that murderer knows."

"But you yourself were not trying to mislead Detective Lipranzer when you gave him your initial impression, were you?"

"Oh no." Painless shakes his head vigorously. He has been prepared for that suggestion.

"You must have been convinced, Doctor, at that time, that birth control had not been used—so convinced that you considered the use of a spermicide to be out of the question?"

"Look, Mr. Stern, I got an opinion. Chemist has results. Opinion changes. Lipranzer know opinion's preliminary."

"Let us consider some alternatives. For example, Dr. Kumagai, you would be convinced that birth control would not be used by a woman who knew she could not bear children, correct?"

"Sure," he says. "But Ms. Polhemus got a child."

"So the evidence has shown," remarks Stern. "But let us not consider the particulars of Ms. Polhemus. Just bear my example in mind. If a woman knew she could not conceive, it would be unreasonable for her to use a spermicide, would it not?"

"Sure. Unreasonable." Painless agrees, but his answers are growing slower. His eyes seem thick. He has no idea where Stern is headed.

"Absurd?"

"I'd say."

"Can you, as a forensic expert, conceive of any reason that such a woman might use a diaphragm or a spermicide?"

"We not talkin about a lady in menopause?"

"We are speaking of a woman who knows without question that she cannot conceive."

"No reason. No medical reason. I think of nothin."

Sandy looks up at Larren. "Your Honor, may the court reporter mark the last five questions and answers so that she can read them back later, if need be?"

Kumagai conducts a slow survey of the courtroom. He looks at the judge, the reporter, finally the prosecutors' table. He is actually frowning now. The trap, whatever it is, has been set. Everyone knows it. The reporter attaches a clip to the narrow sheaf of stenographic notes.

"Is it not your expert opinion, Dr. Kumagai," asks my lawyer, Alejandro Stern, "that Carolyn Polhemus was a woman who knew she could not conceive?"

Kumagai looks out at Stern. He bends over the microphone before the witness chair.

"No," Painless says.

"Please do not rush yourself, Doctor. You did eighteen autopsies in those weeks. Would you not rather consider your original notes?"

"I know the lady use birth control. You stipulate," he says again.

"And I, sir, say once more that we stipulated to the chemist's identification of the specimen that *you* sent."

Stern returns to our table. Kemp is already holding aloft the document Sandy wants. Stern drops a copy with the prosecution and delivers the original to Kumagai.

"Do you recognize the notes of your autopsy of Ms. Polhemus, Dr. Kumagai?"

Painless flips a few pages.

"My signature," he says.

"Would you please read aloud the short passage marked by the paper clip?" Sandy turns to Nico. "Page 2, Counsel."

Kumagai has to change glasses.

" 'The fallopian tubes are ligated and separated. The fimbriated ends appear normal.' " Kumagai looks down at the sheet he has read from. He pages again to the end. He is frowning, deeply now. Finally he shakes his head.

"Not right," he says.

"Your own autopsy notes? You dictate them as you are conducting the procedure, do you not? Surely, Doctor, you are not suggesting you made a contemporaneous error?"

"Not right," he says again.

Stern comes back to the defense table for another piece of paper. I have gotten it by now, I look up to him as he takes the next document from Kemp. I whisper:

"Are you telling me that Carolyn Polhemus had her tubes tied?"

It is Kemp who nods.

The next few seconds are blank. Weirdly, unaccountably, I feel alone, locked in my own teetering sensations. An essential connection has been interrupted. For a moment it is like déjà vu. I cannot make out reasons. What takes place in the courtroom seems remote. I am aware, in a dislocated way, that Painless Kumagai is being devastated. He denies two or three more times that it is possible that Ms. Polhemus had had her fallopian tubes surgically separated to prevent conception. Stern asks if other facts might affect his opinion and pushes into Kumagai's hands the records of the West End gynecologist who performed the tubal ligation six and a half years ago, after Carolyn aborted a pregnancy. It was this doctor, no doubt, whom Kemp went to meet yesterday afternoon.

"I ask you again, sir, would these records alter your expert opinion?"

Kumagai does not answer.

"Sir, is it now your expert opinion that Carolyn Polhemus knew she could not conceive?"

"Apparently." Kumagai looks up from the papers. In my confusion, I find that I actually feel sorry for him. He is slow now, hollow. It is to Molto and Nico he speaks, not Stern or the jury. "I forgot," he tells them.

"Sir, is it not absurd to believe that Carolyn Polhemus used a spermicide on the night of April first?"

Kumagai does not answer.

"Is it not unreasonable to believe that?"

Kumagai does not respond.

"There is no reason known to you that would explain why she might do that, is there, sir?"

Kumagai looks up. There is no way to tell if he is thinking or simply being ravaged by shame. He has taken hold of the beveled rail of the witness stand. He still does not answer.

"Shall I have the court reporter read back your answers to the questions I asked a few moments ago?"

Kumagai shakes his head.

"Is it not clear, Dr. Kumagai, that Carolyn Polhemus did not use a spermicide on April first? Would that not be your expert opinion? Does it not seem to you, sir, as an expert and a scientist, the most obvious reason that no trace of a spermicide could be found in her apartment?"

Kumagai seems to sigh. "I cannot answer your questions, sir," he says with some dignity.

"Well, answer this question, Dr. Kumagai: Is it not clear, given these facts, that the specimen you sent to the chemist was not taken from the body of Carolyn Polhemus?"

Kumagai now sits back. He pushes his glasses back up on his nose.

"I have a regular procedure."

"Are you telling this jury, sir, that you have a clear recollection of taking that specimen, marking it, sending it on?"

"No."

"I repeat: Is it not likely that the specimen containing the spermicide, the specimen identified as containing fluids of Mr. Sabich's blood type, was not taken from the body of Carolyn Polhemus?"

Painless shakes his head again. But this is not denial. He does not know what occurred.

"Sir, is it not likely?"

"It is possible," he finally says.

From the jury box, clear across the courtroom, I can hear one of the men say, "For Chrissake."

"And that specimen, Dr. Kumagai, was sent, was it not, while you were having these regular conversations with Mr. Molto, am I right?"

With this, Kumagai finally rediscovers his spark. He draws himself up in the chair.

"Do you accuse me, Mr. Stern?"

It is some time before Stern speaks.

"We have had enough unsupported accusations for one case," he says. Then, before resuming his chair, Stern nods in the direction of the witness, as if to dismiss him. "Doc-tor Kumagai," he adds.

After court, Jamie Kemp and I sit in Stern's conference room describing Kumagai's cross-examination for a small audience composed of Sandy's secretary, the private investigator Berman, and two law students who work in the office as clerks. Kemp has brought out a bottle of champagne, and one of the young people has turned on a radio. A fine actor, Kemp does a burlesque in which he plays the parts of both Stern and Kumagai. He repeats Stern's most damaging questions in an insistent tone, and then falls in a chair, where he beats his feet and makes the sounds of a person being choked. We are roaring when Stern comes through the door. He has on a tuxedo, or, more properly, part of it: only the striped trousers and the boiled shirt; a red bow tie, not yet knotted, is through his collar. Inspecting the scene he is livid; a fierce anger grips all his features. You can tell that he is struggling to keep himself in check.

"This is inappropriate," he says. He is speaking to Kemp. "Entirely inappropriate. We are on trial. This is not the time to congratulate ourselves. We may not bring a trace of smugness to that courtroom. Juries sense such things intuitively. And they resent it. Now, if you would please clean this up, I wish to speak with my client. Rusty," he says, "when you have a moment."

He wheels and I follow Stern to his office with its soft, almost feminine interior. I suspect that Clara had a hand in the decoration. Everything is done in the same creamy tone. Full-length drapes cover the windows, and furnishings upholstered in Haitian cotton crowd the office, so that it feels as if you are being pushed into a seat. Stern has a heavy crystal ashtray at each corner of his desk.

"It's my fault more than Jamie's," I say when I enter.

"Thank you, but you are not charged with making judgments at this time. He is. That was entirely inappropriate."

"It was a great triumph. He's worked hard. We were enjoying it. He was trying to put your client at ease."

"You need not defend Kemp to me. He is a first-rate attorney and I value his work. Perhaps I am to blame. As a case is headed toward conclusion I always become tense."

"You should savor today, Sandy. No lawyer gets many crosses like that, especially of the state's expert."

"That is so," says Stern, and he indulges in a brief whimsical smile. "What a colossal blunder." He makes a sound, a groan of sorts, and shakes his head. "But that is past now. You have been very insistent and so I wanted to take one moment with you to discuss the case for the defense. I wish there were more time, but I have committed myself months ago to this dinner for Judge Magnuson. Della Guardia will be there, so we will all be evenly disadvantaged." He smiles in appreciation of his own understated humor. "At any rate, your defense: Decisions on these matters are always the client's. If you wish, I will give you my advice. If not, feel free to dictate. I am at your disposal." As I anticipated all along, Sandy has waited until we are clearly ahead on points before allowing me to make my decisions. I know what he would suggest.

"You think we'll even get the chance to offer a defense?"

"You mean, do I think Judge Lyttle will direct a verdict for us tomorrow?"

"In your view, is that possible?"

"I would be surprised." He takes up his cigar from the ashtray. "Realistically, my answer is no."

"What's left that ties me to the crime?"

"Rusty, there is no need for me to lecture you. But you must remember that the inferences at this stage must be taken in the light most favorable to the prosecution. Even Kumagai's direct testimony, preposterous as it now seems, must be credited for purposes of the motion. And the answer to your question is that the evidence, in any light, ties you to the scene. Your fingerprints are there. Carpeting which could be yours is there. The phone records show you were in contact. And all of this was concealed.

"On a more practical level, no judge is eager to usurp the

jury's role as decision maker in a case of this stature. He invites
criticism, and perhaps more importantly, he leaves a sense
abroad that the case was never fairly resolved. I regard the
prosecution evidence, as it stands, as paper-thin. It is likely that
the judge sees it the same way. But he would no doubt prefer to
have the jury discharge you. If, unaccountably, they fail in that
responsibility, he can grant a motion for acquittal post trial,
notwithstanding the verdict. I would consider that far more
likely in this case."

He makes sense, but I was hoping he would say something
else.

"So that brings us to the question of a defense," Stern says.
"Certainly if we proceed we must offer certain documents. We
want to establish that Barbara was at the U., as you claimed. So
we will present the computer log to demonstrate she signed on
shortly after eight o'clock. We want to show that the rent-a-car
and taxi companies have no records to support the notion that
you traveled to the city on the night of April first. The
gynecologist's records we spoke of today must, of course, be
offered. Other odds and ends. I take all of that as given. Whether
we bring on testimony is the question."

"Who would you consider calling?"

"Character witnesses. Certainly Barbara."

"I don't want her to testify," I say at once.

"She is an attractive woman, Rusty, and there are five men on
the jury. She can support your alibi, quite effectively. No doubt
she is willing."

"If I testify, and she's sitting in the first row smiling at me, the
jury will know that she supports my alibi. There's no need for her
to get chewed up."

Stern makes a sound. I have disrupted his plans.

"You don't want me to get up there, do you, Sandy?"

He does not answer at first. Instead, he brushes a trace of
cigar ash from the pleats on his shirt.

"Are you reluctant because of my relationship with Carolyn?"
I ask. "I won't deny it, you know."

"I know that, Rusty. And I do not find that encouraging. I think
it would give a large boost to the state, which they desperately
need. Frankly, we run some risk that the same facts might also
emerge on Barbara's cross-examination. The confidential com-

munications privilege would probably prohibit inquiry into your admissions to your wife about your affair, but one can never be certain. Overall, it is probably not worth the chance." Stern seems casual in admitting that I was right after all—it really does not make much sense to talk about calling Barbara. "But disclosure of these matters is not my principal concern about your testimony," Sandy says, getting to his feet. He feigns stretching, but I know by now that he wants to come sit beside me on the couch, the place where he delivers all the bad news. He adjusts a picture of Clara and the children on the white birch credenza behind his desk; then, most naturally, settles next to me.

"Rusty, I prefer to see the defendant take the stand. No matter how often and how insistently jurors are told that they must not hold a defendant's silence against him, it is an impossible instruction to follow. A jury wants to hear a denial, particularly when the defendant is a person accustomed to presenting himself in public. But in this case I am against it. We both know this, Rusty: Two groups of persons make good witnesses. Those who are essentially truthful. And skilled liars. You are an essentially truthful person and would ordinarily make a fine witness in your own behalf. Certainly, you have years of training in how to communicate with a jury. I have no doubt that if you were to testify to everything you knew you would do so convincingly and that you would be acquitted. Deservingly, I might add."

He looks at me briefly, a quick but penetrating expression. I am not positive whether that is a vote of confidence in my innocence or another comment on the poor quality of the state's case, but I sense the former and I find myself pleasantly surprised. With Stern, of course, it is possible that he has offered that now only to sweeten this pill.

"However," he says, "I am convinced after observing you for several months now that you will not testify to everything you know. Some matters remain your secret. Certainly at this juncture I do not wish to pry. I mean that sincerely. With some clients persuasion is called for. With others you would just as well not know. In a few cases, it is best to leave things undisturbed. That is my sense here. I am confident that the choice you have made is a deliberate one, and well considered.

But be that as it may, when one comes to the witness stand determined to tell less than the truth, he is like a three-legged animal in the wild. You are not a skillful liar. And if Nico blunders into this area of sensitivity, whatever it is, things will go very badly for you."

A pause, a silence just a bit longer than need be, passes between us.

"We must assess the case as it is," Stern says. "We have not had a bad day yet for the defense. Well, perhaps one. But there is not a piece of evidence that stands untarnished. And this afternoon we have dealt a blow from which the state is not likely to recover. It is my best professional judgment that you should not testify. Whatever your chances—and I admit that I think after today they are quite good—whatever your chances, they are best this way.

"Having said all of that, let me remind you that it is your decision. I am your attorney. And I will present your testimony, if you choose to give it, with confidence and conviction—no matter what you choose to say. And certainly no choices need be made tonight. But I wanted to let you begin your period of final reflection with my own views in mind."

He is gone a few moments later, his tie knotted and his perfect jacket removed from its hanger behind the door. I remain in his office, made somber by his remarks. This is the closest Stern and I have come to a heart-to-heart. His candor, after so many months of suppression, is disturbing, no matter how kindly or elegantly phrased.

I wander down the hallway with the thought in mind to have another glass of champagne. Kemp's light is still on. He is at work in his small office. Over one of the filing cabinets, merely pasted to the wall, is a poster. Dropped out against a vibrant red background is a young man in a spangled jacket. He is playing a guitar, and the photo has caught him in motion so that his hair stands on end like a dandelion gone to seed. The word GALACTICS crosses from corner to corner in white caps. I am sure that few people who walk in recognize the Jamie Kemp of a decade ago.

"I got you in some hot water with the boss," I say. "I apologize."

"Shit, that's my own fault." He points to a chair. "He's the most disciplined human being I know."

"And one hell of a lawyer."

"Isn't he? Have you ever seen anything like what went on today?"

"Never," I tell him. "Never in twelve years. How long have you guys had that stuff?"

"Sandy noticed the line in the autopsy Sunday night. We got the records from the gynecologist yesterday. You want to hear something? Stern thinks it was just a mistake. He feels Kumagai does everything half-ass. When he got the chemist's results, he went on from there and forgot about the autopsy. I don't buy that."

"No? What do you think?"

"I think you were set up."

"Well," I say, after an instant, "I've thought that a lot longer than you."

"I believed it," says Kemp. "Most of the time." I am sure he is thinking about the phone records again, but he does not mention them. "Do you know who did it?"

I take a moment with that.

"Why wouldn't I tell my lawyers?"

"What do you think about Molto?"

"Maybe," I say. "Probably."

"What does he get out of it? Keeps you from looking into that file? What do you call it? The B file?"

"The B file," I repeat.

"Except he can't believe you're not going to mention it, if he puts it to you."

"Yeah, but look at the position I'm in. Would you rather be accused by the chief deputy P.A., or some wild man you're trying to nail for murder? Besides, he wouldn't know how far along we were. He'd just want to keep anybody from going forward."

"That's pretty amazing, don't you think? Bizarre?"

"That's probably one reason I don't quite believe it."

"What are the others?"

I shake my head. "I'll have a better idea tonight."

"What's tonight?"

I shake my head again. For Lipranzer's sake I cannot take any chances. This will be between only him and me.

"Is this do-it-yourself night?"

"That it is," I say.

"You better be careful. Don't start doing Della Guardia any favors."

"Don't worry," I say. "I know what I'm doing." I stand up and consider my last statement, one of the most farfetched I have recently made. I bid Kemp good night and go back down the hallway to look for the champagne.

34

Like Santa Claus or the demons that come out in the woods, Lipranzer arrives at my home after midnight. He seems lively and unusually good-humored as Barbara greets him at the door in her nightclothes. Awaiting Lip, I have felt not the slightest inclination to sleep. Instead, the events of the day have combined in such a fashion that for the first time in months I have a sensation which I recognize as something more than hope aborning. It is like the closed eyelids' trembling reception of new daylight. Somewhere inside, there is faith reignited that I am going to be free. In that mellow luminescence, I have passed the most pleasant time in weeks with my wife. Barbara and I have been drinking coffee together for hours, talking about the demise of Painless Kumagai and Nathaniel's scheduled return on Friday, the prospect of a renewed life a balm upon us.

"Downtown they're sayin some wild things," Lipranzer tells both of us. "Right before I pulled out of the Hall, I talked to a guy who had just heard from Glendenning. They say Delay's talkin about dismissin the case and Tommy is kickin and screamin and tryin to think up a new thing. Could that be right?"

"It could be," I say. At the mention of Nico dismissing, Barbara has taken hold of my arm.

"What the hell happened in that courtroom today?" Lip asks.

I start to tell him the story of Kumagai's cross-examination, but he has already heard it.

"I know that," he says. "I mean, how is it possible? I told you that little jerk said the guy was shootin blanks. I don't care how many times he denied it. One thing, Ted Kumagai is history. There ain't a soul in the Hall not sayin he'll be suspended by next week."

As Kemp predicted. By now, I find my feelings of sympathy pinched.

Barbara sees us out the door. "Be careful," she says. Lipranzer and I sit a moment in the driveway in the unmarked Aries. I perked another pot of coffee—this one with caffeine—when Lip arrived, and Barbara has given him a second cup for the road. He is sipping on it as we sit there.

"So where are we going?" I ask.

"I want you to guess," he says. It is, of course, a little late to go visiting. But I learned this approach from the coppers a long time ago. If you've got to find someone, the best time to be looking is in the dead of the night, when almost everybody's at home. "Gimme your shot on Leon," Lip says. "You know, tell me about him."

"I have no idea. He's got some kind of job that he wants to keep. That was clear from the letter. So he has to make a good buck. But he lives on the edge. I don't know. Maybe he owns a restaurant or a bar, with some straight partners. He could be anything semi-respectable. He runs a theater company, how's that? Am I close?"

"You'd never get close. Is he white?"

"Probably. Pretty well off, whatever he is."

"Wrong," says Lipranzer.

"No shit?"

Lipranzer is laughing.

"All right," I say, "twenty questions is over. What's the scoop?"

"Feature this," says Lipranzer. "He's a Night Saint."

"Come on."

"Sheet as long as my arm. Gang crimes has got all kinds of intelligence on him. This guy's like a lieutenant now. Whatever they call them, a deacon. Runs things on two floors in the projects. He's been up there for years. Apparently, he figured that all his hard-ass pals wouldn't think much of him if they found out he's runnin out to the Public Forest to suck white boys' cocks. That's his thing, Mojoleski's got a snitch, gay as a jaybird, teaches high school, who gave him all kinds of information on this jamoche. Seems like he and Leon went sneakin around together for years. This guy was Leon's teacher. Eddie somethin. Nine out of ten, that's the fella who's been writin letters."

"Son of a bitch. So where are we going? Grace Street?"

"Grace Street," says Lipranzer.

The words are still enough to settle a shiver near my heart and my spine. Lionel Kenneally and I spent a few evenings in there. Early mornings, actually. Three a.m., four. The safest time for a white man.

"I give him a call," says Lipranzer. "He's an affluent type. Got a phone and everything. In his own name, by the way. That P.I. Berman did a hell of a job. Anyway, I called about an hour ago. Said I was givin away newspaper subscriptions. He wasn't interested, but he said yeah, when I asked if I was talkin to Leon Wells."

A Night Saint, I think as we drive toward the city. "A Night Saint," I murmur out loud.

I became familiar with the Grace Street projects during my fourth year as a deputy P.A. By then, I had joined Raymond Horgan's fair—haired coterie, and he selected me to lead a large-scale police/grand-jury investigation of the Night Saints. This assault on the city's largest street gang was announced by Raymond just in time to become the centerpiece of his first re-election campaign. For Raymond, it was an ideal issue. Negro gangsters were not popular with anybody in Kindle County, and success would permanently dispel his bleeding-heart image. The Saints investigation was my initial trip to the spotlight, the first time I worked with reporters at my side. It took almost four years of my life. By the time Raymond ran for re-election again, we had convicted 147 identified gang members. The press heralded Raymond Horgan's unprecedented triumph, and never mentioned that more than 700 Saints remained on the street, doing all the old things.

The Saints' genesis would make some sociologist a reasonably good dissertation. Originally they were the Outlaws of the Night, a small, not particularly well-disciplined street gang in the North End. Their leader was Melvin White. Melvin was a fine-looking American, with one sightless eye, milky and wandering, and, for balance perhaps, a dangling turquoise earring, three inches long, in the opposite ear. His hair tended toward the straight and was

worn in Gorgon fashion, resembling, if anything, an unkempt
Rastafarian tangle. Melvin was a thief. He stole hubcaps, guns,
mail, the change from vending machines, and all manner of
motorized vehicles. One night Melvin and three of his pals killed
an Arab gas-station owner who drew on them while they were
emptying his register. They pled to involuntary manslaughter,
and Melvin, who up until then had only visited state youth camp,
went to Rudyard, where he and his three buddies got to meet
men to admire. Melvin emerged four years later in a caftan and
phylacteries and announced that he was now Chief Harukan,
leader of the Order of Nighttime Saints and Demons. Twenty
other bloods dressed just like him settled in the same part of
town, and within the next twelve months they all began, as they
put it, involving themselves in the community. Melvin gathered
his followers to him in a deserted apartment building he called
his ashram. He preached from a loudspeaker on weekends and
evenings. And during the day he taught those inclined how to
steal.

Initially, it was mail. The Saints had people in the post office.
Many, in fact. They stole not only checks and the tickets to
events but account information, so that they could pass forgeries
at any bank. Harukan had what for lack of anything else has to be
called the vision to recognize the principles of capitalist
enterprise, and his profits were reinvested, usually in decimated
real estate in the North End purchased at county scavenger
sales. Eventually entire blocks were Saint-owned. The Saints
drove up and down in their big cars. They blasted their horns
and played their radios. They hustled the daughters of the
neighborhood and made hoodlums, willingly or not, of the sons.
Harukan, in the meantime, emerged as a political figure. The
Saints gave away food on the weekends.

As they became better established, Melvin led the Saints into
smack. Entire buildings became processing centers. Guys with
chemistry degrees would cut the heroin with quinine and lactose
while two dudes with M−16's watched them. In a second area
six women, each one stark naked to prevent any body-cavity
smuggling, made up dime bags, closing them off with seal-a-
meals. Out on the streets in Saintland, high-grade heroin was
sold from stands. There were drive-up windows in garages to
which white kids from the suburbs could come down to score,

and on weekends the traffic was so bad that some mogul in caftan and shades would be down there with a whistle telling people where to go. Once or twice the newspapers tried to write about what was going on, but the coppers didn't like it. There were policemen on the take, something the department has traditionally preferred to ignore, and the cops who weren't taking were just scared. The Saints killed. They shot, they garroted, they stabbed. They murdered, of course, in dope squabbles; but they also killed because of minor differences of opinion, because someone insulted the upholstery in somebody's 'mobile, or because of an innocent brushing of shoulders on the street. They ran six square blocks of this city, their own little Hey Dude fascist arena, a quarter of their terrain occupied by the Grace Street projects.

I have heard it said on many occasions that these projects were drawn from the same architectural plans as the student dormitories at Stanford. Suffice it to say, there is no resemblance now. The small balconies at the rear of each apartment have been curtained off with chicken wire to end the rain of suicides, infants, drunks, and persons pushed, who, over the first five years, became a sauce upon the pavement below. Most of the sliding glass doors to the balconies have been replaced with plywood sheets; and from the balconies themselves a wide variety of objects hang, including laundry, garbage cans, gang banners, old tires, car parts, or, in winter, anything that profits by being kept out of the heat. No sociologist can portray how far the life in these three concrete towers is from the existence most of us know. It is not Sunday school, was Lionel Kenneally's favorite phrase. And he was right; it was not. But it was more than cheap irony or even rabid racism could comprehend. This was a war zone, akin to what was described by the guys I knew who came back from Nam. It was a land where there was no future—a place where there was little real sense of cause and effect. Blood and fury. Hot and cold. Those were terms that had some meaning. But you could not ask anybody to do anything that involved some purchase on what might happen next year, even next week. At times when I listened to my witnesses describe the daily events of project life, in the disconnected way most of them had of doing that, I would wonder if they were hallucinating. Morgan Hobberly, my star, a reformed Saint who, truly, got religion, told me that one morning he rolled out of bed to the sound of gunfire outside his door. When he investigated, he found himself caught between two bloods trying to zap each other with carbines. I asked Morgan what he did. 'Back to sleep, babe. Not my thing. Pulled my pill over my head.'

In truth, my four years of investigation succeeded only because of Morgan Hobberly. The whole heroic incursion into gang life, which Stern has trumpeted before my jury on a dozen occasions, came down to one piece of luck: finding Morgan. An organization like Harukan's did not have the kind of membership who could not be bought. Dozens of them were informants for the police or the federal agencies. But Melvin was smart enough to have a few of them out there doing counter-intelligence work. We were never sure what was right, since we got, through our sources, two or three different stories at any one time.

But Morgan Hobberly was the real thing. He was on the inside. Not particularly because he wanted to be, but because the Saints enjoyed having him around. Everybody knows a Morgan Hobberly. He was born cool, given to grace the way some people are born to music, or horses, or high jumping. His clothes just hung on him right. His movements were lithe. He was not so much beautiful as composed, not so much handsome as present. Aloof was not the right word as much as magical. There was a vibration he stirred in me that somehow reminded me of my feelings for Nat. And because some moral voice that Morgan took for divine told him one morning that Harukan's ways were evil, Morgan secretly went to work for the state. We put a body recorder on him and he sat in the meetings of chieftains. He gave us the numbers of phones that we connected to pen registers and, eventually, tapped. In the seventy days that Morgan Hobberly helped us, we gathered virtually all the evidence for trials that lasted another two years.

He did not make it, of course. The good, they say, never do. It was Kenneally who told me they'd found Morgan. They had a call from the Public Forest district command, he said, and it didn't sound encouraging. When I arrived, there was already that funny scatter of cops and paramedics and reporters familiar to a murder scene. Nobody wants to talk to anybody else; nobody wants to be near the body. People were all over, shot out in different places like spores. I couldn't figure where he was.

Lionel was there already, with his hands dug deep in his windbreaker. He gave me that low look of his, the varlet's eye. We fucked up bad, he was saying; and then his eyes drifted back enough for me to guess the general direction.

He had died of drowning. So Coroner Russell later determined—I would not let Kumagai near the body. He had died of drowning, the coroner found, in the waste pool of a public outhouse. That was where he was. Upside down, with his head, and his two broken shoulders, pushed through the wooden seat. Rigor mortis had set in, so that his legs were spread at a kind of scarecrow angle, and his plain twill workpants and raveled nylon socks and worn oxfords created an atmosphere of unbearably humble address. His skin—the band of flesh visible where the pants and socks didn't meet—was purple, a royal shade. I stood in that tiny wooden shack, where a fly or two still buzzed even though it was now November, where the air was rank even without the summer heat, and contemplated Morgan Hobberly's strange humor and the ether on which I always thought that he could float. I believed less then in angels and ghosts, because I had thought surely that this was one man who, as he made his way through the world, could not be touched.

Lipranzer is looking cold—not unemotional or distant, but actually cold, although the nighttime temperature in August is still verging on the seventies. His shoulders are hunched close and his windbreaker is zipped tight. I know him well enough to recognize this is a sign of discomfort, if not fright. On this turf, I am probably more experienced.

"How you doin, Charlie Chan?" I ask him as we head up the concrete staircase.

"Me no likee this one, boss," he says. "Uh—uh. No fuckee way."

In the projects, a staircase is a building's main thoroughfare. The elevators are seldom operable, and when they are, nobody will get on them anyhow, since there is no mercy for him who finds himself between floors with a carload of Saints. Instead, all commerce is transacted in this stairwell. Dope is sold here; wine is drunk here; love is made. It is near 3 a.m. and still this vertical Ganges is not completely deserted. Near floor 4 two young men are drinking something in a bag and trying to romance a young

woman whose head is lolled back against the cinder blocks.
"How you doin, brother?" they say to a black man who happens
to be climbing up ahead of us. To Lip and me, they say nothing,
but their looks are insolent and cold, and Lip, without missing a
step, flips out his tin as we are going past. He does not want to be
mistaken for an ordinary white man.

At the top of the stairway, the eighth floor, Lip holds a finger
to his lips and quietly pulls the steel fire door back. I follow him
into the corridor, a typical project hallway; brightly lit to
discourage intruders, trash along the sides in isolated pieces, an
uncut smell of human use. About halfway down the wall, the
sheetrock has been smashed out in a shape which for all the
world resembles someone's head. In a hallway like this, one of
Lionel Kenneally's guys shot Melvin White, the night after we
returned the first round of indictments. I was outside to
supervise the arrests, but it was about twenty minutes after we
all heard the gunfire before the coppers would let me go in. By
then the ambulance had arrived, and I went up with the
paramedics. Along with the surgeons, they eventually saved
Melvin's life, making way for his return to Rudyard. When I saw
him, however, Harukan's chances did not seem good. They had
laid him out in the middle of the hallway next to his automatic
rifle. He was making a sound too labored, too desperate to be
called groaning, and his stomach and his arms, which lay upon it,
were painted with blood. Between his hands, a little twisted
purple piece of tissue protruded. And above him stood Stapleton
Hobberly, Morgan's brother, who had begun snitching for us
after Morgan was killed. Stapleton had his penis in his hands. He
was urinating in Melvin White's face while a number of coppers
lounged against the walls and watched.

And what the fuck am I supposed to say if this guy dies of
drowning? one of the paramedics asked me.

Now Lip is rapping on the door.

"Open up, Leon! Wake up! It's the po-lice. Come on, man. We
just wanna talk."

We wait. The building, in a way that is almost beyond the
threshold of detection, seems more silent now. Lip raps again
with the flat of his palm. There is no kicking this door in. They
are all reinforced steel.

Lipranzer shakes his head. And at that moment the door

suddenly, silently, swings open. It is very slow. Inside, the room is totally black, no sign of light. Somehow an extraordinary adrenal rush has begun. If I were to pick out the details that key this response, I could only identify the little metal click, but even before that there is an instantaneous perception of alarm. Danger is palpable in the air, as if the threat of harm were an odor, a stirring like wind. When I hear the sound of the gun being readied, I realize that we are perfect targets, standing backlit in the bright hallway. Yet clear as the thought is, I have no impulse to move. Lipranzer, though, is going. Somewhere along he has said, "Motherfucker," and as he is on the way down, he slides in my direction and cuts my legs out from under me. I land, painfully, on an elbow and roll away. We both end up lying on our bellies on the floor, staring at one another from either side of the door. Lipranzer has his pistol gripped with both hands.

Lip closes his eyes and yells at top volume.

"Leon, I am the po-lice! This man is the po-lice! And if your piece is not out here in ten seconds, I am callin this in, they are blasting your ass away before you can say shit. Now I'm gonna start countin!" Lip gets to his knees and presses his back to the wall. He motions with his chin for me to do the same thing. "One!" he yells.

"Man," we hear, "if you are the po-lice, how am I gone know it. Huh? How am I gone know it?"

Out of his windbreaker, Lip draws his creds—the star and his picture i.d. He inches toward the doorway, then allows only his hand to cross its plane as he pitches them in.

"Two!" Lip yells. He is backing away. He points up at the lit exit sign. We are going to run for it soon. "Three!"

"Man, I'm puttin on the lights now. Okay? Okay? But I'm keepin my piece."

"Four!"

"Okay, okay, okay." The gun scutters over the tiles and lands against the molding of the hallway with a thump. A heavy black item. Until it stopped, I thought it was a rat. Light from the apartment angles out of the threshold.

"Out here, Leon," Lip yells. "Down on your knees."

"Oh, man."

"Down!"

"Shee-it." He comes knee-walking right out the doorway, his

arms extended before him. He is quick and comical now. The cops, man. Always so serious.

Lip pats him down. Then he nods. And the three of us get to our feet. Lip snatches his creds back. Leon has on a black sleeveless T-shirt and a red headband. On the bottom, he is wearing only his Jockey shorts. Apparently we roused him. A smooth-skinned, powerfully built man.

"I'm Detective Lipranzer. Special Command. I'd like to come in and talk."

"And who's he, man?"

"He's my goddamned friend." Lip, who still has his gun in his hand, pushes Leon. "Now get back inside." Leon goes first. Lip covers the doorway; with his gun held by his face, he flashes from post to post, staring inside. Then he goes in to search. After a moment he emerges and motions me in. He holsters his pistol again, at his back, under the coat.

"Man, would we have been a headline," I say to him, my first words since this started. "If he was shooting, you might have saved my life."

Lip makes a face, meant to disparage me. "If he was shooting, you were dead by the time I knocked you down."

Inside, Leon is waiting for us. His apartment is a galley kitchen and a couple of rooms. There is no sound of anyone else, but he is seated on a mattress on the floor of the living room. He has put on his pants. A plastic alarm clock and an ashtray are by the bed at his feet.

"We want to ask you a couple of questions," Lip says. "If you're straight, we're out of your face in five minutes."

"Hey, man. You come in here three clock in the mornin. Come on, man. Gimme a break. Call Charley Davis, man, he's my 'torney, man. Talk to him, Jack, cause I'm tired and I'm goin to sleep." He leans back against the wall and closes his eyes.

"You don't need an attorney, Leon."

Leon, still with his eyes closed, laughs. He has heard that one before.

"You got immunity," Lipranzer tells him. "This guy's a P.A. Aren't you?"

Leon opens his eyes in time to see me nod.

"See, now you have immunity."

"7–7–2," says Leon, "5–8–6–8. That's his number, man.

Charley Davis."

"Leon," says Lip, "about eight, nine years ago you dropped fifteen hundred bucks on a deputy P.A. to make some problems you had go away. Do you know what I'm talking about?"

"No chance, man. Okay? I mean, you come bustin into my home, three clock in the mornin, man, askin me shit like that. Am I a fool, man? Huh? Am I a fuckin fool? I'm gone be talkin to some fuckin white-ass po-liceman about shit like that? Come on, man. Go home. Let me sleep." He closes his eyes again.

Lip makes a sound. For some reason I get the idea that he is going back to his gun, and I have an impulse to stop him, but instead he walks slowly over to Leon. He crouches, right at the head of his bed. Leon has watched him approach, but he closes his eyes once Lipranzer has reached his level. Lip takes his index finger and jabs Leon a couple of times in the forearm. Then Lip points at me.

"See that guy? That guy's Rusty Sabich."

Leon opens his eyes. Captain Saint Killer. Right in his living room.

"Bullshit," says Leon.

"Show him your card," says Lipranzer.

I am hardly prepared for this, and I have to empty the pockets of my sportcoat. In the process I discover that my coat is gray across its entire front with the hallway's soil. I have brought along the documents Lip obtained months ago from Leon's court file, my appointment diary, my wallet. In there I find one dog-eared card. I give it to Lipranzer, who hands it to Leon.

"Rusty Sabich," says Lipranzer again.

"So?" asks Leon.

"Leon," says Lip, "how many of your blood brothers do you think have been on his pad, huh? Twenty-five? Thirty-five? How many Saints do you think he's paid to snitch? You go back to sleep, Leon, and Rusty Sabich is gonna get on the phone tomorrow morning. He's gonna tell every one of them how you go out to the Forest to suck off white boys. He's gonna give them who and when and where. He's gonna tell them how they can find out all about this stone faggot deacon they got, name of Leon Wells. Okay? You think this is bullshit? This is not bullshit, my man. This is the guy who let Stapleton Hobberly take a piss in Harukan's face. Have you heard that story, huh? Now, all we

want is five minutes of your time. You tell us the absolute truth
and we're gonna leave you alone. We gotta know a couple of
things. That's all."

Leon has not moved much, but his eyes are wide open as he
listens to Lipranzer. There is no more play in his expression.

"Yeah, man, and next week, you need somethin else and you
be bustin in the door at three clock in the mornin pullin this shit
again."

"We'll tell you right now if we're ever gonna need anythin else.
Just as soon as you answer our questions." What we'll need is for
Leon to come down to court to testify, if he nails Molto. But Lip
knows the ropes; you don't tell them that for a while. "Now don't
bullshit me, Leon. Here's my first question: Did you or did you
not pay fifteen hundred to make that case go away?"

Leon makes a sound. He sits up straight.

"That fuckin Eddie," he says. "You already know, man. Right?
So why you be botherin me?"

"Leon," says Lip quietly. "You heard my question."

"Yeah, man. I paid fifteen hundred."

My heartbeat has become very solid now. Thump thump. I
expect to see my pocket jumping when I look down at my shirt.

I speak for the first time.

"Did the woman have anything to do with it? Carolyn? The
probation officer?"

Leon laughs. "Yeah, man. You might say that."

"What?"

"Come on, man," he says. "Don't shit me. That bitch set the
whole thing up, man. You know that. She tell me I don't have to
be mopin round, she know how to take care of everythin. Real
smooth. Real smooth. Man, I bet she did it a hundred times. Tell
me where to go. How to bring the bread, man. Very cold lady.
You hear me?"

"I do." I crouch down now like Lipranzer. "And was she there
when you made the drop?"

"Right there. Sittin right there. Very cool. You know, man;
'How you do. Sit right there.' Then the dude start talkin."

"He was behind you?"

"You got it. She be tellin me when I come in. Don't turn round,
just do what the man say."

"And he told you to put it in his desk?"

"No, man. The desk where I was. He say just leave it in the top drawer."

"That's what I mean. It was the P.A.'s desk, right?"

"Yeah. That desk."

"And you paid him, right?" asks Lipranzer. "The P.A.?" Leon looks at him with irritation.

"No, man. I ain't gone be payin no little toad P.A. Am I a fool? He gone take my bread, man, and be sayin, Oh no, can't do it, just got the word from downtown. I heard enough of that shit."

Lipranzer looks over to me. He has not gotten it yet. But I have. Just now. Finally. God, am I dense. Dense.

"So who was it?" asks Lip.

Leon mugs. He does not like to tell a policeman anything he does not already know. I say it for him.

"The judge, Lip. Leon paid the judge. Right?"

Leon nods. "Black dude. Was him, too, man. Behind me? I could tell the voice when I heard him in court. "Leon snaps his fingers, trying to get the name. But there is not any need for him to bother. It's right on the order of dismissal. I take it out of my pocket to check. There's no missing that signature. I've seen it dozens of times in the last two months. It's as distinctive as everything else Larren does.

"So what is it?" Lip asks. It is nearly five now and we are sitting in Wally's, an all-night joint by the river. They used to be famous for doughnut holes, before the national chains got hold of that idea, too. "Larren's porkin her and takin the money to keep her in style?"

Lip is still wired. On the way here, he stopped at some hole in the wall, a blind pig he knew about, and came out with a half pint of peach brandy, of all things. He drank it down like a Coke. He still had not shaken off our initial encounter at the doorway.

God, he said to me. Sometimes I hate bein a cop.

Now I shake my head at his questions. I don't know. The only thing I have figured out for certain in the last hour is that this is what Kenneally didn't want to tell me when I saw him last week. That Larren was taking. That's what pissed off the coppers back then. The judge was doing it, too.

"What about Molto?" asks Lip. "You figure he was in?"

"I figure he was out. I don't see Larren Lyttle in any triangles. Nico said Molto always looked up to Carolyn. She probably asked him to dismiss cases and he just obliged. I'm sure he had the hots for her like everyone else." All very Catholic and suppressed, of course. That would make sense, too. That's the fuel that's kept Molto's engine running at high speed. Unresolved passion.

We talk it over like this for most of an hour. Eventually it gets late enough to have breakfast and we both order eggs. The sun is coming up now, over the river, that spectacular profusion of rosecolored light.

I suddenly think of something and laugh. I laugh too hard, with an embarrassing lack of control. A bout of juvenile hilarity. My thought is ridiculous, not really funny at all. But it has been a long and very odd day.

"What?" Lip asks.

"All these years I've known you, and it never really dawned on me."

"What's that?"

I start laughing again. It's a moment before I can speak.

"I never realized you carry a gun."

Barbara rolls over as I approach the side of the bed in my pajamas.

"Are you getting up now?" She squints toward the clock. It is 6:30. "It's early, isn't it?"

"I'm going to bed," I tell her.

She starts and rolls to her elbow, but I wave that it is not worth talking about. I do not think I will sleep, but I do. I dream of my father in jail.

Barbara waits until the last minute to wake me, and we have to race. The traffic on the bridge is thick, and court is already in session when we arrive. Kemp and the two prosecutors are before the judge. Nico is talking. He looks dour and drawn, and his manner in addressing the judge can only be described as agitated.

I sit down next to Stern. Barbara had called to tell him we would be late, but she diplomatically omitted any mention of why. I spend the first moments of my whispered conference with Sandy assuring him that we are both in good health. Then he explains what is happening:

"The prosecution has entered their hour of desperation. I will tell you about it when the judge breaks. They want Molto to testify."

I thought that was what Nico was talking about. When he is done exhorting the judge, Larren looks down and says simply, "No."

"Your Honor—"

"Mr. Delay Guardia, we went over this carefully the first day of the trial. You may not call Mr. Molto."

"Judge, we had no idea—"

"Mr. Delay Guardia, if I were inclined to allow Mr. Molto to testify, then I oughta declare a mistrial right now, because if this case ever got to the court of appeals—*ever*, I say hypothetically—but if it ever got there, they would turn it around and send it right back. Mr. Stern asked the first day of trial about Mr. Molto's testimony and you said No how and No way, and that's how it stands."

"Judge, you said that we would be entitled to some leeway if the defense proceeded with this frame-up theory. You said that."

"And I allowed you to stand before the jury and make one entirely improper statement in their presence. Do you recall what occurred while Mr. Horgan was on the witness stand? But I should have had more faith in Mr. Stern's professional acumen than to suppose he would venture down that road without reason. I didn't know then, Mr. Della Guardia, that the state's chief piece of evidence was going to disappear after last being seen with Mr. Molto. I didn't know that Mr. Molto and the chief pathologist were going to manufacture evidence, or testimony— and I tell you, sir, that is a reasonable interpretation of the events of yesterday. I'm still considering the question of what happens with Mr. Molto. But one thing that isn't gonna happen is that he gets up on the witness stand and makes matters worse. Now, what's the other thing you wanted to bring up?"

Nico is silent, his head bowed for a second. When he straightens up, he takes an instant to adjust his jacket.

"Judge, we're going to call a new witness."

"Who is that?"

"Dr. Miles Robinson, Mr. Sabich's psychiatrist. He was on our witness list. We omitted him from the order of proof, but I informed Mr. Stern about the change last night."

Beside Stern, I have tensed. He has his hand on my arm to prevent a more precipitous reaction.

"What the hell is this?" I whisper.

"I was going to discuss this with you this morning," says Stern quietly. "I've spoken with the doctor. I will give you my estimate of what the prosecutors are up to in a moment."

"And what's the problem?" asks Larren. "Mr. Stern objects to calling the witness without notice?"

Stern stands. "No, Your Honor. I object to the witness's

testimony, but not on that basis."

"State your objection, Mr. Stern."

"Your Honor. We object on two grounds. Whatever the enlightened view may be of psychotherapy, many persons continue to regard it as a stigma. This testimony therefore risks serious prejudice to Mr. Sabich. More important, I expect that Mr. Molto—who as I understand it will be questioning Dr. Robinson—will elicit material that would violate the physician-patient privilege."

"I see," Larren says again. "Are you moving to suppress?"

Stern looks down at me. Something is on his mind. He leans in my direction, then seems to think better of it.

"Your Honor—my remarks are likely to give offense, for which I apologize. But I believe they are appropriate and necessary to articulating my client's interests. Judge Lyttle, I question the prosecutors' motives in offering this proof. I perceive no factual basis for overcoming the testimonial privilege that prevents a physician, certainly a psychotherapist, from testifying about his treatment-oriented conversations with a patient. I believe that this testimony is offered knowing that the defense must move to suppress it, and that the court must allow that motion. When that occurs, the prosecutors will have someone else to blame when this case reaches the end for which we all now know it is destined."

Nico becomes fiery. He pounds on the podium, incensed by Stern's suggestion that he and Molto are out to trick-bag the judge.

"I deny that," he says. "I deny that! I think that is an outrage!" He does another of his stomping routines, revolving away, and ends up at the prosecutors' table, staring fiercely at Stern as he drinks a cup of water.

Larren is quiet for a long time. When he speaks he makes no comment on what Stern has suggested.

"Mr. Della Guardia, on what basis will you seek to overcome the privilege?"

Nico and Molto confer. "Your Honor, we expect the evidence to show that Mr. Sabich saw Dr. Robinson on only a few occasions. As a result we believe that Mr. Sabich's statements were not for the purpose of seeking treatment and are outside the privilege."

I have heard all I can handle. Aloud, if under my breath, I remark, "What bullshit."

Perhaps the judge hears me. Certainly he looks in my direction.

"Listen here," says Larren, "this case hasn't gone very well for the state. Any jackass would know that, and nobody here is a jackass. But if you think, Mr. Delay Guardia, that I'm gonna let you elicit privileged testimony so that you can try to pull a rabbit out of a hat, you better have another think or two. I can't and I won't allow that. Now, sir, I'm not gonna suppress this testimony, I don't have any comments on Mr. Stern's observations. I don't know whether he's right. I will only say that it is appropriate to adjudicate a claim of privilege on a question-by-question basis. If you wanna put this witness on in the jury's presence, be my guest. But I'll tell you right now that you're on the edge as it is. The conduct of one of the prosecutors has been deplorable. And if he starts attempting to elicit privileged material in the jury's presence, then you're at your peril. Have you conferred with Dr. Robinson so that you know the permissible areas of inquiry?"

"Dr. Robinson has refused to meet with us."

"Well, good for him," says Larren. "You do what you want, Mr. Delay Guardia. But you better have a lot you can get from this witness. Because I can only imagine what this jury is thinkin by now."

Nico asks for a moment to confer. He and Molto walk together to a corner of the courtroom. Tommy is vehement. He has a high color, and he swings his hands emphatically. I am not surprised when Nico announces that they intend to proceed.

So the jury is brought back to the box and Miles Robinson comes to the witness stand. He is in his mid-sixties, trim, with white hair cropped very close. He is soft-spoken and exceedingly dignified. In another era, he would have been called an octaroon. He is fairer than I am, but he is black. I met him briefly many years ago when he was called as a witness in an insanity case. The nation's leading expert on memory loss. He is a full professor at the medical school at the U., co-chair of the Psychiatry Department. When I had my troubles, he seemed pretty clearly to be the best shrink I could think of.

"Do you know Rusty Sabich?" Molto asks, as soon as Robinson has stated his name, his office address, and his profession.

Dr. Robinson turns to the judge.

"Do I have to answer that, Your Honor?"

Larren leans over. He speaks kindly.

"Dr. Robinson, Mr. Stern over there"—he points—"represents Mr. Sabich. Anything he does not think you ought to be obliged to answer, he will object to. Otherwise, you should answer the questions posed. Don't worry now. He's highly qualified."

"We've spoken," says Robinson.

"Very good, then," says the judge. "Reread the question, please," Larren tells the court reporter.

"Yes," says Robinson when that has been done.

"How do you know him?"

"He was my patient."

"How many times did you see him?"

"I checked my records last night. Five times."

"From when to when?"

"February to April of this year. April third was the last time."

"April third?" asks Molto. He faces the jury, who refuse to look at him. He means, however, to call attention to the fact that my last session was two days after the murder.

"Yes, sir."

"Did Mr. Sabich ever discuss Carolyn Polhemus with you?"

The doctor-patient privilege protects conversations, not acts. Up until now Molto has not asked Robinson to repeat anything I have said. With this question, however, Stern quietly comes to his feet.

"Objection," he says.

"Sustained," says the judge distinctly. He has folded his arms over his chest, and he glares down at Molto. It is clear that he shares Sandy's perception of the motives here. And he has conceived of his own politic compromise. He will let Robinson take the stand, and then sustain objections to any questions of consequence.

"Your Honor, may I have the basis of that ruling?" asks Molto. He looks up to the bench defiantly. Lord, how these men hate each other. By now it would require an archaeological dig to get through the sedimentary layers of resentments built up over the years. Some of it has to have been Carolyn. Molto is too primitive not to have been jealous. Did he know, back in their days in the North Branch, about the other dimension to Larren's relations with her? I puzzled on that most of the night. Who knew what about whom back then? And what does Larren think Molto knows now? Tangled webs. Whatever else, it is clear that the dispute between these men by now has nothing to do with me.

"Mr. Molto, you know the basis of the ruling. It was discussed before the jury entered. You have established a physician-patient relationship. Any communications are privileged. And if you question another of my rulings in the jury's presence, sir, your examination will end. Proceed."

"Dr. Robinson, isn't it true that Mr. Sabich stopped seeing you?"

"Yes, sir."

"Your treatment of him ceased?"

"Yes, sir."

"Judge, I submit that these conversations are not privileged."

"You are in contempt, Mr. Molto. Proceed with your examination."

Molto looks over to Nico. Then he lets it all out. He considers his armaments and reaches for the nuclear bomb.

"Did Rusty Sabich ever tell you that he had killed Carolyn Polhemus?" There is the abrupt sound of people gasping throughout the courtroom. But I realize now why Nico was pounding on the podium. This is the question they brought Robinson here to answer. Nothing marginal like whether I used to sleep with her. They are taking one last blind shot. The judge, however, is enraged.

"That is all," he screams. "That is all! I have had it with you, Mr. Molto. Had it! If the other questions are privileged, how isn't that one?"

I whisper to Stern. He says to me, "No," and I say to him, "Yes," and I actually take his elbow and push him to his feet. There is a rare tone of uncertainty as he speaks.

"Your Honor, we would not object to the question, as phrased, being answered."

Larren and Molto are both slow to respond, the judge because of his wrath and Molto in sheer confusion. They both finally comprehend at the same time.

Molto says, "I move to withdraw the question."

But the judge knows what is occurring.

"No, sir. You will not make an inquiry so prejudicial in the presence of the jury and then seek to withdraw it. So the record is clear, Mr. Stern, are you waiving the privilege?"

Stern clears his throat.

"Your Honor, the question does seek to elicit privileged communications, but in my view the question, as framed, can be answered without invading the privilege."

"I see," says Larren. "Well, I suppose that's right. If it goes one way. You ready to take your chances?"

Stern's eyes trail off toward me for an instant, but he responds clearly, "Yes, Your Honor."

"Well, let's listen to the answer, then. We'll know where we stand. Ms. Court Reporter, would you please read back Mr. Molto's last question."

She stands, with the stenographic tape in her hand. She reads in a flat voice:

"Question by Mr. Molto: 'Did Rusty Sabich ever tell you that he had killed Carolyn Polhemus?'"

Larren holds up a hand so that the court reporter can resume her seat and prepare to take down the response. Then the judge nods to the witness.

"The answer to the question," says Robinson in his measured way, "is no. Mr. Sabich never told me anything like that."

The courtroom ruffles in a fashion that it has not to date, with an air of release. The jurors nod. The schoolteacher smiles at me.

Molto will never give up.

"Did you ever speak in any way about the subject of murdering Ms. Polhemus?"

"Objection to that question and to all further questions concerning communication between Mr. Sabich and the doctor."

"The objection is sustained. The objection is taken as a limiting motion and is granted. Any further inquiry being prohibited or irrelevant to these proceedings, I intend to terminate this examination. Dr. Robinson, you are excused."

"Your Honor!" shouts Molto. But Nico instantly has him by the arm. He leads Tommy away from the podium, as they exchange words. Nico nods to humor him, but he seems to have a firmness, a resolve that does not partake of Tommy's outrage.

The judge looks only at Nico.

"Do I take it, Mr. Delay Guardia, that the state rests?"

Nico answers. "Yes, Judge. On behalf of the people of Kindle County, the state rests."

Larren will dismiss the jury now for the weekend and hear the motion for a directed verdict. He turns to them:

"Ladies and gentlemen, I would ordinarily ask you to leave the courtroom at this point in time. But I am not going to do that. Your service in this case is now over—"

I do not understand these words at first, but when I feel Jamie Kemp's arms around me, then Stern's, I know what has occurred. My trial is over. The judge has gone on speaking. He tells the jurors that they may stay if they please. I am weeping. I put my head down on the table for a moment. I am sobbing, but I lift my head to listen, as Larren Lyttle sets me free.

He is addressing the jury:

"I have reflected on this case at length over the last twenty-four hours. At this time, normally a defense lawyer makes a motion for a judgment of acquittal. And most often a judge decides to let the case proceed. Usually there is enough evidence so that a reasonable jury might find a defendant guilty. I think it's fair to say that there ought to be. No man ought to be brought to trial without sufficient evidence that some fair people might conclude beyond a reasonable doubt that he is guilty. I think justice requires that. And I think that in this case justice has not been done. I understand the prosecutors have suspicions. Before yesterday, I might even have said that there were rasonable grounds for suspicion. Now I'm not so sure of that. But I cannot let you deliberate on evidence like this, which is so clearly inadequate. It would be unfair to you and—most importantly—to Mr. Sabich. No person should be held on trial on evidence such as this. I have no doubt that your verdict would be a ringing not guilty. But Mr. Sabich should not have to live with this specter a moment longer. There is no proof of motive here, no concrete evidence that there was ever an intimate relationship. There is no effective proof, so far as I am concerned, after yesterday, to give any reasonable person grounds to believe that Mr. Sabich even had carnal relations with Ms. Polhemus on the night of her death. And, as we have just seen, there is not a shred of direct proof that he murdered Ms. Polhemus. Perhaps he was there that night. The state might be entitled to that inference. If the prosecutors had ever found that glass, I might be more confident. But under all the circumstances, I cannot let the case proceed.

"Your Honor." Nico is on his feet.

"Mr. Della Guardia, I understand you are despairing at this time, but I am speaking and I would like you to hear me out."

"Your Honor—"

"I have a few words to say about Mr. Molto."

"Judge, I want to move to dismiss."

Larren starts, actually draws back. In the courtroom, there is a larger stir and then the serial sound of people moving. I know without looking back that the reporters are fleeing for their phones. The TV guys will have to get their camera vans down here. Nobody was planning for the shit to hit the fan at this point. Larren bangs his gavel and demands order. Then he opens his large hand to indicate that Nico may proceed.

"Judge, I just wanted to say a couple of things. First, it seems like a lot of people have started to think that this case is some kind of frame-up or sham. I deny that. I want to deny that. On behalf of all members of the prosecution. I think we were right to bring this case—"

"You had a motion, Mr. Delay Guardia?"

"Yes, Judge. I hoped when I came to court this morning that you would let the case go to the jury. Some judges would, I think. I think that's the right thing. But some judges probably wouldn't. And since you've apparently made up your mind—"

"I certainly have."

"For Mr. Sabich's sake, I don't think there should be any question about whether this was a proper legal decision on your part or not. I disagree with you. We do disagree. But I don't think it's fair to pretend that I think you're outside the law. And I certainly don't want anyone thinking I'm looking for excuses." Nico turns, if only barely, to look over his shoulder in the direction of Stern. "So for those reasons, I would like to accept your judgment and move to dismiss this case."

"That motion is allowed."

Larren stands.

"Mr. Sabich, you are discharged. I cannot tell you how sorry I am that any of this has taken place. Not even the pleasure of seeing you free can make up for this disgrace to the cause of justice. I wish you Godspeed."

He bangs his gavel. "Case dismissed," he says, and leaves.

36

Turmoil. My wife. My lawyers. Reporters. Onlookers, I do not
know. They all wish to touch me. Barbara is the first. The feeling
of her arms around me so firmly, her breasts girdled against me,
her pelvis squeezed against mine is astonishingly stimulating.
Perhaps this is the first sign of the regeneration of my life.

"I am so glad." She kisses me. "I am so glad for you, Rusty."

She turns from me and hugs Stern.

Today, I elect to make my once-only exit through the heating
plant. I do not wish to face the press's disordered melee. I gather
Barbara, Stern, and Kemp toward the end of the lobby and then
we drop out of sight. But of course there is no escaping. Another
gaggle is waiting when we reach Stern's building. We make our
way upstairs with little comment. From somewhere a luncheon
has appeared in the conference room, but there is no opportunity to eat. The phones ring. And the secretaries soon report that
the reception room is a mob scene, with reporters spilling out
into the halls. The hungry monster must be fed. I cannot deny
Stern this moment. He deserves it, and the consequences of this
kind of success in a celebrated case, in terms of both economics
and professional stature, will enlarge Stern's career for years to
come. He is now a lawyer of national standing.

And so, after half a corned-beef sandwich, we all descend to
the lobby of the building to again confront the jostling, shouting
crowd of reporters, the microphones, the recorders, the brilliant
lights that rise up around me like a dozen new suns. Stern
speaks first, then me. "I don't think that anybody, under these
circumstances, can say anything adequate, especially in a short
period of time. I am very relieved that this is over. I will never

fully understand how it happened in the first place. I am grateful that I was represented by the best lawyer on the face of the earth." I dodge the questions about Della Guardia. I am still not settled in my own mind. There is already a large part of me that is content with the idea that he was merely doing his job. No one asks about Larren, and I do not mention his name. In spite of my gratitude, I doubt that after last night I could bring myself to praise him.

Back upstairs, there is now champagne, the same vintage as Kemp popped the night before. Was Stern preparing for victory, or does he always keep a case on ice? There are still many visitors in the offices. I stand among them with Kemp and Stern and drink toasts to Sandy. Clara is here, Sandy's wife. Mac arrives. She weeps as she embraces me in her chair.

"I never had any doubt," she says.

Barbara finds me to say that she is going to leave. She has some hope that Nat's return can be advanced one day. Perhaps the camp director can arrange a seat on the DC-3 that flies back and forth from Skageon. This will require many phone calls. I see her out through the lobby. She embraces me again. "I am so relieved," she says, "so, so glad it turned out this way." But something between us is impenetrably sad. I cannot, right now, fully imagine Barbara's inner states, but I think that even in this moment of rapturous gratefulness and relief she recognizes that something suspended still remains. In the aftermath of all of this, to go beyond our old troubles will require a treacherous journey across nearly unspannable chasms to grace and forgiveness.

In Stern's offices people keep arriving. A number of cops are here, lawyers around town who have come to congratulate Sandy and me. I feel ill at ease among the many outsiders, so few of whom I know. And my initial euphoria is long past, given way to a suppressed melancholy. At first I believe I am exhausted, and full of pity for myself. But eventually I recognize that my disturbance seems to arise, like black oil percolating from the earth, from something more particular, an idea that seems to demand time for contemplation, and quietly as I can, I leave. I do not say that I am going. I slip out with the excuse that I am finding the head. Then I drift out of the building. It is late afternoon. The shadows are longer and off the river a breeze is up that is rich and full of summer.

The night editions of the papers are on the stands. The *Tribune* head is half a page: JUDGE FREES SABICH. And the kicker: Calls Prosecution 'A Disgrace.' I pay my quarter. "Decrying a 'disgrace to the cause of justice' Kindle County Superior Court Judge Larren Lyttle today dismissed murder charges against Rōzať K. Sabich, former Chief Deputy in the Kindle County Prosecuting Attorney's Office, ending Sabich's eight-day-old trial. Judge Lyttle sharply criticized the case presented by Kindle County Prosecuting Attorney Nico Della Guardia and stated at one point that he believed some of the evidence against Sabich, a former political rival of Della Guardia's, was manufactured by the prosecution." Both papers play it the same way. Nico takes it in the chops. A made-up case against a past political opponent. Ugly stuff. It will run coast to coast. My friend Nico will be doing the hurt dance for a long time to come. The press, blind as ever to half tones or grays, makes no mention of Nico's final gesture of decency in dismissing the case.

I go down to the river. The city is strangely quiet tonight. A new place with outdoor tables on the riverbank is open and I have two beers and a sandwich. I hold the sports page up before me, a way to avoid responding to the lingering gazes of occasional passersby, but for the most part I am engaged in a kind of numb reflection. I call Barbara near six, but there is no answer. I hope she is on the way to the airport. I want to get home to see Nat. But before that there is one stop I have to make.

The front door is open when I return to Stern's office, but the suite is almost deserted. I hear only one voice, which I know just by its word-blank rumble to be Stern's. I follow the sound to Sandy's rich office. From what I hear in the hallway, I take it that he is discussing another lawsuit. The lawyer's life, I think, as I catch sight of him there. This morning Sandy Stern won the best-known case of his career; tonight he is working. There is a brief open before him while he talks on the phone. Copies of the afternoon editions of both papers have been tossed aside onto the sofa.

"Ah yes," he says, "Rusty has just come in now. Yes. No later than ten tomorrow morning. I promise." He replaces the receiver. "A client," he says. "So, I see you returned."

"I'm sorry I ran out."

Sandy raises a hand. No explanation is needed.

"But I wanted to see you," I tell him.

"That happens," says Stern. "I have clients, after trials such as this, very intense experiences, who are coming back for days, weeks really. It is very difficult to believe it is over."

"That's sort of what I'd like to talk about," I say. "May I?" I take one of Sandy's cigars, which he has often offered. He joins me and selects one as I hold his humidor. We smoke, lawyer and client. "I wanted to thank you."

Sandy raises his hand the same way he did before, I tell him how much I admired his defense of me, how seldom I was inclined to second-guess. You are, I say, the very best. This praise appears to run over Sandy with the soothing effect of a bath of warm milk. With this last compliment he does little more than laugh and tip his cigar, one of his courtly gestures, helpless before the truth.

"I also have been thinking about things, and I'd like to know what happened in that courtroom today."

"Today?" asks Sandy. "Today you were acquitted of serious charges."

"No, no," I say, "I want to know what really happened. Yesterday you explained to me why Larren would have to let the case go to the jury. And today he acquitted me, without so much as a motion from the defense."

"Rusty, I made an estimate of what the judge might think. What lawyer do you know who possesses the ability to always correctly predict judicial inclinations? Judge Lyttle decided not to expose you to the risk of an unsupported jury verdict, which might have increased the pressure on him to turn away from what he thought was right. We should both be grateful to him for his perspicacity and his fortitude."

"Last night your estimate was that the state's case was good enough to go to the jury."

"Rusty, I am by nature pessimistic. Certainly you cannot take me to task for my discipline. If I had predicted victory and the result were otherwise, I could understand your concern. This I do not."

"Don't you?"

"We both know that the prosecution's case was not strong to start and that it weakened as it progressed. Some rulings were favorable. Some witnesses balked. Some cross-examinations succeeded. One piece of evidence was unaccounted for. Another was clearly mischaracterized. The state case failed. We have each seen that happen before on many occasions. And matters went from bad to worse for them today. Consider Dr. Robinson's testimony this morning. That was very telling."

"You really think so? I didn't tell him I killed Carolyn. So what? I'm a lawyer. A prosecutor. I know better than to confess to anyone."

"But to visit a psychiatrist two days after the murder, to have the advantage of this most intimate of professional relationships and to make no culpable statement of any kind—Rusty, this was significant proof, elicited by the prosecution, no less. Perhaps if I had known of it, I would have not made the prediction which I did last night." Sandy frowns somewhat; his eyes are slightly averted. "At a moment like this, Rusty, of such sudden change, I have seen persons react strangely. You should not allow your thoughts about events themselves to cloud your appraisal of matters."

Very diplomatic. Don't let the fact that you killed her influence your judgment as a lawyer. This mild betrayal of me, subtle though it is, is so much out of character that I am now certain I am right.

"I've been in these courtrooms a dozen years now, Sandy. Something is wrong."

Stern smiles. He puts down his cigar. He clasps his hands.

"There is nothing wrong here. You are acquitted. The system so operates. Go home to your wife. Is Nathaniel back yet? That should be a marvelous reunion for all of you."

I refuse to be distracted. "Sandy, what accounts for what happened today?"

"The evidence. Your lawyer. The lawyers on the other side. Your own good character, which was well known to the judge. Rusty, what else is it that you think I can tell you?"

"I think you know what I know," I tell him.

"Which, Rusty, is what?"

"About the B file. About Larren and Carolyn. About the fact that she used to carry money to him."

Shock—acute surprise—is not in Sandy Stern's emotional range. His faith in his own worldliness is such that he would never allow anything to so affect him. But his expression now gathers intensity. His mouth draws. And he turns his cigar toward him and considers the ash before he looks back to me.

"Rusty, with all respect, you have been through a great deal. I am your friend. But I am also your lawyer. Lawyer. I keep your secrets. But I do not tell you mine."

"I can handle the facts, Sandy. I assure you I can. I've dealt with a lot the last few months. And as you told me last night, I'm very good at keeping a secret. I just have this bizarre commitment to learning the truth. I'd like my sense of irony complete."

I wait and Stern at last gets to his feet.

"I see the problem. You worry about the judge's integrity."

"With cause, wouldn't you say?"

"No, I would not agree." Stern perches on the sofa arm, a white nubby fabric. He takes a moment to loosen his tie. "Rusty, what I say to you I know. How I know is not a concern for you. I have had many clients. Persons worry. They seek a lawyer's advice at times. That is all. And we speak now tonight and these things are never spoken of again by either of us. For my part, I tell you now, I have never said any of these things. Understood?"

"Very well."

"You doubt Larren's character. You must forgive me, Rusty, a moment of philosophy, but not all human misbehavior is the result of gross defects of character. Circumstances matter, too. Temptation, if you will allow an old-fashioned word. I have known Larren throughout my career and I tell you that he was not himself. His divorce left him in a state of disorder. He was drinking much too heavily. I understood he was gambling. He had fallen into this relationship with a beautiful and self-seeking woman. And his professional life was shattered. He had given up his practice when it was at its zenith, both in terms of his prominence and its financial rewards. I am sure he meant by this change to make up for the reversals in his personal life, and instead he found himself confined as an act of political vengeance in a judicial dumping zone, adjudicating matters of picayune importance which had no relation to what had attracted him to the bench at the outset. Larren is a powerful mind, able, and he heard for years about nothing but traffic tickets, tavern brawls, sexual interludes in the Forest—matters at the periphery of public justice. All of these cases end the same way, with the defendant discharged. It is only a question of labels: Case dismissed. Pre-trial supervision. Post-trial probation. The defendant in any event returns home. And Larren was in an environment whose thoroughgoing corruption was always one of this city's most distressing secrets. The bondsmen. The policemen. The probation officers. The lawyers. The North Branch was a beehive of illicit dealing. Do you think, Rusty, that Larren Lyttle was the first judge in the North Branch courthouse to fall by the wayside?"

"You can't be apologizing for him," I say, and Stern's look becomes fomented—severe.

"Not for a moment," he says strongly. "Not for a moment. I do not for a moment condone what we speak of. It is a disgrace." Our public institutions crumble from such conduct. If such matters had been the object of proper accusation and proof, and were I the judge before whom they were tried, the prison sentences would be lengthy. Probably lifelong. Whatever my affinities or affections.

"But what happened happened in the past. Long in the past. Judge Lyttle, I tell you, would rather die—I mean this sincerely—die rather than corrupt his office in the Superior Court. This judgment is heartfelt and not merely a lawyer's sanctimony about a judge."

"My experience as a prosecutor, Sandy, was that people aren't usually just a little corrupt. It's a progressive disease."

"This is an episode in the past, Rusty."

"You're confident it's over?"

"Very."

"Is that another story, too? How it ended?"

"Rusty, you must understand that I do not have a historian's knowledge. I heard personalized accounts from certain individuals."

"How did it end, Sandy?"

He looks down at me from the vantage of the sofa arm. His hands are on his knees. His face is without humor. Confidences are the core of Sandy Stern's professional life. To him these are intimate and sacred matters.

"My understanding," he says finally, "is that Raymond Horgan became knowledgeable of what was occurring and demanded that it cease. Some police in the 32nd District began to assemble evidence. Other persons with knowledge of that had deep fears that any probing of corruption in the North Branch would ultimately prove the undoing of many persons besides Judge Lyttle. It was frankly from one or two of these concerned persons that I heard this account. At any rate, they determined that the P.A. should properly be advised of an ensuing investigation." Stern looks off for a moment. "Perhaps," he says, with the most remote of smiles, "that was their lawyer's advice. Privately, I'm sure, it was calculated that Horgan would naturally inform his old friend of the perils to which he was exposed and counsel him at all costs to stop. I believe that is what occurred. I emphasize that I do not know whether or not I am correct. As you no doubt perceive, I am most uncomfortable with this kind of conversation, and I have never made any effort to confirm this information."

I should have figured that Horgan was in the middle of this somehow. I take a minute. What is this feeling? Something between disappointment and derision.

"You know," I say, "there was a time when I thought Raymond Horgan and Larren Lyttle were heroes."

"With justification. They did many heroic things, Rusty. Many."

"And what about Molto? Did you ever hear anything about him?"

Stern shakes his head no.

"He was unsuspecting, as far as I know. It is difficult to believe that was really the case. Perhaps he was exposed to others' suspicions and refused to believe them. It is my understanding that he himself was somewhat in Carolyn's thrall. A lapdog. A devotee. I am sure she was able to manipulate him. In Latin America, one sees—or saw, when I was a young man—I have no idea of what transpires now—but when I was young I frequently met women of Carolyn's type, women who used their sensuality with what we might call an aggressive twist. In this day and age, there is something more troubling about a woman with such an old-fashioned and oblique approach to the avenues of power. It seems more sinister. But she was very skillful."

"She was a lot of things," I say. Ah, Carolyn, I suddenly think, with unbearable sadness. What was it that I wanted with you, Carolyn? Something in the moment makes me think that Stern has not quite got her right. Perhaps it is the past ordeal and its extraordinary end today; maybe it's amnesty week in Kindle County—no one may be blamed; perhaps it is only more of the same debased obsession—yet for whatever reason, even after all of it—*all* of it—as I sit here amid the cigar smoke and soft furniture, I still feel for her, and feel most of all now sympathy. It is possible that I misjudged Carolyn entirely. Perhaps she suffered from some birth defect, like a newborn come into the world with certain organs missing. Perhaps the feeling parts were absent in her, or subject to some congenital atrophy. But I do not believe that. She was, I think, like so many of the hurt and maimed who have passed before me: the synapses and receptors were in working order on her heart and feelings—but they were overloaded by the need to give solace to herself. Her pain. Her pain! She was like a spider caught in her own web. In the end, in her own monumental way, she must have been in torment. Surely that was no accident. I can only guess about the causes; what forge of cruelty produced her. I do not know. But there was some form of abuse, some long-practiced meanness from which she clearly meant to escape. She sought to re-create herself. She took on every lustrous role. A moll. A star. A person of causes. A conquistadora of wayward passion. A clever, hard-nosed prosecutrix, determined to master and punish those lesser types who could not contain ugly and violent impulse. But no disguise could change her. The heredity of abuse is so often more abuse. Whatever cruelty made her, she took in and, with self-delusion, wild excuses, but always, I would think, some straining residuum of pain, turned it back out into the world.

"And so," asks Stern. "Are you better satisfied?"

"About Larren?"

"What else?" He has apparently misinterpreted my moment of reflection.

"I'm hardly satisfied, Sandy. He had no business presiding over this case. He should have excused himself the minute it was assigned to him."

"Perhaps that is so, Rusty, but let me remind you that Judge Lyttle had no idea when this case began that that file—the B file, as you call it—was going to be an element of your defense."

"You did."

"Me?" Stern waves at some of the smoke and passes a remark in Spanish that I do not understand. "Am I, too, the target of complaint? Certainly you do not think that I planned to focus on that file at the threshold? And even then, Rusty, was I to make a motion for Judge Lyttle to excuse himself? How would you have framed it? The defendant asks the court to recuse itself because the alleged victim was once Your Honor's lover and partner in crime? Some matters are not for courtroom pleading. Really, Rusty. I do not mean to appear the cynic. And I share your concern for professional standards. But I suggest again that you are reacting to the shock of events. This punctiliousness, under the circumstances, is a bit surprising."

"I don't mean to be a prig. If I am, I apologize. But I'm not concerned about form or technicalities. I have the feeling things were bent well out of shape."

Stern draws back, removing his cigar. It is a long, slow motion meant to show surprise. But it is no longer opening night. I have seen all of Sandy Stern's best moves a number of times and I don't buy this one.

"Sandy, I've been thinking hard about things in the last few hours. Larren Lyttle's career was over if the circumstances of the B file were fully explored. And you used every opportunity to tell him that you intended to do just that."

"Really, Rusty. You must know things that I do not. I saw nothing to indicate that Judge Lyttle fully understood the import of that file. You must remember that its contents were never described in testimony. The file itself was never even in the courtroom."

"Sandy, would you be offended if I told you that I still don't think you're sharing everything with me?"

"Ah," says Stern. "We have been too long together on this case. You begin, Rusty, to sound something like Clara." He smiles, but I again refuse to be dissuaded.

"Sandy, it took a long time for this to sink in. I admit that. For a while I thought that it was just a bizarre coincidence. You know, I thought it was just lucky that your harping on that file took advantage of Larren's vulnerability. But, I realize now, that's not possible. You *meant* to catch the judge's attention. There was no other reason for you to keep referring to that file. The last time you did it—when Lip was on the stand?—we were way past the point where you needed to raise doubts about Tommy. By then, you knew all about Kumagai. You knew you were going to blow Molto away with that. But you went out of your way again to tell the judge we were going to offer proof about the file the first chance we got. You must have told him that, one way or the other, half a dozen times. You wanted Larren to believe that we were hell-bent on turning that file inside out in public. That's why you mentioned that whole business of a frame-up while Horgan was on cross. You wanted to create a record in which Larren would think he had no proper way to keep you from going ahead. And yet when you sat down with me to talk about a defense, you didn't mention word one about the file. We had nothing to offer."

Stern is silent. "You are a fine investigator, Rusty," he says at last.

"And you're very flattering. Actually, I've had the feeling lately that I was fairly dull. There are still a lot of things I haven't figured out. Like what you mentioned a second ago. How *did* you know that Larren would realize that the B file concerned a case where he'd been dirty? What else is there to the story?"

Stern and I stare at each other for a moment. His look is deeper and more complex than ever. If he is disconcerted, it is well concealed.

"There is no more to tell, Rusty," he says at last. "I made certain assumptions, particularly when I saw the judge's reactions with Horgan on the witness stand. They are very close, of course, and as I say, it is my understanding that Raymond would have been quite sensitive to the implications of that file. It seemed likely to me that he and Larren must have communicated about it sometime in the past. But I have no special knowledge. Just a lawyer's intuition."

Horgan. That was what I missed. Raymond had to have told Larren about that file long ago. Stern is correct. For a moment I spin out the further calculations that follow. But that is not for now. I want to clear the books first with Stern.

"So let me see if I get it," I tell him. "You wouldn't dream of directly threatening the judge with exposure. That could be counterproductive, even disastrous. And it's simply not Stern's style. You had to find your own perfect and subtle way of doing things. You wanted Larren to worry about the file, but to believe that he alone perceived his problem. And so, at all moments you made it appear that the defense was in pursuit of Tommy Molto. You acted as if you thought he was the bad guy the file would expose. And the judge bought it. He did his best to steer us in the wrong direction. He did everything he could to make Tommy's zeal look sinister. Larren derided Molto's character. He held him in contempt. Accused him of manufacturing evidence, of signaling witnesses. But that was a double edge. The worse Tommy looked, the stronger your argument for going into the B file became, because it began to seem like this really was a frame-up, engineered by Molto to keep Sabich from discovering Tommy's twisted past. And so it was more and more important for Larren to end the trial. He could never take the chance of letting you go into that file, as you kept saying you wanted to do. Larren didn't know what would come out, but the worst thing, of course, was the truth. He could bet the ranch that whatever Tommy knew about the bad old past in the North Branch, he wouldn't keep it to himself. Molto might hold back to protect Carolyn and her memory—but not to save Larren's ass, at the cost of his own. And so, without so much as a motion from us, Judge Lyttle declares a TKO and sends me home. And, Sandy, there was one man in the courtroom who knew that was what had to happen. You figured it was coming all along."

Stern's eyes are large and clear and somberly brown.

"Do you judge me so harshly, Rusty?"

"No. I share the Stern outlook. No one is above temptation." Sandy smiles at that, somewhat sadly.

"Just so," he tells me.

"But tolerance doesn't require an absence of standards. I know I sound like a world-class ingrate, but I have to tell you I don't approve."

"I did not act for my own benefit, Rusty." He looks at me in that familiar way, lowering his chin so he can observe me from beneath his drawn brow. "It was a situation in which I—in which we—found ourselves. I did not create it. My own recollection of some of the matters you refer to was refreshed as we proceeded. I dwelt on Molto initially because he was so much easier a target than Della Guardia. It was necessary to develop this theme of past rivalries, somehow. When certain other matters came to mind, it was convenient to continue in the fashion that you have described. But I did not mean to coerce the judge. It was for that reason that I made Molto our straw culprit, so that Judge Lyttle would not feel impelled to do something rash. Was I aware that this might create certain subterranean pressures on Larren as well?" Stern gestures—he nearly smiles. Again there is that mysterious Latin look, used this time as the most reluctant, if philosophical, form of acquiescence. "As you put it, I assessed a point of vulnerability. But I think overall, in your analysis, you credit me with an intricacy of mind that no human being—certainly not I—possesses. I made certain judgments, instantaneously. This was not a charted course. It remained a matter of intuition and estimation throughout."

"I'll always wonder, you know. About the outcome."

"That would be inappropriate, Rusty. I understand your concern now. But I would hesitate before I accepted your view of the judge's ultimate ruling. His handling of this case was, I believe, evenhanded on the whole. Certainly, if he was seeking a convenient way to terminate the proceedings, he could have prohibited the prosecution from offering their fingerprint testimony, in the absence of the glass. Even Della Guardia, disappointed as he was, conceded that Larren's decision today was within the realm of the judge's legitimate discretion. Do you think Nico would have made that handsome gesture of dismissing the case if he believed Larren's assessment was unfounded? Judge Lyttle entered a proper decision, and had he not, I am confident you would have been acquitted. Isn't that what the jurors told the press?"

That is indeed what the papers reported. Three jurors told the media on the courthouse steps that they would not have voted to convict. But Sandy and I both know that the seat-of-the-pants impression of three laymen who have learned that the judge on the case called it a loser are worth very little—and are hardly determinative of what nine other people would have done, in any event.

Stern continues.

"As I say, I made judgments. If, in retrospect, either one of us regards them as questionable, then that should be a burden on my conscience, not yours. Your role is to accept your good fortune on its face, without further reflection. This is the legal significance of an acquittal. This matter is now entirely disposed of. I urge you to move forward. You will overcome this shadow on your career. You are a gifted lawyer, Rusty. I always regarded you as one of the finest of Horgan's prosecutors, probably the best. I was quite disappointed that Raymond did not have the sense to step aside last year and attempt to make the appropriate political arrangements so that you could have succeeded him."

With that I smile. Now I know that the worst is really over. I have not heard that old saw in many months.

"I believe you are going to be all right, Rusty. I sense that." For my part, I sense that Stern is about to say something regrettable; even, perhaps, that I have profited from this experience. I spare him the chance. I pick up my briefcase, which had been left here. Stern sees me to the door. We stand at the threshold, shaking hands, promising to speak, knowing that, whatever else, in the future we will have very little to say to one another.

FALL

37

Only the poets can truly write of liberty, that sweet, exhilarant thing. In my life, I have not known an ecstasy as dulcet or complete as the occasional instants of shivering delight when I again realize this peril is behind me. Over. Done. Whatever the collateral consequences, whatever the smirking, the unvoiced accusations, the contumely or scorn with which others might treat me, to my face or, more certainly, behind my back—whatever they say, the terror is over; the sleepless early-morning hours I spent trying to catapult myself ahead in time, envisioning a life of mindless toil during the day, and nights working like half the other inmates on my endless train of *habeas corpus* petitions and, finally, the wary fearful hours of half-sleep on some prison bunk, awaiting whatever perverse terror the night would bring—that horror is past me. And with a sense of earned relief. Every sin of my life seems truly expiated. My society has judged; no punishment is due. Every sticky cliché is right: an enormous weight has been lifted; I feel as if I could fly, like a million bucks, ten feet tall. I feel free.

And then, of course, the shadow moves, and I think what I have been through, with enormous anger and bitterness and a swooping descent into depression. As a prosecutor I lost cases, more, naturally, than I would have liked, and had my chance to observe the acquitted defendant in the instant of victory. Most wept; the guiltier they were, the harder they cried. I always thought it was relief, and guilt. But it is, I tell you, this disbelief that this ordeal, this—think of the word—trial has been endured for no apparent point but your disgrace, and your uncompensable damage.

The return to life is slow: an island on which a soft wind moves. The first two days the phone does not stop. How people who did not speak to me for the last four months can imagine that I could accept their glib congratulations astounds me. But they call. And I am calculating enough to know they may be needed again; I accept their good wishes with some aplomb. But I spend most of my time alone. I am overwhelmed by the desire to be out in the waning summer and the stirring fall. One day I hold Nat out of school and we go fishing from a canoe. The day passes and we say almost nothing; but I am content to be with my boy and I feel he knows it. Other days I walk in the forest for hours. Very slowly, I begin to see things and therefore notice what I did not see before. My life for four months has been an oblivion, a hopeless storm of feeling so wild that there was nothing outside it. Every face that presented itself to my imagination did so with cyclonic impact in my interior reaches, which now, gradually, are growing still, and which, I finally realize, will in time again require movement.

For the present, I remain at home. My neighbors say that I should write a book, but I am not ready yet for any enterprise. It becomes clear quickly that Barbara finds my presence disconcerting. Her irritation with me, held so long in check, now returns in a peculiar fashion. She clearly feels unable to speak her mind. There are no overt complaints, no instants of shrill sarcasm. As a result she seems even more confined within herself than ever. I find her staring at me with an intense look, troubled, angry, I think. "What?" I ask. Her chin dimples in disapproval. She sighs. She turns away.

"Are you ever going back to work?" she asks me one day. "I can't get anything done with you around here."

"I'm not bothering you."

"You're a distraction."

"By sitting in the living room? By working in the garden?" I admit that I am trying to provoke her.

She lifts her eyes to heaven; she walks away. Now she never rises to the bait. This battle, such as it is, must be fought in silence.

It is true that I have made no effort to secure employment. The checks continue to arrive every two weeks from the P.A.'s office. Della Guardia, of course, has no justifiable cause to fire me. And it would turn the office on its head were I to return to work. Nico is under siege from the press. The national reports have increased the sense of local embarrassment. What might ordinarily have passed as mere incompetence in the administration of county affairs has been magnified into a major scandal through the lens of coast-to-coast attention. Nico Della Guardia has made us in Kindle County look to the world like benighted backwoods buffoons. The editorial writers and even the few local politicians of the opposing political party demand that Nico appoint a special prosecutor to investigate Tommy Molto. The local Bar Association has opened an inquiry to determine whether Tommy should be disbarred. The common belief is that Nico, in his ambition to vault himself into the mayor's office, pressed too hard and that in response Molto manufactured evidence, in league with Painless Kumagai. Nico's dismissal of the case is widely read as a confession. Only on occasion are other motivations suggested. I saw a Sunday piece by Stew Dubinsky which mentioned the B file and the aroma that surrounded the North Branch courthouse during those years. But nothing ever followed. Whatever the general understanding, I am not inclined to correct it. I will not exculpate Nico or Tommy or Painless. I still have no wish to tell what I know: that it was my seed taken from Carolyn; that those surely were my prints found on that glass in the apartment; that the carpet fibers detected were from my home; that all the calls the records showed were made from my phone. I will never be ready to brook the costs of these admissions. And there is a rough justice in this. Let Tommy Molto enjoy the experience of attempting to disprove what circumstance seemingly makes obvious. I accept the checks.

It is Mac's last act as chief administrative deputy in the P.A.'s office, before taking the bench, to negotiate a date at which my stipend may end. Nico has suggested six more months. I demand an additional year as reparations. Nine months is ultimately agreed. In our final conversation on this subject, Mac honors our friendship mightily by asking me to speak at her induction. This is my first public outing. Ed Mumphrey, who presides in the ceremonial courtroom, introduces me as "a man who knows a great deal about justice," and the three or four hundred persons who have assembled to watch Mac become a judge rise to their feet to applaud me. I am now a local hero. Kindle County's Dreyfus. People regret some of the pleasure that they felt watching me be flogged. Yet it is not possible for me to forget how out of place I feel in society. The trial is still like a shell around me. I cannot reach out.

Because I am one of the three speakers at the ceremony, Nico is not present. But Horgan could not appropriately stay away. I attempt to avoid him, but later, amid the jostling by the hors d'oeuvres tables at the hotel reception, I feel a hand upon my arm.

Raymond has that blarney smile. He does not take the risk of offering his hand.

"How've you been?" he asks in a hearty way.

"I'm fine."

"We should have lunch."

"Raymond, I'll never do another thing in my life that you tell me I should." I turn, but he follows me.

"I put that badly. I would really appreciate it, Rusty, if you would have lunch with me. Please."

Old affections. Old connections. So hard to break; for what else do we have? I give him a date and walk away.

I meet Raymond at his law firm, and he suggests that if I don't mind, we will not go out. Both of us would be better off without some clever item in the I-On-The-Town column about how Raymond H. and acquitted Chiefdep buried the hatchet in Satinay's prime rib. Instead, Raymond has arranged a catered lunch. We eat shrimp rémoulade alone in an enormous conference room on that stone table that seems to be composed of a single quarried piece, a thirty-foot slab, polished and posted here as an auction block for the captains of industry. Raymond asks the obligatory questions about Barbara and Nat, and he talks about the law firm. He asks about me.

"I won't be the same," I say.

"I imagine."

"I doubt you can."

"Are you waiting for me to say I'm sorry?"

"You don't have to be sorry. It doesn't do a damn thing for me, anyway."

"So you don't want me to tell you I'm sorry?"

"I'm done giving you advice, Raymond, on how to behave."

"Because I am."

"You should be."

Raymond does not miss a bite. He was prepared for some rancor.

"You know why I'm sorry? Because Nico and Tommy made me believe it. It never dawned on me that they had fucked around with the evidence. I figured they'd do as they were taught. They're gonna recall him, you know. Della Guardia? They're gonna try. There are petitions circulating right now."

I nod. I have read as much. Nico announced last week that there were no grounds for the appointment of a special prosecutor. He expressed his confidence in Molto. And the papers and the TV editorialists pilloried him again. A state legislator made a speech on the floor of the House. This week's word is Cover-up.

"You know what Nico's problem is, don't you? Bolcarro. Bolcarro won't give him the time of day anymore. Augie's gonna sit on his hands on this recall, too. Nico will have to make it on his own. Bolcarro feels like he gave Nico a boost, and the next thing he knows, Della Guardia's a candidate for mayor. Sound familiar?"

I say, "Mmm−hmm." I want to sound bored. I want to sound petulant. I came here to make my anger plain. I have promised myself that I will not be concerned about how low I sink. If I feel like calling names, I will do it. Throwing punches. Tossing food. There will be no point below which I will not descend.

"Look," he says suddenly, "put yourself in my shoes. This was a hard thing for everybody."

"Raymond," I say, "what in the fuck did you do to me? I ate your shit for twelve years."

"I know."

"You were out to ax me."

"I told you, Nico made me believe it. Once you believe it, I'm sort of a victim in the whole thing."

"Go fuck yourself," I say. "And when you're done fucking yourself, go fuck yourself again." I wipe the corners of my mouth with the linen napkin. But I make no move to leave. This is just the beginning. Raymond watches me, bitterness and consterna-

tion moving through his ruddy face. Finally he clears his throat
and tries to change the subject.

"What are you going to do, Rusty, with your career?"

"I have no idea."

"I want you to know I'll help however I can. If you like, I'll see
what's available here. If there's anything else in town that
interests you, just say so. Whatever I'm able to do, I will."

"The only job outside the P.A.'s office that ever sounded good
to me was something you mentioned—being a judge. Think you
can do that? Do you think you can give me back the life I had?" I
look at him levelly, intent on letting him know that this tear
cannot be repaired. My tone is sardonic: No judicial candidate
can carry the baggage of a murder indictment. But Raymond
does not flinch.

"All right," he says. "Do you want me to explore that? See if I
can find you a seat?"

"You're full of it, Raymond. You don't have that kind of clout
anymore."

"You may be wrong about that, my friend. Augie Bolcarro
thinks I'm his best buddy now. Just as soon as he got me out of
the way, he decided I could be useful. He calls me up with
questions twice a week. I'm not kidding, either. He refers to me
as an elder statesman. Isn't that something? If you'd like, I'll
speak with him. I'll have Larren speak with him."

"Don't do that," I tell him quickly. "I don't want your help. And
I don't want Larren's, either."

"What's wrong with Larren? I would figure you'd worship that
guy."

"He's your friend, for one thing."

Horgan laughs. "Boy, you came up here with one idea in mind,
didn't you? You just want to piss all over me." Raymond pushes
the plate aside. "You want to give me twelve years' backtalk in
five minutes? Fine, go ahead and do it. But listen to me. I didn't
set you up. You want to take a dump on somebody? Tommy
deserves it. So does Nico, as far as I'm concerned. Join the
crowd. If you want, I'm sure you can contact the Bar Association.
They'll move you to head of the line and let you take a public
crap all over both of them."

"They already called. I told them I had nothing to say."

"So why me, huh? I know you didn't like seeing me on the

witness stand, but did I lie up there? I didn't say a goddamn thing
that didn't happen. And you know that, brother."

"You lied to me, Raymond."

"When?" For the first time, he's surprised.

"When you gave me the B file. When you told me how Carolyn
asked for it. When you told me that it was a bullshit allegation."

"Oh," says Horgan slowly. He takes a moment to adjust. But he
does not falter. Raymond Horgan, as I always knew, is tough.
"Okay. Now I get it. Some little birdie has been whispering in
your ear, huh? Who was it? Lionel Kenneally? He was always
your asshole buddy. You know, there are a few things you might
like to hear about him, too. Nobody's a hero, Rusty. You got your
nose bent out of shape about that? Fine. I'm not a hero. Some
other people weren't heroes. That has nothing to do with you
being charged with murder." He points at me, still unflummoxed.

"And how about my getting a fair trial, Raymond? Did you
think about that? Did you know whether or not Larren was going
to tool me because he wanted to keep that thing under wraps?"

"He's not that kind of guy."

"He's not what kind of guy? We're talking about somebody
who sold his robe. Come off it. The only thing he cared about—
or you, for that matter—was making sure nobody found out. Let
me ask you something, Raymond. How was it that my case got
drawn to Larren? Who gave Ed Mumphrey the call?"

"Nobody gave Mumphrey any calls."

"Just dumb luck, huh?"

"So far as I know."

"Did you ever ask?"

"Larren and I didn't talk about your case. Ever. Not once that I
remember. I was a witness, and as strange as it may sound to
you, we both behaved properly. Look," he says. "I know what you
think. I know how it sounds. But, Rusty, you're talking about
bullshit. It's something that happened to the guy nine years ago,
when he had his head stuck completely up his ass."

"How did it happen, Raymond?" I ask, my curiosity for a
moment greater than my anger.

"Rusty, I don't know what the fuck went on. I talked to him
about it exactly once. And the conversation didn't last any
longer than it had to. He was drunk on his ass half the time in
those days. You know, she was the P.O. Guys on bond would give

her their sob story. She started putting in a word with the judge. And he'd go along. I'm sure he thought it'd make her happier to lift her skirt. One day, one of these guys she's helped out gives her a C-note for her troubles. She brings it to Larren to figure out what to do. He thinks it's funny. She does, too. They go out and blow it on dinner. One thing leads to another. They had a high old time, I guess. He always thought it was like a fraternity prank. They both did."

"And you hired her, knowing this?"

"Rusty, that's *how* I hired her. Larren was giving me all this hearts-and-flowers crap about how broke she was from paying off her law school tuition and making 11K a year as a P.O. I said, Fine, I'd double her salary, but knock this shit off. I thought I'd leave her out there as a deputy. Nobody ever liked those assignments. And with two other deputies to watch her, what could she do? And instead, it turns out that she did a helluva job. A hell of a job. She wasn't long on scruples, but the lady had a lot of brains. And I finally got Larren transferred downtown. And he performed with real distinction. I'll go to my grave believing that. No one will ever be able to knock Larren's integrity on his handling of a felony case. A year later they were both so respectable they didn't even talk to one another. If she exchanged ten words with Larren in the last five, six years, I'd be amazed. And, you know, as the time passed, it got to the point that I could see what he saw in her. You know what came of that."

This, of course, is the answer to what puzzled me last spring. Why did Carolyn make her move first for me rather than Raymond, when she perceived the prospective vacuum at the head of the office. It was not my manliness, my dark good looks. I was fresher, nowhere near as wise. She probably figured Raymond would know better. He should have; maybe he even did. Maybe that's why she didn't end up with what she wanted, why Raymond gave no sign of having been pained. He saw her coming. He knew what to look for.

"Well, isn't that nice," I say. "Everything worked out. Until you get a certain piece of anonymous correspondence. And so you gave her that file to trunk."

"No, sir. No way. I gave it to her. I didn't know what it was. I told her to look at it. And to bear in mind that she could never tell who might come looking over her shoulder. That's all I said. What do you want from me, Rusty? I'm seeing the gal by then. Am I supposed to pretend? If I was such a bum, I'd have done just what you said. Headed for the shredder with the thing."

I shake my head. We both know he is much too careful for that. No way to tell who may come looking for the letter. That's the kind of job that a Medici like Raymond knows he should hand off. And with instructions that will never bounce back on him. Very artful. Investigate. See what's going on. And what goes unspoken is that if it has to do with Larren and you, clean the mess up very carefully. Carolyn certainly tried. I don't have to wonder anymore who had Leon's arrest file from the 32nd District.

"And when she got cooled, you ran and collected the file?"

"When she got 'cooled,' as you put it, I got a call from His Honor. You know, I had told him about the letter when the thing came in. So he's on the phone the day they find the body. Pure Larren, too. He's always been a sanctimonious asshole. He says to me, It might be politically sensitive, why don't I collect that file?" Raymond laughs. Alone. I do not relax my severe expression. "Listen, Rusty, when you asked me, I gave you the thing."

"You had no choice. And you tried to mislead me anyway."

"Look," he says, "he's my friend."

And the key to Raymond's black support. If Raymond had ever prosecuted Larren Lyttle, or let somebody else do it, he could have just as well resigned as run for re-election. But I don't mention that. Disgust has finally displaced some of my anger.

I stand up to leave.

"Rusty," he says to me, "I meant what I said. I want to help you. You give me the high sign and I'll do whatever you want. You want me to kiss Augie Bolcarro's ass in Wentham Square at noon so he'll make you a judge, I'll do it. You want to work for the big bucks, I'll try to arrange that, too. I know I owe you."

What he means is that he wants to keep me happy, now more than ever. But his genuflection is still soothing in a way. You cannot continue pounding a man who's on his knees. I say nothing, but I nod.

On the way to the door, Raymond again points out all the modern art along the walls. He apparently has forgotten that he gave the same dime lecture to Stern and me. As we're parting by the elevator, he reaches for me and tries to take me into an embrace.

"It was a terrible thing," he says.

I break away. I actually shove him slightly. But there are people around and Horgan pretends not to have noticed. The elevator arrives. Horgan snaps his fingers. Something has come to mind.

"You know," he says quietly, "there was one thing I promised myself I was gonna ask you today."

"What's that, Raymond?" I ask as I step inside.

"Who killed her? I mean, who do you think?"

I say nothing. I remain impassive. Then, as the elevator doors begin to close, I nod to Raymond Horgan in a gentlemanly way.

38

One day in October I am working in the yard and I feel an odd stirring. I am fixing the fence—removing the posts, sinking new ones in cement, nailing on the beeftail. For a moment I consider the tool with which I am working. A Whatchamacallit. It is an inheritance of sorts from my father-in-law. After his death, Barbara's mother brought all his yard and home equipment over here. The Whatchamacallit is a piece of black iron, a kind of cross between a hammer's claw and a crowbar. You can use it for anything. On the night of April 1, it was used to kill Carolyn Polhemus.

Right after the trial I noticed that there was still a crust of blood and one blond hair clinging to the edge of one of the two teeth. I stared at the Whatchamacallit for a long time, then I took it to the basement and washed it in the laundry tub. Barbara came downstairs as I was doing it. She stopped dead on the stairway when she saw me, but I tried to appear jovial. I reached for the hot water and began to whistle.

I have picked it up a dozen times since then. I want to observe no fetishes, no taboos. And after a moment for reflection, I decide it is not the Whatchamacallit singing to me like a ghost. Instead, as I consider the grass, the roses and their thorns, the vegetable bed that I helped Barbara put in this spring, there is the sense of something in this house, this land that is irretrievably used up and old. I am finally ready for some considered changes. I find Barbara in the dining room, where she is grading papers. They are stacked across the table like my mother's magazines and notecards from her era as a radio personality. I sit down on the other side.

"We should think about moving back into the city," I tell her.

I expect, of course, that this concession will bring from Barbara the radiance of victory. She has advocated this move for many years. Instead, Barbara puts down her pen and holds her forehead. She says, "Oh, God."

I wait. I know something awful is going to happen. I am not scared.

"I didn't want to talk about this yet, Rusty."

"What?"

"The future," she says, and adds, "I didn't think that it would be fair to you. So soon."

"All right," I say. "You've nodded in the direction of good taste. Why don't you tell me what's on your mind?"

"Rusty, don't be like that."

"I'm like that. I'd like to hear."

She folds her hands.

"I've taken a job for the January term at Wayne State."

Wayne State is not in Kindle County. Wayne State is not within four hundred miles of here. Wayne State, as I recall, is in a city I have visited once, which is called Detroit.

"Detroit, right?"

"Right," she says.

"You're leaving me?"

"I wouldn't put it like that. I'm taking a job. Rusty, I hate to do this to you now. But I feel I have to. They had hired me for the September term. I was going to tell you in April, but then all that craziness began—" She shivers her head with her eyes closed. "Anyway, they were nice enough to give me an extension. I've changed my mind half a dozen times. But I've decided it's for the best."

"Where's Nat going to be?"

"With me, of course," she answers, her look suddenly fierce and aquiline. On this point, she means to say, there must not be even a thought that she might yield. It occurs to me, as a sort of reflex, that I could probably go to court and try to prevent that. But just now I have had enough of litigation. In its odd way, the thought inspires a smile, rueful and brief, a reaction which brings a vaguely hopeful look to Barbara.

"What do you mean you're not leaving me, you're taking a job?" I ask. "Am I invited to Detroit?"

"Would you come?"

"I might. This isn't a bad time for me to start over. There are a few unpleasant things following me around here."

Barbara immediately tries to correct me. She has thought all of this through, perhaps to salve her conscience, probably because there are always these geometries in her head.

"You're a hero," Barbara says. "They wrote about you in *The New York Times* and *The Washington Post.* I've been expecting you to tell me any day that you're going to run for office."

I laugh out loud, but this is a sad remark. More than anything Barbara has said, it proves how far we have already drifted. We have again ceased communication. I have not told her enough for her to understand my own thoroughgoing revulsion with what has gone on in the interest of politics.

"Would it offend you if I moved somewhere closer than here so that I can see my son? Granting that we're not about to live in the same house."

She looks at me.

"No," she says.

I consider the wall for a moment. My God, I think. What happens in a life. And then I think once more of how this all began and pine, as I have so often lately. Oh, Carolyn, I think. What did I want with you? What did I do? But it is not as if I am entirely without an account.

I am nearly forty now. I can no longer pretend that the world is unknown to me, or that I like most of what I've seen. I am my father's son. That is my inheritance—the grimness of outlook bred of knowing that there is more cruelty in life than simple wits can comprehend. I do not claim that my own sufferings have been legion. But I have seen so much. I saw my father's hobbled soul, maimed by one of history's great crimes; I saw the torment and the need, the random and passionate anger that brings such varied and horrible misbehavior to our own streets. As a prosecutor I meant to combat it, to declare myself a sworn enemy of the crippled spirit that commits each trespass with force and arms. But of course, it overcame me. Who can observe that panorama of negative capacity and maintain any sense of optimism? It would be easier if the world were not so full of casual misfortune. Golan Scharf, a neighbor, has a son born blind. Mac and her husband, in a moment of revelry, turn a corner and plunge into the river. And even if luck, and luck alone, spares us the worst, life nonetheless wears so many of us down. Young men of talent dull it and drink it all away. Young women of spirit bear children, broaden in the hips, and shrink in hope as middle years close in upon them. Every life, like every snowflake, seemed to me then unique in the shape of its miseries, and in the rarity and mildness of its pleasures. The lights go out, grow dim. And a soul can stand only so much darkness. I reached for Carolyn. With all deliberation and intent. I cannot pretend it was an accident, or serendipity. It was what I wanted. It was what I wanted to do. I reached for Carolyn.

And so now, still gazing at the wall, I begin to speak, saying aloud things that I had promised myself would never be spoken.

"I've thought a lot about the reasons," I say. "Not that anyone can fully comprehend them. Whatever you call that insane mix of rage and lunacy that leads one human being to kill another—it's not the kind of thing that's easy to understand in any ultimate way. I doubt anybody—not the person who does it or anyone else—can really grasp the whole thing. But I've tried. I really have tried. I mean, one thing I should say to start, Barbara, is that I apologize to you. I think a lot of people would find that laughable. That I would say that. But I do.

"And one more thing you've got to know. You have to believe it: she was never more important to me than you are. Never. I guess, to be unflinchingly honest, there must have been something there that I didn't believe I could find anywhere else. That was *my* failing. I admit it. But as you've told me yourself, I was absolutely obsessed with her. It would take hours to explain why. She had that power; I had that weakness. But I know goddamn well that I wouldn't have gotten over her for years, and probably never, as long as she was walking around. I mean, there is no such thing as justification here, or excuse. I'm not trying to pretend there is. But at least we should both acknowledge the circumstances.

"I always figured it wasn't going to do anybody much good to talk about it. And I assumed that was what you'd figured. What happened happened. But naturally I've spent a lot of time thinking about exactly how it occurred. I could hardly help that. I guess every prosecutor learns that we live closer than we want to believe to real evildoing. Fantasy is a lot more dangerous than people like to say. You get this idea, this careful elaborate plan, it becomes actually stimulating to think about it, it titillates and thrills you, you dwell on it, and you take the first step toward carrying it out, and that is thrilling and titillating, too, and you go on. And in the end, once you edge up to it that way, telling yourself all along that no real damage has been done, it takes just one extraordinary moment, when you revel in the excitement, in the feeling of flying free, for the whole thing actually to occur."

I finally look back. Barbara is on her feet now, standing behind her chair. Her look is quick and alarmed, as well it might be. No doubt she never wanted to hear this. But I go on.

"As I said, I really never thought I'd have to talk about this, but I raise it now, because I think once and for all it ought to be said aloud. There's no threat here. There's not even the shadow of a threat, okay? God knows what somebody in your position might think, Barbara, but there is not a threat. I just want the cards on the table. I don't want there to be wondering about what either of us knows or thinks. I don't want that to be a factor in whatever it is we're going to do. Because all in all, even though you're probably amazed to hear me say all of this, and then say this, too, I expected, I guess the word is wanted, is *want*, to go on. There are a lot of reasons. Nat, first of all. Of course. And I also want to minimize the damage to our lives. But more than that, I do not want that mad act to have had no decent consequence. And basically, in trying to explain to myself how and why this woman was murdered—for what little rational impulses have to do with it, and for what little they are worth as explanations—I suppose I always thought that in part it was for us. For us. For the good of us. God knows a lot of it was simply for my benefit, to—if conscience can stand those words—get even. But I thought some of it was for us, too. And so I wanted to say that, to see if all of this means anything to you or makes any difference."

I am finished at last, and feel strangely satisfied. I have done as well with this as I ever could have imagined. Barbara, my wife, is crying, very hard, and silently. She is looking downward while the tears simply fall. She heaves and catches her breath.

"Rusty, I don't think there is anything worth saying, except I'm sorry. I hope you believe me someday. I really am so sorry."

"I understand," I tell her. "I believe you now."

"And I was prepared to tell the truth. At any time. Right up to the end. If I was called as a witness, I would have told what happened."

"I understand that, too. But I didn't want that. Frankly, Barbara, it wouldn't have done a bit of good. It would have sounded like some desperate excuse. Like you were making a bizarre effort to save me. Nobody ever would have believed that you were the one who killed her."

These words bring fresh tears, and then, finally, control. It has been said and she is, in a measure, relieved. Barbara wipes each eye with the back of her hands. She breathes deeply. She speaks, looking down at the table.

"Do you know what it feels like to be crazy, Rusty? Really crazy? To not be able to get any hold of who you are? You never feel safe. I feel like every step I take, the ground is soft. That I'm going to fall through it. And I can't go on that way. I don't think that I can be a normal person again if I'm living with you. I know how horrible that is. But it's horrible for me, too. No matter what I thought, nobody goes back to the way things used to be after something like this. All I can say, Rusty, is that nothing turned out the way I expected. I never understood the reality of any of it until the trial. Until I sat there. Until I saw what was happening to you, and finally felt how much I didn't want that to be happening. But that's part of what I can't get over. I have no life here, except being sorry. And afraid. And, of course— 'ashamed' is not the word. 'Guilty'?" She shakes her head slowly, looking down at the table. "There isn't a word."

"We could try to share that, you know. The blame," I say. Somehow, in spite of myself, this remark has a whimsical quality. Barbara gasps a bit. She bites her lip suddenly. She looks the other way for a second, and, in a momentary exhalation, cries. Then she shakes her head again.

"I don't think that's right," she says. "The trial came out the way it should have, Rusty."

That's all she says. I might have hoped for more, but it's enough. She starts to leave the room, but stops and lets me hold her for a moment, actually a long moment as she lingers with me, but finally she breaks away. I hear her go upstairs. I know Barbara. She will lie on our bed and weep a while longer. And then she is going to get back on her feet. And begin packing to leave.

39

One day, right after Thanksgiving, when I've come to town for Christmas shopping, I see Nico Della Guardia walking down Kindle Boulevard. He holds his raincoat drawn closed around the collar and he has a worried brow. He seems to be looking up and down the street. He is coming in my direction, but I am quite certain he has not seen me yet. I think of ducking into a building, not because I am afraid of his response, or mine, but simply because I think it might be easier for both of us to avoid this meeting. By then, however, he has caught sight of me and he is heading deliberately my way. He does not smile, but he offers his hand first, and I take it. For that instant only, I am rifled by a shot of terrible emotion—hot pain and grief—but it quickly passes and I stand there, looking affably at the man who, in any practical sense, tried to take my life from me. One person, a man in a felt hat, apparently aware of the momentousness of this meeting, turns to stare as he continues on his way, but otherwise the pedestrian traffic merely divides about us.

Nico asks me how I am. He has the earnest tone people lately have tended to adopt, so I know that he has heard. I tell him anyway.

"Barbara and I split up," I say.

"I heard that," he says. "I'm sorry. I really am. Divorce is a bitch. Well, you know. You had me crying on your shoulder. And I didn't have the kid. Maybe you guys can work it out."

"I doubt that. Nat's with me for the time being, but only until Barbara gets settled in Detroit."

"Too bad," he says. "Really. Too bad." Old Nico, I think, still repeating everything.

I turn to let him go on his way. I offer my hand first this time. And when he takes it, he steps closer and squeezes up his face so that I know that what he is about to say is something he finds painful.

"I didn't set you up," he says. "I know what people think. But I didn't have anybody screw with the evidence. Not Tommy. Not Kumagai." I almost wince at the thought of Painless. He has resigned now from the police department. He had no refuge. He could only claim collusion or incompetence, and so he chose the lesser—and I believe more apt—of the two evils. He did not botch the semen specimen, of course, but I've come to believe that no one would have been indicted if he'd looked back at his autopsy notes. Nobody could have put it all together. Maybe Tommy's also to blame for pushing too hard to bring a marginal case. I suppose he thought my hide would still his grief—or envy—whatever state it was that Carolyn had left him in which so riled his passions.

Nico in the meantime continues, sincere as ever. "I really didn't," he says. "I know what you think. But I have to tell you that. I didn't do that."

"I know you didn't, Delay," I say. And then I tell him what I think is the truth. "You did your job the way you thought you were supposed to. You just relied on the wrong people."

He watches me.

"Well, it's probably not going to be my job much longer. You've heard about this recall thing?" he asks. He is looking up and down the street again. "Of course you have. Everybody has. Well, what's the difference? They all tell me my career is over."

He is not looking for sympathy. He just wants me to know that the waves of calamity have spread and washed over him as well. Carolyn has pulled all of us down in her black wake. I find myself encouraging him.

"You can't tell, Delay. You never know how things'll turn out."

He shakes his head.

"No, no," he says. "No, you're the hero, I'm the goat. It's great." Nico smiles, in a sudden way, so that you know he finds his own thoughts weird, inappropriate. "A year ago, you could have beat me in the election, and you could do it today. Isn't that great?" Nico Della Guardia laughs out loud, pinched by his own ironies, the peculiar readings from his own terms of reference. He spreads his arms here in the middle of Kindle Boulevard. "Nothing," he says, "has changed."

40

In the front room of the home in which I have lived for better than eight years there is complete disorder. Open boxes, half packed, are everywhere, and items removed from shelves and drawers are strewn in all directions. The furniture is gone. I never cared much for the sofa or the love seat, and Barbara wanted them for her condo outside Detroit. I'll move January 2 to an apartment in the city. Not a bad place. The realtor said I was lucky to get it. The house is up for rent. I've decided that each step should be slow.

Now that Nat has left, the job of packing seems to take forever. I move from room to room. Every item reminds me of something. Each corner seems to contain its quotient of pain and melancholy. When I reach my limit, I start working somewhere else. I think often of my father and that scene I recalled for Marty Polhemus, in which I found my old man, the week after my mother's death, packing up the apartment he had abandoned a few years before. He worked in a sleeveless undervest, and he had a brazen manner as he pitched the remains of his adult life into crates and boxes. He kicked the cartons from his path as he moved about the rooms.

I heard from Marty just last week. He sent a Christmas card. "Glad to hear everything worked out for you." I laughed aloud when I read his message. Lord, that kid really has the knack. I threw the card away. But the toll of loneliness is greater than I imagined. A couple of hours ago, I went rummaging through the boxes of trash in the living room, looking for the envelope. I need the address to write him back.

I never wrote my father. After he left for Arizona, I did not see him again. I called on occasion, but only because Barbara dialed the number and put the receiver in my hand. He was so deliberately uncommunicative, so chary with the details of his life, that it was never worth the effort. I knew he was living with a woman by then, that he worked three days a week in a local bakery. He found Arizona hot.

The woman, Wanda, called to tell me he was dead. That was more than eight years ago now, but the shock of it, in a way, is with me every day. He was strong and fit; I had taken it for granted that he would live to be a hundred, that there would always be this far-off target for my bitterness. He had already been cremated. Wanda only found my number as she was cleaning out the trailer and she insisted I come West to settle the rest of his affairs. Barbara was eight months pregnant then and we both regarded this trip West as my father's final imposition. Wanda, it turned out, was from New York City, in her late fifties, tall, not bad-looking. She did not hesitate to speak ill of the dead. Actually, she told me when I arrived, she had moved out on him six months before. They called her from the bakery, where he collapsed with the coronary, because they knew no one else. 'I don't know why I do these things. Really, I have to tell you,' she said, after a couple of drinks, 'he was mostly a prick.'

She did not think it was funny when I suggested her phrase was what should be carved on the stone.

She left me alone to pick through the trailer. On his bed were red socks. In the chifforobe, I found another six or seven dozen pairs of men's hose. Red and yellow. Striped. Dotted. Argyles. In his last years, my father had finally found an indulgence.

The doorbell rings. I feel the faintest surge of anticipation. I look forward to a moment's conversation with the postal carrier or the man from UPS.

"Lip," I say through the storm door. He enters and stomps the snow off his feet.

"Nice and homey," Lip says, surveying the disaster in the living room. As he stands on the doormat, he hands me a small package, not much wider than the satin bow on top.

"Christmas present," he says.

"That's awfully nice," I say. We've never done this before.

"I figured you could use a pick-me-up. Nat get off okay?"

I nod. I took him to the airport yesterday. They allowed him to be seated first. I wanted to go with him onto the plane, but Nat would not permit it. From the doorway, I watched him go down the jetway in his dark blue NFL parka, alone and already lost in dreams. He is his father's son. He did not turn to wave. I want, I thought quite distinctly, I want the life I had.

Lip and I spend a moment looking at each other. I still have not taken his coat. God, it is awkward, and it is like this with everyone, people on the street or people I know well. So much has happened to me that I never counted on. And how are people to respond? Somehow it does not fit into any recognized conversational pattern to say, It's tough about your wife, but at least they didn't get you for that murder.

I finally offer him a beer.

"If you're drinkin," he answers, and follows me to the kitchen. Here, too, half the housewares are in boxes.

As I'm taking a glass out of the cabinet, Lipranzer points to the package he brought, which I've set down on the table.

"I wanna see you open that. I been savin it a while."

He has done a careful job with the paper.

"I never saw a gift wrapped before," I say, "with hospital corners."

Crumpled inside a small white box is a manila envelope ribboned with red-and-white evidence tape. I tear through that and find the glass that turned up missing during the trial, the tumbler from Carolyn's bar. I put it all down on the table and take a step away. This is one guess where I would never have been close.

Lip fishes in his pocket and comes out with his lighter. He holds a corner of the evidence envelope in the flame until he's sure it's burning, then flips in into the sink. The glass he hands to me. The blue ninhydrin powder is still all over it, the three partial prints etched there, a kind of surrealistic delft. I hold the glass up to the window light for a moment, trying for reasons I cannot discern to figure which of the tiny networks of lines are the marks of my right thumb and my third right middle finger, the former telltale signs. I am still looking at the glass when I start talking to Lipranzer.

"There's a genuine question here, whether I should be touched," I say, and now finally catch his eye, "or *real* pissed off."

"How's that?"

"It's a felony in this state to secrete evidence of a crime. You hung your ass out a good long way on this one, Lipper."

"No one around who'll ever know." Lip pours the beer that I've just opened. "Besides, I didn't do a goddamn thing. It was them that fucked up. Remember they got Schmidt to come grab all the evidence? The glass wasn't there. I'd took the thing down to Dickerman. Next day I get a call from the lab, the test is done, I can come pick up my glass. When I get down there somebody's signed the receipt 'Returned to Evidence.' You know, the idea is that I'll put it back in. Only I don't got any way to put it anywhere, since it's not my goddamn case anymore. So I tossed it in a drawer. Figured sooner or later somebody's gotta ask me. Nobody did. In the meantime, Molto's like every other half-ass deputy. Signs off on all the receipts without matchin em against the evidence. Three months later he's got himself a bucket of shit. But that's his problem." Lip lifts his glass and drains most of it. "None of them ever had the most screwed-up idea where the thing went. They tell stories about the way Nico tore his office apart. He had them pick up the tacked-down carpet, I hear."

We laugh, both of us, knowing Nico. When he gets very excited you can see his scalp redden where the hair has thinned. His freckles seem to stand out more as well. After the laughter is done, we wait through a little hollow moment of silence.

"You know why I'm pissed, don't you?" I finally ask.

Lip shrugs and raises his beer.

"You thought I killed her, " I say.

He's prepared for this and does not even flinch. He belches before he answers.

"Lady was bad news."

"Which makes it okay if I killed her?"

"Did you?" asks Lip.

That, of course, is what he's come to find out. If he just wanted to be a soul brother, he'd have taken the glass with him the last time he went fishing and dropped it in the Crown Falls, which rages so magnificently up there near Skageon. But it must be eating at him. That's why he's offered the glass, so I know that we're in it together.

"You think I did, don't you?"

He drinks his beer.

"It's possible."

"Screw off. You're gonna stick your neck out like that cause it's just a little possibility, like life on Mars?"

Lip looks straight at me, his eyes clear and gray.

"I'm not wearin a wire, you know."

"I wouldn't care if you were. I've been tried and acquitted. Double-jeopardy clause says that's all she wrote. I could publish my confession in the *Trib* tomorrow and nobody could try me again for murder. Only we both know, Lip"—I take a slug of the beer I've opened for myself—"they never do admit it, do they?"

Lip looks across the kitchen toward something that isn't there. "Forget it," he says.

"I'm not going to forget it. Just tell me what you think, okay? You think I cooled her. That's not just for the sporting life that a fifteen-year copper hikes the evidence in the biggest case in town. Right?"

"Right. It ain't just sportin life." My friend Dan Lipranzer looks at me. "I think you killed her."

"How? I mean, you must have worked it out in your head." He does not hesitate as long as I would have thought.

"I figure you cracked her in anger. The rest was just to make it look good. There wouldn't be much point in sayin you were sorry once she was dead."

"And why was I so pissed off?"

"I don't know. Who knows? She dumped you, right? For Raymond. That's enough to be pissed about."

Slowly, I remove the beer glass from Lipranzer's hand. I can see his apprehension when I do that. He is prepared for me to fling it. Instead, I put it on the kitchen table next to the one he brought, the one they found on Carolyn's bar, the one with my prints. They are identical. Then I go to the cabinet and take down the rest of the set, until there are a dozen glasses standing there in two rows, one sudsed with beer foam at the head on the left, one dusted with blue powder at the front of the line next to it. It is a rare moment, in which Lipranzer wears none of his hipped-up wise-guy look.

I run the water in the sink, washing down the ashes, then fill the basin with suds. I start talking while I do that.

"Imagine a woman, Lip, a strange woman, with a very precise mathematical mind. Very internal. To herself. Angry and

depressed. Most of the time she is volcanically pissed. With life.
With her husband. With the miserable, sad affair he had in which
he gave away everything she wanted. She wanted to be his
obsession and instead he's hung up on this manipulative slut,
who anyone but he could see regarded him as sport. This
woman, Lip, the wife, is sick in spirit and in the heart, and maybe
in the head, if we're going to be laying all the cards out on the
table.

"She's mixed up. She is seriously on the fence about this
marriage. Some days she's sure she's going to leave him. Some
days she wants to stay. Either way she has to do something. The
whole thing's eating at her, destroying her. And either way, she
has a wish, a wild secret hope that the woman he was sleeping
with could end up dead. When the wife's rage is at a peak, she's
ready to abandon her husband, head for open spaces. But there
would be no satisfaction in that if the other woman is alive,
because the husband, helpless slob that he is, will just go
crawling back to her and end up with what his wife thinks he
wants. The wife can get even only if the other woman is gone.

"But, of course, you always hurt the one you love. And in her
down moods, she longs for everything they had, to find some
way to bring them back to old times. But even in these moods, it
seems that life would be better if the other woman were dead.
With no choice, he will finally give up his obsession. Maybe then
they can recycle things, build on the wreckage."

The sink by now is full of suds. The ninhydrin comes off the
glass easily, although there is a sulfurous stink when it hits the
water. Then I take down a towel and wipe the glass clean. When I
am finished, I get a box and begin wrapping up the set. Lip helps.
He separates the sheets of newsprint that the movers have
provided. He is not talking yet.

"And so the idea is there. Day after day. All the wife thinks
about is killing the other woman. Whether she is in the peak of
rage or the dungeons of self-pity, there is that thrilling notion.

"And, of course, as the idea takes hold, there is another twist.
The husband must know. When she is raging, when she's on the
way out the door, it is a kind of delicious vengeance to think of
him bereft and knowing just who left him in that condition. And
in her softer moods, when the thought is of somehow saving this
marriage, she wants him to appreciate this monumental act of

commitment and devotion, her effort at finding the miracle cure. It will have no meaning to him if he thinks it's just an accident.

"So that becomes part of the compulsion. To kill. And to let him know that she has done it. How is that to be accomplished? It is a magnificent puzzle to a woman capable of the most intricate levels of complex thought. Obviously she can't just tell him. For one thing, half the time she's planning to be gone. And, of course, on the basic level, there is a risk that—to put it mildly—her husband might not approve. He may go tattling. She has to take that option from him. And how best to do that? Fortunately, it is predictable that the husband will investigate this crime. The head of the Homicide Section has taken a powder. The acting head is a person no one trusts. And the husband is the P.A.'s favorite son. He will be the one collecting evidence, him and his pal, the all-star homicide dick Lipranzer. And as the husband proceeds, detail by detail, he will discover that the culprit for all the world appears to be him. He'll know of course that it was not. And he'll know who it was, because there is only one person in the world who has access to this glass, or to his seed. But he'll never convince anybody else of that. He will suffer in lonely silence when she leaves him. Or kiss her bloody hand with new devotion when she stays. In the act itself, there will be purification and discovery. With the other woman gone, she will be able to find just what it is she wants to do.

"But it must be a crime that the rest of the world can reasonably regard as unsolved, when hubby declares that to be the case. It must be a crime in which he alone will realize what has occurred. That's why she decides to make it look like a rape. And so the plan proceeds. Something that must be utilized is one of these glasses."

I show the tumbler I am wrapping to Lip. He is seated on one of the kitchen chairs now, listening with an open look that mediates between rough horror and a kind of wonder.

"It was a glass just like this one that her husband picked up and wept over, the night he told her of his affair. The self-centered sap sat there and devastated her with the truth and cried because their glasses were just like the other woman's. That will be the perfect calling card, the perfect way to tell him, You know who. He drinks a beer one night while he watches the ball game. She hides the glass away. Now she has his fingerprints.

"And then on a few mornings she saves the gooey mess that comes out when she removes her diaphragm. Puts it in a plastic bag, I figure, which probably sat a while in the basement freezer.

"And that's how it's done. April first. Ha ha. That's to help him get it. She makes a phone call from the residence an hour before the event. Hubby is at home, babysitting, but, as Nico would have argued if Stern had ever pointed out that Barbara might have been here when I made that call, you can use the phone in Barbara's study without being heard downstairs."

Lip's chair makes a sudden screech as it jerks back across the floor.

"Whoa," he says. "Run that by again. Who called? Really. Not what Delay was thinkin. Her?"

"Her," I say. "That time."

"That time?"

"That time. Not before."

"You before?"

"Me before."

"Hmm," says Lip, and his eyes dull as he reflects, no doubt, on that day in April when I asked him for what surely seemed a harmless favor, a trivial indiscretion, to skip retrieving my home tolls. "Hmm," he says again, and actually laughs out loud. I do not understand at first, but when I see his somewhat cheerful look I realize he is satisfied. We can only be who we can be. Detective Lipranzer is pleased to know that he was not completely wrong to judge me guilty of some margin of bad faith. "So she called that night?"

"Right."

"Knowin you'd done it before?"

"I'm not sure of that. She couldn't have overheard me, because there was nothing to hear. But if you want a guess, I think she knew. That was my sense. I probably left the phone directory from the P.A.'s office open to the page one time when I called Carolyn. That's the kind of thing Barbara would notice. You know how fixated she is with details, especially around the house. That may even have been what kicked her over the edge. But I don't know for sure. It could have been a coincidence. She had to get in touch with Carolyn somehow. She couldn't just show up."

"What'd she tell her on the phone?"

"Who knows? Something. Bullshit. She asked to drop by."

"And killed her dead," says Lip.

"And killed her dead," say I. "But not without a stop first at the U. She logged into the computer. Nobody ever checked, but I'll bet she loaded on some brainbusting program. I'd guarantee that machine was churning out paper for two hours. Every clever killer needs an alibi, and Barbara, you might say, had considered a detail or two. Then she drives over to Carolyn's, who by now is waiting for her to arrive. Carolyn lets her in. And when she turns her head, Barbara serenely bashes it in with a little item called a Whatchamacallit, which is just small enough to fit inside a lady's purse. Then she gets out the cord she's brought along and does some tying. Leaves the calling-card glass on the bar. And then takes a syringe and the knowledge gained from her readings in artificial insemination and injects the contents of her little Ziploc bag, full of male fluid. She unlocks the doors and windows before she leaves.

"Of course, criminal detection is a little more complicated than Barbara knew. There are entire fields of inquiry unknown to her. Like fiber analysis. She leaves traces she never counted on. The fibers from the carpets in her home, which are clinging to the hem of her skirt. Or a few hairs of her own. Remember how Hair and Fiber didn't bother with the female hair they picked up at the scene? I'm sure she never figured anybody was going to do so detailed an analysis of the sperm specimen. And I would bet that Barbara had no idea about MUD records, and was astonished when it turned out that her call was traced back to our phone. She drew more of an arrow toward herself than she intended. Same thing with that third fingerprint on the glass— probably a moment of carelessness. And of course none of us ever figured that Carolyn had tied her tubes.

"There's the rub, of course. Life, it seems, does not follow the invariable rules of mathematics. Things do not turn out as she had planned. Molto is shadowing the investigation. He picks up on everything she never meant to leave behind, and items like the fingerprints that she had probably figured I could shove under the rug. Things turn very dark for hubby. The world falls in around him. He seems completely fuddled. Maybe he doesn't even know who set him up. And now she finds herself in the one place she never counted on being: she feels sorry for him. He has suffered in ways she never intended, and in the cold light of reality, she is full of shame. She nurses him through his ordeal. She is ready at any moment to save him with the truth, until it fortunately proves unnecessary. But of course there are no happy endings. This story is a tragedy. Things are better now between the husband and the wife. Passion and feeling have been rediscovered. But now The Act stands between them. There are things he cannot say to her. Things she cannot say to him. And worst of all, she cannot stand her own guilt—or the recollection of her insanity."

When I am done, I look at Lip. And Lip looks at me. I ask him if he wants another beer.

"No, sir," he says. "I need whiskey." He stands up to wash his glass. Then he puts it in the box with the other eleven. He holds the box closed while I apply the tape.

I pour him his shot and he stands, drinking.

"When'd you figure all this out?" he asks.

"The big picture? I think I pick up pieces of it every day. There have been days, Lip, while Nat was at school when I've done nothing but sit in the dark and work over the details. Again and again."

"I mean, when did you know what happened?"

"When did I know she did Carolyn? It crossed my mind when I heard there was a phone call from here the night she was murdered. But I thought Tommy must have diddled the phone records. I didn't really know until I saw the glasses again in Carolyn's apartment and realized all of hers were there."

Lip makes a noise, a little too ironic to be called a groan. "How'd that one make you feel?"

"Weird." I shake my head. "You know, I'd look at her. Here she is—cooking dinner for me. For Nat. *Touching* me, for Chrissake. Then, you know, it would all come clear to me: I was out of my fucking mind. I wouldn't believe it at all. For days, I wouldn't believe it. Sometimes I was positive that Tommy set me up. Making me think it was Barbara was part of his scam. I thought that a lot. I would have loved to hear Leon lay it all on Molto. But, you know, at the end, when I knew what it was, I wasn't surprised at all."

"Don't you wanna see her burn?"

I pout my lip. Slowly, I shake my head.

"I couldn't do it, Lip. I couldn't do it to Nat. We've all had more than enough. *I* couldn't take it. I don't owe anybody that much."

"And you don't worry about the kid? With her?"

"No," I say. "Not that. That's one thing I don't worry about. She's in better shape with him. It pulls her back. Barbara needs someone around who really cares about her. And Nat does. I always knew I couldn't split them up—it would be the worst thing I could do to either one of them."

"Least I don't gotta wonder why you threw her out." Lip makes that noise again. "Whew," he says.

I've sat down now in the kitchen chair Lip formerly occupied. I am thus in the middle of the room alone as I speak.

"I'll tell you something that will blow your mind: she's the one who took the powder. I didn't ask her to leave. I suppose six months from now I could have woken up and strangled her in her sleep. But I was willing to try it. I really wanted to try. Crazy as she is, wild and nuts, no matter how many times you turn it upside down, you still have to say she did it because of me. Certainly not out of love. But for it. I wouldn't call it even, but we'd have both had our share to make up for."

Lip laughs at that.

"Boy," he says. "You really got a way with the ladies."

"You think I'd have been out of my mind to stay with her?"

"You askin my opinion?"

"I seem to be."

"You're better off without her. You're givin her way too much credit. You're believin in a whole lot of accidents."

"How's that?"

"The way you're lookin at this whole thing."

"For instance?"

"Your prints. They're on the glass, right?"

"Right."

"And only you would know? You can't make an i.d. yourself. Gotta get the lab to do it. That means somebody else comes up with your name."

"Yeah, but I'm a big dummy. I was supposed to recognize the glass—not ask for prints."

"In a major murder case you ain't gonna ask for prints?"

I take a moment. "Maybe she didn't know they could make a

laser match. My prints are there just to keep me from dropping a dime on her."

"Sure," says Lip. "And in the meantime the lab is lookin at the gism, figurin things out. And they got your carpet fibers."

"Nobody ties those things to me."

"What about your phone records, if somebody should think to look? You said yourself she probably knew you'd been usin this phone to call Carolyn. Why's she dial from here, while you're around the house? Why take that chance instead of goin to a pay phone? You don't think that lady knows from MUDs? Or fibers? Or whose prints are on file? After twelve years of listenin to your stories?" Lip chucks down the rest of his whiskey. "Champ, you don't got this figured right."

"No? What do you figure?"

"I figure she wanted Carolyn dead and you in the slammer for doin it. I'd say the only thing that happened that she never counted on was that you beat it. Maybe two things."

Lipranzer grabs one of the kitchen chairs and sits down astride it. We are now face to face.

"I bet she was world-class pissed when you ended up with this case. She'd have never guessed that on the front end. You're the chief deputy. You don't horse around these days with homicides. You don't have the time. You got a fuckin office to run while Horgan's tryin to save his butt. The only thing she'd know is Raymond would be tear-ass—he'd want to keep this thing in-house, right under his thumb. Anybody'd know Raymond would make damn certain the police assignment was Special Command. I think she figured that some smart homicide dick was gonna nail you. Somebody who'd look at too many doors and windows open, who'd get a report about what was in the wad and see it was all a setup— somebody who'd go lookin for a real bright guy who'd know just how to do it. That's what she was countin on—somebody who knows you real good. Somebody who goes with you to the Red Cross drive and knows your blood type. Maybe even knows you well enough to think you were keepin company with a certain dead lady. Knows what color carpet you got at home." Lip suddenly, and inappropriately, yawns as he looks out to the living room. "Yeah," he says, "when I come for you with the cuffs, that'd put the knife in pretty deep. That's what I figure."

Lipranzer eyes me sagely. Then he nods, convincing himself.

"That's possible," I say, after a moment. "I've thought of that. But she said things didn't go the way she'd expected."

"Meanin what?" he asks. "They didn't fry your ass? I mean, what else you gonna hear but hearts and flowers: Honey, I'da saved you if I had to. What would you do? Say, Go head and turn me in?"

"I don't know, Lip." I look at him, then I slug him softly in the shoulder. "Fifteen minutes ago you thought I was the one who killed her."

In response he makes his sound.

"I don't know," I say again. "I believe two things. She did it. And she was sorry. I'll always believe she was sorry." I straighten up. "And anyway, it never would have done me any good to tell."

"Speakin of tellin, did you let your lawyers know, at least?"

"Nope. Neither one. Right at the end I had this idea Sandy might have figured it out. He talked to me one night about putting Barbara on the stand—and I got a clear feeling he didn't have the slightest interest in really doing it. And the kid, Kemp, had some notion, too. He knew something was out of whack with the phone records. But I'd never have put either one of them in that position, having to choose between my wife and me. I didn't want to be defended that way. Like I said, I couldn't see taking his mother from my son. And besides, it would never wash. If Barbara really figured all this out, Lip, then she knew that, too. Nico had a beautiful argument if I got up there and accused her. He would have said this was the perfect crime. An unhappy marriage. A prosecutor who knows the system inside out. A guy who's become a misogynist. He despises Carolyn. He hates his wife. But he loves the boy. If he and his wife split, he'll never get custody. He'd have said I planned it this way. Made it look like her set-up. Right down to getting her fingerprints on the glass or injecting the spermicide. Maybe he'd say I was using Barbara as a fail-safe, the person I'd like to see nabbed in case the whole house of cards fell in on me. There are plenty of juries that might buy that."

"But it isn't true," says Lip.

I look at him. I can tell that I have left him out there again, floating uneasily in the ether regions of disbelief.

"No," I tell him, "that isn't true."

But there is that flicker there, the brief light of an idle doubt. What is harder? Knowing the truth or finding it, telling it or being believed?

Closing
Argument

When Raymond called, I told him the idea was absurd.

"Instant rehabilitation," he said.

"It is impossible," I answered.

"Rusty," he said, "give a guilty conscience a chance." I was not sure if he was referring to himself or everyone in Kindle County. But he insisted it could happen, and at last I told him that if everything could be arranged I would think seriously about it.

In January, as a result of the petition drive the City Council authorized a recall election. Bolcarro could have prevented it, but he displayed a marked neutrality toward Della Guardia. Nico campaigned actively to retain his office and he nearly pulled it out. He fired Tommy Molto with about two weeks left, but various civic leaders, including Raymond, Larren, and Judge Mumphrey, came out against him, and Della Guardia was recalled with a margin of about 2,000 votes. He has not given up. He is going to run for City Council from the South End, and I expect him to win.

Bolcarro formed a citizens' commission to make recommendations on the new P.A. Raymond was a member. That was what led him to call me. Rumour has it that Mac was the first choice, but she refused to leave the bench. Raymond promised me that the papers had been sounded and that I would receive universal support. I could not think of a good reason to say no. On March 28, four days short of the anniversary of Carolyn Polhemus's murder, I became the acting Kindle County prosecuting attorney.

I took the position with the understanding that I will not

run for re-election. The mayor has told me a couple of times he thinks I'll make a fine judge, but he has not put that on paper. Right now I enjoy the job I have. The news stories refer to me as 'the caretaker P.A.' My relations with lots of people have all kinds of peculiar strains and edges, but it is no worse at work than when I walk down from my apartment to buy a dozen eggs. I accepted that this would be the case when I did not leave Kindle County. It is not that I am brave, or even stubborn. I just don't think the problems of a new life somewhere else would be any easier than dealing with what is here. I will always be a kind of museum piece. Rusty Sabich. The biggest bullshit thing you've ever seen. Set up, no question about it, and then Della Guardia covered Molto. Really pathetic, the whole business. The guy is not quite the same.

The murder of Carolyn Polhemus, of course, remains unsolved. No one talks about pursuing it, surely not with me, and it's a practical impossiblity anyway to try two people for the same crime. A few months ago they had some jailhouse crank who was trying to confess. I sent Lipranzer over to take his statement. Lip quickly reported to the department his judgment that it was a bunch of crap.

I go to Detroit on many weekends. With this job, it is harder than I planned, but when I cannot make it, Barbara sends Nathaniel down. On my second trip up there, Barbara suggested I stay with them. One thing led to another and we have, in a sort of half-ass way, been reconciled. She is not likely to come back here. Her job has worked out well, and the truth, I think, is that she enjoys the distance from me and the reminders. Neither of us expects the present arrangement to last. Sooner or later the swelling will recede and one of us will meet somebody else. When I think about that, I hope it's a woman a few years younger. I would like to have another child. But that's the kind of thing no one can plan. For the present, Nat seems to take comfort from the fact that his mother and I are still married, not divorced.

At times, I admit, I still think of Carolyn. There is none of that crazy longing left, none of the bizarre fixation. I guess she has finally found her place of rest for me. But I puzzle on the experience now and then. What was it, I still think. What

was it I wanted with her? What seemed so imperative about
it all? In the end, it must have had something to do with my
sense of the torment, the agonies which drove her. That
legacy of pain was openly displayed—in her hard-shell
manner, her hipped-up weariness, her ardent courtroom
spokesmanship for the likes of Wendell McGaffen, the
assailed and woebegone. She was herself someone who had
suffered vastly—and who claimed in every visible aspect of
her being to have triumphed over it all. That was not true.
She could no more leave the horrible weight of her past
behind than those Greek heroes could fly close to the sun. But
does that mean it is impossible for all of us?

I reached for Carolyn. In a part of me, I knew my gesture
was ill-fated. I must have recognized her troubled vanity, the
poverty of feeling that reduced her soul. I must have known
that what she offered was only the grandest of illusions. But
still I fell for that legend she had made up about herself. The
glory. The glamour. The courage. All her determined grace.
To fly above this obscure world of anguish, this black
universe of pain! For me there will always be that struggle to
escape darkness. I reached for Carolyn. I adored her, as the
faith healer is adored by the halt and lame. But I wanted
with wild, wild abandon, with a surging, defiant, emboldened desire, I wanted the extreme—the exultation, the passion
and the moment, the fire, the light. I reached for Carolyn. In
hope. Hope. Everlasting hope.

THE
BURDEN
OF PROOF

For Annett

*[Our] decisions have respected the private realm of family
life which the state cannot enter.*

Prince v. Massachusetts, 321 U.S. 158, 166 (1944),
an opinion of the United States Supreme Court

*I once undertook to improve the marriage relations of a very
intelligent man.... He continually occupied himself with the
thought of a separation, which he repeatedly rejected
because he dearly loved his two small children.... One day,
the man related to me a slight occurrence which had
extremely frightened him. He was sporting with the older
child, by far his favourite. He tossed it high in the air and
repeated the tossing until finally he thrust it so high that its
head almost struck the massive gas chandelier.... [The child]
became dizzy with fright.... The particular facility of this
careless movement.... suggested to me to look upon this
accident as a symbolic action....*

*There was indeed a powerful determinant in a memory
from the patient's childhood: it referred to the death of a little
brother, which the mother laid to the father's negligence, and
which led to serious quarrels with threats of separation
between the parents. The continued course of my patient's
life, as well as the therapeutic success, confirmed my
analysis.*

SIGMUND FREUD
The Psychopathology of Everday Life

PART ONE

1

They had been married for thirty-one years, and the following spring, full of resolve and a measure of hope, he would marry again. But that day, on a late afternoon near the end of March, Mr. Alejandro Stern had returned home and, with his attaché case and garment bag still in hand, called out somewhat absently from the front entry for Clara, his wife. He was fifty-six years old, stout and bald, and never particularly good-looking, and he found himself in a mood of intense preoccupation.

For two days he had been in Chicago—that city of rough souls—on behalf of his most difficult client. Dixon Hartnell was callous, self-centered, and generally scornful of his lawyers' advice; worst of all, representing him was a permanent engagement. Dixon was Stern's brother-in-law, married to Silvia, his sister, Stern's sole living immediate relation and the enduring object of his affections. For Dixon, of course, his feelings were hardly as pure. In the early years, when Stern's practice amounted to little more than the decorous hustling of clients in the hallways of the misdemeanor courts, serving Dixon's unpredictable needs had paid Stern's rent. Now it was one of those imponderable duties, darkly rooted in the hard soil of Stern's own sense of filial and professional obligation.

It was also steady work. The proprietor of a vast commodity-futures trading empire, a brokerage house he had named, in youth, Maison Dixon, and a series of interlocked subsidiaries, all called MD-this and -that, Dixon was routinely in trouble. Exchange officials, federal regulators, the IRS—they'd all had Dixon's number for years. Stern stood up for him in these scrapes.

But the present order of business was of greater concern. A federal grand jury sitting here in Kindle County had been issuing subpoenas out of town to select MD clients. Word of these subpoenas, served by the usual grim-faced minions of the FBI, had been trailing back to MD for a week now, and Stern, at the conclusion of his most recent trial, had flown at once to Chicago to meet privately with the attorneys representing two of these customers and to review the records the government required from them. The lawyers reported that the Assistant United States Attorney assigned to the matter, a young woman named Klonsky, declined to say precisely who was under suspicion, beyond exonerating the customers themselves. But to a practiced eye, this all had an ominous look. The out-of-town subpoenas reflected a contemplated effort at secrecy. The investigators knew what they were seeking and seemed intent on quietly encircling Dixon, or his companies, or someone close to him.

So Stern stood travel-weary and vexed in the slate foyer of the home where Clara and he had lived for nearly two decades. And yet, what was it that wrested his attention so thoroughly, so suddenly? The silence, he would always say. Not a tap running, a radio mumbling, not one of the household machines in operation. An isolated man, he drew, always, a certain comfort from stillness. But this was not the silence of rest or interruption. He left his bags on the black tiles and stepped smartly through the foyer.

"Clara?" he called again.

He found her in the garage. When he opened the door, the odor of putrefaction overwhelmed him, a powerful high sour smell which dizzied him with the first breath and drove up sickness like a fist. The car, a black Seville, the current model, had been backed in; the driver's door was open. The auto's white dome light remained on, so that in the dark garage she was wanly spotlit. From the doorway he could see her leg extended toward the concrete floor, and the hem of a bright floral shirtwaist dress. He could tell from the glint that she was wearing hosiery.

Slowly, he stepped down. The heat in the garage and the smell which increased revoltingly with each step were overpowering, and in the dark his fear left him weak. When he could see her through the open door of the car, he advanced no farther. She was reclined on the camel-colored leather of the front seat. Her skin, which he noticed first, was burnished with an unnatural peachish glow, and her eyes were closed. It seemed she had meant to appear neat and composed. Her left hand, faultlessly manicured, was placed almost ceremonially across her abdomen, and the flesh had swollen slightly beneath her wedding rings. She had brought nothing with her. No jacket. No purse. And she had not fallen back completely; her other arm was rigidly extended toward the wheel, and her head was pinned against the seat at a hopeless, impossible angle. Her mouth was open, her tongue extruded, her face dead, motionless, absolutely still. In the whitewashed laundry room adjoining the garage he was immediately sick in one of the porcelain basins, and he washed away all traces before calling in quick order 911 and then his son.

"You must come straightaway," he said to Peter. He had found him at home. "Straightaway." As usual in stress, he heard some faint accentuation of the persistent Hispanic traces in his speech; the accent was always there, an enduring deficit as he thought of it, like a limp.

"Something is wrong with Mother," Peter said. Stern had mentioned nothing like that, but his son's feeling for these things was sure. "What happened in Chicago?"

When Stern answered that she had not been with him, Peter, true to his first instincts, began to quarrel.

"How could she not be with you? I spoke to her the morning you were leaving."

A shot of terrible sympathy for himself tore through Stern. He was lost, the emotional pathways hopelessly tangled. Hours later, toward morning, as he was sitting alone beneath a single light, sipping sherry as he revisited, reparsed every solemn moment of the day, he would take in the full significance of Peter's remark. But that eluded him now. He felt only, as ever, a deep central impatience with his son, a suffering, suppressed volcanic force, while somewhere else his heart read the first clues in what Peter had told him, and a sickening unspeakable chasm of regret began to open.

"You must come now, Peter. I have no idea precisely what has occurred. I believe, Peter, that your mother is dead."

His son, a man of thirty, let forth a brief high sound, a cry full of desolation. "You *believe* it?"

"Please, Peter. I require your assistance. This is a terrible moment. Come ahead. You may interrogate me later."

"For Chrissake, what in the hell is happening there? What in the hell is this? Where are you?"

"I am home, Peter. I cannot answer your questions now. Please do as I ask. I cannot attend to this alone." He hung up the phone abruptly. His hands were trembling and he leaned once more against the laundry basin. He had seemed so coldly composed only an instant before. Now some terrible sore element in him was on the rise. He presumed he was about to faint. He removed his tie first, then his jacket. He returned for an instant to the garage door; but he could not push it open. If he waited, just a moment, it seemed he would understand.

*   *   *

The house was soon full of people he did not know. The police came first, in pairs, parking their cars at haphazard angles in the drive, then the paramedics and the ambulance. Through the windows Stern saw a gaggle of his neighbors gathering on the lawn across the way. They leaned toward the house with the arrival of each vehicle and spoke among themselves, held behind the line of squad cars with their revolving beacons. Within the house, policemen roamed about with their usual regrettable arrogance. Their walkie-talkies blared with occasional eruptions of harsh static. They went in and out of the garage to gawk at the body and talked about events as if he were not there. They studied the Sterns' rich possessions with an envy that was disconcertingly apparent.

The first cop into the garage had lifted his radio to summon the lieutenant as soon as he emerged.

"She's cooked," the officer told the dispatcher. "Tell him he better come with masks and gloves." Only then did he notice Stern lurking in a fashion in the dark hall outside the laundry room. Abashed, the policeman began at once to explain. "Looks like that car run all day. It's on empty now. Catalytic converter gets hotter than a barbecue—six, seven hundred degrees. You run that engine twelve hours in a closed space, you're generating real heat. That didn't do her any good. You the husband?"

He was, said Stern.

"Condolences," said the cop. "Terrible thing."

They waited.

"Do you have any idea, Officer, what occurred?" He did not know what he thought just now, except that it would be a kind of treachery to believe the worst too soon. The cop considered Stern in silence. He was ruddy and thick, and his weight probably made him look older than he was.

"Keys in the ignition. On position. Garage door's closed." Stern nodded.

"It dudn't look like any accident to me," the cop said finally. "You can't be sure till the autopsy. You know, could be she had a heart attack or somethin right when she turned the key.

"Maybe it's one of them freak things, too," the cop said. "Turns the car on and she's thinkin about somethin else, you know, fixin her hair and makeup, whatever. Sometimes you never know. Didn't find a note, right?"

A note. Stern had spent the moments awaiting the various authorities here in this hallway, keeping his stupefied watch beside the door. The thought of a note, some communication, provided, against all reason, a surge of hope.

"You'd just as well stay out of there," the policeman said, gesturing vaguely behind him.

Stern nodded with the instruction, but after an instant he took a single step forward.

"Once more," he said.

The policeman waited only a moment before opening the door.

* * *

He was known as Sandy, a name he had adopted shortly after his mother and sister and he had arrived here in 1947, driven from Argentina by unending calamities—the death of his older brother, and then his father; the rise of Perón. It was his mother who had urged him to use this nickname, but he was never wholly at ease with it. There was a jaunty, comic air to the name; it fit him poorly, like someone else's clothing, and, therefore, seemed to betray all that helpless immigrant yearning for acceptance which he so ardently sought to conceal, and which had been in truth perhaps his most incorrigible passion.

To be an *American*. Having come of age here in the 1950s, he would always hear the whisper of special obligations in the word. He had never bought a foreign car; and he had forsaken Spanish years ago. Occasionally, in surprise, a few words, a favored expression might escape him, but he had arrived here determined to master the American tongue. In his parents' home there was no single language—his mother addressed them in Yiddish; with each other, the children used Spanish; his father talked principally to himself in windy high-flown German, which sounded to Stern as a child like some rumbling machine. In Argentina, with its deep Anglophile traditions, he had learned to speak the English of an Eton schoolboy. But here the idioms of everyday life flashed in his mind like coins, the currency of real Americans. From the first, he could not bear to use them. Pride and shame, fire and ice, burned away at him always; he could not endure the sniggering that seemed to follow even the slightest accented misuse. But in his dreams he spoke a rich American argot, savory as any jazzman's.

American optimism, on the other hand, he had never absorbed. He could not leave aside the gloomy lessons of foreign experience, of his parents' lives—emigrants, exiles, souls fleeing despots, never at rest. Certain simple propositions he took as articles of faith: things would often turn out badly. Seated in the living room in an overstuffed chair, amid Clara's raiku vases and Chinese tapestries, he accepted this like the coming true of an evil spell. He had the inkling of various tasks that were somehow imperative, but for the time being he had no thought to move; his limbs were weak from shock, and his heart seemed to labor.

Peter arrived not long after the paramedics. They had already rolled their white-sheeted cart into the garage to remove the body. Wiry and always intense, Peter had burst into the house, disregarding the policemen at the front door. Why was it, Stern wondered, that he was so appalled by his son's hysteria, this hyperthyroid look of uncontrollable panic? Peter was immaculately kempt, a bone-thin young man with a highly fashionable hairdo. He wore a blousy French shirt with broad turquoise stripes; his pants were olive, but of a style never worn in any army, ballooning widely near the knee. Stern, even now, could not restrict a critical impulse. It was remarkable, really, that this man whose face was rigid with distress had taken the time to dress.

Rising finally, he encountered his son in the hallway leading from the foyer to the kitchen.

"I just can't believe this." Peter, like Stern, seemed to have no idea how to behave; he moved a single step toward his father, but neither man reached out. "My God," he said, "look at it. It's a carnival outside. Half the neighborhood's there."

"Do they know what happened?"

"I told Fiona Cawley." The Cawleys had lived next door to the Sterns for nineteen years. "She more or less demanded it. You know how she is."

"Ah," Stern said. He battled himself, but he found that a selfish shame, juvenile in its intensity, struck at him. This terrible fact was out now, news now, known. Stern could see the canny deliberations taking place behind Fiona Cawley's deadly yellow eyes.

"Where is she?" Peter demanded. "Is she still here?"

As soon as Peter had gone off to the garage, Stern recalled that he had meant to speak with him about calling his sisters.

"Mr. Stern?" The policeman who had gone into the garage was standing there. "Couple of the fellas wanted a word, if you don't mind."

They were in Stern's first-floor den, a tiny room that he kept largely to himself. Clara had painted the walls hunter green and the room was crowded with furniture, including a large desk on which certain household papers were carefully laid. It disturbed Stern to see the police stationing themselves in this room which had always been his most private place. Two policemen in uniform, a man and a woman, stood, while a plainclothes officer occupied the sofa. This third one, a detective apparently, rose desultorily to offer his hand.

"Nogalski," he said. He gripped Stern's hand tepidly and did not bother to look at him. He was a thick man, wearing a tweed sport coat. A hard type. They all were. The detective motioned to a facing easy chair. Behind Stern, the female officer mumbled something into her radio: We're talkin' to him now.

"You up to a few questions, Sandy?"

"Of what nature?"

"The usual. You know. We got a report to make. Lieutenant's on the way. Gotta fill him in. This come as a big surprise to you?" the cop asked.

Stern waited.

"Very much," he said.

"She the type to get all depressed and unhappy, the missus?"

This survey of Clara's character, to be attempted in a few sentences, was for the moment well beyond him.

"She was a serious person, Detective. You would not describe her as a blithe personality."

"But was she seeing shrinks, you know, anything like that?"

"Not to my knowledge. My wife was not of a complaining nature, Detective. She was very private."

"She wasn't threatening to do this?"

"No."

The detective, mostly bald, looked directly at Stern for the first time. It was evident he did not believe him.

"We haven't found a note yet, you know."

Stern stirred a hand weakly. He could not explain.

"And where have you been?" one of the cops behind Stern asked.

"Chicago."

"For?"

"Legal business. I met with a number of lawyers." The fact that Dixon might be in very serious difficulties, so sorely troubling only an hour ago, recurred to Stern now with a disconcerting novelty. The urgency of that situation waved to him like a hand disappearing in the deep, out of reach for the time being.

"How long you gone?" Nogalski asked.

"I left very early yesterday."

"You talk to her?"

"I tried last night, but there was no answer. We have a symphony series. I assumed she had gone for coffee afterwards with friends."

"Who spoke to her last, so far as you know?"

Stern deliberated. Peter's shrill manner would quickly antagonize the police.

"My son might have."

"He out there?"

"He is quite emotional at the moment."

Nogalski, for whatever reason, allowed himself a brief, disparaging smile.

"You do that often?" one of the cops behind him asked. "What is that, Officer?"

"Travel. Out of town?"

"Occasionally it is necessary."

"Where'd you stay?" the woman asked. Stern tried not to react to the drift of the questions. The officers, of course, knew by now who he was and reacted accordingly—they despised most criminal defense lawyers, who hindered the police at every turn and were often richly rewarded for their efforts. To the police, this was a natural opportunity—a chance to pester an adversary and to indulge their customary nasty fancies about foul play and motives. Maybe the spick was humping his girlfriend in Chi while somebody for hire set this up. You never know unless you ask.

"On this occasion, I was at the Ritz." Stern stood. "May I go? My son and I have yet to speak with his sisters."

Nogalski was watching him.

"This doesn't make much sense," said the detective.

It made no sense, the man said. This was his professional opinion. Stern looked intently at Nogalski. It was one of the hazards of Stern's calling that he seldom felt grateful to the police.

Coming back down the hall, Stern could hear Peter's voice. He was carrying on about something. The same ruddy-faced cop who had shown Stern into the garage was listening impassively. Stern took his son by the elbow to draw him away. This was intolerable. Intolerable! Some tough element of resistance within him was wearing away.

"My God, they're going to do an autopsy—did you know that?" asked Peter as soon as they were alone in the corridor. Peter was an M.D. and today apparently he was haunted by his past, the pathological exams he had practiced on the bums turned up in gutters, the gruesome med school humor as six or seven students studied the innards of the deceased. Peter suffered with the thought of his mother as another mound of lifeless anatomy awaiting the coroner's saw. "You're not going to allow that, are you?"

A good deal shorter than his son, Stern observed Peter. Was it only with his father that this craven hysteria occurred? Stern wondered. The climate of their relations did not seem to have changed for years. Always there was this lamenting hortatory quality, too insistent to be passed off as mere whining. Stern had wondered for so long what it was his son expected him to do.

"It is routine, Peter. The coroner must determine the cause of death."

" 'The cause of death'? Do they think it was an accident? Are they going to do a brain scan and figure out what she was thinking? For God sake, we won't have a body left to bury. It's obvious. She killed herself." No one yet had said that aloud. Stern registered Peter's directness as a kind of discourtesy—too coarse, too blunt. But no part of him riled up in shock.

This was not, he said, the moment to cross swords with the police. They were, as usual, being idiotic, conducting some kind of homicide investigation. They might wish to speak next to him.

"Me? About what?"

"Your last conversations with your mother, I assume. I told them you were too distressed at the moment."

In his great misery, Peter broke forth with a brief, childish smile. "Good," he said. Such a remarkably strange man. A peculiar moment passed between Stern and his son, a legion of things not understood. Then he reminded Peter that they needed to call his sisters.

"Right," said Peter. A more sober cast came into his eye. Whatever his differences with his father, he was a faithful older brother.

Down the hall, Stern heard someone say, "The lieutenant's here." A large man ducked into the corridor, peering toward them. He was somewhere near Stern's age, but time seemed to have had a different effect on him. He was large and broad, and like a farmer or someone who worked outdoors, he appeared to have maintained most of the physical strength of youth. He wore a light brown suit, a rumpled, synthetic garment, and a rayon shirt that hung loosely; when he turned around for a second, Stern could see an edge of shirttail trailing out beneath his jacket. He had a large rosy face and very little hair, a few thick gray clumps drawn across his scalp.

He dropped his chin toward Stern in a knowing fashion. "Sandy," he said.

"Lieutenant," Stern answered. He had no memory of this man, except having seen him before. Some case. Some time. He was not thinking well at the moment.

"When you get a chance," the lieutenant said.

Some confusion rose up between Stern and his son.

"You talk to him. I'll call," said Peter. "You know, Marta and Kate. It's better from me."

With a sudden lucid turn, the kind of epiphanal instant he might have expected at a time of high distress, Stern recognized a traditional family drama taking place. As his children had marched toward adulthood, Peter had assumed a peculiar leadership in the family—he was the one to whom his sisters and mother often turned. He had forged intensive secret bonds with each of them—Stern did not know how, because the same alliances were never formed with him. This terrible duty, Stern realized, should be his, but the paths of weakness were well worn.

"Please say I shall speak to them soon."

"Sure." A certain reflective light had come over Peter; he leaned against the wall for an instant, absorbing it all, worn out by his own high emotions. "Life," he observed, "is full of surprises."

In Stern's den, the lieutenant was receiving a report from his officers. Nogalski had come strolling up as Stern emerged from the hallway. The lieutenant wanted to know what the policemen had been doing. Nogalski spoke. The others knew they had no place to answer.

"I was asking a few questions, Lieutenant."

"Think you've asked enough?" Nogalski took a beat on that. They did not get along, the detective and the lieutenant—you could see that. "Maybe you could lend a hand outside. There's a real bunch of gawkers."

When the other officers were gone, the lieutenant gestured for Stern. He knocked at the door with the back of his hand so that it closed part way.

"Well, you got a shitpot of troubles here, don't you, Sandy? I'm sorry to see you again, under the circumstances." The lieutenant's name was Radczyk, Stern remembered suddenly. Ray, he thought. "You holdin' up?" he asked.

"For the time being. My son is having some difficulty. The

prospect of an autopsy for some reason upsets him."

The cop, shifting around the room, seemed to shrug.

"We find a note someplace, we could do without it, I guess. I could probably fix it up with Russell's office." He was referring to the coroner. "They can always measure the C.O. in the blood." The old policeman looked at Stern directly then, aware probably that he was being too graphic. "I owe, you know," he said.

Stern nodded. He had no idea what Radczyk was talking about.

The policeman sat down.

"The fellas go over all the usual with you?"

He nodded again. Whatever that was.

"They were very thorough," said Stern.

The lieutenant understood at once.

"Nogalski's okay. He pushes, he's okay. Rough around the edges." The lieutenant looked out the door. He was the type someone must have called a big oaf when he was younger. Before he had a badge and a gun. "It's a tough thing. I feel terrible for you. Just come home and found her, right?"

The lieutenant was doing it all again. He was just much better at it than Nogalski.

"She sick?" the lieutenant asked.

"Her health was excellent. The usual middle-age complaints. One of her knees was quite arthritic. She could not garden as much as she liked. Nothing else." From the study window, Stern could see the neighbors parting to let the ambulance pass. It rolled slowly through the crowd. The beacon, Stern noticed, was not turning. No point to that. He watched until the vehicle carrying Clara had disappeared in the fullness of the apple tree, just coming to leaf, at the far corner of the lot, then he brought himself back to the conversation. The left knee, Stern thought.

"You don't know of any reason?"

"Lieutenant, it should be evident that I failed to observe something I should have." He expected to get through this, but he did not. His voice quaked and he closed his eyes. The thought of actually breaking down before this policeman revolted him, but something in him was bleeding away. He was going to say that he had much to regret right now. But he was sure he could not muster that with any dignity. He said, "I am sorry, I cannot help you."

Radczyk was studying him, trying to decide, in all likelihood, if Stern was telling the truth.

A policeman leaned into the room through the half-open door.

"Lieutenant, Nogalski asked me to tell you they found something. Up in the bedroom. He didn't want to touch it till you seen it."

"What is that?" asked Stern.

The cop looked at Stern, unsure if he should answer.

"The note," the officer said at last.

It was there on Stern's highboy, jotted on a single sheet of her stationery, laid out beside a pile of handkerchiefs which the housekeeper had ironed. Like the grocery list or a reminder to get the cleaning. Unassuming. Harmless. Stern picked up the sheet, overcome by this evidence of her presence. The lieutenant stood at his shoulder. But there was very little to see. Just one line. No date. No salutation. Only four words.

"Can you forgive me?"

2

In the dark early morning the day of the funeral, a dream seized Stern from sleep. He was wandering in a large house. Clara was there, but she was in a closet and would not come out. She clung shyly to one of the hanging garments, a woman in her fifties whose knees knocked in a pose of childish bashfulness. His mother called him, and his older brother, Jacobo, voices from other rooms. When he moved to answer them, Clara told him they were dead, and his body rushed with panic.

From the bed, he contemplated the illuminated digits on the clock radio. 4:58. He would not sleep again, too frightened by the thronging images of his dream. There had been such a peculiar look on Clara's face when she told him Jacobo was dead, such a sly, calculating gleam.

About him the house, fully occupied, seemed to have taken on an inert, slumbering weight. His older daughter, Marta—twenty-eight, a Legal Aid lawyer in New York—had flown back the first night and slept now down the hall, in the room which had been hers as a child. His younger daughter, Kate, and her husband, John, who lived in a distant suburb, had also spent the night, rather than fight the unpredictable morning traffic over the river bridges. Silvia, Stern's sister, was in the guest room, come from her country house to minister to her brother and to organize the house of grief. Only the two men, Peter and, of course, Dixon—forever the lone wolf—were missing.

Last night, the task of mourning in its grimmest ceremonial aspects had begun. The formal period of visitation would follow the funeral, but Stern, always ambivalent about religious formalities, had opened the house to various heartsore friends who seemed to need to comfort him—neighbors, two young lawyers from Stern's office, his circle from the courthouse and the synagogue; Clara was an only child, but two separate pairs of her cousins had arrived from Cleveland. Stern received them all with as much grace as he could manage. At these times, one responded according to the most deeply trained impulses. To Stern's mother, gone for decades but still in his dreams, matters of social form had been sacred.

But after the house had emptied and the family had trailed off to sleep, Stern had closed himself up in the bathroom off the bedroom he had shared with Clara, racked for the second time that evening by a wrenching, breathless bout of tears. He sat on the toilet, from which the frilled skirting that Clara had placed there decades before still hung, with a towel forced to his mouth, howling actually, uncontrolled, hoping no one would hear him. 'What did I do?' he asked repeatedly in a tiny stillborn voice as a rushing storm of grief blew through him. Oh, Clara, Clara, what did I do?

Now, examining himself in the bathroom mirrors, he found his face puffy, his eyes bloodshot and sore. For the moment he had regained some numbed remoteness, but he knew the limits of his strength. What a terrible day this would become. Terrible. He dressed fully, except for his suit coat, and made himself a single boiled egg, then sat alone, watching the glint of the sunrise enlarge on the glossy surface of the mahogany dining table, until he felt some new incision of grief beginning to knife through him. Desperately—futilely—he tried to calm himself.

How, he thought again, *how* could he have failed to notice in the bed beside him a woman who in every figurative sense was screaming in pain? How could he be so dull, his inner ear so deafened? The signs were such, Stern knew, that even in his usual state of feverish distraction he could have taken note. Clara was normally a person of intense privacy. For years, she had made a completely personal study of Japan; he knew nothing about it except the titles of the books that occasionally showed up on her desk. At other moments, she would read a musical score; the entire symphony would rage along inside her. Barely perceptible, her chin might drop; but not a bar, a note was so much as whispered aloud.

But this was something more. Two or three nights recently he had returned home late, preoccupied with the case he was trying—a messy racketeering conspiracy—to find Clara sitting in the dark; there was no book or magazine, not even the TV's vapid flickering. It was her expression that frightened him most. Not vacant. Absent. Removed. Her mouth a solemn line, her eyes hard as agates. It seemed a contemplation beyond words. There had been such spells before. Between them, they were referred to as moods and allowed to pass. For years, he prided himself on his discretion.

Driven now, he moved restlessly about the house, holding the items she had held, examining them as if for clues. In the powder room, he touched a tortoiseshell comb, a Lalique dish, the dozen cylinders of lipstick that were lined up like shotgun shells beside the sink. My God! He squeezed one of the gold tubes in his hands as if it were an amulet. On a narrow wig stand in the foyer, three days' mail was piled. Stern fingered the envelopes, neatly stacked. Bills, bills—they were painful to behold. These prosaic acts, visiting the cleaner or department store, humbly bespoke her hopes. On the sixth of March, Clara expected life to continue. What had intervened?

"Westlab Medical Center." Stern considered the envelope. It was directed to Clara Stern at their address. Inside, he found an invoice. The services, identified by a computer code, had been rendered six weeks ago and were described simply as "Test." Stern was still. Then he moved directly to the kitchen, already counseling himself to reason, exerting his will powerfully to contain the shameful outbreak of grateful feelings. But he was certain, positive, she had made no mention of doctors or of tests. Clara recorded her appointments in a leather book beside the telephone. Luncheons. The inevitable musical occasions. The dinner dates and synagogue and bar affairs of their social life. He had brought the bill and matched its date against the book. "9:45 Test." He paged back and forth. On the thirteenth there was another entry. "3:30 Dr." He searched further. On the twenty-first, the same. "Dr." "Test." "Dr."

Cancer. Was that it? Something advanced. Had she resolved to make her departure without allowing the family to beg her, for their sake as much as hers, to undergo the oncologist's life-prolonging tortures? *That* would be like Clara. To declare that zone of ultimate sovereignty. Her mark of dignity, decorum, intense belief was here.

Pacing, he had arrived once more in the dining room, and he heard movement on the second floor, above him. With even an instant's distraction, he felt suddenly that, for all the blind willingness with which his heart ran to this solution, he had been caught up in fantasy. There was some explanation of these medical events more mundane, less heroic. Somehow he found the suspicion chilling. Last night, blundering about in their bathroom, searching for tissue, he had come across a bottle of hair coloring hidden in the dark corner of a drawer. He had no idea how long she had concealed this harmless vanity. Months. Or years? It made no difference. But mortification shuddered through him. He had the same thought now: so much he had not noticed, did not know about that person, this woman, his wife.

* * *

"Daddy?" Stern's daughter Kate, his youngest child, was at the foot of the stairs. She was in her nightgown, a tall stalk of a young woman, slender and heartbreakingly beautiful.

"*Cara*," he answered. He had always used this endearment with the girls at times. Stern was still holding the lab bill, and he pressed the envelope into the back pocket of his trousers. This was not a matter to discuss with the children, not today, at any event, when the thought would foment even greater anguish, and certainly not with Kate. Beauty, Stern suspected, had made the world too simple for Kate. She seemed to drift along, buffered by her uncommon good looks and a kindly disposition. Perhaps that apportioned blame unfairly. Much must have happened here, at home. Clara had concentrated so on Peter; Stern in turn shared a natural intensity with his older daughter, Marta. Kate had never been irradiated by the most intense energies of the mysterious family dynamic.

As a youngster, she had displayed the same intellectual talents as her brother and sister; and she had Clara's musical talent. But all of that had withered. In high school she had met John, a sweet, Gentile lunk, an almost laughable prototype, a football player and a paragon of blond male beauty with his apple-pie face and hapless manner. A year after college, in spite of her parents' gentle discouragement, she had married him.

John started out in his father's printshop, but it was soon clear the business could not sustain two families, and so Dixon had put him to work at MD, where, after some false starts, John seemed to be making do, one more ex-jock jostling about on the playing field of the markets. Kate herself taught school. She loved her husband with a pitiable tender innocence, but Stern at moments could feel his heart rub itself raw with worry at the prospect of the moment Kate finally learned about the wallops the world could deliver. Now she touched his hand.

"Daddy, I want you to know something. We weren't going to say anything for another month, but everyone is so sad—" Kate's mouth trembled slightly.

Dear God, thought Stern, she is pregnant.

She lifted her face proudly. Kate said, "We're going to have a baby."

"Oh my," said Stern. He grasped her hand. "My," he said again, smiling bravely and trying to recall exactly how he would be expected to reflect his delight. He kissed her first on the temple, then took her in his arms. He did so only rarely, and here in her thin nightgown he was amazed by the feel of his daughter, her narrowness, the loose movement of her breasts against him. Kate wept with sudden abandon, then drew back.

"We couldn't say anything," she explained to her father. "It wasn't safe yet. We'd had some problems. And now I keep thinking, What if Mommy knew?" Once more she became uncontrollable. Once more Stern took his dark, beautiful daughter in his arms. But even as he held Kate, he found there was an abrupt adjustment in his own vision of things. Clara had abandoned the children, too. He had viewed this last act of hers as aimed exclusively at him. But the children, grown but troubled, were still not past the point where they required occasional assistance. Would it have made a difference, had Clara known Kate's secret? Or had she decided that they too'd had the last of what she could stand to give?

Above them there was stirring. Marta was on the stairs, a smaller woman, also dark, with wire-rimmed glasses and a bosky do of untamed black hair. She regarded the scene below with a vulnerable look of her own.

"Group cry?" she asked.

Stern awaited Kate's lead. She squared her shoulders and

dabbed her eyes. The entire family was to know. As he prepared for her declaration, entirely unexpected, an arrow of joy shot forth from the leaden-like mass of his interior and he was overcome by a startlingly exact recollection of the abrupt ways a baby's hands and legs would move, random and sudden as life itself.

"I just told Daddy. I'm going to have a baby."

Marta's shriek split the household. A self-serious person, she carried on mindlessly. She embraced her sister, hugged her father. The two young women sat together holding hands. Peter arrived then, coming early to beat the traffic, and was informed. With the commotion John emerged, and everyone rose to hug him. In response to his reticence, they were always excessive. They had labored for years to make John feel accepted in a situation where, for many reasons, he knew he never would be. The group by then had migrated together to the living room. Silvia entered in her housecoat, looking grave; clearly she had taken their hoopla as the noise of one more calamity. Silvia and Dixon had never had a family of their own, much to Silvia's despair, and the news, so unexpected, brought Silvia, too, to tears. It was barely past seven and the family, overcome by all of this, clung to one another. And there in the living room, Stern, at last, longed for Clara. He had been waiting for it. More than the disorder and the loss, at this moment there was the absence.

When he looked up, Marta was watching. It had savaged Stern with sorrow to see her the night she had arrived. Marta, brave Marta, his boldest child, trod soldier-like up the walk, a canvas bag slung over her shoulder, weeping openly as soon as she climbed from the taxi. Stern embraced her at the door. 'Daddy, I never thought she was a happy person, but—' Throttled by emotion, Marta got no further. Stern held her and suffered privately the unequivocal nature of his daughter's estimate of her mother. She had always held Clara at greater distance than the other two; as a result, perhaps, she had more to regret.

Across the room, his daughter, with her father's tiny close-set eyes, looked at him sadly now.

I miss her, too, she mouthed.

* * *

Stern, a frequent morning chef, cooked for the entire group. He fried eggs and flapjacks, and Marta squeezed grapefruit for juice, a family tradition. By nine, an hour before the mortician's limousine was to arrive, they were all fed and dressed, quietly gathered once more in the living room.

"How about bridge?" Marta asked. She prided herself on being unrestrained by convention. In most things, Marta styled herself in the ways of the late sixties. She had been a child then and took it as a time of great romance; she went about in flowing gowns and high-laced boots, with her wind-sprung hair. "Mom liked it when we played."

"Oh, sure," said Peter. "She liked it when we square-danced, too, while we were kids. We can do-si-do to the chapel."

Marta whispered to her brother, Oh fuck off, but smiled. Marta had always tempered her rivalry with Peter, and she granted him special liberties now. Kate's tears were constant, but Peter, of the three, seemed the hardest hit, morose, pensive, persistently out of balance. He went off by himself at many moments but returned inevitably to the comfort of his sisters. Close-knit, Stern's children appeared to take strength from each other.

Marta again mentioned bridge. "Daddy, would you mind?" Stern lifted his palms, not quite an answer.

"Will you play?" Kate asked her father.

Silvia motioned Stern forward, encouraging him.

"I have a few things to look after for later." She was preparing the household for the crush of callers that would follow the funeral.

"I shall help Aunt Silvia. You four play."

"I'll help Aunt Silvia," said John. He was on his feet already, a huge young man, a mountainous blond with a neck thick as a tire rim. He had never mastered the game, like so many other things attached to his in-laws. The Sterns with their quiet intense ways had mystified John for most of a decade.

"Come on," Marta called. She was in the sun room, already looking for cards. Stern understood his daughter's excitement. For an instant, it would be as when she was seventeen and the children were all safe from the world of grownup difficulties. Stern, as ever, found himself chafed and touched by his Marta and her impulses.

"Katy, I will play with you," Stern announced. He was always a partner with one of the girls, usually Kate. He and Peter squabbled when they played together. Stern had spent much of the little time he had at home playing one game or another with his children. Chutes and Ladders. Monopoly. Word games when they were in the primary grades. The four of them spent hours around a game table in the sun room. Clara seldom participated. Often she would sit in a fifth chair, with hands and ankles primly crossed, watching or, when necessary, assisting Kate. But she was not obtrusive. This, for better or worse—rules, moves, strategies—was Alejandro's time.

Peter made the cards and handed them to Stern to deal. The sun room—referred to in the old architect's plans, drawn in the twenties, as 'the solarium'—was a narrow area, rimmed with windows, floored in slate. From here they looked directly at Clara's garden. It was the time of year when she would have begun to turn the soil. The stalks of last year's gladioli, trimmed neatly almost to the soil, rose in rows, survivors of the mild winter.

Stern bid a weak club. He played all conventions. Anything but hand signals, Clara said.

"Are you going back to work after the baby?" Marta asked her sister.

Kate seemed a bit puzzled. Her future, such as it was, was apparently beyond her. Within, Stern seemed to cringe. This child with a child! By John, no less. *Vey iz mir*. Kate told Marta that they did not know yet how the money would work out or how she would feel about leaving the baby.

"Oh, it'll be your first," said Peter. "You'll want to give it lots of attention. It will always be special."

The doorbell rang. Through the front panes, Stern saw his brother-in-law. Dixon had returned to town last night. He had been in New York on pressing business and had delayed going home. Stern had felt slighted—the usual with Dixon—and he was taken aback, therefore, at his relief at seeing Dixon on the threshold with his bags yesterday evening. His brother-in-law, a large, solid man, had thrown his arms about Stern and made a good show of great sorrow. One could seldom be certain how Dixon truly felt. That was part of his genius—he was like a forest, full of many colors. He could greet you at any instant with a salesman's blather or the gruffest truths.

This morning, however, Dixon's attention had returned more typically to himself. As Stern took his coat, Dixon lowered his voice discreetly.

"When you're back at the stand, Stern, I'd like to ask you a question or two."

Dixon always addressed him military fashion, last name only. They had met originally in the service, which had led, by turns, to Dixon's making Silvia's acquaintance and to his becoming in time her suitor, a development to which Stern was still not fully adjusted, three decades after the fact.

"Business questions?" he asked Dixon.

"That kind of item. I don't need to trouble you now. I want to hear about your trip to Chicago."

Ah yes, thought Stern, the paths of ego were deep and the living needed to go on.

"I understand your concern, Dixon. The situation may be somewhat involved, however. It is best that we discuss it another time."

A shadow passed, predictably, over Dixon. Fifty-five years old, he was tan, trim, and, even with this darkened look, the image of vitality. He was a powerful man; he worked out every day with weight equipment. Dixon worshipped at the same altar as so many others in America: the body and its uses. His dark brass-colored hair had grown paler and more brittle with age, but was cleverly barbered to give him a mannerly business-like look.

"You didn't like what you heard?" he asked Stern.

In fact, Stern had learned little of substance. The documents he had examined in Chicago, account statements and trading records of the clients for an eight- or nine-month period, had been unrevealing. There was no telling what offense the government was investigating, or even who had suggested to them the prospect of a crime.

"There may be a problem, Dixon. It is too early to become greatly alarmed."

"Sure." Dixon drew a cigarette from an inside pocket. He was smoking heavily again, an old bad habit recently grown worse, which Stern took as a sign of concern. Three years ago the IRS set up a full-scale encampment in Dixon's conference room, with barely a riffle in his breezy style. This time, however, Dixon was on edge. With word of the first subpoena, he had been on the phone to Stern, demanding that the government be stopped. For the present, however, Stern was loath to contact Ms. Klonsky, the Assistant United States Attorney. At the U.S. Attorney's Office they seldom told you more than they wanted you to know. Moreover, Stern feared that a call from him might somehow focus the government's attention on Dixon, whose name as yet had gone unmentioned. Perhaps the grand jury was looking at a number of brokerage houses. Perhaps something besides MD connected the customers. For the present it was best to tiptoe about, observing the government from cover. "They're always looking for something," Dixon said bravely now, and went off to find Silvia.

In the sun room, Stern's children were still speaking about the baby.

"Will John help out?" Marta asked. "Change diapers and stuff?"

Kate reared back, astonished.

"Of course. He's in heaven. Why wouldn't he?"

Marta shrugged. At moments like this, it concerned Stern that she seemed so dumbfounded by men. Her father's daughter, Marta, regrettably, was not a pretty woman. She had Stern's broad nose and small dark eyes. Worse still, she shared his figure. Stern and his daughter were short, with a tendency to gather weight in their lower parts. Marta submitted herself almost masochistically to the rigors of diet and exercise, but you could never escape what nature had provided. It was not, she was apt to say, the form favored by fashion magazines. Notwithstanding, Marta had always attracted her admirers—but there seemed an inevitable doom in her relations. In her conversation there were, by idle reference, a procession of men who came and went. Older, younger. Things always foundered. Marta, in the meantime, now came to her own defense.

"Daddy didn't change diapers," she said.

"I did not?" asked Stern. Surprisingly, he could not recall precisely.

"How could you have changed diapers?" asked Peter, awakened somewhat by the opportunity to challenge his father. "You were never here. I remember I couldn't figure out what a trial was. I thought it was like a place you went. Another city."

Marta called out for John: "Are you going to change the baby's diapers?"

John, carrying a thirty-cup percolator, entered the sun room for a moment. He looked as bad as everyone else, baffled and grieved. He shrugged gently in response to Marta's question. John was a taciturn fellow. He had few opinions that he was willing to express.

In another room the telephone rang. It had been pealing incessantly for two days now. Stern seldom spoke. The children answered, responding tersely with the time and place of the funeral, promising to share the condolences with their father. Most of these conversations seemed to end the same way, with a labored pause before the instrument was cradled. 'Yes, it's true,' one of them would quickly answer. 'We have no idea why.'

Silvia emerged from the kitchen, wiping her hands on her apron, beckoning to Stern. This call, apparently, he could not avoid. In passing, he touched his sister's hand. A woman with a staff of three at home, Silvia had been here toiling tirelessly for three days, running, organizing, taking care.

"Ah, Sandy. What a sad occasion. My deepest sympathy." Stern had gone up to their bedroom, still dark and shuttered, to take the phone. He recognized the voice of Cal Hopkinson. Cal was a lawyer. When Sandy's beloved friend Harry Fagel had died two years ago, Cal, Harry's partner, had become the Sterns' personal lawyer. He updated their wills and each year filed tax returns for the trusts left for Clara. Cal was a practical fellow, amiable if not particularly appealing, and he came rather quickly to the point. Since Marta was in town, he wondered if Stern might want to come down with the children in the next few days to discuss Clara's will.

"Is that necessary, Cal?"

Cal pondered in silence. Perhaps he was somewhat offended. He was one of those attorneys who lived for details, mowing them down each day in the belief that if they went untended they would overgrow the world.

"It's not necessary, Sandy, but it sometimes helps to prevent questions later. Clara left a large estate, you know."

Did he know? Yes, it came back to him that he did. If the truth were told, in these moments in which he was too harrowed and weak to avoid it, he could barely see Clara through the glimmer of gold when he had married her. Poor boy weds rich girl. It was a dream as thrilling and illicit as pornography. And in keeping, he had practiced the usual cruel repression. Early on, Stern stilled Henry Mittler's obvious suspicions with a vow to his father-in-law that Clara and he would live solely on his income. Thirty years passed in which Stern feigned not to care about Clara's fortune, in which he left the details of management to her and those he suggested she employ, and at the end, in the sorest irony, the lie was truth.

"Is there some surprise in Clara's affairs of which you wish us to be aware, Cal?"

A lawyer's pause here, the habit of a man who had learned to measure every sentence before he spoke. Cal probably considered it unprofessional to answer.

"Nothing to *shock* you," he said at last. "I'm sure you have the general picture. There are probably one or two points we should discuss." Cal had laid just enough emphasis on "shock." Surprise but not devastation, in other words. Now what? he thought. A careful, tidy person always, Clara had left behind her, with no sign of concern, a murky, littered wake. Stern said he would speak to the children and prepared to end the conversation.

"Sandy," said Cal abruptly. Merely from the tone, Stern could tell what was coming. "This is such upsetting news. You must forgive me for asking, but was there any sign?"

No, he said quickly, no sign. He clapped down the phone in a barely suppressed temper. Cal really was a clod, he thought. Stern closed his eyes and took a further moment of retreat in the dark bedroom, listening to the harsh chorus of mingling voices that rang up the stairwell. He was in his soul too solitary to brook this continuing intrusion. It was as if there were some large ear pressed to him, attuned to every breath. The thought of the funeral was suddenly unbearable. A death of this nature would stimulate lurid interest in many. They would be there in teams, in droves, associates and friends and neighbors, come to observe the toll of grief and to eye Stern in a subtle accusatory fashion. Even in those he knew best who had come last night, he could detect that grim curiosity. What was the story? they all wondered. What exactly had he done to her? Clara's suicide had exposed some dark grisly secret, as if there were a grotesque deformity which previously lay hidden on the body of their married life. Not certain if it was the loss or simply the humiliation, Stern remained a few more minutes, weeping in the dark.

* * *

"Do you want a boy or a girl?" Marta was asking as Stern returned to the card table.

Some confusion swam across Kate's fine dark features. This was the first time, of course, that anyone had put the question.

"We both want a healthy baby," said Kate.

"Naturally, you do," Marta said. "But if you could pick, what would it be—a healthy boy or a healthy girl?"

"Marta," Stern said, with his cards fanned before him. He had been counting his points again—it was as if he had never seen the hand. "This is not the kind of question a mother-to-be can always answer." Kate had been thinking. "I'd like a girl." She smiled at all of them. "Girls are nicer."

"Do they let girls on football teams now?" Peter asked. "How far have things gone?"

"John would love a girl," Kate responded instantly.

"Of course," said Stern.

Peter touched his sister's hand to reassure her—he was merely being himself.

"Mothers always say that girls are harder in the end," Marta volunteered.

"That's not what Mommy said," Kate answered.

"That's what she said to me," said Marta. With that utterance, the two sisters stared at one another, some darkling learning looming up between them. For all her brash convictions, Marta was a person of humbling doubts about herself and her place in the world, and she had dwelled more openly than any of them in the last few days on memories of Clara. Much unfinished business, Stern estimated. For the moment, she turned to her father for help. "Isn't that what she said, Dad?"

"Your mother," Stern said, "took the rearing of each of you seriously. Which means that from time to time she felt challenged." Stern smiled diplomatically at Marta. "I believe I said a club."

"Pass," said Marta.

Kate passed.

Peter was quiet, his face closed within the same stormy, anguished look of the last few days. He was wondering, perhaps, what his mother had said about boys. Eventually, he became aware of the three of them watching.

"A heart," he said, when the bidding had been reviewed for him.

"Well, I hear congratulations are in order!" Dixon had emerged from the kitchen, where he had been with Silvia. His arms were wide and he was full, as usual, of stuff and personal ceremony. He had missed Kate and John last night and now crushed Kate to his side, where she received her uncle's embrace, stiffly. "Where's that husband of yours! I didn't think he had it in him." Dixon wandered off, presumably to look for John. Kate shot a starchy look at his back, seemingly unimpressed by her uncle's coarse humor or his jokes at her husband's expense.

The truth, Stern knew, was that he tolerated Dixon more freely than anyone else in the family. Dixon's base side had always impelled in Clara some clear negative response, which, out of loyalty to Silvia, had grown more pointed after the period six or seven years ago when some aspect of Dixon's sportive sexual life—the details were never shared by Silvia—had led Stern's sister briefly to dismiss him from their household. With Dixon, as in most things, the children had tended to follow Clara's lead. Peter and Marta and most especially Kate had always enjoyed an intimate bond with their aunt, who, childless, had showered them with favor. But that attachment had never run to their uncle.

In response, Dixon adhered to the example of potentates throughout the centuries: he purchased indulgence. Over the years, he had taken every opportunity to employ the members of Stern's family. He had Stern and John on his payroll now, and each of the children had worked as a runner for MD on the floor of the Kindle County Futures Exchange during school vacations. When Peter had gone into private practice, Dixon had enrolled MD with Peter's HMO, and even made a short-lived attempt to utilize Peter as his personal physician, although, predictably, they did not get along, quarreling over Dixon's smoking and his general unwillingness to follow advice. Perhaps, Stern had long thought, all this family employment represented Dixon's best efforts—a way to share his imposing wealth, with which he himself was so involved, while maintaining the centrality that he desired in any circumstance.

"Will you name her for Mommy?" Marta inquired of Kate. She seemed more absorbed than her sister with this baby. Silvia, passing through the solarium, frowned at Marta's directness, but both young women were accustomed to it. Marta had always had her way with Kate.

"I suppose," said Kate. "Either a boy or a girl. Unless you would mind, Daddy."

Stern looked up from his cards—but he had not missed a word.

"It would please me if you chose to do this." He smiled gently at Kate. In his tie, he felt a sudden closeness in the room. Dear God, the turmoil. Things seemed to come at him from all directions. He felt like those paintings he would sometimes see in museums and churches, of St. Sebastian shot full of arrows and holes, bleeding like a leaking hose. To his enormous chagrin and surprise, he found he had started, silently, to cry again. The tears ran down both sides of his nose. Around him, his children watched, but made no comment. The days, he supposed, would go like this. He removed his handkerchief from his back pocket and found the medical laboratory bill he had examined early this morning. He had entirely forgotten it.

"I shall return in a moment." He headed off to find a Kleenex. Better jam his pockets. From the kitchen, he looked back to the sun room, where his children, grown up but wounded by their grief, awaited him.

Oh, how these children had mattered to Clara! he thought suddenly. What a worshipful passion. She had been raised with servants, by well-intentioned but limited nannies and governesses. She would have none of that with her own. Again an image: Coming home, one of those occasional evenings when he was here before they were all in bed, to find her on her knees in the kitchen. Peter sat at the table reading; Marta was crying; Kate was having her dress hemmed. The little girl, her shins blotched, stood motionless as her mother fingered the garment. On the stove, a pot was boiling over. Lord, the clamor and the ferment. Clara looked up to greet him and puckered out a lip to blow a stray lock that had fallen down into her eyes. She smiled, smiled.

It was miserable, hard work, as it had always been, a numbing routine of humdrum tasks, but Clara found music in the banging and tumult of family life. Stern, in his simpleminded way, thought little of this. Only now could he see that she made herself a devoted audience to their sounds—their needs—as a distraction from that dismal bleat that must have always whistled away within her.

"Sender?" Silvia was standing beside him, concerned. His sister wore her hair in her usual upswept hairdo, a person of simple, graceful beauty her entire life, still smooth-faced and radiant at the age of fifty-one. She had always called him by his Yiddish name, as their mother had.

He smiled faintly to reassure her, then cast his eyes down. The medical invoice, he noticed, was still in his hand and he passed it with little thought to Silvia, addressing her in a circumspect tone. He asked if Clara had ever spoken of this.

Once more, the doorbell rang. Down the long hall, Stern saw Marta admit two young men in sport coats. They waited inside the foyer, as Marta called out for Dixon. One of the two looked familiar. Henchmen or flunkies, Stern estimated. Dixon had retainers around him like a Mafia don. His business never ceased and his need to learn what was occurring was constant. The one Stern thought he'd seen before was carrying an envelope and a blue vinyl briefcase. Papers to sign, perhaps? Dixon was going to do a deal on the casket.

Silvia, in the interval, had examined the bill and handed it back. Alone they communicated as they always had, few words.

"Dr. Cawley, Nate, next door—he would know, no?" she asked.

Of course. Trust Silvia. Nate Cawley, their next-door neighbor, a gynecologist, was Clara's principal physician. He certainly should have the answer. Stern thought of phoning right now, then recollected that Fiona, Nate's wife, who had been among the visitors last evening, had mentioned, in her usual notable lament, that he was gone for a week on a medical conference. He reminded Silvia.

"Yes, yes." His sister, light-eyed and still striking, studied him earnestly. Apparently, she now shared some of the same thoughts Stern had had earlier.

Through the breakfast-room window, Stern saw the funeral parlor's limousine, dove-gray, swing smoothly into the circular drive before the house, parking behind the dark sedan of Dixon's visitors. Silvia headed off to summon the family. Girding himself, Stern stood.

But down the hall the commotion of angry voices suddenly rose. An alarming scene was taking place near the front door. Dixon was shouting. "What is this?" he yelled at the two men who had arrived only moments before. "What *is* this!" Above his head, he waved a sheet or two of paper.

Halfway there, Stern realized what had taken place. Now this! He could not manage the sudden ignition of anger; it had waited for days so near at hand, and now his heart felt as if it would fly out of his breast, like some NASA rocket trailing flame.

"You crummy so-and-sos!" yelled Dixon. "You couldn't wait?"

Stern rushed to place himself between Dixon and the two men. He had realized where he'd seen the man he recognized— in the federal courthouse, not Dixon's offices. His name was Kyle Horn, and he was a special agent of the FBI.

Dixon was still carrying on. Stern by now had seized the paper from his hand and bulled Dixon a few steps farther back into the foyer. Then he briefly examined the grand jury subpoena. All as usual: a printed form embossed with the court seal. It was directed to Dixon Hartnell, Chairman MD Holdings, and commanded his appearance before a United States grand jury here, four days from now, at 2 p.m. Investigation 89–86. Attached was a long list of documents Dixon was to have in hand. The initials of Sonia Klonsky, the Assistant United States Attorney, appeared at the bottom of the page.

"I refuse to allow this to take place," said Stern. Half a foot shorter than the agents, he maintained, in rage, the erect bearing of a martinet. "If you call my office next week, I shall accept service there. But not at this time. I require you to leave. Immediately. You may tell Assistant United States Attorney Klonsky that I deplore these tactics and shall not abide them." Stern opened the front door.

Horn was past forty. He looked like all the other FBI agents, with a cheap sport coat and a carefully trimmed haircut, but there was a weathered, leathery look to the skin about his eyes: too much sun, or alcohol. He had a bad reputation, the wrong type of agent, a petty tyrant full of resentments.

"No, sir," he said. He gestured toward the subpoena, which

Stern had returned to its envelope and was now extending toward him. "That sucker is served."

"If you file a return of service with the court, I shall move to have you both held in contempt." It occurred to Stern vaguely that this threat was ludicrous, but he gave no ground. "Have you no idea of the nature of this occasion?"

Horn made no move. For a moment, none of the four men moved. Marta had crept to the edge of the living room and watched in grim amazement.

"We are preparing to depart for a funeral," Stern said at last. He pointed out the front windows to the mortuary limousine and the driver in his dead-black suit. "Of Mr. Hartnell's sister-in-law," said Stern. "My wife."

The second agent, a younger man with blond hair, straightened up.

"I didn't know that," he said, then turned to Horn. "Did you know that?"

Horn stared at Stern.

"I know I can't seem to get a call back from Dixon Hartnell. That's what I know," Horn said. "I know I come by the front door and he's gone out the back."

"I'm sorry," the younger agent said. He touched his chest. "All I knew was they said this was where we could find him." The agents, thwarted, had undoubtedly employed their usual techniques. A pretext call, as they referred to it. 'This is the Bank of Boston. We have a problem with a million-dollar wire transfer for Mr. Hartnell. Where can we find him?' The courts for decades had allowed the use of this kind of adolescent cunning.

"Hey," said Horn to his colleague, "shit happens." He took the subpoena without looking at Stern. Then Horn tapped the envelope. "This guy'll be in your office Monday morning, nine sharp."

Stern applied both hands to the front door to close it behind the agents. Peter had drawn Marta away, but Dixon remained in the foyer. He had lit a cigarette and was grinning.

"Got you fired up, didn't they?"

"How long have they been trying to serve you, Dixon?"

Dixon meditatively watched a plume of smoke drift away. He was always disturbed when Stern saw through him.

"Elise says men have been calling for a week or two. I didn't know what it was about," said Dixon. "Honestly." His mouth shifted as Stern looked at him. "I really wasn't sure. That's one of the things I've been meaning to talk with you about."

"Ah, Dixon," said Stern. It was unbelievable. A man who earned $2 million last year, who called himself a business leader, creeping down the back halls and thinking he could hide from the FBI. Stern put one foot on the stairwell, trying to focus on the enormous task at hand. He needed his coat. It was time, he told himself. Time. He was dizzy and faint at heart.

Family, he thought, with despair.

3

Four days after the funeral, Stern returned to the office. He wore
no tie, a means to signify that he was not formally present. He
would look at the mail, answer questions. What was the term?
Touch base.

He had occupied this space for nearly a decade and had
cultivated it with almost the same attention as his home. Small
as it might be, this was Stern's empire, and there was inevitably
some tonic effect in the electronic chatter of the telephones and
business machines, the energetic movements of the dozen
people he employed. Not, of course, today. The office, like
everything else, seemed flattened, depleted, less color, less
music. Entering through the back door, he stood by the desk of
Claudia, his secretary, as he considered his lost universe. He
looked for something hopeful in the mail.

"Mr. Hartnell is here."

The agents, as promised, had arrived with the subpoena
yesterday. Over the phone, Stern had dictated a letter to
prosecutor Klonsky, stating that he represented Dixon and his
company, and directing the government to contact Stern if it
wanted to speak with anyone who worked for MD—a request
the government would inevitably not follow. Then Stern had
summoned Dixon for this meeting. His brother-in-law waited in
Stern's office, his feet on the sofa, the *Tribune* open before him,
while he smoked one of Stern's cigars. His sport coat—double-
breasted, with its many glittering buttons—had been tossed
aside, and his thick forearms, still dark from an island vacation,
were revealed. He rose and welcomed Stern to his own office.

"I made myself at home."

"Of course." Stern apologized for being late, then, removing his sport coat, surveyed. Given his trip to Chicago, it had been more than a week since he had been here, but it all looked the same. He was not sure if he was comforted or horrified by the constancy. Stern's office was decorated in cream-colored tones. Clara had insisted on hiring someone's favorite interior decorator, and the result, Stern often thought, would have been more appropriate to the bedroom of some sophisticated adolescent. There was a sofa with plush pillows, pull-up chairs in the same nubby beige material, and drapes to match. Behind his desk was an English cabinet of dark walnut—a recent addition and more Stern's taste—but his desk was not a desk at all, rather four chromed standards topped by an inch-thick slab of smoky glass. Stern, years later, was still not accustomed to looking down and seeing the soft expanse of his lap. Now he was at liberty to refurnish. The thought came to him plainly and he closed his eyes and made a small sound. He reached for a pad.

"What is this about, Dixon? Have you any idea?"

Dixon shook his large head. "I'm really not sure."

Dixon did not say he did not know. Only that he was not certain. Using the intercom, Stern asked Claudia to get Assistant United States Attorney Klonsky on the phone. She had left a number of phone messages, and Stern wanted to arrange an extension of the date when they would have to comply with her subpoena.

"We must answer certain questions at the threshold, Dixon. What are they investigating? Who is it they seek to prosecute? Is it, in particular, you!"

"Do you think this thing's about me?"

"Probably," said Stern evenly.

Dixon did not flinch, but he took his cigar from his mouth and very carefully removed the ash. He finally made a sound, quiet and ruminative.

"This is a subpoena *duces tecum*, Dixon—a request for records. Ordinarily, the government would not send two agents to serve it. The prosecutors were attempting to deliver a message."

"They want to scare the shit out of me."

"As you would have it." Stern nodded. "I imagine they felt you would soon hear of the investigation. No doubt, had I not intervened, the agents would have sought to interrogate you while you were carrying on."

Dixon mulled. He was so full of himself that one seldom gave full credit to Dixon's subtlety. He studied people largely for his own advantage, but that did not mean he was not observant. Certainly, he was familiar enough with Stern's nuances to realize he was being told again that he had been a fool.

"How bad will this be?" Dixon asked.

"I think that you should not compare this with your prior encounters with the IRS and the CFTC." The Commodities Futures Trading Commission was the federal agency that regulated the futures industry, the equivalent of the SEC. "They are bureaucrats and their first love is their own rules. Their minds do not run automatically to prosecution. Federal grand juries sit to indict. This is a serious business, Dixon."

Dixon mugged up. There was a handsome, weathered look to his eyes.

"Can I ask a dumb question?"

"As many as you like," said Stern.

"What's a grand jury? Really. Besides something that's supposed to make you wet your shorts."

Stern nodded, more or less pleased that Dixon was taking things seriously enough to ask. The grand jury, he explained, was convened by the court to investigate possible federal crimes. In this case, the jurors gathered, by the court's order, every other week, alternating Tuesdays and Thursdays, for eighteen months. They were directed by the United States Attorney's Office, which, in the name of the grand jury, subpoenaed documents and witnesses to be examined at each session. The proceedings were secret. Only the witnesses who testified could reveal what happened. If they chose to. Few individuals, of course, wished to trumpet the fact that they had been haled before a federal grand jury.

"And what kind of chance do I stand with them?" asked Dixon. "This grand jury."

"Very little. Not if the prosecutor decides to indict. It is the U.S. Attorney's Office we must persuade. Inside the grand jury room, the burden of proof on the government is minimal—they need merely convince a bare majority of the jurors that there is probable cause to believe a crime has taken place. The prosecutors may introduce hearsay, and the target and his lawyer have no right to learn what has taken place or to offer any refutation. It is not what you would describe as evenhanded."

"I'd say," answered Dixon. "Whose idea was this?"

"The framers of the Constitution of the United States," answered Stern. "To protect the innocent."

"Oh, sure," said Dixon. All things considered, especially given the havoc of a few days ago, he was taking this with stoical calm. But he was, after all, a person of considerable strength. There was no point in not admiring Dixon. He was one of those fellows Americans had always loved. Dixon had come from one of those bleak Illinois coal-mining towns near the Kentucky border. Stern had paid his college and law school bills by driving a punchboard route throughout the Middle West, and when he was out on the road in the fifties, Stern had seen these towns—colorless, square, plain as the prairies, the air sooted with coal dust— placed amid the sensuous pink forms of the earth which had been stripped and raised in the search for coal. Dixon's father was a German immigrant, a Lutheran minister, a spare, unforgiving, tight-fisted type who had died when Dixon was nine. The mother, sweet-natured but easily trod upon, had depended unnaturally on her son. Stern had not learned any of this from Dixon, but only from his relatives, the spinster aunts and one warmhearted cousin who spoke with admiration of Dixon's early sense that he was destined for more than the numb labored slavery of the coal town.

Behind Stern, the intercom buzzed. No answer at the U.S. Attorney's Office, Claudia announced. It was two in the afternoon, but the prosecutors answered the phone only when they wanted to. Keep trying, Stern told her.

"One other thing we must determine," he said to Dixon, "is how the government came to launch their investigation. We must try to identify the source of whatever allegations they have decided to examine."

"You mean, who fingered me?"

"If you are the target, yes. When we know who spoke against you, we will have some insight into the limitations on the government's information. Have you any idea?"

"Not a clue," said Dixon succinctly, letting his hands flutter up futilely. No doubt he had half a dozen areas in mind where the government might question him, but he would never share any of that with Stern, who would hector him about correcting each infraction. "Probably the compliance people from the Exchange," said Dixon at last. "They're always bitching to someone about me." The suggestion sounded halfhearted, at best.

The telephone rang: Stern's inside line, a different tone, like a cricket. Only his family had this number; it was Clara whom he would generally expect. That reflex rose in him and foundered while he absorbed the second ring.

"Sender?" asked his sister. A welcome voice. Stern's love for Silvia was like his feelings for no one else—purer, less burdened. She had been seventeen when their mother died, and Stern, five years the elder, had assumed that his role toward her would become somewhat parental, but their needs, like everyone's, had been less predictable than that. They looked after one another; they filled in what was lost. Stern and his sister, by the habit of a lifetime, spoke each day. Their conversations lasted barely a minute. 'So, busy?' 'Yes, of course. You?' They spoke of their health, the children, the whirlwind of life. Today she said immediately, "Back at work. This is good, I believe."

"The best alternative." He covered the receiver and to Dixon mouthed "Silvia." He was not certain if Dixon would want her to know he was here, but his brother-in-law pointed to himself to indicate that he would like to speak with her when Stern was finished. Stern told her they were together.

"Discussing this stupid business of the other day?"

"Just so."

She emitted a sigh of sorts but made no further inquiry. His sister and he rarely engaged in any lingering discussions of Dixon, neither the rough and smooth of her marriage nor her husband's complex business affairs. That was more or less the compact of thirty years ago, when Stern had so vehemently opposed their marriage. He had cited religious differences, but only as the best excuse. How could you tell your sister that this fellow who called himself your friend had the sharp look, with his double-breasted suits and pomaded hair, of a carnival barker? In those days, Stern would have wagered that Dixon would be gone when the circus left town. But he'd had greater staying power than that. He was brighter than Stern was willing to acknowledge, and more industrious. And perhaps America was a place where virtue was less spontaneously rewarded than Stern—and everyone else—had believed in those days.

"Matters are well in hand," said Stern simply. They spoke briefly of each of his children, and with that done, he extended the phone to Dixon, who spent a few moments chatting happily with his wife. In his own fashion, Dixon was uxorious. He was covetous of Silvia's beauty and loved to see her pampered and expensively dressed. Roses arrived for her every Friday, and you could not walk down the street with Dixon without him spying some item in a rich store window that he decided would look smashing on Silvia. He was oddly preoccupied with his wife; if Silvia had a cold, it was on Dixon's mind. He called her four times a day. Yet this same doting husband had hot pants when any female between the ages of fifteen and sixty-five passed by, and he was always in pursuit.

"Now work hard," said Silvia to Stern when Dixon handed back the phone. Her efforts at humor were inevitably awkward. And in this case she was only trying to mask her real concerns. Silvia, for all her occasional anguish, remained enthralled by Dixon, as dazzled as she had been as a sorority girl. His swagger embarrassed her at moments; his wandering broke her heart. But he remained her life's romance, a figure the size of a monument, the man who still seemed to her half a dream.

"Well in hand," said Stern again, but, having spoken, felt momentarily put out with himself. With work of this kind, it was his practice never to predict favorable outcomes. The general pattern of results, and the evidence, seldom merited that; and he found clients easier to satisfy if he had dampened their expectations. He replaced the phone in that mood of conflict, reminding himself that this was, after all, his sister, her husband.

*   *   *

Stern found a copy of the grand jury subpoena in the in box on the cabinet behind his desk. He reread it and Dixon came to stand over his shoulder, bringing Stern's humidor with him. In the office, Stern usually lit his first cigar by nine-thirty or ten in the morning, and one was always burning thereafter until he left for the day. Clara had never approved. She complained about the odor in his clothing and on his hands and during an exceptional period of high irritability some years ago had refused to permit cigars inside their home. The humidor had been his father's, inlaid with mother-of-pearl and lined in velvet; his father, a quiet, proper man of fragile character, had placed great stock in certain objects. Stern looked into the humidor with admiration, but for the moment some freighted sense of obligation toward Clara caused him to decline.

"What does this show you?" Dixon asked, tapping the subpoena.

Stern, still reading, lifted a hand. To the first page of the subpoena was stapled a lengthy attachment describing the documents the government sought. Dixon, on behalf of his company and subsidiaries, was required to produce a variety of records—order tickets, trading cards, clearing documents—relating to a lengthy list of futures trades. The transactions, identified by date, commodity, number of contracts, month of delivery, and customer account, seemed to have been listed at random. The columns of figures marched down half the page, but the trades appeared to have been sorted neither chronologically nor by client. Stern counted for a moment. There were thirty-seven transactions.

"Let us start from the beginning, Dixon. Tell me about these documents. How are they generated?"

"You understand my business, Stern."

"Indulge me," he answered. The truth, of course, was that he could keep none of it straight. Other lawyers—a huge firm with offices here and in Chicago—attended to Dixon's regular business affairs. Stern learned what little piece he needed to deal with each problem that came his way and, at its conclusion, let all of it—practices, regulations, terms of art—fly from his mind, as in the aftermath of an exam. Oh, he knew the rudiments, the definitions: a futures contract was a transferable obligation to buy or sell a standard amount of a particular commodity for an agreed price at a fixed date in the future. But the markets had moved well past the point they were at when Dixon had started decades ago, and only farmers sold futures to secure harvest prices. Today the play, as Dixon put it, was in money; the markets sold futures on the markets: on bond and currency prices, on stock indices, options on futures themselves. The talk out in the trading room when Stern visited Dixon's offices was well beyond him, about basis trades and hedging yield curves. For all the arcana, Stern tended to recall Dixon's confession that the first people known to write futures on the stock market's prices were the bookies in Vegas.

"Take the first trade here, for Chicago Ovens," said Stern, pointing to the subpoena. This client was a huge bakery concern, part of International Provisions, which produced a third of the bread one saw on supermarket shelves. Stern had visited with their lawyers in Chicago. "As I understand it, this is a typical transaction. They wanted to be certain they can buy wheat in December at a favorable price. So they instructed you to buy them ten million bushels of wheat for December delivery. Correct? Now what happens at MD?"

"Okay," said Dixon. "Every order we get, no matter where it comes from, gets written up on our central order desk, which is here in our offices in the Kindle Exchange. Then they transmit the order to our booth on the trading floor at whatever exchange the future is traded on. Grains and financials in Chicago. Food and fibers in New York. Small lots we'll do here. This one obviously went to Chicago. The order goes into the pit and our broker yells it out till he finds traders who want to sell December wheat. Maybe they're selling for farmers, maybe speculators. Doesn't matter. Then at night the exchange clears the trades—you know, matches them to make sure that MD bought ten million Dec. wheat and someone else sold it. Next day we send our confirm to the client and make sure they've got enough margin money on deposit with us to cover the position. That's the whole story. There a million variations. But that's the basic. Right? That's the paper trail they're following."

Stern nodded: all quite familiar. He studied the subpoena again, then asked what sense Dixon made of the list of trades, but his brother-in-law merely shook his head. They had been placed by five different institutional customers over a number of months. Stern had spoken last week in Chicago with the lawyers for two of these customers—a large rural bank in Iowa, and the baker, Chicago Ovens. It seemed likely, therefore, that the government had subpoenaed trading records from the other three customers as well. Stern told Dixon he would have to contact them.

"What for?" he demanded. It did not attract business to tell customers that a federal grand jury was raking through your records.

"To determine what information they provided." One of the perpetual problems of a grand jury investigation was developing even a rough estimate of what the government knew. Most companies or individuals were not bold enough to disregard the FBI's usual request to keep the agents' questioning secret.

Dixon continued to venture mild objections, but eventually he gave in. His defense of his business was instinctive. He had started extolling futures in the little rural communities, and over three decades had made Maison Dixon a colossus with corporate clients, commodities pools, managed accounts. MD was a clearing member of all the major exchanges in Chicago and New York, and maintained large offices with humming telephone banks in both cities as well as here.

In the meantime, in the late 1960s, Dixon had led a group of local futures merchants in the formation of a small commodities exchange in Kindle County. Dixon's notion was to trade in lot sizes that were more in keeping with the needs of smaller retail customers. The Chicago Exchange would not trade a contract for the future delivery of wheat or soybeans of less than five thousand bushels. In Kindle, you could trade five hundred at prices that followed Chicago's, tick for tick. The Kindle County Futures Exchange—the KCFE—had established its 'minimarket' in all the most popular contracts, and Dixon continued to press his fellow directors for innovations. For the last two years, he had been relentlessly courting the approvals needed to trade a future on the Consumer Price Index. Dixon had made not one smart play in his lifetime but half a dozen. He was regarded with the usual mix of awe and distaste in the financial community. A maverick. A shark. Shrewd. Unreliable. But talented. He had fierce enemies and many admirers.

"Who are these customers, Dixon? What do they have in common."

"Nothing. *Nada.* Different commodities. Different strategies. The only thing I'd say is, they're probably the five biggest customers I have." He uttered this with considerable resentment. The government was attacking at a vulnerable spot.

"And what have you to do with these accounts, Dixon?"

"Not much. Those are big trades they're looking at," said

Dixon. "House rule is that I'm notified on anything that size. But that's it."

"Big trades?" asked Stern.

"Look at 'em," said Dixon. "Everything there is fifteen hundred contracts, two thousand contracts. Pit's gonna jump with those kinds of orders."

"Explain, please."

"You understand this, Stern. Take pork bellies. One car of bellies—one contract—is 40,000 pounds. I get a customer who wants fifteen hundred cars, that's a whole lot of bacon. The price is gonna take off like a rocket. It's supply and demand. You know, we try every gimmick known to man to slow things down. We lay off trades to friendly brokers. We buy the cash commodity and sell the future. But you can't stop it completely. It's like changing nature."

"Ah-ha," said Stern. So they did know something. The government was investigating large trades, trades which MD handled, trades which Dixon knew about, trades which, when placed, had had a significant impact on prices. "And is there nothing else which occurs to you?"

Dixon shook his head gravely. Nope, nothing, he didn't know a thing. Stern laid his thick finger again across his lips. Even with this news, it remained difficult to assay the government's suspicions. The records called for could relate to a number of schemes, particularly on the futures exchanges where knavery of all kinds was rife. Were Stern to guess, his estimate would be that Ms. Klonsky and her colleagues suspected market manipulation of some kind. There were all manner of baroque ploys. A month or two ago, the papers had been full of stories about a foreign government with a failing sugar crop which had tried to force down the world sugar-futures price so the government could buy and fulfill upcoming delivery commitments more cheaply. They had circulated authoritative rumors that something called 'left-handed sugar,' a no-calorie form of natural sugar, had been perfected. For three days prices plummeted, then the futures commissions merchants across the country had discerned what was occurring and bid prices out of sight. Dixon, perhaps, had found some less obvious—but equally illegal—way to tamper with the markets' responses to these huge transactions he handled for his customers. Dixon, however, continued to point up signs that he was in the clear.

"That subpoena doesn't even mention my name," he said. "That has to be good, doesn't it?"

The absence was superficially encouraging. But there would have been little reason for the agents to be so obvious in their pursuit of Dixon last week—or to have gone out of town with their initial subpoenas—unless they believed he would quickly recognize the meaning of these inquiries. His client, Stern decided, was keeping things to himself—not unprecedented in these circumstances, and, Lord knew, the general course with Dixon. Today, however, was probably not the time to press.

On his feet again, Stern, as he often did, took a moment to stare from his window in Morgan Towers, the city's tallest building, down to the Kindle River, whose swift waters ran here, through various tributaries, out of the Mississippi. With its shining, silvery face, the Kindle had been first named La Chandelle, the candle, by the French trader Jean-Baptiste DuSable, who had tarried here on his way from New Orleans to what eventually became Chicago. DuSable's trading post, named after him, was now by far the largest part of a consolidated tri-city municipality of almost a million. Just south, where the river branched and rejoined, two other towns, Moreland, settled by the English, who had Anglicized the river's name, and Kewahnee, once an Indian encampment, had grown up from barge ports and had been merged into DuSable in the mid-1930s. In this era of urban sprawl, the entire area, including the tri-cities, was usually referred to by the name of the surrounding county—Kindle—a hodgepodge megalopolis of city and suburb, prosperity and blight, home in total to almost three million people. The willingness of locals to see their city known by the county name had probably not been dampened by the rediscovery during the 1960s that DuSable, traditionally referred to as the first white man in these parts, had been black.

Dixon was speaking behind him. He wanted to know if they were obliged to turn over all the records the government required. Most of the trades, given their size, had been executed in Chicago, and the search for documents would occupy days for Margy Allison, Dixon's executive vice president, who ran the Chicago office, three hundred miles from here.

"I see no choice," said Stern. "I shall complain to the

prosecutor bitterly about the burdens of production. Tell her your business will be brought to a standstill. And I must have some time to look at the records, to see if I can make out what the government suspects. But eventually we must produce. We cannot challenge the subpoena as overbroad—it is quite precise."

"Whatever happened to the Fifth Amendment?" That was Dixon for you, cavalier where other executives would stammer before the words could come from their mouths. Stern explained that the subpoena sought records which belonged in law to the corporation rather than to Dixon himself. The corporation, not an individual, had no Fifth Amendment rights. Dixon could refuse to testify about the records; but the papers themselves would have to be handed over.

Claudia buzzed. She had Klonsky. Dixon, in the meanwhile, chewed on his cigar and puzzled over the mysterious logic of the law.

*   *   *

"Ms. Klonsky," he said.

"Mr. Stern," she answered. A clear, self-assured voice. They had never met, but Stern had seen her in the courtroom when she approached the podium for status calls. She was in her late thirties, Stern thought, a robust-appearing woman with broad shoulders, dark hair, strong hands. In court, she had emitted the forbidding persona familiar to many Assistants, including a number of the women; eager to prove themselves as tough as their male counterparts, they often came across as humorless and driven, citizens of the late century who saw brutality as a necessary mode in female style. It was largely a pose, but under the circumstances, Stern saw little reason to be retiring.

"Two of your storm troopers arrived at my home a few days ago with a subpoena for my client Dixon Hartnell."

An instant passed without sound. Storm troopers. Stern himself was surprised by the ruffian edge in his voice. Ordinarily, he prided himself on his civility. In the meantime, Dixon, across the desk, was beaming. He had rarely been exposed to Stern when he was so pointed.

"Perhaps I need to explain the circumstances," Stern said.

"I understand the circumstances," Ms. Klonsky shot back. She was bristling already.

No doubt, everyone understood the circumstances, Stern thought. He had many friends in the prosecuting offices, both the Kindle County Prosecutor's and the United States Attorney's Offlce, but they were adversaries, too—and human. It was delicious gossip. Did you hear? About Stern's wife? Here again, as he contemplated this, the world seemed to open, and the force of painful emotion rushed up at him out of his own breast. How, how was it possible? It was such an unreasoning mess. He closed his eyes, which were burning, and he could sense Dixon stirring. It was a sad comment that his shame, more than anything else, brought on these moments, and that the same pride carried him through—some forward-struggling thing impelled him to go on with dignity. Where, damn it, was his cigar? When he spoke, there was no tremor in his voice.

"If you understood, I must say I find your conduct deplorable. Perhaps I should speak to Mr. Sennett." Stan Sennett, a career prosecutor, had been U.S. Attorney for two or three years now. He was the toughest and most humorless of all, and far from an ally of Stern's. Sennett was unlikely to become exercised—the agents, after all, were just doing their jobs—but Klonsky could not say that.

"Look, Mr. Stern, this was an honest mistake. It might even be," she said, "that if you gave me half a chance, I would have apologized. I've been calling you for days now." Stern, rebuked, still chose not to answer. She had been an Assistant for only a year, following a clerkship in the U.S. court of appeals, and, presumably, a distinguished law school career, and he sensed an advantage in her inexperience. She had acquired a reputation as bright but phlegmatic, even flaky, the kind to blow hot and cold. He did not wish to lend her any reassurance.

"Tell me, Ms. Klonsky," said Stern, shifting the subject, "what is the nature of your investigation?"

"I'd prefer not to say right now."

"Are other agencies involved besides the FBI?" Stern wanted to know about the IRS in particular. They were always trouble. And if the federal regulators were involved—the Commodities Futures Trading Commission—he might gain some idea how the charges originated.

"I can't answer," said Klonsky.

"What about Mr. Hartnell? Are you willing to say whether or not he is a target?"

She paused, being careful. Klonsky had had her share of bad experiences with the defense bar already.

"I can't tell you he's not."

"I see." Stern thought. "When will you be able to be more precise about his status?"

"Perhaps after we look at the documents we've subpoenaed. They're due today."

"Well, I am afraid that we shall be a bit late providing them. You are basically asking that Mr. Hartnell and his employees stop running his business and look for records for weeks."

"It's not that bad," said Klonsky.

"I am assured it is."

Klonsky sighed. She was tiring of the conversation. "How long?"

"We need an extension of at least three weeks," he said. Dixon was looking on approvingly. He had his cigar tucked in his cheek, and a large enthusiastic smile. This was better than TV. "No, I am sorry," said Stern, "I had not consulted Mr. Hartnell. Best make it a full month."

"That's ridiculous. These records are probably in a few cabinets."

"I am informed otherwise, Ms. Klonsky. This is a federal grand jury investigation. I represent both the corporation and Mr. Hartnell personally. You will not identify your targets. I must be alert to conflicts at the same time that I try to be certain that our compliance with your subpoena is exact. I am required to make at least one trip to Chicago, if not more, to do that. If you wish to limit your requests, or tell me what is needed first, I would try to oblige." She was silent. If she narrowed her request, she might disclose her interests. "If you think I am being unreasonable, make a motion to compel. I shall be happy to explain all this to Judge Winchell."

Chief Judge Winchell, a former prosecutor, would rule for the government eventually. But no judge in the federal courthouse would set strict deadlines for Sandy Stern this month. His personal circumstances required no mention here. Ms. Klonsky knew the score.

"No further extensions," she said. She gave him a date—the second of May. "I'll send you a letter."

"Very well," said Stern. "I shall look forward to meeting with you, after you have reviewed what we provide."

"Right," she said.

"And, of course, Ms. Klonsky, I do accept your apology."

Klonsky, pierced, hesitated, but thought better of whatever she had in mind.

"Right," she said again and clapped down the phone.

Stern could not restrain his satisfaction. That had gone well. Ms. Klonsky was high-strung and ill-humored and he had gotten the better of her. When the month was over, they could ask for another week or two, if need be.

Dixon was laughing, delighted to see the government bashed. He asked what she had told him.

"Very little. Except that she would not rule out the possibility that you are a target of her investigation."

Dixon drew on his cigar. He was instantly far more subdued, but he shrugged gallantly.

"You slowed her down," he said.

Stern listed what he would be doing near-term: the other customers he would contact; his trip to Chicago to look over the records for the subpoena as soon as they had been gathered.

"In the meantime, you know how these things go, Dixon. Discuss this with no one but me. Act on the assumption that everyone around you is wearing a tape recorder. It would not be surprising if one of them is."

For the first time today, Dixon briefly sported a look of discomfort: he buttoned up his lips and shook his head. Then he ground out the cigar and stood.

"I'm sorry this comes up now, Stern," Dixon said. "I hate to be the thing that drags you back into the office."

Stern raised a hand. "I suspect I shall be here a good deal." He said this somewhat heroically, but that lost feeling came over him again. He had no notion, really, of the immediate future, or even, for that matter, of what lay further ahead. A few images had stirred themselves: figures of stillness and order. He would mind the office and his clients in a state of settled dotage.

Dixon, of course, had different thoughts in mind.

"Oh, you'll have other distractions eventually." He glanced

down at his stubbed cigar with the most minute salaciousness. Stern recoiled a bit, but he knew that Dixon was merely crude enough to say what others were thinking. Even in tear-stained eyes thick with grief and sympathy, Stern could see he was already differently regarded. A single man. Certain facts were elemental. In his present mood, Stern was persistently repelled by contemplation of this subject. More to the point, he knew that his circumstance was hardly ordinary. What woman of even modest sense would be eager for the company of a man with whom another female had literally found life not worth living?

"I assume this will cost a fortune," Dixon said as he picked his sport coat off the sofa arm.

"It will be expensive," said Stern, barely able to suppress a smile. Dixon was rich. His business was worth millions, and he paid himself a seven-figure salary each year, but he maintained the typical frugality of a man who had struggled. He groused unremittingly about the appalling level of his legal fees. But years ago, in Stern's salad days, during that period when Dixon was still attempting to win Stern back after marrying Silvia, Dixon had obligingly urged Stern to bill him like any other client, and Stern had never forgotten the instruction. One more peculiar harmonic had been established between them. Dixon paid for Stern's tolerance, and Stern was willing to allow it to be purchased. And always the concern on either side about who was getting the better of the deal. "I can leave some of the documents to the younger lawyers to examine," Stern said, "but we know too little. I must do most of this myself. Ms. Klonsky will take priority over other matters."

"Please," said Dixon. Once more, he looked around the room. The weight of things had begun to settle on him. He was unhappy. "I don't want to fuck around with this."

Stern considered his brother-in-law with his manifold secrets. Clara's voice, as ever now, came into his mind. Little as she cared for Dixon, she had never seemed surprised by their alliance. Stern had complained often that he did not know Dixon, was not sure he had ever gotten through to him, found the man at times as elusive as smoke.

'I imagine,' she had answered, 'that he says the same of you.'

4

In the mock-chippendale reception room of Barstow Zahn and Hanks, a huge law firm, Stern sat with his children, awaiting Cal Hopkinson, with whom they had an appointment to learn the details of Clara's will. Stern regarded this event with the same maelstrom of contradictory emotions that lingering concentration on Clara's wealth had always prompted, but for the moment most of that was lost in the strong feelings—regretful, fond, salutary—of having his children near at hand.

Tomorrow, Marta would leave. She had stayed a week following the funeral. Work was slow, she said, and Kate and she had planned to sift through Clara's things. Instead, Marta had spent hours alone, looking dreamily about her own room, poking through the house as if it were a new location. She had already mentioned that she would need to return soon to finish.

With the departure of Marta—the child who liked him best, or, more correctly, feared him least—Stern would be alone. His children had offered him what comfort they could in the last weeks, but he felt them drawn away by the onrush of their lives and their plain bewilderment at having to deal with him on their own. With all the children, Clara had been his mediator; they had far less direct experience of him. Oh, he had cared. Deeply. But, in his compulsive orderly way, in its place. No matter how late he returned home from the office, in a routine as fixed as prayer, he received from Clara each night news of the children, the disturbances and triumphs, the unfolding of each small life. Somehow, at the time, he thought they would know that a portion of her interest was his own. When they reached their teens, he was baffled and stung as, one by one, they took up attitudes which silently accused him of being aloof, uninvolved. The lines of attachment were to their mother. As in old-time law, he saw now, the benefits ran only to those in direct contact, in privity.

Cal appeared at last. He shook everybody's hand, precise as a clockmaker, and apologized for the wait. Cal was an unremarkable fellow—temperate, genial, a journeyman of sorts. The most impressive thing about him was a single physical feature: an inch or so behind his left ear, just below his hairline, was a round depression that darkened and appeared to head straight into his skull, as if someone had stuck a little finger into a ball of dough. The mark looked for all the world like a bullet hole—and that was what it was, a war wound from Korea, a medical marvel. The shot had passed straight through, with the only damage to Cal's outer skull. Once noticed, it was the kind of thing you could not keep your eyes off of. Stern spent his meetings with Cal awaiting the instant when he would turn away and Stern could stare freely.

Cal ushered the family toward a wainscoted conference room. Stern was the last to enter, and Cal detained him at the door.

"Before we start, Sandy— As I told you on the phone last week, there's a question or two I wanted to ask you about Clara's estate—some peculiarities I imagine you're aware of."

"Me?" Over the years, his commerce with Clara about her finances was limited to those rare occasions when she raised the subject, and usually he referred her to her bankers or attorneys.

They were interrupted by the arrival of Cal's associate, a young woman with spectacles and straight brown hair named Van Zandt. Marta poked her head out the door to see what the holdup was, and at Stern's suggestion they all proceeded into the conference room, where they were seated around the long walnut table. Little plate engravings, precious caricatures of various legal scenes, ringed the walls, and there was the usual majestic view of the city—the law firms and the corporate headquarters gobbled up all the best space. Harry Fagel had tried years ago to lure Stern into this modern Versailles, but he would have none of it.

"I think," said Cal, "I should just start at the beginning and tell you all about Clara's estate."

Stern nodded. Marta nodded. Everyone agreed this was

appropriate. Van Zandt handed Cal a document—a memo, no doubt, summarizing the will—and Cal solemnly began. Like most sophisticated estate plans, Clara's had been composed with the first eye on the tax laws. As the result of her father's providence decades before, and careful advice since, Clara had been able to dispose of a significant fortune without the payment of a single penny in federal estate tax. Cal disclosed this fact with a refulgent smile of minor triumph.

The great bulk of Clara's wealth had never been transferred to her directly. Her inheritance from her father, mother, and maiden aunt had been placed in a series of trusts that Henry Mittler had established at the River National Bank; these trusts would endure for generations, spilling out income and preserving corpus, in the venerated fashion of old money. When he was younger, Stern had believed that Henry had made these elaborate arrangements because he feared that his son-in-law was some kind of bounder. Now Stern knew that Henry's faith was simpler: any discretion, no matter how constrained, was liable to abuse. This brass-knuckled cynicism had made Henry a formidable attorney, although the same qualities of character also probably contributed to his daughter's lifetime discontent with him. Clara's fiercest internal struggles had been with her father, a clever, domineering, willful man. Now Clara was interred in the synagogue's small cemetery, in the sight of the large monument that Henry Mittler had erected to himself and Clara's mother, Pauline, by the terms of the same will that had created the trusts. The earth reclaimed them all, and their passions, while their bank accounts survived. Stern, never without an appreciation for money, nonetheless contemplated these sad facts with amazement.

"According to our notes," said Cal, "when we revised the estate plan after the most recent changes in the tax laws, the trusts were valued at a little over $7 million. Clara's own estate," he said, referring to the interest spun off to Clara by the trusts over the years which, largely unspent, had been invested for her by the bank, "was in the neighborhood of $2 million. Of course, there have been changes, with the stock market crash and other financial developments, but you have the general picture." Cal had taken his time getting to this point, and you could see that he enjoyed the effect the numbers had on his listeners. Kate's eyes widened and Peter whistled out loud. It was something of an achievement, Stern determined, to have kept the children in the dark about this. He himself was neither shocked by the figures nor far off in the estimates he had made on the way down today, or periodically over the years, concerning these dollars he had seldom deigned to touch.

Clara's will left simple directions. Stern was named executor. The rights to the trusts' income passed in equal divided portions to the children—"share and share alike," as Cal put it. Out of Clara's own fortune, a number of substantial gifts were made to the children and charities; the rest was left in trust for Stern to use as he saw fit.

Having outlined the will, Cal bored in on the details. As he described the provisions, he used the third person—"spouse Alejandro," "children Peter, Marta, and Kate"—and did not bother to translate many of the technical terms. Nonetheless, the inevitable calculations seemed after an interval to take place around the table, and Kate suddenly began to weep. The children could expect to divide among themselves an annual income of about half a million dollars. To this was added a cash bequest to each of $200,000, not to mention the prospect of a good deal more when Stern departed the scene. It occurred to Stern that if he could keep Dixon out of trouble long enough, he would probably be a fitting financial adviser for his nieces and nephew. As to himself, Stern, for reasons he could hardly articulate, felt few compunctions about accepting his wife's gift; perhaps, perversely, because his own estate had grown well past the point where he needed it; or because, after all this, he felt it was his due. By Stern's quick estimate, the residue of the estate left in trust for him—what would remain of Clara's stocks and bonds at the bank—would total about a million dollars.

Going through the details of the trust provision, Cal paused to eye Stern.

"Clara directed specifically that you would remain the beneficiary for life, regardless of any remarriage."

"I see," said Stern.

Cal smiled briefly, delighted by this exacting management of the future, but the children seemed nonplussed by their mother's forethought—a pulse of discomfort traveled the room. None of them had yet raised this subject with Stern. No question they had thought of it; everyone had. Even Clara. But it was disconcerting to one and all—to Stern, as well—to learn that she had formally resolved any objections.

Cal had gone on, but Stern interrupted.

"Is it this trust for me, Cal, that prompted these concerns you raised in the hall?" On reflection, it occurred to him why Cal wanted to speak one-on-one. There might be some conflict between Clara's desire to provide for him and the restrictions Henry Mittler had set down decades ago.

"I'm not concerned, Sandy. I have a question."

"But about this trust for my benefit?"

"More or less. Just give me a moment." Cal dandled a hand; he was too fussy to step out of order. He had been discussing Clara's charitable gifts and he returned to the subject. Kate was crying with fervor. Van Zandt, the big-firm associate, ever prepared, had come armed with a box of tissue and offered another to Kate, while Cal continued with the details he adored.

"Clara also made a bequest of $500,000 to the Riverside Reformed Congregation, half of which she asked to be used to support the Inner-City Arts Program."

The children took this in, still dazzled by the fountain of money spilling forth, but Stern—who might otherwise have received the funds—found Clara's charity characteristic and commendable. For Stern, the notion of himself as a Jew was an absolute and fixed point of reference, the North Pole, as it were, on his personal compass, against which all other issues of identity were judged. Clara and he shared a belief in the importance of the children's religious education, the observance of the High Holy Days. But her religion was far more institutionalized than his. To Clara the synagogue which her maternal grandparents had helped found was a significant anchor, and against all reason she was devoted to the rabbi, a smug self-promoter, and to his many community projects. At Rabbi Weigel's urging, Clara had taught music appreciation as a volunteer for three or four years in the Inner-City Arts Program, an interfaith effort to enhance the curricula of DuSable's most impoverished schools. Clara admired the culture and civility of the well-to-do, but not their sense of privilege. She had always been a person of conscience.

"That's more or less it." Cal was done. He put down his memo and looked about the table, as if for applause.

"The problem," said Stern, referring once more to the trust Clara had left for him. Cal already seemed to have forgotten.

"Oh," said Cal. "As I say, just one question, Sandy: we've been wondering what became of it."

"It?"

"The money. You understand." Cal leaned forward. "Don't you?"

"I had taken it, Cal, from the figures you'd been using that there was another million in the estate." As soon as the words were out he regretted them, particularly the precision with which he seemed to have calculated.

"Well, not quite," said Cal, mincing as ever. "Clara's holdings haven't made it all the way back from the crash. But it's the $850,000 that's gone from her investment account I'm talking about."

No one, for a moment, said anything.

"Gone?" asked Stern finally.

"Removed," said Cal.

The two men considered each other.

"You're not telling us there has been a defalcation, are you?"

"Lord, no!" Cal turned to Van Zandt, as if for help. "We get a consolidated statement from the bank each quarter on the trusts and Clara's investment account. When we heard the news, we looked, of course, and I saw that this sum had been withdrawn last month. I assumed, Sandy—I was certain she would have discussed this with you." Cal paused. "I called."

Stern only now understood.

"You believe Clara spent this money?"

"What else? I took it she'd made an investment on her own, bought a summer home—" Cal's hand trailed off.

Marta spoke up.

"What would she do with $850,000? That's bizarre."

Stern, strongly inclined to agree, began to add his voice to Marta's. But some better instinct saved him. He was rising to a treacherous pass. He had no business predicting what was possible or impossible with Clara in these latter days. Perhaps she was funding a hippie sect. Or feeding a drug habit.

"Cal, I am not certain I understand how this could have occurred."

"I presume Clara went to the bank, dissolved the great bulk of her portfolio, and took the money. It was hers, after all."

"Have you checked with them?"

"Sandy, I wanted to speak with you first. That's why I called." Cal was in excruciating discomfort. Probate lawyers dealt with a world of fixed intentions. They were not suited to surprise. Clearly, he feared that the family might blame him, and had descended already to the sweaty depths of lawyerly justification. "I took it you would know about this. It didn't occur to me—" Cal cut himself off. He seemed to recognize that he was merely doing harm by reemphasizing how shocked he was that Clara had acted without consulting her husband. Cal's sudden—and uncharacteristic—sensitivity seemed by some improbable logic to awaken Stern to his own distress. He was, in fact, reeling. Oh, it was absolutely childish, a response greedy as a six-year-old's, but he could not stifle the thought. She had seen to the children; she had fattened the rabbi and his favorite charity. Only he, in her last days, had been deprived. Shame and anguish, the same venomous mix, rose in him once more.

Cal had gone on talking.

"Now that you tell me you have no idea what this is about, I'll call Jack Wagoner over at the bank at once. We'll track it all down. The probate court will require it." These vows seemed to do little to comfort Cal himself, who sat there worried and deflated, licking his lips. He made it sound as if the money had run away on its own.

"When was this transaction?" asked Marta. "How late in the month?" Cal turned to Van Zandt, who had the date—five days before the afternoon Stern had come home to find Clara. Van Zandt handed a paper, the statement, to Marta; she then offered it to her father, who pushed it aside. The thought of embezzlement, some kind of foul play, occurred to Stern again, but that was unlikely—worse, absurd.

He looked up at a sound: Kate had begun burbling again. Twenty-six years old, with her face tear-blotched and her makeup washed away, she looked half her age. She lolled back on the arm of her brother, who had been largely silent throughout, still laid low by the contemplation of his mother. Stern, in his present state, found himself easily irritated by Peter's solicitude. How was it, he wondered, that the women always seemed to turn to Peter? None of them would tell you that he was untroubled; but they all seemed to adore his quiet sulkiness. He was available. Reliable. A person you could count on. Peter had undermined his father in the most insidious way— by exceeding him. By being what it mattered most that Stern was not. This sudden incisive view into the odd mechanisms of his family did nothing to stem the rising tide of his grief.

He shook hands with Cal and Van Zandt. His children stood, too, but seemed to have no idea how to proceed, whether to stay or go, or even if they ought to move. Stern realized suddenly that he was the center of attention. They were all watching him—his children, the lawyers—looking for signals. What to do, how to respond. But he had little to offer by way of instruction. Here in these elegant surroundings his soul again plummeted toward misery. Suicide. Money. Disease. Clara had left behind an unreconstructed mess.

He was accosted, more or less unaccountably, by a memory of her, as he happened to have observed her one day on her way to her teaching assignment in the Inner-City Arts Program. Stern and the children had long expressed concerns for her safety, but Clara twice a week drove her Seville to the city's depleted neighborhoods for the morning. Coming by to swap cars so he could take hers to the shop, Stern had caught sight of her marching boldly to the school doors—a determined middle-aged lady with a noble look, reddish hair, a substantial bosom. She carried no purse. Her hands were jammed into the pockets of her plain coat and her head was erect, as she ignored occasional quarreling glances. In that split-second, he recognized something essential: not that she was fearless, but rather that he had seen the same expression often before and that for Clara every trip beyond her home apparently required the same effort to master her anxieties. There were all those inner demons which she conquered only by persuading herself they were not real. Somehow, at the end, they had come to life, surrounded and devoured her. A taciturn, mannerly, dignified woman, Clara Stern had gotten herself caught in the world's muck, and it had sucked her down, like one of those prehistoric creatures whose bones were found in the tar pits. He knew that sooner or later he was going to stumble into the very heart of it, too, enduring all the same nightmare horrors she had.

They reached the street before Kate, briefly under control, began crying once more.

5

How does one give up a life? At night, Stern wandered in the large house, looking for answers. In the closets, much of Clara's clothing still hung. With the doors thrown open, he stared at the garments; they seemed as mystical as relics. The empty hangers, remaining from the items Kate and Marta had packed away, waited now like the skeletons of birds.

After Marta left, he moved into her room to sleep. His own bedroom seemed disturbed, torn apart; here he felt by some bare margin more at peace. When he entered the master bedroom to gather up an item or two, the stillness was overpowering. With even a few days of disuse, a shrouded, dusty quietude had come over it. It was like examining a photograph: a bounded portion of an unreachable past, inanimate but preserved. He took his socks, his collar stays, and rushed back out the door.

He was shown a ceremonial kindness by neighbors and families from the synagogue. The suicide's spouse was too gruesome for the dinner table—how do you explain to the children? But the women came by with pots of stew, various chicken dishes, for him to consume alone. The freezer was jammed. Most evenings, he would place something in the microwave, open a bottle of wine, eat and drink, and roam about the household.

On the refrigerator was a note to phone Nate Cawley. He had tried a number of times, hoping to dispel the question of Clara's medical bill, but Nate, busy after his week away at the medical conference in Canada, had not yet responded. Softened by the wine, Stern took calls—friends or Marta or Kate checking in—

and then resumed his movements. He sat in chairs he had not bothered with for years. He went from room to room, stared at the furnishings, the pictures. This tiny porcelain bird. Where had it come from?

Occasionally he was asked out, generally in groups, and usually by other lawyers, a kind of conventional solicitude that reflected more his stature in the legal community than any particular intimacy. This was the sort of social commerce which the Sterns had always minimized. Clara, with her quiet, firm manner, had no interest in people or occasions that offered little substance. Now free to go on his own, he could not bring himself to the pretense these encounters would demand, an evening of vagrant chatter in which everyone would stare at him with unvoiced questions about his wife.

The only outings which he made willingly were to be with his children. In the first two weeks after Marta's departure, he went to Kate's house twice for dinner, and she and John met him once downtown. But the suburban sprawl of Kindle County meant that they were almost an hour apart, and in the work week the travel was exhausting, particularly for Kate, who was wearied by the early phases of her pregnancy. And even with her, he sensed that her attentions required some self-conscious effort; Kate, always unreflectively loving, now seemed vaguely frightened to deal with her father on his own.

Peter, no doubt acting at the instruction of his sisters, also called, and at Stern's suggestion they had dinner one evening. "Something quick," as Peter put it, accepting. They met at a delicatessen downtown, but Clara's absence loomed between them, enormous, agonizing. She had been pained by their estrangement—and for her sake they had always done their best. Now it was suddenly clear that the tie had not survived her; they were both playing roles in a production which had closed. After a few minutes ill at ease they lapsed completely into silence amid the ringing plates and voices of the restaurant.

So for the most part he was alone. One night there was an unexpected interruption. A woman from the neighborhood phoned, claiming to be a friend of Clara's. She went on without a pause to describe her husband's repeated failures in the bedroom—the man had many problems—and ended their conversation saying, simply, "Call me." Stern, of course, did not.

Yet the incident provoked a storm of odd feeling. He had heard the same stories as everyone else, of the unattached females who accosted widowers with striking boldness, but given the circumstances of Clara's passing, he was sure that would not happen to him. Oh, perhaps there had been a card or two, a few calls of sympathy from widows and divorcees of somewhat remote connection. Yet, suddenly, something seemed clarified. People were lonely; women, in particular, were lonely like him. But who knew about all of that—women? Certainly not he. And to what purpose, anyway? The thought of all this left him feeling worse, baffled and inept, stuck within himself, like something buried.

Whatever the distractions, these evenings in the end always found him roaming. He drank wine, told himself he would work, and wandered about the house. As soon as this routine began, he realized that this, not working, was the primary business of his day. He suffered terribly—at sea with tender recollections and volumes of harsh self-recrimination—and yet he receded to these moments almost urgently, as the years swam over him.

His memory of the past was of a million pages observed by a single incandescent light, and of doors falling open as he arrived, burdened with heavy cases, in a hundred different courtrooms. In the decades he recalled, it was always late at night or the morning of a trial, his emotions an intense admixture of determined concentration and stilled anxiety. He puzzled in his hours at home; his children spoke and went unanswered as he nursed motions in his mind, a particular careful tack for crossexamination, and reached forth with a tender hand, meant to hush them, while he thought of something else. Oh, he had achieved. He was in his office with his cigars, his books, his phone, his clients, from seven in the morning until nine or ten at night. He came home then to a quiet house. The children were bedded down, gone. Clara waited with a book on her lap in the quiet living room, the aroma of his warming dinner through the house: an image of order, resourcefulness, sufficiency.

Was he persuaded by that pose? For how many years had he comforted himself with the thought that they did not quarrel, that she seldom voiced the criticisms of other wives? That would have struck Clara as common. True, he treated her with unsparing courtesy. He rarely disregarded her wishes. But, of course, he had chosen wisely, for she seldom spoke up in her own behalf. Oh, they had had their rough spots. Who didn't? The period when the children had gone off to college was one of intense disruption for Clara. When Kate, the last, departed, there were times when he found her in the dark, in tears. It was there each day, the quiet insinuation, throbbing like a bruise: she did not like her life, no part of it. When he tried to soothe her, she turned on him openly, livid with decades of previously unspoken complaints. But they had stumbled on, and Clara had eventually reverted to her strict self-control, her taut smile, and her insistence that she was bearing up. She was like some Swedish minister enduring existential torment in silence and low light.

On these evenings when he wandered, the wine made him sleepy—he had never been a drinker. He jolted awake to find himself upright in a chair, dry-mouthed, the lights blazing. One night a particularly vivid dream startled him out of his sleep. He was bathing at Wolf's Point in the Kindle River. Unnoticed, the water grew turbulent, and soon he was kicking and struggling while the white froth seethed about him. On the shore, amid the trees, his mother, father, and older brother, dressed in heavy dark woolens, watched, each immobile as a statue. Although he was moving backwards, he somehow caught sight of Clara and the children through the bare branches. They were in a schoolroom. The children were seated at desks while Clara, with a finger raised, offered instruction. Churning his limbs in the powerful waters, he called, but they did not notice him fighting off the current, being driven farther and farther away.

*　*　*

Fiona Cawley, his next-door neighbor, greeted him, highball glass in hand.

"Sandy!" she cried. From the first word, Stern knew she was drunk. Fiona let her front door fly open and stood with her arms thrown wide, backlit by the burning lamps of the living room. Nate, Fiona's husband, also drank more than he should have. Perhaps that was what kept them together. For the present, Stern was struck uncannily by a sudden understanding of what motivated Fiona. Loosened by the liquor, she was more attractive; her posture had an alluring pliancy. Clearly, she savored her liberty. She was handsomely dressed as ever in a robin's-egg knit suit that showed off her small figure to advantage. Her hair and makeup were flawless, and she wore jewelry for her evening at home, a large diamond piece between the clavicles. Fiona spent her days caring for herself. She shooed the dog away and pulled Stern into the house by the hand, assuring him, in response to his question, that he was not interrupting dinner. She seemed delighted to see him.

"How *are* you, Sandy." She touched his face, a drunken, excessive gesture. "We think so much about you."

Already he had taken up certain inscrutable mannerisms in response. He had always been good at this, wordless flexing of the brow to suggest complex feelings. Now his look was more pinched, more allusive of pain.

"I am as well as could be expected, Fiona. Is Nate about for just a moment? I was hoping to have a word with him." A personal appearance, Stern had decided, might catch Nate's attention. After hearing from Cal, Stern was determined to be more direct in attempting to unravel Clara's knotted affairs.

"Hasn't he called you? I gave him the message twenty times. Well, he's out for the evening, Sandy, but stay for a second. Have a drink with me. There's something I wanted to ask you about. I'm glad you're here."

Without awaiting an answer, she walked halfway down the hall to drive the dog back to the kitchen. Fiona was one of those people who always got what they wanted. She'd given him no chance to make an excuse.

For nineteen years, the Sterns had lived beside the Cawleys. They had watched the Cawleys' modern ranch go through three separate expansions, so that it now wore a somewhat awkward-looking second story, resembling a small top hat on a large-headed man. They had witnessed the coming of age of the Cawley children, both of whom were now in college. They had enjoyed weekend conversations over the fence; an occasional drink or barbecue; two decades of holding mail and exchanging garden tools—but the Cawleys as a couple, like many others, were treated with reserve. Years before, with the retirement of the obstetrician who had delivered the Sterns' children, Clara had begun to visit Nate as her gynecologist and principal physician. In an emergency—a fall from a tree, a minor infection—he was the unofficial medical adviser to the entire family. Somehow, this professional relationship suited the Sterns well, since it offered a diplomatic means of enjoying Nate without Fiona. As a doctor, he was knowledgeable, relaxed, and affable; at home, he was apt to be overwhelmed by his wife. Younger, Fiona had no doubt been a great beauty, and she was still a fine-looking woman, handsomely slender, with arresting light eyes that were almost yellow. But she was, in a phrase, hard to take: nervous, high-pitched, forever striving, striving. Fiona nursed a hothouse conservatory of internal competitions and visible resentments. A good person to avoid.

"Highball?" Fiona asked now.

Stern put himself down on a love seat upholstered in a fabric of peonies. The Cawleys' living room was decorated in what Stern took to be Irish modern fashion, a self-conscious upgrading of American colonial style. The rooms were crowded with dark tables and commodes, most of the pieces beset with shawls of lace. Fiona occupied herself in a small adjoining den, where she'd set up a tea cart with booze. She drank in elegance; the liquor was in cut-glass snifters, and a large sterling-silver ice bucket had been set down like a centerpiece.

"Some dry sherry, if it is there, Fiona. On a cube of ice. I really must do some work this evening."

"Work?" she asked. "Already? Sandy, you should give yourself a chance."

This was a frequent comment. But no one mentioned alternatives. Dancing? Nightclubs? He must have missed the boat somewhere. What was the etiquette of grieving? To disdain useful labor and watch addlepated fare on TV? Really, Stern was tiring already of these conventional efforts to orchestrate his feelings.

As she handed him his drink, he asked if she was well.

"Oh, me? I'm just ducky," said Fiona, and looked into her glass. Stern recalled now that he had determined years ago, without reflection, not to ask Fiona such questions. The dog was pawing about and growling in the kitchen, where he had been shut up; you could hear his claws racing on the tiles. "What is it you wanted with Nate?"

"I merely had a question or two concerning Clara. Tell him I need only a moment. I wanted to know if he was treating her for any ailment."

"There was something," said Fiona. She used her glass and gestured with a rummy lushness.

"Was there?"

"He used to stop over there in the morning. She needed medication or something." Fiona waved her free hand about, suggesting the way Nate, probably, had put her off.

"Ah-ha." As he suspected. Stern held still. Then, fortified to learn he was right, rose to go.

"Oh, you can't leave yet. Remember? I wanted to ask you something."

"Just so," said Stern. He had indeed forgotten.

She went into another room and returned with a small package.

"Sandy, you're probably not ready for this yet, but when you are, you have to let me introduce you to Phoebe Brower. She is charming. And you'd have things in common. Her husband, you know—" Fiona fiddled a hand and wriggled her features. "Sleeping pills."

He could not quite remain silent—some sound escaped him, a noise of sorts. If Fiona were not drunk, or Fiona, he might have actually taken offense. Perhaps she thought he was starting a club. Unbearable Spouses Anonymous. He recognized the wrapper of the local camera store on the package Fiona was holding. Photos, too? There should be a sign up on his house. Decommissioned. Shipwrecked. Out of use.

"As you say, Fiona. It is much too soon."

She shrugged. "I would think that's something most men would look forward to. Being on the loose again."

Well, they had done fairly well until now, but Fiona was veering off the road. Stern slapped his thighs, a sign he was ready to be on his way.

"Perhaps you are correct, Fiona. Women always know better about men."

"Don't humor me, Sandy. You do that too much. I have a reason for asking."

She was masterful, no doubt about that. Stern sat silent, watching, as Fiona at last drew herself together.

"Sandy, I want you to look at this. I need to ask you a question." She offered the package.

"What is it, Fiona?"

She shook her head. Just look at it, she said. She had no wish to explain. Somehow he had a powerful sense of Clara's absence. This scene could never have taken place a few weeks ago. Fiona, even drunk, would have felt less free to prevail upon him.

When he opened the package, he found a videocassette.

"Watch it." She gestured through an arch toward the small adjoining family room. Stern, thinking of resisting further, abandoned the notion. With Fiona, there was no point.

He found the VCR and pushed the buttons; he was good with machines. The images jerked onto the screen in the midst of some sequence. The picture was of poor quality, homemade. The skin tones were far too rosy. But they showed enough. The first frames were of a young woman. She zoomed in and out of focus, but she remained naked as the day of her birth. She was slender and small-breasted—seated on a bed, and smiling at the camera in a harmless way. He was too taken aback at first to understand what consequence this naked woman could be to Fiona. But then he recognized Nate's voice on the sound track; the words were not clear, and Stern, as he stood there, suddenly nipping at his sherry, had no wish to boost the volume and further intrude. He understood enough: Nate was the cameraman.

Strangely, his first impulse was to feel sorry for his neighbor. How could he have done this to himself? There was nothing particularly salacious about the girl's poses. She crossed a leg casually at one point; she had on black high-heeled shoes, and as Nate moved the camera about her, the dark pubic triangle was more visible, split with the bright pink lick of her labia. There was something almost innocent about these pictures. Certainly relaxed. Nate and the young lady, whoever she was, were well acquainted. She smiled as if she were on a beach.

Then, as Stern had a finger poised over the stop button, the picture flipped; the screen went black, then raced with fuzz, and finally filled once more with figures. It took him an instant to sort things out, and a sense of disturbance preceded his willingness to name what he was seeing. Nate, it seemed, had turned the camera on himself. Out of focus, the white shaft of his erect penis was nonetheless recognizable; perspectives were hard to discern, but Nate appeared to be a man of generous proportions. Then, without warning, the image jumped again and settled finally on what Nate likely had been meaning to portray all along. The distances were too short for the camera's focal range, and you saw mostly the young woman's hair, which, blurred, looked like some matted bathroom rug. But there was no mistaking her reddened lips fixed over the end of Nate's member. "This is great," Nate said on the tape. "This is great." Stern could understand that much. Nate's blow job was preserved forever.

"I see," said Stern. He had stopped the recorder.

Fiona had remained by the tea cart, with her back to the screen.

"Pretty nasty, don't you think? The son of a bitch told me he was going to AA at night. How do you like that?"

"Fiona—" he said, but he had no clue as to what else he should add.

"Here's what I want to know, Sandy." She threw cubes quickly into her glass; she still had not faced him. "If I file for divorce, can I use that in court?"

Stern at once turned elusive. He was not about to get caught between his neighbors. His practice did not include matrimonial work, he told her. Different courts often followed different procedures.

She interrupted, making no effort to hide her harsh look.

"Don't give me a song and dance, Sandy. Yes or no? What do you think? I want to know where I stand."

He realized that he was highly alarmed. The tape had upset him. And it bothered him more than he would have expected to find that the Cawleys, one more fixture in his life, were coming apart. Eventually, however, he answered.

"I would think it is likely to be admitted in court." There was really no question. Any lawyer with half a brain could think up a dozen ways to get the tape into evidence.

"Well, he'll be a sorry little *bastard* that day, won't he? I've told Nate for years he can't *afford* to divorce me. Now he'll really see what that means." Fiona had her chin erect; defiant. It was hard not to be frightened by her obvious relish in the pain she meant to inflict. "Do you know where I was the first time I saw that, Sandy? At the store. Nate actually asked me to take the camera in to have it fixed. And the boy behind the counter showed me the cassette in there and said, 'What's this? ' He played it in the camera—you know how you can do that?—and he gave me this look. This twenty-year-old kid. And you know what I did? You won't believe it. I pretended, Sandy. I couldn't think of anything else. I actually pretended they were pictures of me."

She cried then. Stern was surprised she had held up as long as she had. It struck him that Fiona was right. The young woman looked a good deal like her. The same slender, high-cheeked prettiness. Was that a hopeful sign, or something dismal? Or just one more indication that some people always made the same mistake? Certainly there was no wondering now what distractions had kept Nate from returning his calls.

"Fiona, you are upset," said Stern.

"Of course, I'm upset!" she screamed. "Don't patronize me, damn it."

Thinking he might soothe her, he had started to edge forward. But now he held his place.

"Nate doesn't know I've seen this. I couldn't *stand* to listen to him explain." She looked fiercely at Stern. "And you don't say a thing. I'm still not sure what I'm going to do."

"No, no, of course not," answered Stern, although it was difficult to think that Nate, who after all had handed her the camera, was innocent at every level. But Fiona was not one to adhere to complicated views of human intention. She had a narrow vantage, a limited range—her emotions moved only between mild hostility and absolute rage. She was at the point now of flailing, and was likely as a result to do herself serious harm, as she had just now by urging Stern to look at this tape, thinking she would shame Nate before the respectable neighbors, and finding instead that the humiliation was worse than she could bear. It probably was best that she avoid the confrontation with her husband. In humor, Clara and he had promised over the years that they would never disclose their infidelities to one another. A joke, but not without its point. It was hard to imagine a loving explanation of this sort of business. At any rate, he had been lucky enough to limp through his marriage without unfaithfulness—at least, not of the carnal variety.

Stern tried to be solicitous. Couples have gone on, he told Fiona, but she was paying no attention. She sat on the corner of a lounger, a few feet from where he was standing, sobbing into her drink. He could see the spots of rouge on her cheeks, the perfect part in her colored hair.

"You know what I resent the most? That he would do this now. Now. Twenty years ago, there was always some fellow around. I got out of the car and men watched me walk down the street. They ogled me." She pronounced it with a soft *o*, so that the word rhymed with 'google.' "I could feel it," said Fiona. "But he has to go looking for the fountain of youth. For what? What does he think is so wonderful? What does this do for him? Can you believe that last business? The big goddamn stud." Fiona cried harder. She held the highball glass up to her cheek. "Don't you think I can do that, too? I always thought he wanted me to have some dignity. I can do that. I'll let him take movies. I don't care. Pull your pants down, Sandy, I'll do it to you. Here."

For the faintest instant, Fiona's look became far more purposeful than the liquor would have seemed to allow, and Stern was convinced that she meant to move toward him. Perhaps she even started and he faltered. Something happened—the quickest moment, in which he did not observe things clearly, given his sense of alarm.

"Oh, what do you care," she murmured. She had come to her feet, but she sank down now. He was not sure precisely what she meant by the remark—probably that he was without compassion; but there was some strange insinuation in her voice, in her usual domineering tone, an odd suggestion that he was an abject thing with no right to resist.

"Fiona," he said.

She waved a hand. "Go home, Sandy. I'm losing my mind."

He waited a moment or two until she had composed herself a bit.

"I'll tell Nate you were looking for him."

"Yes, please," he answered, and they parted on that odd note of propriety.

* * *

That night, he could not sleep. Throughout their marriage, Clara had suffered prolonged bouts of insomnia, and often went through the days with a worried look and smarting eyes. Occasionally, in the depth of night, he would rouse himself to find her wide-awake beneath the reading lamp on her side of the bed. In the early years, he had asked what ailed her. Her reply was always reassuring but elliptical, and in time he responded to these episodes only by muttering that she should turn out the light. She complied, but sat upright in the dark. Now and then, when this went on for nights, he had made the mildest suggestions, but Clara was much too circumspect to lay her head, or troubles, on any psychiatrist's couch. She, like Stern, believed that, in the end, one must master these matters on one's own. So be it. Now the troubled nights were his.

He sat up with his pillow propped against the headboard, the single directed beam on his bedside lamp the only light in the house. He took up a Braudel history, and then replaced it on the night table. This episode with Fiona would not pass easily. From his body a mild force field seemed to rise, an almost electrical aura. In the dark he made his way to the sun room for a drink. Vodka and soda, something he had seen a client order in a bar. He pushed aside the curtain, looking to the Cawleys'. Nate's BMW was in the circular drive, and the only light was borrowed from the street lamps and the moon crazing the dark windows. Was Fiona also restless, or did she sleep soundly, spent by ire and impulse?

He roamed back to the bedroom with the drink. With the liquor, the sensations had become stronger and more localized. His genitals were almost singing. With a certain shyness, he reiterated in his mind the tape recording. One image seemed to fascinate him, a peculiar lateral alignment in the camera's eye as it looked down to the woman's head in Nate's lap and caught the white part in her hair, the shining ridge of her nose, and the glistening pale stalk growing out between her lips as she drew back. Slightly drunk, he had no power to resist his own excitement. His organ throbbed, lifting the bedcovers. Three weeks ago, he would have assumed that he was dead forever to such stimulation.

He thought suddenly: What happened there at the end? If anger and despair had emboldened her wildly, would he have stopped her? 'Oh, what do you care?' He still had no idea what Fiona had meant, but recollected, her remark set up a shiver, as if it were a tantalizing message of libertine permission. What *did* he care?

"Absurd," he said aloud, and tried to sleep, galled to think that he was taken up with half-drunk fantasies of Fiona. Fiona! She was one of those creatures he had never found appealing. But now, as he crept in and out of a dusky night-town on the borders of sleep, she appeared in his mind alarmingly confused with the young woman for whom Nate had spurned her. Clara had been twenty pounds overweight since Peter's birth, and Stern did not recall wishing even for a second that that were not so. But now he dwelled on the slim body of that much younger woman, transposed in dreaming moments to Fiona. Near five he slept solidly and then bolted awake. He had had the crudest and most direct of dreams that he had supplanted Nate; his penis stood erect, burning with sexual and urinary urgency. What nimble gesture, he wondered with sudden languor, would have been utilized to speed his response? He imagined, somehow, the fingering of a flute.

Before six, he drove down to the office. The sky was beginning to be colored, gray and rose, a certain prairie feel to it. The night of sleeplessness left him feeling shattered; he concentrated poorly, while the sensations of his smoky dreams persisted, leaking over him. Behind his desk, he remained stimulated, so that even his fingertips, the hairs atop his knuckles, were quick with sensation. And he heard, remote but insistent, that insinuating voice:

Oh, what do you care?

6

Three years ago, Stern had been retained to represent the chief deputy in the Kindle County Prosecutor's Office, who was charged with murdering a female colleague. It had been the tri-cities' trial of the decade, revealing tawdry passions and political intrigues, and Stern's role had briefly riveted attention on him across the nation. In the aftermath, his practice, never insubstantial, had grown significantly. While formerly he'd had one associate, Stern now employed three younger lawyers, all of whom insisted lately that at least one more attorney was needed. One of the lawyers working for Stern, Alec Vestos, dealt exclusively with civil matters and was largely on his own; Stern, even three decades along, felt little confidence with the endless rigmarole of civil procedure—depositions, interrogatories, and requests to admit. The other two lawyers—Raphael Moya and Sondra Duhaney—were both former state defenders and had come to Stern about the same time, two years ago. They followed criminal files in the state court, while Stern usually took principal responsibility for the federal criminal work.

Alec, Raphael, and Sondra were capable of handling most matters without guidance, and since Clara's death, they had been piloting the ship. Stern's hours here were significantly reduced. After his broken nights, he would find himself in the mornings stricken by morose visions from his dreams, often too forbidding to fully recollect. He would lie in bed, feeling as if he were coated by film, seeing himself in a distant, abstracted way as some figure on air, like one of the dybbuks dancing through the background of a Chagall, or an astronaut barely tethered to his capsule, someone who was nowhere, in no field of gravity, able at any instant to drift off forever into the limitless universe. When he managed to rouse himself, he felt enervated as soon as he passed through the office door.

The dispositions of a lifetime made it impossible for him to treat legal problems with indifference; the law would ever amaze him, the way some children were always fascinated by a certain toy. Even now, his abilities struck him as unimpaired; yet his commitments were lagging. Clients with their problems, their urgencies—it all seemed beyond his present reserves. There was a limited number of matters to which Stern was inalterably committed. The rest were shifted to the younger lawyers. Each day here he would receive reports from his associates, meet with those clients he was required to see, examine pleadings, make the necessary phone calls or court appearances, and spend the remainder of the day in aimless desultory reflection. He would say he was thinking of Clara, but that was not completely so. He meditated on virtually anything: TV advertisements, graffiti on an alley wall; the children and their miseries; groceries he needed; bills; planting he still had time to do; the four or five occasions he had promised to return with Clara to Japan and had failed to make the trip, or even preparations. Last week he had read brochures on a new word-processing system for an entire day.

He had closed the cover on his case, preparing for his night of wandering at home, when Alec appeared with a telecopy that had just arrived in the mailroom. It was near seven, and the office was still, only the lawyers present, surveying what remained now that the phones had stopped ringing. The message Stern had received—a cover sheet and a letter—identified Dixon as its sender, transmitting from his magnificent stone home in Greenwood County, where his study was replete with gadgets: fax, computers, tickers, modems. A modern executive, Dixon was never out of touch. The phone rang then, Stern's private number.

"You get that?" Dixon asked.

"I am studying it now." As promised, Dixon's case was one of the few matters to which Stern had given continuing attention. He had tracked down the three clients of Dixon's mentioned in the government's subpoena whom he had not reached before. Their lawyers confirmed that each had been contacted by the

FBI, but only one was willing to provide Stern with copies of the records the grand jury had subpoenaed. Then, earlier this week, Al Greco, from Dixon's office here in DuSable, had called with the names of two large local customers who had received subpoenas for the same kinds of documents. The government's specific concerns were no more apparent.

The letter Dixon had faxed, however, offered some insight. It was from his personal banker at First Kindle, who announced that yet another grand jury subpoena had been served on the bank more than a month ago. According to the letter, agents had visited the bank and briefly reviewed the statements for Dixon's checking accounts. Then, pursuant to the subpoena's command, they had required copies of all items Dixon had deposited and the checks he had written over the last year. This was an exhaustive task, requiring clerks to search through reels of microfilm, but the bank was scheduled to finally produce these items next week. The FBI, as usual, had requested confidentiality, yet the banker, after consultation with his lawyers, had determined to advise Dixon should he wish to venture any objection. The letter portrayed this gesture as an act of heroic defiance in behalf of a valued customer, but it was, in truth, routine.

"What does it mean?" asked Dixon.

Many things, Stern knew. Certainly that Dixon was the target of the government's inquiry; and that somehow they had figured out where Dixon banked. At this point, a few months ago, Stern would have lit a cigar as a way to gather a moment to think. His fingers still wandered toward the handsome crystal ashtray on his desk, as if the nerves had some instinct of their own. It was twenty-nine days, by his calculation, since he'd had his last cigar, the day he flew off to Chicago. This was a lugubrious South American notion, he knew, the idea of a penance, moth-eaten Catholic baggage he was still lugging around from his adolescence, and he a Jew at that. It was typical of the entirely unpredictable ways that Argentina would episodically haunt him.

"It means, I would think," said Stern, "that the government is attempting to trace money. They believe, Dixon, that you somehow unlawfully profited from these enormous trades they are scrutinizing."

Dixon was quiet.

"It's a bunch of crap," he said finally. "What do they think? I stole all this money and mailed it right into my checking account so I could be sure someone would notice? How stupid am I supposed to be?"

Stern did not answer. In his indignation Dixon was convincing, but the sequence of events described by the banker—the fact that the agents had reviewed the statements first—gave every indication that they believed they were on the right track. Dixon had admitted last time that the orders the government was investigating were large enough to significantly alter market prices. Perhaps Dixon had been paid off by traders on the market floor for informing them about his customers' plans. That would fit. The prosecutor would want to examine any personal checks Dixon had received from other members of the exchanges.

"And if they're tracing money I deposit, what do they need my goddamn canceled checks for?" Dixon asked.

"Generally, your checks are desired not for what is on the front but on the back." Dixon did not seem to understand. "By examining the endorsements, Dixon, they are able to identify other accounts, other financial institutions with whom you have dealings. If they do not find what they are seeking in this account, they will move on to the others."

"Great," said Dixon. He went quiet again. Stern, in the interim, scribbled a quick draft of a letter to the bank, asking for copies of the subpoena and whatever they produced to the government. As the bankers' lawyers well knew, there were no grounds to prevent the bank from complying.

"This gal is really a pistol," Dixon said. He was speaking apparently of Klonsky. "She wants everything. Margy told me the records they subpoenaed already take up half a room." A few boxes, is what Margy had said to Stern, but he would see for himself. He was going to Chicago next week to review the documents before turning them over to the government. "You know what they call her, don't you?" Dixon asked. "Klonstadt? Have you heard this? The Titless Wonder." Dixon laughed. On Friday nights at Gil's, within whose mock-elegant foil walls the federal practitioners gathered to pass information about ongoing trials and the tribulations of practice, Stern had heard the nickname. That kind of cruel humor had never been much to his taste.

Dixon was deeply aggrieved. Aggravated. Hounded. Ms. Klonsky's resourcefulness exceeded his expectations. And in his gruff effort to insist that this vulgarity was funny, Stern, for the first time, detected a familiar tone. Stern had listened to it for decades. The willies or the creeps. Call it what you like. It was the sound of incipient internal corrosion, of inner fortifications giving way. That abandoned edge in Dixon's voice touched Stern himself with the cold trickle of something close to fright. Clearly, given his new knowledge of the prosecutor's nickname, Dixon had found himself unable to obey Stern's advice not to talk about the investigation. Instead, in the steam bath at the club, or in some corner of the locker room where he usually talked grain prices or the girls on the floor he'd like to screw, Dixon had bellied out his troubles to somebody—a lawyer probably, given the information he had retrieved. One could only hope it was someone discreet.

"Do you know what the latest is?" Dixon asked. "I'm not supposed to have heard this, but two FBI agents have been up at Datatech all week looking over records on one of the MD accounts. I picked that up today."

Stern made a deeper sound. No wonder Dixon was feeling surrounded. Datatech was Dixon's data-processing vender, which prepared the computer tabulations on all of MD's accounts.

"Which account, Dixon?"

"The house error account."

"What is that, please?"

"Just what it sounds like. Where we clear up mistakes. Customer wants to buy two cans of beans and we buy him corn instead. When we notice what we've done, we'll buy him beans and move the corn into the house error account, so we end up owning the corn instead of the customer."

"And the government wants the records of this account?"

"Better than that. The jokers asked Datatech to put together a special computer run. They just want errors made on trades on the KCFE." The Kindle County Futures Exchange.

"Kindle?" asked Stern.

"Right. It doesn't make sense, does it?"

"No," answered Stern simply. The customer trades about which the government had been subpoenaing information previously had all been executed on the Chicago Exchange. The errors which the government now wished to examine arose, according to Dixon's information, from trades placed on the smaller exchange here. It was like investigating transactions on the New York Stock Exchange by requesting records from the Pacific Stock Exchange in San Francisco. Baffling. But there was something in Dixon's uneasy tenor which suggested to Stern that the government was on the right trail. "From whom do you hear these things, Dixon? About the FBI at Datatech?"

"I got that on the QT. They fouled their britches over at Datatech when they saw the subpoena. I pay those jagoffs three hundred thousand dollars a year, and now they promise to keep this a secret from me."

"Just so," said Stern. "But you have reason to believe in the accuracy of this information?"

"A young lady," said Dixon finally. "I've known her for some time. She wouldn't give me any malarkey. I promised this wouldn't come back on her. I don't want Titless hearing about it."

"Of course." For Dixon, like the others on the exchanges, his word given was exalted. To someone's back a knife could be freely applied, but a deal made eye to eye could not be broken.

"How long is she going to keep this up, anyway," Dixon asked, "what's-her-name, Kronstadt?"

"Klonsky," said Stern. "There is no telling."

"Months?"

"Years, in theory."

"Jesus. And they can just go on sending out one subpoena after another? Even to me?"

"If there is any legitimate investigative purpose, yes." Across the phone lines, Stern heard the little metal click of Dixon's lighter. "Do I take it you have a particular concern, Dixon?"

"It's nothing," he said. He emitted a heavy breath. "Can they get anything with a subpoena?"

"I am not following, Dixon."

"Suppose I have some personal stuff. Can they subpoena that?" Stern waited. What was Dixon telling him?

"Where are these private items housed, Dixon?"

Stern could hear his brother-in-law drawing on his cigarette, weighing how much to admit.

"My office. You know. There's a small safe. It fits in the bottom of my credenza."

"And what is in it?"

Dixon made an equivocal sound.

"Generally," said Stern.

"Personal," said Dixon. "Stuff."

Stern ran his tongue along his mouth. Dixon needed no education in being less chatty. At times, there was a peculiar fellowship between Stern and his brother-in-law. Dixon was a clever man with a winning sense of humor; it was easy at moments to enjoy his company. He and Stern attended ball games together; engaged in such athletic competitions as Stern could manage. Both men were lovers of gadgets, and there were two stores on East Charles which they visited only together, one afternoon a year. And yet there had always been absolute boundaries, guarded by some rumbling unspeaking rivalry, disapproval, distrust. Stern was content to let Dixon leave him often in the dark. He did not want a rundown on Dixon's illicit rendezvous or his borderline business practices. Over the years, this relation of lawyer and client had proved more agreeable to both of them than some jovial effort to feign any kind of filial intimacy. Stern asked (only what the law in its rigors and proprieties demanded, and Dixon listened carefully and answered narrowly, and as he liked.

"Are we speaking of truly personal materials, Dixon? Items which are yours alone and not the corporation's, which were prepared outside the corporation and to which you do not give corporate personnel access?"

"Right. Can they get that with a subpoena?"

Stern pondered. He never liked providing these kinds of saddleback opinions. The client was always holding on to some detail which changed everything.

"In general, you cannot be compelled to produce personal items, absent a grant of immunity. That is not likely to occur at this point in the investigation. A search warrant, of course, is another matter."

"A search warrant?"

"These investigations of brokerage houses are sometimes most unpleasant. Depending on what the prosecutors are seeking, they may find it convenient to attempt to grab up all your records at once. If they start in the office and believe items are missing, your home would be next."

"I better move this stuff? Is that what you're telling me?"

"Only if you're concerned about it falling into the government's hands. If that thought troubles you for some reason, you might think about storing your safe somewhere less likely to be searched."

"Which is where?"

"How big is it?" Stern asked.

A foot square, Dixon said.

"You could send it here, then. Federal prosecutors are more reluctant, even these days, to search attorneys' offices. The warrant requires special approval from the Justice Department in Washington, and the conduct smacks of a violation of the right to counsel. It is very untidy, from their perspective."

"And how do I get to the safe, if I need something?"

Stern declined to state the obvious. Dixon had already made it clear that he had no wish to share the contents.

"I shall give you a key to the office. Come and look as you like. Or better yet, what about another lawyer who is not involved in this present matter? Wally Marmon's office would serve excellently." This was the large firm which represented Dixon on the routine business matters that Stern declined to handle, but Dixon grunted at the notion.

"He'll charge me rent," Dixon said, "by the hour. And he'd get too nervous. You know Wally."

On reflection, Dixon was probably correct about that.

"If this arrangement makes you uncomfortable, then leave the safe where it is, Dixon. Or take it home. As your lawyer, I prefer to see it here."

It would be best to have Dixon's zone of privacy clearly bounded. Lord only knew where they'd end up if Dixon had continuing access to some black box into which he could stuff any document the government sought whose contents made him uncomfortable. Both the client and the lawyer could come to substantial grief that way.

Dixon at last said that he would send the safe next week.

"Handle the arrangements yourself," said Stern. "If no one but you knows where the safe is, no one can tell the government where to search for it."

"What does that mean?" asked Dixon.

Stern waited again. He did not want to alarm him. On the other hand.

"Dixon, I must tell you, I am convinced the government has an informant."

"An informant?"

"Someone close to you or the business. The government's information is too precise. The trades. Where you bank. Who your data-processing vender is. And there is an odd order to what they are willing to have known. I suspect they are interested in misleading you about their sources of information."

"I think they're interested in showing how fucking clever they are," said Dixon.

"You must reflect on this matter, Dixon. The identity of this informant could be of great significance to us."

"Forget it, Stern. You don't have the picture. Every jackal at the Kindle Exchange that's ever wanted to sink his fangs in my hindquarter is probably feeding stuff to those guys." Dixon's tone was bitter as he spoke of his critics and competitors. "And I'll have the last laugh. You mark my words. Just wait," he said. "I'll keep my mouth shut now, because you say I've got to. But when this thing is done, I'll still be standing here. And there'll be some bills coming due."

Dixon was unaccustomed to being vulnerable—or restrained. The need for both enraged him. He hung on the line a moment longer, with the heavy breath of a bull. His bold promises of triumph and revenge behind him, he seemed to have no more to say. Perhaps he recognized their futility. The government would go on, notwithstanding, demanding his records, scaring his clients, courting his enemies, prying into every worldly connection he valued. Across the distance of two counties, Dixon seemed to consider his world of dwindling secrets. That was what had always protected him—not his friendships or alliances; he had few—not even his wealth or the power of his personality. Dixon was like Caliban or God—unknowable. The insult of his present circumstance was profound.

"Just wait," said Dixon once more before he put down the phone.

7

"Don't do anything," the woman said at the other end of the line. "I'm bringing you dinner."

"Who is this?" asked Stern. "Helen?"

"Yes, of course, it's Helen. Will that be a bother? I'll just drop it off and go. I have a meeting."

She must have been calling at fifteen-minute intervals, for he had been home only moments.

"You are most kind," said Stern, eyeing the unidentifiable casserole dish already thawing on the counter. "Come ahead."

So, thought Stern, the female nation heard from, once again. Helen Dudak, of course, probably had no interest in being forward. The Dudaks and the Sterns had been exchanging favors for twenty years. As couples, they had been connected principally by their children. Kate, through most of her life, was the best friend of Helen's oldest, Maxine. The two families had the same ideas about things that seemed to matter substantially when you were rearing a family: about asking to be excused before leaving the table; the number of sweets allowed in a day; the right age to drive alone or to go out for the evening with a boy. The Dudaks were fine people, principled, with reasonable values, and concern for their children. So the relationship had stood on this solid, if narrow, footing. His knowledge of Helen's inner realm was nodding, at best. Clara had never seemed to regard Miles and Helen as an interesting couple, and in the last few years, in the face of many changes, relations had drifted a bit. Maxine had gone to business school, married, and worked in St. Louis; and Helen had been divorced from Miles Dudak for three years now. She had a wised-up, funny, independent air, resolved to exceed the bathos and humiliation of the sad circumstance in which her husband of twenty-odd years, the wealthy owner of a box-manufacturing concern, had moved out and, only a few months later, married his thirty-year-old secretary.

From the kitchen window, Stern observed her arriving with a large purse and an armory of aluminum-foil containers. Buy bauxite, Stern thought as he watched her under flag, proceeding to the front door with the trays pyramided beneath her chin.

"Helen, my Lord, I am one person." Stern unburdened her and showed her to the kitchen. "There's enough here for six. Sixteen." Peeling the foil wrapper back from a tray of chicken, he was braced by the aroma. Garlic and thyme. Had he been required to wager, he would have bet that Helen Dudak was a good cook. It was part of her image of substance. "You must join me. It would be a pity to see all of this consumed from the freezer. Do you have time for dinner before your meeting? Please stay. I would welcome your company."

Helen faltered, but eventually was persuaded to surrender her coat. Had this been planned? Stern doubted it. Helen was not a schemer, although she was clearly pleased to be asked. He took her raincoat to the closet, a fawn-toned garment with a famous label—Miles had not bought his freedom cheaply. She'd already found plates and flatware and was setting the kitchen table when Stern returned. He admired Helen's good sense in not promoting this into a more auspicious encounter in the dining room, but, notwithstanding, there was a certain animated excitement as Helen traveled from the cabinets to the table. Here they were, people in their middle years. His wife was five weeks dead. But he was single, she was unattached, and because of that, they both seemed strangely, almost painfully enlivened.

And he was interested; there was no concealing that from himself. Since his evening at Fiona's, he was aroused in some measure by every woman he saw. For Stern, it was a disconcerting fixation. As he put it to himself, he had not recently tuned in this channel. Oh, he thought, of course. He admired a hundred women in a day, just moving about downtown. But he had practiced such deliberate oblivion. He was one of those men glad for middle years, the settled portion of life, when sexual preoccupation could comfortably be left behind without some slur on masculinity. Now he received, almost in spite of himself, an eager, exhilarant message from his own systems. He could not truly envision himself as the companion of another woman—it was much too soon—but he nonetheless cast a somewhat naughty eye on Helen when he went down the corridor to draw a bottle from the wine closet.

She was, all in all, a handsome person—her midriff had given way somewhat, but Stern could hardly be critical on that score—and even if she looked a little roughened by experience, there was something in that which was admittedly attractive. Her hair was reddish, the color of a fox, enhanced somewhat by a coloring agent these days, but drying with age and verging therefore on a kind of unmanageableness. Her legs were well turned; she had no bottom to speak of; her face was large-pored, heavily made up, but in its own way comely. Helen had her well-worn look— humor, anguish, and dignity. Stern's impression was that she had been utterly lost when Miles departed, but she was a strong person, perhaps not an intellect, but well grounded. She had carried on bravely, rightly convinced that she was not deserving of abuse.

"Well, this is an unanticipated pleasure," he said when the meal was set out before them both. "What did you do to these potatoes, Helen? Really. They are quite remarkable."

Helen described the process. Stern listened carefully. He was fond of potatoes.

She told him about her business. She had been trained as a travel agent along the way, but longed for something less mundane and had become a convention planner. Large organizations hired her to arrange sites, hotels, presentations. She worked out of her home, with a fax machine and a telephone console. A rocky start, but now she was well under way. She delivered the tale with good humor, an entertaining talker and willing to take the lead in maintaining this fragile, convivial air.

The doorbell rang. Glancing through the panes beside the front door, he saw Nate Cawley. Stern seemed to have caught him in a moment of reflection. On the slate stoop, he had turned to look into the wind. He was a smallish man, narrow. His hair was gray and most of it was gone; a few longer hairs stood up straight now in the breeze. Rain was in the offing; late April here was always wet. Nate had run out without a coat and he jiggled a bit to keep himself warm. He wore a golf cardigan and a pair of blue plaid slacks.

"Welcome, Nate." Helen had stood up from the table in the breakfast nook, and peered down the hall toward Stern and Nate in the foyer. In spite of the distance, Stern attempted the introduction. "Do you know Helen Dudak?" asked Stern.

"Certainly." A moment of decided awkwardness occurred. Nate did not move. Clearly, he thought he had interrupted, and Stern had an instant aversive response, old-fashioned but strong, that he was not happy to be seen alone with a woman in his home. This was not the message he wanted Nate to take back to Fiona, who would put it out promptly over the neighborhood wire. Stern swung out a hand magisterially, a hammy bit, to gather some forward momentum.

"We are in the midst of a splendid repast Helen has provided, Nate. Do you care for some wonderful Chicken Vesuvio, or may I get you a drink?"

"No, Sandy. I just ran over for a second. Fiona said you were looking for me." Nate apologized for being hard to reach. Much, he said, was going on. Yes, indeed, thought Stern. The Lord only knew what Fiona said they had discussed, but clearly she had offered an edited version. Preoccupied as he seemed, Nate did not wear the predictable air of a man who knew you and his wife had spent a moment commenting on videos of his erection.

Stern showed him to his study, where he had filed the lab's bill.

"Have you any idea what that might have been for?"

"Huh," said Nate. "Westlab." He studied the invoice at length before handing it back. "I don't use them much."

"Apparently, Clara had visited a physician in the last month."

Nate took a second to absorb that. "Where do you get that idea?"

Stern explained the notations on Clara's calendar. "Frankly, Nate, I assumed it was you. I found no doctor's bills." Nate, a physician and neighbor in the old tradition, often worked on the cuff, billing Clara episodically, if at all. After the meeting in Cal's office, Stern had been through Clara's checkbook carefully. And, necessarily, he had also sifted through the mail. It had occurred to him, he offered, that Clara might have been ill. "Something grave," said Stern, then added, more quietly, "Unendurable."

Nate, mercifully, picked up the thread. A softer look came over him, the gentle eye of a practiced bedside manner.

"No, no, Sandy, there was nothing like that, nothing I know of."

"I see." They faced one another in the study, under a strangely burdened air. Perhaps Nate found Stern's rummaging through his wife's papers unseemly; or he may have been discomfited by Helen's presence. "I was misled, I suppose, by Fiona's mention that you had brought Clara medication from time to time."

"Fiona," said Nate, and a distinct expression of distaste passed by swifty. It was an error, Stern saw, to have repeated any of her intoxicated blather. "Clara's knee gave her some trouble this winter, Sandy. I dropped off an anti-inflammatory."

"Ah," said Stern. The two men continued to look at one another.

"Sandy, why don't I give Westlab a call for you? I'll find out what's cookin'."

"I can do that, Nate."

"Neh," said Cawley. "Let me. They'd be happier to talk to me than you. Assuming they'll talk to anybody. If it wasn't for you guys—" Nate, in his gentle, familiar way, was about to assail Stern with a doctor's typical complaints about the legal profession and its recent impact on medical practice, but he cut himself off. "You know," he said, "could be just a mistake. I've seen billings get awful bollixed up. Maybe they crossed one Stern with another."

The idea struck Stern as farfetched. Then, just as quickly, it was all entirely clear.

"Oh, my." Stern covered his mouth with one hand. "I have a thought." Clara had received the bill—but not the test. That would have been, as Nate's point suggested, for someone else— for Kate. Pre-pregnancy. Pre-something. Kate had said that there had been problems along the way. She had probably shared them with her mother, who, as she often did, would have insisted on helping with the expenses. That was another reason that Kate was so sabered that Clara had died not knowing there had been a medical success—and why no doctor's bill had arrived here. Something rose, something sank, but it all settled in him with the solidity of a correct answer. "I suspect, Nate, this may have had something to do with Katy's pregnancy."

"Oh, sure," said Nate. He brightened considerably. "That must be it." He headed at once for the door, happy to have the matter resolved.

"Perhaps, Nate, if I have further questions, I might ask you to call the lab nonetheless."

"Sure thing," said Nate. "No problem. Just give me a buzz."

On his way out, Nate turned back to wave briefly to Helen. She still had one hand raised, with a sad look of her own, as Stern approached. She had sat alone, not eating. She seemed to know that whatever spell had loomed was broken. The conspicuous presence of Clara's mystery, the many complications were obvious about him. He was a fish in a net. Nothing now would change that.

"I apologize," said Stern. "Questions I was required to ask. He was Clara's doctor."

"Mine, too," said Helen.

"Ah," said Stern, "so that is your acquaintance."

Helen began to eat. There was music from the radio, Brahms. He sat in the caned chair with a full sense of his weight, his earthly substance. As so often, grief was here in its essential character.

"Had Clara been sick, Sandy? I didn't know that."

"Apparently not." He explained briefly. The bill. His thoughts. Helen, who had known them both so long, nodded with each word, eyes quick, intent.

"I see," she said. They were both silent.

"I have no idea why this occurred, you know," Stern told her abruptly. To the thousands of other inquiries, tacit and overt, he had maintained a dignified silence which implied, not falsely, that he found the subject too painful for discussion. Helen Dudak, however, was too trustworthy a soul, too familiar, to be dealt with so briefly. "I take it people talk about this?" He had wanted to ask someone that question for some time.

"Would you believe me if I told you they didn't?"

He smiled wanly. "And they say what?"

"Dumb things. Nice things. Who knows about anybody's life, Sandy? Really. At the core. People are baffled, naturally. No one is quite certain they knew Clara. She was very contained."

"Just so," said Stern softly. He allowed himself the traces of a wry expression.

Helen, wisely, took her time with the remark.

"You must be very angry," she said at last.

To the wheel of seething emotion, the bristling anxiety, the dense miserable sensations, Stern had not heretofore put that name. But of course she was correct. Buried deep in his bones, like a dose of radiation, he could feel the burning away of intense high-level emotion, and anger was the right word for it. It was not a feeling with which he had taken much conscious comfort throughout his life. Being the son of his mother, the brother of Jacobo, he had grown up believing that anger was an emotion allotted to others by prior arrangement. He was the steady one. Now a certain decorousness made him reluctant to fully agree.

"I suppose," he said.

"It would be understandable," Helen continued.

Chewing slightly, he shook his head.

"That, however, is not what predominates," he said.

"No?"

He shook his head again. The powerful volatility of his emotions, the way they were always at hand, made it impossible to observe his usual reserve.

"I doubt myself," he told her. "I failed," he said and, with the words, and their deadeye accuracy, felt as if he had shot himself through with an arrow. "Quite obviously."

"And what about her?" asked Helen. She looked up adroitly, over her fork, but he could see that she was measuring her questions, testing the regions of tenderness to see how far she might probe. It was, Stern decided, an impressive performance.

"Did Clara fail?"

Helen did not answer. She looked on while he considered the question. He understood her suggestion, but he was unable to say aloud the word somehow hanging here like smoke: betrayal. The mystery of it was deeper than that to him, and more complicated. He realized then, for the first time, how much he had dedicated himself to making no judgments in this matter for the present. Again, wordlessly, he wobbled his head: something not to know or to say.

Helen waited an instant.

"You can't let everything rest on the end, Sandy."

Stern nodded. That was a thought, too.

"I speak from experience. You accomplished a great deal with one another. And you made a marvelous couple."

"Oh, yes," said Stern. "I loved to speak, and she did not."

Helen smiled, but leaned back to regard him from a distance. "You're too harsh with yourself." She took his wrist and he reacted, even in this mood, to the sensations of a female touch. "How good a friend am I? May I make a suggestion?" Her hands were tan and strong, the nails unpolished. "Are you seeing someone, Sandy?"

Lord, again! What was contemporary morality?

"Helen, certainly not."

Looking into her plate, Helen Dudak suppressed a smile. "I meant a therapist."

"Ah," he said. His initial impulse was categorical, but he answered simply, "Not for now."

"It might help," she said.

"Is that an informed opinion?"

"Of course. A middle-aged divorce is harder than a hockey match."

Her delivery was lighthearted and Stern smiled. He could see that Helen was from the self-improvement school of life. Very much a citizen of the late century. She believed in the power of Will, or, as it was thought of in contemporary terms, self-determination. Existentialists one and all, we could be whomever we chose, with proper instruction. Something about yourself that bugs you? Chuck it out. Let the shrink refurnish. A deeply conservative strain in Stern distrusted these conclusions. It was all a good deal harder to bear than that. He could see that Helen and he subscribed to different philosophical services. He chose a joke as a diplomatic exit.

"I shall talk to you, instead."

"Sold," said Helen.

They smiled, celebrating the survival of a difficult instant, but then lingered a few seconds in the gloom. Helen at last asked about Kate. For the remainder of the meal, they trod reliable ground, speaking of their children.

At nine, promptly, she stood. She was late for her meeting. Stern saw her to the door, thanking her lavishly for the meal.

"You are a friend, Helen."

"I mean to be," she answered.

"This was the most pleasant evening I have had in some time." He found, upon saying this, that it was a considerable truth and, out of a sudden swell of gratitude, added, "We must do it again."

"Let's," responded Helen. They stood looking at one another. He was too new to this business to have realized before he spoke what he had gotten himself into, and now, otherwise at a loss, he took her hand and in the briefest, politest way kissed it.

Helen rolled her eyes as she opened the door.

"Oh, my God," she said. "Charming, char-ming!" She shook her head and, with her large purse and fawn-colored coat, went off laughing down the walk.

8

To the distant subdivision where Kate and John had bought a compact suburban home, newly constructed and as weakly made as a child's toy, Stern ventured on occasion for a meal. This house was so far from the urban center that there were still cornfields about, and the clods ran clear to the front door, as Kate and John had not yet been able to afford sod. In the front lawn, near the parkway, a single skinny sapling stood, its tiny leaves riffling like a fringe whenever there was wind.

Kate scurried about her father, attempting to comfort him, but as ever, the best of her attention went to her husband. Every now and then, the newspapers reported on twins so preoccupied with one another that they developed a language of their own. So, too, Kate and John. They were forever lost in their small sounds: whispers, murmurs, Katy's wispy laugh. A universe of two. Stern had known other couples like this, tuned in to each other's peculiarities like some strange music, and high on it like opium smoke. They had been together since high school and, so far as Stern could tell, were the only man or woman the other had ever really known. This naïveté had its own beauty. To one another they were the entire realm of otherness: Adam and Eve. Yin and Yang.

It was difficult to imagine the entry of a child into this world of two dimensions, but Kate's pregnancy, if anything, seemed to have intensified the thrill of love. John raced behind his wife's chair to help her up, kissed her with abandon as they slid into the kitchen, clearing plates. Watching his daughter's dark eyes fast upon her husband, Stern felt strangely affected by her love for him. Poor John was a schlepper of the first order. His most important achievement to the world at large would probably remain having been the best tight end in a decade at a high school that traditionally fielded mediocre teams. The higher-powered jocks, with greedy visions of agents, bonuses, and the NFL, had literally run over him at the University of Wisconsin. John, the coaches said, had the size and talent, but not the drive. This was hardly news to Stern, who had come back with his own scouting report years before. But here was an important late addendum: he treated his wife with unfailing kindness. In a hard world, where decency seldom thrived, a realm full of the brutish, the harsh—or even those well-meaning but emotionally land-locked, like Stern himself—John was a standout, a man of gentle disposition and great tenderness. If he had failed to find in himself a killer's ruthlessness, he had discovered something else, which he nurtured with Kate. Who among us might not be willing to trade?

As John trekked through the yard with the evening trash, Stern stood with his daughter in the kitchen. She and John had just finished washing up the dinner dishes and she sopped a cloth.

"*Cara*, I have been meaning to ask," said Stern. "An item came through in the mail the other day which made me wonder if there was any recent occasion when your mother went with you to the doctor?"

Kate looked at him uncomprehendingly. Even in sandals, she was an inch or two taller than he, dark and beautiful, with her straight hair and perfect features.

"Recently?"

"Within the last few months."

"No. Of course not. I told you, she had no idea."

"But perhaps—is there no way your mother might have received the bill for one of your tests, some procedure?"

"Daddy, what in the world?" Kate had stepped back from the sink. She remained tense and emotional at any mention of Clara, and he suddenly thought better of going on. She had provided a sufficient answer.

He touched her on the shoulder to soothe her and stepped into the family room, still furnished with boxes and card chairs, and joined John, who had gone straight to the TV set upon reentering the house. At these instants Stern found himself full of almost religious gratitude for the invention of television sports, which could occupy the few moments he felt obliged to pass with his son-in-law. Tonight, the Trappers, the tri-cities' traditionally woeful big-league baseball team, were on the air, and Stern and John swapped thoughts about the prospects for the season just under way. The story with the Trappers was always the same: young stars traded away when their salaries increased, pitchers who hit it big as soon as they escaped the Trappers' pocket-sized park. Stern, who had made baseball one of his most passionate studies in learning the American way of life, enjoyed his son-in-law's insights. John had an athlete's eye for the nuances of physical performance: the shortstop threw off-balance. Tenack, the magnificent right fielder, was trying, as he did each April, to upper-cut the ball. Wearing glasses for his TV viewing, John poked his frames back up on his nose from time to time as the images of the green field floated on his lenses. He appeared transfixed, childlike, still bound heart and soul by the grace and glory of the fields of play; when John watched, you could almost hear the hot roar of the stadium crowd in his ears.

Long moments passed while Stern awaited John's occasional observations, to which he could add some knowing comment of his own. Stern rarely asked John about work; it had become clear long ago that he would never answer honestly, fearing that his responses, which were likely to verge on complaint, would find their way to Dixon. John had had a slow start at MD, passing bewilderedly through the accounting and compliance departments before finding a home on the order desk, where, Stern took it, his performance was still not stellar. They sat on either side of the glowing screen, John's zombie-like attention to the game undoubtedly increased due to the presence of his father-in-law, while Stern recalled similar dumbstruck reactions, at the same period in his life, to his own imposing father-in-law, Henry Mittler. In these reflections, he felt for John, especially since at heart Stern always remained half ready to revile him for not being better, smarter, more adept, more able to rouse in Kate something laudable, rather than, as it seemed, allowing her to drift to rest on the soft seabed of the commonplace.

A sufficient time passed to suit all proprieties, he bade John good night and, ready to be on his way, found Kate in the kitchen. Seeing her, though, it occurred to him once more how vexed his last exchange with her had left him. If the bill from Westlab was not for Kate, then what? He was back to point zero.

"Katy," he said, releasing her from his parting embrace, "are you quite sure there was no bill for you that might have come to your mother?"

"Daddy, there is no way. What's wrong with you?" She looked at him, incredulous, and he shrugged, somewhat defensively. It had seemed so obvious, so characteristic of Clara that the children were involved.

With the next thought, Stern, halfway across the kitchen, stood absolutely still.

He knew now.

He had blundered past it. But he knew now why Clara had received no doctor's bill; why Peter had been so overwrought that day about the prospect of an autopsy. Because it was he, Stern's son, who was the physician, Peter who had ordered the lab test, and Peter who remained, even now, resolved to honor some prior commitment of confidence he had made to his mother. Stern understood the need to maintain professional secrets, but he could not help suspecting that his son would enjoy this advantage over his father, having exclusive hold, in the end, of one last scrap of her life. Might the others know as well?

"Katy." She was facing him, her attention evidently drawn by her father's abstracted look. "Do you know anything of your mother receiving medical care from Peter?"

"What?" Her mouth had fallen open a bit and her face was rigid with alarm. She obviously took the suggestion as baroque. The question that rose in her eyes was easily discerned: Was her father derailed, off his trolley, losing hold? She looked gravely concerned that these ideas, wild and improbable, were coming from him, one after another.

Was he wrong? The kitchen light seemed suddenly intense. For the first time in his life, he felt a sensation of dislocation, which he knew, instinctively, was typical of the elderly. Kate was correct. Given over to his preoccupations, he had lost his bearings. What had happened to his lifelong habits of caution, tact, discretion? He could not simply run with this knuckleheaded notion and confront his son. If Peter was wrongly accused by his father of even the most well-intentioned manipulations, his predictable response would be outrage; the reverberations would shake what little family structure remained. He would have to hunt down Nate Cawley once again and ask him to make inquiries at the lab. That was the best and most discreet alternative.

"An idle thought," he said to Kate. "Allow it to pass." He took his daughter's hand and kissed her on the temple. He thanked her for dinner and waved off her inquiries about whether he was all right. But he found himself increasingly irritated as he walked into the mild night. Driving along the highway in his Cadillac—this was his car, a Sedan de Ville; Clara's had been towed away by the dealer in part of that procession of changing scenes and backdrops at the time of her death which he recalled now like a cinema montage—he felt the same rise of difficult emotion. He was tiring of Clara's gruesome surprises, her hidden world, with enormous sums expended and secret illnesses. In his confusion, he had now even begun to suspect his children. This was her fault, Stern thought suddenly, her fault! The declaration almost rang in him.

Still in this mood, he stopped near home at a convenience store. Certain household tasks remained beyond him. Claudia called in his grocery list from the office and the store obligingly delivered the bags to the back door. But there were always items missing: cream cheese, milk. He never had enough orange juice. Waiting in line, he observed with admiration two young black women who were ahead of him, in halter tops despite the chill of spring, talking high-speed bebop slang, disarmingly casual with their obvious sexuality. He felt again the high-voltage transmissions of sensual energy. What was all this? he wondered. Signs of life, he told himself; natural, he thought, but there was something wild and unpredictable in this urgency. He was so deeply stimulated by virtually any female. Was it some racist conceit to think that he would be as strange as some Martian to these women? He imagined, nonetheless. What really was the look and feel of those heavy brown breasts, smooth-skinned, heavy-nippled? His imagination rushed on to these thoughts. He stood unmoving in the store, his mouth slightly agape, aroused.

Back in the parking lot, he sat in the car, a bit shocked at

himself. How could he really? You would think, observing his
adolescent eagerness, that he'd had no passionate life with Clara,
which was not true. As a young man he had craved her—more, in
fact, after they were married than before, when so much else
seemed to be involved; and even as age and time had tempered
the pulse of things, that hunger had never been wholly lost. A
man and a woman in the end were always that to each other,
opposites and mysterious, and in the act, with its joining and
exploring, things more magical and solemn than the most
ancient ritual forever resided. Certain other couples, his age and
older, made allusions to the extinction of these impulses. Dick
Harrison, a neighbor, remarked to Stern one night, 'I hold it up,
the sunlight passes through.' But three or four times a month
Clara and he struck this fundamental compact—creaky, lumpy
old bodies as she said, moving toward each other across the bed
and, as ten thousand times before, melting together. Lately, he
had tried to recall the last occasion and found, almost certainly,
that it had been more than a month before her death. One more
sign of what he should have noticed. But he was on trial, fraught
and distracted, and who after the years does not know better
than to foment small crises? They move apart and then rejoin.
The image is of some X-ray shadow, a form in negative space;
opening and breathing, closing, clinging, like the wings of a moth
in the dark, the walls of the heart.

Now that same woman had turned him loose in late-century
America, where standards for sexual performance were touted
on the covers of the magazines sold at the checkout stand right
there behind the broad store window. Was he prepared for this?
The uncomfortable truth was that he had no past to brag about,
no comforting memory of the wild oats sown by young Alejandro
Stern. Geography, as he thought of it, had been against him.
Argentina, with its gauchos and machos and so forth, probably
would have been a more propitious place to pass his adolescence. Male lust was better accepted there, a legacy of the
nation's Italian and Spanish forebears. His brother, even at the
age of fifteen and sixteen, was an impressive roué. He had many
women, or at least claimed to: whores, Indian girls, older women
lusting for youthful energy. Stern could still clearly recollect
listening awestruck to Jacobo's account of his initiation, at the
age of thirteen, with a very thin young woman attired in a black

strapless evening gown, who had met him in the lobby of the Roma, a seedy downtown hotel in B.A. Months later, Jacobo contended he recognized her on the street in a habit, walking with her sunken eyes, amid a row of novices leaving the Convent of Santa Margarita. Stern, forty-five years after the fact, found the thought of this woman as imagined, with her sunken eyes and small breasts, disturbingly provocative.

But his youth in America in the fifties had contained nothing so exotic. The Puritans reigned once more here, and sexuality seemed to be a particularly unbecoming trait for a dark foreigner, a suspect impulse like fellow traveling. Lust was one more wild hunger that he willingly constrained for future satisfaction, even with Clara, with whom he would not have slept before their wedding but for her insistence that they were more likely to enjoy the honeymoon if they could leave this particular anxiety behind. And so, two weeks before the ceremony, in Pauline Mittler's parlor full of Oriental brocades and Viennese glass, with all the lights still burning for fear that someone in the house might notice, Clara had wriggled from her girdle and her hose, lifted her skirt, and lain back on her mother's red divan. For many reasons, that had struck Stern as an act of astonishing trust. And he? He was terrified and, because of that, also somewhat affronted, angered by the indignity of these shabby mechanics. Thirty-one years later, those emotions remained real to him, near at hand in the dark auto, the peculiar residue of a night of high feeling in which he had been confused and put out. But he had proceeded; he remembered that as well. He had fiddled interminably to release his erect penis from the bindings of his trousers, and Clara Mittler had become the first—the only—woman in his life.

9

Stern had first seen Chicago when he was thirteen, near the end of the overland passage his mother and Silvia and he had made from Argentina. That journey had been impelled by his mother's involvement with a man named Gruengehl, a lawyer who had been showing her great interest since, it seemed the moment of his father's death. Gruengehl was a figure in one of the few anti-Peronist unions, and following his jailing, his friends and colleagues had swept into his mother's house to help them pack, their route for exile already arranged. In 1947, with displaced persons throughout Europe clamoring for entry to the United States, and Argentina's diplomatic ties to the U.S. questionable after the war, legal immigration was problematic. Instead, they traveled by train to Mexico City, and then were driven across the border, looking like one more family of *braceros*. In Brownsville they boarded a train North.

Stern, even so young, had known that Argentina was not his destiny. His father, a physician, had left Germany in 1928 and forever mourned that the Nazis prevented his return. Papa always unfavorably compared life in Argentina to what he had known before: the quality of goods, of music, of building materials, of people was sadly lacking in his eyes. Jacobo, whom Stern admired, had become an ardent Zionist and preached from the time Stern was nine or so the glory of Eretz Israel. When Stern stepped off the train in Chicago, he believed his life had started. They went on to Kindle County, where cousins of his father's were waiting, but Chicago would always be what he thought of as America, with its massive, soot-smeared buildings of brick and stone and granite, full of smokestack arms and sullen, teeming throngs, the land of Gary Gooper, of steel, skyscrapers, automobiles. He recognized in every face that day the striving children of immigrants.

More than four decades later, Mr. Alejandro Stern returned, a man of prominence with his own troubles. On the fifth floor of the Chicago Exchange, he sat in the walnut conference room at Maison Dixon, thumbing thrrough documents he could not comprehend. Outside, the vast trading room of MD burned on, eighty young men and women, casually dressed, each behind a telephone console blinking with the action on twenty lines , and a pillar of cathode-ray tubes. Across these glowing screens darted figures, flashing by briefly like fish in the sea, a matrix of dollars and cents, beans and oil, fast markets and bulletin items, high, low, open, volume, change. The telephones chirped like crickets, and different voices occasionally gained ascendance. "Anybody here want to buy old bonds at 6 plus?" "It's moving, it's moving." "I'm going to hedge you up on the D-marks." Between calls, these young people, working customer and managed accounts, would offer to the entire room a hip, sardonic commentary. One fellow whined in a mock accent of some kind, "Oh, the market, she is just like a woo-man, first she wants you, then she don't, she won't never make up her mind." An attractive young blonde beside him inclined her middle finger in response.

"Got it all figured out?" Margy Allison, Dixon's chief operating officer, had returned for a moment to check on his progress. She had been in this business most of her adult life, almost exclusively for Maison Dixon, and, apparently, still found it thrilling. Nothin' to it, she seemed to suggest, as she motioned to the stacks of paper around Stern—even a silly old Okie gal could git it. Margy loved to do routines like that, for the amusement of her friends up North. An M.B.A., she preferred to come on like an oilfield roughneck. 'Mar-gee,' she would say, when introducing herself. 'Hard *g*. Hard girl.'

"I believe we shall need an accountant," Stern told her.

Margy made a face. She was the paymaster in these parts and a legend for her tightfistedness. Every time she signed a check, she told you what a dollar used to buy in the country.

"I can put all that stuff together for you."

She was capable, no question, but unlikely to find the time.

With the advent of overseas trading, and night sessions of the markets, Maison Dixon was open twenty-four hours a day, and there were problems to solve at every juncture. At her door at any hour, there was usually a line: clerks and secretaries and boys up from the floor in the unstructured jackets with the large square plastic badges on the pockets. Stern, accordingly, told her she could not afford to spend the hours this job would require.

"If you're billin' us your usual hourly rate, Sandy, I can afford a lotta time." She smiled, but her point, of course, was made. "I'm sure you got one of those hotel rooms like you usually do when we're payin, big enough to hold the opera with the elephants. We can take this whole mess there and look it over. Assumin a' course"—Margy hooded her shadowed eyes—"you're willing to chance bein alone with me." She cast herself in a vampy role, a female sexual braggart. It was part of her low routine, coming on tough and crude, like the kind of woman you imagined finding smoking a cigarette at the bar of some mid-city lounge. Stern had no idea where the truth resided, but she had laid it on thick with him over the years, perhaps as a way to flatter him, or simply on the assumption he was harmless. Now, of course, the mere suggestion inflamed his new libidinal itch. Being himself, he changed the subject.

"Do any of these records, Margy, have anything to do with the house error account?" He had Dixon's recent phone call in mind.

"They want that now, too?" Margy, nearly as irritated as Dixon by the government's persistence, went off at once to find a clerk to gather the records. This was why he traveled to the documents, Stern thought. Something else was always needed.

Stern took it that, sometime in the past twenty years, Margy had been one of Dixon's women. She was far too attractive not to have drawn Dixon's attention. But it had not gone along happily. The amount of surmise and conjecture which Stern had quietly made about this matter surprised even him. Gradually, he had filled in the blanks, tested these guesses against what was observable, and taken them as true. He had long assumed that Margy had waited interminably for Dixon to leave Silvia; that she was somehow the focus of the crisis that had erupted years ago when Silvia briefly ejected Dixon from the household; and that she had declared the struggle lost when Dixon moved back in with his wife. For a year or two, Margy had disappeared to work for another house. But there really was no way to run MD without her. Even Silvia would have recognized that. Instead, she was offered Chicago as a domain of her own, and the title of president of half a dozen of the subsidiaries, not to mention an enormous annual salary. So she had labored under those terms, devoted to Dixon's business, and probably still to him, the deprived and rejected heroic woman of one of the country ballads she had grown up humming. That was whom Margy reminded you of—those down-home ladies who stood onstage, with their twangy voices, their coiffed hair and stage makeup, sad and glamorous, hard and wise.

Eventually, the clerk arrived. The records of the house error account were laid on the table with the rest. Stern glanced through the papers, but he knew he was getting nowhere. Every time Stern found himself facing a room full of documents, he cursed the avarice that led him to do what was decorously referred to as white-collar work, and to a clientele of con artists in suits and ties who hid their crimes by laying waste to forests.

Margy reappeared in time, placing her face against a brightly manicured hand and leaning languorously on the metal doorframe. His bemusement was apparent, but Margy smiled indulgently; she had always liked Stern.

"You want me to help you out? I really am willin. We'll do like I said. Get the hell out of here. Gimme fifteen minutes."

It was more than an hour and a half, but eventually one of the messengers had brought down four transfer cases of documents and loaded them into Margy's car. She tore off down the Loop streets for the Ritz. She handled her automobile, a red foreign model, like a stock-car driver. His mother had been high-strung, hysterical. Clara was soft and dignified. That, to Stern, comprised the familiar range for female behavior. This woman, if truth be told, was stronger than he was. She could sprint an obstacle course faster or hold out longer in the face of torture. Watching her behind the wheel, he felt admiring and daunted.

This evidence of Margy's capacities was, Stern suddenly thought, instructive about Dixon. It was a mistake to see him merely as some smutty conquistador seeking notches on his gun, butterflies for his collection. Dixon valued women, trusted them, counted on their counsel. In a woman's presence, his charm and humor, and an enormous, almost electrical human force beset him. Even Stern, whatever his innate sense of rivalry, felt he liked Dixon more. And women responded to Dixon's attention. It was one of the symmetries of nature.

Of course, this interest was not detached. With Dixon, one was always well advised to remember the base elements. The markets, the pits, tense, fast, trying, were full of cokeheads and types lost in the bottle; Dixon's release was more natural: fucking. The quickest zipper in the West, someone had once called him. Not that Stern was often treated to the details. He was the brother-in-law, Silvia's blood ally, and Dixon had better sense than to test Stern's loyalties. But no one, least of all Dixon, could make a complete secret of so persistent a preoccupation. Occasionally, his pure delight overcame him, and he confided to Stern, as he did to so many other men. Dixon, for example, engaged in a personal sport in which he kept track of the exact number of women he saw in a day who inspired his most basic fantasies. 'Thirty-one,' he'd say to you, as you were greeted by a hotel clerk. 'Thirty-two,' when he looked out the window to see a woman getting on a bus. At the Rose Bowl one year, amid the coeds and cheerleaders, he claimed to have reached two sixty-three by half-time, despite giving complete attention to the game.

Usually, the extent of Dixon's interest was less amusing. Stern had been with him at the airport, passing through the metal detector, when Dixon emptied his pockets into the tray meant to receive valuables and tossed in a package of prophylactics as naturally as a pack of gum. This was a few years ago, when such items were still not the subject of polite discussion. From subsequent commentary, Stern took it that in these matters of personal hygiene, as in so many other things, Dixon was a pioneer, meticulous about protecting himself long before the current mania. But the security guard, a young woman, reddened noticeably, far more horrified than if Dixon had pulled a knife. Even Dixon, walking toward the airport gate, was chagrined. 'I should just have my thing coated in plastic.' Like a membership card or a snapshot. Neither abstinence nor restraint apparently suggested themselves as alternatives.

Witnessing these misadventures, Stern attempted to evince no interest. But he paid attention. Who wouldn't? It sometimes seemed as if he could recollect the details of each one of Dixon's randy stories. And Dixon, never one to miss a point of vulnerability, had made note of Stern's penchant long before. Once, when the two of them were traveling in New York, Dixon carried on with special animation with a young waitress, a smooth-featured young Puerto Rican woman of haunting beauty who seemed to be responding to Dixon's sly smiles and lascivious humor. He watched her trail away from the table and caught in Stern a look not much different from his own.

'Do you know what it feels like to touch a woman that age?'

'Dixon, please.'

'It's different.'

'Dixon!'

Stern recollected that he took his knife and fork to what was on his plate with particular vigor, chewing with bovine single-mindedness. But when he glanced up, Dixon was still watching, shrewd and handsome, made merry by the sight of the disturbance he had caused.

* * *

At the hotel, Margy made herself at home. She had kicked off her shoes before the bellman had dropped the cases, and threw the straw-colored silk jacket to her tailored suit on the bed. Grabbing a menu, she called room service for dinner, then opened the minibar. "God, do I need a drink!" she declared. Stern asked for sherry, but they had none, and so he drank Scotch with Margy.

As Stern began emptying the document cases, she took his hand.

"So how you doin, Sandy Stern?" She had a sweet solicitous look, seated on the bed. No mention had been made of Clara's death; Stern had wondered if she even knew. Now, at once, she seemed soft enough to cry on, with the beckoning availability of an open field. He was never quite sure what to make of her. She had an imposing appearance, the kind other women referred to as 'put together.' Her hair was frosted and curled; she was expensively dressed. Her eyebrows were penciled so that they extended almost to the corners of her eyes, lending her the mysterious look of a Siamese cat. She was a large, handsome

woman, strongly built, with a pleasant, expansive bottom—
something happened across Margy's hips that Stern, for whatever reason, had found notable for a number of years, watching her
march about in her tweed skirts or bend over a cabinet. She was
bright and ambitious; in her career, she'd moved from secretary
to top executive. But she had a look of being written on by life. I
am the blank slate. Inscribe. The message left was sad.

"I am making do. Margy," Stern said. "There have been better
times, of course. It seems to be a matter of adjustment. Day by
day."

"That's right," said Margy. She nodded. You could tell that she
regarded herself as an expert on tragedy, well informed. "You
are a sweet fella, Sandy. It's always the ones that don't deserve it
that get all of life's troubles."

This country formulation made Stern smile. He looked at
Margy, slumped somewhat and sitting on the bedside in her
stocking feet.

"I shall survive," he said. Even this prediction, he recognized,
struck some note of improvement.

"Shore," she told him. After a second, she dropped his hand.
"Life goes on. You're gonna have all those softhearted old gals
just hoverin around pretty soon, so you don't feel so lonely. You
know, widows and divorcées just stopping to say Hi, hope you
ain't too blue, on their way home from the beauty parlor."

Margy always thought she had everybody's number. Stern
laughed out loud. In spite of himself, he recalled Helen Dudak's
visit. Even Margy, it seemed, was more flirtatious than she would
have been two months ago. In any event, he, was unaccustomed
to this kind of attention. Women had always found him solid and
charming in a social way, but he had never sensed any allure.

They worked for some time before dinner arrived. Stern
stacked the documents on the carpeting in the categories called
for by the subpoena and showed them to her. She lay casually on
the bed, chin down, shoes off, tossing her legs around girlishly.
She had found a can of pistachio nuts in the minibar, and she
pried them open with her bright fingernails, the shells making a
tinny drumming noise as each hit the bottom of the wastebasket.
Arriving with dinner, the room-service waiter rolled in a small
cart and lifted the sides to form a table. Margy had ordered wine,
too. The waiter attempted to pour Stern a glass, but his head was

whirling already from the Scotch.

She threw the documents down and began as soon as the waiter lifted the steel warming top on her dish, eating robustly. People teased her, she said, about how fast she ate, but she had grown up with four older brothers and had learned better than to wait. Done, she threw her napkin down on the bed and pushed herself back.

"So what-all is this thing about?" she asked. "I can't get much out of Dixon."

Stern, with his mouth full, shook his head. He was enjoying his meal, lingering. He seldom of late had anything worth eating at this hour, when he preferred it.

"You think he got his toe in the bear trap? That old boy is too smart to let them catch him." Margy, like anyone else who knew Dixon well, did not presume that he walked straight lines. They all knew better.

"My concern," said Stern, "is not so much with Dixon's discretion as with that of others." Margy cocked her head, not comprehending. "From the precision with which the government is moving, I suspect they have an informant."

"Those Exchange compliance types," said Margy, "they do a lot with their computers."

"That is what Dixon assumes. But they have too much personal information. I would look to someone who once enjoyed Dixon's confidence. A business colleague." As evenly as he could, Stern added, "A friend." A part of him, on guard, watched her for any telltale response; in this sort of matter, no one was ever above suspicion.

"Naw," said Margy. "I don't think you'll find a lot of folks on the street too eager to take out after Mr. Dixon there. They all heard the story. They know better'n that."

"What story is that?" asked Stern.

"Mean you never heard that?" Margy hooted. She poured more wine for both of them. Stern demurred but picked up his glass as soon as it was filled. It seemed to him she had drunk a great deal, three Scotches before dinner and most of the wine, but you would hardly notice. "This is a great one." She laughed again.

"I am the brother-in-law," said Stern. "Over the years, I have no doubt missed many stories."

"You can bet on that," said Margy with a knowing, heavy-lidded look. She sat up on the bed, legs crossed, seemingly indifferent to her daytime image of the businesswoman vamp, her touseled hair, heavy makeup, and perfume. Instead, she seemed jazzed up, high, inspired, Stern realized, to be speaking confidentially about Dixon. "Let me tell you about Mr. Dixon Hartnell. Old Dixon, he can take care of himself, Sandy. You remember the IRS thing? You were the attorney, right?"

The problem, as Dixon liked to put it, was that his wife had refurnished, as the cost of readmitting Dixon to the household. When Silvia was done, the decorator presented them with a final bill, not counting payments along the way, for $175,000; according to the financial records of both Dixon and the decorator, this sum was never paid. Instead, the decorator, an amiable, high-strung fellow who annually spent every sou that passed through his hands, inexplicably took an interest in the currency futures markets and opened a Maison Dixon account in which an astonishing flurry of activity took place. In a ten-day period, he traded sixty times. When the dust settled, $15,000 equity was now $190,000 and change, a clear profit of $175,000, most of it a long-term capital gain, taxed at two-fifths the rate it would have been had Dixon simply written the decorator a check. The IRS spent nearly two years trying to unravel the devices they suspected Dixon of employing—the intervening brokers, the offshore trusts—before giving up. Dixon remained cheerful throughout, while Stern was on pins and needles, having discovered, as the IRS had not, that Dixon's Mercedes dealer and the contractor who had added an addition to his home had also gone unpaid, while experiencing great success as traders of futures in heating oil and cotton, respectively.

"You know how that thing got itself started? You ever hear that tale?" asked Margy.

"I did not receive what I would call vivid detail," said Stern. "As I recall, it was Dixon's position that the Service had received information from an employee. A tip. Brady? Was that his name?"

"Right. You remember Merle. With this little mustache sort of split in two. He ran all our operations for a while. A computer wizard, hack-off, hacker, whatever that is." Margy flapped a hand. "Remember?"

Stern shrugged: vaguely. Dixon's people came and went. So far as Stern recalled, Merle's departure, in a dispute over a raise, had been oddly timed with the start of the IRS inquiry. Apparently, he had fulminated and delivered threats before he left: What I know, what I can do. He was out to scuttle Dixon's ship.

"My assumption," said Stern, "was that Merle must have been the person who received certain critical instructions."

"No, no," said Margy, with an evasive smile. "Dixon isn't the kind to hand anyone a rope. But Brady, you know, he'd look at that little ol' cathode-ray tube. He'd figure out all sorts of everything. That's how he got Dixon's number."

Stern uttered a sound. This made sense. Brady knew enough to make trouble, but not to deliver the *coup de grâce*.

"Anyway, fast forward two years. The IRS has done its ol' proctoscopy on Dixon—"

"His term," said Stern.

"His term," she said. They smiled at one another. Dixon, with his quirks and passions, and his well-concealed inner core, was secret terrain they had both explored. They were initiates. Acolytes. In their shared understanding of this phenomenon, there was a strange intimacy.

"This, as they say back home, this is the good part." Port, she said "One day Dixon's in the Union League Club in DuSable, and guess who's there? Why, it's ol' Brady. You'd think Dixon'd pick up an ashtray or somethin and bang this boy on the head, but no, sir, he's downright friendly. Dixon shakes his hand. Tells him how glad he is to see him, too, sorry they lost touch, all kinds of buddy-boy sweet-talk. Old Brady, you know, he's like everybody else, he never knew whether to smile or pee in his pants when Dixon showed up, he's quite relieved. Dixon takes his business card. Brady's working as a back office consultant, and Dixon starts sending Brady work. I couldn't believe it when I saw the checks, I got on the phone, I said, 'Dixon, what the hell are you doin now?' He just says, you know, 'Leave me be, lady, I know my business.' I figure maybe he's had a character transplant or somethin, he's become forgiving, maybe he's been hearin Billy Graham."

She took a drink and Stern lifted his glass with her. He had never seen this side of Margy before. She was a storyteller in the old tradition. She needed a porch and a jug of corn whiskey. He had a sense, listening to her, of the way she had grown up watching men, admiring them, taken in by them in a certain way. That perhaps was the key to her longtime attachment to Dixon and the swashbuckling privateers of the markets.

"Anyway, next thing I hear, Dixon and Brady are quite chummy again. They're goin out, them and the wives. Brady's one of these types married to a skinny little lady who always wants more. You know what I'm talking about? She's got to make up for something. I don't know what it is. But they're at plays, havin dinner. I tell you. Maybe they went out with you and Clara."

"I never heard a word," said Stern.

"No," said Margy, correcting herself, "I wouldn't think. Then one day I'm talkin to some ol' boy, I don't remember who, and he says, 'Word is Brady's comin back to MD to run your operations in Kindle.' Dixon won't answer me, you know how he gets, but I check, everybody's heard it. Sure enough, word comes from the Kindle office, there's gonna be a big announcement. Dixon sets up this fancy luncheon over at Fina's. He gets all his key people around. I flew my little Oklahoma fanny in there. You know, we're all sittin there havin a nice time. Then ol' Dixon looks at Brady. 'By the way,' he says, right in front of everyone. Cheerful as a chickadee." Margy took a drink and looked straight at Stern with her bright, hard eyes. "I fucked your wife last night." Just like that. And he had, too. No doubt about that with good-buddy Dixon. Can you imagine this? He's got eight folks around the table to hear this. Lunch was over before they served the soup. I'm not kiddin. Believe me, that made some ripples around here. So that's why I'm tellin you: nobody's sayin diddly-doo about Dixon."

Stern was quiet. He took the bottle and finished off the wine. "Remarkable," he said at last. He meant it. The story filled him with a peculiar sense of alarm. The truth about Dixon was always uglier than Stern could quite conceive of on his own.

"Ain't it, though. Ol' Dixon, boy, sometimes I think he oughta have himself a peckerectomy. He's got an unusual way of doin things."

Stern chuckled, but Margy passed him a meaningful look, liquor-loosened and reproving, as if to warn him of the amount he did not understand. This woman, he knew, comprehended things about men and women, about carnality, that were remote from him.

"Let's get goin with these boring old papers." She smiled, sat up, smoothed her skirt and blouse. But she was not quite done. She looked lost for a moment, glancing away. Somewhere along in the telling, much of her own pain about Dixon had emerged from hiding. Distress had reduced her good looks, brought a wincing closeness to her features. "That son of a bitch," she said suddenly. Stern was somehow penetrated by her forlorn tone and the thought of glamorous Margy, here in her forties, with her career and life in the shadow of Dixon's mountain.

Stern reached out and briefly held her hand.

"Well, you're a kindly ol' boy, ain't you?" she asked.

Stern knew what was going to happen now. Now that he'd had enough to drink, he realized that he'd known for hours, since she looked at him that way and asked with apparent disinterest about the women hovering around him. Beneath it all perhaps was the polar tug of loneliness, the sore yearning of the isolated soul, but now, adrift on the ether of the alcohol, he was suddenly filled by the hot itch of anticipation. There was a racing tempo in his hands as he waited for the next move.

He did not have to wait long. Margy reverted for a few moments to the papers; she spoke; mumbled; then suddenly peered at him with a drunken intense look of heat, appetite, disorder. If he had been sober, perhaps he might have found it comic, a woman turning a gaze on him hot enough to scale paint. But he wasn't. He simply held his ground and watched as she stood and then leaned down and kissed him as he sat in the brocaded hotel armchair. Her lips were chapped, and, as he would have imagined, somehow crusted hard. There was a taste of salt from the meal she had eaten.

"How do you like that?" She laid his head against her breast. Dove-soft. The strong sweet smell of her perfume was all around him, and on his cheek he felt a silky undergarment shifting beneath her blouse. He did not move. He was certain he would receive further instruction.

She kissed him again, then released him and strode off to the bathroom, the water splashed. Stern moved to the edge of the bed, bracing himself. Dear God, he was drunk. The room had not begun to move, but he sensed that it was unglued, starting to become slippery in the peripheral world just beyond the corners of his eyes. What was the old line? A drop of courage. Well, he felt courageous. He was willing.

The lights went out. Margy was poised by the switch. She wore nothing now but her jasmine-colored silk blouse, which was unbuttoned and parted an inch or two over her chest and hung at the length of a negligee. Her legs were bare, her hair was down, and without her fashionable attire and high-heeled shoes, she looked far more delicate. Her skirt and a silky flag of lingerie were bundled in her hand. She tilted her head.

"Well, look who's gettin lucky," Margy said.

Stern turned off the lamp behind him. Moving across the room to meet her, Stern kicked through two or three piles of records. She was much smaller than she appeared, an inch or two shorter than he, but solid in his arms. Her mouth was raw and smoky.

How strange and friendly this all seemed. She even drew back at one point to laugh. He swept aside her shirt, touched her breast, and then bent gallantly to kiss the small dark button where his years with Clara had taught him to expect more. Drunk as he was, this was awkward, and they rolled almost at once onto the bed. Body to body, there was in the small details— the texture of flesh, the precise location of elbows and knees— the exciting news of contact with a different female structure, but over him swam, surprisingly, the sensation of something familiar; he was more relaxed at this than he would ever have imagined. It was this old mysterious human thing relived, man and woman, nothing larger than that. She worked off his tie, opened his shirt. Her leg was up over him as she embarked on this enterprise, and almost casually his hand came up to the warm slick arena at her bottom. She had washed there and his fingertips slid in a bit, and this, this ancient sweet warm feel, this! sent a spectacular surge through him so that he suddenly groaned.

In a few minutes they were joined. Margy for her part slid into a transport of her own. Her eyes were closed, and as Stern rolled, she made a peculiar internal hum, pulling herself down into him with every stroke. There was something oddly practiced and isolated about it; Margy knew how to look after herself. Near the end, she put one hand on his butt and held him where she wanted him, dove onto him a final time and then approached the peak and reached it with a terrible tremolo whinny, setting both hands and their long red nails groping in his back. The thought of those crimson-tipped hands pressed into the loose pale flesh of his own back—the image reached him as something remarkably tantalizing, and that, as much as Margy's agitation, the rising pace of her breath, set him off finally, so that he momentarily lost track of her, still struggling against him, and then waked to her, this soft, sweet-smelling woman beneath him going still at almost the same second as he did. She pulled him to her in a kind of gratified, comradely hug. "Terrific," she said, a remark which Stern heard as praise of the process really, rather than him. Her eyes were still closed and she smiled faintly; her makeup was messed. Her familiarity with all this, her comfort in a strange man's arms, was a phenomenon. Somewhere long ago she had vowed to take whatever was to be had for herself.

She kissed him beside the ear and rolled away, grabbing the pillows on her side of the bed. Familiar as any man's wife, she arranged her rump solidly, so that it found some part of his flank, and then she disappeared into sleep, so quickly that Stern somehow recognized that, more than anything which had gone before, it was this moment of refuge which had been the goal for Margy. To her, he was a man she could calmly sleep beside. In her drowse, she murmured. The light, Stern supposed. He leaned closer to the strange, intimate smell of her, to catch her whisper.

"Oh, God," he said when he heard her, and then embraced her, fit himself to her, and, once the lights were out, slept.

Don't bill us, she had whispered. Don't bill us for the time.

*   *   *

Sometime he woke. He bolted upright, staring blindly in the dark. He had no idea, no inkling where he was, until he recognized a chair where his suit hung and remembered the hotel, Chicago, Margy. He could still feel the weight of her form beside him, but he dared not reach for her. There was a distinct line of pain boring inward from his temple. He groped for his watch on the bedside table, then realized he could read the hieroglyphics of the blue digital numbers on the clock radio: 3:45. That was not what struck him, though. It was the calendar, also there in smaller figures.

He sat at the edge of the bed, calculating as Margy's heavy sounds came to him in the dark.

Forty, he thought. Since the day he came home to find her. Forty days, exactly.

10

When he woke, she was sitting on the bed, legs crossed, wearing his shirt. Pillars of photocopied records had slid into a slatternly mess before her. Margy's head was on one hand.

"Well, I figured it out," she said. "He's a peckerhead, okay."

Stern, naked, found his shorts beside the bed, and narrowly parted the drapes. The sun had only begun to rise in an overcast sky. He went briefly to the bathroom. There was a woolen feeling in his mouth and head. A hangover? He groped in his jacket pocket for his reading glasses.

"Now, what is this?"

"House error account doesn't look very good." Margy flopped over onto her belly. Her bottom was bare and her position on the bed pressed up an appealing décolletage. Stern for a second tried to take account of events. He was a widower, in his underwear, engaged in a business conference, and his penis was already growing firm. She picked up a copy of the subpoena and penciled check marks beside four trades, large positions, four different dates. "Now, these guys are gonna move the market, right?"

Perhaps because of the distraction, he was momentarily confused. Then he recalled Dixon's explanation last month: large orders, a thousand contracts at a time, would cause a sharp movement in the price of the future.

"Supply and demand," said Stern.

"Right," she said. "Now, suppose you got a customer's gonna be comin into the pit with a huge buy order that'll run up prices through the roof. And you're a big peckerhead and wanna make a buck or two. What'd you do?"

Stern thought. "Purchase what the customer intends to buy?"

"Dang right."

"Prior to the customer?"

"Dang right."

"And then sell once the market has risen."

"You betchum. They got all kinds of names for it. 'Front runnin.' 'Tradin ahead of the customer.' But they been playin this game ever since there was a market." Margy looked up. Ungroomed, her hair was darker, and her eyes seemed bloated a bit by the short night. She remained, however, a pretty sight, this large hearty woman, smart and energetic. Stern noticed that she had never removed her earrings, little berries of gold.

"I would assume that the compliance staff of the Exchange is alert to this?"

"Shore. Exchange catches you at it, you're out on your keester in a big goddamn hurry. And they're always lookin."

"And how, then, were such precautions avoided here?"

"Error account."

"The error account," said Stern, merely for the sake of repetition. Somehow, as she snaked along on her belly, the shirt had came away completely from one breast, which rested pale and round on the bedclothes. He had momentarily fallen into their discussion, but this new sight revived other inclinations. Libido was like a rusty gate, he decided; finally open, it was difficult to close. He picked up a piece of paper on the bed and casually hid his erection.

"I gotta give it to ol' peckerhead. I'd never have figured this one. The house error account is where we clean up mistakes. Right? Sometimes we buy or sell a contract on one commodity, customer wanted another. We buy three cars, customer only asked for two. Any dumb ol' mistake. Account number isn't right or somethin. Soon as somebody notices the error, down on the floor or in accounting or when the customer complains, trade gets moved to the error account. If we can't get the trade where it belongs, we close out the position—you know, sell what we bought or buy what we sold. Okay?"

Okay, said Stern.

"Now suppose I'm a real clever peckerhead and I wanna trade ahead of my customers and I don't wanna get caught. I buy a little in Kindle of what I know they're gonna buy a lot of in

Chicago. Price'll move tick for tick in both places. All I gotta do is wait for the market to jump. And I don't do it in my name. I make a mistake. Deliberately. Wrong account number, say. Then, after the market runs up, I sell out the position."

"Once more, with a wrong account number?"

"Right. Couple days later, when the smoke clears, both trades are sittin over in the house error account. Compliance'll never be lookin at Kindle, and even if they do, they won't find anybody buyin ahead of the market. All they see is some dumb ol' mistake. But when we close out the two positions, the buy and the sell, we got a hell of a nice little profit in the error account."

Stern wagged his head in amazement. How nice a profit, he wanted to know.

Margy shrugged. "I haven't finished lookin yet. Four trades here made close to a hundred thousand, though. I'd say you probably got six times that. Not bad, you know, for a few phone calls while you're scratchin your fanny."

Six hundred thousand, thought Stern. Ms. Klonsky was not pursuing a petty offense.

"Only thing," said Margy, "is this little scam still doesn't seem much like our friendly peckerhead."

That had been Stern's thought as well, that the rewards were not worth the risks for a man of Dixon's wealth. But Margy laughed at the idea when Stern said that.

"Oh, he'd screw you in the ground for a buck and a quarter, let alone half a million. Naw, it isn't that. Just doesn't seem like Dixon. Our customers! That's his religion. I can't figure him makin them suckers. He's loyal." Lawl. She grabbed Stern's hands. "But I know he done it," she said.

"Because he must be informed before any large order is traded?" This fact, which Dixon had admitted in Stern's office, had already come to mind.

"That's one thing. But lotsa folks in house know what we're doin. Only, if I stole five, six hundred thousand bucks, am I gonna hide it in your pocket? It's the *house* error account. And ol' Dixon Hartnell is shore enough the house. He owns MD Clearing Corp, MD Holding Corp, Maison Dixon. The whole shootin' match is his. This is probably some dumb old game he was playin, seein' if he could get a laugh or two up his sleeve."

Stern contemplated the notion of Dixon committing crimes

for his own amusement. It was not impossible. With Dixon, of course, nothing was.

"And what became of the money?" Stern was thinking about the subpoenas the government was serving at Dixon's bank.

Margy turned onto her back and wobbled her head a bit to indicate that she did not know. Her breasts went loose and splayed against her chest; beneath her chin, where the blush-on ended, a pale rim of flesh was visible, oddly pallid, as if the years of cosmetic treatments had drained her complexion of color. These flaws meant little to Stern; he remained in heat.

"I can't tell without a lot more lookin. But you want my guess about what he did with the money?"

"Please."

"Nothin."

"Nothing?"

"Nothin. Just leaves it there. That's what I'd do. Error account always runs at a deficit. That's because when you goof on an order and the customer makes money on it, he won't tell you it's an error. He just accepts the trade. You only hear about the losers. And that's okay. Cost of doin business. But you can lose forty thousand a month, and if you start makin some profits, all of a sudden you're only losin two thousand a month. See? Nobody knows the difference. Except ol' peckerhead. Cause, at the end of the year, that six hundred thousand's gonna end up on the bottom line. Sort of like he give himself a bonus."

"Very clever," said Stern of the entire scheme. "And quite adept of you, Margy, to figure all this out." He kissed the back of each of her hands.

"Oh, I am a clever harlot," she said, smiling up at him. Stern wondered whose phrase that was, who had called her that before; it seemed to be something she was repeating. He, naturally, might guess. "But I'm not the smartest one."

"No?" asked Stern, sitting beside her now on the bed, where she waited sunny-side up to face him. "Who is that?"

"Ol' you-know-who. They won't never catch him. All he had to do was call the order desk to put on these positions that ended up in the error account. He only does that twenty times a day. Nobody's gonna remember him doin it. And there isn't one piece of paper in this mess with so much as his initials on it. He's gonna point to forty other people coulda done it instead of him. Phone clerks. Customers' reps. Coulda been me." Margy smiled then. "They may think it's him. They may know it's him. But they ain't gonna *prove* it's him." Margy had watched television, heard these lines; perhaps she was imitating Stern. She had certainly convinced herself. Dixon was confident too, Stern thought, recalling Dixon's predictions of vindication on the phone. His client was fortified by his prior successes with the IRS and his knowledge that the government had run off to ransack his checking accounts when the money had never really left the company. Stern, however, was hardly as sanguine. The Assistant U.S. Attorneys were often adroit financial investigators. They might blunder about at first, but if Margy was right in her suspicions about how Dixon had handled his ill-gotten gains, the prosecutors would find them eventually, in his hands, and draw the same conclusions as she had about who was responsible. Dixon remained at substantial risk.

"I should speak to the MD employees in Kindle who received these orders on the desk to be certain their memories are as vague as you suppose," said Stern. It would be wise to remind whoever might have dealt directly with Dixon of how long ago these events occurred, and the confounding volume of orders received each day; Stern would have to do that promptly, before the FBI unearthed contrary recollections. Margy promised to recall the order tickets from storage and have them sent to Stern; he could identify the order takers and contact them directly. She would send a memo to Kindle, asking all employees on the desk to cooperate with their lawyer.

"Course, this still isn't what I'd call comical," said Margy. "The Exchange'll bang the bullpucky out of the company. They'll give us a whole bunch of fines and censures and make a big stink. Then they'll hand it over to the CFTC and let them make some stink, too. But ol' you-know-who, he'll be okay. He'll be fussin and stinkin along with the rest of them, makin out like how'd this awful thing happen right under my nose. And then he'll turn around and fire someone to cover his hillbilly fanny." Margy inclined her head slightly so that she was more or less eye to eye with the excited area of Stern's shorts. Looking back, she gave him a little knowing grin, which he thought was at his expense, but it was not. She was still thinking about whom Dixon would fire. "Prob'ly me," she said with a sad little buttoned-up smile.

"Probably me," she repeated, and laughed then, laughed and raised her arms to Stern again and pulled him down to her for comfort.

*   *   *

Parting at the hotel-room door, he promised to call her. "That'd be nice," Margy answered simply. Clearly, she did not believe him; men said that all the time. As soon as the cab had deposited him at O'Hare, he thumbed through the yellow pages and sent an enormous bouquet, without a card, to her office. Seated in the cramped booth, behind the perforated stainless-steel partitions, he was visited by images of the night and morning and he almost shivered with the staggering thrill of it all. Had that truly been he, Alejandro Stern, gentleman lawyer, child of a Catholic country, humping his brains out a few hours ago? Yes, indeed. His spirit was on alert, his flag unfurled. He had Margy's smoky taste on his lips, the touch of her silks in his palm. When was he returning? He laughed out loud at himself, so that a woman in a booth across the way actually looked straight at him. Slightly shamed, he found suddenly the splinter of something more abiding buried closer to his heart. Gratitude. Oh yes, he was grateful to Margy, to the entire race of women, who, unbelievably, had seen fit to take him in once more. With his hand still on the telephone, he pondered the sheer blessing of another human being's embrace.

At the gate, the attendant announced that the plane for his short flight back to the tri-cities was delayed. "Equipment problems." As usual! Stern, even in his buoyant mood, could not pull free of his hatred for this airport, with its endless corridors and sickly light, its teeming, hurtling bodies and worried faces. He located the airline's executive lounge, all black leather and granite, and telephoned his office.

"Claudia, please call Ms. Klonsky and schedule an appointment for Friday. Tell her I wish to deliver the documents she has subpoenaed from MD." Stern had not spoken with the prosecutor in a month now. Raphael had called to beg an additional week on the return date, and reported that Klonsky sounded on the verge of rage. Stern did not like to beard the Assistants—it was not his style, and more to the point, enmity among lawyers complicated a case. He would have to make amends somehow with Klonsky. The lawyer's life, he thought, always toadying. Judges. Prosecutors. Certain clients.

"You want your messages?"

Stern was seated on a sofa; the telephone console was cleverly inserted in the granite top of a cocktail table. Claudia reported a call from Remo Cavarelli, an old hustler under indictment, who wanted the status date for his next appearance before Judge Winchell. There was also a message from a Ms. Helen Dudak, who wanted to speak to Stern: a personal matter. And Cal Hopkinson had phoned. Developments, he thought with a sudden surge of something undefined, interest or apprehension, when he heard Cal's name. He had Claudia put him through, but Cal's secretary said he was on another call. Stern held a bit, then decided to call back and punched in the number Helen had left. She had told him she worked at home, with a headset plugged into the phone-connected earpieces and a tiny suspended mike, smaller than a thimble. He imagined her like that.

"I'm picking up on the end of our conversation the other night," said Helen.

"Yes, of course," he answered, not truly certain what she meant.

"I wanted to invite you to dinner here. Two weeks from Saturday. The two of us."

"Ah," said Stern, and felt his heart palpably squirm. Now what? Helen meant well, he thought. And she was charming. But could he manage these complications? Yes, said some voice suddenly. Yes, indeed.

Yet, having accepted, he dwelled on Margy and quarreled with himself as he put down the phone. Eating, after all, was not a form of sexual intercourse. But then again, he slyly thought, he was becoming quite a fellow. In the crowded airport lounge, with the stalled travelers murmuring around him, he once more laughed aloud.

This time he got through to Cal.

"Sandy!" Cal cried. "Where are you?" Cal told him the story of his most recent unscheduled layover at O'Hare. Stern eventually asked about the bank.

"That's why I was calling," said Cal. "Just to let you know the story." River National, Cal said, was being perfectly neurotic about this transaction in Clara's investment account. Any time a will was involved, the bank worried over everything: the probate court, the Attorney General's Office. They insisted on retrieving every single piece of paper before they would meet. Cal was pressing for a conference in the next week. He spoke with the self-congratulatory air that Stern himself often assumed with clients, describing his communications with the bankers and file clerks as if it were mortal combat.

"Really, Cal," said Stern. He did not want to be one more complaining client, and ended the conversation rather than speak his mind. Cal was too fussy to be forceful—he, too, would want to see each paper—and besides, he was probably in no position with the bankers, who in all likelihood sent him business—wealthy customers who needed trusts drawn, wills updated. But it was unfair, Stern decided in a moment, to blame Cal for the complications Clara had made. Stern had lived decades never wholly knowing what was occurring behind Clara's composed and gracious façade. And still the wondering went on. All that old simmering frustration was boiling up in him again.

He redialed his secretary's number.

"Claudia, did Dr. Cawley return my call?" Following his evening at Kate and John's, Stern had chased Nate about, leaving word at the office, the hospital, at home, asking Nate to call the lab. It was not clear that Nate had even gotten the messages, and Stern remained unsure that he would follow through, in any event. Nate, after all, had other worries.

"Should I try someone at his office?" asked Claudia.

Stern drummed his fingers on the tabletop and did not answer. Out the window, the view was obstructed by a 747 which was being washed by workers mounted on a series of movable scaffolds—Stern was reminded of zookeepers and a giraffe. He certainly could venture to Westlab himself—wherever it might be. As Clara's executor, he had a legal right to inquire. But if the administrators at Westlab were sticklers about privacy, as Nate suspected, Stern would need credentials, which would mean involving Cal. Better patience, Stern thought. Nate would get to it eventually.

But there was a soreness here, more persistent than his curiosity about Clara, which seemed to rise and fall with the tide of his grief. It took Stern an instant to fix upon it: Peter. The suspicion born at Kate and John's that he had been outdone by his son had not proved easy to put aside. Oh, he knew it was unfair, unlikely, unbecoming to believe that Peter in his great anguish had had the presence of mind, or the cunning, to manipulate his father about the autopsy. But Peter, to Stern's memory, had been so insistent—he could still recall his voice resounding down the corridors at its wailing pitch as he upbraided that poor bewildered cop, the frantic glint in Peter's eyes. Questions lingered. With Peter, Stern supposed, questions always would.

"Claudia, connect me, please, with the general switchboard of the Kindle Municipal Police." As soon as Stern said it, he knew it was probably an error. Throughout his professional career, he had been alert for any opportunity to avoid the police. They always made trouble in the end. He gave the operator who answered the name and precinct he wanted and comforted himself with the thought that the old policeman was probably not there. As the saying went, They never were.

"Ray Radczyk."

"Alejandro Stern, Lieutenant."

"I'll be damned. How are you, Sandy?"

"Continuing." He heard the beep on the line then, over the usual tumbling of the police station in the background. The old cop sounded positively alight to have heard from him. For the life of him, Stern could still not recall the connection. He had puzzled on it once or twice, a vagrant thought that came along with many others when he remembered that late afternoon. "Do you still have that file with my name on it, Lieutenant?"

"Hey, come on," said Radczyk, and laughed. "I got a job, just like you. Never was a file. You know that."

"Of course," said Stern. This Radczyk, he recalled, was not really a bad fellow. Minding his profession, naturally.

"Say, where you at? Sounds like we're talkin over two tin cans."

Stern explained: O'Hare. Stuck.

"Oh, sure," said Radczyk.

"Lieutenant, there is a question with which I would probably never bother you were I not waylaid with a moment on my hands."

"No bother," said the cop. "Shoot."

Stern paused.

"I was wondering if the coroner reported anything unusual in connection with his examination of my wife?"

"Huh," said Radczyk. Listening to himself, Stern realized how extraordinary this question would sound, arriving out of the blue. Radczyk took his time. "I know he ruled it suicide, a' course. I was gonna give you a call, then I thought, hell—"

"Certainly," said Stern. Neither of them, for an instant, spoke. Stern waved off a waiter in white coat who approached to offer him a drink. "I realize this is a peculiar inquiry—"

"No problem. Lemme dig up the case report. Just come back from dictation a week or two ago. Gimme a number. I'll be back to you in two shakes." Stern read the number from the console. What would Radczyk do? Perhaps he would motion for someone else to pick up the other extension; or check to be sure the call-taping system was functioning.

A woman passed by, tall, near fifty, dressed entirely in red— she wore a silk suit with a tight straight skirt and a black-welted bolero hat which matched her outfit; her hosiery was black; a handsome figure. She looked vaguely in Stern's direction, then turned away, but even the instant of contact with her dark eyes somehow reminded him of Margy, and he fell back fully into her grasp, as if he suddenly had passed through the doors of a movie and was flooded over by the light and images of the screen: Margy, as she stood by the light switch, bare-legged and heavy-bottomed, her blouse undone, the black triangle visible below; her bright fingernails roaming to certain of his parts; the way her mouth lolled open, and her hue, in the profuse light of the morning, increased even across the frail skin of her closed eyes as she traveled along the channels of sensation.

A peculiar sound arose, a beeping: the telephone, he realized.

"Here we are," said Radczyk. "Let's see. Now wha'dya need?"

"It is merely curiosity, Lieutenant. I thought there may have been something unusual the coroner remarked on."

"Not much here. No autopsy. That's what you wanted. I told him there was religious objections. Couldn't figure out anything else."

Stern realized then that Radczyk had called back on a private line. No beeping signal; no tape. Supposedly, at any rate. Stern made no response.

"It's short and sweet, Sandy. Blood test with a C.O. level. And a copy of the note. And the coroner's ruling. Nothin' in the police reports. I looked at them when they come through."

"I see."

Radczyk took a breath. "Mind if I ask what's up?"

"A minor matter, Lieutenant. It's unimportant."

"Sure," said Radczyk. "What kinda matter?" With these questions, he assumed a certain authority. He was, after all, a policeman, and this was, after all, his case. Stern cursed himself and then launched into a concertedly tidy explanation: a medical-laboratory bill had arrived and could not be accounted for. It was, Stern said again, no doubt unimportant.

"I could go over there and check for ya," Radczyk said.

Stern found the idea startling—particularly its appeal. In theory, medical records were not to be disclosed without a subpoena. But most hearts knocked at the sight of a policeman's star. Records clerks would tell a cop most anything, if not surrender the paper. Radczyk could learn as much as Nate, perhaps more. But Stern was too much on edge with the policeman, especially his peculiar would-be intimacy. "I could not trouble you, Lieutenant."

"No trouble," said Radczyk, then lowered his voice somewhat. "I still owe ya, you know."

Stern hung on the line.

"Westlab, right?" asked Radczyk. "I'll go over there myself, Sandy. Keep it between you and me that way. I'll find out what's doin. Gotta get all the loose ends tied up for the case report, right?"

Stern waited. "Certainly," he said.

"Sure," said Radczyk. "Should have something Friday, Monday latest. I'll call. Good trip back."

Stern cradled the phone gently. There was a sharpness to the objects—ashtrays, lamps—he saw about the lounge. He had the congested feeling he had known all the way back to childhood.

He was certain he had just done something wrong.

11

The reception area of the U.S. Attorney's Office was shabby. From the looks, one would have thought he was visiting a solo practitioner down on his luck. The shag carpet was reminiscent of an animal afflicted with the mange; the wooden arms of the rectilinear furniture had begun to splinter; and the inhabitants were the usual town-square gathering. A nut or two sat huddled in the corners, glancing about furtively and writing out lengthy, incomprehensible complaints about various politicians or the FCC's plot to lobotomize them through the airwaves. Witnesses and prospective defendants, too poor or too untutored to be accompanied by lawyers, sat with grand jury subpoenas in their hands, awaiting the Assistants who would make use of them. Now and then federal agents, or an occasional defense lawyer, looking hangdog and disappointed, would emerge from the offices. And of course today Mr. Alejandro Stern, prominent member of the federal criminal bar, sat here as well, surrounded by two ponderous document cases as he awaited Ms. Klonsky, who the receptionist said was on the phone.

This office had always struck Stern as a happy place. The lawyers were young and inspired, and almost all of them knew they were merely passing through. They did not remain AUSAs for long—five years, six was the average. Enough time to learn to try a jury case, for each to feel she or he had made a sincere effort to improve community well-being, before the greener glades of the private sector, of what Stern still thought of as real practice, beckoned. It was a good job, Stern thought. He had lost the best younger lawyer he'd ever had, Jamie Kemp, to the U.S. Attorney's Office in Manhattan, where Kemp had gone to try cases on his own and work on a rock musical which resurrected certain songs Kemp had composed two decades before when he had briefly been some kind of musical star.

Kemp was quite nearly not the only one to join federal employment. Before the present United States Attorney, Stan Sennett, had been returned here from San Diego by the Justice Department, Stern had been approached about taking the job. The top aide of the state's senior senator had invited Stern to breakfast at one of the downtown clubs. This young man, who looked something like the singing star Garfunkel, with a head of shocked whitish hair that stood erect like a dandelion gone to seed, had thrown around every corny platitude known to man; it was worse than an obituary. This offer was a compliment to Stern's abilities, the young man insisted, and to the wisdom, Stern knew, of a life in which he had never been politically aligned. While Mayor Bolcarro was not allowed by the senator to reward his retainers with federal appointments, his known enemies were rarely elevated.

For Stern, the prospect of being the federal prosecutor was not easily dismissed. This was an advocate's job of sweeping power. For four years Stern could command the non-uniformed armies of the IRS, the DEA, the FBI, and deploy them as he saw fit. No more of the drug agents' gruesome shenanigans. An end to the heartless prosecutions of widows and firemen for failing to report the income from part-time jobs or CDs. But, of course, he would have to be a prosecutor. Stern would have to dedicate himself to apprehension, accusation, punishment, that triad of unmentionables that by long-nurtured reflex he despised. Could Alejandro Stern rise magisterially in court and excite a jury's ugly passions, could he beg them to inflict suffering they would quail to bear themselves? He could not. No. Could not. The imagery unloosed in Stern a real feeling of illness. Oh, he did not hate prosecutors. He had gotten over that early in his career. He admired at times the incandescent zeal of these young people as they attempted to smite evil for the sake of life on the straight and narrow. But that was not his role, not his calling. He was Sandy Stern—a proud apologist for deviation. No person Argentine by birth, a Jew alive to hear of the Holocaust could march in the jackboots of authority without intense self-doubt; better to keep his voice among the voices, to speak out daily for these frail liberties, so misunderstood, whose existence, far more than any prosecution, marked us all as decent, civilized, as human. He could not abandon the credo of a lifetime now.

Ms. Klonsky was off the phone. Beyond the single office door, opened electronically by a solemn guardian behind yellow-tinged bulletproof glass, lay a half block of clatter. Telephones pealed; telewriters, still used in this era of word processing, banged. The Assistant United States Attorneys, distinguished young lawyers with law-review backgrounds, were made into ruffians by the atmosphere and stood in the hallways shouting to one another.

Stern came to this office often, generally with a singular mission: to hinder, to thwart, to delay. On occasions—rare occasions, usually at the very start of an investigation—he arrived to offer an openhearted portrayal of what he believed to be the truth. But most often the defense was one of avoidance. It was his goal to learn as much as possible while revealing only what the prosecutor already knew, would never care about, or which might trouble or distract her. There were those prosecutors who believed in candor, who would lay their case out as a bare challenge. But, for most, the appeal of secretiveness was irresistible. Stern could merely float notions, ask questions, lighting from fact to fact, like some pest nibbling at fruit.

"My best wishes to you," said Stern to Ms. Klonsky, as he entered her small office. Robust-looking and dark, she had come to her feet to greet him. To Stern's surprise, she wore a maternity dress, a blue cotton jumper of plain finish which as yet hung loosely. Observed in an abstracted way, Ms. Klonsky was quite attractive—large eyes, a straight nose, prominent cheekbones, the sort of routine good looks one would expect to see in a restaurant hostess. She presented a full figure of peasant proportions, strong legs and arms, and an ample bust, although the latter feature, according to nasty bruiting, was somewhat misleading. At Gil's it was said that Ms. Klonsky had undergone a single mastectomy while she was a law student. Ergo, the Titless Wonder. Stern had never been convinced of the verity of this information—at Gil's the jokes at the prosecutors' expense seemed to grow crueler as the night wore on—and his doubts rose again now. Would a former cancer patient risk pregnancy, with its hormonal surges and vast bodily changes?

"My daughter is also in this wonderful condition," he said. "Our first grandchild." Stern heard himself say 'our,' but had no will to correct himself. He would have to search some time to know how else to put it.

Klonsky also appeared to take in this odd note. She congratulated Stern, and inquired about Kate's condition—Stern had noticed long ago that the affinity of women for each other was never greater than in the process of childbearing, this circle no man could enter. But then she added, by the unpredictable logic that always brought people to it, "My condolences on your loss."

He nodded without a word. The two document cases, each the size of an accordion, were beside him. They waited, amenities exhausted, on the outskirts of adversity. He took a seat before her desk.

"You seem, Ms. Klonsky, to have misconceptions about my client."

She summoned a small, sealed smile, meant to reflect poise and fearlessness. As the years had passed, Stern found himself practicing against young men and women close to his children's ages. In general, it was his impression that they found him charming; his accumulated attainments lent him an almost statesmanlike stature. The Assistants were often deferential, without abandoning the poses required by conflict. At moments, Stern would find himself wondering how Peter or Marta would react if they could see the naturalness, the virtual honesty he brought to his relations with persons just like them. What would they think? Would this be the stuff of epiphany, or would they seize on the obvious? These people were not his children.

"In what way, Mr. Stern?"

"I know you suspect him of a crime. Yes?" She seemed to nod. "Tell me, Ms. Klonsky—"

"You can call me Sonia, Mr. Stern."

Stern took her graciousness as a sign that she believed she could hold her own.

"You must do the same, then. Please call me Sandy."

"Thank you."

"Certainly."

She smiled at him so suddenly, with a flash of such remarkable open amusement at their maneuvering, that Stern himself was taken aback.

"You are inclined to tell me nothing?"

"I can't, Sandy."

"Is there an informant? Is that the reason for your hesitation?"

"No comment."

"Because I have already assumed as much."

"If there's an informant, Sandy, I haven't the foggiest idea who it is."

This, Stern knew, was a clever response. The Assistants were often in the dark about the identity of informants, particularly those who had been promised they would never have to testify. The secret remained with the FBI agents, who would conduct covert meetings with their source and write reports to the U.S. Attorneys identifying the "c/i"—cooperating individual—only by a number assigned at Bureau headquarters in D.C.

"Mr. Hartnell is not a retiring sort," said Stern. "The business landscape is no doubt replete with those he has offended. Persons fired. Jealous competitors. You are aware, I am sure, that the comments of such persons have to be evaluated carefully."

Ms. Klonsky laid her pretty face daintily upon her fingertips and smiled agreeably. She was taking it all in, watching him work.

"He's had his troubles before," she said. "The CFTC. One of the exchanges, or was it two?" She took a beat. "Not to mention the IRS."

Oh yes, thought Stern, she had developed a thick file. To be expected.

"I represented Dixon on all of those occasions. There are times that he has put business expansion before recordkeeping. Candidly, Ms. Klonsky, the Exchanges and the IRS enforce a punctiliousness that the U.S. Attorney's Office itself would have difficulty adhering to." Stern gestured out the door. At times, in this office, you could learn the gravest grand jury secret simply by moving at deliberate speed in the corridors. The young Assistants stood in their doorways, gossiping about investigations. Names were tossed about. Old files were stacked like refuse, without regard to the confidences they contained. Some years ago Stern had seen two large accordion folders with the name of Mayor Bolcarro on them, waiting for storage, and felt a painful twinge of regret for the government's apparent lack of success. His observation made Ms. Klonsky laugh.

"You are wonderful. Stan Sennett said you'd walk through the door and just charm the pants off me, and here you are doing it."

"Me?" He maintained a look of humble innocence, but he registered the mention of Sennett's name with some concern. Stern and the present United States Attorney were not mutual admirers. The relationship went back at least a dozen years, to the period when Sennett was a state court prosecutor and could not seem to win a jury trial when Stern was defending. If anything, the wound had deepened of late. In one of his rare courtroom appearances, Sennett, in January, had prosecuted a case in which Stern represented a local city councilman charged with extorting sexual favors and cash payments from members of his staff. Stern had vilified the government's chief witness, whom he characterized as a professional informant, a so-called private investigator who seemed to find someone prominent to tattle on whenever his own questionable activities brought him to grief. The councilman was convicted only of one count—a tax misdemeanor—and remained in office, while Sennett lamely claimed victory, a boast openly scoffed at in the press.

In passing, they were cordial—Stern was with everyone—but Stan's memory was long and the rancor deep. As meaningful, for present purposes, was Ms. Klonsky's inadvertent admission that the U.S. Attorney had been consulted about this case. With five hundred indictments every year, and three times the number of grand jury investigations, only matters of prime significance reached the front office. All in all, this was a most unwelcome word. Dixon was making the wrong enemies.

Ms. Klonsky asked for the documents she had subpoenaed, and Stern lifted the cases onto the desk one by one. She rose with some awkwardness, apparently no longer able to judge her body's dimensions confidently, and headed to the hallway to retrieve her file. Left by himself, Stern circumspectly examined the possessions in her narrow office. Working the endless hours of a young trial lawyer, she observed no distinction between home and workplace; the passions of her private life spilled out here. Amid the inevitable diplomas and licenses, a large Kandinsky-like oil hung, and a banner from a world-peace parade was stretched across her bookcases. The books them-selves were not merely the usual ponderous legal treatises and casebooks, but also rows of paperbacks. There seemed to be a good deal of Continental fiction and many political works. Stern saw the name of Betty Friedan a number of times; also Carl Jung. The bottom shelf appeared to be the place of honor. On one side was a single photograph of Ms. Klonsky and a broad, curly-headed man, noticeably younger than she. Four books were centered between silver bookends: three slim volumes that had the look of poetry, all by a man named Charles, and a hardcover book called *Illness As Metaphor*. On the other side, in a Lucite frame, was a snapshot of a gap-toothed boy; taped to it was a bright, sloppy child's drawing of a figure, over awkward lettering: S, O, N, N, Y. Both N's were drawn backwards.

"Your son?" asked Stern, gesturing to the boy's picture when Klonsky returned. She lugged a brown expandable file across her body. As Stern feared, it was of considerable bulk.

"Sam is my husband's son. He lives with his mother. This is our first."

Wonderful, said Stern. A special joy. He remained deeply attuned to his desire to move onto a friendly footing with her.

"Wonderful or crazy," she said. "I refer to this as a geriatric pregnancy. My obstetrician is absolutely paralyzed. A forty-one-year-old lawyer with a medical history! He's afraid his malpractice premiums will double."

Stern smiled amiably, but naturally offered no comment. A medical history, he noted.

"Sometimes I think I'm nuts getting started at this age."

"Well, you say your husband is experienced."

"Oh, Charlie? I'm not sure he's noticed that I'm pregnant." She laughed, but her eyes veered away as she measured some private thought, so that Stern knew they had abruptly reached the end of this road.

Instead, she reached for the documents, sorted and rubber-banded, which Stern had piled on the desk. They had been organized trade by trade, and she checked them off the subpoena. As she worked, Stern again began quietly asking questions. He had closely examined the records, he said. They disclosed nothing exceptional. No apparent market manipulation, no passing off bad trades to discretionary accounts, no double-charging of customers, no bucketing, by which the customer would pay a worse price than the house had on the floor.

"It is most difficult from these documents to imagine what your informant is alleging. You have not subpoenaed records of a single account that Dixon controls. Nothing here is tied to him." There was some flicker, a reflexive contraction within her serious brown eyes. Stern made no mention of the house error account, or the documents that Klonsky was trying to obtain from Dixon's bank. He would never belie the impression that he was as ignorant as the government wished to keep him.

"Can I ask?" she said abruptly.

"Of course."

"Why does it matter whether there's an informant? Assume there is."

Indeed, thought Stern.

"Do you not think your target is entitled to know what wrongdoing this informant is claiming against him?" He was about to use her name, but he did not feel comfortable with 'Sonia' and thought it would be too stiff reverting to 'Ms. Klonsky.' "Is Mr. Hartnell obliged to stand by idly while the government determines if it can puzzle together one scrap of paper here, another there, until it has its case and is ready, quite literally, to destroy his livelihood and his life?"

"I don't see how he'll be hurt by waiting now."

"He may assist. If I understand what your informant says, I might be able to bring pertinent matters to your attention."

"And you might also be able to identify the witnesses in advance, try to influence them, and do your best to control the flow of information."

He stared at her a second.

"Just so," said Stern quietly. He could not prevent a momentary scowl. The barroom wags were right about her. Not that she was incorrect in her estimate of Stern's intentions; hardly. But there was something naïve in the way she presumed to inhibit him. Whether Ms. Klonsky knew it or not, she was engaged in a contest, a process, not the search for the Holy Grail. When she brought witnesses quailing into the grand jury room, where their lawyers could not accompany them, where the thought of every indiscretion, every lapse, accosted them like bogeymen, so that these persons were slavish in their eagerness to please the prosecutors, this, per Klonsky, was not influence. It was the government at work. But if the target's lawyer spoke to the witnesses himself, reviewed their records, and tried to keep their recollections balanced, that bordered on subornation. The problem was simple: she was still new to her job. Poor Sonia Klonsky. Past forty and still so much to learn. He found himself quite disappointed.

"You're angry," she said.

"Not so."

"I wasn't suggesting that you would do anything unethical."

"Nor did I take it that way."

Stern spent a further moment unloading his cases, withdrawing bundles of documents with their blackened edges of copier murk. Ms. Klonsky was still disconcerted by the change of mood.

"I thought we were having"—she waved a hand—"an exchange."

"We disagree," said Stern. "Consider it a matter of obligation, of our respective roles." He stood. "Where might I expect you to go next?"

She looked at him a moment.

"I don't feel satisfied, Sandy."

How in the world had Stan Sennett hired this woman? Did she want to have sensitivity sessions in the grand jury? What a remarkable person. In spite of his reluctance to admit it, she had some quality of magnetism. Her smile, especially in its sly aspect, was endearing; a deep, serious intelligence glinted in her eyes. But he felt braced by the recognition of a moment before. With Sonia Klonsky, one had the sense that, for all her woman-on-the-go composedness, a fragment of her soul remained on the verge of hysteria. There was something seething, molten, uncontrolled, unknown. That had a touching quality as well—a woman past forty, still on the voyages of a teenager.

"Ms. Klonsky," he said, "we really do not need to engage in hand-wringing. I assure you, we shall remain on cordial terms." He offered his hand. Instead, she sank down in the chair behind her desk, her face still dark and troubled, and rattled open a drawer.

"There's one other thing. Since you represent Mr. Hartnell, we can't agree to serve you when we subpoena other witnesses from MD. The potential for conflict is too great."

Something new was coming, Stern realized. Klonsky was

saying, in effect, that she would soon be setting sails for Dixon's employees, attempting to get them to testify against the boss. If the government had its way, each would have a different lawyer. This was the prosecutors' usual stance. Divide and conquer. Under the guise of concern about professional ethics, they tried to ensure that anyone who might have something to blab to them would not be under the influence of the target's lawyer. Stern agreed wholeheartedly about the ethical precepts, but believed that the right to determine conflicts in the first instance was his, not the U.S. Attorney's. He protested now, but Ms. Klonsky reverted to her firm look, forbidding further discussion.

"Anyway," she said, "Stan thought there was one subpoena that should be served on you. As a courtesy." Klonsky opened a manila folder and removed a single sheet of paper, offering it to Stern. "We gave him a long date—almost a month—so you'll have plenty of time to help him arrange for separate counsel." Dumbly, Stern nodded. When he looked back, Klonsky was filling out a return of service on the back of her file copy, recording on whom and when the subpoena had been served.

He had been having such a buoyant spell, Stern thought with sudden forlornness, gibing with this able young woman, assaying her character. Now this. His arms, as he looked at the subpoena, were leaden with alarm. Some primitive curse rose up in him against Dixon and his inevitably tortured courses. From the way this was being handled, the acknowledged special treatment, Stern suspected at once what was afoot.

"Are there other persons from the order desk whom you expect to call?" he asked offhandedly, hoping the import of the question would slip past her, and Klonsky simply shook her head no as she wrote. Stern, at once, felt his condition grow worse. The order tickets Margy had promised to request from the Kindle office had not yet reached him, but he knew now what they would show. Dixon had not called just anyone on the order desk to trade ahead, as Margy had speculated; that, apparently, would have entailed too much risk, the chance that someone shrewd and less obedient might speak up, object. Instead, Dixon had conveyed the orders to a single compliant sap, the only soul on the order desk with whom the government needed to speak. And, of course, his daughter had married him. Stern folded the subpoena into three even parts. "John Granum" had been typed on the dotted lines reserved for name and address. His son-in-law now had a date certain for grand jury testimony. Klonsky's guile, her fear of undue influence on the critical witnesses, was growing more understandable.

"Is he a target?" asked Stern.

"Maybe he has something to tell us."

"Immunity is a possibility?"

"I think so." Klonsky once more glanced downward; she was saying too much. "I understand your interest, Sandy. But this would be more appropriate with whoever represents him. As I say, this is a courtesy to you. Stan didn't want another incident like the one at your home."

"Most considerate," said Stern. "My thanks to both of you." He did not wish to sound particularly curt, but he was experiencing a fading lack of control.

Ms. Klonsky looked at him sadly. He could see who he was to her—a home-wrecked widower with one more enormous family problem. He had her sympathy, which was not at all what he had come here expecting to obtain.

* * *

Outside the U.S. Attorney's Office, the elevator arrived, opened, and then refused to move. Stern, still spinning with anger, threw down his empty cases and pounded on all the buttons. Up. Down. Door open. Door close. The new federal building had been completed ten years ago, with every contract sprinkled down on cronies from the fingertips of Mayor Bolcarro like a confectionery topping. The structure had been intended as a courthouse, but the judges, after a brief period of occupancy, issued various orders and injunctions and moved themselves back into the ancient Federal Square building across the street. Nothing here worked. The elevators. The heat. The windows popped out in high winds or low temperatures and showered glass on the pedestrians below. It had taken six years to complete construction, and the litigation was still ongoing a decade later. The architect, the engineers, the general contractor, and virtually every tradesman who had touched the place were co-plaintiffs, co-defendants, or cross-parties in four or five separate suits. Now and then, Stern would see the herd of lawyers arrive for the various status calls. They would stand before the judge, twenty and thirty abreast, and bicker. In the meantime, the building grew so brisk during the occasional periods of Arctic cold that gripped this city that one federal judge, during the short period when court had been held here, mounted the bench in mittens and instructed the lawyers that they were not required to remove their hats.

At last, the steel box began to move. After the delay, it stopped at every floor. Stern, who had an appointment to meet Lieutenant Radczyk for lunch, simmered at the edge of outburst. Dixon. John. *Gevalt.* what an ugly mess his brother-in-law had made!

Headed down, with lunch at hand, the tiny space was jammed. The elevators, naturally, had been stintingly designed, too small for the building's population. In his state of high agitation, crushed against the rear partitions, Stern took an instant to react when a woman in front of him, a tall brunette in her thirties, stepped back and made contact. Indeed, that put matters somewhat delicately, for she had not merely brushed against him or inadvertently driven her spike heel into his toes. Rather, this young woman had laid the cleave of her rear end firmly against his hand. And would the Sandy Stern of a month ago have politely pulled away? No question. Today he remained still; he was certain that she took him for the wall. But at the next stop the elevator stuttered on its cable, minutely rocking. And did she ease back even farther? So it seemed. And did Stern, as the floors went by, find himself, almost involuntarily, inclining his hand by the most subtle degree? He did. He did, so that by floor 4, his fingers, two or three, were delicately pressed against the parting of her buttocks and the filmy folds of her green dress and the elastic ridges of her undergarments below. By the natural movement of the car, this arrangement provided the most discreet stroking each time the elevator jolted to a halt.

From behind, Stern tried to study this young woman. Was she one of his casual courthouse acquaintances, another lawyer having fun in an offbeat fashion? He did not recognize her. Her eyes were green; one cheek was blemished. A professional person, he assumed, in an expensive green silk dress, carrying her briefcase. With each stop, she seemed to lean back a little more. Her jaw was set in a largely abstracted manner, but save for paralysis, there was no way she might not have noticed what was occurring. At the ground level, she let all her weight come back into him, so that for the briefest instant his hand fit snugly inside and—possible?—was vaguely squeezed before she stepped forward to exit. Across the metal threshold, she looked about for bearings, and when her view crossed his, her expression was far too indefinite to be called a smile. Hiking away, she reached back and gave a quick jerk at her skirt to free it from the rear cleavage where the material was gathered.

Dizzy and aroused, impressed, even inspired by this boldness, Stern followed her from the elevator. So this was the life of men and women in the modern day! It was Cincinnatus who was called back to battle from the plowfield; rearmored, remounted, and placed in charge of war and strategy. That was Stern— except that Cincinnatus had been a hero and an officer in his youth and Stern was never more than a buck private. He'd had more diverse sexual experience in the last four days than in his entire prior lifetime. And there was no hiding his pleasure from himself. His sweet interlude with Margy had revived him like a dose of water on a thirsting plant—he felt the strength of his own vitality from root to leaf. No wonder people so easily made fools of themselves. If he'd never known, he did now—this was *fun*. How did one pursue these leads? Coffee. A hotel room? What happened next? Amazed by himself, still toting his cases, he actually followed the young woman for a block before he recalled Radczyk. She never once looked back; apparently, she took her gratification from teasing. And yet, even when he'd stopped, he had no sure knowledge of his own capacities. He did not know what excesses were within him; he might sprout wings and fly, he might dance naked in the intersection. He felt like some soaring bubble, a thin surface containing the exciting weightlessness of freedom.

12

By the Kindle river, near the docks on the Kewahnee side, an underground world had grown up. Stern always marched down the iron stairwell from the boulevards above with a sense of significant descent, somehow related to entering darkness in the daytime. These piers where the bargemen would unload their cargoes of fruit, rice, and coal brought up from the South retained an economic importance for Kindle County well into this century. In the 1920s, the local movers and shakers, full of the improbable hope that the tri-cities, like an urban Cinderella, could be made to resemble Paris, decided to pretend the docks were not here. On concrete pilings driven down into the sandy banks of the Kindle, the downtown section of Kewahnee was extended; great roads were built and modest skyscrapers rose. Beneath, the gritty dockmen and barge hands continued to work in a netherworld barely reached by daylight, while the suit-and-tie crowd rushed about above, dealing, suing, buying and selling the labor and commodities being delivered to the city in the dark below.

These days, Lower River, as this area was known, was eerie with the garish yellow glow of sulfur lamps. Abutting the streets, the docks of the trucking concerns which had located here originally to carry off what the barges brought and which eventually had supplanted them were littered with crates and spoiling produce. The air sang with the racing pitch of tires on the roads above and the windy commotion of that traffic. For many years, this was the locale where bodies were dumped and drug deals done. The flow of hot merchandise across the trucking piers, by rumor, was still steady. In his early years in practice, Stern was always going about down here to visit one crime scene or another. A thousand people passing by and nobody knew nothin'. The situation was usually far more frustrating to the police than to Stern.

Rather than joust in the noontime traffic, he had walked across the bridge, carrying his two large empty cases. He met Radczyk at a place called Wally's. It was hardly scenic. As with each establishment in Lower River, one entered from the rear. The windows at the back of the restaurant faced the river, which was otherwise inaccessible, looking out to the pilings and the iron underpinnings of the roads. Toward the top of the horizon, a line of daylight broke through and, depending on the angle of the sun, sometimes lit the slaty surface of the water brightly enough to show the floating silt and the industrial debris. Radczyk was at a table smoking a cigarette and, for unknown reasons, studying his shirt when Stern approached.

"Ah, Sandy!" The copper's ruddy country-boy face was radiant. This warmth, whose source Stern still could not recollect, continued to make him uneasy. Radczyk had phoned this morning, saying he had some results. He suggested Wally's, a policemen's hangout, which suited Stern, who was always just as happy not to walk into the station house. Here Stern was more impressed by the size of the man than he had been in his home; Radczyk barely fit into his chair, a hulking figure being slowly diminished by age. He wore a tweed sport coat and the bright red golfing shirt he had been examining when Stern arrived. He explained now that it was an Easter gift from his children. "You get the grandkids over and they tear the place apart, makes you glad you can send them home."

Stern smiled obligingly. It occurred to him that he, too, would soon be entitled to these fond complaints. The prospect today seemed considerably less consoling. The thought of John briefly scuffed at Stern's heart.

"So," said Stern. "You had success?" He sought to bring Radczyk to the subject. He was the kind who would chat about anything else.

The old cop reached to the inside pocket of his sport coat and came up with a single grayish page, a copy of something. He put on his reading glasses and considered the paper as if he had never seen it before. Then he removed his eyeglasses and pointed the temple at Stern.

"You give any thought to talkin with her doctors? That's what I'd do in your shoes."

Immediately, Stern felt the same vexation that had overcome him on his way from the U.S. Attorney's Office. Why had he bothered with this policeman? He was old, and probably never terrifically competent. Trust Radczyk to suggest a starting point where Stern had already been. He was not fully able to conceal his irritation.

"Lieutenant, I am afraid I have already attempted that course."

"Mind if I ask what come of it?" asked Radczyk.

"What came of it," said Stern, "was that Clara's personal doctor tells me he did not order this test, and I have been unable to determine which physician did."

"Huh." Radczyk looked back down to the sheet he held. "No name here," he said. "Suppose I coulda asked when I was out there." The notion that the name of the treating physician might have been relevant occurred to Radczyk remotely, a far-off idea, like the notion of life on the planets. Stern was finding it increasingly difficult to stifle himself.

"You were at Westlab?"

"Oh, sure, sure. Done just like I told you. Went out there, got the administrator, you know, showed her my star. Nice gal. Liz something or other. Very professional, you know. Looked to be a little Mexican or Italian gal. I said I was doin routine follow-up, what records did they have? She showed me the whole file right there in her office. Give me a copy of the results." Radczyk hoisted the paper in his hand, and Stern, without invitation, reached across the table and quietly took it.

The hangdog waitress came by with her green pad, saying only "Yours?" to each man. Stern ordered as he studied the copy. It was a half sheet on the letterhead of Westlab. The rest of it contained computer-printed figures. Numbers. Codes. A meaningless scramble. In his frustration, Stern nearly groaned.

"Did they tell you, Lieutenant, what this test was for?"

"Sure," he said. " 'Viral culture.' " He took the paper back and with a dirty fingernail showed Stern a tiny box which had been x'd.

"A virus?"

Radczyk nodded.

Stern took this in: Clara had seen the doctor for a virus. So here was the outcome of nearly two months' pursuit. His wife had the sniffles. A persistent cough. No wonder she had bothered only Peter. He smiled faintly. For all the pain, it had the quality of a burlesque.

"And they had no more to report?"

Radczyk seemed to have settled himself elsewhere. He considered Stern with his pleasant, rosy look and huddled closer.

"Still don't remember me, do you?"

Stern, who would ordinarily go to considerable lengths to avoid admitting something so unflattering, simply shrugged. He had better sense than to try to fool an old policeman.

"Didn't think so." The cop edged forward. "Marv Jacoby."

It hit Stern like lightning. "The brother," said Stern. The orphan, he thought. "That was some time ago."

Childishly pleased to be recalled, Radczyk sat there smiling. "Hadn't taken the tags off my sergeant's stripes yet."

So this was the orphan. Stern instantly recalled the entire tale. Radczyk had been raised by his grandfather, who ran a paper stand, one of those metal shanties on a street corner; in the winter, they took heat from a fire in an oil drum. One day two young neighborhood hoods, looking for nickels and dimes, tried to stick up the grandfather, and ended up shooting him dead. The beat cop was Harold Jacoby—Jews did not become lieutenants in those days—and he took the grandson home and raised him with his own. Harold had two natural sons, as Stern remembered, and all three became policemen. Ray was the eldest. Eddie eventually quit the force and went to California, where he'd done well in the security business. It was the youngest son, Marvin, who became Stern's client.

Lord, what a thug he was, Stern thought when he remembered Marvin. Gum-chewing, wisecracking, with little black eyes and, as they said on the street, an attitude. Marvin was a wrong cop from the day he got his star. And a daily heartache to Ray here, who took over Marvin's guidance when the father passed away.

Almost a dozen years ago, certain police officers, disgruntled by the usual departmental rivalries, had begun to assemble evidence of wrongdoing in the city's North Branch district. This effort required no intrepidness. The North Branch was wide open: cops on the pad; bail bondsmen steering cases; judges on the take. Marvin was not the worst offender, but one of the least popular, and at the time he first met Stern he had a subpoena to appear before a state grand jury that was looking into allegations that Marvin had taken monthly payments from certain narcotics dealers to warn them of ensuing police raids.

"I still owe you for all of that," said Radczyk.

Stern shook his head. It had not been much. He had simply touched the pressure points. Like someone who knew jujitsu. Stern had paid discreet visits to certain politicians whose alliances he'd estimated would be disturbed by sudden havoc in the North End. The county prosecutor, Raymond Horgan, who had friends like everybody else, had seen fit to quash the investigation. For these efforts, Radczyk had been unreasonably grateful; he had attended each of Marvin's visits, fretting like a mother; he was as garrulous then as now. Marvin simply sat there in his uniform, cracking his gum, while Ray went on reinterpreting every remark and arguing in behalf of Marvin's exculpation. He seemed determined not to believe the worst, the kind of devoted big brother every man should have. None of it had done any good for Marvin, who was discovered a few years later in the trunk of a car being towed from a parking lot in the North End. As Stern heard it, Marvin was stark naked, with blowtorch holes burned black through his privates.

Stern said that out loud, that he might not have been much help to Marvin in the end.

"Gave him a chance," said Radczyk. "He was three times seven. Can only give a fella a chance." Stern and he both pondered that observation. "I shoulda known he'd never make a cop. Hell," said Radczyk, "I don't even know what kind of cop I made." Radczyk, caught in his own tender reflections, smiled crookedly. There was something unavoidably touching about this confession—the very plainness of it. Radczyk was pushing retirement but remained in doubt about these fundamental judgments. His woe Stern did not feel; he had no question about his fitness for his calling, no regrets about what he would have done with greater diligence or harder work. It was the costs of that kind of dedication he was now attempting to assess. The thought brought him back to where they had started. Glancing about to find his cases, Stern stood.

"I thank you for all your good work on this matter, Lieutenant. I am in your debt."

Still apparently anchored in the past, Radczyk considered Stern with a tentative, saddened look and for the first time had no comment.

"Did my wife have a virus, by the way?" Stern asked. He wondered how remote the glimmer was that he had been chasing.

In answer, Radczyk showed the paper. His thick finger lay in the findings section of the form. Stern squinted across the table: "HSV-2 Positive." When Stern looked to him inquiringly, Radczyk shrugged. Whatever that meant. Medical gibberish.

"Maybe I oughta go back there and get that doc's name for you," said Radczyk.

This time Stern caught it, a savvy flash that passed through Radczyk's worn cheerful face, sharp and sudden as the reflection off a blade—something you see, then don't. He had seen this clever gleam in Radczyk before, Stern realized, and let it go by. It amazed him, after all these years, that he could still be taken in by the police.

Stern set down his cases and resumed his seat. He spoke precisely, as he would in court.

"You must excuse me, Lieutenant, but I believe you did not answer my question."

Radczyk's happy mug took on an oafish expression. Caught, he looked both ways and weighed something, probably an impulse to try another feint: What question? He did not do that.

"Yea, verily," said Radczyk at last. "I did not."

"What was this test for?"

"Oh," said Radczyk. He pushed the few clumped strands of hair over his red scalp. "That's what the doctor should be telling you, Sandy. I'd rather not."

"I see. Are you refusing?"

The policeman looked around, big and unhappy.

"No, I ain't refusin' you, Sandy. You ask, I'll tell ya the truth."

"Well, then?"

Radczyk's old face was soft and drained.

"Herpes," Radczyk said.

"Herpes?"

"I asked the lady. That's what she told me. Herpes." Radczyk passed his hand over his mouth, wiping it in a fashion, and said, "Genital herpes."

Stern found himself pondering the dirty river, the flecks of wood pulp, disintegrating cardboard, whitish foam that floated by. He had felt just this way recently, he thought with idle precision. When was it? Then he remembered opening the door to the garage. Peering down, he noticed that one of his hands was gripping the dirty gray table by the edge.

"The test was positive?" he asked. Of course, he knew what the paper had said.

"Sandy, you're askin a guy who don't know a thing. I'm repeating what the lady told me. Who knows? Who knows what we're talkin about? I'm goin right back there. I'm gonna get this doc's name, I'll have it for you in no time flat."

"Please do not bother, Lieutenant."

"No bother."

"You have done enough." Of course, it came out the wrong way. Stern stood there, reeling, suffering, unable just now to do anything to make amends.

My God, Clara, he thought.

Stern insisted on paying the check. He grabbed the old policeman's rough hand and shook it solemnly, and Radczyk, in some kind of conciliatory gesture, took the copied page and placed it in the pocket of Stern's suit. Then Mr. Alejandro Stern, with his empty cases, turned to go, wondering where so early in the day he could find a place to be alone.

PART TWO

13

Clara Mittler was already too old when she met him. It was 1956.

Their acquaintance was first struck in the auspicious climate of her father's law office, where Stern had let one room in Henry Mittler's suite. In those years Stern revered Henry; by the end, he saw his father-in-law as a man with too little justice in him to be admired. But in 1956, with his large and sometimes volcanic personality, and, more pertinently, his influence and wealth, Henry Mittler loomed before Stern, fresh from Easton Law School, like some diorama giant, a majestic emblem of the attainments possible in a life at the bar. He was a sizable fellow, with a formidable belly and whitish hair pushed straight back from a widow's peak, distinct as an arrow, and his manner was, by turns, shrewd and scholarly and ruthless. In many ways, Henry was the most refined of gentlemen; he collected stamps, and for many years thereafter Stern would watch with amazement as Henry, with his jeweler's glass and tweezers, studied, stored, and filed. In other moods, he was a person of gutter commonness. Whatever his temper, he projected the imposing aura of an orchestral maestro.

This impressive congregation of qualities—and, as Stern learned later, a fortunate marriage to a woman of significant standing—had made him a business counselor whose insight and discretion were prized throughout the city's small but wealthy German Jewish community. Two of the larger independent banks downtown were his clients; so were the Hartzog and Bergstein families, only then conquering the

*first terrains in their future kingdoms in air travel and
hostelry. Henry had come of ae in an era when those he
served stood for sweatshops and union busting and heartless
home foreclosures—the entire pristine empire of wealth,
accepted as being in the Order of Things. It was a different
world now; Caplial no longer equaled Power in America in
the same brute fashion. But Henry, no less than anyone else,
was the image of his times, when it was expected that a
business lawyer of his eminence be a gentleman to his
clients and a son of a bitch to everyone else.*

*Seven young attorneys worked for Henry in paneled suites
in the old LeSueur building, with its Art Deco features of
heavy turned brass. Graduating from law school, Stern had
responded to an ad in one of the lawyers' gazettes and rented
a single room. It was a promising arrangement. Henry did
not go to court himself. There would be occasional matters of
small consequence that he might refer to Stern. Collections,
liens, attachments. Small divorces, perhaps. Minor personal-
injury matters, or traffic tickets. It made little difference. If
the flow was steady enough, Stern could satisfy his rent of
$35 a month.*

*For this sum, Stern acquired use of Mittler's law library—
which had seemed an impressive concession, although the
gilt-trimmed treatises on commercial matters contributed
nothing to the criminal practice that Stern wished to
establish—and Mittler's secretary took his phone messages.
In those first months, he could not afford a telephone of his
own. Stern's calls were received on Mittler's general number
and returned, a dime apiece, from a wooden phone booth in
the lobby thirty-two floors below.*

*This arrangement, comfortable to Stern, was soon unaccept-
able to Henry. He had no complaints with Stern's handling of
the matters he referred. But he did not care for the clientele
that Stern brought back from police court, where once or
twice a week he would stand in the corridors in the hopes of
drumming up some kind fo a practice. After two or three
barren attempts, he had attracted the attention of a police
sergeant named Blonder, and for a fee of $5 for each success,
Blonder had begun carrying on in lyrical fashion about
Stern's many triumphs and passing out his card to the*

detainees being ferried in the police paddy wagon. These clients—gypsies, shoplifters, drinkers who had become embroiled in barroom disputes—would come to the oak-wainscoted offices of Henry Mittler to wait for Mr. Stern, beside Henry's client, Buckner Levy, in pince-nez and fedora, the president of the Cleveland Street Commercial Bank. There were no incidents, but the sight of these toughs, who sat in their undervests smoking cigarettes and, on one or two occasions, mistaking the ashtrays for spittoons, drove Henry wild. By the time Stern happened to meet Clara, his clients had been relegated to a bench in the hallway, while Henry comtemplated a more complete eviction for Stern himself. In fact, in his initial rage, Henry had directed Stern to initiate the search for new quarters, although afterwards no more was said of that.

As for Clara, she was employed in her father's office two or three days a week. Stern's first sight of her was from the hallway as he was passing. She was a slender young woman of erect carriage who sat before Henry Mittler with a green stenographic pad in hand. Stern paused; something was not in place. She has a finished look, expensively dressed in a silk blouse and a brown skirt of fine wool; she wore pearls. Then he notice that she was seated not on a chair but on the footstool of Mittler's easy chair.

"Yes, Stern." Henry had caught sight of him in the doorway. Stern, who had not meant stop, said he would come back later, but Mittler was in an expansive mood and more or less ordered him into the office. "My daughter," he said, with his hand raised, while he looked across his desk for something else.

Her hair, a muted reddish shade like finished cherrywood, was cut unfashionably short; her complexion, flawed by one or two livid marks near one cheekbone, was generally pallid; and Stern on first impression could not tell if she was pretty or plain. Her expression certainly seemed deadened. She nodded to Stern with no more interest than she would show a stick of furniture.

It was his pipe Henry had been searching for.

"I suppose you've made other arrangements by now," he said as he shot fire into the meerschaum bowl.

"Not just yet," said Stern.

Years later, Stern could still remember the shocking speed with which he had calculated the advantages of winning this young woman's attention. It was Henry, however, not Stern, who had gotten them started.

"Stern is from Argentina," said her father.

She brightened. "From?" she asked.

In 1956 most Americans regarded foreigners of all kinds with apprehension; about Argentina they wished to learn no more than the tango. Stern was grateful for her interest.

"B.A., principally. We lived in different parts. My father was able to turn the practice of medicine into an itinerant trade."

"Your father was a doctor?" asked Henry. "You've always made out like you were some impoverished son of a bitch. Pardon, Clara."

"Regrettably true," said Stern.

"This is the one who goes down to the lobby to use the telephone," said Henry.

"Ah," said Clara.

The heat of shame rushed up on poor Stern. Clara seized his arm.

"Daddy, you're embarrassing Mr. Stern."

Henry made a face. It was no matter to him.

From these first instants some elements seemed incomprehensible. She was too sophisticated—too rich—a young woman to be a stenographer, but she appeared two or three times a week, typng and answering the phone. When Stern happened by, she would smile idly, a self-contained human being, hard to decipher beyond a heavy hearted stoical exterior.

"You are a student?" he asked her one day, impulsively, when he was in the hallway near the small interior office that she shared with two other women.

"Me? No. I finished college three years ago. Four. Why would you ask?"

"I imagined—" said Stern. He was lost, as usual, for the proper word.

"That I was younger," she said.

"Oh, no." This truly had not entered his mind, but the

young woman seemed to shrink from him. She had embarrassed herself by exposing this vulnerability. "I wondered simply how you were otherwise engaged, when you were not here."

"You think I have something better to do than my father's typing?"

"Miss," said Stern, but he saw then that she was attempting to be coquettish and was, simply, awkward at it. "I am certain you are capable of many things."

She did not answer. He turned away, morose. Truly, he was doomed with this family. A few days later, however, as he was passing in the hall, she called.

"Mr. Stern?" *He looked in, not certain that it was her voice he'd heard. Her eyes were down as she pecked at the typewriter, a substantial mass of black cast iron. Eventually, she spoke, though it seemed to require considerable deliberation.* "Tell me, Mr. Stern, what did you suppose I studied?"

Oh, dear. Now what? He seized on something likely to be inoffensive.

"My estimate, I suppose, is that you were a musician."

Her immediate look of pleasure was incandescent.

"My father told you."

"No," said Stern, enormously relieved.

"You enjoy music?"

"Very much." *This was not really a lie. Who did not like music? She had studied the piano for many years, she said. She mentioned composers whom Stern knew merely by name. Vaguely, they agreed to enjoy music together on some future occasion. Yet, as Stern came away from the conversation, he was struck again by how peculiar this young woman seemed. College educated and half-idle, full of such taut sensitivity. How old was she? Twenty-four or twenty-five, Stern calculated, a year or two older than he. Old for a girl not to be married, even in the States.*

The next week, Henry called him to his office. On his way, Stern feared that his eviction was about to be consummated, but he could tell at once, from the way Henry groused and pawed about, that he had something else on his mind. If Henry were revoking a license at will, he would do it without hesitation.

"We can't use these," Mittler said. "Pauline and I."
Symphony tickets. He held them forth. "I'm sure Clara would
like to go." Stern was too dumbfounded for Mittler to take any
chances. "You know," he said, "Clara put me up to this. She
was too bashful to ask herself."

"This is very kind, Mr. Mittler. I am most pleased."

"Sure you are," said Henry. "Look, I have no goddamned
judgment about my daughter, Stern. I don't know if this is
the right thing to do or not. You may think she's bright, but
she has no idea of what she's up to half the time. Believe me. I
assured her mother there would be no problem here. I told
her you were harmless." Mittler's eyes had a yellowish cast
and he fixed Stern directly.

Should he have turned away? Decades later, in the depths
of grief, he could pose the question, but he would never damn
them both with an affirmative response. He had taken the
two tickets from Henry's hand, while answering the assessment of his harmlessness in a murmur. Anyone listening
would have thought he had agreed.

14

As soon as Peter laid eyes on him, Stern could tell that his son was unsettled. It was a familiar look, something not too far from panic, which, in a blinking, was put aside by the work of adult will. Peter glanced about his reception room, seeking to determine who else was present, and then asked quietly, "What's wrong?"

Stern had never been to his son's office. While Peter was a resident, Clara and Stern had met him for dinner once or twice in the university hospital cafeteria. In his green togs, with his stethoscope lumped into a pocket, he seemed vital, smart, remarkably at ease. Peter's mastery of his place had touched Stern; he was happy for his son, who was so often overwrought. But apparently the meetings had not been as uncomfortable for Peter. In the year and a half he had been in private practice, he had never invited his father to come by. Clara, certainly, had been here for lunch. But Stern had wandered around the suburban office center today for some time looking for the place, a smaller HMO, feeling various qualms, certain that at any instant impatience and anxiety would lead him to turn around. They had not. Unfortunately, there were real needs here, a genuine quandary.

"I require your advice on a matter," Stern told his son. "Something somewhat delicate."

At a loss, Peter took him back through a warren of garishly painted corridors to a small office, not much bigger than a cubicle. In these surroundings, Peter had largely surrendered to the mundane. His desk was clean, dustless, occupied by only a few odds and ends supplied by the drug companies: an onyx pen set, an octagonal plastic thing which turned out to be a calender. There was some grass cloth on one wall, an unimpressive silkscreen; his diplomas were lined up typically along one plaster column. On the top bookshelf, Stern saw the only photograph in the office, a small oval-framed picture of Clara taken a few years ago. A recent addition, probably. Grown men of Peter's generation did not display their mothers' photos, even that discreetly, while they lived.

"So what is this?" Peter asked. "Are you all right?"

"Generally," said Stern.

"Kate said Claudia told her that you don't show up some mornings."

Stern had no idea his daughter and his secretary spoke. It was touching that they took it upon themselves to communicate about his well-being—and typical of Peter that their secret would be casually betrayed. Stern had missed the remainder of the day after seeing Radczyk, and yesterday, Monday, as well. Even today, he had not been certain he could rouse himself. But he had not come here seeking sympathy. He said simply that he was as well as could be expected, and Peter nodded. Amenities passed, his son was not obliged to inquire further.

And would he have answered if Peter had? Stern, pointed by his son to a small upholstered chair, settled in it with a certain morose heaviness. No, he would not have. Somewhere in Stern's heart there was a perfect Peter, the son whom every man wanted, full of ready unspeaking sympathies, and inclinations in all matters of consequence exactly like his father's. But this figure was no more than a shadow, so removed from every day that he did not even have an imagined form. Stern dealt with the real man as best he could. He respected Peter's abilities; he was bright—always the star student—and meanly clever. Like the women, Stern was willing to call on Peter when he was in need. But he was unwilling—unable—to yield something in return. That was truth. Have it. Peter reacted; Stern sat like a stone. It was all as it would ever be.

"Is it something else with Mom's will?"

"No," said Stern. He could hear the impatience in his voice, but Peter virtually demanded that his father state his business. Here, the dispenser of treatment and knowledge, his son was sovereign. This was clearly an unwelcome intrusion.

"There are questions, Peter, which I need to put to someone. I trust your discretion."

"Medical questions, you mean?" As he asked, Peter moved behind his desk, the dashing young doctor, with his center-parted hair and long white coat. Even considering Kate, it was possible that Peter was the best-looking of the children. He appeared to be in peak physical condition, razor-thin and athletic.

"Yes. Medical questions. Technical questions."

"What happened to Nate?"

A reasonable inquiry. Stern himself had spent the weekend phoning Nate, who remained the first choice as medical adviser. But Dr. Cawley's personal life appeared to have rendered him as unreliable as a teenager, and Stern had tired of leaving messages.

"This is a matter with a contemporary flavor, Peter. I presumed that I could bother you. If another time would be preferable—"

Peter waved off the suggestion. "I was just wondering. So what is it?"

Stern felt his mouth drawing, preconsciously. Various cycles of discomfort started up in different regions of his body. Yet he was determined to proceed. The fact was he required information, not just to feed a grisly appetite for knowledge, but also because it had dawned on him over the weekend that his own well-being might be in doubt. There were other physicians he knew. But it was hard to single out just anyone for questions of this nature. And in the end the most villainous side of his character was awakened by his son, especially in regard to his relations with his mother. Rationally, Stern could not brook any real suspicions. Never mind Clara Stern. He had lost, sometime last Friday, any authority to predict her behavior. But no woman of Clara's social class, of her experience or temperamental reserve, no *mother* could have turned to her son for treatment of a problem of this nature. But here Stern sat, nonetheless, eager, among other things, to dash any final doubts.

"I wish information."

"For yourself?"

"I am asking the questions."

"I see that."

"Take it that I am inquiring in behalf of someone with a need to know." Peter, as was generally the case with his father, wore his emotions visibly. He puckered up his mouth sourly to indicate he found this delicacy stupid. Stern, as usual, said no more. He meant simply to follow that tack, suggesting that a troubled client needed these answers. Assuming his son was uninvolved, Stern would never mention Clara—for Peter's sake as well as his own. In prospect, he foresaw this meeting very much like the encounter with a critical witness—one of those daring tightrope walks of courtroom life, exposing the witness's ugliest misconduct without giving the remotest hint that his client had shared in the behavior.

"Peter, does your practice make you familiar with the full variety of—" What word? "In my day, the phrase was venereal disease, but I believe that is no longer popular terminology."

"Sexually transmitted diseases," said Peter.

"Just so," said Stern.

"Which one?"

"Herpes," said Stern. Somehow, as this discussion had begun, Peter's aspect had changed. He had reverted to his role as clinician. He sat up straight in his chair, his brow compressed, his expression somber. Now, with the word, his calculations seemed far more intricate. His hands remained folded with doctorly exactness, but his eyes rolled through changes of color like the sea, so that Stern had the fleeting intuition that his suspicions were well placed, after all. "This is a subject in which you are versed?"

"I'm versed," said Peter. "What's the problem?"

"If one is exposed," said Stern.

"Yes," said his son.

"How long before the disease appears?"

Peter waited.

"Look, Dad. This is not the kind of thing you screw around with. Do you think you have herpes?"

Stern attempted to remain impassive, but within he felt some failing motion—like the fluttering of wings. With his brooding days, his tortured emotions, he had failed to estimate accurately what would transpire here. With Peter staring him down, that was only too obvious now. They knew each other too well. Peter had recognized, naturally, instantly that his father was the party in interest—and like any doctor, any son, had predictable concerns. If he was shocked, it was only because his mother was barely two months dead and the paterfamilias was here, already asking for a full scouting report on the wages of sin. The atmosphere of charged discomfort slowly increased between them, while Stern gradually realized that if worst came to worst he would have no choice but to further his son's misimpressions. Meanwhile, he tried once again to steer the conversation onto more neutral ground.

"The facts which concern me, Peter, are basic. A woman is infected. A man is with her. I merely wish to know what the prospects are that he, too, will contract the disease."

"Look, that's too vague," Peter said, and once more considered his father. "Let's talk about a person, okay? This person. How does he know there's a problem?"

"Assume the proof is positive. She has been tested."

"Tested. I see." Peter stopped for quite some time. "And you're informed?" Peter shook his head. "He's informed?"

"Just so."

"By this woman?" From Peter's tone, it was clear that he envisaged some wanton courtesan.

"As I say, assume an authoritative report."

"Right," said Peter. "And she's active at the time of contact? The virus is shedding?"

"Meaning?"

"Florid signs of the illness. Lesions. Blisters. Ulcers. A rash."

Stern, in spite of himself, recoiled somewhat. He had noticed nothing like that. But by now he had realized it was no accident that he could not recall his last encounters with Clara.

"I am afraid that my information is not that exact, Peter."

"Can you ask?"

"I would think not."

"You would think not?" Peter peered at his father. This imaginary assignation, Stern recognized, was beginning to sound as if it had taken place in an alley. Peter, disquieted, looked down to his folded hands. "The disease is only communicated by direct skin-to-skin contact with someone who is actively infected, or prodromal—that is, about to begin. Onset of the infection is two to twenty days from contact. Far more frequently, within the first week. If you get it. Some people are effectively immune. If you're beyond those periods, without symptoms, you're probably all right. Probably," his son repeated.

"I see," said Stern. Peter was watching carefully to see how this news affected him. "And if one is infected, how long does it last?"

"The initial efflorescence is usually three to six weeks at the outside. But this is one of those viral infections that can come back. I'm sure you've heard that. It's usually seven to ten days on recurrence."

"And how, Peter, does one know if he is infected?"

"Well, the first thing you do is look."

"For what?" asked Stern.

Peter rested his hand on his chin, with his sour expression. At last, he stood up from behind his desk and closed the door. Then he pointed at his father.

"Take down your trousers."

"Peter—"

"Fuck this nonsense. Stand up. Let's go." He was far too positive to allow any quarreling. Somehow, Stern was struck, either in irony or longing, by the recollection of the why he had foreseen this meeting, with himself in complete control.

"Peter," he said weakly again.

"Chop-chop." Peter clapped his hands. He was disinterested and positive. His eyes were already lowered to Stern's belt line.

As a moment, it passed without incident. Body things, as he was learning, had an intense factitiousness about them, an irreducibility. Peter dropped to one knee and removed a slender flashlight from his pocket. He gave instructions like a dance instructor. Left, right. Pull this, pull that. His bedside manner was entirely antiseptic, his look of scrutiny intense and pure.

"Any irritation?"

"No."

"Burning at any time?"

"None."

"Any functional problems of any kind? Urination? Emission?"

Stern decided to forgo remarks about the problems of age. He answered no.

"Any kind of discharge?"

"None."

"Swelling."

I wish. "No."

Peter touched him once, precisely and momentarily, in the groin, probing his lymph glands.

The examination ended after Stern stood with his organ extended like a fish by the tail, dorsal side facing, and Peter ran his light the length of the limp column and over the scrotum.

"You look clean," he stated and motioned for Stern to recover himself. Then he added, "Hold on a sec." He slipped out the door discreetly, then returned with a small plastic beaker. "I'd like a specimen," he said.

Stern objected. Was this necessary?

"It's a good idea, Pa. There are occasions, rare ones, where patients, particularly males, can contract HSV-2 without the usual symptoms. You could go walking around with an infection in the prostate or urinary tract, and end up spreading it." Peter looked at him pointedly, then added that he also wanted to draw blood for something called a serum viral titer test, in which his father's present antibody levels could be compared with those in five or six weeks, to ensure there had been no infection.

"Is all this necessary?" Stern asked again.

Peter simply pointed to the small john down the hall. Stern went, as directed. He stood in the tiny room, petting his organ for stimulation, experiencing the usual difficulty of performing on command. Immediately outside the door, two nurses gabbed about a patient.

Was Peter gay? The question, a familiar one, struck like lightning, timed to arrive, as usual, so that it would inspire maximum discomfort. Nevertheless, there was no putting off the thought. The young man was thirty years old, and his sisters and mother had always seemed to be the only women in his life. He had never had a live-in girlfriend; indeed, when his parents saw him he rarely, if ever, had a female companion. That did not mean much. Who willingly exposed an outsider to the neurotic fun house of his family? Nonetheless, Stern, at moments, saw what in an amateurish and bigoted fashion he took for signs: Peter's close attachment to his mother. A certain prissiness. Well, even this speculation was vicious. And, if for no one else, inappropriate from a parent. The fact was—and here at last was the truth with its contained explosive effect, like a charge set off in a strongbox—that the thought always managed to please

Stern vaguely. It would be a permanent advantage. It would serve Peter right. Stern, with little consciousness, shook his head while this river of resentment poured forth. Today in this smelly closed space the clarity of his ill feelings was bleakly, unremittingly sad.

Back in Peter's consultation room, his son waited with an elastic strap and a syringe. After the beaker was relegated to a nurse, Peter knelt beside his father and inserted the needle. In the meantime, Stern gathered himself for another question he knew was required.

"I take it this is the kind of matter which ought to be shared with partners?"

When Stern looked back, his son's mouth was parted and his eyes were widened. Unable to master his own pretense, Stern had not thought about the impression this question would make. There was woman number one who had the problem. Now he was speaking of other partners—using the plural. It had been quite a couple of months.

"It would probably be advisable," Peter said at last. "Overall. If the blood work would be quicker, I'd say that you could save yourself the embarrassment. But five, six weeks." Peter shook his head. "You'd better say something, just in case. Ninety-nine out of a hundred, you're fine. But if something were to show up, you'd want them to know what it is."

"I see." Well, the Lord only knew what Margy had heard in her time, but the thought of informing her still made Stern shudder. He would never explain the true circumstances to her any more than to anyone else. It would appear to her to be another example of the bad faith men were always capable of. "And I take it, for the present you recommend abstinence?" he asked almost hopefully. He had resolved over the weekend to revert to retirement.

Peter smiled in a quickly fading trace, amused by the thought of his father with a sex life, or, more likely, by the fact that he had the right to govern it.

"Well, you're not active. And we'll know soon whether or not you're prodromal. If it's subclinical, a sheath is adequate to protect your partner. All in all, I'd think that's enough. Assuming you're consistent."

"Yes, of course." Stern fluttered a hand to show that this

conversation was purely speculative. Truly, he no longer cared.

Peter withdrew the lavender-topped vial from the syringe. He shook the blood, eyed it, and went back to his desk to make various notes. While he busied himself, Stern pondered his final inquiry.

"This disease cannot be contracted by accident, can it, Peter?" He could not keep himself from asking, but the question sounded, even to him, lame and pathetic.

"Is that how you're afraid you got it, Pa?" Peter's amusement, when he glanced up, was clearly no longer guarded. Not that this remark seemed particularly rancorous. Peter was always waspish, sarcastic. But Stern realized that there was little chance that his daughters would not hear of some of this. Peter's professional confidence could be expected to reach only so far. This tidbit was far too delicious. Details would be sparing, but something telling would be said. Kate, for example, needed some comfort. 'You know how concerned you were because Pa was coming in late in the morning?' The tittering, at least, would be fondly inspired—and far from the real problem.

"I was not thinking of myself."

"Your ladyfriend?"

Stern made a noise of assent. His ladyfriend. Peter took a second, intent on labeling the tube.

"I would love to help you harbor illusions, but the odds are pretty slim. If your friend has been tested, that means a viral culture, and if it's HSV type 2 that's been identified, then sexual contact is almost certainly the source. You know, the old toilet-seat thing—" Peter didn't finish the sentence. Instead, he simply made a face.

In spite of himself, Stern sighed. He had been prepared for that verdict. Clara Stern, as he had known her, was a woman of attractive bearing and, as she herself was inclined to acknowledge, looks that had improved with age. As adipose and crow's feet, all the usual corporeal failings had overcome others, Clara maintained her pleasant eternal look, dignified and composed. Stern had always admired her because at any age she was a far handsomer person than he. But certain women, married women, mothers prototypically, became too involved with the dense network of their activities—the nurturing, organizing, doing, and attending—to broadcast any ostensible sexual interest. In thirty-odd years, he could not recall an instant of conscious jealousy, a man whose attentions, for whatever reason, had seemed to excite her. She was a person who defined by her daily conduct what was not wayward. She was on a higher plane than that.

Thus, even days later, Radczyk's news remained unfathomable. It went, somehow, beyond right and wrong. The idea of a fifty-eight-year-old woman—this fifty-eight-year-old woman, on the eve of grandmaternity—with a sexually transmitted disease was as horrifying as some freak-show grotesque. Would the antecedent practices erupt only in late middle age? Perhaps he had spent a married lifetime playing the fool. He refused to believe it. It was like the concept of a fourth or fifth dimension. Beyond the capacities of an ordinary mind—or at least of his. Call it machismo or personal limitation, he could not envision his wife, as she clearly had been, with another man.

And it was for this reason that she had done what she had. In his ravaged state of the last few days—amid the torment, the anger, the reviling and utter disbelief—that fact had not been lost. Her intent had been to spare him. This was not sentimentality or self-delusion. After all the calculations, the conclusion remained the same. There was a lapse here, a monumental breach of faith which in life, perhaps, she might never have lived to see him forgive. She had saved herself great pain as well. But in the end her kindness, her fundamental kindness, remained her lodestar, her guiding light.

Oh, Clara! On the chair, with his sleeve rolled and his bled arm still vaguely atingle, Stern teetered for an instant on the verge of tears. With that, his life, what was left of it, the many small illusions, would disappear. Peter would have to be told, or might even guess. He saw that and, in the sluices of powerful remorse, for a moment did not care. Then his pride, with the grinding precision of a huge laboring machine, engaged once more and brought him fully about. He rolled down his sleeve over the gauze Peter had taped inside his elbow.

"And if this illness were to appear," Stern asked, "there is no treatment?"

"There's a drug called acyclovir. Ointment or pills. It's very successful in reducing the active period, and in many people it even prevents recurrence. Generally, the disease retreats into the nerve ganglia and waits to rear its ugly little head.

Sometimes it never does. Sometimes it returns every few months, in ever-weakening episodes. That's the usual course. But there are all kinds of extraordinary clinical histories. Acute cases. Florid recurrences years apart. The most difficult part of it is prodromal—you're in a contagious phase for a day or two before the visual signs appear, and short of a culture, you can never be completely certain that you won't infect someone else. It can mess up your life pretty well. In addition to being extremely uncomfortable."

"Yes," said Stern. His mind remained on Clara. All told, the weight of events seemed again to have settled on him with all their dead-star density. The facts, the facts. He had always placed his faith in particulars. Well, now he had them, lots of them. Many facts and, he supposed, certain inevitable conclusions.

He stood up and, without allowing time for reaction, touched his son's smooth face.

"You are a good doctor, Peter. I appreciate your concern."

Wise and sad, Peter nodded. His eyes did not leave his father. His son seemed to have a gift, a sense for the human nuance, the pathos that trailed along with each disease, mortality's dismal gossamer. Stern was pleased to find him so worldly. In their relationship, there was rarely anything subtle.

"Look, I'm sure you're okay," Peter said. "We'll just watch it. All right?"

"Very good," said Stern. He tossed on his suit coat. "I am grateful. And sorry, Peter, to have involved you in such a disagreeable business."

"Oh, hell," said Peter. "You know what they say."

"What is that?" asked Stern. He was at the door.

"Life is full of surprises." His son was smiling. No doubt, he was thinking already about telling his sisters.

15

Dixon, predictably, enjoyed competion and for years had utilized every excuse to lure Stern into joining him in various sports. As Stern was apt to say, a business meeting with Dixon generally meant he would sweat. When Stern was younger, and considerably thinner, they had played handball at Dixon's downtown club. Stern was more nimble than his appearance might suggest, but he was no match for his brother-in-law. Larger, stronger, and far more athletic, Dixon never seemed to tire of winning. In season, he would bring Stern out on Lake Fowler to fish. Stern would foul his line and cast into the bushes and lily pads; back on shore, Dixon would describe Stern's ineptness to everyone they met. 'The only man who ever went fishing and nearly took a bird. I kid you not. Cardinal up in a tree? Stern missed hooking him by inches.' Stern often told Clara that he was the trophy Dixon wanted stuffed and mounted.

By now, Stern had limited this rivalry to golf. Stern had more feel for this game; he was better on land than sea. But, as usual, he did not play often enough to offer any serious competition for Dixon, who was virtually a scratch golfer. Dixon was a daring trouble player; he loved the shots where he had to rest one foot in the crotch of a tree or fade the ball around a light pole, and he was particularly reckless here on his home course. The Greenwood Country Club was cut a century before into these rolling hills, nearly forty miles from the city. This was horse country, with hills deep in elm and oak, poplar and pine. Easton University was no more than ten minutes away. Here, with Lake Fowler, the well-to-do breathed cooler air and pretended that the city that kept them rich was nowhere near. Dixon adored this life, like every other badge of status, and had his principal home nearby, a huge stone house which sat on twenty acres on the lakeshore.

They played from an electric cart, accompanied by a forecaddy. Dixon usually had one or two favorites, high-school-age boys, hardscrabble types with whom Dixon could josh about their sex lives, offering them his golfing theories after each successful shot. Dixon treated these boys kindly and tipped them shamefully well. Today they were accompanied by a young man named Ralph Peters, a black kid who lived in DuSable and traveled nearly an hour and a half by train to reach the Greenwood Club on the weekends. Next year, Dixon was going to get a golf scholarship for Ralph, who was the caddy champion. With Dixon, this was not just talk. If need be, he would endow the scholarship himself. But he would also expect a chorus of appreciation and various acts of reverence befitting a beneficent king.

Stern waited until the third tee to talk about the investigation. "I visited with Margy."

"So I heard," said Dixon. He was practicing his swing, but Stern thought he detected something whimsical in Dixon's expression. On the other hand, he could not doubt Margy's discretion.

This hole, like most at Greenwood, was short and narrow, a little dogleg cut into the woods, about 330 yards. The green was set to the right of the fairway, so that the hole, sketched on the back of the scorecard, looked like a lowercase p. Dixon waggled his driver mightily over the ball, then pulled his shot deeply into the trees.

"Shit. Well, Ralph will find it. There." He pointed the driver toward the hollow below where Ralph had emerged from the woods to indicate that the ball had been located.

Stern took the ground on his drive, but the ball hopped down the fairway. With the angle, Dixon would be away. He floored the cart and they zoomed down the hill together. Stern, wearing a tam, held it and yelled a bit over the wind.

"I looked at the records the government wanted, before turning them over. And I also examined what I presume the agents assembled at Datatech."

"And?"

"And I am concerned."

Dixon glanced back, very briefly. He drove the cart up to Ralph. "Right there, Mr. Hartnell. You better punch out."

Dixon tromped in and out of the bushes. Stern could not see the lie, but had no urge to follow. He'd seen it before: Dixon making faces, muttering, conferring with Ralph with the gravity of a general.

"I'm going for broke," Dixon yelled.

What else was new? Ralph could be heard quarreling. He was telling Dixon he could never do it. The sun gleamed through the foliage behind the two figures.

The shot, bedded on dried leaves and twigs, sounded cleanly, but a second or two on in its course took a tree with the round musical sound of marimbas. The ball rattled around in the wooded heights, breaking branches, then suddenly fell heavily to earth, like a gift from heaven, only twenty or thirty yards from the green. Dixon came crashing out of the bushes in time to see the ball drop. He turned back to Stern with a magnificent smile.

"Member's bounce."

Ralph followed along, carrying the club and shaking his head.

Watching Dixon march across the fairway toward the cart as he continued congratulating himself, Stern was taken by an intimation, soft as a whisper, of the young soldier he had met decades ago, during basic training in the desert at Fort Grambel. They had encountered one another somehow—in the barracks or the latrines. At this point Stern would have preferred some auspicious recollection of their meeting, but he remembered little, only the predictable bad judgment of youth. He had liked Dixon; worse, he had admired him. Dixon was one of those large commanding figures that Stern could never be—a shrewd country boy, a good talker with a distinct, twangy hill accent, who looked like a million in his uniform, square-shouldered and jut-jawed, with wavy dark blond hair. With the advent of war and the death of his mother, Dixon, full of red-hot ambition, had joined up. The service, with its grand traditions, its medals, its legends, was like a cast for an ingot. Dixon saw himself as an American hero in the making.

Stern had enlisted, too, but with ambitions less grand. When he was honorably discharged, he would automatically become a citizen and thus put to rest the family's perpetual concerns about their outdated visas. He was twenty years old and already a college graduate, having raced through school, a dark sunken-cheeked sort with heavy black hair, much slimmer than today's model. He had done better in the service than those who knew him now might expect; he had scaled the walls and carried the packs without relish, but he was dull to discomfort of most kinds in those days. His hungers inspired him.

Stern was never certain what there was about him that had drawn Dixon's interest—probably the fact that Stern was college-educated and quickly marked for OCS. It mattered not. The alliances of a soldier's life were easily founded, and in 1953 a hillbilly, or a Jew with a Latin accent, picked from limited entrees on the American social smorgasbord. There was a night when he and Dixon had sat on a bunk, passing back and forth a smuggled bottle of Jack Daniel's and a pack of Camels, talking. About what? The future, Stern believed. They both had plans.

For Stern, the future was nearer than he imagined. One day, at the end of basic training, as he was readying to ship out for Officer Candidate School, his major announced that Stern was required at home. The officer did not explain, but the orders Stern was handed had a typical military brusqueness. In a blank was written, "Hardship furlough—mother critical." She had had a stroke. In the hospital, he found her paralyzed and unable to speak. Her dark roaming eyes seemed to search his face meaningfully, but he was never certain that she recognized him. She was dead within a week, and Stern, now Silvia's sole support, was honorably discharged. He never returned to Fort Grambel. All of it was left behind, his kit and duffel bag, the sadistic sergeants, OCS—and Dixon Hartnell. By now, over thirty years later, Dixon had as many faces to Stern as a totem pole—Silvia's husband, an important client, a local powerhouse in the avenues of commerce, one of the few men Stern knew well whose accomplishments he thought of as markedly overshadowing his own. He seldom remembered that yearning young man who had attached himself to him in that vaguely supplicating fashion.

Dixon hopped back in the cart, still radiant at his miracle shot. He would never willingly return to the subject of the investigation. Like someone who learned in his sleep, however, he expected Stern to force him to listen. They were at the stage now where Dixon—any client—had to recognize he was in mounting jeopardy.

"Dixon, this is a grave matter. These records are very damaging."

"Maybe I should have taken a look at them before you turned them over," said Dixon. "Some of the problems might have disappeared." He smiled tersely.

"Dixon, I suggest you abandon such thoughts. If you follow that course, you may as well walk straight to the penitentiary and skip the intervening steps. Too many people have seen your business records. The company that put them on microfiche. Margy. Me." Stern let that sink in. "Not to mention the chatty fellow who told the government to look for them in the first place."

Dixon looked at Stern directly, full face. His eyes were greenish-gray, a color hard to name.

"My thing get there?" Dixon asked. Eventually, Stern realized he was referring to the safe. He decided not to ask why the present discussion brought it to mind.

"Quite secure," Stern answered.

"I did it the way you said. Handled it myself. I even got Margy to cut a check in Chicago to pay the trucking company." The trucker, characteristically, had refused to take the safe any farther than the very center of Stern's office. Not much more than a foot square, the gunmetal cube must have weighed 150 pounds. After a week, Stern and Claudia had struggled to get the safe as far as it was now, behind his desk. Out of an arch impulse, Stern had begun using it as a footrest.

"Where's my key, by the way? You said you'd send one."

"Shortly," said Stern. He would have to remind Claudia, inasmuchas Dixon remained intent on keeping the contents to himself. The dial of chrome and steel on the safe looked as if it could withstand a dynamite charge. At odd moments, Stern had examined it already. Dixon, meanwhile, had floored the cart, racing toward Stern's ball. Stern held his hat again and yelled over the wind, "I warn you, this situation is perilous."

"You've said that about other situations."

"And I was correct. You were fortunate."

"So I'll be fortunate again." Near Stern's ball, they came abruptly to a halt. "Can't you do something, file something? Make some kind of motion?"

"There are no credible motions to make for the time being,

Dixon. Judge Winchell will not put up with delaying tactics. It would be unwise to irritate her, as we may need her patience later."

Dixon dismounted from the cart and lit a cigarette, his back to Stern as he suddenly took to studying the woods. Stern went on, notwithstanding.

"Dixon, your records give clear indication that someone at MD was trading ahead of your largest customer orders."

Dixon pivoted. With his chin lowered, he looked like a glowering fighter on a magazine cover, the whites of his eyes showing large and luminous with a smoldering shrewd anger. He never enjoyed being found out, one of many reasons that Stern had avoided any further mention of Margy.

"No kidding," said Dixon.

"Indeed, I am not," said Stern. "It was very cleverly done. Smaller orders were placed on the Kindle Exchange just before you went into the Chicago markets with large orders that would affect prices everywhere. And these Kindle orders were always written with botched account numbers, so that, after clearing, they would end up being credited in the house error account. Countervailing buys and sells, leaving a profit just a few pennies shy of $600,000. It was a brilliant scheme."

"Six hundred thousand," said Dixon. He pointed to the ball. "Your shot."

Ralph was behind the cart a respectful distance with Stern's five iron. Stern's drive had traveled downhill, but it had trailed to the right of the fairway—the wrong place to be on this hole—so that Stern was required to play left. He sliced naturally and positioned himself at an angle to the hole.

Dixon credited misfortune to various deities, like wood elves. Losses on the trading floor belonged to the bean god. Here he paid homage to the god of balls.

"Ball god!" screamed Dixon as Stern's shot tore off for the deepest woods. Ralph turned to watch it go, like an outfielder pining after a homer.

Stern took another from his pocket and hit his shot cleanly. The ball faded, not quite sufficiently, toward an area left of the green, hit the uneven ground there, and kicked, as if drawn magnetically, into a sand trap.

"Beach," said Dixon, in case Stern had not noticed.

They parked the cart in the left rough while Ralph crashed around in the woods, making a hopeless search for Stern's ball.

"So what happens?" asked Dixon. "With this thing? They want the money back, right?"

"That is merely the starting point, Dixon. If the prosecutors employ the RICO statute, as I expect, the government will attempt to forfeit the racketeering enterprise—you understand: take it from you as punishment."

"What's the racketeering enterprise?"

"MD."

"The whole fucking business?"

"Potentially. Not to mention a term in the penitentiary."

"Oh, sure," said Dixon, jumping down from the cart again for his shot, "you couldn't expect them to go easy."

Dixon's bravery was admirable. Stern had actually been asked twice in his career by other clients facing the rigors of forfeiture about the legal consequence of suicide: could the government still grab their dough if they were dead? Stern avoided answering, fearing the consequences of a truthful response, since all phases of a criminal prosecution were, in fact, terminated by death. With Dixon, of course, there was no risk of self-destruction. He probably could not conceive of a world he did not inhabit. But Stern knew nonetheless that he had struck a nerve. To threaten Dixon's business was to toy with the obsession of a lifetime. He had begun thirty-some years ago, driving all over the Middle West in search of clients, soliciting the small-town businessmen whose livelihoods depended on farm prices—the merchants, the feed-lot owners, the rural banks which could use commodity futures to hedge their loan portfolios. Dixon's strategy, he explained to Stern later, was to sign up the fire chief. The firemen were volunteers, fought flame and death together; the fire chief was the captain of their souls. If he liked something, all would. No trick was too low for Dixon. He carried a fireman's helmet in his trunk.

Now he flew between the coasts, doing deals, but his first love remained sitting in the office, plotting strategies for the managed accounts, the commodities pools, the large customer orders. He made money and lost it with every tick, in each future, but Dixon never lost his interest in the game, a mixture of street savvy and balls poker. Three or four times a year, he would grab his dark jacket and badge and go to the floor for part of the day. Even in the chaos of the trading floor, the news would go out that he was there. He stepped into the tiered levels of the pits, shaking hands and tossing greetings like Frank Sinatra onstage, commanding the same reverence, or, in some quarters, subverted loathing. Dixon did not care. Stern had been in the Kindle office one day when Dixon had lost $40,000 in less than half an hour and he was still exhilarated by the tumult of the floor, the jumping and shouting of the trading crowd, what he took as an essential moment in life.

Dixon lofted his ball between the extended foliage of two tree boughs. The ball did not bite well and ran about twelve feet past the cup.

"Tough par," said Dixon, thinking of his putt.

Ralph stood at the edge of the sand trap like a well-armed soldier, Stern's sand wedge in one hand and the rake in the other. Stern trod down dutifully into the pit, then bedded himself in, dog-like, shaking his fanny. These shots, hit an inch behind the ball, were all acts of faith. Stern thought of fluid motion, then swung. Amid an aura of sand, the ball rose from the bunker. It traveled almost sideways when it hit the green, but it came to rest within two yards of the flag.

"Making it hard on me," Dixon said. Stern had a stroke on each hole.

Ralph handed them their putters, then drove the cart off toward the next tee.

"They have to prove it's me, don't they?" Dixon asked as the two men stood on the green. "All this crap, taking the business—they don't take my business away because somebody else did this without me knowing. Right?"

"Correct," said Stern. He moved his putter near his shoes. "If that is what occurred."

"Look, Stern, everybody in the place puts on trades that end up in the error account. There are a hundred, hundred fifty trades a month that go through there." This was the point which Margy had seized on. "Maybe somebody's trying to screw me, make me look like a bad guy."

"I see," said Stern. "The government, Dixon, not to mention a jury, is rarely persuaded that an employee is willing to steal hundreds of thousands of dollars and then give it to his employer out of spite."

"Me?"

"It is your account, Dixon."

"Oh, bullshit, it's the house account."

"It is your house, Dixon. And it is logical to attribute all of this to you, if the money remains in the account."

Dixon suddenly showed a quick, scornful smile.

"Is that what they think?" he asked. He tossed away his cigarette and removed a piece of tobacco from his tongue, while he fixed Stern with a dry look." The message was plain: I am not that dumb. Apparently, Dixon had exercised more care than Margy had made out. There was another layer of involvement in Dixon's scheme, one that somehow isolated the error account and the unlawful profits. A flash of something, say a smile, passed between the two men before they moved off on either side of the flag.

Dixon putted first, and swore freely as the ball danced around the cup. Stern, with a short putt to halve the whole, shocked himself by making it.

"Goddamn it," said Dixon, not for the first time.

They moved onto the next tee and sat on a bench under a tree, holding their drivers, while the foursome ahead approached their second shots. The fairway was long, gleaming under the sun on the par-five hole. There were ten traps—Stern called this hole 'the march across the desert.' Idling there, he briefly reconsidered the government's scrutiny of Dixon's bank account. Perhaps that had to do with the devices Dixon had used to conceal the money. In all likelihood. They were still looking.

"There is another problem," Stern said.

"Naturally," his brother-in-law responded.

Stern told him that John had been subpoenaed.

"Meaning what?"

"They want to ask him questions about this matter."

"So? He's a good kid. Let them ask questions."

"They are suggesting that they may grant him immunity." Dixon squinted and studied Stern.

"What are you telling me?"

"I'm telling you that they believe he has critical knowledge. They are interested in making him a witness against you."

"And what am I supposed to say?"

"Is that prospect of concern to you?"

Dixon, perpetually cryptic, made a face—a philosopher could not have done better. Who knows what about whom?

"It might be."

"I see." Stern briefly looked away. But he had known this was coming. The tickets from the orders that had been entered in Kindle ahead of the large Chicago trades had reached his office yesterday, and John's awkward scrawl, even his initials sometimes, were on each form. The prosecutors' hopes for John were obvious: they wanted him to finger Dixon as the man who'd called the Kindle orders in each time. But it was not clear yet that John could oblige. He took hundreds of orders a day. The possibility remained that Dixon had used John regularly because he was as unimpressionable as a stone, the man on the desk most likely to forget, and that there had been nothing memorable or overt in their dealings that would ignite John's recollections now. There was no point in asking Dixon. He could not say what John remembered, and would never answer precisely, in any event.

"Then we had best find him another lawyer," Stern said at last.

"If you think so."

"I do. I cannot represent someone whose best interests may lie in testifying against you. How could I be loyal to John and loyal to you? It would be a hopeless conflict of interests."

For an instant the bleak morass of family difficulties, framed in this way, confronted both men. Even Dixon, Stern thought, had a mildly sheepish look.

"Who will you get for him?"

"The choice is John's. I will suggest some names. Lawyers I am familiar with." Lawyers who would talk to Stern, who would do their best to moderate the danger of John's testimony. This was very delicate. Stern, in spite of everything, smiled at his next thought. "Your employees' manual provides that he will be indemnified for his legal fees."

Dixon rolled his eyes. "Great."

The momentary humor, however, seemed to do nothing to allay the heavy mood between them.

"Look," said Dixon. He was about to explain, but he caught something in Stern's look that stopped him. Suddenly it was obvious to them both how harshly Stern judged him for leading

John into this swamp. Dixon endured this reproof another instant before turning away.

Ralph, by the cart, mentioned that they could hit. Dixon strode to the tee, swung mightily, and hooked his shot miserably, deep into the trees. He walked across the tee, outraged, slamming his club head repeatedly into the sod, and finally flung the wood away.

Stern was standing when he returned.

"Do you have something to say?" Dixon demanded.

There was no pretense he might have been referring to his shot.

"My fee does not include lectures, Dixon."

"You think it was a stupid-ass thing to do, right? The whole fucking idea. Dumb, as bad as anything else. And you'd expect me at least to be smarter."

Stern waited.

"Just so," he answered.

With his driver, he began walking forward on the tee, but Dixon caught his arm with his gloved hand before his brother-in-law could pass. He suddenly seemed too put out for courtesies. He presented his natural self, large, rough, expansive. Since Stern had known it all along, he admitted his nasty secret—in spite of his expensive haircut and Sea Island cotton shirts, Dixon was a vulgarian. He pointed.

"Stern, do you know why a dog licks his balls?"

Stern considered that a moment.

"No, Dixon, I do not."

"Because he can," said Dixon, and looked at his brother-in-law squarely. Before he headed toward the cart, alone, he repeated it. "Because he can."

16

Someone had once observed that when a man was wearing a hat it is harder to tell his troubles. Stern found surprising accuracy in this peculiar commonplace. Under a bright straw boater, with a brilliant red, white, and blue band, he proceeded down the avenues toward the River National Bank, where he would meet with Cal Hopkinson and the officer in charge of Clara's trust accounts. The day was bright, the perfect sweet late May you expected in Kindle County.

The hat was Marta's—from a high-school play a decade ago. Stern had found it in her room, and during one of the lengthy long-distance conversations they had recently been having late at night, she had urged him to wear it, hoping it might improve his mood. He was certain he would feel like a clown as soon as he set foot outside the house. Instead, it proved oddly heartening to think that people who knew him well might not recognize him, could believe he was someone else.

Across the marble lobby of River National, Cal Hopkinson waved. Together, he and Stern found the office of the bank vice president, Jack Wagoner. Wagoner was your usual inoffensive gentleman in banking, immaculately groomed and well mannered. Henry Mittler, long ago, had permanently damaged all bankers in Stern's estimate with his grudging private opinions of the banking clients who had made him rich.

Whatever disparaging bromide Henry might have employed about Jack, he was smart enough to know there was a problem. His mission was to explain to a man what his wife had done, without his knowledge, with most of a million dollars. Furthermore, the man was a lawyer. A suicide was involved. A will was

in question. Bad medicine for a banker, or anyone else. The air in
Wagoner's office full of antique reproductions and a good Oriental
rug was decidedly uneasy. A single file folder lay in the center of
Wagoner's otherwise immaculate desk.

"Mrs. Stern issued written instructions to dissolve at least
$850,000 in assets in her investment account on March 20th."
With that, Wagoner produced a handwritten letter on Clara's
stationery. Cal and Stern looked it over together on the corner of
Wagoner's desk, then Stern took up the document himself. The
hand was strong and clear. She wrote a one-sentence direction,
setting forth the amount and granting the bank the discretion to
liquidate those securities it deemed best. Holding the note, he
recalled the other piece of correspondence Clara had set herself
to a few days after. Many messages left behind, but no long
explanations. Stern, without thinking, briefly worried his head.

"May I ask who dealt with her?"

Wagoner knew all the answers. His assistant, Betty Fiori, had
received Mrs. Stern's call and told her that written instructions
were necessary with an amount of that size.

"And what then became of those funds?" asked Stern.

"They were disbursed," said Jack, "pursuant to Mrs. Stern's
directions."

"How?" asked Cal.

"By certified check drawn against her investment account."
Wagoner had obviously spoken to his lawyer and was answering
only as questions were asked. He now presented a white slip by
which Clara had requested certification; she had wanted to
reassure someone that her check would be good. Stern recognized her signature on the form, but the amount, a little over
$850,000, was written in another hand.

"Whose writing?" he asked, pointing.

"Betty's."

"And to whom," asked Stern, "was this check made payable?"

"We looked for the canceled check." He pushed a button on his
telephone console and asked that Ms. Fiori be summoned. She
appeared at once, another person in a dark blue suit. She recited
the steps she had taken to find the wayward check. Their own
check-reconciliation department had searched; their bank; the
Fed. The trust officers, who normally received the canceled
checks and statements on this account, had looked high and low.

It was this tracing process, clearly, which had gone on while the bank had been holding Cal at bay.

"I'm positive it hasn't cleared," Ms. Fiori said.

"Can we stop it?" asked Cal.

"Stop?" asked Wagoner. "It's a certified check. We've guaranteed payment."

"It hasn't been presented."

"How could we stop it?" asked Wagoner.

"It's stale, isn't it?"

Stern spoke up. The question he had asked before had not yet been answered.

"To whom was this check made payable?"

Ms. Fiori looked to Wagoner.

"We don't ordinarily make a record of that," he said. "We have no reason to."

"You do not know?" Stern spoke to Ms. Fiori. Wagoner might never answer directly.

"We don't know," she said. "Usually, you have the returned check. Sometimes we'll put a note on the requisition. It wasn't made payable to Mrs. Stern, if it helps. I remember that."

"You do?" asked Stern.

"Yes."

"Clearly?"

"Yes."

He was in the mode of cross-examination now. Familiar ground. Something, he suspected, had made an impression on her.

"There is a particular reason you recall?"

She shrugged. "Not really."

"You remember the name?"

"I don't, Mr. Stern. I've racked my brain."

"But it was not an entity? A corporation? Partnership?"

"No, I'm sure of that."

"Not a charity or a foundation?"

"No."

"An individual?"

"I believe so."

"I see," said Stern. He knew the rest. It was obvious now why she remembered. "A man's name," said Stern finally.

Ms. Fiori, involuntarily, allowed her teeth to close a bit against her upper lip.

"Yes," she said.

Yes, thought Stern. Of course.

For a moment no one in the room spoke.

"So some fellow is walking around with my wife's check for $850,000 in his pocket?"

It was absurd, of course, but the humiliation was unbearable. It raced through him, like acrid fumes, and seemed to force its way to his eyes. He knew he was flushed.

Cal at last said something.

"Jack, there has to be a way to stop that check."

"Cal, it's certified. We'd be buying ourselves a lawsuit for wrongful dishonor. We don't know what kind of transaction was involved here." Wagoner, provoked by Cal, glanced as an afterthought at Stern. He had been indelicate. "I promise you this much. We'll let you know when the check is presented. If you want to get an injunction at that point, God bless you."

Stern was already on his feet. He spoke to Wagoner and Ms. Fiori, thanking them for their assistance, told Cal he would be in touch, then left the office. He was—again—reeling.

Outside the bank's revolving doors, he placed Marta's skimmer on his head and watched as the wind took the hat away and bounced it down the pavement, weaving among the pedestrians. When he turned, Cal was beside him, watching it go.

"I'll chase it," Cal said, but did not move.

Stern gestured that he ought not bother. They walked in the direction of the hat without speaking.

"I'll bet," said Cal at last, "when everything is said and done, we'll still have a chance to unwind that transaction. She couldn't have had the slightest idea of the tax implications of what she was doing."

Stern barely contained himself. What a numskull Cal was, always congratulating himself at length because he was not even dumber. Who gave a damn about the money? Here at last, three decades along, Clara had found the way to curtail his interest in her wealth. When he turned back, Stern found his eyes fastening on the dark spot behind Cal's ear.

"I am not concerned, Cal. Whatever it was, shall be." He caught sight of the banner on his hat; it was resting against a mesh trash bin a hundred yards away.

He took a step in that direction, and then stood still while that ugly interrogatory suddenly burned through him: *Who?* Oh yes, it was time for that again. Who was it? In the first few days, Stern with considerable discipline, and an aversion to pain, had refused to lower himself to this debased parlor game. But eventually the outrage boiled up in him and he could not suppress his dismal curiosity. It would have been more noble to be able to claim that it was vengeance for Clara's sake he was after—to find and punish the heartless scoundrel who'd inflicted what became a mortal disease. But his needs were more basic, and entirely his own. Whether or not it was a lurid interest, he simply had to fill in the picture.

In these moods, he suspected virtually every man who came into his view. Was it the mailman or, as in some filthy story, a salesman traveling door-to-door? Today he'd learned that it was someone who needed money—perhaps an impoverished student of hers whom she had fallen for and sought to mother; or a struggling musician in a garret who wanted a permanent endowment? Perhaps a young man starting out in business. Or an older, married fellow who needed cash to finance his divorce?

Once or twice, at home, he'd picked up Clara's leather-covered address book and had gone through it page by page, weighing prospects with every male's name, no matter how unlikely. Any man would do. How about Cal? Perhaps his surprise at the money's disappearance was only an elaborate act. With a lover's gratitude, Clara had made a gift of what Cal had long superintended. But Ms. Fiori surely could not have failed to recall Cal's name with him seated right there. Perhaps it was Dixon. Of course, Clara's distaste for him seemed so sincere, and Dixon with his plastic-coated penis was, by Peter's evidence, not likely to be spreading—or contracting—any such disease. Nor had Dixon the need for anybody else's money. How about Nate Cawley? He had the sex life of a chimpanzee. Perhaps all his skulking about was a reflection of guilt. Or the pompous rabbi at the temple? He certainly was an object of Clara's esteem and generosity.

Abjectly, unwillingly, Stern on the street corner placed his hand across his heart. Cal was down the avenue waving Stern's hat to show it had been safely recovered. Stern studied the throng of suited men striding the street. Who? he thought, seething with hatred, weakened by shame. *Who?*

17

In MD's offices in the Kindle County Futures Exchange, Stern asked the receptionist for John Granum and took a seat. Dixon had a showpiece office a few blocks south of here, a place with exposed brick walls and banners and baffles used for sound deadening that was often pictured in architectural magazines; that was the site of MD's local trading room and central executive offices. But the order desk and back office remained here in a bright, functional-looking space in the KCFE.

After a few moments Al Greco, Dixon's number-two person in Kindle, affable, half bald, too fat, greeted him. Dreading this meeting, Stern had put it off much longer than he should have. Finally, this morning he had left a message that he was coming, but John apparently had been needed on the floor. They would have to go get him. From his desk drawer, Al grabbed his red plastic trading badge, engraved with his initials and MD's clearing number, and pulled his navy-blue floor jacket off a hook. Downstairs, at a security desk, Stern was signed onto the floor for fifteen minutes. Two years ago, a fellow in a wig had placed dozens of trades and disappeared without settling the losing transactions. Now, if Stern exceeded his granted time by more than a minute, a cadre of security officers would spill across the floor and pull him out as unceremoniously as a spy.

This was an exciting place. On the Exchange floor, the profusion of color and the volume were exceptional. It was like being on the playing field in a thronged athletic stadium. The huge black tote boards thirty feet overhead flashed in optic shades of orange, red, green, and yellow as their digits fell, while a red band of local and national news raced by below. Young people—runners, traders, order clerks—dashed about in their colored coats and corduroys, each looking purposeful, hyped-up, singleminded. The floor was confettied with discarded orders. In the meantime, in the tiered trading pits, the fundamental business went on, the brokers, the locals, the top stair men, forty and fifty deep, buying and selling in a screaming melee of surging hands. Fingers up and out; beckoning or refusing. From their black wrought-iron observation posts, the pit reporters overhead copied down each fill. For all the electronic circuitry, the phones and faxes and computers that took information to and from this place, at the junction point one still depended on physical skills: visual acuity, strong lungs, and good ears. The din, the fierce voices, rang out incredibly. At the windows three stories above, various gawkers stood with their faces pressed to the glass.

In this world, greed had annealed with some kind of benighted manliness, so that there was at times an atmosphere of savagery. Young men—too many of them Jewish for Stern's comfort—moved about with astonishing swagger. Twenty-eight years old, thirty. Kids who had barely scraped their way through high school had bought seats on the Exchange and traded for their own accounts, often making millions. Others would lose their shirts or trade away an accumulated fortune in a matter of days. It made no difference. Those who went into the pits wore the macho pride of bullfighters. Like cavemen they lived on the unpredictable whims of wind and rain, markets, seasons. This, they believed, made them tough. The risk made them high. Stern had heard stories, amusing if not true, of handjobs delivered in the jostling trading pits by certain female clerks. Verity was not the point of these tales. They emphasized the exhilarated air that many believed they breathed here. They had it better than ordinary drips—money, the blood of life, was always passing through their hands in staggering amounts. Once, years ago, when Dixon was still often on the floor, Stern had met him for lunch and found him conferring with four younger colleagues, all traders.

'I got this one,' a man had said, moving in front of one of the elevators.

'For what?' a second asked.

'A bill.'

'A big bill?'

'Right.'

Dixon laughed and dug through his pockets. He stepped before the second elevator.

Eventually, the five of them passed the stakes down to Stern. A thousand dollars a man. In cash. They were betting on which elevator would come first.

Al, a dozen feet ahead of Stern on the floor, pointed to John in the MD trading booth, a narrow gray counter space that looked like a hotel newsstand. Between the pits, the various clearing corps had these tiny preserves where orders and fills could be phoned back and forth from the floor. Every inch down here was precious. Ten people would work in quarters closer than steerage.

John was on the phone now, writing furiously, talking back. Upstairs at the other end of the line, Dixon, doing his ugly deeds, had found him. He must have asked for John by name. Was he counting on John's loyalty or his ignorance? Probably both. John was eager to please him. Dixon had mentioned that John had asked repeatedly to be advanced into the hurly-burly of the trading pits. He was not ready, Dixon said, had not been around long enough. He kept John on the order desk, although John filled in down here whenever he could. Like all the runners, the clerks, this business's perpetual flotsam and jetsam, John apparently shared the common dream: Get experience. Get a seat. Get rich. The pits remained one of the few places left where an unpromising young person, a high-school loser, a kid without an electric guitar or four-three speed could still hit it big. John, Stern took it, wanted one more chance to make it.

John slid out of the booth while Al took his place. His son-in-law greeted Stern with much the same look of dismay Peter had recently. After a futile effort at conversation, they returned to MD's office. The only space John had of his own was a desk in the midst of the tumultuous back office. John stopped there to throw down various papers, then directed Stern to a conference room. A magnificent photo of Kate stood on the desk amid John's piles. His daughter, Stern thought again, was an exceptional beauty.

Even chatting with his father-in-law, John looked childishly uncomfortable. His huge shoulders sloped, and he idly fingered an envelope on the desk. He wore the uniform of the floor, MD's unstructured navy cotton jacket, corduroys, and a knotted tie dragged three or four inches below his open collar. A photo ID hung from his pocket.

What was there about this young man that Stern found so infuriating? He was reminiscent sometimes of a comic-strip oaf, so large and amiable that he deserved a balloon over his head: *Duh*. He was not dumb. Clara, for years, had been at pains to make that point. He had had no difficulty finishing college, long after his athletic career had ended. But there was a fecklessness about him. Large, apple-cheeked, blond, plumper than in his playing days, he looked like an inflated two-year-old, with as little guile. Stern was convinced that the present matter would render him numb. He would have no intuition about how to proceed and few resources with which to manage the strain of the coming months. Stern had seen these situations throughout his professional life: a family member, a business colleague, thrown a rope by a prosecutor, offered freedom in exchange for testimony. Some tossed it back, with royal indifference. But not many. Most tried to save themselves, bargaining with the truth and appealing to those they implicated for understanding. They ended up scorned by everyone. It was hard to imagine John having the suppleness to endure this storm.

Stern had stood to close the door and after a brief preface came to the point.

"Dixon Hartnell is being investigated by a federal grand jury."

"Ooo," said John. He looked like a carpenter who had just walloped his thumb.

"Yes. It is very unpleasant."

"What for?"

"Well, I think I should let someone else explain the details to you. In general, the government seems to suspect some form of improper trading ahead of customer orders. Has anyone from the FBI attempted to speak with you? A chap named Kyle Horn?"

John shook his head. He didn't think so. "What does he look like?"

"Big fellow." Big blond goyishe-looking lunk in a cheap sport coat, thought Stern. But that would not do.

John again shook his head uncertainly. You would think FBI

credentials might make an impression, even on John, but there was never any telling. Stern removed the subpoena from his briefcase and tried to explain what it meant.

"Due to our relationship—yours and mine—the prosecutors were courteous enough to allow me to receive this for you. However, because I already represent Dixon, you should consult with another lawyer before you answer the government's questions."

"What kind of questions?"

"I could speculate, John, but that would probably not be best."

John squinted. He didn't get it, of course. Stern explained that the government believed he had valuable information.

"They want to use me to get him?"

"Exactly."

The large baffled look Stern would have predicted rose up in John's eyes. A deer in the road. He had no idea what to do. The conflicts were between all the simple things that he took as harmonious. Loyalty. Truthfulness. Self-preservation.

"John, you and your lawyer must decide whether you wish to negotiate with the government for immunity. If that is the case, then your lawyer will give the prosecutors a prediction, a proffer, of what you would say."

"Yeah," said John, "but what if I don't want to talk?"

"Again, John, that is a good question for you to put to your lawyer. But the government can always choose to grant you immunity without regard to your desires, in which event your choices are between answering questions and jail."

"Jail?" John took this in, too, with continuing ponderous reflection. "I really don't know that much."

As this conversation proceeded, Stern had gradually felt his heart declining, and with this response, it plunged the remaining distance. 'Not that much,' said John. But more than nothing at all. Dixon would be safe only with virtual amnesia on John's part. Even the vaguest memory of who was behind the trades would do for the government, especially if they succeeded in tracing the profits into Dixon's hands. And sitting here, his son-in-law exhibited a discomfort most telling to a practiced eye. There was no outraged inquiry from John about what this trading ahead had to do with him, or how the prosecutors might have gotten his name. He knew the government's interest in him was well placed.

"What does he say about all this? Dixon? Can you say?"

Stern shook his head. But he felt for an instant like holding his breath. A moment of the most delicate sort had arisen. With somebody else, another employee, Stern would have ventured a comment whose direction was as faint but discernible as an idling wind: 'This is, of course, a critical matter for Dixon, his entire life and business are at stake.' But John was without subtlety. He might ask an impossible question—'You mean I should lie?'—or, even worse, take Stern's comments as a commandment. In all, Dixon—and Stern—would have to trust John's lawyer to make the appropriate assessments and to offer the correct guidance.

"Where am I going to get this lawyer from?" John asked.

"I have some names I might suggest, if you would like."

"Oh, sure."

"MD will indemnify you—pay your expenses—so you need not worry about that."

Stern was working on the list right now, writing on a piece of office stationery, names and phone numbers. George Mason. Raymond Horgan. No one would quite manage to reconcile the diverse needs of John's circumstances as well as he could have, but that was out of the question, and Stern, in any event, saw the wisdom of his not serving as scoutmaster on this trail. Just these few minutes had changed his estimate of John for good.

John took the list and shrugged. He had better get back to the floor, he said. He continued to wear his usual look, furtive and confused. Watching John hulk off to the elevator, Stern felt a ruthless anger with Dixon gathering again. How could he? How could he have embroiled this boy in the usual piggish market high jinks? But the answer was too obvious. Dixon with his infallible calculation of what was best for himself had no doubt recognized that his greatest protection was in a family member less experienced in the business. Easiest probably to give sotto-voce instructions, knowing they would not be questioned, or, if the time came, willingly recalled. Soon, Stern was going to have to turn his attention to the issue of when and how to get out of the case. If there was an indictment and John was a government witness, Stern could never handle the matter at trial. Cross-examining his daughter's husband was unthinkable. Perhaps he should also give a list of lawyers to Dixon and exit post haste. But he recognized his own lack of conviction. Just now, Stern was not eager to sever any other long-term relations. And he had resisted breaking with Dixon for many years.

Part of that, of course, was for Silvia's sake. Nor should one overlook the force of gratitude. Much of Stern's present practice, in which he most often represented lawyers and bankers and corporate officials, could be attributed to the fact that he had become known as Dixon's lawyer. It had been his exit from the grimy world of the police courts into the arena of high-class crime—embezzlements and frauds, tax matters, bribery, and now and then a murder of passion. Dixon—a classy borderline operator—had, by the peculiar logic of these things, elevated Stern, and it was virtually an instinct in him never to give short shrift to anyone who had helped him in his practice.

Yet he knew that the things that attached him to Dixon were not simply external. After thirty-two years practicing law, though his acquaintances were legion, his admirers many, Stern, in a way he seldom felt inclined to meditate upon, was apt at times to feel somehow abandoned—left to himself. Oh, there were hundreds of persons he cared for, whose lives and ideas interested him, and with whom he felt an eager mutuality. He got on the elevator in the courthouse and there were always half a dozen people to greet him. He was well known, likable, eager to please, and reluctant to give offense. Stern had his circle, mostly men near his age, primarily lawyers and judges, a number of them Yiddish speakers like his mother, subtle, clever people whose talk of books and sports and business gossip he regularly shared over lunch and sincerely valued. Good company. But he had in mind more than that. He meant the kind of unguarded male affinity that young men on teams, in gangs, on street corners had. Did women, domestication, destroy that? Or the fierce struggles of the daily world where every man was your enemy? Who knew? Yet Dixon remained. He was present. Stern could pay him no further compliment. But, like a granite marker beside the road, Dixon seemed to be the man who had always been nearby.

My brother-in-law, thought Stern, alone in the tiny room where John had abandoned him. Brother. In. Law. What kind of peculiar term was that?

18

To Kindle County Symphony Hall, with its wedding-cake balconies and ceiling frosted with wreaths of gold, where Clara Mittler and Alejandro Stern had passed their initial evening together, Stern now came on his first night out with Helen Dudak. The coincidence did not strike him until Adolph Fronz, the elderly conductor, raised his baton, and then the thought quickly added to Stern's discomfort. He had very nearly broken this engagement; only his kindly impulses toward Helen and his reluctance to offend her had made him carry through. It was a sad fact, shameful, awful—choose your pejorative adjective— but Radczyk's report had taken something from him that even the moment in the garage doorway had not. He had been a larger and more essential failure than he had imagined. Sex mattered. Ever and always. This he was learning, and his feelings now— alternating between vertiginous rage and desolation—left him deeply disinclined toward any female. The notion of spending an entire night attempting to be the charming, alluring gentleman of a few weeks before was simply out of the question. At the last moment, having spied tonight's tickets for one of Clara's many symphony series thumbtacked to the kitchen bulletin board, he had phoned Helen to propose this change.

'I cooked,' Helen said simply.

Music, then supper later, perhaps?

'All right.' Helen was obliging. He found himself enormously relieved. In the dark hall, while Fronz twirled and the players strummed and tooted, he would be alone, free from the need to prattle. Afterwards, the weariness of the work week could overcome him.

"I don't quite know why," Helen told him at intermission, "but I wouldn't have picked you for symphonic music. More quartets," she said, "or a single guitar." They stood in the lobby, blinking in the sudden lights. Couples Clara and he had seen here for years lifted their hands in greeting. But no one came near. With an entirely unpredictable force, a gust of grief and remorse blew into Stern, as he realized he had started his new life. For Helen, he smiled ruefully.

"I am indiscriminate." Stern touched his ear. "Tone deaf. I cannot tell the difference between the Kindle symphony and the high-school band." He had kept this fact from Clara for thirty-some years, though when it turned out that Marta could not tell one note from another, she must have entertained suspicions.

"Oh, Sandy." Helen held his wrist as they laughed together at his failings. Why was it that he always forgot how much he liked Helen Dudak until he was beside her? She looked marvelous. Her fox-colored hair had a crisp outline that betrayed a trip to the beauty shop, and she wore a simple black dress peeled back from her shoulders. Against all expectation, as the lights went down once more, he found himself pleased to be here.

"So you went to the symphony for all those years and never knew what you were listening to?" asked Helen, as they were driving off afterwards. She was turned fully about to face him, seated girlishly on her knees. It was typical of Helen and her instinct for important nuance that she had returned to this subject. They were headed toward her home for dinner. In the end, there was no way to say no. Besides, Helen's company was soothing. And after all his laments over the untrustworthiness of women, he was now full of a more familiar feeling which they had always reliably satisfied: he was extremely hungry.

"Clara enjoyed it."

"I recall. But—" Helen said, then stopped.

"Yes?"

"It's nothing."

"Please."

"I guess I was wondering why you would go now."

"Ah," said Stern, hoping to conjure up some tactful response, and vaguely frightened to find her so astute. Out the window, the center city flashed by, uninhabited, ghostly in the isolated pools of mercury light, the doorways dark. Helen, to his relief, continued on her own.

"I suppose I was going to give you advice."

"Feel free."

"No," she said. "There's really no comparison between my circumstance and yours."

"Duly noted," Stern said. "You were thinking?"

"Oh, just that, as awful as it is, there are things to enjoy in being alone again. The liberty of it. Finding what's your own." As the streetlights flowed across her, Helen turned back to measure his response. "I'm sure this is terribly offensive."

"No, no," said Stern. He was eager to agree, pleased to show that he understood her good intentions, and happy to foster the thought that he had suggested the symphony out of some unthinking reflex. And, in fact, this was a valuable notion. A good solid person of real judgment, Helen had hit on something that he otherwise would have missed. Whatever his misery, parts— large parts of him—had accepted his new bachelorhood with relish. Not just the brief period of cavorting. The moment right now was one more instance—relaxed, at ease, and able to speak about himself in a way Clara seldom encouraged. Clara had her minute agendas, her quiet steps which she always danced. For many years (Too many years! he thought, and felt again the accustomed iron point of guilt) he had recognized in some unspoken way that she utilized all this silent planning as a means to escape torpor and depression. But the point was that she had done it, he had known it, adjusted to it, and now it was no longer there, like a ticking metronome gone silent. Wounded and reeling, his soul had nonetheless expanded in the recent circumstance, reentering regions closed off for years.

Helen served a splendid supper. She made a salad of shrimp rémoulade, and cooked a small piece of blackened fish. She stood over the iron skillet with the smoke rising, drinking her wine and chatting, like a cooking-show host. Rick, her younger child, a sophomore now at Easton, dreamed, like many nineteen-year-olds, of being a criminal defense lawyer. Helen relayed his questions. Did Stern believe most of his clients were innocent? How could he defend them if he didn't? How did he feel when he found out they were guilty?

These were old questions, the puzzles of a lifetime, and Stern enjoyed answering Helen, who listened alertly. Some spoke of the nobility of the law. Stern did not believe in that. Too much of the grubby boneshop, the odor of the abattoir, emanated from every courtroom he had entered. It was often a nasty business. But the law, at least, sought to govern misfortune, the slights and injuries of our social existence that were otherwise wholly random. The law's object was to let the seas engulf only those who had been selected for drowning on an orderly basis. In human affairs, reason would never fully triumph; but there was no better cause to champion. Helen sat back, drinking her wine, attentive.

For dessert, she brought out berries. She lifted the wine bottle toward Stern, but he shook it off. Helen had drunk freely; Stern had had a single glass. He was drinking too much lately, which never before had been his habit; his head was sore on many occasions.

"As usual," he said, "I have done all the talking, and about myself."

"You're wonderful to listen to, Sandy. You know that."

"Do I? Well, I appreciate a receptive audience."

Helen looked at him directly.

"You have one here," she said somewhat softly. They were silent, considering one another. "Look," said Helen Dudak. "You know it. I know it. So I'll say it. I'm available. All right?"

"Why, certainly."

She raised her dark eyebrows. "In all senses."

For an instant, Stern's heart actually seemed to shiver. What was it about Helen? She had a way with facts which could be utterly disarming. She laid out what was on her mind with no more ceremony than a butcher tossing meat onto the scale. But they both knew they had come to an auspicious pass.

"You're not ready," she said immediately. "I understand that." She reached for her wine and quaffed it, her first overtly nervous gesture. "But when you are, you are. We're on our way to the twenty-first century, Sandy. There are no proprieties left about this kind of thing. Not everyone goes nerve-dead in mourning."

He was not sure what he'd say if she gave him the chance. Certainly it would not do to explain his circumstances to Helen, that like a vampire he had been out ravishing when he was supposed to be dead, while now he had been laid into his crypt with a stake right through the heart. Fortunately, however, explanation did not appear necessary. This was, Stern sensed, well scripted, and Helen had assigned herself all the lines. She had a missionary role. She was going to heal Stern, sell him on himself. In a second she would be telling him that he was still attractive. He had known Helen for decades now and recognized this forwardness as uncharacteristic. This was not Helen's true nature, but rather the new and improved model, head-shrunk and reorganized. So much of this seemed self-consciously political. The formerly colonized nations should engage in self-determination. Speak your mind. Admit your desires. You were equal and entitled. He was less hopeful than she about the virtues of this revolution. But, for tonight, it was just as well. He would play his part. Here sits Mr. Alejandro Stern, history's first bald coquette.

"You're quite an attractive man, Sandy."

He could not suppress his smile. Again, she misunderstood.

"Do you think that the only thing women find attractive is a twenty-year-old body?"

Here was one of the five or six highest-order mysteries of life. What *did* women find attractive? Attention. That he knew. Strength of one kind or another, he had long supposed. But the physical element entered somewhere as well.

"Whatever that might be, Helen, I think I lack some of the essential ingredients."

"I don't think so. I think you have all the essential ingredients. Maybe some of the inessentials—" Her hand trailed off in space and they both laughed merrily.

God knows, there was no sense in pretending he did not enjoy this. He did. Given the frame of mind with which he had started the evening, her honesty, affection, her excitement in his presence seemed a heartening miracle. He took her hand.

"Helen, this is a charming offer. I am sure it will obsess me." As usual, he enjoyed being elusive. He was back to his essential aspect, the foreigner, unknown and hard to figure. His ambiguous look was apparently too much for her. She shrank back and shook her head.

"God, I've made a hash of this."

"Nonsense."

"Oh, Sandy." She covered her face with both hands. "I'm drunk. I can't believe this." She sat, eyes closed, suddenly flushed, suffering intensely. The sight of dear, honest Helen so humiliated moved him terribly. He was beginning to take on the emotional lability of an adolescent. For now, no matter. He stood at once and from behind her chair wrapped his arms around her.

"Helen," he said.

"I'm drunk," she repeated. "I let myself come on like a lush sitting at a bar."

"You appeared the true, kind soul you are. I am positively alight with flattered pride. And," he said, "I am enormously interested."

"You are?" She craned her neck straight back, so that she was looking at him upside down, a cute maneuver somehow befitting a person half her age. Her smile, too, was girlish.

"I am," said Mr. Alejandro Stern. He cared for her much too much not to embrace her. He leaned down to meet her, full of kind intentions and wholly unprepared for the spectacular jolt that lit him from the first contact. Helen, too, felt this and actually groaned. He came around the chair, took her in his arms. He touched both her breasts.

"Upstairs," she said, after a moment. She took him by the hand and led him to her bedroom. There he opened Helen's dress, pulled down the bodice, and helped her remove her brassiere. Her breasts were wide-set and flattened somewhat by age and the toils of female experience, but the sight, to Stern, remained deeply exciting. She left him to begin turning down the spread. Helen had loosened his tie and he pulled it from his collar.

It was then that he remembered Peter's caution. Stern remained stock-still. He was without indispensable equipment. This would be terrible.

"Helen," he said. She looked at him, but his mouth seemed merely to grope. "Helen, I find this most embarrassing—"

"Ohhh," said Helen. "Aren't you contemporary?" She pointed across the bed to a nightstand. "The top drawer."

Amid the pantyhose there was a package of condoms. He tried not to start. Helen, who had slipped her arms back into the top of her dress, so that it was languorously draped, smiled faintly.

"I'm not offended, if you're not. To tell you the truth, it's a necessity." He did not understand. "Birth control," she said.

"Why, Helen," said Stern. This news, somehow, pleased him.

"Don't get too excited," she said and tossed aside the

bedcover. "I'm in menopause. Like everyone else. Just not as far along."

Stern fingered the package. The economy size. Twenty-four and most of them gone. Dear Lord, modern life was disconcerting. Helen had come back around the bed to him. She pushed her arms free of each sleeve.

"Where were we?" she asked.

Afterwards, he lay with Helen in her bed. Somehow, tonight, he had been less adept. He had fumbled with that stupid latex thing, and their nervousness expressed itself as an almost comic courtesy. 'Is that all right?' 'Oh yes, yes, please.' Nonetheless, they lay here, quiet and adhering to one another, fully content. At some point, he thought, he was supposed to leave. But not just now. In an idle way, it occurred to him that he was a truly vile creature, one of those sly, conscienceless rapscallions out of some French bedroom farce, vowing chastity and then throwing himself on the first woman that passed into sight. What was wrong with him?

But he did not feel vile—or wrong. He had supposed from listening to TV and the movies and cocktail talk—from wherever it was these ideas came—that these couplings, called casual, were supposed to be loveless and numb. But here in the soft dark he found himself aswarm with gentle feelings. This woman, like Margy, would be dear to him for life. Was that self-deception? Or had pop mythology just missed the point. Was it intimacy and connection that everyone was seeking? He thought, oddly, of Dixon. Did the master swordsman also experience his thousand interludes this way? Yes. Probably. Even for Dixon there must have been more to his wandering than the chance to brag. He craved acceptance, tenderness, female succor, before returning to the world made harsh by men. So, too, Mr. Alejandro Stern. His life as he had always known it was gone, and the road down which he marched was largely unknown to him. What was ahead? The last months, he recognized quite suddenly, had been rife with fear. But not right now. For the moment, with Helen curled in the crook of his arm, her breathing against him slowing as she dove near sleep, he had stepped aside, taken time out, cooled himself in the refreshed air of night. For today, tonight, for the first fraction of time since it had happened, he was able to declare himself, however briefly, at peace.

For the occasion, Stern borrowed the 1954 Chevy of his law school classmate George Murray. At this time in America, automobiles had only recently ceased being shaped like teakettles and Stern regarded this vehicle, which came equipped merely with a heater, as sleek and impressive. He had not made the acquaintance of many girls in the United States; there seemed to be so few opportunities. For years, he had been ahead of himself in school and, accordingly, was of little interest to the young women around him. And since he was seventeen, he had worked each weekend, driving a punchboard route that took him all about the Middle West in a dilapidated, foul-smelling truck owned by Milkie, his grubby one-eyed boss. Over time, his inexperience seemed to compound itself. Foreign-born, Hispanic-accented, Jewish, he was apt in female company to feel like something set down here from another universe.

So he was grateful for Clara's ease with him. He crossed his feet trying to race her to the car door, but she remained amused and casual. Somehow, he made this dour young woman comfortable. As much as he aspired to her, blindly and instinctively, she perhaps thought he was all that she deserved.

"You know," she said, as soon as he was seated, "this was really my idea. I begged my father to ask you."

"This," said Stern, gesturing to the two of them, "was my idea. You, however, put it into action."

"Oh, you are smooth." She smiled. "Daddy says that. He thinks you're very bright."

"Does he?" Stern, unaccustomed to city driving, watched the road in desperation. If this car suffered any injury, he would have to flee the state. Murray had made that clear.

"What do you think of him?" she asked. "My father?"

Stern, in spite of himself, was too distracted to prevent himself from groaning.

Clara laughed out loud. She touched his arm as he moved the gearshift along the column.

"I'm terrible, aren't I? I'm not like this, Mr. Stern. It's all your fault. Do you know that I am usually so quiet? People will tell you that about me."

"What else would they tell me?" Stern asked. He had fallen

into a companionable mood. She smiled, but it was the wrong question.

"Tell me about Argentina," she said after a moment.

The concert was Ravel. She spoke to him about the music, making offhand reference to passage that she supposed were as plain to him as if they were words written on the page. At the intermission, he bought orange juice. Only one bottle, for her. His normal penury had guided him without reflection and he saw at once that he had disconterted her by making his lack of means so plain. But she refused to be flustered. She offered him the straw that had been punched down through the cardboard bottle cap and made him take a sip. And there something occurred. The concert hall was crowded; the grand acoustics of the building amplified the hubbub, and the lobby lights were stingingly bright after the prior hour in darkness. But the moment to Stern grew more intimate than an embrace. Somehow her character had become as clear to him as the notes which had been played: she was kind. Committedly. Unceasingly. She cared more for kindness than social grace. This vision of her overtook him, and Stern, in a kind of swoon, felt himself suddenly immersed in that warm current and his heart swimming toward her.

"That was wonderful," she told him as they moved along beneath the theater lights after the concert. She had carried her coat out the door, and they stood, buffeted by passersby, as she struggled with one sleeve. Summoning himself, Stern asked her to accompany him to Chinatown for dinner. He had contemplated this moment all week. He would have to take her somewhere. Chinatown, he eventually decided, answered the imperatives of economics and romance, and the thought of the meal—he was thin in those years and always hungry—had tantalized him for days. She refused, however. The money, surely, on her mind.

"I must tell you, Miss Mittler, that I intend to take a telephone next week." This was true. He had held off only because he was not certain Henry would allow him to keep his office. But the remark, spoken in jest, succeeded in amusing her. This, Stern recognized at once, was a kind of rare power with her. Under the marquee lights, Clara Mittler easily laughed. She was wearing a tiny pink hat, with a trimming of

white veil, and she reached up to hold it.

"Next week," she said. "We'll make a separate outing of it.
Why rush ourselves tonight?"

Agreed. He offered her his arm and she took it. They strode
off together through the sumphony crowd, the men in over-
coats, the women in fur stoles and jewels. Stern felt a swell of
pleasure. He was certain that someone there looked up and
thought, What a handsome young American couple.

19

The phone message said "Margy Allison." If it had read, simply, "Margy" he would have realized who it was an instant sooner and felt a lesser pang. He had not had a word with her since they had parted at the hotel. No more flowers—not a call to say hello or, more pertinently, to mention that he might have inflicted a social disease. He'd had every intention. But it would have been easier to have the Department of Public Health send a postcard than explain this matter by phone. And how was he to account for the underlying facts, while protecting Clara's privacy—and his own? Peter had already called to report that the specimen tested spotlessly; after the second blood test, due in a couple of weeks, he'd have a clean bill of health and nothing to tell her. Better to wait, he had thought. But now, with the message in hand, he was cornered. Well, he had gone the great circle in a few months, from faithful husband to complete cad. He sighed and asked Claudia to get Margy on the phone.

"Hi, there," she said. Stern thought he detected a chord of good cheer in her voice, but his hopes were soon dashed. She was being ironic. "Long time, no nothin'," Margy added.

The line gathered sound. What had ever made him think he had skill with women?

"If I said I am horribly embarrassed, would you believe me?"

"Shore," said Margy. "I'd believe that. I'd believe that makes a lotta sense."

She was angry. Indignant. Stern sank a little lower in his chair, trying to hold himself together around a livid core of guilty feelings. She was going to give it to him. He had it coming.

"I am afraid—" he said, then stopped. He was going to say that he was new to all of this and, accordingly, confused. But it was much too pathetic an excuse.

"Of what?" said Margy. "You gonna tell me there's somethin you're scared of?" Skeered.

"Margy, I am truly sorry. Truly. You are much too fine a person to be treated so shabbily."

"You bet I am," she said.

"I know that. I really—"

"But here I am callin you."

"I am very pleased you did so."

"I didn't call you to please you. I got somethin you better see."

"Me?"

"Yeah, you. Like it or not, I figure you're the guy I gotta talk to about this."

When the thought came to him, it was like being stabbed. Oh God, he thought. Oh God. He closed his eyes. She had it.

"I sat there lookin at this goddamn thing and that's what I thought—well, I'm gonna be talkin to that rascal now."

"Oh, Margy," said Stern. He waited a moment in unbearable shame. "When did this appear?"

"Yesterday."

Naturally. Count on Peter to get it all wrong.

"This is my responsibility," said Stern. "You should have no doubt about that."

"Why would I have any doubt about it? I'm callin you, ain't I?"

Stern continued to keep his eyes closed. Never in his life had he undergone a moment like this. Never. He had always treasured his honor. One hand crept absently along the desk until he recollected that this furtive search was futile. He was going to buy cigars today. That was a promise to himself. A sworn oath.

When he did not speak, she said, "I need you to tell me whatall I gotta do."

"Of course."

"How long is this goddamn thang gonna last, anyway?"

What was it that Peter had said? Three weeks to a lifetime. He told her simply that one could never be certain. He had no wish to get into details.

"That's great. I suppose I gotta come down there?"

"Here?"

"Where else?" She was apparently confused about treatment or diagnosis.

"I would think everything necessary can be done in Chicago."

"Well, I'd think so, too," she said, "but it ain't gonna be like that."

He had no idea what outraged impulse she was giving vent to now.

When the thought of Helen came to him abruptly, he could not breathe. He sat back in the chair rigidly, dumb. Surely, there could not be a problem there, too. Peter had virtually promised. And if he was wrong twice? Stern's eyes were now open wide.

Margy asked if he was there.

"I am sorry." He asked her for a moment and pulled himself closer to the desk, gripping the glass by its green edge. All that control he had exerted, that excessive, ugly compulsive grasp he always had on himself and had always quietly despised—it had a purpose. He saw that now.

"You know I only got three weeks," Margy said.

"Three weeks?" he asked.

"Till I'm supposed to be there. This thing says June 27th."

What thing, he almost said. But he did not. A miracle process of reconstruction was immediately at work. Oh, he was still alive. He understood now: she had been served with a grand jury subpoena. He slapped himself on the chest, where he could feel his heart pounding.

Answering his questions, she provided a short account of events the day before. The subpoena had been served by Chicago FBI agents, local functionaries uninvolved in the investigation, who merely dropped off the paper, telling her she would have to testify on the twenty-seventh about the documents called for.

"You are quite right," said Stern. "You must come here. I was thinking for a moment that they might not require a personal appearance before the grand jury, but since they told you otherwise—" He was lying fabulously now—in an instant he would have the entire conversation retooled. "So you say the twenty-seventh." He reached for his appointment book, but Claudia had it. He did not bother to retrieve it. "Yes, that is fine. Well, I shall see you here then."

"That's all?" she asked.

"No, no," said Stern, "of course not. I must meet with you, review the documents , determine why they have bothered you."

"But you're my lawyer. It won't be like John. Like you said you're responsible."

"I must check with the Assistant United States Attorney to be certain. But I must say—" Stop, he told himself. Cease. He was blathering, still electric with relief. "Margy, put the subpoena on the fax machine. Right now." For a moment they were on the line together, unspeaking, difficult small things gathering in the hushed whirring. Then Stern announced that Claudia was summoning him to another call, a fiction out of whole cloth, and placed Margy on hold until the subpoena copy was laid on his desk. It sought corporate records and, properly, should have been served on him as the corporation's lawyer. He had not taken Klonsky's warning to mean they would go this far. But Chief Judge Winchell had let the prosecutors get away with this tactic in other cases where they had argued it was necessary to be sure that employees would be exacting in producing documents. And as usual, Stern noted, the government's informant had been on target in identifying who would know MD's records best.

The contents of the subpoena were in most regards predict-able. Listed first were approximately two dozen dates; the government wanted every ticket written on the central order desk those days. By asking for records of all of MD's business on each date, the government was continuing its effort to obscure its interests by not focusing on individual transactions. But amid this volume of papers would be the tickets John had written at Dixon's instruction for the orders that had ended up booked to the error account. Once again, the informant was right on the mark.

In the subpoena's second paragraph, the grand jury requested all MD's canceled checks for amounts over $250 written in the first four months of the year. This, Stern took it, was a continuing step in the government's efforts to trace into Dixon's hands the illegal profits made trading ahead. It was also an encouraging sign; apparently, as Dixon predicted, the subpoena to his bank had been unavailing. Stern had spent an evening or two examining copies of the records the bank had produced and could see nothing more noteworthy than the occasional six-figure personal checks for investments and purchases that were part of Dixon's millionaire life-style. Certainly, there were no large deposits from unexplained sources.

"What is this last item?" Stern asked Margy, as he got back on the line. His pulse had retreated to normal. He read: " 'All account opening documents, purchase and sale records, confirmations and monthly statements for account 06894412, the Wunderkind Account.' Do we know what that might be?"

"I been lookin at that," said Margy.

"And?"

"And he's a clever old dog. You got the error-account statements I gave you?"

Stern put her on hold a moment while Claudia pulled the file.

"Look at Jan 24," she instructed. "You see where the error account's got a buy and a sell of fifty thousand bushels of oats?"

He saw it. Dixon—someone, to indulge the formal presumptions—had bracketed these orders around a surge in oat prices caused when Chicago Ovens bought more than two million bushels that day in Chicago.

"Trades make a profit of about forty-six thousand, right?"

He was in no position to follow, let alone challenge her arithmetic. He simply agreed.

"Now look at the next day. You see where there's a buy of two April 90 silver contacts in the error account?"

"Yes." According to the posting notes in the error account statement, this trade, like the oat transactions the day before, had been made under an account number of which MD had no record. Therefore, all the trades had been set over in the error account.

"Now guess what the cash value of the silver is? Surprise you that it's a little under forty-seven thousand?"

Everything was a surprise at this point, but Stern, recognizing his role, merely said "No."

"Now look down the error account statement," she said. "See the two silver contracts again?"

" 'Journal transfer to A/C 06894412.' " Stern read the note from the statement, then looked again at the subpoena. This was the number of the Wunderkind account. As usual, he did not understand.

"See, he used the profit he made in oats on the twenty-fourth to buy silver on the twenty-fifth. The cost of the silver gets debited to the error account, and after it's paid for, he makes accounting entries and journals the silver into this other account, Wunderkind. See? He's turned the profit into silver and he's got it in his hot little hand."

"And does anything similar happen on other occasions?"

"Far as I can see, it's every doggone time. Makes some money tradin ahead, then he throws on an error position to absorb the profit and shifts it over to the same account."

"Wunderkind?"

"You betchum."

Stern explained it to himself to be sure he understood: it was a complicated device to move the profits made by trading ahead out of the error account. Once the profit was in hand, he could buy new contracts, making some mistake that would also put the new trade in the error account; after the error account paid for the new position, it was transferred to the account of Wunderkind—whatever or whoever he was. This was why Dixon had given him that sly look on the golf course.

"And what happens to all the positions which this Wunder account holds?"

"Dunno, cause I ain't got the records yet. He probably closed them right out and put the money in his pocket."

"And Wunderkind denotes what?"

"Beats me. Maybe it's the name on the account. Only thing is, I can see from the number it's a corporate account."

Stern nodded. So this race was heading into its home stretch. If the government could show that Dixon controlled this Wunderkind account, they would have the link they needed to blame all this on him. But from his expression on the golf course, it was probably a fair bet that Dixon had some final feint in store, another clever dodge to keep the feds from tracing these dirty dollars to him. A corporate account, Margy said. Perhaps the corporation's stock was held in trust, and the trust was controlled and funded from offshore. In the course of the IRS investigation a few years ago, Stern had seen Dixon utilize ploys like this, cagey maneuvers that would have done the CIA proud. It was John who remained the principal concern—what would he say to the government? If he stonewalled them or went halvesies with the truth, Klonsky and Sennett would threaten to prosecute John—and mean it. Stern shook his head again over the delicacy of his son-in-law's situation.

Stern asked Margy to be sure she had the records pulled together by the Monday before her appearance.

"Shore. I'll just work all weekend. What else is new? Think maybe I'll get in there Sunday night," said Margy in a leisurely way. "Stay over by the Gresham."

"Ah, yes," said Stern. "I see Claudia waving. It must be most urgent. Many thanks," he told Margy, "many thanks," and put down the phone, feeling queasy and grateful and free.

20

Twice in the last week, Stern had gone home in the morning to change for work and to look over the mail from the day before, having spent the night at Helen's. They had been out three times since their evening at the symphony—dinner, the theater—and she demonstrated on each occasion her ability to make him sweep aside the vexing detritus of his wrecked life. With Helen, he tended to hear only her beguiling musical laughter, her clear firm voice, and to feel, of course, the urgent throb of his reinvigorated romantic life. Dear, sweet Helen—she remained intent on improving him.

In yesterday's mail, Stern this morning found another copy of Westlab's bill, a pink form this time, bearing a red block-letter stamp which said OVERDUE. Yes, indeed, he thought at once. His most recent speculation was that, given the nature of the problem, Clara had consulted a female physician; he had gone paging through her phone book once again, looking for a name, even while he felt it would be fruitless. What could this doctor tell him? What could she change? But his curiosity was not all a matter of reason. He took this overdue notice as a direction from fate, and with Westlab's bill and his checkbook in hand he set out, as soon as he was dressed, to find the place where, in the middle days of February, a specimen from Clara Stern was cultured, examined, and, with clinical exactness, named. What if it was a mistake? he thought suddenly as he was driving, and then realized, as he had a hundred times before, that diagnosis was not the final issue. Clara had had a reason to suspect a problem. Only in the Bible and the tales of King Arthur did the virtuous have relations in their sleep.

Stern had never recognized the lab's address, but his street guide placed it on a small court tucked between two prominent commercial avenues, no more than five or six blocks from the Sterns' home in the Riverside neighborhood. And there it was, a low, flat-roofed brick building with casement windows, a construction style of the 1950s. He had been driving by Westlab for twenty years and never noticed. Within the building's glass doors there was little public space, a small waiting area with four plastic bucket seats bolted to a bar of steel, and a glass partition. At this window, he asked for Liz. She was beckoned and came forth, just as Radczyk had described her, dark and small, with short black hair cut into a fringe around her face. She wore gray slacks and heavy makeup; liner was glopped below her bottom lashes as well. She smiled attractively, accustomed, you could tell, to dealing with the public.

"I am Mr. Stern," he said. "This bill was sent to my wife before she passed away in late March. In the confusion of events, I am afraid I neglected it."

"Oh, *that's* all right," said Liz emphatically. A hand proffering absolution, casual but complete, passed vaguely by her nose.

He waited just an instant.

"There was probably a doctor's bill as well. Either we never received it or it was misplaced. I would like to contact the doctor to be sure the bill has not been overlooked, but I am not certain who that was. Could you give me the name of the physician who ordered the test? I am the executor of my wife's estate, if there is any concern—"

"Oh, no." Liz waved a hand the same way and, with Stern's copy of Westlab's statement was gone at once, receding into the visible office space, illuminated as in most buildings of that era by too much glaring fluorescence. From somewhere farther back came a vague antiseptic smell. Banging through the file drawers, Liz called out to another woman about something else, then returned, paging through a folder. She had not quite arrived at the window when she spoke.

'Calling,' he thought she had said.

"Pardon?"

"Do you know him? Dr. Nathaniel Cawley? His office is over on Grove. About three blocks. Here's the address." By now she had laid the folder down before Stern and showed him the test requisition, a long form of small type and boxes which had been filled out in the usual indecipherable doctorly hand. Nate's name and office address were stamped at the top of the form, but there was no question he had been the one to give the orders: he had signed, in a scribble, and had written "Viral culture for HSV-2" in a block for comments at the bottom of the page.

Weak and suddenly chill, Stern glanced up to find Liz looking at him oddly. Perhaps she was reacting to his dumb response or had recollected Radczyk, or had finally noticed what the test was for. His first impulse, however, was that he must continue to pretend, and he removed the gold pen from his inside suit pocket to write down Nate's address. There was no paper around, however, and instead, without speaking, he turned away.

"Did you want to pay this?" Liz was holding the bill.

He wrote out the check falteringly. He could not get the numbers right and had to tear up his first effort.

Nate! Outside, Stern fell heavily onto the cherry-colored leather of the front seat of the Cadillac. There was undoubtedly a way to explain. Drinking too much, or overcome by the involvements of his personal life, Nate had allowed this to skip his mind. Nonetheless, Stern was badly shaken. Nate was fuddled at times but steady. It alarmed him for incomprehensible reasons to think of a doctor as unreliable or inexact. He reached for the car phone; this model had come equipped with one. Stern had no use for it—his daily drive to the office was no more than ten minutes, and he could walk to both courthouses—but out of his love for gizmos and toys, he had let Claudia get him a number and he used the phone on any occasion. Now he flipped on the ignition, dialed information and then Nate's office.

"He's not in. Can I help you, Mr. Stern?"

"I must speak with him." He had shown Nate courtesy enough; he felt entitled to an immediate response. "It's something of an emergency."

The nurse paused. You could tell what she was thinking: Patients—everything was a crisis.

"He's at the hospital." She repeated the number. "Try to page him. He's in the middle of rounds, though. I'm not sure you'll get him."

He left his numbers—office, car, home—then dialed University Hospital. When he reached the page operator, he described the call as urgent. Behind him, near the doors of Westlab, a mother was dragging a screaming child up the walk toward the building. Stern turned about fully to watch this scene. The little boy apparently knew what was coming, for he was carrying on fiercely, almost lying on the ground. The mother herself was overcome; eventually Stern noticed that she was crying, too.

"This is Dr. Cawley."

"Nate, Sandy Stern."

"Sandy?" In his voice of something, frustration or disbelief.

"I shall be only a moment. It was important that I speak to you about Clara."

"Clara? Jesus, Sandy, I'm in the middle of grand rounds." Nate took a second to contain himself. "Sandy, can I talk to you about this later?"

"Nate, I apologize, but—"

"Look, Sandy, is it on this Westlab thing? Is that why you're calling? I've gotten your messages."

Nate, as he'd anticipated, was going to explain. In a prescient moment, Stern saw how compulsive and foolish he would look.

"I know it is a silly obsession, Nate, but—"

In a rush, Nate interrupted again.

"No, no, Sandy, it's my fault. I'm sorry I've made you chase me around, but I did look into it. Okay? I checked my files, I called Westlab, nobody knows what it's about. They have no records of any kind over there, and I don't either, so I don't know what to tell you. It's just a mistake, I'm sure. Okay? We've all checked thoroughly. Just let it go. All right?"

Stern found himself looking down at one palm, pink and completely empty. What is it? he thought. What now? But there was already something moving through him in a subdued rumble, so that it was only another instant before he finally made the connection: Nate was lying. He had been lying all along. For just the faintest second, Stern needed to remind himself to breathe as he listened to Nate's words go stumbling on. What more was he missing? he wondered. And then, as so often of late, he decided that he had no wish to know.

Afterwards, he was unsure how the conversation had ended. The receiver, with the lighted touch pad on its back, was recradled and he was looking at his hand on it before he had

recovered. He started to redial, but a sage voice urged him to
gather himself first. He had learned something in the courtroom.
A liar, called out, lied about that. Nate would deny misleading
him. If confronted, he would tell Stern that, no matter what the
form said, it was wrong. He needed to be composed—far more
than he was now—to deal with this.

He slowly placed the car in gear and pulled out of the lot.
When he had driven a block or two, under the large stout trees
that rose up along the parkways in this part of town, the thought
drove through him, sharp and sudden, as if he had been impaled:
She had hated him. Despised him. That, somehow, was what
animated all this deceit. He could understand what motivated
Nate; that had taken only a few minutes' reflection. He was lying
out of cowardice—because he did not want to face Stern with
the facts. Not merely Clara's unfaithfulness. That was the
symptom, not the cause. But the disease, a kind of brutal and
unremitting spousal discontent, was too painful to disclose. And
yet it was obvious in every act, in the reeking mess she had left
behind for her husband to discover. Never able to speak her
mind, she had settled for a graphic demonstration—a life, a
home, bespattered and fouled.

And was he to pretend now that he never knew this? Along
River Drive, he was approaching one of many vista points, a
space of concrete, with an old Greystone wall bordering the
river, and a line of park benches looking out toward the green
hills of Moreland and the fashionable suburbs on the western
bank. Abruptly he parked and crossed the street. He leaned over
the thick wall, watching the swift waters sluicing by with their
hidden, welling currents, twinkling, lambent—La Chandelle—
then fell back onto one of the benches.

Only in the years when the children had gone off one by one to
college was anything apparent. By the time Kate departed, a
brooding desperate quality had come over Clara, a suffering
lightlessness that would not yield. Unfalteringly polite, she was
regularly out of sorts, and he was unable to soothe her. In the
most indirect of approaches, he had suggested counseling, which
she instantly rebuffed. Always mute about her discontent, Clara
complained now periodically about his unavailability. The office.
His trials. His cigars—it was during this time that he was
forbidden to smoke at home. The message in retrospect was

clear: He still had his life, in which she had never been included. She had little left. Shocked to be rebuked so directly, Stern had avoided her. He accepted a series of engagements out of town— a lengthy trial in Kansas City, seminars and demonstrations of courtroom techniques. He had gone flying across America for months, until he had shrewdly suggested the irresistible, a trip together to the Far East. In Japan, with its monstrous cities and mysterious gardens, they came together again.

But before that, during the Kansas City trial, on one of his rare days at home, he had had what he saw now was the opportunity to look into her heart. The trial, concerning a nasty conspiracy of politicians and union officials, had gone on for fourteen weeks. Stern would fly home on Friday nights, leave again midday Sunday. He was present in body only; he spoke on the phone most of the weekend, or worked at the office downtown preparing for the upcoming government witnesses. On one of those Sundays, Clara had asked him to come with her to a showing of Japanese pots, raiku—ceramics fired directly in the blaze, then rolled in straw for markings. Clara was a passionate admirer of all the Japanese arts. Stern did not have time for this outing, but he agreed, hoping to appease her, knowing she would feel free to buy a substantial piece only if he was along. She pointed at one pot after another. Did he like it? Once or twice, he made the mistake of allowing his impatience to show. When he saw the effect of this, he began to gesture toward the shelves himself. This one? That? She found his sudden eagerness patronizing and abruptly suggested they leave. 'Certainly there must be one,' he said. She yearned for few physical possessions.

Tersely, Clara shook her head and went ahead of him out the door. A moment, like so many of late, of wholly different aspirations. At the head of the staircase in the dark gallery building, he stumbled and reached back for her hand. The iron newel saved him. When he looked up, Clara had her brow drawn down wearily in irritation, and a rare edge was in her eye. She might as well have proceeded with the pronouncement: He did not please her, in a deep abiding way. The hand he had reached back for, he remembered, had remained at her side.

He had believed that was past. Instead, it seemed now that this was to be Clara's parting look. Guilt had overcome her in the end and she had left behind a message begging forgiveness. But

she apologized only for her conduct. The rest could not be
changed. Clara's heart, too, had been set to the fire and inscribed
with this hideous grudge. Better she should have torn apart the
house, broken all the china, slashed the pictures on the walls.
Instead, full of rage and despair, she had smashed and destroyed
herself, and left him to wound himself whenever he stooped for
any of the pieces.

He spoke to her of Argentina.

*His father had come from Berlin in 1928 to serve as a
doctor in the agricultural settlements of Russian Jews who
had arrived in the 1880s and put down near Santa Fe. There
Bruno Stern had met Marta Walinsky. From subsequent
comments, Stern took it that his mother believed she had
acquired the sum of life's meaningful attainments by
marrying a physician. Jacobo came at once, and four years
later Alejandro; Silvia five years after that.*

*In the same way some actors are always on stage, Papa
was always a doctor. He wore a full beard and he was
wedded by the heat of fierce anxiety to his professional
manner. He walked through the streets of Entre Ríos in his
white coat and brought it home to Mama to launder. He wore
three-piece woolen suits in every season. His fingernails
were carefully pared and his hands were whitish and bathed
at the start of every day in lavender cologne. He hung his
stethoscope about his neck, picked up his medical bag, and
walked down two streets to his infirmary each morning.
Mama told him that Papa was important. He made people
better. They respected him. Papa loved respect. Something
about respect—Stern never knew the precise dimension of
his father's failure—brought the family when Stern was
almost five to Buenos Aires, with its gracious, cosmopolitan
air. One more unfortunate move. The city folk took them for
rubes, and Mama's country relatives treated them at once as
disagreeable porteños.*

*In the United States, word that Stern had grown up as a
Jew in Argentina was taken as suggesting dangers only
slightly less than if his father had stayed on in Berlin. To be
sure, among the Argentines there were many anti-Semites.*

Mama's cousin Ritella recalled from her rocking chair with emphatic flourishes the Semana Trágica, *tragic week, when she was in her teens and roving mobs had entered the Jewish quarter in Buenos Aires with iron bars and barrel staves, beating any Bolshevik they found, which was taken loosely to include virtually any Jew. But for the most part, the years in B.A. that Stern recalled were not dramatically different from what he might have experienced growing up in Chicago or New York. In the area north and west of Corrientes and Callas, nearly 300,000 Jews—many of them, like his mother, the children of Russian immigrants who had come to the Littoral province late in the nineteenth century—maintained a full community life. There were three Yiddish dailies, kosher butcher shops and bakeries, the tiny storefront synagogues. These were poor people— shopkeepers and factory workers, dockhands and meatpackers—who, as Mama put it, sold their labor to survive.*

To Clara, as she sat across from him in the Chinese restaurant in a booth whose sides were magnificently tooled with red-eyed dragons with green tails, the familiar details were not emphasized. He spoke of the Indians who trod barefoot in Entre Ríos; the country's uncouth gauchos. He explained the crazy quilt of Argentine culture, with its diverse European element of British uprightness, Italian amplitude, and Hispanic bravery and guilt. The excitement of a far-off place and its customs thrilled her; you could see it in her face, but she sat silent as a cat. At times, you would think she was not capable of speaking. He, in the meantime, carried on with animation about what he most often felt inclined to hide. Her luminous look felt to Stern like a kind of homage.

Afterwards, she accepted his arm and they walked through the park back to George Murray's Chevy.

"You really must stop calling me Mr. Stern."

"Very well. What are you called, then. Alejandro, is it?"

"Most people call me Sandy."

"Very good," she said. "Sandy." Even with her perfect manners, he could tell that she struggled not to react to the inanity of the name. He joked that at last they had been

introduced.

"Oh, I knew who you were."

"Pardon?"

"I recognized you. From Easton."

"Did you?" He was quite surprised. By his private calculations, she was too old to have been at the college while he was in law school, and he was certain she had not been a law student. There had been only nine women to enter in his three years and he had decided she was quite attractive and not liable to be forgotten.

"I'm sure it was you. I saw you in the law school library all the time. You never seemed to leave."

"Ah, yes," he said forlornly, "that certainly was me." He asked what had brought her to the law school.

"A fellow." She looked down at the walk. "He was in your class. He was like you. He'd been in the service." Stern asked his name, but she flapped her hand. No account. "He didn't make it through."

Stern uttered a sympathetic sound. Of his class of three hundred, only about 120 had received degrees. The overheated atmosphere of law school and its occasional terror still returned to him at times in dreams. They had reached the car and Stern held the door.

"I am shocked to find I was so memorable," he remarked inside.

"Oh." She smiled a bit. "You had a GI haircut."

"Ah," said Stern. He could read her thought: he had appeared so terribly out of place. The story of his life. Foreign-born scholarship boy with government haircut. At Easton he would have looked like an arrival straight from the immigration dock. She touched his arm. It did not surprise him that she already recognized the large place ocupied in him by pride.

She said merely, "Please."

He tried to save the moment. "I am flattered that I made any impression."

She looked down at her lap. So he saw it for the first time: Clara Mittler biting back her words. She knew a difficult social pass and had an infallible intuition for when to withdraw. He had learned to imitate her at this, in the way married couples will after decades, how to keep his silence when it was best, but he never had the same mastery as she. The subject drifted past; the sting receded. He started the car and drove, again tensely studying the streets.

"Did you enjoy law school?"

"To endure," said Stern, "not to enjoy."

"That's what my father says. I used to study in the law school library when I was an undergraduate. I wanted to go myelf, but he wouldn't hear of it." She labored with the thought. "And what about Easton, Sandy?" She used his name deliberately. "Did you find it a pleasure to be out in the hills?"

Here Stern showed more caution. This was apparently her alma mater. What could he say? There in the rolling countryside, thirty miles from the hub of Kindle County, Easton University had been built in the 1870s as an Episcopal alternative to the land-grant universities. By now, it had a magnificent faculty and a world-class reputation. But it was full of foppish fellows in tweed coats, boys from from Brooklyn and Iowa who carried on as if they were princes and dukes. Easton was more Yale than Yale, a palace of pretensions. It had been an astonishing three years to Stern. Some people took him as exotic; others as a waif.

"Easton," said Stern, "I found to be much farther from the city than mere geography might suggest."

"Oh, yes." She nodded heartily. "I used to think the same thing all the time when I was teaching."

"Teaching?" asked Stern. For a few moments, he learned a thing or two about her. It turned out that after college she had been a grade-school teacher at the Prescott School in DuSable. The students were almost exclusively black— "colored," they said in 1956—poor youngsters whose poverty surrounded them like a vast gulf between them and the rest of the world. On the coldest mornings, attendance was down substantially because of the number of children who did not own coats.

"Nothing was wasted," she said. "Every moment was worthwhile. Whether you succeeded or failed."

"What caused you to stop?" asked Stern.

In the dark car, she made a heavy sound. "I quit almost

two years ago."

Move to strike as nonresponsive, Stern thought. The nomenclature of the courtroom was always in his mind these days, one more American dialect he wished to faultlessly master.

"*For a particular reason?*"

"*I thought I had something better to do.*"

In George's car, they both became silent.

When he said good night to her beside the iron standards of the pointed fence that bounded Henry Mittler's handsome Georgian home in Riverside, she shook his hand and smiled against her will, and made him promise to call her about dinner next week. He watched her dash up the stairs, full skirt and petticoats hoisted. She ran through the doors of the house, which were large enough to front a mission, without turning back. Was she close to tears? Something had happened. She had been here, then gone, aswarm in her own troubles. A fascinating young woman, bright and tenderhearted, and from the eagerness with which she spoke of seeing him again, he was sure that no snub had been intended. But as he stared up in the dark at the ocher brick and iron flower boxes that hung on Henry Mittler's home, the weight of grim conviction settled on him. He would never really know what lay inside.

21

With his usual abject look, Remo Cavarelli waited in the marble corridor outside the courtroom of United States District Court Judge Moira Winchell. Stern hung on to Remo like an old tie—one too garish and oddly proportioned to accompany any part of the current wardrobe. With his coarse hands and North End speech, Remo was an embarrassment to the young lawyers in Stern's office, who were accustomed to Stern's current trade—business people and professionals overcome by material appetites or caught up in ambiguous circumstances. But Remo had been a client for nearly three decades, and Stern would not abandon him. He had first approached Stern in the teeming halls of the North End police court and reappeared every few years in the midst of one scrape or another, a tough block of a man with the roughened brown face of a mariner.

Remo was a thief. He stole as a profession, with attitudes not unlike a professional hunter's. He admired what he stole; he enjoyed taking it; he looked forward to doing it again. And he regarded apprehension as part of his calling. Each time he went to jail—and he had done three stretches already—he lamented the effect on his family. On the last occasion, Stern remembered, Remo had wept wildly as he contemplated separation from his young son. But he had come of age among men who made bluff pronouncements about the time they had done. And so, when he was caught, Remo Cavarelli pled guilty.

That was how he intended to answer the indictment pending against him here for conspiring to loot an interstate shipment. Not today, of course. Like a man with a toothache, the only thing that Remo regarded as worse than his present predicament was its solution. But sooner or later, after Stern had arranged another continuance or two, Remo would approach the bar and publicly admit his culpability. And this time it would be against the advice of his lawyer. The government's case was extremely weak—a conspiracy depending entirely on Remo's coincidental appearance at the site where a hijacked refrigerator truck was being unloaded of its cargo of beef sides. Stern had encouraged Remo to go to trial, even offered to adjust his fee, but Remo was not interested. Trials were for people who had a gripe. Remo had none. At this point, with his fourth conviction, Remo was likely to be gone for a number of years. But he remained resolute.

Before the courtroom door, Remo pumped Stern's hand and Stern took a moment to explain what would happen today. The period for pre-trial motions was now past, and Judge Winchell would set a trial date. Remo was to do nothing more than stand at Stern's side before the bench. His appearance was not required, but Stern urged Remo to attend nonetheless. He would look like a tamed ruffian beside the lawyers as they spoke a language he could not understand. His coat hung on him with an evident foreignness; his broad tie formed a huge knot and elevated the collar points on Remo's polyester shirt. Remo's head would list slightly throughout, and his large rough hands would cling to his sides pathetically, as if, like awkward sensors, they could feel the cold weight of the bars. Stern had seen Remo perform this routine before, and standing beside Sandy, he would break even the hardest heart.

Today he would get the chance. Moira Winchell had started out as a federal prosecutor, and went on to spend a number of years as a big-firm litigator, one of those lawyers who attended to complex civil lawsuits, trading Himalayan masses of documents and seldom bringing cases to trial. Ten years ago, she had been the first woman named a federal judge in this district; by now, she had been elevated by her colleagues to chief. Moira was rightfully celebrated as the triumphal conqueror of generations of discrimination. But, alas, there was a reason Moira had succeeded when others had not. She was a tough cookie. And the bench had made her tougher. Facing the manifold burdens of life as a federal judge—crowded dockets, churlish lawyers, middling pay, and almost unlimited power—some people did not respond well. They came to the bench thrilled by the acclaim of their peers and became, in a short period of time, as temperamental as Caligula. Moira Winchell was one of them—snappish, sarcastic, even, at moments, downright mean. Stern had tried cases against Moira years ago, during the time she was a prosecutor, and forged with her a relationship of mutual regard. More recently, the judge and her husband, Jason, a law school professor, had passed occasional intermissions with Stern and Clara at the symphony. There, soothed by the music, Moira was amiable, if a little haughty. But in her courtroom she was harder than granite.

"Mr. Stern, where are we going with this matter?"

From the substantial height of the dark bench, Judge Winchell addressed him as soon as the clerk called the case for status. She gave no apparent attention to Moses Appleton, the Assistant United States Attorney who stood beside Stern on the shoulder opposite Remo. Moses, a young black man, was a crackerjack lawyer—he figured for great things—but the prosecutors, all of them, were like cigar-store Indians to many of the judges: fungible young functionaries routinely clamoring for vengeance.

Stern promptly complained about the prosecution, claiming that they had not provided enough information on the case for him to determine whether it should be "resolved without trial," an oblique reference to a guilty plea. Judge Winchell, who had heard it all before, motioned him silent. In the large old courtroom, lawyers, each awaiting his or her turn at the podium, sat by the dozens on the dark-lacquered benches, attending to the judge like a reverent congregation and all the while registering legal fees in six-minute increments.

"Two weeks for the government to file a Rule 801 statement, supported by 302s and grand jury testimony. We'll set the trial for two weeks thereafter. No continuances. Give them a date," said Judge Winchell to her minute clerk, who sat almost at ground level, four feet below. The clerk, Wilbur, who took his cues from the judge, called out a date next month like an announcement of doom.

Remo, beside Stern, spoke up for the first time.

"So soon?" he whispered.

"Hush," said Stern.

On the bench, Judge Winchell whipped her straight dark hair back over her shoulder.

"Mr. Stern, might I have a word with you?" She started down the stairway beside the bench and, as Stern approached, waved Appleton away. He was unneeded. Stern knew what was coming.

"Sandy," said Moira Winchell, suddenly beside him at his height, "I was terribly sorry to hear about Clara. We all think of you." She placed her long hand on Stern's shoulder and gave him a level look of real sadness. He found himself oddly moved by the judge's sincerity. Here in the strong light of the courtroom, where Moira did not bother with makeup, Stern was impressed by the toll reflected in her features. Her pretty Irish face was deeply lined now; her eyes held no amusement. One tended to forget the earnestness that underlay all her efforts. The world watched her, she knew, waiting for a serious mistake.

"Your Honor is most kind."

"Call," she said. "We'll have lunch."

Then she drew her black robe around her again as she ascended to her superior place. Her face was already wrinkled with its familiar look of irritation. More lawyers. More disputes. More decisions. Onward.

Both Appleton and Remo had waited a few feet away.

"Moses," said Stern in the corridor, "I shall speak with you." Then he led Remo into the attorneys' room, a serene chamber with ancient oak desks and black-and-white photos of various judges of the court of decades past, all floured with dust and askew on the wall. Stern quickly summarized what had occurred. The judge would soon demand a final decision about whether Remo would plead guilty. Stern, again, urged him to proceed to trial, but Remo was clearly indifferent to this advice.

"This here thing," Remo said, "is Friday time. You know what I mean?"

Stern did not. He shook his head.

"What's your religion?" asked Remo. "Catholic, right?" Stern shook his head once more. With his Latin accent, he had long found that Remo's mistake was often made. After all these years, he was certain that it would shock poor Remo to learn the truth. But Remo made no further inquiry. He was caught up with what he was saying.

"See, in the Roman Catholic religion, for all the time I was growin up, the priests say, No meat on Friday, don't eat meat on Friday. You know? Fish, that's okay. Jell-O mold, that's okay. But no meat. See, but guys done it. Lotsa guys. Sometimes you'd slip up or somethin, you know. You'd be eatin a steak, then you'd think like, Jesus, what day is this? Sometimes it'd be on purpose. I remember, when I was at St. Viator's, there's a group a us, we'd go for burgers *just* on Fridays. We'd sit in a booth in the window and wave to the Sisters when they went walkin by. I'm not kiddin." Remo laughed to himself, and wobbled his large dark face. "Oh, we was bad."

"Then all the sudden the priests change their minds. See? It's okay now. Have whatever you like, no problem. But what happened to all the guys who's down burnin in hell for eatin meat on Fridays, huh? You think they let them out? I asked the Father, you know, cause I'm wonderin. I asked, Those guys get out or what? Oh no, he says. God's rules is God's rules. You don't fuck with them. You know. I mean, he don't say you don't fuck with them, but you get what I'm sayin."

"So that's this here thing—it's Friday time. It's bullshit. I didn't do nothin. Honest to God, I cross my heart, it wasn't my job. You know, I heard about this thing, so I shown up and all, I figured could be I'd get a piece.

"But maybe these guys and I, maybe we done some things before. See? So that's how it works out. It's Friday time, on account of what we done before. So what can you do?"

Remo shifted his large shoulders and raised his hands. He did not control God's universe; he merely understood a few of its rules. In his mild brown eyes the look of conviction was deep. Stern, inclined to quarrel, stifled himself. Behind Remo he saw Sonia Klonsky, burdened with numerous case files, drifting by. He called after her and quickly shook hands with his client, leaving behind the one man in the courthouse who had no doubts about justice.

* * *

"I must have a word with you about Margy Allison," he said, coming abreast of her. Klonsky had apparently spent a typical morning for a trial Assistant: shifting between courtrooms, leaving messages with the clerks and other young prosecutors so that her cases, up for status or motions, could be passed while she ran between court calls. Stern attempted to complain about the government's conduct in not serving him with Margy's subpoena, but she showed no remorse.

"You knew what our position was." Klonsky strolled ahead, intent on her next court appearance. "Who's going to be her lawyer?"

"Is she a subject?"

"Not at present."

"Then I intend to represent her."

Klonsky was prepared for this, too. "Stan thinks there's a risk of conflict."

"Can you explain that?"

"No."

"Then you may thank the United States Attorney for his ethical vigilance on my behalf and inform him that I shall be Ms. Allison's lawyer." His smile was personable; he meant to be firm, not snippy. "May I ask, as Margy's counsel, a few questions?"

"If you insist."

"What do you wish from her?"

"Some documents." Klonsky smiled but did not slow her pace. "Some questions. I have to go to Pivin." She pointed to the courtroom of Judge Albert Pivin, seventy-eight years old and still presiding over an active calendar. Stern followed her inside, but the clerk saw her and called her case immediately and Stern went outside to wait across the hall from the courtroom doors. Emerging a few minutes later, she greeted him with a somewhat rankled look. Apparently, she had thought she was free of him.

"Sandy, look. Personally, I don't care what I tell you. But you know how Stan gets. He's running a tight ship."

Stern followed her to the cloakroom, where she retrieved a light raincoat, then proceeded down the central alabaster staircase of the courthouse. Her business here was apparently concluded.

"What exactly is it Stan Sennett has told you about me?"

"Oh, don't be like that. He has a great deal of respect for you. Everybody there does. You know that. Frankly, he looked very concerned the first time I told him you were involved in this case. I'm not supposed to admit that, am I?"

"Oh, Mr. Sennett has no fear of me," said Stern. "Old prosecutors merely love to praise their opponents. It adds immeasurably to the thrill of victory." This gallantry, of course, was intended for the U.S. Attorney's consumption. Like all men lacking self-confidence, Sennett was easily flattered and the South American in Stern was always alert to appease those in power.

Klonsky was laughing out loud.

"Come on," she said. "We're just taking you as seriously as we should." She pushed out the doors of the courthouse. Spring was in its finale, the winds still sweet and the air light, just before it took on the burdens of summer.

"What you are doing," said Stern, "is limiting the information I receive, in order to protect your informant."

From her look, he could tell she felt he was trying to bait her. She did not answer.

"Please," said Stern. He took her by the arm momentarily. "I must ask you one or two more questions about Margy. Allow me to buy you coffee. I did not eat breakfast." He pointed to a little restaurant on the corner called Duke's, and to his surprise she came along wiihout complaint. He meant what he said—he was hungry—and he found Ms. Klonsky, in spite of himself, pleasant and challenging company. Primarily, of course, he hoped that in a more amiable atmosphere she might be less resolute about guarding America's secrets. Ms. Klonsky, as she had just demonstrated with her remark about Sennett, was not really equipped to be discreet. She understood the role, but her large, expansive character was still not comfortably confined by lawyerly proprieties. Like many young attorneys, she was imitating the mentor—Sennett, in this case—rather than making allowances for herself.

Duke's was little more than a lunch counter, a greasy spoon with an open grill under a spattered aluminum hood, and a number of old Formica tables. Klonsky set her files down when they were seated and lifted her face to the frying smells.

"Wonderful," she said.

"That is an overstatement. Reliable will suffice. You have never been?"

She shook her head.

"The proprietor," said Stern, "is the little dark fellow you see in the kitchen. A Rumanian. He is best known for his sausage, which he makes himself and which he aptly refers to on the menu as 'Ruination.' Will you eat?" Stern already had the menu in hand.

"I shouldn't," she said. "I've put on twelve pounds already." But she picked up the laminated card nonetheless. "Your son-in-law got a lawyer, you know. I was a little surprised by your referral."

"Oh, well," said Stern, and smiled fleetly. He, on the other hand, was well practiced in appearing agreeable yet remaining silent; how John chose his lawyer was not the prosecutor's business. He had been troubled not to have heard something from his son-in-law, but Klonsky's remark made it clear that he had followed Stern's advice and retained Raymond Horgan. There were many people in the legal community puzzled by Stern's affinity with Horgan. They'd had celebrated battles while Raymond was the Kindle County Prosecuting Attorney, culminating in some uncomfortable moments three years ago when Stern had cross-examined Horgan, who appeared as a prosecution witness at the murder trial of Rusty Sabich, Raymond's former Chief Deputy. But the law, much like politics, made its own strange bedfellows. Horgan's large firm liked to send cases they could not handle due to conflicts to Stern, who could not compete for the other legal work of the big corporate clients, and he naturally reciprocated.

"What's really good?" she asked.

"The sausage, if you have the stomach for it. I am not certain it is suited to your present condition."

"I doubt it," she said. "I've just started eating meat again. For the protein."

"A vegetarian?"

"Oh, I've been very careful for years about what I eat. I was once very sick." She looked directly at Stern, the hinge of some tentativeness clear in her eye. "Cancer," she said.

The waitress came then, saving Stern from a response. Ms. Klonsky had a disconcerting directness, a willingness to proceed past the recognized borders with little thought, a trait which made Stern uneasy. She asked for a single scrambled egg, while he ordered an omelette and two servings of the sausage. He promised her a bite.

"What was I saying?" she asked. Stern did not answer, but she remembered herself and said simply, "Oh, yes."

"You appear a picture of health now."

"I think I am. I mean, I wouldn't be in this condition—" She lifted a hand. "But so much of it is outlook. You really never forget about it. You tell yourself you're well. You search for signs that you're not, and when you don't find them, you rejoice and tell yourself that you can go back to believing that you're infinite, the way you did before."

"How old were you?"

She raised her eyes to remember. "Thirty-five, thirty-six just about."

Stern shook his head. That was young, he said, for that sort of thing.

"Well, you know how it is. You get to the hospital feeling why me, how me, and then there are plenty of people in the same condition, and worse." She had asked for tea and interrupted herself to fish the bag in and out of the cup when the waitress brought it. "It didn't seem so unusual there. But I was a very young thirty-six. My life was in chaos. I was in law school, but it was the fourth postgraduate education I'd started. I had no idea what I was doing. My relationship with Charlie was going through its one millionth crisis—" She raised her hands for emphasis, one wrist today bedecked with a row of bright plastic bracelets. "It just seemed so unbelievable to me that I was being shown the door, when I didn't even feel I'd arrived."

The expression made Stern laugh. "What were your other postgraduate programs?"

"Let's see." She raised her hands to count and again lifted her eyes to the grim acoustical tiles of Duke's ceiling. "From college, I went out to California for graduate school in philosophy, but I wasn't ready for that, so I enrolled in the Peace Corps—remember that?—and was in the Philippines for two years. When I came back, I started graduate school in English, which is where I met Charlie. I left that because I couldn't imagine actually writing a dissertation. But, of course, I'd finished *all* the class work before I figured that out. Then I taught for about a year and a half, then I went back to the U. as a graduate student in education. Then I gave up on the educational bureaucracy as hopeless. Naturally, I owed a fortune in student loans at that point. So I began thinking about getting a decent-paying job. Which led to law. There were some things in between, but they didn't last long enough to mention."

"I see," said Stern. "It does sound as if you had a hard time getting started."

"Not starting," she said. "That was no problem at all. Finishing was hard. I always believed that I was not an achievement-oriented person, but when I got sick, I was really unhappy that I didn't have a single thing I could look back to that I'd completed. It was as if I'd passed through and never even left tracks. It was pathetic. I was getting radiation. I was lying there with my hair falling out, recovering from surgery, and I had Charlie bringing me volumes of Hart Crane. I actually started writing my dissertation right there. And, naturally, one morning I vomited all over it. That, needless to say, was a low point." She sat back, gripped by her own story. She picked up a dull steel fork off the table and stared at it. "I'm talking too much," she said.

"You are charming, Sonia," he answered, and immediately felt he had been drawn into her habit of saying more than one should. He rushed on to something more neutral. "So you became a health-food person in the wake of your illness? My daughter, who is a lawyer in New York, comes home with a knapsack full of bags and bottles of such things. I've learned to ask no questions."

"Oh, yes. That's me. Ms. Natural here. We drive around all day on Saturday and shop. Charlie has written poems about it. It really is better for you. But the doctor has been dropping some pretty broad hints about more protein."

"Your husband is a poet?"

"A living, breathing, write-every-day poet. He actually puts it in our tax return: 'Poet.' He has another job, naturally. You have to. Charlie likes to say we have the same employer." She smiled. "He's a postal clerk. He was an instructor in the English Department at the U. for years, but he couldn't hack the politics. And he makes more money this way and gets more time to write. It's an absolutely impossible, impractical life, to which he's completely devoted." She smiled once more, somewhat fitfully this time. Perhaps she felt she was being disloyal. She looked again at the silverware and took a second to praise her husband's verse.

The eggs came then.

"God," said Klonsky, "what is that black lump?"

"Ruination," he said. "What else?" Stern cut a piece and lifted it toward her, but she made a horrible face and raised both hands.

"It makes me queasy just to see it. It looks like something excreted."

Stern dropped his fork to the plate.

"Young woman," he said darkly, "this is my breakfast."

She began to laugh then, a fine trilling note full of joy and congratulation. He laughed himself and she got caught up in her own amusement and went on until she had to use her napkin to wipe her eyes. She managed to say, "Bon appetit," and began to laugh again.

He started to eat in spite of her.

"That's right," she said. "Don't let it get cold."

"It happens to be good. And I am quite hungry."

"You must be." She broke down one more time. She tried, with a few false starts, to control herself.

"Are you sure you will not try some?" He lifted his fork in a perfect deadpan, and set her off once more. This time he laughed himself for quite some time.

She told him he was a good sport.

"I am accustomed," Stern told her. "My daughter in New York lectures me about meat. She has ruined a number of meals."

"What's her name?"

Stern told her.

"Marta. That's beautiful. I'm thinking about names all the time now. It seems so important. The first thing. And I don't want my child to feel that I've done what my mother did to me."

"You do not care for Sonia?"

"I hated it as a child. My mother was this very heavy lefty? A big-deal labor type, until her union threw out the Commies. I was named for a Russian revolutionary killed in the revolt of 1905 and I resented being somebody else's symbol. I wanted to be called Sonny. Which threw my mother into a rage. She thought I was being anti-feminist. Then I got to be forty years old and a lawyer, and all of a sudden I wanted a name that would sound professional. So I'm Sonia in the office. And my old friends still call me Sonny." She laughed at herself. "That's a little like what you do. You say Alejandro in court, but you introduce yourself as Sandy."

Stern smiled in an allusive way, reflecting his own inscrutability, but he was flattered to think he had been so closely observed. It was natural really, he told himself, for her to keep watch on a likely adversary.

"My mother was an obliging sort. She called us by different names, depending on the locale. I had a Yiddish name. A Spanish name. And, of course, she desperately wanted me to fit in here. Even at the age of thirteen, I could recognize that it was not an optimal period for Alejandros in the U.S. I suppose you may take my using Sandy as a sign of weakness on my part." This was very much as he thought of it—that he had yielded. His mother was a powerful person in her home. He seldom spoke of her but she was still with him every day, with her dark shrewd eyes, her teeming social ambitions, and her desperate pained hope that his father would somehow become the man she had envisioned instead of the poor wounded thing he was. Stern tended to remember her as she appeared on the nights she and his father went to the opera. The rich gown made a somewhat opulent display of her large proportions; her reddish hair was held in place by a diamond-studded comb, and her entire figure appeared gripped by her fierce determination to be seen, and remembered. He had always known that every fiber of strength in him derived from her.

"So how did you settle on Marta?" Klonksy asked. "Was it a better world for Alejandros by then?"

"She is named for my mother," said Stern. He laughed at that and shared a look with her, the complexities of these facts seemingly lost on neither of them. Then he lifted his fork. "Last bite," said Stern.

She covered her mouth amid a muffled retching sound and Stern played along.

"I'll have you know, young woman, this is the best breakfast I've had for days." For effect, he rang the tines of the fork against the dish, but the remark, intended in jest, somehow carried a forlorn suggestion of his personal plight. Ms. Klonsky gave him a sideways look, sweet and sad and lingering, and Stern suddenly was deeply embarrassed. He had disciplined himself to avoid this approach to anyone: Pity me. Feel for me. He looked down once more at his plate.

"You were going to tell me what you wished with Margy," he said. He heard her sigh. But when he looked up, she had folded her hands and gathered herself.

She corrected him: "You were going to ask some questions."

"I thought you might tell me about the Wunderkind account."

"The number's on the subpoena."

"Why is it, Sonia, that this account is of such interest?"

She shook her head firmly.

"No can do, Sandy."

"You expect me to bring this woman to the grand jury without any idea what she may be venturing into?"

"I've told you, she's not a subject. I'll be happy to put that in writing. If she tells us the truth, she has nothing to worry about. You know the drill, Sandy."

"But the secretiveness—"

"Doctor's orders," she said. "That's how we're doing it." She was speaking again of Sennett. Stern, despite himself, made a sound. This had seemed from the inception to be too significant a matter for an inexperienced Assistant. Now he could see quite clearly that Stan Sennett was behind the scenes, pulling the strings, pumping the levers, palpitating at the thought of a case that would get his name in *The Wall Street Journal* and bring a moment of disquiet to that den of thieves in the Exchange, as he saw them, with their granite palace along the river.

Sennett was a wiry, humorless little man, with the narrow, bird-boned physique of a runner. He was married to a probate lawyer named Nora, an ascetic type with a fixed jaw. Stern always imagined the two of them in a home with no dust and little furniture, eating carefully and going out for weekend runs. Stan had started out as the Chief Deputy Prosecuting Attorney in Kindle County under Ray Horgan, but he had gotten a yen for California and joined the Justice Department in San Diego. As the choice for U.S. Attorney he had been roundly welcomed— Stan was intelligent, experienced, and more or less independent of the mayor and his dark cabal.

It was, however, one of the sad facts of political reform everywhere that incorruptibility was not the sole attribute of good government. Sennett was the kind of grim bureaucrat, a person of strong discipline and limited vision and courage, who seemed to turn up too often in prosecutors' offices. Everybody's chief deputy, he never quite seemed to believe he had assumed the mantle himself. In Stern's judgment, he had a dangerous

mixture of attributes for a man in power: he was vainglorious
and insecure, quick to make judgments that were not always
correct, and entirely beyond persuasion once he had done so.
When you sat with him, presenting a problem, pleading for
mercy or simply trying to make a point, his small shining eyes
would follow you while his expression remained forbidding. 'No,'
he would say the instant you had finished a ten-minute
presentation. 'No can do.' Few words of explanation, little
warmth. No argument. He would stand and shake your hand and
see you to the door.

Now he was using Klonsky as his cat's-paw. That was for
appearances, but the fact was, this was his case. Stern wondered
if Klonsky knew how quickly he would push her aside when the
lights of the videocams filled the room. In the meantime, a dark,
high-density fluid of regret poured through Stern, the stuff of
gloom. Sennett would be dogged in the hunt; Dixon, whatever
his evasive maneuvers, was in for a long, bloody fight. Lost in
these reflections, Stern reached forward and picked up the
check.

"Oh, no," she said. As they walked to the door, Klonsky
insisted on paying her share. Stern eventually recognized that
this was a point of propriety and took two dollars from her.
Duke, with his fried-up hair, received their money and bade
them, with heavy accent, to return.

Outside, he shook her hand and told her that Margy and he
would see her the following Tuesday. She faced him with what
was already becoming a familiar look of ambiguity and regret.

"Thank you for asking me. I enjoyed our conversation."

"As well." He made a brief, cutaway bow, Mr. Alejandro Stern,
the foreign gentleman. She smiled at that and, with her heavy
files slung across her body, went off toward the new federal
building down the block. Pigeons with their shining gray heads
arose fluttering in her path, and a rush of underground air,
breathed up through a grate in the walk, ruffled her skirt. As he
watched her go, it came to him again, an intimation clear as the
arrival of spring, that he was alone. The usual affairs of the day,
the courthouse, his children—they did not seem to do. Like
nausea or hunger, a deep-sprung bodily response, the sense of
his own unconnectedness overcame him, just as it did certain
mornings, and to his surprise he stood for some time watching

the figure of Sonia Klonsky whittled by distance and the phenomenon of aging vision, until she was no longer distinct amid the dark forms on the street.

22

At night, he saw Helen—more often, each week. The logic seemed irrefutable. Why should he be home in an empty house when Helen, a charming dinner companion, was available? Various adolescent intuitions told him that he was moving with too much dispatch toward an undesired destination. But she was such pleasant company, and who, reasonably, would choose loneliness? He was fifty-six and going steady.

And, like some teenager, he was also screwing his brains out. In fin de siècle America, it seemed, this was how men and women paid respects. The hell with notes and flowers. Let's get it on! One afternoon, Helen met him for lunch at his club in Morgan Towers. In that upright atmosphere, with the waiters in frogged coats and the bankers and business folk waxing genial, Helen grasped his hand and said, "Fuck me, Sandy." She had had a glass of wine and her eyes looked very green.

And did he resist? Not on your life. Mr. Alejandro Stern, at 1:27 in the afternoon, rented a room in his own name across the street in the Hotel Gresham. They were at the elevator when Stern recollected that he lacked a necessary item. In the hotel's sundry shop, the attendant proved, of course—of course!—to be an older woman, with a heavy tailored suit and a strong German accent. Already giddy from the loss of inhibition and the lunch-time wine, Stern stuck up his courage and was able to clearly pronounce, "Prophylactics."

"Of course." The woman nodded ponderously as she searched through the warren of old-fashioned cupboards where the rubbers were hidden. Eventually, she offered an entire box of different brands. "Good to use them," she added, in the most cordial hotel style. In the elevator, Stern and Helen had been unable to contain their laughter. Thereafter, that was their watchword. At the most intimate moment, Helen was apt to drone, "Good to use them."

Making love to Helen was inevitably that kind of good-spirited enterprise, and often highly educational. She had read all the books; she had practiced every maneuver. There was nothing she was going to miss. Some developments that took Stern by surprise were, naturally, the result of thirty years with one lover in which the zones of exploration had been long established. He was mystified the first time Helen had extricated herself from his embrace and nudged him onto his back, then moved below. His first thought was that he was the object of a visual inspection, a prospect which he found far more exciting than he would have imagined, but she was soon otherwise occupied, busy with her mouth and fingertips.

"Did you like that?" she asked afterwards.

He answered slowly. "The wings of a dove."

Yet, even making allowances for his lack of prior experience, he still found in Helen a disconcertingly determined interest in the sexual act. This was not a roundabout complaint concerning Clara. Whatever inadequacies she may have felt—and who could doubt the evidence?—he had never been dissatisfied. But for Helen the actual moment of encounter, the performance, was supreme and seemed to acquire a detached dreamlike rapture that Stern sometimes experienced in museums. They were, both of them, the thing observed, pure phenomenon: her body, his, with their rosy tumescent glow and throbbing veinous parts, the glistening pinkish shaft probing and disappearing. He watched with Helen's bold approval. She slipped her hand down to provide yet one more stimulant.

Like a door prize, there was always something new. One day she tweaked the nipples of his chest while he worked above her. Another time, she lifted her legs and gently moved his hands so that his thumbs kneaded at the delicate little bead which he could reach as he pumped inside her. She presented herself from the rear, the side. She faced him and sat athwart Stern on a diningroom chair. Naked, stimulated, he would drag around the furniture as she instructed as a prelude to the latest innovation. He told her afterwards that the combination of sexual exertion and stoop labor threatened a coronary occlusion.

"You're in good shape," Helen said and reached below to pet him admiringly.

Stern could tell that Helen was immensely proud of her role as pathfinder and instructor. But occasionally the unlikelihood of these antics would overcome him. In the hotel room the afternoon they had received the peculiar blessings of the German lady in the sundries shop, Helen stood upon two dressers and Stern caught the sight of their forms on the dull slate-green surface of the television tube: a short man, with the tip of his erect penis nipping up just above the bottom of his white belly, which hung on him like a flour sack, his hands dug into the flattened shapes of Helen's buttocks, crouching slightly and pressing face and tongue upward into the wet odoriferous reaches of that mystical passage. It looked like a circus trick or the played-out fantasy of a cheap pornographer. The image remained with him for hours, lurid, fascinating, but nonetheless disturbing. Was this some more essential self, or a brainless imitation of what others aspired to? Who were they supposed to be? A part of him remained ill at ease with this emphasis on the physical, not what he'd thought of as his best realm. But whatever his misgivings after the fact, he enjoyed these encounters as they were occurring. He admired Helen's lack of restraint, and her agility. When he thought of her, it was with appreciation and desire, even while he discouraged himself from pressing for exact answers about the true state of his feelings for her.

His friends and acquaintances welcomed Helen openly. It made for fewer reminders of Clara and her passing, which no one wished to contemplate. The Hartnells invited Stern and Helen to a ritzy summer cotillion that Silvia had organized at the Greenwood Club. At first delighted to be included, Helen became uncomfortable with the pretense of the evening once she had arrived. Whenever backs were turned, she rolled her eyes at Stern and made faces, conduct which upset him, with his lifetime adherence to certain rigid courtesies. "You don't like all this schmaltz," she murmured to him at one point. Helen's honesty was wonderful and endearing, but he also realized how uncertain it made him. She could set him on edge a dozen times a night with her straightforward observations, particularly of him. Was he brave enough to face Helen and her facts? She wanted to know everything about him and then make it better. At one point, turning away from the bar and looking across the enormous tent that had been pitched for this affair, he observed her in animated conversation with Silvia and found himself alarmed. This was a mismatch, Stern thought suddenly. His sister was a woman guarded by layers of the most protective refinements, much as the petals lay about the center of a rose. His first impulse was that she was somehow in danger. He whisked Silvia away to dance.

"So?" asked Stern. His sister had known Helen only remotely over the years, having encountered her principally at family affairs.

"A charming person," Silvia answered, somewhat formally. He would have expected a similar response from Clara, who, no doubt, would have thought a contessa or professor a more fitting companion for Stern. At that point, Helen came whirling by in Dixon's arms, looking happier than she had all evening. Helen, like most women, enjoyed Dixon's company.

"Is he the one who is in so much trouble?" she asked Stern as they were driving home on the highway cut between the dark hills.

"He is," said Stern simply. With her unfailing sense for what was important to him, Helen listened carefully to everything he told her about his practice, but he could not recall exactly what he'd said which led her to piece this together.

"Well, you'd never know it," Helen said. "He's quite entertaining."

"When he wishes to be," said Stern.

In the dark, she placed her head on his shoulder. Clara, raised in the fading era of rigid female posture, would never have been capable of this gesture, and he drove the hour back to the city with Helen drowsing, a warm, comforting weight upon him.

Two nights later, they had a different kind of evening. Helen's daughter, Maxine, came to town with Rob Golbus, her husband of only a few months. Maxine had been Kate's childhood friend, and Helen proposed an evening out with all three couples—Kate and John, Maxine and Rob, Stern and her. With the perfect resourcefulness one expected from Helen, she figured out entertainment pleasing to everyone and bought tickets to a

Trappers game. Stern was always delighted to spend a night in the handsome old park with its brick outfield walls and cantilevered upper decks, where skied fly balls occasionally came to rest as homers. But there was soon an irritating undertone. Too much seemed to be assumed. Maxine spoke repeatedly of Helen and him visiting St. Louis, so that he began to feel both put upon and cornered, while Kate seemed coltish and jumpy all evening. When Helen casually—too casually—mentioned a remark Stern had made to her one morning this week at breakfast, Kate burst into the unnerved tittering one would have expected from an early adolescent. When John offered to go downstairs for refreshments, Stern eagerly rose to lend a hand.

With their order placed at the counter beneath the stands, they stood in silence. His son-in-law, laconic as ever, put on his glasses to watch the televised version of the game on the screen above the old fry grill.

"How is the matter proceeding?" asked Stern eventually, desperate for some topic of conversation. He thought, perhaps, to ask if Kate was bearing up; it had occurred to him that the stress of John's problems might have contributed to her worn look and high-strung mood.

"The matter?" John looked at him.

"The grand jury business." Stern had lowered his voice slightly.

"Oh." John poked his glasses back up on his nose and reverted to the TV. "Okay."

"Klonsky, the Assistant United States Attorney, tells me you have found a lawyer."

"I guess." John hitched a shoulder. It was time for sports; the rest of this was bad news, workaday stuff.

"You are in excellent hands. Raymond is very experienced." John removed his glasses.

"Oh, I didn't end up with him. I've got a guy named Mel."

"Mel?" asked Stern. "Mel Tooley?" It was an article of professional decorum never to speak ill of another lawyer to his client, but Stern could not restrain the note of contempt. Mel Tooley had not been on the list Stern had given John. The only list of Stern's where Tooley might appear would be one naming the despised of the earth. Tooley, who had been the chief of the

Special Investigations Division in the United States Attorney's Office until he entered private practice approximately a year ago, was one of those lawyers who seemed to be attracted to the profession because it legitimized certain forms of deceit. Stern's disagreements with Tooley over the years were celebrated; legendary. No wonder Klonsky had said she was surprised by the referral. How had John wandered into the clutches of a creature like that?

His son-in-law had already gathered up the box containing the tissued dogs and the beers and was mounting the concrete steps back to the boxes. Fraught with paternal anxieties and lawyerly rules, Stern followed, lecturing himself. It was, in a word, none of his business how John had chosen his counsel—even Mel Tooley.

Halfway up the stairs he ran into Kate, literally, jostled against her as she was on her way down. They both exclaimed. Stern laughed, but she seemed startled to see him and jumped back. Here in the stairwell, better lit than the stands, he again noticed her appearance. She was nicely turned out in a sort of maternity sailor suit with a large red bow, but she looked drawn and, most shockingly, seemed to lack her childish blush. It was more than pregnancy, Stern suspected. John's situation was taking its toll. He instantly had the thought that this was the face of Kate's true adulthood. Whatever he had long expected was now in its onset. He touched her hand.

"Katy, are you all right?"

Fine, she answered, just on her way to the ladies' room. She touched her stomach and added that it was for the third time.

"But is everything else—?"

"You mean John?" When he nodded, she seemed to wince fleetingly and touched her stomach again. She began to speak, then stopped herself. "I shouldn't say anything."

Kate had been briefed, he saw, fully informed. She had the facts, the procedures. In all likelihood, she knew a good deal more than he did.

"I quite agree. I merely wanted to reassure you."

"Daddy—"

"I have seen these situations often, Kate. Trust me. It will turn out all right."

"I only wish, Daddy."

"You must be patient. It will all probably go on longer than any of us like. But you should not worry."

"Daddy, please. You're starting to sound like Mommy. She never wanted me to worry. 'Don't worry, Katy, don't worry.'" She had lifted her hands in imitation, quick, bird-like shapes. "Sometimes I wonder: Did she think if I worried I was going to break or something?"

He considered this lament, so unlike her, not sure how to respond.

"Daddy, it's not that easy. Believe me." With that, she sighed, a despairing sound, and took another step down. "I *have* to go to the bathroom," she announced, and moved off in that direction. Stern watched her depart. What was that last bit about? But he thought he could read the portents in her mood clearly. She was worried not merely for her husband—but by him. Kate, not unlike her father, had learned more from John, and about him, than she had cared to know. John lumbered on, he slept nights, but his wife now had her eyes open. To himself, Stern briefly groaned and muttered one of his mother's Yiddish phrases. As he emerged into the open night air, the crowd was roaring over a fabulous catch by the right fielder Tenack. Ascending, Stern had seen the ball go by like a shooting star.

By prior arrangement, Rob and Maxine went off to spend the night at Kate and John's—a chance for a more intimate visit. Helen begged Stern to stay with her. "Just to sleep," said Helen, who had barely been able to rouse herself in the car. The large, somewhat secluded house which Miles and she had built only a year or two before the end of their marriage seemed to haunt her at times, especially after one of the children visited.

In her room, Helen without ceremony shed her clothes, leaving them on the floor in a single heap, and threw herself down naked on the bed. The intimacy pleased her, he knew: to be able to bare herself without reflection or fear of his scrutiny under the strong overhead light. See what you like. Helen had clearly done her best, but in truth she still looked somewhat pounded-on by experience—blotched and slackened here and there, her legs varicose-etched right up to her seat. Not that any of these observations were critical. He was hardly a physical example himself, and he had not withstood two pregnancies. He had been oddly troubled of late to find white hairs growing in his pubic region. But he and Helen were approaching the same point—not quite on last legs, but battered, wobbling, losing the battle to the major forces of physics, gravity, and time. This was one set of facts beyond the power of even Helen's will.

Stern, who had developed his own routine here, covered Helen in bed, shooed out the cat, and locked the doors. Yet for reasons he could not fathom he was not at ease. He was disturbed at moments by the thought of what it might spell for Dixon to have John in the hands of unfriendly counsel; but these were the kinds of worries that for decades he had been able to quell at night. Dozing off, he thought for an instant about Kate, looking transformed by the world of adult woe, then Nate Cawley, still to be cornered. Tomorrow he would catch him. Soon. And yet each time Stern felt himself gentling down to sleep, he rose like some float in the water. Eventually, it became a night of restless dreams. In the one that he remembered, Stern, from ground level, had seen a bird, lifeless in the snow, beneath the needled boughs of an evergreen. This bird, an old ragged thing with plumage of black and white, was gently lifted by a female hand. She stroked the old bird's chest, stated that his wing, which was held erect from his body, was broken but would mend. Her voice struck a note of joy and congratulation. Waking in Helen's room, with the strong morning light haloing the edges of the heavy drapes, Stern recalled nothing of this woman but that encouraging prediction, Helen continued in the shallow breath of sleep. He reached over to touch her shoulder. But he was certain that the voice he had heard when he was dreaming had not been hers.

23

Kate had bought Stern an answering machine. For all his love of gadgets, he'd sworn that this was one he'd never own. He was a slave to the telephone as it was. More to the point, it always pained him to listen to his voice on tape; his accent sounded so much more distinct than he imagined. But he could not spurn his daughter's generosity. On the machine, Kate most days left a bright message or two (lately, as John's problems had deepened, Stern thought he could occasionally detect a leaden undertone in Kate's greeting); Helen also often recorded a pleasant word, so that Stern, despite himself, looked forward to coming home and fiddling with the buttons. Tonight, however, the first voice he heard was Peter's. "It's time to schedule your blood test." Typically blunt—and indiscreet. Stern, in the empty house, actually reached to the side of the machine to lower the volume.

But the message was a familiar reminder. He lurked by the window, awaiting Nate Cawley. He had spent a number of evenings working at the dining-room table in the hopes of spying Nate as he drove up; Stern had given up on reaching him by phone. While he waited, he opened his mail. There was a brief note from Marta reminding him that she would be home in a couple of weeks, over the Fourth of July, to continue sifting through Clara's things.

On paper, Marta was terse, but she had taken to calling late at night, on the verge of sleep, sometimes even waking Stern for long, meditative conversations. Marta had continued to dwell on Clara's death—she recognized it as an enormous passage. And in her casting about, which she willingly shared, Stern, as usual, found much common ground with his older daughter. Sitting up in bed, he listened to her talk, mumbling responses, half-drowsed but intent.

Marta had always been a person of somber character; Stern could not remember her as frolicsome. Even at seven or eight, she seemed perplexed by the fundamental nature of things. Why does a woman marry only one man? Why do we eat animals if it is wrong to treat them cruelly? Can God see inside things or merely their surfaces? Stern, much more than Clara, valued Marta's dark, contemplative side and was, inevitably, moved by her internal struggles. She was the child with whom he felt most in touch. Second in his own family, he understood her occasional mighty battles with Peter, her unrestrained—if momentary—resentment of him.

He had been so pleased when she went to law school, not merely because he was flattered to be imitated, but more because the law, with its substance, its venerated traditions, and its relentless contemplation of social relations, seemed capable of providing one set of proposed answers to the questions with which Marta had been so long preoccupied. But neither law school nor practice seemed to have lessened her brooding or uncertainty. She took the bar exam in four states before deciding to remain in New York; she'd found three different jobs before accepting the present one, the lowest paying, most tenuous, least promising. She was a single professional in New York, caught up in the usual New York swirl of consumption—the latest restaurants, stores, and events—but late at night there was an unguarded tone of deprivation. She was unsuccessful in her relations with men, stalled in her career, baffled by life, and more or less alone. Stern looked down to her note, with strong sensations of her. Marta's quest—soulful, troubled, yearning—was nowhere near its end.

Out the window in the lengthening evening, against a magnificent streaked sky, the BMW at last circled around the Cawleys' drive. Stern was out the door and halfway to the auto before he saw that Fiona was driving. He stopped in his tracks.

"Sandy." She smiled and stepped from the car, carrying a small bright sack from some shop.

Stern stood in the grass. He wore his suit pants and a handmade shirt, monogrammed over the pocket; he had removed his tie. Glancing down, he noticed he was still carrying

Marta's note. Stern explained to Fiona that he had mistaken her for Nate.

"I took his car today. Mine's conking out whenever I use the air."

"Ah," said Stern, and rocked on his toes. With Fiona and him, it was always awkward.

"Actually," she said, "there's something I've been meaning to show you. Come in for a minute." Fiona set off for the front door, keys in hand, without allowing him the chance to refuse. Stern moved reluctantly in her wake up the pea-gravel walk. What new treachery of Nate's did she wish to disclose? Fiona set her package down on a candle table near the doorway and snapped on some lights. Stern said he had an appointment shortly, a remark which Fiona, predictably, feigned not to hear.

"This is really the most curious thing," she said. "Come upstairs. I want you to see this." Fiona stopped to release the collie from the kitchen. Stern declined her offer of a drink, but Fiona paused to pour a bourbon over ice, and quaffed half of it at once, easy as water. "It's so hot," she said. The dog, in the meantime, jumped all over them both, then, rebuked, followed placidly as they walked toward the staircase.

Upstairs, Fiona opened the door to the bedroom and passed down a hall into the bath. Stern hung back, hesitant to follow. There was a certain stimulating intimacy in being with a woman in her bedroom. It was not the bed so much as the privacy of the scene. The room was clearly Fiona's, finished to her taste in crepe de Chine and ambiguous pinkish shades. The strong scents of powders and colognes, too sweet American smells, rose here. A long umber negligee lay as a sort of inviting preconscious thought, discarded beside the bed on an upholstered chair arm, suggesting a languorous form.

"Here," said Fiona, "this is it. Come here." She was in the bathroom, the door partly closed. When Stern pushed it open, Fiona was studying a tiny paper bag. Her drink had been set down on the counter. "I saw this last week. I couldn't understand why Nate would keep something with Clara's name on it in his medicine cabinet."

In his surprise, he virtually snatched it from her—the small patterned bag from a local chain pharmacy. Two computer-generated prescription receipts, little tags that conveniently assembled all the information required by Medicare or insurers, were stapled to the lip of the bag, overlapping one another. On the top one, Clara's name, address, and phone number were printed. Stern could feel a large vial inside the sack. It was pointless to ask what Fiona was doing roaming in her husband's medicine chest. Undoubtedly there had been many such expeditions: the pockets of his suits, his daily diary, his wastebasket. Fiona would have no trouble with the kind of low tactics divorce-court hostilities required.

"Indomethacin," Stern read the tag. "This is for Clara's arthritis, I believe. Nate told me he had brought some to her."

Fiona passed him an odd look.

"If he brought it to her, how come it's still in the bag?"

Stern made a sound. She was right about that. But the answer was obvious. Nate had had two prescriptions filled: that was why there were two tags. When Stern flipped to the lower one, he saw the word "Acyclovir" and his heart skipped. Quickly, he withdrew the clear brown container from the bag. What in the world would Nate Cawley need with this stuff?

"What is it?" asked Fiona.

Stern was intent on the label on the bottle. In the blank following the word "Patient," "Dr. Nathan Cawley, M.D.," was listed, and Nate's office address and phone were also printed there. 85 ACYCLOVIR 200 MG CAPSULES. TWO (2) CAPSULES FIVE TIMES DAILY FOR FIVE DAYS, REMAINDER ONE (1) CAPSULE FIVE TIMES DAILY, IF NEEDED.

When the thought came to him, Stern's face shot around to Fiona.

"Does Nate take these pills?"

She shrugged. "I'd imagine. This is his medicine cabinet. What are they?"

"Acyclovir," answered Stern, pronouncing it just as Peter had when he explained that the drug was often successful in reducing the active period of the infection. The herpes infection. Dr. Nate had prescribed for himself.

She reached for the bottle, and Stern, without thinking, pulled it farther away. The prescription was dated two days before Clara's death. He shook the container. Almost empty. Wrenching off the cap, he spilled the contents onto a piece of tissue and counted six capsules remaining. Seventy-nine consumed. Stern contemplated the numbers: Nate was taking these pills more than a week and a half after Clara's death. He stared down at the little yellow capsules with an unremitting intensity. The brand name of the drug was printed right on them.

Fiona spoke to him again. "Sandy, what is this for?"

Oh yes, thought Stern. He had known this, had he not? It was all right here before him. Nate's lying, all his dodging and running—they were classic signs. There was clearly something Nate wanted neither discovered nor discussed. And it was here. Right here. Not simply what had ailed Clara. But the fact that Nate, who went on serenely consuming these capsules after she was laid to rest, had spread the disease. It had taken a real act of will, a high-minded deliberate obdurateness, not to recognize Nate's role. After all, there had been obvious opportunities for initiation of this dalliance. 'Please remove your clothes and put on the smock. Doctor will be with you in a moment.' A man as wrathfully henpecked as Nate would probably find Clara's quiet, inscrutable bearing irresistible. Yes, and it still seemed, still—if he could claim he knew anything about this woman's nature— that anything of this character with Clara would have required time, exposure, trust, a gradual erosion. It was inevitably someone she knew well. Oh, yes. Nate had visited Clara in the mornings, Fiona had said long ago.

"Sandy," said Fiona, "for Godsake. What are the pills for?"

He continued to hold the bottle in his hand and he looked again at the label. The woman, he supposed, was entitled to know.

"Herpes," he said.

"*Her*-pes," said Fiona. Her jaw flew open and she stepped six inches back. "Why, that son of a bitch." With a sudden snuffling sound, Fiona, as unpredictably as last time, began to cry.

"Let us sit down a moment." Stern swept up the pills and replaced the bottle on a shelf within Nate's cabinet. Then Stern steered Fiona around the corner into the bedroom and sat with her on the edge of the Cawleys' perfectly made bed. The tailored spread was of a heavy mauve material, welted on the edges. Fiona was attempting to recover. She dabbed the backs of both hands at the heavy purple shadow over her eyes. Stern extended an arm in comfort, and she laid her narrow body against him for a moment, bringing close the rosy odor of her various perfumes.

As soon as his hand was clapped across the thin cap of her shoulder, he had the first inkling. He had no notion from where the idea came. Some vicious instinct, he supposed, although it seemed that the plan had been present, unformed, for some time.

Fiona got up to find a tissue, but sat down again beside him on the bed. "Herpes," she muttered to herself. Stern, from the corner of his eye, could see the barest trace of a smile as the clear thought crossed Fiona's mind: Served him right. Served the bastard right. Then she looked at Stern directly.

"Am I going to catch this?"

"I am afraid that it depends."

"On what?"

"Your contact."

"Contact?" Fiona did not get it and looked at him with irritation.

Stern awaited the right words. Oh dear, this was difficult. Divorce lawyers must ask all the time. Probably, they were crude and direct. 'When was the last time you let him plug you, honey?'

"I do not mean to be indelicate—"

"Are you talking about our sex life, Sandy?"

"Just so."

"Not much."

"I see."

"It's not as if I don't like it, Sandy, I do," she added quickly, fearing, as always, the poor judgment of others. "But you know how that can get. I haven't let him come near me since I saw that thing." She gestured toward the floor, the family room, the television set. "Not that he seemed to care."

"And when was that, Fiona?"

"March?" She dipped a shoulder. "I don't take notes, Sandy."

"No, of course not."

"Frankly, I think he'd given up trying by then. He gets like that." She smiled again, grimly.

Stern imagined that Nate had given up long before. He had his own predicament. Not that it was much excuse. Nonetheless, here in Fiona's precise bedroom, Stern was overcome by the mystery of anyone's marriage. It was like culture or prehistory— a billion unwritten understandings. Nate and Fiona. What an unlikely couple, he mild and casual, and she so severe. She was always pretty, however. Her good looks must have mattered to Nate, been his pride. His treasure was at home while he went tomcatting all over the neighborhood, catching infections and fucking everybody's wife—Stern's wife, too. The recognition brought him to a kind of momentary delirium. Always reluctant to consciously anger, he felt drilled by the urge for revenge, high and mighty, powerful as a prizefighter. The thought passed over him again like a wave of fever. Was he really capable of this? Oh, yes. He felt excited, inspired, and nasty.

"So am I?" asked Fiona. "Going to catch this?"

"I see little chance of that, Fiona, given what you describe."

She pondered. "I suppose I should be grateful he left me alone."

Still seated beside her, Stern slowly said, "I should say he did a great injustice, Fiona."

Her head listed to a dubious angle, as if he had gone loony. Stern smiled bravely.

"A great injustice," he repeated and gradually lifted his hand. He grasped the top button of Fiona's knit dress and leaned over to kiss the brown area at the top of her chest.

She drew back at once. But she was smiling. "San-dy," she said.

His own look was intent; he meant serious business. He opened the button he had grasped and pulled the garment back slightly to caress her again.

"Oh, my," said Fiona, and laughed out loud. "I don't believe this." Fiona, it seemed, found it hard to contain herself; this was screamingly funny. The choices here, he knew, were entirely his own. She would not stop him. Fiona was a weak person. Her only resilience was in her brittleness of character, but she had no convictions. Taken by surprise, she would laugh her way along, not knowing what else to do. And he? How did he feel now? Odd, very odd, my American friends. Oh, this was wild and improbable and absurd. But sexual daring was more exciting than flying. He quietly touched her breast and felt blessedly, remarkably, fantastically, that he was no longer himself.

He opened another button and pulled her brassiere down. Her breast, small and white, seemed as startling as a fish darting by in water, and he bent to kiss her on the small button of her nipple—

Someone was looking at him!

On the bedside, Stern jolted. He actually found himself standing halfway, his arms raised defensively. The collie, cowed, had also jumped back, dragging its front paws, but did not utter a sound.

When he looked back, Fiona had risen and stood directly before him; her brassiere remained pushed down, so that her white breast looked like a package partly unwrapped. When he met her glance, something happened—perhaps his fear, even momentary, had dissuaded her, or, more simply, time had brought her back to herself. But he saw a point of contraction sharpening in her eyes, and then her arm moved. He knew what was coming but it seemed undignified to defend himself. There was a flash of pain as she struck him open-handed on the side of the face, and he felt instantly that one of his front teeth, which had knocked together, might have chipped.

"You're not any better than he is," said Fiona. "You son of a bitch."

Her back to him, she fiddled with her clothing. He felt obliged to respond, but for the time being was not capable. He sat on the bedside again, suddenly melting in shame.

"Forgive me," he said.

"Jesus," said Fiona.

He was going to tell her she was an attractive woman, but that sounded the wrong note.

"I was overcome," said Stern instead, one of his usual ambiguous formulations.

"You were taking advantage." This thought, when uttered, caused her, with as little warning as usual, to cry once more. She sat down in a white wicker chair by the window and crushed the ball of tissue to the center of her face. She'd found her drink, and she drained it for comfort, then stood, probably wanting another. She gave Stern a fiery look—one more unspoken curse—but, without further words, departed. The collie loped along behind her as she disappeared down the hall.

Listening to her clump down the stairs, he looked up at the Cawleys' bedroom ceiling. Cobwebs hung from the stylish fixture. Oh God, he was full of loathing and self-reproach. He had that underwater feeling of being very drunk, so that he knew it would be even worse whenever the adrenaline passed and a feeling of normality returned. What in the world could he have been thinking? Oh, he was going to despise himself. He did already.

He walked over to the chair Fiona had sat in. Through the mullioned window, he could see his own house. In the twenty years he had lived here, he had never viewed it from this angle, and he looked down for some time on the variegated slate roof of the bedroom wing, taken by the sight. When he recognized the gable of his own room, he actually tried to imagine Nate and Clara enwrapped about each other there, but the image, mercifully, refused to flourish.

What about the money? he thought suddenly. What in God's name did Nate need with 850,000 bucks? But Fiona had given him the answer to that weeks ago: for years she had threatened Nate with financial ruin as the cost of a divorce. She would fight like a terrier for every penny, for the sheer sake of vengeance. But with Clara's fortune squirreled away, Nate could afford Fiona's wrath. Did that mean there was a pact between them, Nate and Clara? Were they each to abandon their spouses? Did she mean to leave Stern lonesome, wandering—the way he was?

Downstairs, he heard the front door slam. Fiona was gone—perhaps to take a drunken drive about the city, rattling on to herself about the viciousness of men; or simply to give him a moment to slink off in shame. The collie, deserted by his mistress, trotted back into the room. The animal tilted its head, gazing with luminous greenish eyes. Imagine the dog's life, always on the seeming verge of comprehension.

This time, with the new thought, Stern was unable to move. This truly was Clara's legacy to him, instants of horror as he made out the hidden forms in the mess she left behind. In his line of work, he was always attempting to puzzle out precisely what had occurred in the past. The participants, clients or government witnesses, rarely provided reliable accounts. They were knocked off course by winds of fear, blame-shifting, self-justification. But occasionally, as he worked over a case, Stern himself would recognize what had happened. A word, here or there, a piece of paper. The jigsawed pieces fit.

Weak and light-headed, he had the same sensation now. Poor Clara. Now he understood. She had bestowed her enormous gift as the groundwork of whatever plan she and Nate had laid and, only after that, had learned the nature of her new medical predicament. Perhaps it was the first Nate knew of the problem. But in the circumstance he would have had no choice but to admit his other interest—probably the young lady in the video downstairs. Infidelity among the unfaithful. Oh, yes. Stern saw it now. What a drama. It was as tragic as *Madama Butterfly*. Bilked. Jilted. Diseased. Shame and loss at every window, every door, the future an endless refraction of ugly events: a husband's wrath, a lover's departure, and the excruciating knowledge of a fortune squandered in order to buy her boyfriend the freedom he intended to spend in other pursuits. What humiliation! Like a heroine of myth, Clara had lost everything through pride and desire. Sitting now on Fiona's expensive bedspread, Stern placed one hand over his heart; it felt rough and sore, pumping away within his chest.

He would have to call Cal. At once. What a story this would be to tell. Lawyer Hopkinson would drill another hole in his head. Stern wanted the papers drawn now. With the check, Nate was in a tricky position. His plan from the start must have been to hold it in order to hide the funds from Fiona and her divorce lawyer. But now, with Clara's death, with bankers and executors, with probate, he would have to move, fearing that someone might soon learn of the transaction and attempt to see it undone. The day Nate found the nerve to present his check, Stern would sue. There would be smoke and fragments everywhere. He would grind Nate Cawley like a seed beneath a stone.

In this burst of vicious impulse, Stern was smitten suddenly, overpoweringly, with the sensation of how preposterous this was. None of this had occurred. He thought that clearly. Any second, groping for the switch, he would find the light and see where he really was. But when he turned about, the collie was truly there, still watching, and the house he had lived in for twenty years was out the window, viewed at this angle from which he had never seen it before. His lip was beginning to thicken and welt from the impact of one of Fiona's rings. He found his way down, closed the dog in the kitchen, and then, feeling that something he could never recall was utterly lost, let himself out the door.

*For him, the most evocative memories of their courtship
were of the times he sat in the parlour of the Mittler home
while Clara played the piano. Her soft reddish hair followed
just behind the occasional downward movements of her
head; her eyes were fast upon the keyboard, or closed, as she
turned herself over to the music. Her high intelligence sang
through the instrument. The first time she performed for
him, he had no idea what to say. He had come to the door to
collect her and she invited him to step inside a moment.
Neither of her parents was home and apparently she felt free
to show him about. "My piano," she said. He asked her to
play, and instead of demurring as he expected, she set herself
free. He sat on the red plush divan in his scarf and overcoat,
utterly ignorant of the music, but overcome by the conviction
with which she struck the keys. He admired her intensely.*

"Magnificent," he said.

*She stood shyly beside the instrument, absorbing his
praise.*

*They went then to the show. The movie—he still
remembered—was the subject of some excitement. Marty. The
story of this lonely, inept man, full of longing, stirred Stern.
That was him, him! Afterwards, walking to George Murray's
Chevy, parked far down the block, he recognized that Clara,
too, had been sadly moved. She clung to him firmly as they
strolled, speaking of certain harrowing moments lived out
on the screen.*

*When they reached the car, Stern could not help himself.
He cried out and doubled over for a moment.*

"Oh, George," he said.

*Whoever had sideswiped George Murray's car had left a
number of victims. The scratches began behind the door,
growing in a broadening trail until the point of impact on
the front fender. There the metal was cruelly withered and
the filament of the front headlamp hung down from a single
wire. The auto ahead was worse; the entire trunk was folded
up like a smash carton.*

*"Oh, God," she said when she finally saw it. She grabbed
his arm. "This isn't your car, is it?"*

*"Oh, no." The loss seemed incalculable. His mind fumbled
ahead futilely for some way it all could be restored.*

"I'm so sorry."

He shrugged, staring at the wreckage.

"No telephone this month," he said.

He was required to call the police. They walked to a drugstore and the police were there by the time they had returned to the car. George Murray, thankfully, was not home. Somehow Stern felt he could tolerate all this, except telling him. This girl and her sympathy seemed to give him courage. The cop was an amiable type, an older white-haired man who had been put out to pasture. He asked Stern about his accent in an honest, inquisitive way and then lay in the boulevard hauling on the bumper in order to straighten it out so that Stern did not dirty his suit. Stern sat behind the wheel, turning it as the policeman pulled on the dimpled sheet metal.

"Good enough to drive," the cop finally announced. "Save you a penny or two on the tow. Those fellas are pirates."

The policeman, Leary, tipped his hat when they drove away. Stern had no idea where they were going.

"Shall I take you home?" he asked her.

"Oh, not yet," she said, so emphatically that Stern was taken by surprise. The car had no radio, but there was a clock. It was five past midnight. "I have to be certain you're well. Are you?"

He made a sound. He was badly shaken. Yet it was amazing how buoyed he was by female attention. He reminded himself of the cartoons he saw in the theater of Popeye when he ate his spinach. With her, before he faced George and the months of bills, he felt almost invincible.

"Where shall we go, then?" he asked. "Are you hungry?"

"Really, no. I couldn't, not now. I lost whatever appetite I had. I don't take a drink very often, but I could use one now. You, too?"

He answered her again with a sound. "Under the circumstances, I could drink," he said.

"You know what would be nice? Why don't you stop at a package store and we can sit out by the river. There's a lovely spot. I'll show you."

So that is what they did. They bought a bottle of Southern Comfort and two cheap tumblers and drove a few blocks to a parking lot on a low bluff over the river. The river was wide here, black and wild with sound beneath them. The moon was up, high in the trees, filling Kindle with racing light.

As she opened the bottle, he cautioned her.

"George," he said, "expects his car to be returned in mint condition."

She eyed him over the cap, unimpressed on this occasion by his mild humor.

"You're going to suffer terribly over this, aren't you?"

He hesitated, then shook his head bravely.

"You wouldn't consider letting me pay for this, would you?" she asked.

He shook his head again.

"I could, you know. I have quite a bit of money. My mother's sister left a trust. It was available after I was twenty-five and it just sits there."

"And what would your father think of that?"

"I don't care what my father thinks."

Stern again made his sound. He thought of her as he first saw her, on Henry's footstool.

"Do you care?" she asked. "About him?"

"I am afraid I do."

"I do, too," she said, after a moment. "I'd rather say I don't, but I do. I think most girls care more about their mothers, but my mother worships him. Is your family like that?"

Stern laughed, thinking of his father as he came to know him toward the end, an agitated, feckless human being on the verge of one breakdown or another.

"No," he said.

"Do you like my father?"

Stern contemplated the question. The engine was running, a throaty rumble, so they could have heat.

"I believe I am too afraid of him to know the answer."

She laughed out loud.

"Do you know what I like about you, Sandy? You don't remind me of anyone."

He was tempted to remark about making virtues out of faults. But he realized that this pleased him. He was who he was. The car, the disaster, had allowed a remarkable candor between them. Moreover, as was usually true on the rare occasions when anyone could inspire him to straightforward response, he learned a good deal about himself.

"And how do you feel about your father?"

"The same as you," she said. "I admire him. When I was a girl, I wanted to be just like him. Before I realized that he wouldn't let me. I resent him, I suppose. It's hard to know. My parents have been quite angry with me for some time."

Stern sat back against the door to look at her. The liquor had begun to make him warm and somewhat drunk.

"What is the story you seem to have to tell? I sense great unhappiness."

"Do you?"

"You must forgive me. I suppose that was rather blunt."

"Rather," she said. In the dark, fear reached up to seize him. He had gone too far. He was on a cliff with this girl. At any moment this atmosphere of intimacy could fade and she could revert to being the daughter of a wealthy man, well beyond him. He knew that was what she meant before—that she did not know how to regard him. Like any person born to great wealth, she was proficient with an offhanded officiousness—she could instantly push him off to a million-mile distance, if she wanted to.

"I don't think of myself as a happy person," she said. "I'm very shy. Except around you." She smiled. "Are you happy?"

"I enjoy my work. I care for my sister. But no, I do not consider myself a cheerful person by disposition."

"I didn't think so," she said. They were both quiet. "I'm going to tell you everything," Clara Mittler said presently.

He waited a moment in the dark before he said, "All right."

24

"Mel? Sandy Stern," he said into the telephone.

"San-dy!" cried Mel in return, the usual trumpet blast: hail fellow well met. Face forward, Tooley had a single expression, a beaming countenance of unlimited goodwill. Turn your back, however, and the knives came out, the mischief started. An insidious fellow. Tooley claimed to be Irish—it was in this city, like many others, a political advantage, particularly at the bar— but he had the swarthy look of a more Southerly heritage. Mel wore a wig—profuse, dark, and curly as the coat of a poodle—a trait which Stern, in spite of his efforts at tolerance, found shabby and insincere. The man was always sweating and, in consequence, bathed in cologne. And he was overweight—not that Stern was the kind to criticize this fault; but Mel, cut to the dimensions of certain cattle, still favored double-breasted suits and flashy pocket hankies, and refused to accept biology as fate. He squeezed himself into tapered shirts and sat with his dark hairy gut bulging between the buttons, his oily smile suggesting an unambiguous belief that he was suave.

Stern had dealt with Mel for years when Tooley was a prosecutor, a prickly relation marked by many bitter struggles. Mel, in a word, was underhanded, an exception in an office in which most of the lawyers were overly aggressive but generally respectful of rules and rights. Stern's most serious run-in with Mel had occurred five years ago, when Stern represented a contractor whom Tooley desperately wanted to testify against two gentlemen whose names ended in vowels. The contractor had been granted immunity, but he persisted in a version of events which even Stern, privately, regarded as improbable.

When he and his client showed up for his grand jury appearance, the contractor, a hardboiled, tight-lipped kind, suddenly paled; the sweat on his scalp looked like rain. He was a Knights of Columbus man, the father of nine, and Tooley had the contractor's former mistress seated primly on the sofa outside the grand jury room. For the sake of his client, Stern, always reluctant to publicly criticize any attorney, had to file a disciplinary complaint with the District Court Executive Committee. The judges had clucked their tongues and chastised Mel, but in the end the contractor testified, and just as Mel liked. Tooley had the last laugh. Face to face, he claimed to bear no grudges and was quick to praise Stern's ability. But in a world where ego mattered so, one knew better than to believe that. Stern wondered again how it was John had wandered into Tooley's hands.

Tooley, now, said he had been about to call, a remark which Stern took as being within striking distance of the truth. Tooley naturally was interested in making arrangements for MD to pay his fee. He wanted a $15,000 retainer—on the high side for a fellow of Tooley's age, but what Stern might have expected. They chatted as best they could about the case. Stern said nothing to Tooley about the house error account; he had to assume that every word would go back to the prosecutors, to be used however Tooley saw fit, for John's advantage or simply as some way to curry favor for the future. Stern described the customer orders that the government was tracing, said the prosecutors seemed to think that Dixon had made some sort of improper profit.

"I take it that they believe the orders were placed with John," said Stern.

"Were they?" inquired Tooley, as if he did not have a client to ask. "I mean, I don't have any documents to look at. I wouldn't mind seeing whatever you've turned over."

Stern made a note and said that he would send them.

"Well, of course," said Stern, "he may have received these orders but might be unable to recall them, given the crush of daily business. I have no idea whether or not that is a possibility, but a reasonable person might understand that." Tooley was very quick—he would not miss the hint—but he did not answer, which Stern regarded as unpromising. Stern went on: "What exactly is it that Klonsky tells you she wants with him?"

"Actually," said Tooley, "I haven't dealt with Sonny. I've talked just a little bit to Stan." Sennett again. Stern shook his head. "He's got his hand on the throttle on this one. Did you know that?" asked Tooley. He would have been delighted to one-up Stern with the news.

"I have gotten that drift. I imagine he has his own agenda."

"He always does," said Tooley, joining in brotherly fashion in the familiar complaints defense lawyers had with the present United States Attorney. From Tooley, this was mostly show. He had worked for Sennett for more than a year before entering private practice, and in that time Stan had promoted Tooley to chief of the office's Special Investigations Division. Stan had made Mel a big *macher*. There was a reason Tooley had chosen him as his point of contact. "So, how you like dealing with Funny Sonny?" Mel asked, obviously skirting. "She's a piece of work, isn't she?"

"Ms. Klonsky?" asked Stern. "I hadn't heard that name."

"That's what I call her," said Mel. "Everybody calls her something. She's my fault, you know. I hired her, right before I left the office. I mean, Stan did. But I interviewed her. I thought she had some balls. You know?"

"Yes," said Stern simply. He understood the point.

"But I don't think she's a real star there yet. What's the word? Ambivalent. They can't get her to decide anything. She's always wringing her hands. You know. Tries a good case, though. Nice-looking woman has got a hell of an advantage in front of a jury, don't you think?"

Stern uttered a sound. Perhaps. Mel went on. Clearly, he had little interest in speaking about John.

"Y'know, I should blame you for hiring her. I say she's my fault, but she's really yours."

"Mine?" asked Stern. "Klonsky?"

"I just remembered this. I asked her why she wanted to be a trial lawyer and she told me this story about when she was in her first year of law school, how she saw every day of the Sabich trial. She loved watching you work. I forgot how she described you. 'Sleight of hand,' I think. I thought it was a cute way to put it."

Indeed, thought Stern. Tooley must have held his sides.

"So you see, you're her idol, Sandy. I bet she gets hot flashes whenever you call."

"There is hardly any sign of that."

"Who knows with her? Very emotional person. She been telling you yet about her goofy husband?"

"Not really," said Stern. He felt, more acutely now, some alliance with Klonsky. Mel was improving his opinion of her the longer he went on.

"She will," said Mel. "She tells everybody. You know about this guy? He's a mailman. I'm not kidding. He writes poetry and delivers mail. The guy thinks he's Omar Khayyam or something. Apparently he's nuttier than she is. Every second day while I was there she was in the head bawling her eyes out, saying she was going to divorce this guy. And now she's p.g. because her biological clock is going ding-dong. Oh, well," said Mel, finally tired of the subject. "Be kind to her, Sandy."

"More the reverse," said Stern, trying in the mildest way to say something in Klonsky's behalf.

"I'm sure Sennett's watching her like a hawk."

"So it seems," said Stern. "Might I ask what he tells you?"

"Not clear," said Mel. "Not clear. I believe they're looking for immunity. I'm not certain for what."

Stern hung there, feeling for all the world like a small insect humming its wings in a formidable breeze. There was little more that he could ask. Given pride, and fear of what might go back to the government, he was reluctant to discuss the blank spots in his knowledge of the investigation. And there were few other avenues of inquiry. What John had told Mel, if anything, was out of bounds in this kind of situation. Many defense lawyers blurted out their client's confidences like bits of witless news posted on some local bulletin board, but Stern had never shared that inclination. In a situation of potential adversity, he neither asked for nor shared his client's private words, his rigidity on this point of ethics accepted as one more part of Sandy Stern and his formal foreign manner, like the hedgerow and iron fence about certain older homes.

"I'm just getting into this thing," Tooley said. "Maybe I can give you a call next week when I get my bearings."

"Yes, of course," said Stern. He would never hear from Tooley, not until a day or two before the indictment was returned, when

Mel would describe vaguely the factors that required John to ax Dixon. Stern had faced similar dilemmas himself when he represented witnesses. But he tried to give his colleagues what little help he could along the way. Stern prepared to conclude the call, going over the list of things that Tooley wanted from him. Mel, slyly, had put the shoe on the other foot and was the one receiving all the information.

"He's a nice kid," Tooley said in conclusion. "Maybe not a rocket scientist, but he should come out okay."

"One hopes," said Stern, nettled nonetheless by the feeling that Tooley had gone out of his way to provide this dim assessment of his son-in-law.

"It's crazy how he came to me. You gave him a couple names, I take it."

"A few," said Stern. Neither he nor Tooley harbored illusions about whether Mel would have been included.

"He called those guys, but nobody was in. Apparently you put the fear of God in him. Felt he just had to get a lawyer lickitysplit. So he called everybody he knew and ended up getting my name from your son."

"From Peter?"

"My brother Alan and Peter were like this in high school. Remember Alan? I have to give Pete a call and thank him."

Alan was a handsome, wholesome, genial kid. It seemed impossible that the same home could have produced something as viperous as Mel Tooley. Stern held his head while he absorbed the latest news. Peter again! It was as inevitable as the seasons, however, that he would have mixed in if asked. Ignorant or not, his son considered any family problem part of his domain. Meanwhile, Stern imagined Mel across town, in his flashy office, smirking. He had Stern's client paying his fee while John considered laying Dixon low, and Stern's own son was the source of his employment. Quite a tickle.

Chalk up one more for the government, thought Stern, as he put down the phone. There were lawyers friendly to the target or his counsel, or naturally disinclined to help the prosecution, who would go over the situation with John two or three times and remind him of how large the gaps were in his memory, how unrewarding testimony for the government might be. But that clearly was not Mel's plan. He would offer John up freely to the prosecutors, encouraging him to be forthcoming with the vaguest hunch or suspicion. And John—if Stern could correctly read Tooley's silence and the signs in his own conversations with his son-in-law—apparently had much to tell.

Idly, he contemplated how it must have gone between John and Dixon. It was not likely that Dixon had announced what he was up to; he was too secretive for that. He issued commands, which John was afraid to countermand. But a certain furtiveness must have accompanied this scheme. Just between me and you. Don't tell. As Clara always said, John was not dumb. Sooner or later, he must have known that these trades were being handled differently from others. So they went on in the usual murky world of collaboration and deceit, each with some unspoken ground of disrespect for the other: You are weak. You are dishonest. His son-in-law was the classic stuff of the government witness, an unquestioning lower-down with the convictions of a noodle. As soon as Tooley explained the facts of life to him—that his commodities registration and his right to do business on the financial markets in the future hung in the balance—he would reduce his level of actual suspicions to none at all. By the time he got to the witness stand, he would be one more wanton soul testifying that he had merely followed orders, without a minute for reflection. With his look of childish innocence, and his relative inexperience, John would carry this act off better than most.

Thinking of all this and the way the situation was gradually spinning out of control, Stern felt queasy. For just an instant, he fell beneath a quirky vision of his entire family down at the federal courthouse, testifying, pointing fingers, hopelessly involved. In that scene, he somehow was the victim, not the man accused but the one left out in the cold. Everybody knew more than he did. He shook the notion off, but looked down to the phone, full again of that sense of coming injury which could not be prevented.

25

Margy seemed to have done something with her hair. Near her shoulder it sprayed up in a froth of curls, and its blondish tint seemed brighter when she came into the light. She looked bigger than Stern recalled—a hale, large person full of life. He refused at once to allow recollection or imagination to take him any further.

"Fine," she answered when he inquired about her flight. "Nice hotel," she added. "Slept good." A simple declarative utterance ripe in implication: all was forgotten, forgiven, swept aside. Margy was good at this, pretending that nothing had ever occurred; she had done it, Stern sensed, dozens of times. Whatever the writhing inside, the internal outcry, the reverberations would never touch the surface. She sat there all dolled up, wearing a raw-silk suit and an orange blouse with a huge bow. She had come into Stern's office carrying a large briefcase and a garment bag slung from her shoulder, and had been savvy enough to extend her hand, with its long red nails, while his secretary was still present, so that neither of them would be discomfited by the opportunity for some more intimate hello. The Oklahoma businesswoman, determined and composed. Hi y'all.

Behind his smoky glass desk, Stern spent a moment describing the day's agenda. He and Margy each drank coffee. Together, they would scrutinize the documents the government had subpoenaed and attempt to anticipate Ms. Klonsky's questions. Then they would proceed to the U.S. Attorney's Office, where Klonsky would interrogate Margy in preparation for her appearance before the grand jury, which would immediately follow.

"Do I gotta do that," Margy asked, "siddown and have this chat with her?"

"No, but it is routine. It suits both sides. I am not allowed inside the grand jury room, so by submitting to an interview, we learn in advance what the prosecutor has in mind and I will have the chance to help in any troublesome areas. Ms. Klonsky, in turn, finds which questions she would rather not ask you on the record."

"I get it." Margy was satisfied. She asked where he wanted to start, and he pointed to the briefcase.

"The hard part," said Margy with a smile. Hard port.

"A problem?" asked Stern. He did not care for the sound of this. He put down the coffee cup and removed the subpoena from the file. Margy unloaded first the checks the government had demanded—all those written in the first four months af the year for amounts exceeding $250. She had them literally tied up in string, nine stacks, each the size of a brick, with the severed perforations lending, from the side, a striated look, like certain fish.

"What-all they gonna do with these?"

"They are looking, I assume, for funds being transferred to Dixon. Is there any evidence of that?"

"Shore," she said. "Lots of it. Salary. Bonus."

"Anything else?"

"*Nada.*"

"Did any companies or accounts you know him to control receive money?"

"Nothin," said Margy.

Good, he thought. He flipped through the stacks, more to get the feel of the checks than anything else. She had made two copies, a set for Stern and a set for herself, and had a clerk stamp an identification number on each. You did not need to teach Margy anything twice.

Stern referred again to the subpoena. Because many of the records were already here, Stern last week had taken responsibility for assembling the trading records which the prosecutors had asked for. The remaining documents had been delivered to Stern's Office, and in preparation for today he had carefully gone into each pile and replaced, just where he had found them, the order tickets the government was surely seeking—the four or five dozen which John had written. The bundle of documents, copied and numbered like the checks, waited now in a white transfer case. He showed them to Margy, then had Claudia summon one of the young men in the office, who would deliver the records to the grand jury room prior to their arrival.

Stern read aloud the government's last request for records of the Wunderkind Associates account.

"The strange port." Margy had her briefcase on her lap and removed a manila folder. Maison Dixon, like many houses, used what was called a consolidated statement, in which purchases and sales, confirmations, margin requirements, and positions were all reported together. The computer spat out a single form, which was mailed to the customer any time there was account activity. The second leaf of that computer form remained at MD and was microfilmed. Opening the folder, Stern was surprised to find the original statements which should have gone to Wunderkind.

"It's strange," she said. "See the address."

The documents said "Wunderkind Associates" at the top, and "[HOLD]." He asked what the notation meant.

"Hold," she said. "You know. Like 'Don't mail it, I'll pick it up.' "

"Does that occur often?"

"Sometimes. Fella's gettin a divorce and don't want his wife countin up everything he owns on her fingers or toes. Or he thinks the IRS is openin his mail. Or he don't think much of the mailman in his neighborhood. Lotsa reasons."

Stern nodded. "And these were never picked up?"

"They were sittin right in the file."

"Chicago account?"

"Kindle," she said. "05." She lifted her bottom from one of the cream-colored chairs to point to the account number. "Greco found them."

"Peculiar," said Stern.

"Oh, that ain't what's strange."

"No?"

"Look through 'em."

He did, and as usual noticed nothing.

"Look at the activity. Look at the balance. Remember? This is where he's puttin all that money he makes tradin ahead. I thought for sure he'd be cashin out these positions he's transferrin in, havin us cut him one check after another. You know: take the money and run."

Clearly, however, that was not what had occurred. The statements portrayed frequent trading, two or three movements a day. There was no unusual concentration of positions. T-bonds. Silver. Beans. Sugar. Yen. Those were the favorites, but all were frequently traded, often with multiple moves each day. Stern read to the end in February of that year.

"He lost money?" asked Stern.

"Not just money," said Margy. "Everything. There ain't a red centavo that got stole that didn't end up goin right back into the market. Hell, he didn't just lose all that. He lost more. Look at the last statement."

Stern turned the pages again. On the final statement, in bold-face, there was a deficit balance reflected of slightly more than $250,000. Trading on margin—borrowing money from the house to put on positions worth more than what you had invested in the account—it was always possible to lose large amounts quickly, and it had happened here to a fare-thee-well. Everything had been sunk into sugar contracts, which had come to ruin over several days in February when the market ran wild. By the time Mr. Wunderkind had extricated himself, the loss was enormous, a quarter of a million dollars more than the equity he'd had in the account to start with.

"The debit balance was paid off?" he asked.

"That's what the statement says. All 250,000 bucks. I never heard nothin about it."

"Should you have?"

"You betchum," said Margy. She sat up a little straighter. "Deficit balance over a hundred grand? Either I hear about it or it goes straight down to Dixon from accounting."

"Ah," said Stern. He wondered. Dixon could have probably written off a debt to the house like this with a single stroke of the pen. But the statement showed funds received—Wunderkind had paid off the money he owed MD.

Stern stared at the papers and, with the familiar frozen precision of his most single-minded attempts to understand, went over it all aloud. Margy nodded each step of the way. The man had self-consciously placed orders ahead of customers, a major infraction. In order to hide that, erroneous account numbers were used and the transactions, taken for mistakes, were moved to the house error account, where substantial profits of tens of thousands of dollars on every pair of trades accumulated. Then, in order to gain control of these illegal profits, the man had placed additional orders, once again making deliberate errors in the account information. The result was that the error account paid for the trade. Then the new position was moved by various accounting entries to this new account.

"Wunderkind Associates," said Margy.

"Wunderkind Associates," said Stern. "And then, instead of simply closing his positions and making off with all these illgotten gains, he traded on them. Repeatedly. And badly."

"Right."

"So that, at the end, the net result of dozens of unlawful transactions, all of them wickedly clever, is that they have cost him approximately a quarter of a million dollars."

"That's what the paper says."

"Not right," said Stern resolutely. He knew, with a conviction durable as steel, there was more to it than this. These shenanigans in the Wunderkind account were one more interim link in the long, twisted chain. Stealing this money had turned into a sport for Dixon, his version of the steeplechase. How many hurdles could he take at a canter? Stern decided at once that the losses had to be phony. There was ample precedent for that. From what Stern understood, at the end of every year there were dozens of such transactions on the Exchanges, designed to fool the IRS. In violation of every rule, trades were arranged off the floor and then carried out in the pit as a kind of second-rate pantomime, so that a loss was recorded for tax purposes, while the position, through one device or another, eventually returned to its original owner. No doubt, something like that was involved here. Perhaps there was some record Dixon meant to set: most laws broken in a single theft. Stern sat there shaking his head, convinced he could never work through the final intricacies of this scheme. On the other hand, it was possible the prosecutors would not manage that either.

"I am not certain, Margy," said Stern at last, "that I see this as the problem you do."

"Oh," she said, "this ain't the bad port. This is the strange port."

"Ah," said Stern, and felt his internal elevator descend another floor or two, not as far or as steeply as he might have expected. He was growing accustomed to this. "And what, Margy, is the bad news?"

"This thing"—she hied half out of her seat to indicate the subpoena—"asks for all the account information. You know, the account application, risk disclosure statement, signature documents."

"Yes. They want to prove whose account this is."

"See, that's why we got a little problem here, Buster Brown. Cause I can't find even an itty-bitty scrap of paper to show who these Wunderkinds are."

"No," said Stern simply.

"I'm tellin you," she said. "It's all gone. All those forms go on microfiche. Fiche for the month that account opened last year ain't to be found. Three copies. Then we got a little computer screen on every customer. You know: name, address, social security. Somebody's gone in on the system and zapped it out. You put in that account number, you get nothin but a blinkin light. And a' course, the hard copy on all the forms—they been swiped right out of the file."

"And where were those records kept?"

"Depends. Central microfiche is in Chicago, but we got a backup here. Hard copy for this account'd be here. Computer you can get on anywhere. If you know what you're doin."

"And would Dixon have access to these records?" The question, even to Stern's own ear, sounded weak. The answer was obvious. Margy put it her own way.

"Honey, there ain't nothin in three cities that Dixon don't have access to from the receptionist's be-hind to the drawer where I keep my Maalox. It's Maison Dixon. You askin me if somebody saw him piddlin around in a file cabinet they'd say, Hey there, watcha doin? No chance. I told you. They're all scared a' him."

"You searched thoroughly, Margy?"

"I went through the files here myself last night."

"I see." He flipped up the humidor and looked at the cigars, snug in their brown jackets like military men at ease. Last week, he'd had Claudia fill the box, but he had not yet lit or even pressed his teeth into a cigar. "Of course," said Stern, "there have been times that records have been lost in the process of copying for microfiche, correct?"

"Shore."

"And accidental erasures of computer information probably occur daily?"

"Maybe," said Margy.

"And if you have no microfiche in either city, perhaps you never had one in the first place?"

Margy looked at Stern with outthrust chin and gimlet eye, as he made these efforts in the mode of piercing cross-examination. Her expression was easy to read: No sale.

Stern took a long swallow of his coffee and turned to the window. From here on the thirty-eighth floor of Morgan Towers, the river held a liquid gleam. Some days it was leaden and murky. In high winds, the current increased and the water spit and lashed at the brown standards used to moor barges and other slow-moving hauling craft that sometimes made their way upstream. Over time he'd come to know the meaning of its changing tones. Stern could tell from the density of color if the barometer was dropping, if the cloud cover was heavy or likely soon to lift. That was the value of experience, he supposed, to be able to read the meaning of signs, to know the large impact signaled by small things.

This would go badly with the government. Quite badly. He had been warning Dixon against this for months now, to no apparent avail. Dixon was shrewd enough to recognize that even if the prosecutors could not figure out what he had done with the money, they would have a case if they could prove he had stolen it—and proof that he controlled this Wunderkind account would suffice. But it was a desperate response to destroy the documents. The government could barely avoid proving Dixon was responsible. As Margy said, there was probably no other person in the company who could have gone into the files in two cities with the same impunity. As the government showed Dixon's access to each missing record, the circumstantial web would take on a taut, sinister look. And for that kind of action there was never an innocent explanation. Stern was good. He could refer to error accounts and margin calls and limit drops and make a jury dizzy. But when the prosecutors wheeled the MD shredder into the courtroom, there would be no way to cross-examine the machine. Dixon might as well have jumped inside. You could never save clients from themselves, Stern thought. Never.

So begins the last act in the tableau of Dixon Hartnell, smalltown boy made good, gone bad. For Stern, in every case which came to grief there was a moment when his knowledge of a gruesome future fact became firm and thoroughly delineated. Occasionally, it was not until the jury spoke; but more often there was some telling instant along the way as when Stern, as the saying went, could see beyond the curve. In the matter of Dixon Hartnell, husband to his sister, client, compatriot, sporting and military companion, today was the day. Too much was accumulating here—knowledge, motive, opportunity; the error account, John's recollections, the documents gone. Today he knew the end of the story.

Dixon was going to the penitentiary.

*   *   *

He took a few minutes to coach Margy on the basics of dealing with Klonsky: Listen to the question. Answer it narrowly and precisely. Volunteer nothing. Never say no when asked if particular events occurred; answer, rather, I do not recollect. Name, rank, serial number. Hard facts. No opinions. If asked to speculate, decline to. And in the grand jury, remember that Stern literally would be at the door. She had an absolute right to consult with counsel at any time and should ask to speak to her lawyer if there was any question, no matter how trivial, for which she felt remotely unprepared.

He helped her pack the documents back into her briefcase and slipped into his suit coat by the door. He picked up her bag and asked if she was ready. Margy lingered in the chair.

"I was pretty tough on you," she said quietly. She looked at her coffee cup, against which she rested one bright nail. "When we were talkin a few weeks ago?"

"Not without warrant."

"You know, Sandy, I got lots of calluses." She looked up briefly and smiled almost shyly. "The only thing a gal wants is for you to pretend a little bit."

Stern moved a step or two closer. As usual with Margy, the thought of her boss was not far away. Dixon was probably very good at pretending, resorting to every corny gesture; he would throw his coat down in a puddle if need be, or croon outside the window. And here was Margy telling him that women liked that sort of thing. Stern waited, summoning himself. The best he could manage was diplomacy.

"Margy, this has been a time of extraordinary turmoil. Many unexpected developments."

"Shore." Margy smiled stiffly and tilted the cup, garishly rimmed with her lipstick, gazing down with great interest at her cold coffee. "Shore," she said again.

Well, thought Stern, here one could begin to understand her dilemma. Margy wanted her gentlemen friends to pretend—so that she could tell them coldly that she did not believe them. Stern was certain that he had now arrived at an essential vision. He had heard the pitch, found the harmonics of a perfect composition in the scale of personal pain. Margy's creation was as clever as Chinese handcuffs. Constrained, however you moved. His heart, as usual, went out to her.

And so, out of some impulse of tenderness, he told her what he took to be the truth. "I have lately been seeing a good deal of a woman who was a friend of ours for many years." Very brief. To the point. He was not quite certain what he meant to accomplish by this eruption of candor, except the virtue of honesty itself. Indeed, after his bizarre interlude with Fiona, in which Helen had not been so much as a momentary thought, he had no idea whether this fact was any better than convenient. But clarification was called for, and Margy, whatever his admiration, was not his destiny. The news had the predictable effect. Her pupils took on the contracted look they might have in strong light. He had cast her again in her inevitable role: once more, the loser; the flop-and-drop gal, She was not pleased. Margy, like everyone else, wanted a better life than the one she had.

"Nice for you," said Margy. She snatched her purse, closed her case, smoothed her skirt as she rose, grazing him with a tight, penetrating smile. What was the poet's phrase? Zero at the bone. She had put on again her blank tough-guy look that she brought to business meetings, once more Dixon Hartnell's hard-ass hired hand.

They walked the three blocks to the courthouse in virtual silence. Stern's only remarks were directions: Just up there we

turn. They were escorted back to Klonsky's narrow office at
once and Margy settled herself in the old oak armchair like a
rider in the rodeo. She was ready.

"Margy," she said, when Klonsky asked what she liked to be
called. "Hard *g*." Hard *g*, indeed, thought Stern. Like a diamond
drill.

They had arrived late, and Klonsky cast an eye up at the clock.
Time before the grand jury was assigned by a deputy court clerk
in quarter-hour intervals and was zealously guarded by the
Assistants, who were always pressed to get their business done
in the period allotted. Klonsky began questioning Margy, even
while Stern was reviewing her non-subject letter. It was signed
by the U.S. Attorney himself and assured Margy that she was not
suspected of any criminal involvement, assuming she told the
truth before the grand jury. Stern put the letter in his case and
looked on as Klonsky worked. She asked Margy questions, all of
them routine, and wrote down the answers on a yellow pad.
Wearing her prosecutor's hat, Sonia was like most of her
colleagues, relentless, humorless, intense. Her pace was sufficiently methodical that Stern actually grew hopeful that the
matter of the missing documents might not come up. That would
allow him to have a pointed conversation first with Mr. Hartnell.
But with only a few minutes remaining before they were
scheduled to appear at the grand jury, Klonsky removed her
tissue copy of the subpoena from the file and went through it,
item by item. When Margy handed over the statements for the
Wunderkind account, she added brightly, "That's it."

"That's it?" asked Klonsky, with an immediate look of
apprehension. She glanced back to her papers.

Stern, for the first time, spoke up. Somewhere, he said, there
was a misunderstanding. The various account-opening
documents—signature forms, applications, et cetera—seemed
to have been misplaced and could not presently be located. A
diligent search had been conducted by Ms. Allison and would be
continued, Stern stated, under his direction.

"They're gone?" asked Klonsky. "Trashed?"

Margy started to speak, but Stern reached out to grab her
wrist where a heavy bracelet lay. It was far too early, said Stern,
to assume the documents could not be located. The subpoena
had been served barely three weeks ago, and MD was a

substantial company with hundreds of employees and more than one office.

"I don't believe this," Klonsky said. She largely ignored Stern and put a series of questions to Margy, identifying the documents, the copies, the places they were stored. She extracted, in more precision than Stern had, the details of Margy's search. Conducting this inquiry, Klonsky was rigid and intent behind her desk. Whatever her occasional geniality, Ms. Klonsky, when provoked, was quick to anger.

She looked at Stern. "I'm going to have to talk to Stan about this."

"Sonia," said Stern, "again, I think you are leaping unnecessarily—"

She cut him off with an ill-tempered wave of her hand. Clad in her familiar blue jumper, she bumped her belly a bit against her desk as she climbed out from behind her chair and led the way downstairs to the grand jury.

When the judges had deserted the new federal building, they left the grand jury behind. The defense lawyers protested this propinquity to the United States Attorney's Office, but it was recognized as vain posturing. For all practical purposes, the grand jury belonged to the prosecutors. An unmarked door in the corridor a floor below led into what looked like a doctor's reception room; it held the same inexpensive furniture, with cigarette burns and splintered veneers, as in the U.S. Attorney's Office upstairs. Behind two additional doors lay the grand jury rooms themselves. Stern had often peeked inside. It did not look like much: a tiny raised bench at the front of the room and rows of tiered seats, like a small classroom. The twenty-three grand jurors, who had been called out of the regular jury pool to help the prosecutors determine whether they had enough evidence to try someone for a crime, tended to be union workers of one kind or another who had no store to mind, or else the retired, women at home who could manage the time, or frequently those out of work who valued the $30 daily fee.

To Stern, the grand jury, purportedly intended to protect the innocent, remained one of the preeminent fictions of the criminal-justice scheme. Occasionally, the defense bar was warmed by tales of a renegade grand jury that returned a no bill or two, or quarreled with the prosecutors about a case. But usually the jurors deferred, as one would expect, to the diligent young faces of the U.S. Attorney's Office. By all reports, the grand jurors sat knitting, reading papers, picking at their nails, while a given individual, brought here by the might and majesty of the United States, was grilled at will by the Assistants.

"Remember I am here," he told Margy. She strolled inside, hauling her briefcase, and did not look back. She remained in poor humor with him. Klonsky also was put out, and, perhaps without meaning to, slammed the door on Stern as she called the session to order.

The proceedings were secret. The room had no windows and a single door. The grand jurors, the prosecutors, the court reporter could not disclose what had occurred, unless there was a trial, when the government was required to reveal the prior testimony of witnesses. In this federal district, commendably, there were seldom leaks of grand jury matters and much went on here that was never heard about again, a comforting fact for those subjected to baseless or even unprovable allegations. But it was the same respectable principle of secrecy that was cited to bar the witness's lawyer from attending; Stern had only the right to wait at the door, in the fashion of a well-trained dog. The witness, under no bans of confidentiality, could leave if need be after every question to ask the lawyer's advice. But intimidated by the setting, and eager to appease the interrogator, they seldom did so. His clients usually left Stern maintaining his vigil at the door, his case and hat in hand, his stomach grinding.

Sometimes, particularly with male voices of a certain timbre, Stern found that the seat nearest to the grand jury room enabled him, if he moderated his breathing and others outside were not gabbing, to overhear the proceedings word for word. Today he was not as fortunate. Barney Hill, the deputy court clerk who slotted time and filled out attendance forms for witnesses, chatted to Stern about the Trappers, and the women's voices did not seem to carry as well through the heavy door. He could hear Klonsky at a certain pitch and the confident tone of Margy's response. After fifteen minutes, the door banged open and both women emerged. They were finished. Predictably, Margy had chosen not to visit with her lawyer.

"I'm still concerned about those documents," said Klonsky from the threshold of the grand jury room, with a number of the grand jurors milling about behind her. "Ms. Allison's going to be looking for them again."

"Of course," said Stern.

"As far I'm concerned, we're beginning an investigation for an O.O.J." Obstruction of Justice.

Stern once more attempted to mollify her, but Klonsky, with half a smile at his familiar excuses, waved him off. She repeated again that she was going to talk to the U.S. Attorney, and headed out, apparently to do just that.

Stern, left with Margy, pointed her to one of the narrow rooms immediately beside the grand jury chamber which were set aside for witnesses' consultations with their counsel. The room, six by ten, was bare; it contained a worn table and two chairs, and the gray walls were marred and filthy. Stern's practice, invariable over the decades, was to debrief his clients right here, while their memories were fresh, question by question.

Stern closed the door and Margy sat, frosty with him but otherwise calm. He asked how it had been.

"Fine," she said serenely. "I lied."

Stern stood with his hand on the knob of the door. This happened now and then, of course. Not as often as was commonly imagined. But now and then. A client chucks up her chin and frankly admits to committing a felony. Notwithstanding, he promptly felt feverish, weak.

He sat down, facing her. She remained bitter and cross.

"May I ask," said Stern, "in what manner you provided incorrect information?"

She flipped her white hand, her bracelets and long nails.

"I don't know. She asked if I had any idea where the records went."

Realizing that he was somehow the target of all this, he tried to avoid showing his relief. Barring further stupidity—an outright confession—the government would never make a case for perjury based on the fact that Margy had kept her opinions to herself.

"She asked if I knew anything about this Wunderkind account from any other source."

"You told her no?"

"Right."

"That was untrue?"

"Yep."

Stern had not been bright enough to ask that question in his office. Perhaps Margy might have responded fully then. Certainly she was not likely to expand now.

"Anything further?"

"She asked if I talked to Dixon about the documents. I told her no to that, too."

"But you had?"

"Shore."

What made him think he was wily when he had neglected the obvious? Naturally, she talked to Dixon about this. Who else would know where the records had gone? In all probability he had ventured a few suggestions concerning what she ought to say to the government—and to Stern. In truth, he had no desire to learn exactly what Dixon had told her. It was sure to enrage him—and at any rate, the conflict of interests which the U.S. Attorney had so gratuitously predicted had now come to pass. Margy's lying, from a coarse perspective, almost certainly advanced Dixon's cause; Stern could no longer counsel both clients. He knew he had himself to blame for that predicament. In thirty years, his personal relationships had never interfered with his professional obligations, but one way or another, his widower's priapism had brought him here—if nowhere else, to the point that Margy was furious enough with him to admit what she had done. For the present, however, his humiliation was subordinate to his duties, which were clear.

"Margy, I would like to introduce you to another lawyer, who, I believe, will counsel you to return to the grand jury at once and recant."

" 'Recant'?"

"Correct the record. If it is done immediately, no harm will come to you."

"I've been there and I'm gone." She had a terrible sour expression and got to her feet. Anger increased her substance— her hair, her frills, her bright nails, high heels, her smoothly glinting hosiery. Margy was a person of many pieces carefully assembled, but right now every layer was galvanized by her temper. "You don't have any goddamn idea what's goin on here, do you?" The way her eyes fixed on him, as she looked down, was frightening—not just the harshness, but the disrespect. She had made, apparently, certain assumptions that to her chagrin she now recognized were incorrect.

"I should like to know," he said hollowly. At the moment, he found himself gripped strongly by fear—for Margy's predicament, and more, by the way she took him to task for his ignorance. So much was swimming beyond his knowledge or control. John. Dixon. Margy herself. They were like bits of matter drifting off into space.

"Nah," she said. She shook her head, its many curls. "Not from here, Jackson. You know who you gotta talk to. I got a plane to catch." She hitched her bag to her shoulder and picked up her purse and her briefcase. "This here thing is a fool contest: who's the biggest fool. You remember you got told that by Margaret Jane Allison of Polk's Cowl, Oklahoma." With bags in both hands, she used a foot to prop open the door, and without a backward glance went through it.

26

Some defense lawyers said the worst moments came after indictment, when you saw the evidence assembled by the state—the mountain you could never climb. But Stern always welcomed that challenge; once you knew the prosecutors' direction, every other angle became a line of escape. It was the times in the midst of an investigation that could be the most unbearable for him. Usually, there were people to interview, records to look at, motions to make. But, on occasion, he was frozen by realization: the government knew something and he knew nothing at all. Lawyer's terror, he called it—and at the moment it was as bad as it had ever been. Blind and ignorant, you fear that any move will be wrong, the one to send you tumbling from the cliff. And so woeful, beleaguered—the right word, in all respects, was defenseless—you hang there, immobile, in darkness, awaiting the storm, hearing the winds build, feeling the air growing chill. He sat in the witness room, slumped, weary, aware of his weight, his age. He was terrified for Dixon.

When he looked up, Klonsky was posed in the doorframe, leaning upon it and taking him in.

"Sonia."

"Sonny to my friends." She smiled; he must have looked pitiable to have softened her so quickly. But he welcomed her kindness. Sonny, then. She sat down in the card chair where Margy had been. "Stan wanted me to see if I could find you."

"And you succeeded." He smiled cordially. "We may speak lawyer to lawyer, Sonny?"

"Of course."

"I was as dismayed as you to learn that those documents were not where they were expected to be."

"I assumed as much, Sandy. But it's a very serious situation for your client."

He smiled gently, in order to indicate that he did not need the pointer.

"That's what I was talking to Stan about," she said.

"Ah, yes," said Stern. "The mighty United States Attorney." Just now, in his present mood, he found his feelings much harder to suppress: the thought of Sennett, tight-fisted, rancorous, was the flint against his stone. He cautioned himself to assume a more amiable tone in speaking of her boss. "What does he tell us?"

"He tells us," said Sonny, "that he believes you can find the documents."

"Does he?" said Stern. "Imagine having fifty-four Assistants to supervise and still taking the time to do my job as well."

She smiled in spite of herself. "He says he has a message."

"Very well."

"Find the safe."

Nothing moved; not a twitch was allowed; perhaps, for some infinitesimal time, the blood did not flow. This was the training of the courtroom: Betray nothing.

"Do you understand this remark?" he asked her finally.

"Do I?" asked Sonny. "Do you think I should answer that?"

She did not have to; it was clear. Sennett was using her as no more than the messenger. Stern knew what that spelled. ¡Ay, carajo! old words, a curse from childhood. Mr. Sennett and his informant. They seemed to know everything. Perhaps it was not an informant at all? Rather a wiretap. A mike in the wall. A hidden camera. Stern drew a breath. If anything, his fears for Dixon were greater. In company he smiled, a primitive reflex.

"What's funny?" she asked.

"Oh," he said, "I do not believe that I have handled a matter for some time that has frightened me more."

"Frightened?"

"The correct word." He nodded. "I have never been in an investigation where I have received less information."

"From the government?"

"Certainly from the government. You have never even formally confirmed who is being investigated or for what crime."

"Sandy, there's no rule—"

"Rules are not the point. I speak of fairness. Of what is commonplace." Having given himself berth to speak, he could not contain his indignation. "Do you not believe that some basic accounting of the government's suspicions is appropriate by now? Rather than engaging in these highly selective and minimal disclosures in the hope I can be sent scurrying in one direction, then another? Do you think I cannot recognize that these subpoenas are composed with the obvious intention of hiding any scrap of information about the prosecution's knowledge and interests?"

"Sandy—look, you know I'm not in charge."

"You sit here now. You have been an Assistant long enough to know what is customary—and what is not. Give me just a word or two."

"Sandy, Sennett is really hinky on this thing."

"Please, I do not ask you to breach any rule of secrecy or standard of propriety. I shall settle for whatever information you can comfortably provide. If you would prefer, I shall tell you what I suspect about your investigation, and you need only state whether I am right or I am wrong. No more. There is no special harm in that, no confidences breached. You may do that, no?"

Could she? The uncertainty swam across her face. Sonny's strength would never lie in hiding her feelings.

"Sonny, please. You are a warm individual and I sense a friendship between us. I do not mean to overreach that. But I have no idea any longer where to turn."

"Sandy, maybe I know less than you think."

"Certainly it is more than I."

They considered one another across the table.

"I have a million things to do," she said at last. "I'll think about what you've said."

"I would need ten minutes. Fifteen at the most."

"Look, Sandy, to tell you the truth, I don't have a second to breathe. I've got four cases going to trial in the next two months. Plus this thing. We've had plans since March to take Charlie's son up to his family's place in Dulin and stay there over the Fourth to pick strawberries. Now I have to come back here on Monday, and I had to move heaven and earth just to get the weekend free. So you'll have to forgive me if I tell you that I'm a little bit pressed."

"I see," said Stern, "you have no time to be fair?"

"Oh, come on, Sandy." She was frustrated by him, exasperated. He was plucking every chord. "If it's so important to you to spend fifteen minutes asking me a bunch of questions I'll never answer, you can drive a hundred miles up to Dulin on Saturday. That's the best I can do."

When he asked her for the directions, she laughed out loud. "You're really going to come?"

"At this point, I must pursue any avenue. Saturday afternoon?"

"God," Sonny said. It was on County D, six miles north of Route 60. Brace's Cabin. She described it as a glamorized shack. As he jotted this down, she pointed at him.

"Sandy, I'm not kidding. Maybe I don't agree with everything Stan's done, but it's his show. Don't think I'll get out in the sunshine and do something I wouldn't do here."

"Of course not. I shall speak. You need only listen. If you wish, you may take notes and repeat every word I say to Sennett."

"It's a long trip for nothing."

"Perhaps not." Most unexpectedly, he had found again a trace of whimsy. He spoke in the greedy whisper of a child. He was, he said, so very fond of strawberries.

*　*　*

On the phone, Stern could hear Silvia's voice resounding down the long, stone corridors of Dixon's home as she went to summon her husband. Lately, whenever he spoke to his sister, he detected a note of apprehension. But by their long understanding, she would never discuss Dixon's business with Stern. And Silvia, if the truth were told, was one of those women, come of age in a bygone era, who would never willingly set foot in the sphere they saw reserved to men.

"What's up?" Dixon was not reluctant to be brusque. "I'm on the social fast track. Your sister's got us entertaining half the Museum Board in fifteen minutes." Silvia, her mother's daughter, never tired of the involvements of a high-toned social life: women's auxiliaries, charity committees, the country club. Dixon mocked her rather than admit out loud that he loved doing what he imagined rich people did, but their nights were absorbed with charity balls and fund-raising occasions, gallery openings, exclusive parties. Stern often caught their picture in the papers, a remarkably handsome couple, looking smooth, stately, carefree. Silvia over the years had become preoccupied—as Dixon wished her to be—with acting her part, adjourning by limousine to the city for a luncheon, a trunk show at a tony ladies' shop, the typical flesh-touching exercises with the wives of other very wealthy men who had welcomed the Hartnells into their company. Other days, she played golf or tennis, or even rode.

Were it someone else, Stern would have been inclined to disparage the frivolity of this life-style, but there was no flaw in his sister which he had not wholeheartedly forgiven. In some ways, Silvia reminded him of Kate, with whom, in fact, she was uncommonly close—she had allowed beauty to be her fate. She had been treated to a privileged education and it had led her to Dixon. End of story. Even in the years when Dixon was out tromping in the cornfields to establish his clientele, he had commanded her not to work, and Silvia, with no apparent misgivings, complied.

Yet Silvia was graced—redeemed—by kindness. She remained an extraordinary person whose generosity far outran the customary or typical. Clara, who had little use for empty vessels, loved and valued Silvia. They talked two or three times a week, met for lunch, lectures at the County Art Museum, theater matinees. For decades, they had attended the symphony's Wednesday afternoon performances together. And whatever motivated others, Stern could voice no complaints. Silvia, as no one else in the world, adored her brother. In certain moods, she sent him brief notes, bought him gifts. She called every day and he continued to speak to her in a way he shared with no others. Difficult to define, but there was a pitch to their exchanges as easy as humming. He remained the moon to her, the stars—galaxies, a universe. How was Stern to describe as deficient a life in which he still played such a stellar part?

"We need to see one another," said Stern to Silvia's husband now. "The sooner, the better."

"Problems?"

"Many."

"Give me a hint."

"I would rather do this in person, Dixon. We have a great deal to discuss."

"I'm on my way to New York on the 5:45 tomorrow morning. I'll be there the rest of the week." Dixon, again, was hoping for a breakthrough on the Consumer Price Index future, going to meetings in New York or Washington twice each week. "Then Silvia and I are going to the island over the Fourth." He was referring to another of their homes, one in the Caribbean, a serene cliffside refuge on a tax-haven island; the IRS, during its investigation a few years ago, had been driven to a frenzy by the inability to trace so much as a penny going down there. Stern, in his office behind his glass desk, drummed his fingers. Dixon, apparently, did not have time to be in trouble.

"I spent the day with Margy and Ms. Klonsky."

"I heard that was happening."

"Yes," said Stern. Of course, Dixon had heard. That was the point. Stern felt at a terrible disadvantage over the phone. "There were a number of disturbing developments."

"Such as?"

"The prosecutors seem to know about your safe, for one. I believe they will be looking for it shortly, if they are not right now."

On the other end of the line, Dixon did not stir.

"Where the fuck do they find out about that?"

Where, indeed? Stern had not needed Dixon for that question. There was a certain obvious, if disquieting logic: Margy goes into the grand jury and the records are missing; Margy comes out and the government mentions the safe. In her anger, Margy could have disclosed anything. Perhaps Dixon had been prudent enough never to mention the safe or its movements to her, but that was doubtful. In his present mood of dark suspicion it had even struck Stern that Margy might have been the government's source of information all along. A ridiculous thought, really, but one that continued to reemerge. In that scenario, everything today and for many days—and nights—before had been no more than well-acted melodrama. Highly unlikely, of course. But such charades had occurred in the past. There were cases where the government had indicted their informants to maintain their cover. Stern at this point ruled out nothing.

"I was hoping, Dixon, you could shed some light."

"Hardly," said Dixon.

"Would John—"

"John? John's still lookin for the men's room, Stern. Come on." Both men breathed into the phone.

"There are also some records, Dixon, that seem to have disappeared."

"Records?" asked Dixon, far less impulsively.

"Concerning the Wunderkind account. Are you aware of that?"

"Aware of what?"

"The account. The documents. Their disappearance?"

"I'm not sure I'm following you. We'll have to talk about this next week."

"Dixon, it is quite clearly the disappearance of these records that is inspiring the government's interest in the safe."

"So?"

"If the records could be located—"

"No chance," Dixon said harshly. For an instant again, both men were silent, equally set back, it seemed, by the many implications of this remark and its tone. Then Dixon went on, making a token effort to be more ambiguous. "I don't think there's much hope that'll happen."

"Dixon, this will go very badly for you. Very badly. I have told you before, it is the absolute zenith of stupidity." With Dixon's lapse, Stern found himself able to be more direct; he imagined a certain air of affront on the other end, but he continued. "In the current atmosphere, Dixon, if this safe is accurately traced, it will provoke many difficulties. Not to mention that it would be sorely embarrassing to me."

"Embarrassing?"

"Damaging to my credibility. You understand. And the blame will be laid to you, nevertheless. The prosecutors will know the safe did not fall to its present location from the sky." On the phone, Stern felt obliged to exercise some circumspection. Even with a wiretap, the government was prohibited from overhearing this kind of conversation between an attorney and his client. But you could never tell, particularly in a house as large as Dixon's, who might inadvertently pick up an extension.

"You mean, after telling me to hand the thing over, you want to give it back?"

"Not at all. I am telling you that you are exercising poor judgment and creating a perilous circumstance."

"I'll take it. Send it back."

"Dixon."

"Listen, I have to put on my fricking tuxedo. I'll be back on the sixth."

"Dixon, this is not an opportune time for a vacation. I must ask you to return as soon as your business is concluded in New York."

"Come on. To me it sounds like a great time to get away. It's a few days. This'll hold. Law things always do."

"Dixon, I have many questions and I expect plain answers."

"Sure," said Dixon. "Right. Coming," he yelled, as if Silvia was calling, though Stern heard not the faintest echo of his sister's voice.

27

Arriving home late Friday night, Stern stood in the foyer of his empty home. Helen was out of town, jetted off to someplace in Texas to inspect a convention site; she would not be back until Sunday. With a certain resolve, Stern prepared to undergo the weekend by himself. While a leftover chop warmed, he wandered about the house, read the mail, and hung in the eddies of various dissatisfactions. A trying week.

Before the huge windows of the solarium, he paused. By grace of prior work and fortuitous rain, Clara's garden had flourished. The bulbs that had gone into the ground last fall now rose in glory—round peonies, lilies expressive as hands. Stern, utterly oblivious all these months, was suddenly struck by the perfect rows and stepped out into the mild evening air. Then in the fading light and rain—sweet breeze, he froze, lurching a bit as he came to a complete halt. Across the hedgerow, he caught sight of Fiona Cawley stooping in her yard.

To say that he had avoided Fiona was not correct. He had hidden from her; he sneaked in and out of his own home like a commando. To his present mind, that incident had absolutely not occurred. Only with the prospect of confrontation did it recur to him with a harrowing pang. What had he done? What grand figure of macho revenge had he thought to imitate? Now, a week later, he was unwilling to accept the image of Alejandro Stern as a reprobate, a bounder making unwelcome passes at the neighborhood wives. Other men might have been more casual with their honor, but since a few hours afterwards, everything surrounding the episode seemed to have been smashed into storage. He had never phoned Cal. He had stopped searching for

Nate, and even felt somewhat relieved of his urge, so great a
week ago, to grind Dr. Cawley like pumice. No doubt, he'd have it
out with Nate sooner or later. But only when Stern had accepted
his own conduct, when he was ready to chat, one cad to another;
only, frankly, when he had a better grip on himself and the
mysterious world of his intentions.

Now he stood stock-still, like some creature in the wild, but
something, the scent of fear perhaps, gave him away. Fiona
reared her head, saw him, and with the cruel curl of a powerful
unpleasant expression advanced on the horny row of privet that
marked the property line between the Cawleys' and the Sterns'.
She had huge rusty garden shears in hand and was dressed in
what she took to be gardening clothes, a monochrome outfit that
was the green of an avocado, slacks and a clingy top. Her hair,
usually smooth as a helmet, was windblown and hung in clumps,
holding a few small brown leaves and twigs. She leaned across
the privet, gesturing, hissing actually: Come here.

"Sandy, I need to talk to you." She advanced along the row. "I
don't want you avoiding me."

Stern at last stood his ground. He had no idea who he was, but
the person inhabiting the skin of Sandy Stern was going to get it.
His smile was appeasing. Fiona, in the meantime, seemed
wordstruck. She had him where she wanted, and now had no
idea what to say.

"I need to talk to you," she repeated.

Determined to make it easy for her, Stern said, "Of course."

At that moment, behind her, Stern caught sight of Nate. He
appeared to have just arrived home; his tie was wrung down
from his collar and he was still carrying his case. He peeked
about the shingled corner of his house and stared with a wide
look on his pale narrow face. Fiona, following Stern's eye, turned.
As soon as she recognized her husband, her face shot about
again with a grieving, stricken expression.

"Oh God." She put both hands on her cheeks in a childish way.

Stern waited to see who would speak. He had once again the
sensation of something momentous. And then, through the mild
night, he heard the pealing of his telephone, clearly audible to all
of them as it carried from the open French door of the solarium.
Stern begged off without words; he threw up his hands futilely—
Marcel Marceau could not have done better—and trotted a bit as

he went toward the house, delighted, actually thrilled, to have escaped. But some intimation of the likely outcome of the scene he had left behind slowed his pace and eventually the thought came to form: Fiona would tell him. If she had not already. Think of the advantage she'd gain. With her tale of refusal, she could lord a superior moral character, while still punishing Nate by hinting that she, too, was not beyond temptation. With his growing sense of the Cawley marriage—nasty, competitive, and pained—Stern knew Fiona could never keep this episode to herself. In the darkness of the house, he stood still while the phone went on ringing, and his spirit gathered blackly about a hard seed of apprehension and shame.

Oh, he thought, this was preposterous. What had he to fear from Nate Cawley? What apology could Nate demand from Stern, of all people—Nate, who had *shtupped* his wife and stripped her fortune? He withered in anxiety at the prospect, nonetheless. He saw suddenly that he would look across whatever space he shared with Nate Cawley and confront the very figure of all the failures in his own marriage. He was not sure he was ready for that, even now.

The machine had answered the phone. Through the lightless house Stern heard the amplified voice, made deliberately husky and sinister: " 'I vant your blood.' " It was Peter. Stern picked up the extension.

"So you *are* there," his son said. They waited the usual agitated instant before either spoke again. "Well, are we going to do this or what?"

Stern, who had begun to think the test was unnecessary, found that he did not have the strength to argue.

"I am at your convenience."

"I've got my average exciting Friday night going, dictating charts. You can come over right now, if you've got the time. Or are you seeing Helen?"

Peter liked Helen. On the few recent occasions when they had all been together, Peter seemed to have imposed some self-conscious restraint on his usual inappropriate or acerbic remarks. Stern explained that she was gone until Sunday and said he would come ahead now. Closing the sun-room door, he paused. The Cawleys were together in their yard, standing close, arguing. When Fiona's hand swept up in the direction of the

Sterns' house, he jumped away from the door and waited, pressed against the wall, while he quietly lowered the blind.

* * *

Perhaps it was the effect of Peter's joke on the phone, but there were few places as eerie as a darkened office building on a weekend evening. Stern found both sets of plate-glass doors at the front still open, but inside, he was at once drilled to the core by the sensation of being alone; the large, darkened building hulked about him. The pharmacy on the first floor was black-grated and closed. He rode the elevator up and, disembarking, found the long, tiled corridor lit in each direction only by a single fluorescent fixture, offering not much more illumination than a child's night-light.

What had Peter said? His average Friday night. As unpredictably as most of his feelings about his son, the stark sadness of this declaration overcame him. The stylish admiring friends of Peter's college and high-school years seemed to have faded away. There was no one Stern knew of besides Kate who regularly shared Peter's company. How did he spend his time? Stern had little idea. He had inherited his mother's tastes for music; he cycled; he worked. When he came to visit his parents, as he had done now and then while Clara was living, he liked to go running through the public forests in the Riverside neighborhood. Afterwards, dripping with sweat, he would sit in the kitchen and read the newspaper aloud to his mother, making various caustic remarks about events. Clara served him soft drinks, puttered with dinner. Stern witnessed these scenes largely as an outsider, struck by the very oddness of his son. Peter would be affronted to think he had his father's sympathy; his tightly wound personality also reflected a kind of strength. But approaching the office door, Stern felt the blackish wellspring of Peter's sarcasm, aloofness: his pain.

How, Stern thought to himself, how had it become this way? He had in mind suddenly not merely Peter but the girls as well.

Somehow these children had come into being—emerged with that strange agglomeration of talents and temperament he recognized as being essential to each. By three or four years of age, they had left behind the indefiniteness of infancy and were as fully formed as tulips on a stalk, ready to unfold. As a parent, he seemed so often to be no more than a spectator, applauding the expanding capacities, silently concerned by other developments. When Peter was six, his parents began to notice certain traits. Moodiness. A quietude that seemed to border on despair. Peter, who now fashioned himself a renegade, had the unyielding character of a steel soldier. And in time his sisters manifested, each in her way, discontents of their own. Marta, outwardly engaging, was known to become lost—so much like someone else—in impenetrable sulky dreams. Katy, who Clara always privately insisted was the brightest of the three, remained sunny and affable, but almost clinically indisposed to strive for any form of achievement.

Stern to this day found all this shocking. In his childhood, there had been such remarkable disorder born of his father's fragile condition, and the consistent watchful eye the entire family maintained on free-floating Argentine hostilities. But the home that Clara and he created was peaceful, prosperous— normal insofar as Stern understood the word. The children were cared for—and loved. Loved. Oh, he may have had failings as a parent—at his best, he was undoubtedly too contained with the kids for American tastes—but even in his dimmest, most distracted state his love for his children was genuine, glinting like some fiery gemstone in his breast. And no person would ever be able to measure the bounds of Clara's dedication. Thus, as a younger man, it had stunned him to learn that every good fortune the world could offer wasn't enough: his children suffered, nevertheless. Their difficulties became one more thing over the years to note about each and, with whatever halting efforts, to attempt to embrace. *Geh Gezunderhayt*, as his mother would have put it. Let them go in health, in peace.

Peter showed him inside with little ceremony. With the office closed, he was free to take his father into an examining room, a tiny tiled space with an antiseptic smell and a leather patient's table, test equipment, and instruments.

"Roll up ze sleeve, *bitte*," said Peter. Tonight it was accents. Stern complied, and his son precisely, instantly inserted the needle. "You okay?"

Stern nodded. "And you, Peter?"

His son, equivocally, opened his palm: Who knew, who could

say. They spoke of Marta, expected in town any day. Stern asked about Kate.

"I thought you went to the ball game with her the other night. Looks great, doesn't she?"

"Actually, her looks concerned me," said Stern. "There is a difficult situation at hand. The circumstances are such that I must be somewhat removed, but I fear it is affecting her."

"I've heard about that," said Peter quietly. Stern had come with no intention of raising the matter of Tooley. What was done was done, and besides, it would be unprofessional for Stern to complain. Yet they proceeded into disagreement as if commanded by nature. It turned out that Kate in her concern for her husband had involved her brother. The thought that the situation had required her to turn to Peter rather than him wounded Stern unexpectedly.

"John wanted a name, I gave him a name," said Peter. He withdrew the needle and flicked the vial with a certain pesky discontent. "Mel's competent, isn't he? What did I do wrong? You already told John you didn't want to get involved."

How typical, Stern thought. His fault, his shortcomings. A quarreling voice, in which Stern would explain the ethical concerns that had led him to treat John as he had, died unuttered. What was the point? He had already come out second best again with his family.

He had some thought of suggesting dinner, but Peter showed him out directly, taking Stern past the small consultation room, where the medical charts were heaped on his desk, weighed down by the black-corded dictaphone handset. Outside, in the parking lot, Stern was struck by the sight of Peter's office, now the only bright window in the black solid square of the medical center.

As a child, Peter had had a magnificent singing voice—sweet and pure like some perfect liquid. His vocal range was reduced by adolescence, when his sound became rougher and quavering. But at the age of seven or eight Peter often performed in school plays and community theaters. With his musical talents, he had found one more way to beguile Clara. She became a genuine stage mother who attended each performance in a quiet nervous heat. Stern came along now and then, uncertain about how to behave. From the back of the auditorium, he would watch the small figure onstage. By some vestigial parental instinct, Stern believed that those had been the happiest moments of Peter's life, alone, admired, standing within the sole spot of light in the dark room, and bringing forth that lilting, expressive voice—he controlled every word, every note, filling his song with an emotional range unusual for a child of his age.

That was the past, Peter's past, that time of expression, attention, performance. Through the dark, Stern looked up to the light where his son; hard on the way through his own adulthood, would go on into the night, alone, the only sound his roughened voice mumbling out the details of the medical charts.

28

Brace's cabin was built along a wash. From the roadside, you saw only the roof coated with moss, glowing chartreuse in the brilliant sun, and the tin chimney pipe. Bumping along in his Cadillac in an astonishing fog of dust, Stern would have gone past it, except for the wooden sign knocked at an angle into the yellow ground. He had already been down and up, rapping on the door, nosing to the window, where he saw nothing but darkness. Below, by the house, the cover of the trees—oak, pine, cottonwood, birch—was deep, the forest floor dark and moist, barely penetrated by light. As he climbed back up to the road, the sun was intense. In the gravel parking area, Stern searched for other tire tracks. The red flag stood raised on the round aluminum mailbox.

What was he doing here? He had awakened with a hopeful spurt. The thought of driving north through the sloping valleys, beyond the state line and the congested blight of urban life—his urban life—inspired expansive feelings. Now in the heat, far more intense here on the plains, he was full of doubts. Had he really driven two hours for a fifteen-minute conversation that in all likelihood would not occur? He would accomplish nothing beyond a moment's discomfort for both of them. Thinking better of that, Sonny had probably decided not to come. He sat up on the car trunk with his face to the sun—the first lick of scorching summer heat he had felt—and then, when he grew uncomfortably warm, trudged down again and scouted about the cabin.

It could not have been more than three rooms, perhaps only two. Down in the wash, it was bordered on two sides by a deep veranda in which half the punky boards had been replaced; the roof was supported by greenish treated standards. At the farthest corner, where the wild bushes and other growth of the ravine rose against the house, a round contraption had been carved into the porch. Stern bent to inspect the knobs and rubber hoses; there was a canvas cover across it.

He was there when he heard the gravel spurned above. By the time he walked around, Sonny Klonsky was charging down the stairs from the roadside. Her arms were full, with two grocery bags and half a dozen children's books, and seeing Stern, she bothered with no greeting but threw him, rather, a harried conspiratorial look of complete exasperation. The door to the cabin proved to be unlocked and she ran inside. The ride apparently had been a long one for a woman midterm.

When Stern turned about, a boy was watching him, five or six years old, wearing a striped T-shirt and blue jeans, a dark-eyed, freckle-faced fellow with a bowl-shaped do of perfect silky hair and a look of cheerless curiosity.

"Sam?" asked Stern. He never had any idea how he remembered these things.

The boy toed the dirt and shied away. Stern climbed the ties braced into the earth, which formed the stairway up, prepared to greet Sam's father. The boy had climbed into the front seat of an old yellow Volkswagen, a convertible, where there was no other passenger. Stern asked about his father and the boy murmured an inaudible response.

"Not coming?" asked Stern.

Sam, chin tucked down, waggled his head.

"No." Sonny spoke behind Stern and moved somewhat wearily back into the sun. "The poet's in climacteric, or whatever it is. The grip of inspiration." She pulled Sam by the shoulder from the car and introduced him to Stern, then reached into the back seat. There were two sleeping bags there, more groceries, and a single large piece of soft-sided luggage. Stern helped her carry the items down to the cabin.

"I hope you did not make this trip simply for me."

"I came for Sam," said Sonny. Entering the stale-smelling dark of the cabin, she faced Stern with a look that did not fully contain the nerve of her lingering anger. "And his father can go fuck himself."

"Oh, dear," said Stern.

"Oh, dear," said Sonny. She threw the packages down on a worn table. The cabin was a simple affair. The plank floor had been painted; the studs had been paneled over in knotty pine. The central room was occupied by a cable-spool table and painted chairs, and a double bed with a wrought-iron frame and a clean chenille spread. To the left was a bath and another small room. The old stained toilet with its black seat made a tremendous clatter, recovering from recent use.

In a mewling voice, the boy was pestering her about something.

"Yes, all right." She opened a window, then turned without stopping and went back out the door. Stern heard her moving heavily on the porch, then a deep bowel-like rumble beneath the cabin floor. From the rear window, he could look up to the wooded crest of the ravine, the bosks crowned in light. When the wind blew, there was a wonderful scent.

"Are those raspberries back there?" Stern asked, when she returned.

"Oh, yes. The strawberry field is back that way, too, another hundred yards. Acres of them. They make the air sweet, don't they?"

"The aroma is splendid."

"I hope you don't mind, but I promised Sam I'd take him picking right after lunch. Some of us have had a few disappointments today." Her eyes drifted off to the boy, who must have fussed badly about his father.

"Of course," said Stern.

"You're welcome to come. Or you can look around in town."

He made no response, but he had, he realized, not the slightest inclination to depart. Stern did not have what might be called an outdoor wardrobe. He wore a pair of golf slacks and a cotton placket shirt with some animal embroidered at the breast. Casual attire suited him poorly. Even in the dark colors recommended to the overweight, he cut a figure of awkward proportions and looked a little like a plum. Nonetheless, he was in the out-of-doors, the wilds to him, and ready for adventure.

Sonny stirred among the bags until she found a jar of peanut butter and sat down at the table to prepare the boy's sandwich. She offered Stern lunch, but he had eaten on the road. Watching her move about, you could see the toll of multiple responsibilities: lawyer, caretaker, weekend traveler; pregnant person. The fight with her husband—a bloody one, apparently—had left her drained. Her body seemed to have contracted a bit about her abdomen; she stumbled on, solid-footed, without grace. In the heavy summery air, her cheeks were rosy and her full, pretty face almost radiated heat. She wore shorts and a sleeveless blouse. She lifted her dark hair off her neck at moments to air herself.

Sam, called back in to the table, assailed his food with unwashed hands. He was quiet in a stranger's presence, interrupting his silence only to ask at one point, "Did you?"

"Ye-es," she said, as if she were giving in. Sam was in love with the hot tub, she explained. As the boy ate, Stern asked a bit about the cabin, how often they were here. The property, including the strawberry field, had formerly belonged to Charlie's parents, people of means who used it as a summer retreat. When they moved to Palm Springs, Charlie wanted only this, a shack that had housed migrants before Charlie's father turned it into a refuge for himself. Charlie, Sonny said, had retained the faith of the sixties and believed that owning things was a pain in the ass.

"There's some kind of covenant. When the Braces sold, everybody agreed their family could always harvest the fields they'd planted for personal consumption. You can be the honorary Charlie for today. I'm sure it will be an improvement," she added, in a heavy sarcastic tone he had not heard from her before. She cleared Sam's plate and brought out a number of plastic buckets from below the sink. Sam grabbed his at once and begged her to hurry, but Sonny paused, tying a bandanna across her forehead. She extended a bucket to Stern, then took a ragged straw hat from a shelf and without ceremony placed it on his head. "You'll need this for the sun."

"Shall I look in a mirror?"

"It's magnificent," she said. "Trust me." She reached up again to angle the brim and gave him a merry look. For a second she seemed, despite her heavy form, winsome as a cheerleader, the kind of girl who would be grabbed and whirled about by some fellow, even though there was probably not a moment in her life when she'd been that sort of woman, and Lord knew, he had never been that kind of man. Then he followed Sonny and the boy from the dank cabin, and entered blinking into the potent daylight, his heart flopping about with a kind of febrile stirring.

Pregnant, Sonny nonetheless remained far more agile than he; the boy, of course, climbed like a mountain goat. They plunged briefly into the woods and up a steep trail in the ravine. Stern, straining, puffing a bit, followed them back into the sunlight. After a few hundred feet of deep weeds, burned yellow already, they came to another graveled road. It curved, dry and white, beside the limitless acres of the farm, the low plants rising out of their hummocks in perfect ranks, the berries hanging red and luminous, bright as jewels. Sam reached to Sonny and then, by force of habit, extended the other hand, small and grimy, to Stern, who took it as well. So, he thought, still dazzled by the light and the overpowering heat. He had no sense of direction. The cabin was somewhere behind them, but he had no inclination to look back. Holding Sam's hand, he crossed the road and began walking with them into the strawberry field.

* * *

"When I was twenty," Sonny said, "I wanted to meet somebody who was perfect. Now that I'm past forty, I just wonder if anyone is normal." As they walked into the field, she went on unburdening herself, her gestures emphatic, speaking in her unguarded way about her husband. She seemed to be at one of those impasses in her marriage where she suddenly viewed her husband as she might a neighbor observed from an undisclosed vantage, say a window or a terrace, seeing him only as a peculiar unfathomable individual who lived nearby.

"His passion for what is actually happening is only to the extent he can reduce it to expression. You know?" She looked back to Stern, wearing her bandanna, squinting in the sun. Down the rows of the strawberry field, Sam ran in gym shoes and jeans, his feet kicking out, the yellow bucket bouncing at his side. His thin voice carried back to them in a swell of wind. "And the point of expression is so that he has things in control. I'm sure that's why he's not here."

"What's that?" Stern was losing her, much as he tried. She was speaking for the most part to herself.

"Pure jealousy. Can you believe it?" Trudging along, she

laughed: the notion was ridiculous. Briefly, Stern felt an unidentifiable twinge. "I think the idea of meeting you was more than he could stand. You know, my adversary—it sounds so professional. He can't conceive of me with a life apart from him, paying attention to anyone but him. I don't know how he'll live with a baby."

"I apologize. This is certainly my fault for being so insistent," said Stern.

"Oh, it's my fault," she said. "It's mine. Believe me. I was up all night, realizing that for the one billionth time. I think my mother made me feel obliged to put up with temperamental people."

Listening to Sonny, who was twisted about by impulse and emotion—beseeching, beleaguered, ironic, angry—it struck Stern that Clara and he had had the benefit of certain good fortune. In his time, the definitions were clearer. Men and women of middle-class upbringing anywhere in the Western world desired to marry, to bear and rear children. Et cetera. Everyone traveled along the same ruts in the road. But for Sonny, marrying late in life, in the New Era, everything was a matter of choice. She got up in the morning and started from scratch, wondering about relationships, marriage, men, the erratic fellow she'd chosen—who, from her description, still seemed to be half a boy. He was reminded of Marta, who often said she would find a male companion just as soon as she figured out what she needed one for.

"How long is it you two have known each other, you and your husband?" Stern asked: He was a few feet away from her, kneeling awkwardly to look at the plants.

She gave him instructions on how to harvest the fruit. The overripe berries, dark as blood, looked wonderful but would not hold. "And you may as well roll your pant legs up. There's no pride out here and a lot of dust and mud. What did you ask me?"

He repeated the question.

"We've only been married a few years, if that's what you meant, but I've known him forever. It was a doomed relationship right from the start. I was his T.A. in Freshman English. The people in the English Department were scandalized when I started going out with him. Well, not scandalized. That department wasn't scandalized by anything, but they thought it was pretty odd."

"He was a freshman?"

"An older freshman, in my defense. He'd been in the service. But he was irresistible. He's very dark, very big, very quiet. It was like someone put a mountain down in my classroom." Sonny in the great heat shook her head, apparently overcome by the memory. "Talk about romantic. How could I resist a man who came back from Vietnam with poems hidden in the pockets of his camouflage outfits? I *wanted* to believe that poetry could transform the world, but Charlie really did. Have you ever known anyone like that?"

"My brother, I would say. He was a poet," said Stern, who had just finished rolling his trousers, exposing a row of pale flesh over his black nylon hose. He must have looked worse than a scarecrow. The straw hat she'd given him was too large and rested unevenly on his ears.

"Honestly?"

"Oh yes, a young one. He wrote romantic verse in a number of languages. I believe he was quite gifted. My sister still has Jacobo's poems somewhere. I would like to read them again someday, but just now it would be a melancholy experience." He took on momentarily the stung look he could not avoid from time to time, a close expression of admitted pain.

"He passed away?"

"Long ago. I seldom speak of him, actually. But he was an extraordinary figure—destined for greatness. He was the most remarkable young man. Handsome, bright. He wrote poems. He declaimed in public. He was a prize scholar. And he was also *quite* a rogue. That was an important aspect of his character. Always in the midst of one misadventure or another. Filching fruit from a stand. For a period when he was sixteen, he would sneak out at night to keep company with the mother of one of his friends."

Sonny made a lascivious sound: Oo la la. "He sounds as if he was something."

"That he was," said Stern, and repeated the phrase. "He was the child the world adored. I felt this, of course, as a terrible weight, being the younger brother." In his parents' home, his brother as the first-born and a son had assumed a natural centrality, a regal primogeniture. Handsome, outgoing, willful, Jacobo had in one fashion or another overpowered everyone.

Their mother lived under his spell, basking in each achievement, and their father was no more capable of confronting Jacobo than anyone else. Even as a child, Jacobo had more or less run the household, his moods and passions governing them all like the tolling grandfather clock in the front hall. At the age of fifty-six Stern could still recall his jealousy. There was probably no fury in his life like the rush of emotion Jacobo had inspired. Stern, too, was dominated by him, awestruck but also wildly resentful. Jacobo was often cruel. He relished Alejandro's admiration, but he would not allow any equal in his domain. How many times did they enact the same scene, where Alejandro wept in humiliation and rage, and Jacobo laughed a bit before yielding to comfort him? *Chi, pibe.* "The entire life of my household—my mother's especially—was at an end after he died."

He stood straight and rubbed his knees. In the heat and wind, he felt a dreamy vagueness. The field of fruit, the irrigated furrows and the plants rising from the hills of straw, stretched in all directions into the dusty haze. There was not another soul around, not another voice, except for Sam's, and the birds', and the drone of planes approaching a country airfield ten or twenty miles away. Argentina, he thought suddenly. Its cruel history, its fateful cycles of hope and repression, pained him like a crushing hold applied to a vital place; it was always that way. He seldom thought of any of this, and when he did, the memories filled him with an ardor, fresh as any lover's, for the United States. There were cousins left down there who prospered generally, but had also suffered terribly; they wrote once a year, sending money, which Stern invested for them in bank accounts here.

"How old was he then?" Sonny asked of Jacobo.

"Seventeen years four months."

"How horrible. What happened?"

"One of those terrible tales of impulsive youth. He fell in with a Zionist crowd. Wealthy young Jewish people. My mother was thrilled at first by such impressive comradeship. When she eveutually realized how strong Jacobo's attachments were, it was too late to retrieve him. This was in the midst of World War II. Argentina was supposedly neutral, but tilted toward the Axis, and these were politically dangerous views to hold. Jacobo decided that he would go to Palestine, fight with Haganah. He could not be dissuaded. He knew, like everyone else, that he was destined to be a hero. There were thirty of them. We went down to see them off and the boat truly looked as if it would sink before it left the harbor. My mother wept; she knew she would never see him again. And she did not. The Germans said the Allies had sunk the boat; the Allies blamed the Germans. Perhaps it was a storm. We never knew."

Here amid the acres, thinking of all of this, speaking of what was lost and so momentous, he saw his present life as vulnerable as a paper construction. In Sonny's company, there was, for whatever reason, less sadness. But it was like letting your fingertips drift along the raised features of a relief—he could feel the textures and recognized again his deepest secret, that without Clara, with the children grown, he had been left with no fundamental alliance. He could sense the desperate struggle every day had been, doing what had been done before with a determined effort to give it no reflection. Far from the city and those routines, he was strongly under the influence of this hearty outspoken young woman. The images were of things thriving, unfolding in the torrid early season heat, as if there was some fertile spirit carried from her, like the scent of humus on the occasional spells of warm wind.

"Charlie's not that kind of magnetic personality. He believes in the lives of the poets. A higher essence. He doesn't want to live like everybody else. He's grim and silent and—if you ask his wife—deliberately difficult."

Stern, straddling the row, reared his head to smile at her. He had moved on quite a distance from their starting point, stirring under the leaves and pulling, and Sonny just now was following him along, eating idly from her bucket. The fruit, baked by the sun, was wild with fragrance and incredibly sweet, gliding and soft on the tongue.

"It's not all that funny. We tried to live together for ten years and it never worked. Somebody was always moving out."

"There was a change eventually, I take it."

"When I got sick. Charlie showed up at the hospital with a bunch of posies and begged me to marry him. Begged—and I hardly needed to be begged at that point." She had a few berries in her hand and she stepped over a row to drop them in Stern's bucket. She made a remark: the stooping killed her back. Across her forehead, the bandanna had been darkened by sweat. Sam appeared at just that moment, as he had from time to time, holding aloft a huge berry. Both Stern and she took an instant to extol the prize. "He was very convincing. And you know how it is—it's a crisis, you think you're looking right to the center of things. I figured I loved Charlie, he loved me. The rest of it was details." She shook her head. "Nobody promises us we'll be happy, do they?"

"No," said Stern.

"No," she said. "Anyway, it was very complicated by then."

"I imagine," said Stern quietly. He saw that this Charlie was due some commendation, having the heart to beg for the hand of a woman whose life hung in the balance.

"Oh, it wasn't what you'd think." She seemed to be smiling. "He was married," Sonny said. "I told you: there were details."

"Hmm." Stern took an instant, adjusting. "Sam's mother?"

"That's right. He married her after one of our breakups. As I said, it's been an up-and-down relationship."

"Well, you know the sayings," said Stern.

"Which ones?"

"Many. 'True love never did run smooth'?"

Sonny shrugged. The thought was not consoling.

"How did you meet your wife?"

"Oh, that." Stern lifted a hand, prepared to consign the story to the ineffable, and then thought better of it, that it would be, in a word, unfair. "I worked for Clara's father. He let me office space. One thing led to another."

"And what was not smooth?"

"Most everything. You can imagine the complications when a penniless immigrant falls in love with the boss's daughter."

"Her parents objected?"

Stern made a sound, still not quite able, even thirty years later, to withstand the recollection of the disruption.

"And they never accepted you?"

"On the contrary. After I married Clara, her father offered to take me into his practice. He was quite prominent. I lived in dread of him but envied his success, and was much too callow to refuse."

"So what happened?"

"We learned a bit about each other. Eventually, we had a serious disagreement."

"Over what? Can I ask?"

"Oh, this is a very embarrassing story," said Stern. He stood up to face her, adjusting the hat on his head. The rim was shot round with straw bands that had come loose and scratched his forehead when he moved. "One day my father-in-law called me into his office and told me there was a file he wanted me to steal from the county courthouse. A divorce matter for an important client, in which the husband had managed to sue first. This was thirty years ago, and the request was not quite as unthinkable as it might be today, but it remained a serious matter."

"You're kidding! And your relationship fell apart when you refused?"

"No, our relationship suffered when I did as he asked. We knew much too much about one another then. He knew how craven I was; I knew that he was corrupt. I suppose that having the courage to do that convinced me that I could walk out on Henry, too."

Stern glanced over to Klonsky. He had never told that story to another mortal soul, not even to Clara, whose loyalties, so early in their marriage, he could not fully depend on. Sonny had now sat down with the bucket between her knees, her face bright with the heat, massaging her lower back. It seemed they had passed the point where he could shock her; if he went marauding naked down the rows, she would nod and accept it with the same placid smile as a further exchange of intimacies.

He bent again—the brightest berries were beneath the leaves, resting just above the straw beddings—but he remained under the charm of his own story. For a short time, his image of Henry with his braces and his white widow's peak was as clear as if he were only a row or two over. He had been as brazen in this request as in so many other things, putting it to Stern right in front of the client, a fretful-looking woman in a tight blond hairdo and a dark green suit. Stern had wondered a bit about Henry's relationship with her. It was well known that Henry was not a man of perfect virtue; but that question, like many others, went unanswered. 'Oh, don't look at me that way,' said Henry. 'This stuff is done all the time. I give Griffin McKenna one hundred dollars every Christmas to make sure no one does it on any of the bank's cases, and half the goddamn files disappear anyway.' But you have to sign for the file, Stern noted. 'Are they going to look at your dog tags? Write down a name. Jones. Jablonsky, for Chrissake. Just make damn certain that you don't write down Mittler—or even Stern, for that matter.' For some reason, this recollection seemed to have been edging up on him for days. Then he remembered: John and Dixon. Amid the present amity, the thought was troubling and he immediately put it aside.

"He sounds like he was a pretty tough customer."

"Oh, he was. No question about that. I have not met many men tougher than Henry. He reminded me of certain policemen. In some ways, he seemed to be made of stone. Resolute. This was how it was. *Punkt.*"

"Did Clara like him?"

"Ah, well. Now that is another question." For a moment, he turned his attention to the plant; this picking, hard on the back and thighs, was satisfying work, quickly rewarding, and tempting in its own way. He found a berry large as a small apple and showed it to her. "Clara had strong feelings for him. She sat by his bed weeping when he died. At many other times, in earlier years, she reviled him, and probably in stronger terms than most children criticize or rebuke their parents."

"That sounds like my mother and me," said Sonny. A wind, most welcome, came up then and raised dust in a revenant form down the road. When he looked back to Sonny, she had her eyes closed and both hands placed over the full shape in her middle. He was afraid that she was in pain, but it became clear quickly that it was, instead, resolve which gripped her. "God," she said. "God, I am going to do better." She opened her eyes then and greeted him with a magnificent smile—happy to be here, to have survived it all, to swear her vows and to see him sharing this, their acre of common ground.

29

Late in the afternoon, with Stern carrying all the buckets, the three of them returned from the strawberry field. The wind had turned suddenly, freshened by some northerly impulse. When they reached the cabin, Sonny sat heavily in a chair and laid the backs of her hands across her eyes. Stern suggested she lie down.

"Would you mind?" she asked. "Just for a few minutes? Then you can try to have that talk with me."

"Sam and I shall make do."

"You can wash the strawberries," she said. "Sam enjoys that. And Sam—check the hot tub. Make sure everything is okay."

The kitchen sink was joined unceremoniously to the rear wall, without any cabinetry to hide the plumbing. The boy stood on an old bentwood chair and insisted on holding each berry under the running tap. Laconic when Stern arrived, he now went on with five-year-old officiousness, issuing an unbreaking string of commands.

"Don't take the green thing out till you eat them."

"I see."

"They get rotting."

"I see."

"Then get them dry but don't squish them."

"Certainly not."

When the berries were bagged and refrigerated, Sam offered to show Stern his cave in the ravine. Stern called twice to Sonny but she did not respond and they left the cabin quietly.

Sam's cave was in the hollowed trunk of an old oak. The boy had built a nest of sorts out of dried leaves and twigs and in an empty fliptop cigarette box had stored two or three plastic figures with gargoyle faces and muscular bodies of a resilient resin. Sam told Stern their names—each apparently was an important cartoon star—and spent quite some time heavily engaged in the staging of various interplanetary wars, which Stern observed from the safety of a resting place in the crotch of a birch tree about thirty feet away. Cowboys and Indians, the pastime of his children's early years, was now banned on political grounds. Villains these days were alien species, and, rather than six-guns, firearms were lazer-mazers that evaporated all objects with a bright red beam. The game ended abruptly when the boy turned from his pieces.

"I'm hungry," he said.

"After all those strawberries?"

Sam tossed up his hands and repeated that he was hungry.

"I am sure Sonny will make you some dinner. Shall we see if she is awake?"

Inside the cabin, however, no one was stirring. Stern called to her softly and Sam added his voice at more telling volume. Stern hushed him and, after holding the boy back, crept alone to the small rear room where she lay uncovered on a narrow folding cot, still rosy with the heat but solidly asleep. Her hair was dark against her skin and one leg of her shorts had crept far up her thigh, showing some of the soft weight of pregnancy. Sonia Klonsky, his energetic antagonist, slept with the adorable soft innocence of a child, her pink mouth tenderly parted. Briefly, Stern, without reflection, raised the back of his hand gently to her cheek.

When he turned, Sam was watching from the open doorway.

"I want to to be certain she is not sick," Stern whispered at once. But he felt his heart knocking and he heard an urgent note in his voice. The boy, however, required no explanation.

"I'm hungry," he said again, somewhat pathetically.

Stern raised a finger to his lips and ushered Sam out.

"Do you know how to make dinner?"

"What is it you wish, Sam?"

"Hot dog and potato chips."

"That may be within my range."

They ate two hot dogs apiece. Sam was a garrulous, free-flow talker except when he ate, an activity he undertook briefly but with great concentration. When he was done, he resumed conversation, relating, in response to questions, that he was five and a half, went to all-day kindergarten at the Brementon School, and could read, although he was not supposed to. He was a remarkable child, full of a warm, seeking intelligence. That brightness lit him up like a candle and gave him a physical radiance which, in a person so young, amounted to beauty.

He considered Stern through a single squinted eye. "What's your name again?"

"Sandy."

"Sandy, can I go in the hot tub after dinner?"

"You must ask Sonny, after she is up."

"I *always* go."

"Sam, not so loud. You will wake her."

As the light dwindled, Stern and Sam played Battleship. Sam, most impressively, understood all the rules, although he treated them with occasional indifference. At one point, as Stern marked out the location of one of the boy's destroyers, he erased furiously on his page.

"Sam, I believe your ships must remain where you placed them."

"See, I was really going to put it somewhere else." He pointed to the page.

"I see," said Stern.

"I really was."

"Very well." Peter, Stern recalled, had refused to obey the rules of any game until he was past ten. He cheated with alarming guile and cried furiously whenever he lost, particularly to his father. After Sam's triumph in Battleship, they played a number of hands of Go Fish. Sam was a canny player, but was interested only in making books of picture cards. He did not care to hold ace through ten.

"I wanna go in the hot tub," he told Stern.

"When Sonny wakes up." Stern had checked on her again from the doorway only a few minutes before.

"I'll have to go to bed then."

"I see. What is it you do in the hot tub, Sam?"

"Look at the stars."

"Perhaps we can look at the stars, nonetheless."

"All right." He climbed down from his chair at once, ignoring the hand in play.

On the veranda, Stern found two splintered rockers and they sat side by side. The change of wind had pushed off the haze and the country sky was clear and magnificent. The air, after the heat of the day, was almost brisk. Sam had read a number of books about astronomy and at the age of five spoke about "the heavens." He knew the names of a number of constellations and demanded that Stern orient him to each.

"Where's Cassiopeia?"

Oh dear, thought Stern. Cassiopeia. He had not spent many evenings in his life studying the night skies.

"Over there, I believe."

"That one?"

"Yes."

"Sort of blue?"

"Yes."

"That's a planet."

"Ah," said Stern.

The boy accepted this failure without complaint. Stern had forgotten that—that it was not rivalry or a showdown that Sam was after, just information. If it was unavailable here, there would be better sources soon enough.

"I'm cold."

"Would you like your jacket?"

"Can I sit in your lap?"

"Of course." Stern boosted the boy beneath his arms, and he settled in at once, lolling back against his chest and belly. Dear God, the sensation. He had forgotten. To be able to fold yourself about this life in the making. The small limbs; the waxy odor of his hair after time in the woods. Stern put both arms about the boy and let Sam nestle against him.

"Is the sun a star?" asked Sam.

"So they say."

"Are the stars hot?"

"They must be."

"Could you drive a jet plane through a star if you went real fast?"

"I suspect not, Sam. The stars are hot enough to burn up most anything."

"Anything? Like the whole earth?" Sam now had a troubled

look. Stern wondered if he was telling him more than he should. "What if you poured like jillions and jillions of gallons of water on it?"

"That undoubtedly would work," said Stern.

The boy was still watching him. "Are you joking me?"

"Joking? No. Is that a joke?"

"You're joking me," the boy insisted. He pressed his finger in Stern's belly, as often seemingly had been done to him.

"Well, perhaps a little."

Sam turned around and rested again against his chest.

Was it possible? Stern thought in a swift rush of emotion. Was it truly possible? Could he start again and do it better on this go through? Oh, but this was mad. With the small boy somehow coursing against him, Stern closed his eyes in the great country darkness and wrestled despair. How, truly, could this be occurring? He saw more and more clearly how fixed his feelings were, how set he was on a path of absolute lunacy. He could not prevent a brief sound from escaping.

In a moment, Sam turned back.

"Can I go in the hot tub? Please," he said. "Please please please."

"Sam, I know nothing about hot tubs."

"I do. I'll show you. It's easy." He slithered away and ran down the veranda. "It's full and everything."

Stern drifted over. The tub protruded about a foot above the level of the porch. Sam had already eased off the canvas cover. The water temperature was moderate, apparently for Sam's benefit. What, after all, was the harm?

Sam hugged him the instant he agreed and immediately shed his clothes. Fully naked, he dipped in a toe.

"Come on," he said.

"Pardon me?"

"Come on. Get your clothes off."

"Thank you, Sam. I do not care to get into the hot tub."

The boy gaped. "You have to. Sonny says I can't go in without a grownup. I'm only five years old, you know."

"Yes," said Stern. He stood a moment and stared at the moon, just rising and visible through the fingerlet branches of the trees of the ravine. He had lost control over most everything sometime ago. In the dark, he kicked off his shoes and loosened his belt.

As life had repeatedly shown him, there was usually something to other people's pleasures. However suspect it seemed, the hot tub was enchanting. Little foggy wisps rose in the moonlight and the thin evening air was gentle as a breath. His large body felt lighter, submerged in the dark. Stern sat on a bench inside the tub and Sam crouched beside him to keep his chin above the water's level.

"When is Sonny gonna get up?"

"Soon, Sam. She must have been very tired."

"She's going to have a baby," said Sam. It was the first mention he had made of the subject.

"So I understand," said Stern.

"Is she sick?"

"No," said Stern.

"You said she was sick."

"No, I said I wanted to be sure she was not sick." What would he tell his father of what he observed? Or Sonny, for that matter? For the moment, that concern, like many others, seemed capable of passing.

"Do you go to Sonny's work?"

"In a fashion."

"Sometimes, if someone does something bad, the good people have to tell them they did something bad."

Stern thought of adding a defense perspective but answered finally, "Yes."

Sam suddenly stood straight up, shining like a fish in the moon's light. He hung his head over the edge of the tub.

"Uh-oh," Sam said.

"What?" Stern feared that the tub might be leaking.

"No towels."

Together they groaned in the dark.

It was Stern who, after a brief disagreement, was appointed to return to the cabin. Wearing only his boxer shorts, he saw in the mirror on the back of the bathroom door that his seat was sopping. He could hear Sonny a few feet away, grumbling a bit in her sleep.

Sam was wrapped and dried and placed in his pajamas. Before going to sleep, he demanded a story. In his backpack was a comic book depicting a protracted battle between two television characters, a blond hulk and a hooded creature who resembled a skeleton. They were dressed in medieval costumes but were located in outer space in the distant future and traded threats. The blond triumphed; that much had not changed.

The boy lay down, then drew himself up again, full of the familiar curiosity of bedtime.

"Sandy," he said, "does good always win?"

"Excuse me."

"Does good always win?" the boy repeated.

Stern was not certain if this was apropos of the story or their conversation before. He nearly asked what Sam was referring to but restrained himself with the thought that it was unseemly to be evasive with a five-year-old. Marta used to venture questions like this. Peter did as well, probably, but in his case they were put solely to his mother.

"No," Stern said finally. "Not always."

"It does on TV," the boy said. This was offered in part as refutation.

"Well, it should win," said Stern. "That is what the television is showing you."

"Why doesn't it win?"

"It does not always lose. It wins often. But it does not win every time."

"Why not?"

"Sometimes the other side is stronger. Sometimes both sides are good in part." Sometimes neither, Stern thought. In the midst of this, he could not keep himself from thinking of Dixon. He looked at the boy. "Sam, who talks to you about this, about good winning?"

"It's on TV," said Sam innocently. He had no notion that he had engaged in an abstraction. "How much does good win?" he asked. "A lot?"

"A lot," said Stern. He had meant to answer, As often as it loses. But he felt this was inappropriate and perhaps not even correct. There was no place for brutal honesty with a child. Everyone felt that. It was taken in the Western countries as a rule of nature. So we raise our children with love and comfort for a future they can only find disappointing. He told Sam it was time to sleep.

"Thank you for keeping me company, Sam."

"Sure." He lay down and popped up again. "Wait a second." He clambered from the bed, searched his bag, and came back with a small stuffed bear and a yellow piece of blanket. Passing by, he kissed Stern as naturally as if he had been doing it forever, and then right before Stern's eyes laid himself down and was instantly asleep.

* * *

A child asleep, a woman asleep, and Mr. Alejandro Stern in sole waking possession of a still home. It had been many years since he had felt this particular pleasure. He sat at the cable-spool table and ate a bowl of strawberries, listening to Sam's husky breath and, now and then as a distant counterpoint, a sighing sob from Sonny. Oh, he was pretending. He knew that. Nothing was truly hidden from himself. But he was enjoying it far too much to depart. He again wandered outside to the veranda. His wet underwear had begun to chafe, and after some reflection, he retrieved his towel inside, undressed once more, and hung his shorts on the branch of a tree, hoping the breeze would dry them before the long ride home. Then he resumed his place in the hot tub. The moon had risen fully and loomed over the ravine, full of tricks and magic. All his troubles waited for him in the city, in the daylight. For just this instant, watching the wisps wraith off the water, he was free.

It was only a few minutes before he heard the screen door bang.

"There you are." Her voice in the dark came from somewhere behind him. He turned in one direction, then the other, and still did not see her. "I thought you'd left until I saw the car. How long was I asleep?"

About five hours, he told her.

"Oh God." Sonny was at the corner of the porch, keeping her distance in an effort to be discreet. "I'm so sorry. What did you do with Sam all that time? Did you feed him?"

Stern described their activities. "He is a splendid young fellow. Bright as a firecracker."

"His father's son."

"No doubt."

"I don't think much of Rebecca, his mother. But she's done great things with Sam. I don't quite understand it. It seems like you can't predict who the good parents will be. It frightens me."

"You will fare well, Sonny. I am sure of it."

Gradually, she had approached. She was now a few feet from the tub and took the last few steps at once. She stooped a bit and her hand lingered in the dark water.

"God, it's nice. Sam helped you figure it out?"

"He was quite insistent on getting in here."

"We do everything to encourage him. He doesn't seem to recognize yet that it's the same water that's in the bathtub."

"It was only after I had finally agreed to let him do this that he informed me that I was required to join him. But I must say, it is most pleasant. After he was in bed, I could not let the opportunity pass. Here I am on a Saturday night in the woods. The sky is clear, the moon is full. The solitude is magnificent."

She inclined her head to look, as Stern had, at the stars. She was quiet a second.

"Will you die if I come in there?"

The shock of cold emotion, terror really, went through him like a bolt of iron. He shook his head before he spoke.

"No, no," he said.

"Because, look. I mean, people have different attitudes. You can just say it's too embarrassing."

"No, no," Stern said again. He was not sure he was capable of more.

When she began to slide off her shirt, Stern looked away, studying the tremorous movement of certain dark branches in the wind. But even this effort at discretion was not a full success. In the extended half of the cabin's casement window, he noticed a clear reflection and, turning back, caught, even against his will, just the slightest glimpse of her form, licked in the moon's bluish cast. It was no more than her upper torso as she eased into the bath, the smooth swell of the other life, and the lopsided proportions of her chest, where the fine blue light clung to the smoothness of her scarred left side, the visible ribs looking a bit like piano keys; like all things human, the sight was far more bearable than he had imagined. She settled in the bath and shook her hair free.

"Ah, this is great."

"I feared you had heat stroke."

"Just tired."

She reached over and laid her hand very briefly on his forearm. "It was nice out there."

"Yes."

"I'm glad we've become friends."

"As well."

These things came out of Sonny trippingly; she spoke from the heart as a regular matter. For him, it was all a muddle. He felt, as so often in his life, the important moment, the one of high emotion, deep feeling, sliding beyond him, not merely beyond control but wholly out of reach. He would never stop being himself.

"Can I tell you a story that will embarrass you?" she asked.

"If you believe I can stand it."

"I think you can." She looked off in the darkness. "When I was in law school, I went down to watch you in court. When you were defending Judge Sabich. I was there every day. It was like close-up magic. You know—how it doesn't really matter whether the balls are disappearing, because it truly is magic that human skill can make it look that way? That's how I felt. I didn't care whether he was guilty or innocent. I just wanted to be able to do what you did. What do you think of that?"

"I think you are most kind to tell me." She peered over; he could see she did not understand, and he inched somewhat lower in the tub. "I find it difficult, of late, to think of my professional life as an example to anyone. Given its costs."

"Are you talking about your wife?"

He made a sound.

"Huh," Sonny said. She was quiet. "Is there something you could have done?"

"Paid greater attention."

She did not seem inclined to respond, and he was quickly seized by a fear that she found this morose or, worse, self-pitying. For a second she disappeared, plunging beneath the surface of the water and came up glistening, shedding water and light, bubbling her lips and smoothing her hair.

"You know what I think?" she asked.

"What is that?"

"I think you can only be yourself." She wrung out her hair. Was this the thought for the night? Stern wondered. "I tell myself that a thousand times a day. Everybody's screwed up.

And things happen that screw you up worse. You get cancer. Or somebody dies. But you do your best. I would give anything to be a lawyer as good as you are, to think I did something important that well. I mean, look at what you've done."

"I look," he said, "and feel that I could have done better."

"Then do better next time."

"With the next life?"

"With the next part of this one."

That was, he realized, the only answer, the sole sane response. This, too, seemed to be a repetitive theme.

"And remember," she said, "that you're an example to people like me."

"You flatter me."

"I mean it."

He looked over to Sonny. She had laid her arm on the back of the tub and he touched her most briefly, as she had touched him. Then he went on.

"Apparently, I was not example enough, inasmuch as you chose the wrong side."

She drew back, as he expected. "Is this humor?"

"Of course."

"Oh." She smiled, shirking off the sense of injury. "I always thought I'd become a defense lawyer. But prosecutors have so much power. To do good things, you know—not just bad."

"Of course," he said again. "I admire the rectitude for which prosecutors stand."

"But you wouldn't think of doing it?"

"I have thoughts. But my view—purely an idiosyncratic one, I stress—is that I would only be doing further damage to what is already smashed and broken. Understand, I truly believe yours is a job that must be done—but better not by me."

"Is the story true, then?"

"What story is that?"

"That you turned down the offer to be U.S. Attorney before they gave the job to Stan?"

He waited, reflecting. "Is that worn-out rumor circulating again?"

She knew she was being put off.

"I'm not asking so I can tell someone else." With all her terrible pride, she was, he saw, somewhat offended. "I have a reason for wanting to know."

He described his meeting with the senator's aide in a few sentences. "I was never told that I was the first choice. I have no idea who would have been selected, even had I been disposed."

"You know it would have been you," she said, "and so does Stan. I think that bothers him. A lot," she added.

Stern privately had long harbored the same view. She was pensive, and then dipped again beneath the water.

"I'm getting out," she said when she emerged. "The o.b. doesn't like me in here for more than ten minutes."

Stern turned away to stare at the moon and the darkness.

"When you're ready," she said behind him, "we can have that talk." He heard her pad off and, after telling himself not to, turned to watch her go, with her bundled clothes clutched to her chest, her hair dripping, the broadened lower proportions of her form still a becoming sight, wet and shining, as she retreated.

In a minute, he rose. He was on the edge of the tub, in his full naked glory, when Sonny leaned out the window with another towel. "You should see the look on your face," she said, and hung the towel on the window frame. He could hear her laughing inside as she walked away.

When he came in, she was in a white terry-cloth robe, combing out her hair at the cable-spool table. Un-made-up, undone, she remained herself, strong and pretty, confident of her own appeal. She went to the bed to move Sam to the smaller room, but Stern insisted on carrying him and, with Sonny directing, bore the warm, small form to the cot in the adjacent room. Sam remained miles off in the profound grasp of a child's sleep.

"Strawberries? Cottage cheese?" Sonny was eating and the food was on the table. Stern declined. "So how do we do this? You're going to tell me what you know and I'm going to tell you if you're wrong. Is that the deal?"

"Sonny, I was perhaps too insistent. If—"

"No," she said, seizing a strawberry. "Sennett is screwing you around. I was never sure why before. Your client deserves better treatment. But there's only so much I can do."

"I understand."

"All right," she said. "Shoot."

This was a boundary, a line he preferred not to cross. He went on, merely because he remained grateful for her company, their conversation, for any reason not to depart.

He started with the basics, the large orders, the two exchanges, the error trades. When he mentioned the use of the house error account, she drew back with a marveling smile. "Now, how did you figure that out? Sennett is sure you'll never get it." When he hesitated, she turned the back of her hand. It did not matter. "Go on."

"Can the government show, by the way, that market prices were affected by any of these trades, or that someone was otherwise harmed?" He had been thinking about this point for some time. After indictment, a motion to dismiss on these grounds would be called for, claiming the prosecution could not prove a crime.

"We've looked at the cases," Sonny said. "There's an offense here. If you profit off the customers' information, you're taking something from them, one way or the other. What do you think the customers would say?"

Stern lifted his hands noncommittally. In the abstract, he probably agreed with her. He was more certain a judge would.

"Go on," she told him again.

He described how the accumulating profits, after further manipulations, were invested in the Wunderkind account—where over time they were lost, all of them, not to mention a good deal more.

"And you suspect Dixon of controlling this account."

"Go on," she said yet again. She had offered no other comment when he told her what evidence he thought they might have.

"I am certain the government can explain," said Stern dryly, "why someone would steal $600,000 in order to lose it."

"That's not an element of the offense." She meant that the government could prove the crime without solving that riddle. The fact that the money was lost might not even come into evidence.

"Nonetheless," said Stern.

"Go on," said Sonny. She had become grave and composed and clearly had no interest in debates.

"Right now, you seem to be energetically seeking the documents which show who established the Wunderkind account. Without that, of course, you will have no way to tie Dixon to the account, to the profits, and to the trading ahead."

For the first time, she was completely quiet. Stern waited until he realized that he was being informed he had missed a step.

"Is that where John comes in?"

"I don't know where he fits, Sandy. Honestly."

That matched what Tooley had told him; Mel was dealing strictly with Sennett. Stern wondered if that meant that John was being extraordinarily cooperative or more difficult than expected—or simply that Sennett, as usual, was being high-handed and secretive, even with his own staff. Yet even if John had a perfect recollection of Dixon calling in every dishonest trade, the government would want proof that Dixon controlled the Wunderkind account, where the profits briefly rested. Without that, the prosecutors would have difficulty establishing that Dixon was not acting innocently or at the behest of someone else. Stern repeated this thought aloud.

"But you still require the signature forms in order to establish Dixon's relationship to the Wunderkind account."

Again, she made no answer.

"I am wrong?" asked Stern.

Sonny reached to the bowl and ate another strawberry, while he tried to concentrate. This was ordinarily his strength, picking out the nuances of the evidence. But he had missed something of consequence. He remained quiet.

"Last year," said Sonny, after a bit, "starting out in the office, I prosecuted a lot of dope cases."

"Yes?" He had no idea where she was leading.

"You know how those cases go. DEA sees suspicious activity. There's an informant. They get a warrant, knock down the door of a stash house, find ten keys of cocaine and no one inside it. Then they come to the poor Assistant to issue grand jury subpoenas so they can figure out who owns the house—and the dope."

"Yes," he said again.

"When you get the title to the property, or the lease to the apartment, whatever, it's pointless. It's always some little old lady from the North End with whiskers and a bunch of cats. But we prove it's their house, anyway."

Stern nodded. He was familiar with the government's techniques. They went to the gas company, electric, telephone, and found out who was paying the bills. In one case that Jamie Kemp

had handled before moving to New York, the government proved
control of the house by showing that their client had purchased
the garbage cans in the alley. He took it that Klonsky had issued
a broad hint but for a moment it was lost on him.

"The deficit," said Stern suddenly.

She smiled.

"Dixon paid for the quarter-million-dollar debit balance left in
the Wunderkind account," he told her.

"Go on."

"That is why you subpoenaed his bank records. To find the
check he wrote to cover that debit. You were never tracing the
funds he'd deposited."

"Go on," said Sonny.

"And you have the check?"

"Go on," said Sonny again.

He waited. Dixon, too, had apparently missed the point of the
inquiries at the bank. Protecting its informant, the government
with its various subpoenas had made a convincing show of being
more interested in the money Dixon received than what he'd
paid out.

"So why, then, are you so concerned about the account-
opening documents?"

Of course, she would not answer. Stern subsided again to
silence. What if Dixon had filched those papers? Why would the
government initiate such hot pursuit of what was beside the
point?

Unless the prosecutors knew in advance that Dixon had made
off with the records. Of course. Their informant had once more
led them to the right spot. The prosecutors—Sennett, at least—
never expected the Wunderkind records to turn up in Margy's
hands. That was why Sonny had recovered her good humor after
she had gone to speak with him. She had learned what Sennett
had counted on all along, that the prosecution would end up
with the best of both worlds: evidence that Dixon controlled the
account and proof he was trying to conceal that fact. With that
kind of showing—state-of-mind evidence, as it was called—the
government could cut off any clever conjectural defenses that
might be ventured at trial to suggest a half-sane or innocent
motive for Dixon's conduct. Once the prosecution was able to
establish that Dixon was covering his tracks, there could be little

argument about what he thought of his own activities. John, at this point, remained Dixon's sole hope, and a faint one at that. If John's memory failed in some critical regard about who had instructed him to place the error orders, there might be a minute space in which to turn a sly pirouette. Yet that was not likely. The prosecutors had the critical proof in hand now. The walls were closing in on Dixon, as on some Poe character; the light was growing weak. Here, supercharged by the presence of this young woman, the weight of these developments did not really seem to settle upon Stern fully.

"You really like him, don't you?" Sonny asked, after watching him a moment.

"I care greatly about my sister. Perhaps my feelings for Dixon are merely force of habit. But I am very sad to hear this."

"This is just between us," Sonny said. "Stan would hang me."

"You have told me nothing." He crossed his heart, a schoolboy habit from Argentina, from a time when Gentile friends demanded the gesture, never understanding his reluctance. "There will be no communication. To anyone. No hint. My promise."

He looked at her across the table. He had exhausted the excuse that brought him here. He rose, slapping his sides.

Sonny yawned.

"Believe it or not," she said, "I think I'm going to sleep."

She insisted he take an enormous bag of berries. As they approached the door, he made her promise to say goodbye for him to Sam. Then she grabbed him, applying a quick comradely hug, coming close enough to bump her firm belly against him and sweep her wet hair across his cheek. His arms came together slowly and never reached her before she was gone again. A brief ache of some kind, of deprivation, rose up and subsided.

"You were most kind to have me," he said from the other side of the screen.

"We'll do it again," she said. As he trudged up the stairs, her voice, full of her own ironic laughter, reached him in the dark. She'd had an afterthought.

"If I'm still married to Charlie."

30

He arrived home near one, after traveling down the dark country roads and then the highway, tugged through the night by the beam of his headlights and the heavy currents of his own thoughts. He had tuned the radio to the mumble of a Trappers game, but after a time snapped it off and drove entirely in silence, dominated by sensation—the heat and scent of the strawberry field, the reverberating charge when she had slid so quietly into the water. At moments, of course, he pondered about Dixon. Soon they would have to seriously consider the alternatives. For a few minutes Stern worked at it all in his mind, probing, tangling and untangling, but he saw no avenues of quick escape. He thought, naturally, of his sister then. Silvia would suffer. Full of high emotion in the dark, he endured that pain anew.

Inside the door of his home, Stern plunged his heavy-bottomed body down on the antique milking chair in the front foyer, his thick legs poked out before him. The bag of strawberries, moistened now by their own juice, lay in his lap. Across the hall, he caught a piece of his reflection in the wig-stand mirror and saw how ridiculous he looked; he had been in that tub more than an hour and never let a drop of water touch his head. The little pouches of hair on either side, brittle with the sun, were lifted out like cherub's wings, and two or three dirty streaks of dried sweat ran from his crown to his cheeks. Licking his lips, he could still taste the dried salt gathered in the hollow beneath his nose.

He was exhausted. But there was no resisting in the safety of his home the measure of his own excitement. Here in this known space, close and his alone, something finally gave way, and riding up in him he felt at last the full expression of what had waited thoughout the day. He made a sound out loud as the longing radiated through him and he sat riveted by passion. This was remarkable. His blood carried an electric charge. His heart and male organs were affected by an aura of desire which was not just that deep body-wanting thing, that longing like a stifled moan, but something else, something needier, softer, and more yearning. He wanted, simply, this young woman. To be with her. To hold her and be held. My God! It passed over him in waves as he marveled at the overpowering, transforming feeling of it all. The rest of life did not exist, not simply the boundary lines of circumstance, but the hobbling limits of personality. Here, for a moment, all limitations could be exceeded. He would croon beneath her window or, more simply, confess to this wild yearning. He had half a mind to go directly to the phone, until he recalled that he had seen none in the cabin. This was what drove grown men to shirk their families and young men to foolish daredevil acts. He sat gripping the arms of his chair.

Oh, it made no sense, but that was hardly the point. The empire of dreams, the region where images preceded words and sensation was supreme, had given up this fixation and there was no logical quarreling with it. How much, really, did we ever understand about this? He'd had prescriptions from everyone, advice from every soul on earth about how to run the remainder of his life. But this was what he had been awaiting—to find what was beyond humdrum propriety or custom and to learn his own true ambition. And it was this young woman, troubled but struggling each instant, no matter how else she faltered, to be the real thing, her best and most authentic self.

But, of course, nothing would happen.

The thought swung through him like the closing of a heavy door. Not a thing would actually occur. He had proved that convincingly when he sat inches from her, naked as Adam and Eve, and had been powerless, inert. Her troubled talk of leaving her husband was just that—angry idle talk. She was merely becoming accustomed to the fact that the pathways in her life were, finally, marked out, established. At the age of fifty-six, he had now managed to lead the emotional life of a seventeen-year-old, full of moonstruck fantasies that would never be fulfilled.

The anguish sang through him for a short time with the perfect reverberations of a high note rung from crystal.

And somehow, then, he thought of Clara. The association was not direct, for his thoughts were actually bittersweet, some admiration of the pure sentience of his present state. He had been immobile throughout, but now a new shock passed through him, for he recognized, with a precision that passed beyond the realm of any allowable doubt, what it was that Clara had been seeking when she turned away from him. Just this: the mercy of passion. And here in his chair he was equally certain—sure, if he had learned a thing about her in the decades—sure not merely that she had never found that grace but that she had discovered that for her—in her—it would never be attainable. Never. In this instant, there was not a grain of ill feeling, only comprehension, definite—complete. Eyes wide, he sat, somehow rebuked by the enormous silence of the large home and the harshness of these judgments which he made about himself and his entire life. His blood was coursing; the image of that young woman a hundred miles away still seemed so near, so compelling, that he remained half inclined to lift his hand in greeting. And yet he held that thought of Clara at her ultimate moment, grappling with desperation, as the biblical figures were portrayed in lush oil paintings wrestling God's winged angels of death. Never, she had thought. Never, he thought now. Never.

"I was engaged," said Clara that night as they sat in the dark car over the river, with the sweet julep smell of the liquor around them. "We broke it off a year ago last June." It was nearly December now. The street lamps and scattered light from the sky, vaguely refracted, cast deep shadows; he could see only the movement of her eyes as she looked ahead through the car window. Some spirit of bravery gripped her, though. There was a finer, noble look to her as she spoke; Stern was impressed, as he had been often lately, by her beauty. "His name was Hamilton Kreitzer. Do you remember him? From law school?"

The name meant nothing to Stern. He had the vaguest image of a fellow with a callow, luminescent smile and half a head of wiry blondish hair.

"He's older. Than we are. Than I am. He had left Easton before I started. But, well, he was glamorous. You know, he came driving out on the weekends. He had that little English car, whatever it's called. The roadster. He'd come flying onto campus with the top down in the middle of the winter and his scarf blowing behind him. He went out for some time with Betty Tabourney's sister. He had a terrible reputation. But girls don't ever know what they really like, do they? He's very handsome. You have to give him that. He's got a tiny little mustache like Errol Flynn. And, of course, he's quite well-to-do. His father is one of Daddy's clients. They make candy. You see it in all the five-and-dimes. Packaged stuff. It's been stale whenever I've bought it. At any rate." She stopped to adjust herself in the seat. She was probably not accustomed to speaking at such length. For a moment, even in the dark, Stern could discern some tentative relfex: she was not certain that she wanted to go on. Then she straightened somewhat and continued, looking again through the front window, raising that fine profile. "They call him Ham. Nice name for a Jewish boy." She laughed. "Of course, my parents liked that. You know how they are. They don't like anything to be 'too Jewish,' which means Jewish at all."

Stern made a sound of acknowledgment, assent. He knew what she was saying.

"At any rate, I saw him one night at a dance, the Grover Hospital Cotillion. He was just out of the service, going to law school. I was with another boy, but we spoke, you know how that is, flirted, and he called me up the next week and asked me to be his date at another of these dances. I knew half a dozen girls who had gone out with him, and not one of them had a decent thing to say, but I was so thrilled. Oh." She closed her eyes, she shook her head, overwhelmed. "I was so delighted to have all my friends, everyone I knew, see me with Ham Kreitzer."

She found her drink in her hands—she seemed to have forgotten it—and nipped at it briefly. He could see it was not much to her taste.

"I was quite surprised when he called after that. But he honestly seemed to enjoy my company. He told me how I'd *blossomed since college." She threw a hand in the air for expression, then regained herself and made a sound that led Stern to believe that in the dark she might have blushed. "Well, I had grown up a great deal. I suppose he was attracted to the side of me that didn't think he was all that important. Which was there, even though you wouldn't know it to listen to me now. He enjoyed the challenge of winning me over. And, of course, I listened to him. He liked to talk about himself. So many men do."*

Across the seat from her, Stern smiled, but she was too caught up to find any special meaning in her remark.

"But when you go to know him, he was like everybody else. He had so many schemes. He hates his father, despises the poor man, and naturally, after he was dismissed from law school, he felt he had no other choice, and so he has to work beside his father every day. He wants to break away so desperately and of course he never will." She turned to Stern. *"I felt something for him. And I believe it was mutual. But he was also at the age at which it was expected that he would get married. He'd had his flings or wild oats, or whatever you call it. And I'm socially acceptable. My parents are, that is. So we were engaged. I loved to sit and hold his hand, just watch him. He is such a handsome man. I couldn't believe he was mine. It all seemed so magnificient. My,"* she said. For the first time in the dark, she touched her eyes, but she drew herself together. She had her own momentum now.

"Of course, that's not the end of the story. We were engaged for fourteen months. I had to have a June wedding. Two weeks before the ceremony, I got a phone call. I could tell he was far away. 'Darling,' he said, 'I'm afraid I can't go through with it.' I wasn't surprised. I'd realized by then that he was really quite a little boy. I knew he would be terrified. He didn't say where he was. It turned out that he was on Catalina Island. And that one of the girls had disappeared from the packaging line—I'm sure she was on Catalina Island, too. I didn't care about that. It was me he didn't want. Whether he preferred someone else was beside the point. And then, of course, there was one more problem." Across the seat, she turned in Stern's direction, while the heat purred, pouring up thickly from beneath the dash. *"I was pregnant,"*

she said.

He realized she was watching him to see if she could catch some flicker of his reaction in the dark. And she had judged him correctly. Her news instilled not merely shock but something close to panic. But as a child in a home rife with torment he had learned to save all expression and he showed nothing now; not a ripple to the surface.

"Are you shocked?" she asked.

He drew his breath and reflected.

"Yes," he said at last. There was no avenue for diplomacy.

"I was, too. Not at how it happened, naturally. And I don't want you to think that I was taken advantage of, or that I was left behind like some dirty conquest. We had carried on that way for many months. I think, frankly, that I liked the idea of it better than anything else. The secret. The romance. Wasn't this what the world was supposed to be about?" She stopped. "Well, listen to me." She seemed to consider looking over once more, but even she was not that courageous. Stern fought back the same cold panic. He regretted suddenly that she was telling him all this; but that, he realized, was the point. Somewhere down the bank, voices, a man's and a woman's, were raised, then passed.

"Naturally, I couldn't believe I was in that state. It was only a month. I hoped for a while that something would happen. But it didn't. Then I thought about killing myself. And I very nearly did. I actually got hold of some sleeping pills. I fell asleep one night holding the bottle in my hands, and I remember"—she laughed and tossed her head—"that after an hour or two I jolted awake and I thought I had done it, and I actually accepted it, the whole idea, for just one second, and then was glad I had the chance to think better of it. I was sure that telling my parents would be the worst thing I'd ever done, but it was even more difficult than I'd imagined. Lord," she said suddenly, "I never want to do anything like that again." Again she touched her eyes. "My father was monstrously angry. Monstrously. And of course they wanted me to marry Ham, which was out of the question. We quarreled about that for another week. But finally my father took me to Mexico City. The flight was eleven hours each way. We had to fly through Chicago. And I was so sick coming back, I thought

I would die. But it was taken care of.

"And I really have very little now. I know how silly that sounds. I have so much compared to most people. And even compared to what I had before, there's no real difference. But I feel as if the whole world's changed. I gave up my job before the wedding. Because Ham wanted me to. That's what brings me around the office. And naturally I'm ashamed. I really don't know who's heard about this. I imagine everyone. I go into a movie theater or a store or to the concert hall and I assume that every person knows. That they're whispering. You know how unkind people are.

"So," she said. "That's the story. It's terrible, don't you think?"

"Painful," said Stern.

A breath, almost a sob, rattled through her, and she nodded.

"Do you know what humiliates me most? That I didn't realize what I wanted. That I was almost twenty-five years old and had no idea. I should have know better than to care for the likes of Ham Kreitzer. I did *know* better. And I couldn't help myself." She lifted her arm in the dark to see her watch.

They drove largely in silence. At her home, he began to get out of the car to open her door, then stopped.

"This was a very fine evening."

"Oh, certainly." She laughed. "You'll be indentured to George Murray for the rest of your life and your date turns out to wear a scarlet letter."

Stern looked at her directly.

"I heard the most wonderful music played on the piano."

She reverted to the gestures of the rich, and kissed him, French style, on each cheek. Then she left the car by herself and ran up the concrete stoop of the parents' Georgian home. She waved to him from the doorway.

Driving away, he still felt the liquor. But he knew he would never sleep. There was a briefcase full of work at home. And the problem of the car to be fully contemplated, waiting like some vexing puzzle he knew it was his responsibility to solve. But he could not make his mind work over those things. Even a few blocks away, he recognized his emotions.

He was thrilled. Thrilled. The cool racing beat of high excitement was in his blood. He was thrilled—by her trust, her depth. There was wild, exciting news in her confession of a carnal side. But what thrilled him most, Mr. Alejandro Stern, immigrant American, refined rascal, placid scheming soul—what thrilled him most was that he knew now she was truly available to him.

PART THREE

31

Greeting Helen on Sunday night, he was unprepared for his tender feelings. How welcome the scent of her perfume, her very form, as he lifted his hands to embrace her. Ah, Helen. In her doorway, he took her in his arms and lolled her about. They both laughed. Even now, though, the thought, the ache for Sonny was not far away.

"Tell me of your journey," Stern insisted.

She described Texas, hot and desolate. You drive seventy-five on the highways and the city towers loom ahead through the shimmering heat and seem to come no closer.

"You were bad while I was gone," she said. They were in the kitchen; Helen was tossing a salad and Stern was making a faltering effort at assistance while he drank his wine.

"Me?"

"I called last night and got your machine. At eleven o'clock." She raised an eyebrow.

"I was working," he said. "Dixon's case," he added to enhance his credibility. He had attempted to reach Dixon all day. He wanted the man back in town at once. He phoned the island house directly a number of times, and finally called Elise, Dixon's secretary, at home—she could reach Dixon twenty-four hours a day, like the President. Today, however, Dixon was out of touch, lost under the Caribbean sun. Perhaps he had done the wise thing and decided never to return or, more realistically, wanted to enjoy, unencumbered, the last breath of freedom. Certainly, Dixon knew best how grave his problems were. There was a reason that he felt he had to get away.

In the meantime, Stern stood in Helen's kitchen, if not lying to her, then avoiding the truth. To what point? he wondered. He had no idea what to do. Go on? Long? Suffer? There was at all moments this intense sensation of heat. Sooner or later his resistance would erode; he would seek out Sonny and perform some lunatic act. Today at home, he had been utterly useless. He came to rest, and sat, mouth agape, eyes caught, replaying all the same images in a heart-bursting swoon. He was hopelessly smitten. But what about the present? The world? Here was Helen, decent, capable, and kind. How should he treat her? He had no plans, except a vague inclination to avoid sleeping with her tonight, for the sake of decency perhaps, or more likely because he could not stand further stimulation.

Helen as usual had prepared a splendid meal, shrimp rémoulade, his favorite, with two warm vegetables and potatoes. She wanted this to be a glorious reunion. Just last week, in speaking about Miles, Helen had said in the mildest, most casual fashion that when she divorced she could not imagine marrying again. There was no emphasis, but she clearly intended to describe that state of mind in the past tense. Stern had not missed the point but had prudently allowed the observation to pass. Now, over time, he would have to maneuver gently for distance.

They ate and chatted. He was grateful, even in his punished, overwrought state, for their constant amiability. Stern pushed the potatoes aside with his fork.

"You like those," Helen told him.

A Stern face: a world of emotions too hard to express. "I am contemplating a diet," he admitted.

"Dieting?" Helen took a bite, chewed once, and eyed him acutely. The intelligence flashed in her eye. He felt his stomach sink. What in the world had led him to conceive of her over the years as not bright? "I was right," she said. "You're seeing someone younger, Sandy, aren't you?"

Now what? Why is lying so often the truth? Seeing? Oh yes, he was seeing. On the air, in the sky. A holographic projection. He was seeing someone younger, all the time.

He had been still a few seconds.

"Yes," he said.

Helen looked straight at him. She said, "Shit."

A moment passed.

"Well," said Helen.

He could not think of a single comforting word.

"I'll live," she told him.

Tongue, speak. He merely watched.

Helen got up from the table.

He found her by the island cutting board in the fancy kitchen Miles had built her before he set himself free. Chin high, she watched the darkening sky through a broad window, her view partly obscured by an apple tree that had blossomed magnificently only a few weeks ago.

He touched both her elbows as he came up behind her. "Helen."

She reached around herself to hold his hands.

"I knew this was too soon. I should have let you get over all of it."

"Helen, please do not—" Overreact? "Helen, this is not—"

"Yes, it is," she said. "You're hooked." She looked back at him. "Aren't you?"

He closed his eyes rather than respond.

She turned away and crushed her fist squarely in the middle of her nose. She wanted desperately not to cry.

"I'm really being miserable."

"Of course not," he said.

"You didn't make any promises." She eyed him. "How young?"

He considered avoidance and gave up the thought.

"Forty," he said. "Forty-one." Pregnant. One-breasted. Married to someone else. And not interested in me. The utter madness of it, for a moment, almost drove him to the floor with shame.

Helen shrugged. "At least you're sane."

He nearly groaned.

Eventually, they returned to the table. He offered no details of this new interest—how could he?—and Helen courageously refused to ask. She told him that Maxine, after her day with Kate, had remarked on Kate's drawn look; she did not have the glow of some pregnant women. Hearing the remark, he thought at once of Sonny, then was pierced to see how quick he had been to skip beyond his concerns for his daughter.

As soon as he had his coffee, he went to the closet for his hat.

At the door, he took Helen in his arms, and she held him for a moment.

"You're not going to mind if I tell you I don't want to see you, are you?" she asked. "Under the circumstances?"

"Of course not." He kissed her briefly and walked into the tender night air, toward his auto, full of the pangs of terrible regret. Truly now, he was losing his grip. He had given up the best part of his actual life to indulge a high-school fantasy. But through all this immediate anguish, his heart still rose. One tie that bound, now severed. There were a thousand others, but his intent was clear. He was going to surmount all obstacles, each of them. He felt as valiant as a knight. He walked down the suburban avenue with a determined step, full of momentary pain, and the winging feel of freedom, of wild, improbable dreams.

32

Monday was a day of unexpected communications.

The first was awaiting Stern when he reached the office. Dr. Cawley had called, Claudia said, and needed to see him. She had compared schedules and agreed to a meeting at five o'clock at Nate's office. "He said it was personal," said Claudia, "and that he didn't want to see you at home. That's all."

Personal and not at home. *Mano a mano*, in other words—away from Fiona. Nate had tiptoed around Stern for months. Now he wanted a meet? Stern sorted the possibilities. Had Fiona spoken up, as Stern suspected she would? Were Nate and he about to have a scene? Perhaps Nate was going to clear the air completely—hand Stern the check and declare a lasting peace. His sense of intrigue for once was greater than his anxiety.

Later in the morning, he also heard from Mel Tooley. Stern was on the phone, attempting one last time to persuade AUSA Moses Appleton to soften his position on Remo, when Claudia laid down a note saying Tooley was on hold. Stern ended his conversation with Moses promptly.

"None of this goes any further," Tooley said.

"Of course."

"Sennett's sneaking around like some spook. He hears I talked, he'll go ballistic. You didn't get this here."

Stern once more assured Mel of his confidence.

"My guy is going in the grand jury next week."

"I see. May I ask the terms?"

"Immunity. Letters. Court orders. I got him everything. It was a white sale at the U.S. Attorney's Office."

"And the prognosis for my client?"

"Bad."

"I see."

"Very bad. There's a bunch of papers and tickets my guy wrote and your guy told him how to do it, every i, t, and comma."

"I see. And your client recalls this clearly?"

"Like a vision. My guy was new to the business, didn't know what was going on, so all this stood out." Mel waited. "You know that song and dance."

Stern said nothing. John had done the predictable thing. There was justice in this. Dixon, after all, deserved what he was going to get.

"He really feels like shit about this," Tooley said. "You know, it's family stuff. Very messy. Well, I don't have to tell you."

"No," Stern agreed.

"I keep telling him he's got to think 'Me first.' He doesn't have a long way to wander on this thing. If he fucks around with them, they land on him with both feet." Tooley meant that MD's records implicated John as well. Whatever John's protests that all this had been over his head, the prosecutors knew that no one, no matter how naïve, could have regarded this maneuvering as wholesome. But wanting its case to be ironclad, the government preferred to have John's testimony, rather than a woebegone lower-down sharing the charge and defense table with Dixon. This, too, was an entirely predictable turn of events. "He'll look like a whipped dog up there, if that does you any good." Mel was talking about John's trial testimony. That would be another lawyer's problem, in any event.

"When does he appear before the grand jury, Mel?"

"A week from tomorrow. I don't think the indictment's far away. They've got it all pretty well organized. I imagine they're going to D.C. for RICO approval right now."

"Yes," said Stern again. The racketeering charge, the one by which the government would divest Dixon of the business in which he'd invested a lifetime, required approval in Washington. Stern would have to request an audience at the Department of Justice. The bureaucrats in D.C. would sometimes act with greater restraint than the U.S. Attorney, although there were unlikely to be any soft hearts in this case.

Tooley and he concluded with a vague promise to speak again. It was unlike Mel to be so forthcoming. Usually there was a hidden agenda, two or three of them, in fact. Was it possible he was actually acting at Sennett's instruction? Yes—but it would be hard to mislead Stern about the testimony of his daughter's husband. That probably accounted for Mel's candor, the fact that Stern would inevitably learn about this. Realizing that, Tooley wanted credit for being the first with the news. Stern drummed his fingertips on his desk and picked up a cigar. Of late, he had taken to twirling them between his fingers, unlit, never letting the ends touch his lips. Dixon was going to have to be made to think seriously about a guilty plea. In cases like this, the best that generally could be managed was to agree to a staggering financial penalty in hopes of sharply limiting the time in jail. Whatever was hidden in the islands, many of the visible assets here were in jeopardy—the stone house, the chauffeured cars. Dixon would want to save what he could, for Silvia's sake. Perhaps Stan would accept forfeiture of a discrete sum—millions—and Dixon's resignation from the business in lieu of all the stock.

In the meantime, Stern would have to call Kate—and John—take them to dinner as soon as the grand jury appearance was past. Dixon's wayward path had detoured the life of his family long enough. Stern wanted to be sure that his daughter, and even his son-in-law, knew that he was prepared to go on with this episode in the past. If Dixon decided to resist the government, Stern would help him search for another lawyer; the time was at hand. That, however, would not be a complete solution. It was difficult to imagine a family gathering with Silvia, whose husband was in prison, occupying one corner and John, who sent him there, the other. Stern let a sound of some distress escape him. They would all remember this year.

* * *

Nate's nurse, who showed Stern back to the consultation room seemed familiar—he had seen her timid smile and slender good looks somewhere before. Stern watched the young woman depart and spent an instant trying to place her, before Nate bade him sit in a gooseneck chair of maroon leather.

They asked, conventionally, about one another's health, then lapsed into silence. Stern had never been here and that fact

seemed to underscore the unusual nature of their meeting—
right faces, wrong setting. The atmosphere grew tenebrous. The
consultation room was far more ample than Peter's, furnished,
like the Cawley home, out of Ethan Allen, with an imposing
wallpaper of green vertical stripes and a heavy paddle-shaped
clock on one wall. Nate sat in his long white coat behind a
substantial walnut desk, his certificates arrayed about him,
rocking a bit in his tall leather chair. Eventually, he eased
forward and came to the point.

"I want you to know, Sandy, that I'm going to ask Fiona for a
divorce."

Stern was dumbstruck, not by the news, of course, but by the
notion that this was Nate's revelation.

"Are you asking my advice, Nate?"

"Not really. If you have some, I'll take it."

"No," said Stern, then added wickedly, "It may be expensive."
Nate let the back of his hand drift out in space: no matter. He
could afford it. Stern found his jaw setting harshly, as if there
had been a graft of iron. "Have you told Fiona?"

"Not exactly. I wanted you to know first."

"Me to know?"

"You," said Nate. He fiddled with the little ornaments on his
desktop, an onyx-bladed letter opener, a matching paperweight;
then, eventually, he folded his hands. "Sandy, I don't care," he
said. "About what happened between you and Fiona."

"I see," said Stern.

"She told me."

"Apparently." He had his feet on the floor and his hands in his
lap. So far, he was holding on better than he might have
expected.

"I found a piece of your mail in the john off our bedroom a
couple weeks ago. We ended up having it out then."

"My mail?" asked Stern, but he realized then what Nate
meant: Marta's note, the one Stern had carried out of the house
that night. He had been looking for the letter just the other day,
having been unable to reach Marta by phone and wondering
when she was due to arrive.

"As I said," said Nate. "I don't care. I really don't. It sounds a
little bizarre to say I don't care, but I don't."

"Very well."

"You slept with Fiona, so you slept with her." Nate threw up his hands magnanimously.

Stern found that he had hold of both arms of the chair, his fingers gripped down to the studs; perhaps he feared that the furniture was going to fly. Slept with his wife! What had she done? Fiona's killer instinct, he saw, had taken her far from the facts. Did she think that, by setting them even, she could get a new start with Nate? No, Stern decided, probably not. Fiona had just hunkered down, abandoned all caution, and taken her greatest pleasure—retribution: I want to see the look on the dirty bastard's face.

"Am I to respond?" he asked eventually.

"You don't have to."

"Because, to say the least, Nate, you have not received an accurate portrayal." Stern stopped then, recognizing his dilemma. What were his lines? 'It is not true, Nate, that I fucked your wife. I only attempted to do so.' That would not be an especially stirring defense. Nor, for that matter, did Nate seem to believe him.

"Listen, Sandy, that's not the point of this."

What *was* the point? Stern studied Nate, who did not quite have the fortitude to look back. He had always taken Nate as a person of little malice—a healer, a caring type, with that easy, quiet manner that many women took for masculine gentleness. All in all, in spite of Stern's moments of dizzy rage, those judgments held. Nate had no real will to do injury. Instead, he muddled about, full of warm feelings and covert impulse, inadvertently knocking over lives like plates in a china closet. He had grown up in Wyoming and had come to the big city as a medical student. At times, he still liked to play the befuddled cowboy. Over the years, Stern had decided that pose concealed laziness, sloth, a weakness of spirit. That was why he so easily surrendered to female temptation or, more pertinently, maintained his unsatisfying life with Fiona. The same remained true now. He clearly savored the sheer ease of the solution Fiona's supposed confession presented: You've screwed my wife, and I don't care. Now take her off my hands and let us go on in peace. The matter of Clara was far from his mind—a secret he took to be entombed and thus forgotten. He dealt merely with the present. Fiona could be dismissed and cared for in a single stroke, and at a cheaper price. He would dust off his hands and move on.

Assessing all of this, Stern, amazingly, felt at considerable advantage. Not so much with the facts. That Fiona was lying was almost beside the point. She'd said what she'd said. Go disprove it. But he was much better equipped than Nate to deal with a circumstance of this sort. He saw suddenly, decisively, how this would play out, and knew that Nate, whatever his plans, was about to be badly outflanked. He told him so directly.

"I believe, Nate, you have miscalculated."

Nate pulled a face. He was going to deny any cunning, but thought twice of that and said nothing at all.

"Were I you, Nate, I would proceed to divorce court with caution."

Nate stiffened. Clearly, he had more here than he had bargained for. He flipped his hand again, as he had before.

"Sandy, I—Listen, this isn't a holdup. Or whatever you think. Don't take it that way."

"No, of course not," said Stern. "I know you would not mean to threaten me. Nor I you."

"You?" asked Nate.

"I," said Stern. "But let me offer a word of warning, nonetheless. Do not, Nate, attempt to involve me in your bloodbath with Fiona. Do not dare. After all, we both know, I am not a witness to your good character or your veracity."

Nate wound his head about as if he'd been kicked.

"Jesus," he said.

"If I am placed under oath, Nate, I shall speak truthfully about all matters. Including those most painful to me. Do not think that pride will prevent me from disclosing the manner in which you and Clara deceived me."

Nate for an instant was absolutely still, his mouth open in a small dark o. Then he took his hand and covered his eyes. He heaved a bit.

"Look." Nate eyed his desktop, considered his thumb. "Look," he said again.

"Yes?" said Stern. He had known, instinctively, that Nate would be helpless. "As long as you have chosen to speak plainly, Nate, let me do the same: there is a large check which I believe you owe Clara's estate." Nothing—no scruple, no sense of taste, not even the recollection of his own discomfort—could dull Stern's delight in this moment. With a whetted look of absolute malice, he considered Nate, who sat back in his tall chair, his sparse hair in disarray from the sudden pulling at his face and scalp, looking overwhelmed, sorely confounded, scared.

"I was afraid you were going to say that," said Nate.

"I have a lawyer looking into this matter."

"I was afraid of that, too."

Stern nodded. He finally understood Nate's plan. He'd held the check, not merely to hide it from Fiona's future attorney, but from Cal now. He wanted to see if the coast was clear or if he'd been discovered.

"I would suggest you do the same, and have the attorneys make contact," said Stern.

Nate absorbed that in silence, but finally looked at Stern.

"I knew you'd find out eventually," said Nate. "I've eaten myself up alive about this whole thing. You may not believe that, but I have. Really. It's on my mind every day. I know you probably think I'm responsible for what she did. At the end."

"I do not blame you solely, Nate. I offer you that solace. I am sure that the ultimate denouement was a shock to you as well. But I bear you heavy resentment, notwithstanding. Clara's choice to take a lover was, of course, her own. But as a doctor, Nate, particularly one experienced with this sort of"—Stern waited, then fastened something down in himself and pushed on—"this sort of sexually transmitted disease and its course, I would certainly have expected you to have exercised greater care. And I take it from what I see that you were entirely indifferent to Clara's needs at the end."

"You think I mistreated her?"

"How else am I to feel?"

With an unhappy look, slumped in his chair, Nate nodded, mostly to himself.

"Not to mention the fact that you abused me, Nate, and our friendship. You lied to me. Quite boldly."

Nate again closed his eyes, then licked his lips so he could speak.

"I was afraid of what you would do when you found out. I admit that. But I want you to know something—I followed her lead. At all times. I did what she wanted."

Cornered, cowed, Nate took a coward's response. He blamed Clara. He was too weak perhaps to focus upon the sheer nasty bite of these words. But this meanness, intended or not, hit Stern like a blow. Yes, of course. This was the rebuke he had coming: she liked it. For an instant, he was close to responding with gutter obscenities. Even when he recovered, his accent, to his own ear, suddenly seemed peculiarly distinct.

"Nate, you are a scoundrel."

"Jesus," Nate said again.

Stern resumed his feet. This confrontation, long imagined, like so much else, seemed far more difficult in actuality than in prospect. He had no wish to prolong it. But Nate's comment still left a wake of ruthless emotion.

"One last word, Nate," said Stern. "A piece of friendly advice." Nate, who, all in all, looked thoroughly wrecked by this conversation, sat up on alert: he knew something else was coming. And he was certainly correct, for Stern had had a flash of the insight that for three decades had saved his life in the courtroom, some adrenalized ability of the synapses to suddenly connect, no more explicable than the gift of tongues or flight. "I suggest you fire your nurse before you head off for divorce court. Fiona has some damaging evidence, and the cross-examination will be even nastier if that young woman remains on your payroll."

The nurse was there, fiddling with some charts, when Stern threw open the office door. She had taken a message from his office and handed Stern the slip. He did not bother examining it now. He was in a courtroom mode, playing for appearance, knowing his behavior would be carefully recounted. He looked her up and down, just like that, an entire once-over, which she took in almost innocently, with the same uncertain smile, the same unruffled bland beauty. Then he showed himself out, having decided, with Fiona's videotape well in mind, that the young woman belonged to that small class of human beings who look worse with their clothes on.

33

"Claudia called—urgent," read the pink message slip the nurse had handed him. He reached her on the car phone, driving back to the office.

"They got you," said Claudia.

"I have something somewhat pressing of my own. Please find the number at Dr. and Mrs. Cawley's home and patch me through." They were on the line together while it rang a number of times; Fiona was not in. Stern swore—old words—in Spanish.

"Did they give you the message about Ms. Klonsky?"

"Klonsky?"

"That's what's urgent. She's called here three times in the last hour. She says she has to see you today. Personal business. I wasn't sure where you were going from there, but she said she'd go to your house and wait for you. I gave her the address. Is that all right?"

It was nearly six now. Stern slammed on the brakes and jerked the car to the curb. His hands were shaking. He was already turning around.

"Hello?" asked Claudia.

"Yes, yes. How long are you there tonight, Claudia?" Another few hours, she answered, working on a brief for Raphael. Stern asked her to try Mrs. Cawley every fifteen minutes and to give her this message: Mr. Stern apologized for not reaching her directly, but he was unavailable and thought it important that she know Dr. Cawley and he had met this afternoon and had a very thorough and candid discussion. "And then tell her," said Stern, "that I want to know, with all respect, if she has lost her mind. You must repeat it just so."

Claudia was mumbling and laughing as she made notes; she always enjoyed Stern.

He put down the phone then and shot off through the traffic. The auto clock said 6:02. Urgent and personal. Yes! He was flying.

The yellow Volkswagen was in the circular drive of Stern's home. He could see it as he approached, driving too fast down the block. It was an instant before he picked out Sonny. She sat on the slate front steps, her legs spread to make way for her belly, and her face turned to the sun—Ms. Natural, as she had called herself last month. Stern did not bother putting the car in the garage. Instead, he parked behind her and hiked up the drive, exhilarated and self-conscious.

Here he was, he thought, at one of those signal moments in life which come upon you, part of the infinite progression, just like other moments, but with the chance for enormous change. There had been a great deal of that for him lately—but he was prepared. He had probably not felt a thing like this in over thirty years, yet he recognized it at once. A certain border terrain had been crossed, and they waited on the edges of real intimacy— not just social interaction or an exchange of views, but penetration of the most fixed personal boundaries. And here, awaiting that final passage, he felt the full complexity, mystery of her persona. Oh, he knew nothing about the kinds of things that had made her. They came from different ends of the earth, different eras. It would be years before he recognized the imprint of her experience upon her, every layer, like the accumulating pages of a book. But his heart rose to the assignment; and he was confident that the required energy still resided within him. Every corny fatigued metaphor seemed apropos. He was drunk with the prospect, dizzy.

"What an unexpected pleasure," he said, beaming, as she awkwardly stood, brushing the soil from her seat and blinking off the sun.

*   *   *

He had actually opened his arms to embrace her, when he caught her look, pointed and intense, which stopped him cold; he knew at once that he had blundered. From somewhere she had produced a white envelope and she raised it at arm's length, as if to warn him, or even, perhaps, to fend him off.

"This is not for pleasure, Sandy. I came to give you this." She continued to extend the envelope. "I wanted to do it myself."

He stood there, mannequin—still. How had she put it? After forty, she had learned no one was even normal.

"Here."

Eventually he took it. With any reflection, he would have known what it must be, but instead he opened the envelope, fumbling and mindless, and studied the document. It was a grand jury subpoena which she had drafted; her initials were at the foot. Investigation 89—86. He read it over three or four times before the import came home. It was addressed to Stern himself; he had been subpoenaed to appear personally, commanded to attend on Thursday 10 a.m., and then and there produce "a safe transported on or about April 30 from the premises of MD Clearing Corp. and all items in your possession, custody, or control which were contained within said safe as of the time you received it." She had checked both boxes on the form—he was required to testify and to produce the object. As he read, there loomed up in him once more the familiar intimation of yet another disaster.

"I have to tell you," Sonny said, "that I'm really pissed off."

"Oh, Sonny," he said. "This is a misunderstanding. Please. Come inside for a moment." He was already walking up the slate stairs to his home.

"Sandy, there's no point."

"A moment," he said again.

They came into the foyer, and around them the house was dark and cool.

"Sonny, I am constrained, of course, by privilege," he said, meaning that he could not repeat anything Dixon had told him, "but I believe you have a terrible misimpression about this."

"Sandy, I really wouldn't say too much if I were you. I don't know where this thing will end up, and I don't want to have to testify. I can't play the game as hard as you guys do. Any of you."

"Sonny, there are no games involved."

"Oh, please! How can you say that? After you sat there telling me you were going to search for those records, when you had them in your office all the time. And I fell for that routine. That's what I really can't believe. Do you know what I've been wondering all day—what was so important you had to drive a hundred miles to find out about it? What would you have done with those documents if I told you the government's whole case depended on them?"

His mouth parted vaguely as he realized what she was saying: he was being accused. He sat heavily on the milking chair, which was behind him.

"You misunderstand," he said again.

"I understand fine. I thought you were my fucking friend."

"I am your friend."

"Pardon me, but *bullshit*. Friends don't do this to each other. No matter who their clients are. Do you want to know how I found out?"

He nodded mildly, afraid that, if he showed greater interest, in her great anger she might refuse to say.

"I walked in this morning," she said, "feeling sort of cheerful, and there's Kyle Horn waiting for me. He had a nice weekend, too—he went through all the checks from MD what's-her-name brought into the grand jury last week. And guess what he found? A check written out of your client's Chicago office to a cartage company here, with a little note on the bottom: 'DH Personal.' Think DH is trying to hide something, maybe?"

Margy again, thought Stern. Had Horn merely been exhaustive, or had someone provided him a clue about what he might find in those stacks of negotiated checks?

"So, naturally, he wants a grand jury subpoena, and he's out to the cartage company before noon and comes back with the bill of lading and lays it on my desk. 'Your idol,' he says. 'Shit happens.' I'm not naïve, Sandy. I understand you have a job to do. But you don't seem to care a bit about the position you put me in."

"Oh, Sonny, I care enormously." His tone—soulful, plaintive—took even her aback, and she stared at him a moment, weighing his sincerity. Finally she winced and turned for the door.

"My client," he said to her, "will not return until late on Thursday."

She shook her head at once.

"Don't ask for an extension, because you won't get it from Sennett—or from me. You and the safe and everything in it are in the grand jury on Thursday morning."

"That is not possible without conferring with my client."

"Then you better get a lawyer, Sandy. I mean it. This isn't amusing or cute or anything else. Don't put yourself in a vulnerable position with Sennett." She stopped herself, "Jesus, I'm doing it again. Look. You need a lawyer."

"A lawyer?" asked Stern.

Sonny seemed to hear the sounds first and bolted about facing the stairwell. It had not occurred to Stern that they were not alone, but he recognized the wind-sprung hairdo and the flowing gown, even before the face, so much like his own, appeared over the banister.

"Who needs a lawyer?" Marta asked.

34

The ensuing scene at the bottom of the staircase was brief and confusing. Stern, at the height of emotional turmoil, found himself sorely annoyed with Marta for her grand entrance and her failure to announce herself earlier. Never one to brook criticism casually, Marta defended herself stoutly, reminded him that she had written and that she had been letting herself into this house with the same set of keys for nearly twenty years.

"I called Kate. She said she left you a message last night. Don't you even listen to that machine?"

Finally daunted, Stern made no reply. Instead, he noticed Sonny, who seemed awestruck by the unpredicted outbreak of spirited family emotions. He made the introductions, while Marta, in her familiar way, removed the paper from his hand.

"This is a grand jury subpoena," she said.

"Ms. Klonsky has served me this moment."

"Again!" exclaimed Marta. Clearly she recalled the day of the funeral. "You people are too much. Haven't you ever heard of an Office?" She took one step toward Sonny. "Get out," Marta said.

"Oh Lord." Stern held his head. He reached despairingly after Sonny, but she was at the door long before him, and was gone with no further remark than "Thursday," as she pointed at Stern.

"My God, Marta. Your tongue!"

"You mean you're happy about this?"

"Marta, this is a most complicated circumstance."

His daughter tipped her head querulously and her face abruptly took on a new light.

"Is that the girlfriend?"

"Girlfriend?" asked Stern. Flummoxed, he managed to ask

who had spoken to her about his girlfriends. It was a serial connection, as it turned out. Maxine had called Kate last night, after hearing from her mother; Marta had spoken with Kate this afternoon when she had not met Marta here, as planned. Kate said she was not well, but that Stern would be expecting Marta, since she had left a message last night. The discussion of last night apparently brought out the rest.

"Is she?" Marta asked. "Your girlfriend?"

Deeply troubled by all this—Sonny, the subpoena, the image of a tom-tom network of females wailing over his shortcomings late into the night—Stern could not contain his irritation. Why did his children, in their twenties, extend to themselves an irrevocable privilege to be irreverent, even rude?

"Does she appear to be in any condition to be my girlfriend?"

Marta shrugged. Who knew? Who understood proprieties at the end of the century?

Stern, ready for another subject, asked about Kate.

"She says it's nothing physical. She's tired. But she sounds upset. Is something going on around here?"

"*Ay*, Marta," answered Stern, who finally took his daughter in his arms. He asked about her flight, whether she was hungry. They decided to go out for dinner.

"What about this?" asked Marta of the subpoena.

"I should call someone now, I imagine."

"I could represent you," Marta said. "I've had a couple clients get grand jury subpoenas, nothing like this but, you know, you could tell me what to do. I don't have a lot of experience in court, but I'd love to try it. I'm licensed here."

Indeed, thought Stern, not to mention in three other states. Nonetheless, as a holding action, the idea held some appeal. Stern would never feel completely comfortable as the client of one of his competitors. And criminal lawyers gossiped so freely. He would hate to read some clever item in the papers about his visit to the grand jury. All in all, this was the sort of thing he would be just as happy to keep in the family.

"Bring it along," said Stern. "We can speak over dinner."

Marta ran upstairs. There were things of Clara's she had discovered during her afternoon sifting through the dressers that she wanted Stern to see.

* * *

"That," said Stern, "is a cameo your grandfather Henry gave her when she was sixteen. I have not seen it in years." Stern held the pendant above a small silver-stemmed menu light on the table. By the same wan glow, Marta studied the female silhouette.

"It's beautiful."

"Oh, yes. Henry had a fine eye for such things."

"It's strange she never gave it to one of us. Don't you think?"

Perhaps she could not bear to part with it. Or to think about her father. Perhaps this was marked for the first granddaughter. It piqued him to think that Clara had some plan which had gone unfulfilled. He asked Marta what else she had discovered.

"This is amazing." Marta peered into her enormous bag and withdrew a huge ball of tissue, from which she slowly unwrapped a splendid sapphire ring. The stone was very large, guarded by a row of diamonds on either side, the setting platinum or white gold.

"Dear Lord," said Stern as she handed it over. It was the kind of item, so grand, that these days one could not even afford to insure it. He studied the ring at length. "Where on earth did you find these things?"

"There was a little Japanese black lacquer box at the bottom of her second drawer. I guess it was her private place or something." Marta touched the ring. "You don't know where she got that? It looks old."

Her private place, indeed, thought Stern. Could Nate possibly have provided a gift so lavish? Once more, he had that sensation of the earth failing beneath him, as he grappled with Clara's secrets. Then he clenched his eyes, stabbed by guilt. Oh, he was a shabby, suspicious fellow.

"This," said Stern, "is undoubtedly the ring your mother received the first time she was engaged."

"Engaged!" cried Marta.

Stern smiled a bit. "You did not know that your mother married me on the rebound?"

"God, no," said Marta. "Tell me. This sounds juicy." She had leaned across the table and the waitress had to shoo her back in order to set her dinner down before her. The establishment was called Balzini's, a glamorized neighborhood place in Riverside, with an Italianate theme and fake fireplaces and tablecloths of crimson linen. The steaks were reliable. He would always be enough of a son of Argentina to enjoy a piece of grilled beef, but it was hardly what he would have expected Marta to choose. Apparently, however, over the years she had found that they made a generous chopped salad.

He told her Hamilton Kreitzer's name, and that the courtship had ended precipitously. But he said no more. If Clara had not wanted to share this part of the past with her children, it was not his place to do so. Her privacy now remained Clara's final and most valued treasure.

At the same time, Marta was the least likely of the three to be thrown off by any revelations. Marta, whose relations with Clara were most difficult, in some ways knew her best. Stern's most telling recollection of the two would remain seeing Marta at ages four and five, dark-eyed, standing beside her mother at the sink and questioning each habit: Why do you peel the carrots? Why do you wash your hands before you touch the food? What if we just went outside and ate vegetables off the ground? How can germs hurt you if you can't even see them? On and on. Clara, a woman of some patience, was inevitably exhausted. 'Marta, please!' This became the signal, as it were, for more intense inquiry. There were occasions when Marta actually drove Clara from the room.

Having become acquainted early with her mother's vulnerabilities, Marta was less inclined to worship Clara than her brother and sister were; she saw her mother more as others very likely did. These were not, in all measures, pleasant observations; over time, Stern had acquired a strong flavor of Marta's opinions. Her view of her mother probably came down to a single word: weak. Marta had little use for Clara's homebound realm, her music and her garden, and the occasional synagogue functions and teas. She regarded her mother as inert, with her dignified manner and cultivated habits sheltering her from turmoil, inner and outer, that she lacked the spirit to address. Marta saw the world by her father's measure: action, achievement. Her mother was not a doer, and was accordingly diminished in her daughter's eyes. Over time, they had come to have a relationship that could be described as proper. Clara was wounded by Marta's reproaches. Still, she remained available to her. In the universe of relational disasters—Peter and his father, for example—Marta and Clara had managed to make do. They recognized and reverenced, in spite of misgivings, their world of attachments.

"Was this her broken heart?" Marta asked, touching the ring her father held.

"Perhaps. Is that how you saw her, Marta—a person with a broken heart?"

"I don't know. Sometimes." The judgment, like most of Marta's observations, cut him deeply. She went on with no recognition of that. "It's hard for me to think of you guys floundering. Having sad romances. When I was a child, I thought what every kid thinks: that you two were perfectly matched, that you'd just been out there waiting for each other. Silly, huh?" Marta looked up shyly, her small eyes flickering her father's way. No doubt, over time, Marta had also developed an unforgiving view of her parents' marriage. Stern long assumed it had contributed to her ambivalence about men, her shifting attachments. But now, suddenly, her line of sight rose far past Stern, carried off by recollections. "God," she said, "I can remember one night—I must have been eleven or twelve, and I found myself sitting up in bed, in the dark. Kate was sleeping, it was warm and the wind was slapping the blinds, and I thought, Oh, he is out there! This one man, this perfect man. It was so exciting, that thought." She closed her eyes, shook her head, suffering. "Did you ever think like that?"

Stern wondered. His adolescence, as he recalled it, seemed full of other passions: the stalled complex of feelings that arose around the memory of Jacobo; his fiery determination to be American. At night, in bed, he planned: he thought about the clothes he saw—he could remember being preoccupied with a pair of red suspenders for weeks—the way the young men dug their hands into their pockets; he mumbled phrases in English, the same words again and again, with the same sublime frustration, feeling each time that he could not quite hear himself for the sound of his accented voice. There was not much romance in him then, yet he knew what Marta meant: that romance of perfect union: heart on heart; each word, each gesture immediately known; the soul's image reflected, a fit like puzzle pieces. He was still now, his blood suddenly racing as his mind lit once more on the image of Sonny. Already, the picture was fading somewhat, was a fraction more remote. Some bracing principle of reality had begun to intervene, burnishing his heart with much desolate pain and a feeling of injustice. He smiled weakly at his daughter and said, "I understand."

"Now, of course, it's not one man I think about, it's any man. There's something about the whole thing I can't get. Men and women?" As she shook her head, the thick, ungoverned hairdo went in all directions. "Lately, I've been tormenting myself trying to figure out if men and women can be true friends without sex. Do you know the answer to that one?" she asked her father in her natural, direct way.

"I fear I am of the wrong generation. I lack experience. The two women I counted as true friends were your mother and your aunt. No doubt, that is not a valuable perspective."

"But it's always there, isn't it?" asked Marta. "Sex?"

"That seems to be the case," answered Stern, and thought again—fleetingly—of Sonny.

His daughter ate her large salad, ruminating.

"Do you still count Mommy as a friend?" Marta asked. "Even now?"

Well, here certainly was a question for a child to put to a parent. How much hope could he hold out?

"Am I allowed to answer only yes or no?"

For the first time she displayed a look of impatience, displeased by his forensic gambit.

"Marta, we seem to have done a great deal to disappoint you."

"I'm not asking you guys to apologize for your lives. I'm really not. I just wonder. It seems so depressing. You know, you spend thirty years and that's what it comes to—with somebody rotting away in a garage. I think about it. What was she to you at the end? In the beginning? Was she the One? Probably not, huh?"

His first impulse, of course, was not to answer, but Marta in these moments had a sincerity that was unbearable—for all her worldliness, the prickly humor, the boldness, she searched with the same innocent urgency that Sam had manifested gazing at the night sky. It was beyond him not to respond.

"We live in this world, Marta. Nowhere else. As you say, it is disappointing to learn that your parents' lives are no better than your own. You will not be graduating at some point to a higher order of existence." Uttered, these words sounded harsher than he had intended, but she accepted them with the same serious look. "No person speaks accurately of the feelings of years and decades in a few lines. I cannot see your mother apart from the life we had. I had the good fortune of most people who find any contentment to have determined what mattered to me and to have achieved some of it. My work. My family. I adored the three of you—I suspect that was never adequately communicated, but it has always been true. And I cared greatly for your mother. I know I disappointed her terribly, over time. I was not as good a friend to her as she was to me. And she disappointed me as well—particularly at the end. I admit, awful as it may be to do so, that I resent that ending terribly. In my inner sanctum there are many rooms which appear closed to visitors—I acknowledge that. But I believe, after months of reflection, that I am a better and more capable person than she was willing to see me as being." He said this to his daughter stoutly, with his face held high and his voice metered by conviction, even though he realized that Marta had little notion of everything he was referring to. Then he chewed at his steak and swirled his wine. He drank the half glass down, but the tide of strong feeling remained, so that he was unwilling to allow this to be the final word.

"We did our best, Marta. Both of us. Given the vast limitations with which we all deal. We shared an enormous amount. Not just events. But commitments. Values. She was the sum of my entire life. I loved her. Sometimes passionately. And I believe, even today, that she loved me, too. Every parent wishes for his child a life better than his own. But I admit I would be very pleased to see you forge a relationship as enduring."

Marta nodded gravely. He had answered. Stern noticed that he had continued to hold the ring, the fine stone glinting even in the weak light. He admired it again for a moment and handed it back. When Marta lifted her purse, he asked if there were other treasures she had uncovered in her afternoon of searching.

"No more treasures," said Marta. "Just something I wondered about." She brought her face right down to the purse and reached in with both hands. "What kind of medication was she on?"

"Medication?" asked Stern.

It was a silver pillbox, oval, with a hinged lid. It had been in the

Japanese box, too, Marta said. She sprung the cover, but even before it lifted, Stern knew what would be inside. He spilled out the small yellow capsules right on the tablecloth. The brand name was printed on their sides. Seventy-nine of them. He counted twice. The same number he had found missing from the bottle in Nate's medicine cabinet.

Marta looked at Stern in sympathy. His confusion was plain.

"Not possible," Stern said.

"Maybe," Marta offered, "you should ask Nate Cawley."

*　*　*

He sat up late that night. Marta, understandably, preferred her own room, and so Stern, for the first night in months, returned to the bedroom he had shared for twenty years with Clara. Marta had ransacked the bureaus; the drawers hung open, with silky undergarments spilling over the edges. There were a number of cartons on the floor into which items were being sorted—some to be given away, others to keep.

Again, he had difficulty sleeping. The raucous Independence Day eve celebration was going on down by the river. After ten, the racket of the fireworks began, a few miles away; from the window in the gable he could see the shuddering glow reflected at instants against the thin clouds. He was one of those immigrants who still became weak with sentiment—and gratitude—on the Fourth of July. What an idea this country was! The flourishing of the liberal democracies, with their ideal of equality, remained in his eyes, along with advances in medical care and the invention of movable type, humankind's grandest achievement of the millennium. His life in the law—at the criminal bar, in particular—was somehow bound up with those beliefs.

He lay on the bed hoping to slip off. He tried to read, but the turbulence of the day rode with him: his confrontation with Nate; Sonny steaming like some departing ship toward the horizon; the vexing legal complications he was headed for; and the spirits wakened by his conversation with Marta. His daughter asked—demanded—her entire life that her parents speak to her from the soul. It was in some ways the most disturbing event of the day.

At one point he quietly moved downstairs to reexamine the pillbox, but Marta apparently had it with her. Instead, he parted the curtains and stared at the Cawleys'. It was all beyond him now. He would have to speak to Nate once more, but where in God's name did such a conversation even begin? 'Now, Nate, as long as we were on the subject, I had just another question or two about your affair with my wife.' Stern shook his head in the dark.

Then he returned to the bedroom. Even after months, Clara's scent remained here; as much as the unspeaking furnishings, she was present. Lying in the bed, he expected Clara to emerge from the bathroom at any instant, a comely middle-aged person, flattered by the full lines of her nightgown, hair shining, face creamed, distracted as she often was, humming faintly some musical theme.

Ah! he thought without an instant's preparation, ah, how he loved her! His recollection of her was suddenly overpowering, the most particular details returning to him with painful exactness: the soft wave in which she wore her hair for years; the harmless sweet smell of her French bathwater; her pink gardening hat; the tiny peculiar ridge, flange-like, on each side of her nose. He remembered her slow way of lifting her hands, her slender fingers and the slim wedding band—gestures somehow articulate with intelligence and grace. These memories stormed over him so powerfully that he felt he could embrace her, as if in this urgent heartsore fondness he could clutch her from the air. The freshness of his love stunned him; it wrung his heart and left him weak. He had no idea what dark crabbed corner of madness she had wandered off to. He could deal solely with the woman he had lived with, the person he knew. That woman, that person, he missed terribly.

There in that moment, close and potent, he waited until at last the ghost was somewhat faded. Here was what he had attempted to communicate to his daughter, this eternal ocean of feeling. Then he lay under the intense beam of his reading light, wrapped in his Paisley robe, unstirring, holding for this particle of time to what little more he could of the presence— mysterious, defined, animate, deep—of Clara Stern.

35

On Wednesday morning, Marta came down to work with Stern. Claudia and Luke, one of the office men, who had both been with Stern more than a decade, marveled at her—how pretty she was, how mature and poised. Then she and Stern occupied themselves drafting a motion to Chief Judge Winchell, asking that the date of Stern's grand jury appearance be continued. Although it ended up less than three pages long, the motion took hours to compose, because the problems presented, as Marta recognized first, were complex. Ordinarily, communications between a lawyer and his client for the purpose of securing legal advice were privileged—the government could not compel either the attorney or the client to disclose them. But was the privilege properly invoked here?

"That's it?" asked Marta. The safe, a cubic foot of gunmetal, still stood behind Stern's desk. "And you've never opened it?"

"I have no combination, and no permission from your uncle."

Marta set a toe against it; she wore pink socks under her huaraches. Her leg—as much as showed when her billowy skirt fell away—was, Stern noted, dense with hair.

"Jesus, what is this made of? Lead? This thing would survive nuclear war."

"Dixon values his privacy," said Stern simply.

"Well, that's a problem, don't you think? How do we say that you received the contents for the purpose of providing legal advice when you've never seen them?"

Stern, who had not focused previously on this dilemma, reached for his unlit cigar.

"But, on the other hand," said Marta, "doesn't it tend to

disclose confidential communications if you admit you've never opened the safe? Doesn't that reveal the client's instructions and show that the client has, in essence, told the lawyer that the contents are so sensitive he will not or cannot share them? And what about the Fifth Amendment in Dixon's behalf?"

Marta went on a bit about that. She had a large, subtle mind. Stern, well aware of his daughter's brilliance, was nonetheless impressed by her facility with matters to which she previously had had little exposure. She had gone to Stern's library and digested the leading Supreme Court case as soon as they arrived, absorbing its difficult distinctions without lengthy study. Marta was wholly at ease in one of those complex areas where the law's abstractions occasionally became as unavailable as higher mathematics to Stern himself.

Eventually, as they sat together drafting, they determined that their legal position for now was simple: given the potential applicability of attorney-client privilege, Stern could not properly proceed without instructions from Dixon. Accordingly, they asked the court to continue the subpoena briefly to allow Stern to consult with his client when he returned to town. Marta wrote each sentence on a yellow pad, reciting it aloud, and she and Stern edited, trading words. Stern, who by long habit did all such work alone, was delighted by the ease of this collaboration. When the motion was complete, Marta signed it as Stern's lawyer.

"What happens if she orders you to testify tomorrow?" Marta asked. She was referring to Judge Winchell.

"I have to refuse, no?"

"And the government will move to hold you in contempt. She won't put you in jail, will she?"

"Not tomorrow," said Stern. "I would expect the judge to give me time to reconsider, or at least grant a stay, so we could go to the court of appeals. Eventually, of course, if I persist after being ordered to produce—" His hand drifted off. This happened, on occasion, lawyers jailed for resisting court orders detrimental to their clients. Among the defense bar, such imprisonments— usually brief—were regarded as a badge of honor, but Stern had no interest in martyring himself, particularly in Dixon's behalf. "I am in your hands," Stern told his daughter.

"No problem," Marta said, and hugged him. "But be sure you

bring your toothbrush."

* * *

On Thursday morning at ten o'clock, at the precise moment he had been scheduled to appear before the grand jury, Stern and Marta entered the reception area of the chambers of Moira Winchell, chief judge of the federal district court. The allocation of space reflected the proportions of another century; while the judge's chambers were grand and cavernous, the outer rooms constructed for secretaries, clerks, and criers were stinting, the desks and office equipment wedged together a little like a packed trunk. The narrow waiting area was bounded by a hinged balustrade of broad spindles. When they arrived, Sonny Klonsky sat on the sole available seat, flushed and pretty in spite of her grim demeanor. Stern's heart spurted at the sight of her, then settled when she fixed him with a baleful look. He reintroduced Marta.

"We're waiting for Stan," said Klonsky, and with that, the United States Attorney pushed through the door, narrow and flawlessly kempt, humorless as a hatchet blade. Even to Stern, who regarded himself as fastidious about his personal appearance—treating himself to custom-made suits and shirts and even, once a year, a pair of shoes from a bootmaker in New York—Stan was impressive. He was the sort of fellow who did not cross his legs for fear of wrinkling his trousers. He greeted Stern properly, shaking his hand, and managed a smile when he was introduced to Marta.

With that, they were ushered into the chambers of the chief judge. Because of the secrecy of grand jury matters, the hearing—much to Stern's good fortune—could be conducted here in private. Although the judge's court reporter arrived through a side door, carrying his stenotype machine, the transcript would be held under seal, unavailable to reporters, the public, even other lawyers.

In the privacy of her chambers, Moira Winchell was personable. She wore a dark dress—no robe—and came out from behind her enormous mahogany desk, larger than certain small automobiles, to venture a cordial word to each of them. She had met Marta more than a decade ago—Stern had no recollection of this—and greeted her warmly.

"Are you practicing with your father now? How wonderful for him."

The arrangement, Marta indicated, was temporary. As the greetings went on, Sonny ended up at Stern's shoulder. She was almost exactly his height—he had made no note of that before—and he turned, without a thought of resistance, to stare at her, her strong face and handsome features. Like any good trial lawyer's, her attention was entirely on the judge; she took no notice of Stern at first, and when she finally felt his gaze, she provided him with a quick distracted grin and turned away, following the judge's suggestion that they all be seated at the conference table.

The furnishings here were in the ponderous Federal mode, massive pieces of handsome dark woods, ornamented only with deep, many-planed edges, American style, with no European gewgaws. Huge arched windows rose on two sides of the chambers, but the light remained somehow indirect, as if, in the dark style of the late nineteenth century, the architects had turned the building obliquely to the path of the sun. The judge as usual spoke her mind without inviting comment.

"Now look, Stan, I've read this motion. How can you refuse Sandy time to talk to his client?"

Marta, without expression, caught her father's eye.

Sonny, rather than Sennett, answered for the government. The United States Attorney was present merely for emphasis, to let the judge know that the government viewed this as a signal matter. There was a history here, Klonsky said. The government had been seeking the documents it believed were in the safe for many weeks.

"Are you telling the court," asked Marta, "that the grand jury has heard evidence about the contents of the safe?" This was an adroit question, turning the tables on the government in the hope that they might reveal something about their informant in order to support their position. But Klonsky veered at once from that course, saying that she was not commenting at all on what the government or grand jury knew.

"Then on what basis do you even issue the subpoena?"

The two young women went on contending. Stern, who had accepted his daughter's caution to say nothing, sat back with

peculiar detachment. With no speaking part, he did not feel fully
himself. Sennett, at the far end of the table, kept his hands
crossed primly as he listened; he was customarily a person of
few words. The court reporter was taking down nothing,
awaiting the judge's instruction to go on the record. Stern after a
moment realized he had lost track of the argument. Without
looking back, he could not tell which of the young women was
speaking; each had the same heated tone and confident timbre.
The thought, for reasons he could not fathom, made him dizzy
and sick at heart.

"Look. Look," said the judge at last, "let's cut through this.
With documents missing, the government clearly has a broad
right to inquire. So I'm not going to entertain any motion to
quash, if that's what you have in mind next, Marta. But I must say
that the privilege questions here are not simple ones—they
seldom are when an attorney is subpoenaed—and I cannot
conceive of how Sandy could be forced to answer without being
given the opportunity to consult with the client. So that will be
my ruling."

She pointed to the court reporter, who began to type now. The
parties identified themselves for the record, and the judge
permitted Marta and Klonsky to briefly state their positions.
Then she allowed the motion.

"Off the record again," the judge said to the court reporter.
"What date do we fix?" She asked Sonny, "When does the grand
jury meet again?"

"Next Tuesday, Your Honor," she answered, "but that's a
special session called to hear just one witness." She meant John.
The government wanted Stern nowhere near when his son-in-
law went before the grand jury to implicate Dixon. Apparently,
they contemplated lengthy testimony.

After consulting the grand jury's schedule, Judge Winchell set
the subpoena over two weeks. Klonsky looked down the table to
Sennett, who shrugged: nothing to do. Clearly, they had wanted
to move more quickly. The indictment, as Tooley had guessed,
was not far away.

"On the record," said the judge to the court reporter. "Mr.
Stern, you shall appear before the grand jury on July 20. If there
are privileges to be asserted, we'll take them up on a question-
by-question basis. I'll make a note of the date and I will be

available if you need me. So ordered," concluded the judge. The court reporter folded the tripod on his machine.

"One more thing," said the judge, "for all of you." She waved away the court reporter, who had paused, thinking they were going on the record again. "I don't like to see lawyers in the grand jury. It's a dangerous practice for both sides. I encourage you to resolve this among yourselves. Sandy, you're ably represented. Very ably. The same is true of the government. With all these good lawyers, I find it hard to believe you can't arrive at a proper solution among yourselves. I expect reason to prevail." She flexed her brow and looked about the table at each of them. Hell to pay, in other words, for anyone who was unyielding.

In the hallway, the company parted. Sennett, outside the judge's presence, abandoned the semblance of a pleasant demeanor and walked off with a stiff look and no comment. Klonsky tarried only long enough to tell Marta that she would wait to hear from her. Once more, she said nothing to Stern. As the elevator descended, Stern felt the weight of his troubles. Marta, on the other hand, was exuberant.

"What a gas!" she cried on the way from the courthouse. The judge was right; she had done very well. Stern complimented her at length. "Can I come back if we don't work this out?" Her plans were to return to New York tonight.

"You are my lawyer," answered Stern. "I cannot proceed without you."

But he intended to allow no repetition of this scene, exciting as it may have been. He had phoned Dixon's office before they left for the courthouse, and Elise, his secretary, had promised that Stern would be his first call. It was time to play Dixon the music, the short, sad song. This party was over. Stern kissed Marta in the courthouse square and sent her toward home, where she and Kate were to go through the last of Clara's things. He returned to the office, his mind, with customary dolefulness, on his brother-in-law.

36

By five o'clock he had still not heard from Dixon. He had talked to Elise twice in the interval, and on the last occasion, near 3 p.m., she had said that Dixon had a critical problem in New York on the Consumer Price Index future and was flying out again tonight.

"Tell him if he leaves town without making time to see me I shall resign as his lawyer."

Elise, accustomed to trivial banter from Stern, paused, waiting for the punch line, then took the message without comment. Stern called Dixon's home next, but reached only Silvia. They spoke for almost half an hour about the islands, Helen, Marta's arrival. Eventually, Stern asked if Silvia knew where her husband might be. He was due home shortly to pack, she said, and Stern made her promise that Dixon would call.

Late in the day, Stern sat by the telephone, reviewing the FBI reports on Remo Cavarelli's case, which Moses Appleton had provided at last. As Stern expected, the agents' memoranda reflected little hard evidence against Remo. His three cohorts were, as they said, dead bang—caught in the truck with their hands on the beef sides—and each had pled guilty weeks ago. But they were all tough professionals, old school, and would keep their mouths shut. The only proof against Remo was his dimwitted arrival—the agents stated that he literally had walked up to the truck and looked in at the arrest taking place—and the remark by one of the thieves that "our guy made arrangements." The government would claim this referred to Remo, who supposedly was going to dispose of the loot, a role which would account for his late appearance on the scene. So far as Stern could tell, the government had no real basis for their suspicions. Assuming that the prosecutors found no proper excuse to bring out Remo's long criminal record in front of the jury, he stood a reasonable chance of acquittal. The case should be tried. Stern, who had not been to trial in almost four months, since the weeks before Clara's death, welcomed the prospect. The only problem was convincing Remo.

The phone rang. "Stern here."

"Daddy." It was Marta. She and Kate had finished for the day. They were leaving shortly for the airport and wondered if Stern wanted to meet them for dinner before her flight. They hoped to reach Peter, too. Eager to see Kate in particular, Stern agreed. He went down the hall to determine if Sondra could assist on Remo's trial, and to solicit a second opinion from her on the strength of the government's case.

When Stern returned to his office, Dixon was sitting on the cream-toned sofa. Wearing a double-breasted blazer and yellow socks, he had his feet up and was smoking a cigarette. He was brown and wholly at ease; the top of his forehead was peeling. Amazed by his entry, Stern only then noticed the leather key case thrown down on the sofa beside him. He'd forgotten having given Dixon a key.

"Silvia says you broke up with your girlfriend. I thought you had better judgment than that, Stern. She's an interesting gal."

Stern had heard similar criticisms often this week, but he did not care to discuss the matter, especially with Dixon, who only meant to divert him.

"Dixon, have I mentioned before that you are my most difficult client?"

"Yes." He flicked his ashes. The crystal tray was on the sofa beside him. "What's up?"

"Many matters."

Dixon turned his wrist. "I've got ten minutes. The car's downstairs. I have a meeting at LaGuardia at 9 p.m. I spend two years working on this thing and it goes to shit in a week. Honest to God," he said.

Stern considered his brother-in-law with a stark humorless look and sat down behind his desk.

"You are going to prison, Dixon."

"No, I'm not. That's why I hired you."

"I cannot remake the facts. I have no comprehension of your motives. But I understand the proof. It is time we consider the alternatives."

Dixon caught on at once.

"You want me to plead guilty?" He stubbed out his cigarette, eyeing Stern as he did it—there was a yellow cast to his eyes, a hulking feral power. He felt, evidently, he was under attack. "You think I'm guilty?"

This, of course, was one further element of their unspoken compact. Dixon spared Stern the facts; Stern withheld his judgments. He was surprised to find himself even now so reluctant to express himself, but there was no avoiding it.

"Yes," said Stern.

Dixon ran his tongue around inside his mouth.

"Dixon, this matter is taking on hopeless proportions. John has been granted immunity and will testify before the grand jury next week."

Even Dixon was brought up short by that news.

"And he's saying what?"

"That he followed your instructions—each improper order in Kindle came from you. He was a witless sheep led astray. I am sure you can imagine his testimony."

"Did John tell you this?"

"Dixon, as you know, I may not communicate with John about this matter."

"Where do you get this from? His lawyer? What's his name, Toomey? I thought you said he was a snake. Maybe he's bullshitting you to help out his old compadres."

"About the testimony of my own son-in-law? I would think not. No, Tooley has done what he must in this case. He has persuaded John to follow his own interests. He is a young man. He has a pregnant wife. No one, Dixon, would tell him to turn his back on immunity. No one," Stern repeated.

"I won't believe it until I hear it from John." Dixon lifted his chin and dragged on his cigarette. "I could have had a million reasons for placing those orders."

Stern knew that if he asked for one or two Dixon would remain silent for some time.

"Besides," said Dixon, "you've been telling me they have to show I made money through this thing. You said that the profits got shifted into that account—what's its name?"

"Wunderkind."

"They can't find the records," said Dixon.

"I believe they have located them," said Stern.

Dixon abruptly came to his feet. He hitched his trousers and walked behind Stern's desk to check on the safe, on which Stern out of habit had rested a foot.

"No, they didn't," said Dixon. He wagged his head and displayed a broad wiseass smile.

Stern groped on his desk until he found the subpoena. Dixon took some time reading it. When he was done, he was considerably sobered.

"How'd they find out where it was?"

"They have their own story, but I tend to suspect it was by the same means they have found out everything else: their informant. Perhaps you were careless in discussing this."

"The only person around who even knew it was moved was Margy, because she cut the check to the cartage guys. I told you that before."

Had he? If so, Stern had forgotten. The detail had not seemed significant then. Dixon was reexamining the subpoena.

"This thing was due today," he said.

Stern described the hearing.

"You're not going to let them get it, are you?"

"I shall follow any instruction you give me, Dixon, assuming Marta and I agree it is within the law."

"What are you telling me?"

"I can assert the attorney-client privilege."

"And?"

"I doubt I shall have to testify about our conversations."

"What about the safe?"

"That is a complex legal question, Dixon."

"But?"

"When all is said and done, Dixon, I suspect we shall have to produce it."

Dixon whistled. He lit another cigarette.

"Look, Stern, you told me, when I sent it here, those bastards wouldn't be able to get it."

"I told you, Dixon, that your *personal* papers would be more secure."

"Fine," said Dixon. "It's personal. It's all personal shit in there."

Stern shook his head.

"If I say it's personal," said Dixon, "where the hell do you get off saying it's not?"

"No," said Stern. He would not pretend he had never practiced law that way, but he had allowed himself the luxury of a clear conscience for many years and he was not about to become Dixon's winking collaborator. "There is no stretch of the imagination, Dixon, under which internal company documents pertaining to the Wunderkind account do not belong to the corporation. They should have been produced by Margy last week."

"Oh, for cry sake," said Dixon. He stood up and threw off his gold-buttoned blazer. He was wearing a shirt of dark vertical stripes, wide open at the throat, with the white hairs of his chest well displayed; his arms were thick, and dark from the sun. "Get the fuck out of my way." Dixon strode around Stern's desk, bent at the knees, and lifted the safe several inches into the air. Then he began to walk with it.

"Dixon, this subpoena is directed to me, not to you, and I must comply with it. You may not remove the safe from these premises."

With the safe slung between his knees, Dixon started toward the door, lumbering like an ape.

"Dixon, you are placing me in an impossible position."

"Ditto," he said.

"Marta is extremely clever, Dixon. Much more so than I. There are motions to file. With an appeal, we may keep the government at bay for months. I promise you we shall resist by every lawful means.

"You'll lose." He had little breath, but he continued swinging along. "You've already told me you don't have a leg to stand on."

"Dixon, for God's sake. This is madness. You are assuming," said Stern, "that the government has no other way to prove you controlled that account."

Dixon, past the desk, eased the safe to the floor and turned back.

"What other way would they have to prove that?"

"There must be other means," Stern offered lamely. For an

instant he'd had a thought of mentioning the check Dixon had written to cover the deficit balance in the Wunderkind account. But that impulse was past. On a giddy night in the woods, he had made an irrevocable promise. Whatever may have occurred since, he surely would not go back on his word. At best, he could be indirect. "Certainly, Dixon, the account application cannot be the only means to determine who was responsible for the account. Perhaps John knows."

Dixon peered at Stern in determined silence. At length, he shook his head with painstaking slowness, a gesture of absolute refusal.

"No dice," said Dixon. He bent at the knees again and took hold of both sides of the safe.

"Dixon, if I appear without the safe or an explanation for its disappearance, Judge Winchell, I promise you, will remand me to the custody of the marshal."

"Oh, they won't put you in jail. They all think you walk on water."

"Dixon, I insist."

"Me, too."

"I must withdraw, then, as your lawyer."

Dixon took a moment with that.

"So withdraw," he said at last. He adjusted his shoulders and, with a practiced groan, hoisted the safe again.

"Dixon, you are committing a federal offense right before my eyes. And one in which I am implicated. You are forcing me to notify the government."

Dixon, near the door, glanced back over his shoulder with a sullen, challenging darkness.

"Dixon, I mean it." Stern reached for the phone and dialed the U.S. Attorney's Office. At this hour, they were unlikely to answer. "Sonia Klonsky," said Stern into the instrument, while in the earpiece he continued to hear the ring.

By the door, Dixon dropped the safe; he was red-faced, heaving for breath. As Stern replaced the phone, Dixon waved a hand disgustedly. He took a step out, then came back to the sofa and stuffed his cigarettes and his keys into a pocket of his sport coat. He shook a finger at Stern, but he did not yet have enough breath to speak, and left without another word.

Stern had agreed to meet his children at the Bygone, one of those clever chain restaurants plunked down by their corporate parents at commercially availing spots in every major city in America. The one in Dallas looked just like the one in the tri-cities—the same old cast-iron lampposts, bell jars for bar glasses, and little girls' trading cards with pictures of kittens cutely cemented under the urethane tabletops. The restaurant stood on a bluff overlooking the network of highways near the Greater Kindle County Airfield. Stuck in traffic, Stern could see it miles away.

The airport now was what the river had been to Kindle County a century ago, a point of confluence for the vast urges of commerce. Great office buildings—rhomboid shapes of shining glass—had risen in what were hayfields only fifteen years before; enormous warehouses with corrugated doors and various chain hotels constructed of preformed concrete stood at the roadside, and the highway was heavily posted with signs for other projects that would be under development to the end of the century. The traffic at all hours was thick. Stern, stalled intermittently, snapped off the radio in the Cadillac so he could give vent to various thoughts about Dixon.

Perhaps, Stern thought, tracing the trouble back to its roots, if Silvia had felt more secure in the afterrnath of their mother's death, she would have found Dixon less compelling. Stern had done his best, planned carefully for both of them. He sold some of his mother's furniture and two rings to raise capital, and by the following fall, Easton University, the pastoral haven of privileged education in the Middle West, became the refuge of the orphaned Sterns. Silvia, a gifted student, ahead of herself in school like her brother, enrolled in the college on a full scholarship; he attended law school on the G.I. Bill. Stern for the sake of economy, and continuity, lived in their mother's apartment in DuSable, riding the train down each morning, while Silvia was soon invited to join a sorority.

For financial support, Stern resumed the punchboard route he had driven throughout college. The punchboards were minor attractions utilized by small-town merchants; for a dime a chance, customers poked tiny paper rolls out of the board and read a joke or, far less often, word they had won a washer or a TV. On Friday mornings, Stern loaded new boards and the prizes won a week before into the aging truck his boss Milkie provided him, and rambled in fourth gear along the prairie highways, visiting the small-town stores to make his deliveries and split the fees. By the time he returned to the tri−cities late Sunday, Silvia had taken the train up and was in their mother's apartment preparing dinner. These were rewarding, expansive moments, coming off the road with the dust of several states on his suit, and he looked forward to his sister's company, their hours as a family of two.

One Sunday night he turned the key and found Silvia seated at the dining-room table with Dixon Hartnell, who was still in uniform. Passing through the city on leave, he had searched out Stern's address and Silvia had let him in. She claimed to have remembered Dixon's name, but there was no way to be sure. Silvia was smitten with all of Stern's law school friends, and from the first moment you could see that these two young, good-looking people were intent on each other.

Stern was horrified to find Dixon, long consigned to the past, beside his precious sister. Dixon still had the flossy gleam of a cheap suit, and having been shot at in Korea, having served as the commander of other men, he was more brash. Stern treated him correctly, and sent him on his way after dinner, fairly certain they would not see him again.

Dixon's correspondence with Silvia began properly enough with a note thanking his hostess for dinner. It never occurred to Stern to suggest she not answer. Eight months later, when Dixon appeared again, mustered out and enrolled at the U., it had become a romance. Stern had never been Silvia's disciplinarian and he was at a loss as to how to put an end to this disastrous relationship, though he bristled with disapproval whenever the two were together in his presence and barely spoke to Dixon. Finally in Silvia's junior year, a crisis erupted. Stern forbade her to transfer to the U. to be with Dixon. She accepted this edict with typical silent distress, but three months later they announced marriage plans. Silvia and Dixon countered every irate objection Stern raised: Dixon would convert to Judaism; Silvia would not have to leave college; Dixon, indifferent to school anyway, would drop out and take a job with a brokerage house. Stern, long-suffering, denounced Dixon at length: a huckster; a fake; an illusion. They remained resolute. One Sunday night, Dixon appeared at dinner and begged Stern to attend the wedding: he would both give away the bride and be the best man. 'We can't do this without you,' Dixon said. 'We're the only family each of us has got.'

When Dixon completed his conversion course, Silvia and he were married beneath a canopy. Stern stood immediately behind the bride and groom. He began weeping halfway through the ceremony and could not stop. He had not carried on like that in front of others before or since, but his circumstances had overpowered him: he was twenty-four years old now and utterly alone. His search for a wife, never a matter of conscious priority, started at that moment.

As for Dixon and Silvia, there was no saying years later who was right and who was wrong. Silvia relished the comforts time provided and Dixon's almost celestial admiration of her; but her pain, particularly with her husband's wandering, was sometimes intense. Given the history, she never dared speak against him to Stern, except during that short period several years ago when Dixon was banished from the household. One evening then, Stern had come home and found Silvia and Clara at the dining table. There was a sherry snifter between them and he could tell from Clara's warning look that something was amiss. Red-eyed and tipsy, Silvia spoke at once to her brother.

"I always thought it was all because he wanted children so badly," she said, offering her own explanation for Dixon's wanderlust. That barrenness, which the doctors could not explain, was Silvia's heartbreak in those years; she talked of it often to Clara, but only in private, for Dixon was far too humiliated by their failure to bear the thought that anyone else knew. "But he's taking advantage," said Silvia. "He always has. I did not even realize he had been lying to the rabbi until he took off his pants our wedding night."

This remark seemed entirely mysterious at first, and then deeply shocking. The revelations seemed to ripple off, not around Silvia, but about Stern himself. He was being informed of something deeply telling, yet he could not read the message. By then he had engaged in dozens of athletic competitions with Dixon, stood with him time and again in various club locker rooms. Dixon did no fan dance; the fact, as it was, was plainly displayed. He must have assumed that among men, creatures of the here and now, this centuries-old ritual could be disregarded as brutal or passé. Who ever knew exactly what Dixon thought? But certainly he would not believe that Stern had simply not noticed that Dixon had never been circumcised.

* * *

On a knotty-pine bench by the door—the entire restaurant motif was of a basement rec room—Stern's daughters waited for him, drinking club soda, engrossed in one another. Stern took Kate in his arms.

As they were seated, Marta offered Peter's apologies. He had been unable to reschedule his late rounds.

"And where is John?"

Kate's dark eyes skated quickly toward her sister. They had struck some agreement.

"He's with his lawyer," said Kate. "You know where. They have him looking at papers all night." Marta, obviously, had encouraged Kate to be plain, but the subject made her quiet and glum.

"This is a hell of a situation," said Marta in a tone that was largely devoid of blame. She had had many of the details from Stern, but clearly had learned more from Kate during the day.

"If there is not a complete resolution shortly, then I shall be stepping out of the case," said Stern. Marta knew this, but he repeated it for Kate's benefit. Seeing her made him more resolute. He took the hand that Kate had laid on the table beside him. Her eyes smarting, she suddenly hugged her father and brought her face to his shoulder in the small booth.

After debating whether Stern or Kate should be the one to take Marta to the airport, they agreed to go down together in Stern's Cadillac. They left Marta at the metal detectors, then Stern swung back to drop Kate at her car. The parking lot for the Bygone was on the restaurant's roof, and the location offered impressive vistas of the airport, the highways, the hills, and the violet sky being pinched of the last light. Kate kissed her father quickly and was gone, but Stern, sensing he had not said all he meant to, threw open his door and called after her. He trotted a few steps to catch up and took her hand.

"This business with your uncle, Kate—the blame for it does not fall on John. If it is any consolation, you must tell him I said so."

Kate did not answer. She looked all around, in every direction, and for no apparent reason began tapping her foot. Stern's impression was that she was about to cry. She rooted in her purse. It was not until the flame rose in the dark that he realized what she was doing.

"Katy! You smoke?"

"Oh, Daddy." She looked about again, all ways, as she had just done.

"How long is this?"

"Always, Daddy. Just a few puffs. Since college. Exams. You know: heavy stress. It's terrible for the baby. I have to cut it out," she said, but then inhaled deeply and turned her face up into the aura of smoke she released.

"Kate, I realize this has been difficult."

She made a sound, almost laughter, a bit derisive.

"Daddy, I wish it weren't so easy for me to shock you." She spoke almost harshly and stopped herself. They were silent. Then she took a last drag; in the dark he saw the cigarette fall, the lighted bit tumbling end over end and splitting in three on the pavement. She made a long business of crushing out the embers, twisting them repeatedly under her foot. "Look, Daddy, we'll get through this. We have to."

Inches taller than he, she brought her soft cheek against his, then hiked off toward her car, her high heels clacking, her keys jingling in her hand. He stood in the parking lot, poorly lit, watching as she backed her car out quickly, then gunned the Chevy into a turn, leaving behind a ghost of dark smoke.

Who was that, he wondered, that woman? Of all things, the
image that remained with him was of the way she had crushed
out that cigarette, with her toe pivoting so harshly on the
asphalt. There was a certain fierce purpose in that which he had
never been certain existed in her. He thought of her tonight and
as he had seen her at the ballpark and suddenly had the clearest
intimation of how it was with Kate. Her whispering. Her
murmurs with John. She was a person with secrets, with a secret
life. And the greatest secret of all, perhaps, was that she was
someone else—someone different from the beautiful innocent
thing her parents wished her or allowed her to be. Stern's
deepest impression, that she was a person very much like her
aunt, like Silvia—lovely, capable, kind, but limited by choice—
was merely the impression she had found it easiest to leave, so
that she could otherwise elude them, with no trace. Who was
she? he thought again. Really? He stood in the mild summer
night and turned back to where she had been, but even the
smoky cloud of exhaust had cleared away.

* * *

Stern slowly drove home. Approaching the dark house, he was
tense. If he had anywhere else to go, he might not have gone in.
The weeks, months really, he had spent overcome by various
women and the ether of sexuality were, if not at an end, at least
in abeyance for the night. Without that, he felt in some ways
more familiarly himself—round, solitary, solid like a stone. As he
knew it would be, the large house was as wholly empty as it had
been full the night before with that spirit of visitation. Now he
was alone. The silence loomed about him with the power of some
wayward force; he felt his own figure somehow dwindling in the
unoccupied space. He stood in the slate foyer, where he
inevitably seemed to tune in on his own soul, and thought quite
distinctly that his life had gone on without Clara. It was an
absurd notion; what he meant was well beyond expression. The
fact, such as it was, had been clear at one level from the instant
he stood here months ago, white with panic, yet still able to draw
breath. But it seemed that it was not until this very moment that
he actually had believed it. Yet he felt it now, his own life, that
particular strand drawn out of the intricate tangle of mutual

THE BURDEN OF PROOF

things he and his wife had created and shared. It was like electrical work, finding the line that drew power—he could feel the hum of his peculiar, isolated existence, which had continued with the persistent unmusical rhythm of a beating heart—his own heart, lugging on. He was by himself, neither pleased nor embittered, but aware of the fact. His mind lit somehow on Helen then, and he closed his eyes and worried his head a bit, full of regrets.

He slept again that night in the bed he had shared with Clara—solid dreamless sleep, if brief. He was up by six and, reverting to old habits, was at his desk by seven. He went through piles of mail that had gone unread for weeks. He felt calm at the core, purposeful. But in the office something was amiss. It took him at least an hour to notice.

The safe was gone.

38

"This isn't funny," Marta said when he reached her in New York on Friday. "You've got to get it back. I don't know how much of this is privileged, but even if you told the whole story, no one will ever believe he just took the thing without your help. You're going to end up in jail."

Stern, at the end of the line, made a grave sound. Marta's analysis was much the same as his.

"This scares me," she said. "I think you should get a real lawyer."

"You are a real lawyer," said Stern.

"I mean someone who knows what they're doing. With experience."

What kind of experience might that be? asked Stern. There were no defense attorneys expert, so far as he knew, in explaining the disappearance of critical evidence.

"Tell him he's a big fucking asshole," offered Marta near the end of the call.

"If I can get him on the phone," answered Stern.

Dixon avoided Stern until Monday, but when he came on the line, after Stern had made repeated demands of Elise, he was as innocent as a coquette. "I'd file an insurance claim," Dixon suggested. "Notify the cops. There's important stuff in there." With Stern broiling in silence, Stern's brother-in-law pressed on with this shameless routine. "You're not blaming me, are you?"

Stern spoke into the telephone in a mood of absolute violence.

"Dixon, if you insist on convicting yourself with ludicrous antics, so be it. But it is my livelihood and my reputation at stake. The safe must be returned promptly." He pounded down the phone.

The next morning, he came to the office hopeful. But the safe was not there. The Berber carpet where it had rested for weeks was now permanently dimpled with the impress of the four heavy feet.

At moments during the week, he actually indulged the thought that Dixon might not be involved. He had been in New York late that night, Dixon insisted. He had gone to his meeting. How could he have swiped a safe? What about the maintenance people, he asked, the late-night cleaner-uppers? They all had keys. Maybe one of them had noticed the safe after it was moved and decided to carry the thing off, hoping it contained real valuables. The notion, although preposterous, was urged by Dixon relentlessly. Trying to resolve every last doubt, Stern, despite his warnings to himself, offhandedly mentioned the safe to Silvia, in the midst of their daily conversation on Wednesday.

"Oh, that," she said with sudden exasperation. "You would never believe what went on here." She proceeded to describe a scene last week involving Dixon and Rory, their driver. Silvia, recovering from jet lag, had apparently been roused from a sound sleep by the two figures who stood at the closet arguing. The driver, with a heavy German accent, had spoken to Dixon severely, warning him that he was out of breath and should leave the lifting to him, while Silvia sat up in bed, clutching the sheet to her chest, addressing both men, who, she said, ignored her. Dixon was swearing, fuming, carrying on in a violent temper about Stern. He had gone off to the airport to rent a private jet.

"Sender, whatever is going on between you two?"

Stern, who always had an easy time putting Silvia off, did so again. A business disagreement, he told her. Upon reflection, he said it would be best if she made no mention to Dixon of his call. His sister hung on the line, troubled and confounded, caught between the North Pole and the South, the two men who dominated her life. Resting the phone, Stern again regretted having acted impulsively. For one thing, he recognized only now that his conversation with his sister was probably not privileged. He sat scolding himself, while he contemplated the law's obliviousness to family affection. In the worst case, Stern would face ugly choices when he was called before the grand jury: implicating Dixon and abusing Silvia's confidence or, on the other hand, disregarding the oath.

What a trial Dixon could have, Stern thought suddenly. First, his daughter's husband would incriminate Dixon; then the government would call Stern himself. Under the compulsion of a court order to respond, he would describe Dixon's ape-walk with the safe and its disappearance shortly after. Then, for the *coup de grâce*, the prosecutors would try to find an exception to the marital privilege in order to force Silvia to testify about the safe, too. How Stan Sennett would enjoy it. The entire Stern family versus Dixon Hartnell. Looking down at the phone, Stern shuddered. It would breach the faith of a lifetime to testify against a client, any client, let alone Dixon, whatever he was.

* * *

Stern had come of age in the state courts. There in the dim hallways lit with schoolhouse fixtures, with the old wainscoting bearing the intaglio of hundreds of teenagers' initials, with the crotchety political retainers, who displayed an almost pathetic craving for any form of gratuity, he felt at ease. That was a scene of royal characters: Zeb Mayal, the bail bondsman and ward committeeman who, late into the 1960s, still sat in open view at a desk in one branch courtroom issuing instructions to everyone present, including many of the judges called to preside; Wally McTavish, the deputy p.a. who would cross-examine the defendants in death-penalty cases by sneaking close to them and whispering, "*Bzzz*"; and of course the rogues, the thieves— Louie De Vivo, for one, who planted a time bomb in his own car in an effort to distract the judge at his sentencing. Oh God, he loved them, loved them. A staid man, a man of little courage when it came to his own behavior, Stern felt an aesthete's appreciation for the knavishness, the guile, the selfish cleverness of so many of these people who made it possible to embrace human misbehavior for its own miserable creativity.

The federal courts, which were now in a fashion his home, were a more solemn place. This was the forum preferred by the lawyers with fancy law school degrees and prominent clients, and admittedly, it was a more ideal place to practice law. The judges had the time and the inclination to consider the briefs filed before them. Here, unlike the state courts, it was a rarity for lawyers to engage in fistfights in the halls. The clerks and marshals were genial and, in proud contradistinction to their colleagues in the county courthouse, incorruptible. But Stern never left behind the feeling that he was an intruder. He had won his place of prominence across town, watching his backside, avoiding, whenever possible, the questionable dealings in the corridors, proving over time that skill and cleverness could prevail, even in that brassknuckles arena, and he still felt that he belonged there, where the real lawyers of his definition were—in the Kindle County Courthouse, with its grimy corridors and pathetic rococo columns.

These thoughts of one more fugitive border crossed came to Stern in the idle moments before the commencement of the afternoon session in Moira Winchell's courtroom. Remo Cavarelli, cowed and silent, sat beside Stern, biting anxiously at his sloppy mustache and upper lip. Notwithstanding Remo's agitation, the indulgent somnolescent air of the early afternoon had fallen over the courtroom. Judge Winchell, like her colleagues, allowed an hour and a half for lunch—time enough for wine with the meal, a screw on the sneak, a run for the athletic. Then, without warning, a door flew open and Judge Winchell stalked from her chambers and assumed the bench, as Stern and Appleton and Remo and the few elderly spectators came to their feet.

Wilbur, the sad-faced clerk, called Remo's case for trial. In spite of Stern's frequent reassurances that nothing would actually transpire today, Stern could feel Remo quaking at his side. Wilbur already knew there would be a motion for a continuance, and no jury had been summoned.

"Defendant is ready for trial," said Stern, for the sake of the record, as soon as he reached the podium.

Appleton, Stern knew, was not. He was trying a two-pound buy-bust cocaine case before Judge Horka and would need another week or so before he was ready to go on to this case. With an Assistant less cordial than Moses, Stern might have fussed—there were, after all, fifty other prosecutors down the street who could try this matter—but he listened in silence to Appleton's request, adding merely, "I object," at the conclusion of Moses's presentation, a remark which Judge Winchell ignored with the studied indifference she would have applied to a stray sound from the hall.

"How's next Thursday?" asked the judge. "I have a grand jury matter that may require some attention, but that's all." The judge, marking in her docket book, let her dark eyes find Stern. "Mr. Stern," she said with practiced discretion, "as I recall, you have some involvement with that matter. Have the parties resolved their impasse?"

"Not as yet, Your Honor."

"Oh," said the judge, "how disappointing." The arch mannerisms did not conceal the predictable: Moira was displeased.

Klonsky had called Stern first thing that morning. 'I don't have your daughter's number in New York. I thought we better talk. You're in the grand jury next Thursday.' It was Friday today.

Her voice still stimulated wild feelings. How goes it with your husband? he wanted to ask. How do you feel? He read out Marta's number from his book.

'Has the government reconsidered, perhaps?'

'We'll compromise,' said Sonny. 'You deliver the safe and an affidavit that says that it's in the same condition as when you received it, and you won't have to appear before the grand jury.'

'I see.' The government, as usual, would get everything it wanted, but their moderated stance would please the judge.

'I think this is fair, Sandy,' said Sonny. 'I really do. The fact that you have the safe just isn't privileged. All we want is the safe and to know that we have everything that was in it. We'd be entitled to get the thing if he'd left it at MD, where it belonged. We can't allow someone to avoid a *subpoena duces tecum* by conveying what we want to his lawyer.'

Even if he had the safe, Stern might not have agreed, but there was no point in quarreling now. Speaking with Sonny, in fact, made him unbearably sad. The whole situation—all aspects—was impossible.

Stern called Marta to pass on this news, and then at her suggestion drafted a motion to withdraw as Dixon's counsel. It was a simple paper, stating that there were irreconcilable differences between lawyer and client. He sent it to Dixon by messenger just before he left to meet Remo, along with a note saying that he would file the motion next Tuesday, unless the point of difference between them was immediately resolved. The motion was not actually required in a grand jury proceeding, but

Dixon would not realize that, and Marta believed it would be an appropriate prelude with Judge Winchell.

Considering the judge now, as Appleton went on begging for more time, it was clear that some groundwork was in order. When Stern rejected the prosecutors' compromise, offered none of his own, and simply refused to produce the safe—his latest plan—Moira's reaction would be severe. Standing here, Stern saw admirable prescience in Marta's prediction of jail.

The judge made Moses plead miserably, but ultimately set Remo's case down for trial the first week in August.

"And work on that other matter, won't you, Mr. Stern?" she said as she rose from the bench. There, from that considerable height, she smiled in her icy, domineering way, a person accustomed to being obeyed.

In the corridor, Remo again began to quarrel with Stern as soon as they were alone. He was still dead-set against a trial.

"How much more is she gonna give me if I take a trial?" Remo asked. "With this babe," he said, "I could catch a real whack."

Stern again played Remo the music: If he was convicted, he was going to the penitentiary for a lengthy period, in any event, guilty plea or not. The evidence, all factors considered, warranted proceeding to trial.

"Yeah, but what's it cost?" asked Remo. "You don't work for nothin, right?"

That, Stern allowed, was true.

"Sure," said Remo. "Right. No one works for nothin. So what I gotta give you? Five, maybe?" When Stern hesitated, Remo's dark eyes widened. "More? See. I ain' been doin much as it is. You know, few months now, there ain' much." Stern had no idea whether Remo was referring to legitimate endeavors or not, and by long habit was disinclined to ask. From other remarks, he took it that Remo's routine at present was confined to visiting the neighborhood social clubs, drinking aperitifs from eleven in the morning on, and playing backroom card games, throwing down money with great show and cursing in Italian. "What's the odds in that? I go way," said Remo, "there ain't nothin as there is for the old lady and the kid. And I give you five?" Remo had settled the matter of fee with himself. "I don't see it. Neh," he said, then furtively smiled. He stepped closer to Stern and whispered, the trace of Frangelico or something else still on his breath from his idle morning. "Course," he said with a lively look of amusement, "if you had a job or somethin, we could maybe work it out. You know."

Stern peered at Remo.

"You know: Do me, I'll do you. You know. No offense or nothin. You probably ain't that kind of guy." Remo was not at all certain what he had gotten himself into or how to read Stern's expression of almost brutal concentration. "No offense," said Remo again. "Right?"

39

On Saturday night, Stern returned home prepared for another desolate evening. He was beginning to give in to old habits and was once more spending the weekends in the office, trying to swim through the ocean of items neglected for months. He had spoken with Silvia this morning and with spurious innocence asked what their weekend held in store. As he had predicted to Remo, she and Dixon would spend both days at the country club. He refused the invitation to join them; legal work called. With whatever honor he retained, he declined to be more specific about his plans. Besides, he was still not certain he really had the nerve to carry through.

Alone now, facing his empty house, he thought with considerable regret of the invitations he had spurned in April and May. Many people now believed Helen had first call on his time. He would have to send up smoke signals or whatever signs were used by a widower willing to sit at dinner beside the aging maiden cousin. Disheartening, he thought, but better than lonely solitude. He opened the car door and recalled in a dizzying rush that two weeks ago he had believed he was in love.

With a foot in the drive, he stopped. Nate Cawley was across the smooth expanse of lawn between the two homes, tending to his garden. Shirtless in the balmy evening, Nate drove a shovel energetically in the beds of his evergreens. Stern, taken aback, wondered if he truly had the will to deal with this, too. But the moment for decision passed quickly. Nate became aware of his gaze and Stern rose from the auto and the two men faced each other across the short distance. They met a step or two onto the Cawley property.

"Thought maybe I could get you to make me a drink," said Nate. Involuntarily perhaps, he glanced over his shoulder in the direction of his house and, presumably, Fiona. He was glazed with sweat. Grass clippings and specks of dirt clung to the patchy gray hair on his upper body; both hands were caked with dried soil. He briefly developed the courage to look at Stern directly. "Fiona and I had quite a conversation a few nights ago. We probably oughta talk."

"Of course," said Stern and, in spite of himself, swallowed. His heart plunged somewhat and then stalled. It—and he—were not going down any further. Whatever was in store would apparently be absorbed under the existing quota.

Stern showed Nate through the front door and directed him back to the sun room. He asked for a diet soda—Stern recalled Fiona's mention of AA—and was standing there, facing the garden, when Stern returned with the glass. Nate was a slight fellow, narrow across the shoulders and back. His dirty khaki shorts hung down from his seat, and he was sockless in a pair of old loafers. Except for the bald spot, you might have been reminded of a young boy. Perhaps this was what women found so appealing.

Nate raised the glass in salute, and took a great breath. He began.

"First off, I owe you a heckuvan apology."

In the courtroom, Stern had learned to say as little as possible in uncertain terrain. He dropped his chin now in a fashion that might have passed as a nod.

"After twenty—odd years, I should have known better than to believe Fiona. She was so full of vinegar. Probably couldn't enjoy the real thing half as much as she liked telling me." Nate smiled a bit. "And boy, was she ticked off that I talked to you. How dare I." Nate tossed his head about in frank wonderment. "There's only one Fiona," he said.

He had taken a seat on one of the white wicker chairs that surrounded the glass-topped table on which Stern and his children had played cards the morning of the funeral. The late light, almost umber, fell through the broad French windows of the solarium.

"I guess it just suited me to think that something was goin' on. Would have made things easier for me a lot of different ways."

He laughed, a nervous sound which Stern realized he had heard from him on other occasions. "I know I should have thought better of you, Sandy. If I had, I'da realized why Fiona hauled you over there when I found that letter under the medicine cabinet. Instead of thinking one silly thing or another.

"But frankly, even after we talked, it didn't dawn on me that was how you'd put it together. I figured then—" Nate paused, and held his own thought with a quick smile which seemed to be at his own expense. "Well, I didn't figure that. I take it you found Clara's pills in her stuff and asked somebody what they were for. Then when Fiona showed you that bottle, it was just like two and two. She told me you counted the caps." Nate looked up, seeking confirmation apparently, and, receiving nothing, laughed in the same fashion. "She didn't have the damnedest idea what was going on, by the way. She thought you figured *I* had it." Nate laid his thumb against his chest and smiled at the thought. Of course, he enjoyed the notion of Fiona being misled.

To this soliloquy Stern listened with only passing comprehension. But somewhere, as Nate went along, Fiona began to enlarge in Stern's estimation. Recanting, she had apparently mentioned nothing of Stern's advances—or the full nature of their conversations. Perhaps that suited her purposes as well. But all in all, Stern believed she had better motives. Having taken his name falsely once, she had decided not to blacken it again, even with the truth. A gesture of decency—from Fiona, no less. People, thought Stern, could always surprise you.

"So the pills Clara had here came from the bottle in your medicine cabinet?"

"Sure," said Nate. He nodded emphatically. "She wouldn't have them in the house on a bet. She figured you'd know what the pills were for or start asking about 'em. I could never talk her out of that." Nate, downcast, shook his head. "I had to do every damn thing but take the pills for her. Get the prescription, keep the bottle, bring her her caps for the day every morning. Hell, I had to promise I'd write the 'scrip in my name." Nate smiled gently, then looked intently at Stern. "Nothing was more important to Clara than being sure you didn't find out." He took a second to allow that to settle in. "Afterwards," said Nate, "after what happened, I thought it was just as well to keep it to myself. But when you showed up asking questions about that bill, I panicked."

"You were protecting her memory," said Stern.

"That's a nice way to put it, Sandy. But you and I both know I was trying to save my own ass." Bent over, he looked away. On the table beside him, framed photos of the family were arranged in a row. The faces of the children at younger ages, Clara, Stern gazed out in witness.

"Look," said Nate, glancing up at once, "I don't want to get sued. I've just flat-ass decided to tell you that. I've been practicing medicine for twenty years, and I'm one of the few guys I know who doesn't spend half his week with lawyers and depositions. I guess my feeling was that this would be the worst time. After hitting the rocks with Fiona. It's the last thing I need, to see my malpractice premium double. I can't afford it, with two kids in school, not to mention alimony. And more to the point, the thought bothers the hell out of me—being an enemy with your patients. I realize that's the world we live in. The patient died, the doctor mistreated her. What's the term you guys have? The thing speaks for itself. I heard what you said the other day: it's a big check for Clara's estate. I followed you, believe me. That's who sues, right? The estate? I'm sure there's lots of money to be made here. But I wanted to try to explain this to you, since I did a piss-poor job of that the last time we talked. Maybe you'll reconsider."

Stern, who had lost Nate entirely for a moment, like a plane off the radar, suddenly had it all, everything, clearly in focus. Nate was Clara's doctor. Her physician. No more. Stern opened his mouth to speak, but Nate, hanging his head down, remained under way.

"I'm not gonna pretend that I'd handle the situation the same way today. I've looked backwards and I see that there were a hundred different things I could have done. In retrospect, I should have brought a shrink in. That's obvious. Maybe I should have involved you, too. But I was trying to keep her faith."

"Nate," said Stern softly, "I was overwrought during our last conversation. There will be no lawsuit concerning your care of Clara."

"No?" Nate took a moment to adjust to the thought. "That's a hell of a relief."

The two men looked at each other. Nate, chilled by the house's air conditioning, rubbed his arms.

"She spoke to you of this impulse, I take it?" asked Stern. "Ending her life?"

"She did," said Nate. "She had a way of talking about it." Nate posed, studying the air so he could recall. "She said she wanted to put out the noise. Something like that. You know, she didn't always go on that way, but over seven years, when things got bad, I'd hear it once in a while. And I can't pretend I didn't take her seriously."

Nothing, for an instant: no sound; no time. "*Seven years*," the man had said. Looking down, Stern realized he'd taken a chair.

"Seven years, Nate?"

"God—I'd assumed—" Nate stopped. "Well, how would you know?" he asked himself. "Sandy, this wasn't a new condition, It was a recurrence."

"A recurrence?"

"You understand: she wasn't newly infected. This disease in some people returns. About two-thirds of all cases. Usually, it goes on for a couple of years. It gets better and better and finally peters out. But sometimes, pretty rarely, you can have bad episodes a number of years apart. That's what happened to Clara. I treated her originally about seven years ago. I really thought that what happened now was going to happen then. The only thing that kept her from giving up was the fact that you weren't around."

"I was not?" asked Stern. "Where could I have been?"

"Kansas City, as I recall," said Nate. "Some trial?"

"*Ayayay*." Oh, it was terrible. It was the most shameful moment of his life, but he sat there, in his wicker chair, with his eyes closed, thanking God. Seven years ago. That at least neared the periphery of comprehension. Then, eventually, he was taken by a new thought: "My Lord, Nate, after all that time, what was there to hide?"

"Sandy, I think in her eyes it was worse. Because she had said nothing for so long. In some ways, she seemed to feel it was kind of an added deception. And being further from it, she was less accepting of her own behavior. Whatever she'd been thinking back then, she couldn't understand it now. It was this old, awful mistake that she couldn't get away from. And I didn't even know what to tell her anymore."

"You mean medically, Nate? There were no answers?"

"You have to understand the whole history." Nate looked into his glass. "She'd been treated for years with acyclovir. It saved her life originally. I mean it. It got things under control, just like that. She took it preventively for six months. But the drug's toxic enough that they warn against taking it longer. Eventually, she had recurrences. Two tiny ones, about two, three years apart. But with the drug—" Nate snapped his fingers. "We'd put her back on, and then five days from onset, good as new. I mean, it was always a trouble and a worry as far as she was concerned. The faintest sign, and she was in my office. I must have cultured her three times a year. But, you know, it was under control. All in all. I thought it was." Nate, who had raised both hands, made a face and let them fall.

"About six weeks before she died, it flared up again. She took her pills and they didn't help. She had a full, florid course. We see that all the time with other viruses or bacteria—some kind of auto-mutation, so you end up with a resistant strain. She had a bad couple of weeks. And then it came back again. I consulted everybody I knew, but it was so damn unusual, and the virus is unpredictable to begin with. And by then she was talking pretty seriously about doing what she did. I could see her giving up. One time, just kind of like thinking out loud, I said something about talking to you, one of us, and I thought she'd jump right out the window. No way." He repeated that and, as many times before in this talk, shook his head.

"Anyway, I'd thought I'd talked her into trying one more course of medication. Double dosage for five days. That was what was recommended to me. But I had that conference in Montreal. And, to make a long story short, I went. That's where I get really critical of myself." Nate was bent again, almost doubled over, studying his soiled hands. Behind him, out the large windows, the sky was pinking over, and the sun, dying in ember radiance, was masked in thin clouds. "I knew she was in crisis. I talked to her about my going. I gave her the chance to tell me not to, but Clara would never say something like that. You know, she promised me nothing would happen. I gave her all the pills she'd need while I was gone—she said she'd just hide them. And I," said Nate, "I had consulted with another doctor who was aware of the situation, and I hoped he could just kind of watch things for me. But it was my responsibility. If I wanted to play confessor, then I had to know what I was doing."

"Nate," said Stern, "I meant what I said to you in your office. There is blame enough to go around. You need not punish yourself. It was a professional judgment."

"No, it wasn't." Nate drained his glass and looked at Stern. "I took Greta with me. On the sneak. We made our plans. I," said Nate with considerable weight, "was looking forward to that." Greta, Stern realized, was Nate's nurse, the toothsome bland beauty from the videotape. "Still sure you don't want to sue?"

"Yes," said Stern.

"Oh, hell," said Nate. "There I am in Montreal, lying with this girl, when the phone rings and it's Fiona, bawling her eyes out. I thought she was soused for a change, and then suddenly I realize she's talking about Clara. God, what went through my mind. I just figured, if it ever came out—how I left this patient in distress so I could go speak college French and screw my mistress . . ." Nate looked at Stern. "I didn't ever want to have to tell you that."

"Now you have," said Stern.

"I sure have."

The two men hung in the silence.

"And what was the outcome with Fiona?" asked Stern.

"Can't put that genie back in the bottle. We each went and got a lawyer. We're gonna sell the house. Both live there for the time being and not talk to one another. That whole mess."

"I am truly sorry, Nate."

"Yeah, well, I'd say we died a natural death. I think I'm in love with this girl, Sandy. 'Course, I've wanted to be in love with all of them. I'm like the fella in the song. Lookin' in all the wrong places. But I think it's true now. So I'll try it again from the top. Can't do any worse."

"How did Fiona react?"

"Well, she's gonna beat me into the ground financially. She always told me she would, and Fiona'll keep her word, I'm sorry to say. She's got the evidence, all right. I appreciate the warning." He glanced up at Stern. "Pretty goddamn embarrassing," he said. "Lawyer said to me if I really wanted out so bad, I could have saved myself a lot of money by just writing a note."

Stern, in response, could manage only one of his Latin shrugs.

He felt for Nate, though, at the thought of him watching that tape and witnessing all the harm he had done. That truly was not in Nate's character, the inflicting of pain. Oddly, Stern felt a bond to him, joined by the embarrassments which they'd unwittingly shared. He knew Nate's shame, and Nate, of course, had known his for years.

"All in all, I'd say Fiona was actually kind of spunky. You want to know what she said? This'll tickle you. She said men still find her very attractive. She's certain that as soon as we're divorced there'll be all kinds of fellas in hot pursuit. She actually mentioned your name. After tellin' me how she'd been making up stories. Can you beat that?" Nate laughed, but something in Stern's look made him cut himself off. "You can do what you want, you know."

"Of course," said Stern. No more. It made for an uneasy moment, but he felt obliged not to join any conspiracies against Fiona. They had their own compact now, and Stern sensed from what Nate had said that Fiona and he might have matters to sort out. If so, he had only himself to blame.

Stern saw Nate to the door. When he began to castigate himself again, Stern held up a hand.

"I know what it means to maintain a confidence, Nate. Clara had her secret and you were obliged to keep it."

Nate waited. His mind seemed to be working ahead. Stern wondered if there was more that Nate had determined not to tell him out of some vestigial duty to Clara. Nate seemed to read that thought.

"I don't know who it was, Sandy, if that's what you're wondering."

The sound of it was so gross that Stern's impulse was to deny that he had any curiosity. But of course that was not true.

"She told me years ago that the person, whoever, was aware of the problem. That was the only thing I had the right to be concerned about. The relationship was already over when she came to me," Nate looked at him helplessly. "I assume it was a man. These days—" He lifted a hand.

"Yes, of course," said Stern. Of course. This possibility, briefly contemplated, Stern rejected.

They shook hands. When Nate was gone, Stern returned to the solarium and the row of family photos lined up in their frames on the game table. A picture of Clara as a very young woman was at the end. She was dressed in a white blouse and pleated skirt, posing in her page boy with a hand on the newel of the central staircase of the Mittler family home. Her smile looked coaxed at best, a wrinkle of hope managed against deep currents of resistance. The world was at war then, and even at the age of thirteen or fourteen, Clara Mittler seemed to have her doubts about the future.

40

If one thought about it carefully, as Stern had for three days now, this was not a theft. Not legally. The property in question, the safe, was lawfully in his custody, not Dixon's. And the risks of prosecution, in any event, were nil; neither Dixon nor Silvia would ever prefer charges. This action was simply an expediency. He had taken advantage of Silvia by asking about the safe. Involving her in its return, in light of Dixon's iron-headed determination not to yield to the government, would compromise her unforgivably with her husband. This solution was dramatic, effective, and, given Dixon's conduct, richly deserved. But in the car with Remo, driving from the highway through the wooded hills with their subdevelopments and residuum of baronial estates, Stern was beset with considerable anxiety—he had not made a court appearance in twenty years that had frightened him the same way. His bowels and his bladder both seemed on the verge of becoming unpredictable, and throughout his entire upper body there was a palpable tremor. Suppose the brawny German driver came in and resorted to violence? What if the police were somehow advised and entered with guns drawn? Stern, on a dozen occasions, had imagined Remo and him bloodied or massacred.

Remo, driving his old Mercury, was cheerful. He loved his work. He had urged Stern to allow him to do this alone, but that was unthinkable. If someone intruded, Stern, whatever the embarrassment, could explain, but Remo alone might come to real grief. As it was, the risks—at least as they could be calculated—were minimal. The Hartnells would be at the club, Dixon shooting a late round of golf, Silvia sunning herself by the pool, and on a Sunday afternoon no one else would be home. The cook and the houseman were both dismissed at 2 p.m. The driver stayed with the car, cooling his heels behind the clubhouse. As long as the weather was good—and the sky was crystalline as they drove—the plan was flawless.

Behind the wheel, Remo smoked his cigarette and chatted companionably.

"I ain' done houses much," said Remo. "Not since I'm young. There ain't no good guys to work with. Them burglars, they're all crazy. I'll never forget, I'm eighteen, nineteen, a guy got me on a job, one of them places down near the river. You know, real fancy apartment. Knocked the door right off the hinges. Jesus, the stuff these people had, real nice stuff, beautiful." Remo lifted two fingertips to his lips and made a kiss. "We got what we got, and I come in the living room and this son of a buck, Sangretti his name is, he's got his pants down and he's taking a shit, right there on the rug. I says, What the fuck is this? You know, and since, I heard all the time about burglars do stuff like that. In somebody's house, for Chrissake?"

Stern, too nervous to respond directly, nodded and for whatever reason felt obliged to explain again that this was not a burglary. The house was his sister's; it was a practical joke of sorts within the family. An ironic glimmer came into Remo's eyes. He needed no excuses; he knew how it was. Everybody wanted things and did what they had to. Remo was one of those crooks who believe that they are no worse than anyone else.

Sensing this judgment, Stern nearly spoke up in his own defense. He was not one of those lawyers, the state court sharpies with the razor cuts who worked only for the Boys, and who took payment in cocaine, or hot artwork, or, in one instance Stern had heard of years before, a hit on his wife. As a young lawyer, he had done things for money on occasion, some of them nasty enough that he no longer cared to recall them. But one of the clearest grains in his character as a lawyer was the desire to let his clients know that he did not wade in the same polluted waters they did. The utter meanness of this conviction—and its dubious basis—came home to him with sudden disturbing clarity: a visit to yet one more unattractive aspect of his soul. These months of gazing inward had been a little like a trip to a freak show, with the sheer ugliness of what he found never quite overcoming his compulsion to look.

Following Stern's directions, Remo proceeded down the narrow wooded road fronting Dixon and Silvia's home. The house itself, erected more than a century ago of stone and heavy joints of mortar, was below them, behind a quarter mile of lawn, which itself was interrupted by a lighted tennis court. Behind the house, Lake Fowler twinkled, dotted with speedboats and small craft under sail.

"Nice," Remo said. He turned the car around and parked so that it was partially obscured by the untamed shrubbery that grew up with summer lushness along the roadside. They would walk in, Remo said, down the long gravel drive. After they had the safe, one of them could bring the car down. Never park, Remo told him, where it was easy to cut you off. Stern absorbed these lessons in silence, noting that Remo accepted none of his reassurances about the safety of the job.

They walked to the rear of the house, Remo appreciatively examining the grounds. A number of large blue spruce rose throughout the sloping lawn, and the air was freshened somehow by the clear water of the lake. Behind the patio, the gardeners this year had laid out a bright patch of small summer flowers, most so exotic that Stern did not know their names. He looked down to the lake. The boathouse was below and, beside it, a waterfront cottage that Dixon had winterized and filled with athletic equipment. Last year, he had also added a lap pool, and the long finger of still, blue water glimmered. Beside a large screened porch, Remo now looked the great house up and down. Following Remo's eye, Stern saw that it was the power and phone lines, not the architecture, Remo was assessing. He questioned Stern again about the burglar alarm. Remo had a hand on the metal junction box, and he reached to his back pocket for a tool. He worked there awhile, then waved a number of wires that he had pulled free.

"Is that all?" asked Stern across the yard.

"That's it."

Remo entered through the screen porch. He had a slap hammer with him, inserted like the other tools in various pockets and covered by the tails of a long velour shirt. For his day on Lake Fowler, Remo had worn blue jeans and cowboy boots. Stern thought he looked very much like a burglar, thickset, with bulky arms and bowed legs.

Remo had driven the lock through the barrel of the doorknob by the time Stern had followed him onto the porch. The back door was secured by a chain. Remo asked if he should pull it free or break the glass. Whichever was more authentic, Stern answered. It was important that it look like a burglary, not for Dixon's sake—he would know what had happened—but for everyone else's. After the break-in was discovered, the police would comb the house but find nothing missing. Only Dixon, eventually, would recognize what was gone and he was in no position to file a police report admitting that the safe had ever been here. Stern regretted upsetting his sister—he might let her know somehow that he was involved—but Dixon's consternation he would savor. Done in on his own turf. Dixon would be livid, unhinged with rage. Standing in the shade of the porch, Stern actually chuckled.

Remo, preoccupied, raised one heavy boot, bracing himself against the wall of the porch, and gave the door a tremendous kick. It flew open with an explosion of plaster dust and the breaking of glass. "Shit," said Remo. The back window had shattered from the impact as the door sprang back. The first plan, thought Stern in spite of himself, gone awry.

Like much of the house, the hallways were stone; the taps on Remo's heels resounded. He looked about freely as Stern showed him to the staircase. The home had been built in the 1870s, with period elegance—twelve-foot ceilings and tiered moldings. In the dining room a circular mosaic of Venetian tiles was laid in the stone floor. The stillness of the unoccupied house set a shiver in the bottom of Stern's spine. He thought about using the toilet, but he wanted to get in and out quickly. This was a bad idea, he thought suddenly. Terrible. Something was sure to go wrong. Remo leaned into a front parlor to admire the French antiques and the pictures on the walls, English watercolors mounted in heavy frames. "Beautiful, beautiful," said Remo. The wealth of the house, perfectly composed here in its unoccupied state, impressed even Stern.

Upstairs, they moved into the enormous master suite. Dixon years ago had combined three or four rooms to get what he wanted, a bedroom area on the palatial scale of Beverly Hills. There were two baths, his and hers. Dixon's, through which they walked, a cavern of travertine, held a Jacuzzi the size of a small swimming pool, and a one-bay wooden sauna attached to the shower. The bedroom itself was not particularly large, but it was festooned with various gizmos—intercoms, a telescope, an old market ticker, a large projection TV which pivoted on a remote control over the bed. A deck out the French doors provided a commanding view of the lake. On the side of the bed where Dixon slept, the antique night table was stacked with business magazines and a number of thrillers. An ashtray held the butts of three cigarettes. Stern felt oddly thrilled by the chance to spy.

"Here," Remo called. He had entered the walk-in closet on Dixon's side of the room and cleared away his suits. "That it?"

The safe was right there, dull gray, the color of seawater under clouds, turned on its back, so that the silver numerical dial was face up. A set of free weights was beside it, the plates haphazardly stacked; a bar, with three dishes on each side, had been rolled to the wall.

"Just so," said Stern.

"Get back," said Remo. Stern moved into the room. "Oh, my fucking God." Remo swung the safe out the door and set it down promptly. "That's a fuckin ton." He stood up straight to rub his back. "We shoulda brought help."

Both men stared at the safe.

"Thing's open," said Remo. With the safe set on its bottom again, its small door indeed hung open a dark fingerbreadth. Dixon, evidently, had checked the contents, perhaps to be certain that Stern had left them undisturbed. Or could it be that whatever the government was seeking had been removed? With this thought, that the safe had been emptied, Stern knelt immediately and pulled the door wider. The light was poor, but he could see that there was a wad of papers inside, folded, doubled and tripled over.

There, on his hands and knees, even before he made out the sound, Stern could feel the vibration of the garage door opening.

"Oh, my Lord." He rose awkwardly and ran a few steps to the doorway to listen. He faced Remo. "Someone is here." Outside, he had heard the gravel crunching, but by the time he reached the bedroom window he could see only the rear fender of a Mercedes as it pulled into the farthest bay of the four-car garage.

"Oh, for Godsake," said Stern. He had not fully imagined how humiliating this was going to be. It was a shocking breach of decorum—inexcusable, inexplicable—breaking into someone's home.

"Hide," said Stern.

"Hide?" asked Remo. "What for?" An eyebrow lowered. "You mean this ain' really your sister's?"

"Of course it is. But I prefer not to be apprehended in this silly exercise."

"I been caught," said Remo. "Lots. I don't never hide. Guys get shot like that. Just siddown. Be quiet. Maybe they ain't comin upstairs." Following his own advice, Remo found one of the eighteenth-century French chairs beside Silvia's writing desk. He crossed his legs and smiled patiently at Stern. He reached to his pocket for a cigarette, then thought better of that.

Remo was right, Stern thought. His own reactions were juvenile. Particularly if it was the houseman or the driver, there would be real danger in some effort to avoid him. But Stern's skin still crawled. Dixon would never let him live this down. He would ridicule, threaten—whatever advantage he could wring from having caught Stern *in flagrante* burglary would be utilized repeatedly. Stern crept into the carpeted corridor, stepping forward with breathtaking precision, like a pantomime character. In some unconscious japery of this task, he had dressed all in black, in slacks and a cotton golf shirt, and he hung back now in the shadows.

He could hear the steps rapping out in the stone hallways downstairs, an even slapping rather than the sharp clack of a woman's high heels. Would Dixon be violent? His temper with Stern was ordinarily restrained, but this was a much different setting. If someone popped out of the shadows in Stern's home, what would his reaction be? Probably to run. But that was Stern.

The footfalls drew near the stairs. Stern pushed back into one of the doorways. Whoever was down there lingered, then walked away. With a desperate plunge of his heart, Stern recalled the kitchen. The narrow hall from the garage emerged right beside it; if the person who'd entered noticed the broken glass, he would surely hale the police. Stern listened intently; if there was a voice on the phone, he was determined to run. He looked about to see where he was—Dixon's den. Fax, computers, three telephones. The old rolltop desk was heaped with papers, and the shades, for whatever reason, were drawn. A pillow and a blanket were on the sofa. Dixon, he took it, was not sleeping well. This room, more than the rest of the house, was rank with the rancid smell of cigarettes.

The footsteps came back. Then nothing. After a short time, he realized the visitor had started up the carpeted stairs. Stern pushed back farther, so that he could see only the landing. The person was upstairs now, but Stern had not yet caught sight of the figure. Then Silvia, in a graffiti-patterned beach cover-up and flat shoes, passed by, looking about, wholly abstracted, mumbling to herself. She pushed her sunglasses up so they sat atop her upswept hairdo. Like Dixon, she was richly tanned. She was headed for the bedroom where Remo waited.

Stern held his head and, after one more second's faltering, called his sister's name.

She shrieked—not for long, but at a high, hysterical pitch.

"Oh, my God," said Silvia. She had laid one hand, with its polished nails, over her heart and the other touched the wall. She was breathing deeply. "Sender," she said. "You nearly killed me."

"Forgive me."

"What in the world?" she asked.

Stern actually deliberated saying that he had come to go swimming. But enough was enough.

"I am stealing something," he answered.

She took only a second with that. "The safe?"

He nodded. Silvia's expression became cross—powerfully irritated. She spoke to him in Spanish for the first time in probably forty years: What is in the safe?

"*¿Qué es lo que contiene la caja de seguridad?*"

"*No sé.*'" I do not know.

"*¿Esto es para ayudarlo?*" This is to help him?

Stern shrugged. "I believe so," he answered in English. "I must do this, in any event."

"Give me a moment. I want to speak with you about all of this. I came back for a book." She turned again toward her room, but Stern took her hand. There was a man he had brought with him in there, he told her.

"Oh, Alejandro!" She shook her head in severest reproof. "You are like two boys, you and Dixon."

"This is a serious matter."

She made a disgusted sound. She refused to believe it.

Stern led her downstairs to the living room. Silvia, unfailingly polite, offered him a drink, and he asked for soda. She tapped her shoe for a moment on the servant's button in the carpet beside the sofa, then, recalling it was Sunday, went off by herself. Stern looked about the vast living room. Silvia and her decorator had strived for a crowded, almost Egyptian effect; the colors were dark, with many eruptions of gold in the fabrics, and there was furniture in all corners—chaises, heavy drapes, twin antimacassars with a whiskery fringe, adorned, for no apparent reason, with voile shawls. On a table was a huge vase of woolly protea, dark desert plants with a primeval look. The far wall of the room was all stone, like the facing walls of the house, with an enormous hearth of double-width beams. An original oil by a well-known Spanish artist—one of his savage women, purchased years ago by Dixon, with his inevitably astute eye—hung fearsomely over the fireplace. In the winter, logs the size of tree trunks burned here all day. They left, even now, a smoky residue, as if the air had been cured.

"What did you do to my kitchen?" demanded Silvia as she returned. She handed her brother the glass but looked at him scoldingly. Stern made one of his expressions and Silvia smiled, though she went on shaking her head. "Sender," she said, "you must tell me what is occurring."

In her absence, he had pondered how to put this, and he adopted a moderate approach. The government was investigating. They had done so before, but this was a criminal matter and the prosecutors seemed to have hold of evidence of some questionable practices on Dixon's part. The investigation had grown increasingly complex, but Dixon was attempting to put his head in the sand. The government had demanded the safe, and Dixon, against Stern's advice, was endeavoring to hide it, a maneuver which would prejudice not only Dixon but Stern. He spoke allusively, hoping his sister would not gather the full impact, but she understood enough.

"Is he in danger of prison?"

"He is," answered Stern. Silvia sat still, a small woman sparely knitted together. She looked tiny, with her bare legs and flat shoes. She clutched her elbows close to her body and drew her face long to maintain her composure. Stern himself, to his enormous surprise, found himself on the verge of tears in sympathy.

"I have been very concerned for him," Silvia said.

"I as well."

"You have no idea, Sender." She knotted her hands. "He coughs for thirty minutes when he wakes up in the morning. His secretary tells me he is terribly forgetful. He does not sleep. He wanders about at all hours. Or leaves in the middle of the night, headed God knows where. For the last week he has not even slept here once." She glanced up at Stern; this was intended to be a significant remark, referring apparently to something other than Dixon's travel schedule.

"I am attempting to help him, but he is resisting."

"Of course," she said, "but I am afraid he will never survive."

"He will survive," said Stern. "He is one of those types who always survive and triumph." Spoken, the words struck him as merely cordial. He had not realized until now how deep-seated his own fears for Dixon were, even as he felt some swell of resentment rise when he predicted his glory. "I had hoped to come and go today without involving you."

"I shall not tell him," said Silvia.

Stern weighed this, but remained convinced that it would be wrong to force Silvia to take sides. Dixon was entitled to the comforts of home.

"That is not necessary."

"Unless he asks," she offered.

"He is certain to ask once he sees the disorder in the kitchen."

"I shall have it repaired. Tomorrow. Today, if possible. I would be very surprised, at any rate, if he spends the night here." She looked down again at the rug. Years ago, before Silvia had evicted him, Dixon would do this, fail to return. He had an apartment in town where he usually claimed to be, and no doubt often was, enjoying one young woman or another. Once he and Silvia were reunited, however, Dixon seemed to maintain a minimal pretense and confined his roaming to business hours or his many trips out of town. "It is very disturbing," she said.

He nearly uttered a word or two in Dixon's behalf, about the strain recently, but he realized it would be little comfort.

"Do you ask where he goes?"

"Work." She smiled tersely. "Of course, there is no answer when I phone."

"I see." Stern at first said nothing. "I must say, I hope this can be endured. It would be a terrible moment for you both to repeat your separation."

Silvia made a face. "There will be no repetition. I am accustomed." She smiled the same way, briefly, bitterly. "As you know, our difficulty was not only that."

Stern looked at his sister without comprehension.

"Oh, you knew. Clara knew. She told you; I knew she would. You are gallant, Sender, but there is no need to pretend."

"I am not pretending," said Stern.

"Truly?"

"Truly."

"It is long past," she said, and flipped a dark slender hand. She was ready to give up the subject, but she saw that Stern was still puzzled and she came forth with the truth abruptly to satisfy him. "He had come home with an illness. Which I was afraid he had inflicted on me. It was repulsive."

"An illness?"

"A disease. You understand."

His head was ringing now, and his throat and chest felt terribly constricted. He asked, nonetheless, as he knew he was required to.

"Herpes?"

Her mouth opened somewhat and then, to his amazement, Silvia smiled—in a reluctant fashion, part grimace. She would never see through him, she would never understand him. Only from Stern in the entire world might this be tolerable, but if he insisted, she would find humor in the pain of the past. Older brothers, after all, forever reserved the right to tease.

"Oh, Sender," she said to him with a girlish wag, "you knew all along."

41

Eventually, Remo descended the staircase. He had brought the safe with him, and he took each step sideways, in a straddle, lowering one booted foot, then the other. It was slow work and he stopped at one point and rested the safe. He lit a cigarette and eased down the remaining stairs, with the Marlboro tucked in the corner of his mouth and one eye closed to the smoke. From his seat on a living-room settee, Stern could see Remo coming, but he made no move to assist him, nor did he open his mouth to speak. He was capable of movement, no doubt of that; but he was uninterested. Perhaps he would remain here, with his hands folded, for what was left of his life. He did not feel any emotion with particular strength, except that he was no longer himself. His head was still ringing, and his arms were light; but, predominantly, he was beset with the sensation of difference, departure. A new man—not better or worse—but someone else would leave here.

"I heard you talking in the hallway," said Remo when he finally arrived. He knew his presence was no secret.

"Of course," said Stern. "Remo Cavarelli, Silvia Hartnell."

Silvia nodded properly to the man who had broken into her house.

"We goin or what?" asked Remo.

"Sender, are you all right?" asked Silvia. This was not the first time.

"Quite all right." Stern managed a smile. His voice sounded peculiar to him, weak. It was as if his spirit had fled his body and was outside, examining him.

"We still takin this thing?" Remo nodded to the safe at his feet.

Stern, after recalling what he was speaking about, smiled fleetingly again.

"Oh, yes."

Remo departed for the car. Silvia, too, left the room to make a phone call. There was a local fireman who did work around the house and might even be available on Sunday to repair the kitchen.

Stern was left alone with the safe. Remarkable, really, Stern thought, that he had spoken Spanish to Silvia—he would have wagered a large sum that he could not finish a sentence. Occasionally over the years, certain *latino* gentlemen appeared in Stern's office, Cubans usually, who needed the assistance of bilingual counsel. And of course, during the 1970s there were the pathetic impoverished Mexicans who were arrested here by the gross for distributing brown heroin, sad, unlettered men, spewing their *chingas* and begging Stern to take their case at any price. Stern had always declined such representations. It was not the drugs that bothered him; it was the old fear of being recognized for what he feared he was, someone else who did not belong here. But he saw very clearly, as he held off more pressing thoughts, that that period and those attitudes were behind him. Those clients would henceforth be welcome. The words, he was sure, would come back to him over time.

He reached for his soft drink and tasted it. Silvia had said he knew all along. She had meant something else, naturally, but alone here he wondered if the unintended meanings were also correct. A part of him remained solidly composed with the truth; his first faith would always be in the facts. But in another region—someplace silent but still known to him—the toll was mounting, the damages were still being assessed. If he had foreseen this, it was only with that inner eye that always envisions the bad dreams—the worst dreams—coming true. It was clear now that it was *who* much more than *what* that Clara dared not live to tell. Her choice of a lover was no accident; he would never be persuaded otherwise. Clara knew her husband too well. Afterwards, even she must have been frightened by the sheer ferocious spite that had moved her. It was that which she trembled to reveal. Well, at least the evidence of his senses had not failed him. Clara indeed had no use for Dixon after he returned to Silvia. She must have been disgusted with him. And herself. What transpired between them? What conversations? He was back here again, a familiar point of arrival, feeling he would probably rather not know.

Stern hunched forward on the settee and brought a toe to the door of the safe. It was still open and Stern with the sole of his shoe wedged the little door wider. The lump of papers was in there. Oh, why not? he thought. He could put up with anything.

There were two full sheets from a microfilm printer, heavy with toner, each folded in four. As he removed them from the safe, various items, about which the records were wrapped, fell out: two checks and a number of the gray celluloid squares which Stern recognized as microfiche cards.

"The phones are not working," said Silvia, coming back to the living room; she was deeply perturbed. "How can I reach him?"

Remo returned at that moment.

"Who's that?" he asked. "Who's comin?" Remo'd had enough time in the closet to notice the weights and, all things considered, wished to be gone when the man of the house arrived. Silvia explained her difficulty, and they disappeared together so Remo could reconnect the phone lines. In the interval, Stern went through the papers from the safe, studying them for some time. Remo returned first, then Silvia breezed back in.

"He's on his way now," Silvia said. She seemed consoled by the thought that the disorder in her kitchen would be quickly repaired.

"Well, let's get goin," said Remo, a hasty departure still on his mind. He bent over the safe. "Alley—oop," he said.

Stern and his sister followed as he lumbered through the stone hallway. Stern had all the papers from the safe cradled in his hands. Silvia held the screen for Remo, and at his request opened the rear door to the Mercury. Squinting in the brilliant sunshine, Stern and his sister watched as Remo sank to his knees to lower the safe onto the dirty floor of his spring-shot Cougar. He stood up straight and dusted off his hands while he waited to catch his breath. A rill of sweat had run down his temple.

"On second thought," said Stern suddenly, "we shall leave it." Remo's jaw fell open, revealing a mouth full of bad teeth. "If you would, Remo, I shall ask you to replace the safe where we found it."

"No," he said, in disbelief.

"Please," said Stern. He had assumed, without thought, his most commanding manner, and Remo looked at him uncertainly, reluctant to obey but unwilling to object further. Stern turned to Silvia. "It shall all be as it was. You need say nothing."

She, too, appeared confused, but, like Remo, did not know how to respond to the change in his manner.

"Very good," said Stern to both of them. He walked back into the house, turning to ask Remo to bring the safe into the living room for a moment. Stern had continued to hold all the items from the safe, and he sat again on the settee and laid them out on the raw-silk fabric so that he could arrange the papers as he had found them. The two copied pages were first, then the microfiche squares, then, at last, the two checks, one nested inside the other. He studied them again. The first was Dixon's canceled personal check for $252,646 made payable to MD Clearing Corp. The note in the memo section said "Debit A/c 06894412," which was surely the number of the Wunderkind account. This was the check which the government, according to what Sonny had told him in Dulin, had already obtained a microfilm copy of through the subpoena to Dixon's bank.

The other check, the one Stern examined at greater length, was printed on the long green bank stock of River National and was a certified draft drawn on Clara's investment account and made payable to Dixon Hartnell personally. The amount, inscribed correctly in numbers and figures, was $851,198. Stern held the check, full of the strong emotion that contact with Clara's possessions continued often to bring over him. Then he refolded both checks and wrapped them and the microfiche cards in the two printed pages, along the same creases on which they had been folded before. These sheets reproduced the first and last pages from the account agreement for Wunderkind Associates where identifying information for the account holder would appear—name, address, social-security number. On the last page, after dozens of paragraphs of warnings and disclaimers, the customer executed the agreement. Before replacing the papers in the safe, which Remo obediently had set at his feet, Stern peeked again at the final line where in her steady fluid hand Katherine Stern had signed her name.

42

Certainly, he was no happier. Much of what had transpired in the last few days had left him more confused than ever. But somehow an old ability to distract himself with work had revived. Recently, Stern had resumed his habit of being the first person in the office, and in the last week, he had agreed to take on three major new matters—an insider trading case already under indictment; a defense fraud investigation conducted out of Washington; and a county case in which the owner of a waste dump faced possible manslaughter charges. Beleaguered, Sondra and Raphael pleaded that they were too shorthanded for more work. But Stern himself was ready. In the office, he felt an energy and relish that had been previously lacking. The toil of man in society! The rushing about, the telephone calls, the small breaks of light in the tangle of egos and rules. Mr. Alejandro Stern adored the practice of law. His clients, his clients! No siren song was ever more compelling than a call to Stern from someone in dire straits—a tough in the precinct lockup in his early days, or a businessperson with an IRS agent at the door, as happened more commonly now. Either way, it excited him to a kind of heat: 'Speak to no one. I shall be there momentarily.'

What was it? What was this mad devotion to people who balked at paying fees, who scorned him the moment a case was lost, lied to him routinely, withheld critical information, and ignored his instructions? They needed him. Needed him! These weak, injured, even buffoonish characters required the assistance of Alejandro Stern to make their way. Disaster loomed. Life destruction. They wept in his office and swore to murder their turncoat comrades. When sanity returned, they dried their eyes and waited, pathetically, for Stern to tell them what to do. He drew on his cigar. 'Now,' he would say quietly.

In the afternoon on Monday, he found a moment to call Cal.

"Just to let you know," said Stern, "that the matter of the elusive check has been resolved."

"Oh, really?" asked Cal. He waited.

"So, if you would be so kind, Cal, let our friends at River National know that all is well and thank them for their cooperation."

"I will," said Cal, "I will." He cleared his throat. "May I ask?"

"Quite a complicated matter," Stern said.

"The beneficiary, I meant. The payee."

"It is difficult to say," said Stern, striving for a frank tone, "just at the moment. But the matter is well in hand, Cal. Have no doubt. My deepest thanks to you."

"I see," said Cal. He was hurt, of course. He expected greater veneration and confidence from Stern, as a matter of professional courtesy, if nothing else.

Returning home that evening, he found an enormous hanging case in the foyer. He bent to examine the luggage tag. Marta was back. She usually traveled with a backpack and a briefcase, the baggage of her diversified life.

She was not in the house. Instead, after circling the first floor and calling, he spied her out the solarium windows, leaning across the hedge in animated conversation with Fiona. Marta was listening, with far more interest than she generally showed their neighbor. Stern ventured out. When Marta saw him, she broke off to embrace him, and Stern, by some peculiar logic, then reached over the hedge, took Fiona's tanned hand, and kissed her as well. She was in her gardening attire, a few leaves in her hair with stray vegetation, and she seemed to blush at Stern's enthusiasm.

"Doesn't she look wonderful!" Fiona declared, motioning to Marta, who was in the usual formless floor-length frock. Fiona undoubtedly held the private belief that Marta was dressed like one of the women who had walked behind the wagon trains across the prairie. "I was just giving Marta the news," said Fiorna.

"Oh, yes?" asked Stern, with some foreboding.

"About Nate and me," said Fiona more definitely.

"Ah, yes. Nate mentioned that. I am sad to hear it, Fiona."

"We're probably both better off." Like many people on the other side of a dread event, Fiona appeared, as she said, better off—more resilient than one might have expected.

Marta was beginning to slip away toward the house. Stern made a remark about stumbling over her suitcase.

"I'm planning to stay for a while," she told him. "I quit my job."

"You did?" asked her father. "Just like that?"

"A month's notice, but I have some vacation coming. I'll go back for a few days next month to clean up. But last time I was here, I was looking at Katy, how tired she was, and it just sort of dawned on me, she's having a baby and I'm going to be eight hundred miles away for no good reason. Why did I bother taking the bar exam in four states if I don't go where I want to? I'll find a job here. Do you mind?"

"I should say not."

Fiona chimed in: Wonderful, wonderful—how nice for all of them. Stern found his head bobbing in agreement.

"I have to call Kate," Marta said. "I'm supposed to go see John and her later. Do you want to come?"

"Not tonight," said Stern promptly. "Please tell Kate, however, that I wish to have dinner with John and her later this week."

"God," said Marta, "you sound so serious."

He supposed he did. Stern did not answer, and Marta galloped into the house. Both Fiona and he watched her go.

"Did you take it she is planning to live here?" asked Stern.

"It sounds like it."

"Dear me." The thought of Marta and her vitamins and minerals in permanent residence provoked a moment of consternation. Fiona, in the meantime, had crept a bit closer to the hedge.

"I suppose that you're madder than hell at me," she said quietly.

"Hardly, Fiona. In truth, I received what I deserved."

"I was trying to warn you that night. When Nate came home. Honestly." She tested Stern with a glance. "After all, Sandy, I had to say something when he found that letter. You put me in a helluva position. And I couldn't *stand* to tell the little bastard that I'd had some respect for our marriage, when he didn't have a bit. But do you know the worst part? When I told him that ridiculous story, I could see he was actually happy. Do you believe that?" Fiona shook her head gravely. "Why am I always so dumb?" she asked Stern, and looked at him momentarily as if she expected an answer. She stood in her garden, just over the property line, hopelessly lost to the misery of being herself, of making so often, like everyone else, the same mistakes.

"He swears up and down, by the way, that those pills weren't his," Fiona said. "He kept saying they were for a patient. Finally, he told me if I didn't believe him I could call the other doctor who worked on the case. Guess who that was."

Stern lifted his hands: no idea.

"Peter."

"Peter?"

"Your son. Isn't that a coincidence?"

The night was thick. The bugs were out now in mid-July, buzzing and biting, and Stern swung at something close to his ear while he thought of the look Nate had given him the other evening when they were parting. It was obvious what Nate had held back. Stern realized he had been right all along. At the thought of yet another showdown, he nearly groaned. Perhaps with Peter it was unnecessary.

"Anyway, I'm sorry," said Fiona.

"Fiona, the apologies are all mine. As you say, I put you in a difficult position. And you more than made up for it. I appreciate your discretion with Nate when you spoke again."

"Oh hell, I figured what's the point. I couldn't give him any more satisfaction." She remained glum, and continued shaking her head, overwhelmed by divorce, herself, the varied but momentous concessions of defeat that life just now was requiring.

"Nonetheless," said Stern, "I am sorry to have made you the victim of my state of disruption."

"Oh, it wasn't so bad." She looked up then, shyly, teasingly, beneath her penciled brows, a pretty fifty-year-old woman in her avocado gardening outfit, practicing the elusive, winsome look she used to give the boys. "Kind of gave me a boost." Disconcerted by her prior remarks about Peter, Stern nevertheless could not keep himself from laughing aloud.

"You have been very generous, Fiona."

"Oh, sure," she said once more. She considered him pensively, some deliberation evident in the striking yellowish eyes. But he could see they had made their ways. His ship and Fiona's were each headed off for their own channels. His tact, for once of late, had not failed him—truly, he was more and more himself. Moved by all this, he reached out and took Fiona's dirty hand, which rested on the bushes, and kissed her palm.

"Here we go again," said Fiona. She rolled her eyes and walked away. Stern called after her: let him know any way he might help. She waved bravely, then paused by the gray steps to her back porch. "Do you know that little son of a bitch has actually stopped drinking?" she asked Stern across the short distance and then, with the strength of challenge, resentment, her entire complicated persona, shook her head fiercely once more and pulled open the door.

In his kitchen, Marta was replacing the phone.

"How is your sister?" asked Stern.

"Uneasy. There seems to be a lot of strain. She said John testified in the grand jury last week."

"So I understand. I spoke to Tooley today."

Marta asked for a description of John's testimony. She had been reluctant to ask Kate.

"My conversation was as one would expect with Mel. Very evasive. He made it a point to tell me that he had not been in the grand jury room—as if I thought he might have been. It seems, though, that it went very much as we would have thought. John blamed your uncle: Dixon gave all the orders; John carried them out, with no appreciation of their significance."

"Ugh," said Marta.

"Yes, indeed."

"And what about the safe?"

"I do not have it," said Stern simply.

"Have you heard from Uncle Dixon?"

"Not a word."

"Can you figure out what he's up to?"

"At moments I have an idea. Then, again, I am mystified."

"You let him know you'd file that motion tomorrow, didn't you? To withdraw?"

Stern said he had.

"You better go through with it. You have to put some distance between yourself and him. That woman, Sonia, whatever her name is, she's going to be screaming for your scalp. And Judge Winchell may give it to her."

"Yes," said Stern. He had considered that, too.

"So?" asked Marta.

"So we shall see." Stern walked across the kitchen and took his daughter in his arms. "Go meet Kate. Tell her about your change of residence. I am sure she will be delighted."

"What about you? You really don't mind having your nutty daughter come back?"

Stern kissed her. He thought of Peter, of John and Kate. Of Dixon. Clara.

"You will be at home," he said to her.

43

It was not quite seven when Stern arrived at the office on Tuesday morning. He had left Marta a note suggesting she come downtown this afternoon to plan as best they could for his grand jury appearance two days from now. He had heard her return late last night, but he had not risen to greet her. Another day could pass without hearing the latest of Kate and John.

Inside the outer door, Stern waited. A sound? Some sense of disturbance. He paused at the door to his office, which was ordinarily locked but now stood barely ajar. From the threshold, he pushed it wider. Across the room, on Stern's cream-colored sofa, Dixon was asleep. He had stunk up the space with his cigarettes and the effluvium of his slumbers.

Beside him, on the carpeting, stood the safe.

Quietly, Stern slipped behind his desk. He worked there for about fifteen minutes, until a client called, the defendant in the waste-dump investigation, a heavy-bellied fellow named Alvin Blumberg. Alvin was one of those types guilty as sin and paralyzed with fear; he wanted what he would never hear—a promise he would go free. Stern listened as Alvin ventilated, complaining about the prosecutors, his business partners, the intolerance of his wife. After some time, he broke off the call. He would have to introduce Alvin to Sondra. When he replaced the phone, Dixon was just sitting up, stretching out, yawning, rubbing his eyes. He was wearing a simple cotton camp shirt and a pair of pleated trousers; a heavy gold chain was around his neck, and he immediately pounded at his shirt pockets looking for his cigarettes.

"What time is it?"

Stern told him.

"I have to call Silvia. You mind?"

Stern pushed the phone to the corner of the desk and watched as Dixon spoke with his wife: He had come down to Sandy's, there were papers to look at, he had been here all night. "He's sitting right here. He found me asleep. Ask him. You found me asleep, right?" Dixon turned the phone around. Stern, reluctant to be Dixon's prop and his excuse for a night spent God knows where, murmured in the direction of the mouthpiece that Dixon had been asleep. "You see?" Dixon then ran through his schedule for the day with her, every meeting, each person he expected to see. "I love you," said Dixon near the end of the call. Stern watched him, tanned, whiskery, the flesh beneath his jaw slackening. His wavy hair was beginning to thin. Age was overcoming him, but Dixon still brought to his conversation with Silvia all earthly interest. In their waning years, as they slipped into dotage, Dixon and Silvia would maintain their happy fixation on one another, aided, no doubt, by some inevitable dwindling of Dixon's interest in other pursuits. The recognition, as usual, affected Stern: however thwarted or immature Dixon's emotional life, it was no lie when Dixon told Silvia he loved her. After his discoveries on Sunday, Stern would have expected that witnessing this exchange, as he had so often over the years, would have driven him to rage, but his immediate sensation was of absence, pining, the sting of real envy—his own wife was gone.

"You want to go get some breakfast?" Dixon asked him. He had cradled the phone.

"What is it you have brought me, Dixon?"

"You wanted the fucking safe? There's the fucking safe. Are you happy now? Problems all solved?"

"The government also wishes an affidavit from me stating that the contents have not been disturbed."

"So give them the affidavit."

"How am I able to do that?"

"You want to see what's in there?"

"On the contrary. I am simply making a point."

"I want you to look." The safe was facing him and Dixon spun the dial. After reaching in, he threw a single piece of paper down on the glass of the desk. It was Dixon's check, folded in four, the one he had written to cover the debit balance on the

Wunderkind account. Stern found his glasses and made a considerable show of studying the document.

"No more?"

"You know what the fuck you're looking at?" Dixon had given up all sign of his civilized manners. He was his true self now, agitated and profane.

"I believe I understand the significance of the check to the government." If they turned over only this, Sonny Klonsky would accuse Stern of more bad faith, of conforming the contents of the safe to the contours of the government's knowledge. Of course, that would remain one more private grief between them—she would never be able to tell Sennett what she had revealed. "The prosecutors seem to believe that there are account documents somewhere."

"*Are?*" asked Dixon, with one of his roguish smiles. He was stressing the present tense.

"That would be most foolish, Dixon."

"Well, I kind of agree," he said. "I was having a little bonfire, and then I had second thoughts, but that's all I could save." He pointed to the check. "They won't complain. They'll have my head on a platter, anyway, if they ever get hold of that."

"Assuming they have not obtained this check already," said Stern.

"Where would they get it?"

"It is possible, of course, that this was what they were looking for with their subpoenas to your bank."

Absorbing that thought, Dixon proceeded to the obvious: Why bother with the safe if they could already establish Dixon's control of the Wunderkind account? Tactics, Stern explained. Proof that Dixon was withholding documents would provide compelling evidence of his guilty frame of mind.

"You mean I've fallen into their trap?" Dixon asked.

"In all likelihood," said Stern. He had his hands folded. He was relentlessly composed. He had never given a better performance. Dixon, in the meantime, stroked his chin thoughtfully. He sighed, pulled his nose; he shook his head.

"You think I should plead guilty, don't you? That's what you said last time."

"If one is guilty, that is always an alternative that merits serious consideration."

"So what'll happen to me? What kind of deal can you cut?"

"The usual wisdom is to attempt to buy freedom. Negotiate for a heavy financial penalty and a lesser prison term."

"How much time?"

"These days? With the federal sentencing guidelines, probably three years."

"And when do I get paroled?"

"There is no longer parole in the federal system."

"Jesus."

"Very harsh."

"And I voted Republican," said Dixon. He smiled stiffly. "How much do I have to give them to get this three-year bargain?"

"One can only estimate, Dixon. Certainly millions. God only knows how much Stan Sennett will want you to forfeit. Probably some large portion of the value of your interest in MD. It will be very costly."

"Hmm." Again he gripped his chin and, unpredictably, smiled. "They can't forfeit what they can't find, can they?" This thought, of what was hidden in the Caribbean, seemed to fortify Dixon for a moment. Silvia would be well provided for. Stern saw his logic.

Dixon lit a cigarette.

"If you do not mind, Dixon, it would give me a better sense of our negotiating position if I had an idea of what actually transpired."

"You already know," he said, but ran through it quickly: how he was informed of large orders to be executed in Chicago and immediately called the central order desk to place front-running trades in Kindle. He described his use of the house error and Wunderkind accounts to gather and shelter the profits. "Pretty fucking clever," concluded Dixon, "if I do say so myself."

"What about that account, Dixon—Wunderkind? What was that?"

"Just a corporate account. I'd had it set up for this."

"And what was John's role in all of this?"

"John? John is a lunkhead. He did what I told him. John would think it was raining if you pissed in his eyes." Dixon looked at his cigarette and tapped his foot; he was wearing smooth Italian shoes of taupe-colored leather. He seemed at ease.

"A man of your wealth, Dixon. It is—"

"Oh, don't start moralizing, Stern. That's the markets, okay?

Down there, we eat our young. Everybody does it. Shit, the customers do it—the ones who know what's up. It's humanity in the jungle. I got caught with my hand in the cookie jar, that's all. I want to move on. I want to get this fucking thing over with." He slapped his knees and looked at his brother-in-law directly— ruddy, vital, still handsome, Dixon Hartnell, colossus of the marketplace. "I want to plead guilty," he said.

Stern did not answer.

"Okay?" asked Dixon. "What time is it? Give those assholes a call, will you? While I still have my nerve. I want to hear the sound of Sennett, that pompous son of a bitch, falling over from shock."

"I believe, Dixon," said Stern, "that you seek to deceive me."

Dixon jolted visibly.

"Me?"

"Just so."

"You're crazy."

"I believe not."

Dixon's mouth hung open a bit.

"You've been talking to that girl, haven't you? What's her name? Krumke."

"Alas, Dixon, your antics have cost me the confidence of the government. I have not been speaking with Ms. Klonsky."

Dixon stood up. He walked around the office, waving his cigarette.

"You want me to bleed, don't you?"

"I would welcome the truth, Dixon. If you care to tell it."

Wandering, Dixon paused at Stern's spot by the window and looked down to the river, spangled and living in the morning sun.

"There are some things about that account."

"Which account is that?" Stern asked.

"Wunderkind, Inc. Whatever we called it."

"Yes?"

"That was John's account. Or it was supposed to be. I didn't want to move money into an account that would trace to me. So I asked him to open one. You know, a corporate account, because of exchange compliance. It can't be in his name. The KCFE has a rule that member employees can't have their own accounts."

"So whose name did you use, Dixon?"

Dixon turned around. He was in extreme discomfort.

"Kate. She signed the account papers. In her maiden name. I'm sure she didn't know a damn thing about what was going on. Goofball just told her to sign by the x."

"And what did John obtain by accommodating you in this fashion?"

"Oh, he's the village idiot. I ask him to jump, he says, How high. He wants to be a floor trader. He was waiting for me to promote him. Look, he's a kid. He's a noodle. You bend him in whatever shape you want. I told him to do things, he did them."

"You did not promise him even a penny in profit?"

"I never talked to him about it. Frankly, I think he's too dimwitted to ask. And there never was any profit, anyway. Not for long."

"Yes, Dixon, explain that to me. You stole money and then lost it?"

"It was Las Vegas. Who cared? I lost, I got more. It was a fucking amusement, Stern."

"In which you embroiled my daughter and my son-in-law— your niece and nephew. A crime of curiosity in which you proposed to hide behind children—my children?"

Dixon did not answer. He returned to the sofa and fired his lighter for another cigarette.

"Did you not estimate, Dixon, that John would tell the government about that account and how it was established?"

"Yeah, I estimated," he said. "I just wasn't real eager to tell you." Dixon lay back and extended his feet. "I have the records at home. I'll bring them in."

"Did you fear, Dixon, that I would lose respect for you?" He delivered the remark perfectly—a rapier thrust; cold steel.

"Oh, go fuck yourself, Stern. I'm sorry—I did it, I'm guilty, and I'm pleading guilty. I'll have a long time to repent. So call the goddamned prosecutors and let's get this over with."

With one arm over the sofa back, Dixon blew smoke rings in the air.

"You are guilty of a great deal, Dixon. But, regrettably, not this crime."

Dixon sat up straight.

"Are you frigging out of your mind?"

"I believe not. You are innocent, Dixon."

"Oh, please."

"Dixon, you are telling me precisely what you believe the government thinks."

"You're right about that."

"Which you know to be a lie."

Dixon, brought up abruptly, did not answer at first.

"A lie?"

"Let us leave aside, Dixon, the question of motive. You insist that a rich man might steal as willingly as a poor one, and that is often the case. But explain this, please. You tell me that you inveigled John into establishing this account so that, if the day ever came, blame might fall on someone other than yourself. And yet, when the government became aware of the account, you hid the records from them."

"So? I'm not quite as big an asshole as I thought I was. Besides, I told you: I wasn't real interested in explaining that one to you."

"I feel, Dixon, that you had other motives."

"You're smoking dope, Stern."

"Tell me, Dixon, according to your explanation, how is it that the government learned of any of this in the first place? Who is the informant, Dixon?"

Dixon shook his head no. As if he had never even pondered the question.

"Who do you think it is?" he asked.

"After a great deal of reflection, I have concluded that it is Margy, and that you have known that all along, perhaps even directed her activity."

Dixon was absolutely still. His eyes, a lighter shade tending toward gray or green, moved first.

"You've lost your fucking mind. Completely."

"I believe not."

"You really are a piece of work," Dixon said. "Do you know that? You badger me for months to tell you about this. You cross-examine me. You send me frigging motions. You threaten my secretary. And now, when I finally suck it up and let you know what's going on, you call me a liar and make some wild-ass accusation that came to you in a hallucination. Go fuck yourself, Stern."

"A wonderful speech." Stern raised both hands and clapped once.

"I'm pleading guilty."

"To an offense you did not commit?"

"Look, I'm not taking any more of this crap. You're my lawyer, right?"

"At the moment."

"Well, I want to plead guilty. Make a deal. Those are your orders. Instructions. Whatever you call it."

"I am sorry, Dixon. I cannot do that."

"Then I'll fire you."

"Very well."

"You think I won't do this? I'll do it without you. The city is full of lawyers. They all work for pay. It's like blood on the water. I'll have six by the end of the day."

"You are not guilty, Dixon."

Dixon wrenched his face and his voice tore from him at top volume.

"Goddamn you, Stern!"

It was like a cannon blast. Somewhere in the still building Stern could hear movements. Down the hall, a door opened.

"You smug, insufferable little son of a bitch. Has there ever been a minute in your life when you didn't think you were smarter or better than I am?" Dixon had a wild look. He had come within a few feet of Stern, and Stern was afraid for an instant that Dixon might strike him. But at last Dixon turned away and bent toward the safe.

"Leave it be, Dixon. I remain under subpoena. The safe is my responsibility."

Hot rage, nuclear in its intensity, radiated from Dixon's look, but he stepped away.

"Can you fucking imagine?" he asked before he left.

* * *

"Stern here."

"It's Sonny."

He greeted her warmly, asked how she felt. With her voice there was still, if more distantly, the same storm of feeling. Faroff thunder. He looked at the clock built into the telephone. Another of his gadgets. It was well past five.

"Listen," she said. "I just got the most bizarre call. Your client. Mr. Hartnell. He told me he wants to come in to have a meeting with me."

"Ignore him," said Stern at once.

"I tried. I told him I couldn't talk to him, because he had a lawyer. He said he fired you. Is that right?"

After a pause, he told her he was not certain precisely where they stood, that Dixon was extremely emotional at the moment, feeling the stress. "If I withdraw, however, I shall not do so before he has substitute counsel. I must insist, Sonny, that the government not deal with him directly."

"Well, Sandy, I don't know. I mean—"

"I am not criticizing you."

"I understand."

Most judges would react adversely if the government proceeded. With Stern professing that the client was in turmoil, the court would feel that the prosecution had taken unfair advantage. Even Sennett would not take the chance. His case was strong.

Why put it in jeopardy? Sonny, no doubt, was making the same calculations.

"I'll talk to Stan," she said at last. The usual exit from a difficult pass. "Do I take it Mr. Hartnell might be interested in a plea?"

"I would advise him against that," said Stern. "Most emphatically."

"You're bluffing," she said. He could hear the tricks in her voice, the humor. She could not keep herself from a certain bonhomie. She relished being on the same footing with him, proving herself. She was kind enough, however, not to press further. "What about the safe?" she asked. "Have you and Marta talked about our proposal?"

"What is it you want?" Stern asked. He remembered, of course. It was merely a lawyer's device, one of a thousand, hoping the terms might somehow improve when they were repeated. They did not. She offered the same deal: produce the safe and an affidavit that its contents were undisturbed. So here was that moment again, the everyday of the lawyer's life. It was, after all, only a signature. Who besides Stern would know?

"I believe, Sonny, that I shall not be able to comply."

"Look," she said.

"I understand."

"I don't think you do. Stan has very strong feelings."

"Of course."

"Oh, man," she said. She pondered. "I don't like where this is going, Sandy. I really don't. Is your client aware that we can prove he controlled that account? You know, Wunderkind?"

"I cannot tell you what I discussed with my client, Sonny, but I have not breached your trust. I hope you would not assume otherwise."

"I know that. I meant—" she said. "Listen, I have to think this through— If I can see my way clear to let you tell him, do you think that would make a difference?"

"You are very kind, Sonny. But it would make no difference at all."

She hesitated, deliberating. From her silence, he was sure she was lost.

"Sandy, this is nuts. If you think that someone in this building is going to be afraid to put Sandy Stern in jail—"

"I harbor no such illusions. I assure you."

"And there's nothing else anybody can do?"

He waited with the thought, unwilling to prevail upon her again. He had done that in Dulin, and in the end there had been considerable emotional cost to them both.

"What?" she asked.

"No matter."

"What?"

He sighed. "The informant."

She made some sound with her tongue. "What about it?"

"I take it you still do not know the identity."

"I couldn't tell you if I did."

"Of course not."

"So?"

"I believe the United States Attorney has taken particular delight in duping me. I suspect you will find that your source is someone with whom the government knows I have a relationship, one that naturally tends to place that person above my suspicion." He weighed saying "a client," or even giving her Margy's name, but the more specific he was, the more difficult this would become. As she said, she could never confirm an identity. "If my suspicions are misplaced, I would very much like to know that."

"And that's important to you? In connection with this? The subpoena?"

"Critical," he said.

"I'm not making any promises," she said. "If I find out, I find out. I don't know what I'd do."

They waited on the line. It amazed him again—she was such a strong, fine person.

"How is your life?" he asked. He dared not be more precise. Your marriage. Your husband.

"Better," she said.

"Good," he told her.

"Yeah," said Sonny, and waited. "But the law sucks," she told him before she put down the phone.

44

"State your name, please, and spell your last name for the record."

"My name is Alejandro M. Stern. The first name is A, l, e, j, a, n, d, r, o. The last name is S, t, e, r, n."

"M?" asked Klonsky. She would perhaps never wholly resolve her curiosity about him.

"Mordecai."

"Ah." She absorbed that stoically and went back to her notes.

Sonny ran through the usual preamble, one Stern had read in dozens of transcripts. She told him that he was before the Special March 1989 Grand Jury—March being when they had been impaneled—and provided a one-line description of investigation 89–86, which, she said, concerned "alleged violations of Title 18, United States Code, Section 1962." She also mentioned that Stern was not a target and that his lawyer was outside, available to consult with him.

"And her name is Marta Stern, same spelling?"

"Yes," said Stern. He spoke to the court reporter seated before him, Shirley Floss, who formerly had worked in Judge Horka's courtroom: M, a, r, t, a." Shirley smiled as she typed. Proper spellings were the moon and stars of a court reporter's life.

Stern sat in the witness chair, inside the grand jury at last—thirty years of curiosity finally satisfied. Beside him, behind the façade of the raised walnut bench, were the grand jury foreperson and the secretary, two middle-aged women selected from among the grand jurors for this largely ministerial function. A small desk, shared by the court reporter and Klonsky, was immediately before him, and arrayed beyond in the small, tiered room sat the remaining grand jurors: the League of Nations, all races, all ages. Two older men slept; a young thuggish man, with heavy sideburns and long, greasy hair, read the paper. Some listened abjectly. A slender, attractive, middle-aged woman sat with a pad, taking notes for her own benefit. There was no window, no natural light.

"Where do you reside, Mr. Stern?"

He gave his home address, and in response to the next question answered that he was an attorney. Sonny moved to the table.

"Mr. Stern, I show you what the court reporter has marked as G.J. 89—86 Exhibit 192. Do you recognize it?"

It was the subpoena she'd served on him. One hundred ninety-two exhibits, Stern thought. John had been a busy fellow. No question, the investigation was nearly complete, indictment was near. Klonsky established Stern's receipt of the subpoena and had him read the text aloud.

"Now, Mr. Stern, do you have in your possession, custody, or control the safe referred to?"

"I decline to answer."

"On what grounds?"

"The attorney-client privilege."

Klonsky, who expected this, turned to the grand jury foreperson, a gray-haired woman with glasses.

"Ms. Foreperson, please direct the witness to answer."

Abashed by the thought of a speaking part in the drama that occurred routinely before her, the foreperson barely glanced at Stern and said simply, "Answer."

"I decline," said Stern.

"On what grounds?" asked Klonsky.

"As stated."

Sonny, who up until now had been proficient and formidable, appeared to have second thoughts. Her pregnancy had progressed to the point that it had wholly erased her usual solid grace. She waited before him, with her own thoughts and a rankled look. "Mr. Stern, I advise you that I shall have to ask the chief judge to hold you in contempt."

"I intend contempt for no one," said Stern.

Klonsky asked the grand jurors to recess so that Stern and she could proceed to Chief Judge Winchell's chambers. The grand jurors were more or less familiar with this trip, since they strolled down the block en masse and appeared before Judge Winchell each week to return indictments. Stern, now and then, had seen them coming, a covey of happy executioners. It was a function to them, $30 a day, part of the customs of the law as arcane as the habits of the Chinese. For the defendant, it was often the end of a respectable life.

Sonny threw open the jury room door, and Marta, dressed in a dark suit and nylons—nylons!—peered inside.

"What's up?" she asked her father.

"We are on our way to see the chief judge."

On her face, Stern saw his own reflective Latin expression, accepting the inevitable.

The group—Sonny, Sandy, Marta, and Shirley, the court reporter, who was also required—waited silently in the corridor for the tardy elevators of the new federal building.

"I called Stan," said Sonny. "He'll meet us there."

The U.S. Attorney was going to smite his staff and call for justice. It was evident that to a degree Stern had never fully appreciated Sennett hated his guts. Shame, spite, humiliation; the bitter yearning for self-respect. Human beings, thought Stern, were such pitifully predictable creatures.

The small party walked down the teeming avenue in the summery heat. Shirley had packed her machine and notes in a small case, and toted it along on one of the little wheeled carrying racks that airline stewardesses use for their luggage. She talked to Stern about her children. The youngest, in college at the U., hoped for a career in radio and TV. Sonny and Marta, in spite of themselves, got along admirably. They had finished law school at virtually the same time and had mutual acquaintances. A fellow named Jake, a law school friend of Marta's, had clerked with Sonny in the court of appeals.

Sennett, in his flawless blue suit and perfect shirt, waited for them in the judge's anteroom. As they walked through the door, the U.S. Attorney was, literally, studying his nails. He shook Marta's hand, and Stern's. Feeling somewhat surly, Stern did not return his greeting.

After a minute, Moira Winchell's door opened and the chief judge swept a hand to usher them in. She was in a straight skirt, and her hair, more and more visibly shot through with gray, was held back by a headband today, so that she looked a bit schoolgirlish.

"Well, I can't say I'm happy to see any of you." She called out the side door for her own court reporter.

The group was seated again at the judge's conference table, solid as a fortress. The light of the day fell through the heavy windows, long parallelograms of brilliance that gave the rest of the room a kind of prison gloom by contrast. Pure metaphor, thought Stern of the association.

"On the record," Judge Winchell said to her court reporter. "Mr. Sennett, I take it you have a motion?"

Stan raised a hand to Sonny, who drew out of a manila folder a short written motion which had been prepared in advance. It asked that Stern be ordered to reappear before the grand jury and to respond to the questions he had refused to answer. Reappearance was required because the grand jury had no power of its own to compel him to respond. It was only for violating the judge's order to answer that Stern could be found in contempt—and jailed.

Moira put the motion aside.

"All right, let's hear what happened. This is the court reporter?"

Shirley was sworn, and read from the narrow stenotype pad in a singsong voice, stumbling at moments as she interpreted the symbols. The judge's court reporter, Bob, sat beside Shirley, taking it all down on a machine of his own.

"Answer by Mr. Stern," she read at the conclusion, " 'I intend contempt for no one.' "

Stern saw Sennett, at the foot of the table, frown. Stan was not buying any.

"All right, Ms. Stern," said the judge, careful with her record. "What do you say to the motion?"

"We object, Your Honor." Marta said that whether Stern had received or retained the safe were both questions that implicated communications with his client. She asked for a week to present a brief in support of that position, and Sennett, speaking for the government today, objected in his usual tone of suppressed vehemence. Briefs were unnecessary on this issue, he said, and would unfairly delay the grand jury's final action.

Marta fought back bravely, but the judge eventually sided with the government. She would never tolerate briefing each question Stern was asked.

"If you have cases, I'll read them right now," the judge said.

Marta did. From her briefcase, she removed photocopies of various judicial opinions speaking to the breadth of the attorney-client privilege, and passed copies to the judge and the prosecutors. The company, including the two court reporters, sat silently while the judge and the lawyers read.

Stan clearly remained intent on indicting quickly. Yesterday morning, Stern had received a letter from the Department of Justice granting him an appointment with the Organized Crime and Racketeering Section at 9 a.m. next Tuesday in Washington, D.C. If it went as usual, the meeting would be brief, polite, and entirely perfunctory. By two weeks from today at most, prosecution would be approved and Dixon Hartnell would be a former powerhouse, become instead the carcass for a three- or four-day media feeding. That Thursday morning the business pages would banner the rumor of his imminent indictment, as the result of a leak from the man at the end of the table. Then, following return of the charges that day, Stan would hold a news conference and read his press release with a still-eyed intensity that would make him appear properly tough when his sound bite flickered up on the evening news. On Friday morning the indictment would command the front page here, and probably an item in the *Journal* and *The New York Times*. Following that, the weekend papers would run a lengthy rehash, comparing Sennett's initiative im combating corruption on the Kindle County Futures Exchange with others around the nation, or, even worse, recounting the tragic rise and fall of Dixon Hartnell.

And while his reputation was devastated, the actual bricks and mortar of Dixon's business life would begin to collapse. Competitors would vigorously woo Dixon's stunned clients, and key employees would start freshening their résumés. In light of the RICO charges, a restraining order would be entered at once, tying up all of Dixon's visible assets, so that Stern would have to call Klonsky for permission before Dixon could cash a check for spending money. The reporters would lurk outside Dixon's home and call him on his private line at work. And Dixon, everywhere, would see some reflex of aversion or harsh judgment pass behind the eyes of each person he met. To Stern, this remained unfathomable—it was impossible to think of Dixon brought so low or, more pertinently, being able to soldier on in the face of such disgrace.

"Here's what I think," said the judge. She had finished reading Marta's cases and apparently was not even going to allow argument. "I think these opinions are not on point. In this circuit, under decisions like *Feldman* and *Walsh*, an attorney must make a specific showing in support as to each question asked or item sought for which the privilege is claimed. The privilege must actually, not potentially, apply. From this I conclude that the privilege does not protect Mr. Stern or any other witness from answering whether he has a subpoenaed item in his possession. Otherwise, the court and counsel might become embroiled in lengthy proceedings that are, in reality, pointless. Accordingly, Ms. Stern, I am going to overrule your objection and order your client to answer. Now." The judge laid her long hands on the tabletop. She wore no jewelry other than a slim wedding band, and her nails were unpolished. "I would like to know whether or not your client intends to respond, since I'd rather have some time to reflect before dealing with any contempt. Why don't you use my study to confer?"

"I think she's right," said Marta as soon as she had closed the door to the study.

"Of course, she is," said Stern. The room was compact—probably the quarters for a scrivener when the building was first erected. There was a wall of books, and various photos of Jason Winchell, and also a dog, an Irish setter, in the phases of its life from puppyhood to mothering a litter. The dog's eyes were green and eerie in the light of the flash as her pups suckled beneath her. "Your desire is that I answer this question?"

"That's my advice," said his daughter.

They returned to the table. Marta said that Stern would answer. The prosecutors showed nothing, but the judge nodded. She was pleased.

"All right, now," said the judge. "What's the next question going to be? I'd like to avoid wasting the grand jurors' time—I don't want all of you trooping back and forth repeatedly."

"Well, what's the answer to the question?" asked Sennett.

The judge looked at Stern, and Marta raised a hand to prevent her father from speaking.

"I believe my client will indicate that he has the safe in his possession." Marta knew this much, having seen the safe in the office again. But Stern had kept to himself what had further transpired between Dixon and him, and Marta, to her credit, had not inquired. She took seriously her father's obligation to maintain Dixon's confidences.

With the news that Stern had the safe, Sennett wheeled about and gave Klonsky a look. Perhaps he had been betting against that. Sonny did not respond. In the grand jury, she was businesslike, but now, confronting the consequences, she was considerably less animated and seemed increasingly withdrawn from the proceedings, which Sennett was conducting more or less on his own. She was paler, showing less of her usual rosy glow. Stern could not help thinking of Kate or taking small comfort from what he viewed as signs of Sonny's sympathy.

"Next question," said the judge again.

"The next question," said Sennett, "is whether the safe, including its contents, is in the same condition as when Mr. Stern received it or whether, to his knowledge, anything has been removed."

Marta started to object, but the judge was already shaking her head. One question at a time, she told Sennett. He whispered to Klonsky, who somewhat listlessly shrugged.

"The question," he said, "is whether, to the best of Mr. Stern's knowledge, anything has been removed from the safe since the time the subpoena was served."

This, regrettably, was a clever improvement. As reframed, the question followed the lines of the judge's prior ruling and went no further than asking whether Stern had maintained possession of what had been subpoenaed from him. Sennett was working in increments. If Stern answered that nothing had been removed since Sonny served him, Sennett would attempt to move back to the time Stern had received the safe. That might be more objectionable. Of course, Stern realized, he was never going to answer the first question.

"All right now, Ms. Stern, any objection to that question?"

"Asking him if he knows," said Marta, "doesn't distinguish

between what his client might have told him and what he has learned on his own."

"We'll limit the question to exclude any communications with his client," interjected Sennett.

"So the question, then," said the iudge, "is, leaving aside client communications, does Mr. Stern know of anything removed from the safe since the time the subpoena was first served upon him?"

Sennett nodded. That was the question.

"Any further objections?" asked the judge.

Stern whispered to Marta: Assert privilege. She did, stating that the question still called upon knowledge gained in the attorney-client relationship and might reveal the attorney's own mental impressions.

"Very well," said the judge, "I'll overrule those objections. This question, no less than the one before it, simply deals with what is and is not in respondent's possession, without regard to client communications. Therefore, I'll order Mr. Stern to answer. Again, I'd prefer to know now whether he intends to respond." The judge once rnore gestured grandly to her study.

"No," said Stern when they were alone.

"Daddy!"

"I shall not answer."

"Why not?"

"I cannot respond." There was a small sofa, a love seat of heavy brown tweed, and Stern fell down upon it. He suddenly felt quite tired. Marta remained on her feet. "You told me before he took the safe that he'd never let you open it."

"True," said Stern.

"So you don't know if anything has been removed." Marta stared at her father. "How could you know?"

He shook his head—he would not answer.

"Come on," she said.

Stern glanced up at the walls—the judge had various citations there, a medal from a woman's group. As Stern would have guessed, she kept a cluttered desk here in her private space.

"If I were to answer," said Stern, "that to my knowledge the contents of the safe are not the same, what would transpire?"

"They'd ask you what's missing, how you know it's gone, who had access to the safe, where it was located, whether you know who's got what was taken." Marta was counting off the questions on her fingers.

"And would our privilege objections to such questions be sustained?"

"Maybe. To some of them. It depends how you know."

"Perhaps to some. But certainly Judge Winchell would require that I state who had access to the safe or where it may have been located."

"That's a reasonable guess," Marta said. "Are you really telling me that he took something out of there and you know it?"

Once more, he refused to answer her.

"Dad—"

"Marta, if I testify that Dixon took the safe, that Dixon returned the safe, and that some item is missing, what inference will the prosecutors and the grand jury draw?"

"That's obvious."

"Just so," said Stern. "And thus I cannot indulge this line of inquiry. I shall not give answers that imply wrongdoing by my client. Nor, frankly, have I any intention of responding to questions from anyone about the safe's contents."

"On what grounds?"

Stern, baffled, thought an instant. "The right to privacy."

There was no such thing in criminal proceedings. They both understood that. Marta studied her father. Stern knew the internal race taking place, the mind dashing ahead of the emotions. Somewhere, if she was nimble enough, there was an argument to be made that would persuade him, save him from himself. Her small dark eyes were intent.

"You're not being asked any of those questions now," she said. "All they want to know is whether the contents of the safe are the same. Yes or no. If you have a problem later, we'll deal with it then."

"I refuse. Once we start down that road, there is no logical stopping point."

Marta groaned. "What was in the safe?"

Stern shook his head.

"How do you know?"

He shook his head again.

Marta watched him with the same driven concentration.

"Aunt Silvia," she said at last. "She told you. You're protecting her."

"You are brilliant, Marta, but not correct."

"I don't understand this," Marta said. "I don't understand what you think you know. And I don't understand your loyalty to him. Don't you hate him? After all the stuff he's pulled?"

Stern hesitated.

"Come on," said his daughter.

"I have a duty to Dixon. The government can seek evidence against him in every other corner of the world, and seems to have done so. He is entitled to know that his lawyer will not join the melee."

"You don't have a duty to violate court orders. This is a matter of personal philosophy, not law."

"So far as I am concerned, Marta, this is not discretionary. And if it were, I would not use the legal system to settle my differences with Dixon."

Frustrated, Marta threw down her hand.

"What about the Fifth?" she asked suddenly.

"No," said Stern. "In my judgment, Dixon has no Fifth Amendment rights in these circumstances."

"No, no. What about you? You can be innocent and assert the Fifth. If you disclose that something was taken while you were under subpoena, you might be incriminating yourself. You've got a Fifth." Marta was excited. She had convinced herself this was the solution.

Resolutely, Stern differed. If he did as Marta wanted, the prosecutors would promptly obtain a use immunity order dissolving his Fifth Amendment rights. Nothing would have been gained and the judge would feel taunted by the desperate tactics.

Defeated, Marta sat down beside him.

"I don't understand this. How can you do this to yourself, just to suit him?"

"If I were to suit your uncle, I would commit perjury and solve all my problems. Perhaps I am simply too much of a coward to adopt that approach."

"Daddy, please. If you confront her in an area like this, where we have no legitimate grounds to resist, she'll put you in jail."

"Then that is what will occur."

His daughter looked at him for some time.

"Jesus Christ," said Marta. "And you complain about him as a client. What was in the goddanm safe?"

He shook his head again.

They returned to the table. The judge and the court reporters were chatting about movies.

"All right, on the record," said the judge.

Marta folded her hands, placed them squarely on the table before her, and announced that Stern would refuse to answer the question posed, on the grounds of the attorney-client privilege and the Sixth Amendment's guarantee of the right to counsel. The judge, the prosecutors, even the court reporters took a second to absorb this.

"Move contempt," said Sennett at last.

"My client believes that the government is attempting to use him as a witness against his client," added Marta.

"Whether that is true or not," said Judge Winchell, whose eyes were cast to the floor, "he must answer. Neither the attorney-client privilege nor the Constitution allows him a basis to refuse."

"He will not respond," said Marta. She leaned toward the judge with erect posture and an implacable look. She betrayed not an iota of doubt. Marvelous, Stern thought, in spite of everything else.

The judge covered her eyes with one hand.

"Well," she said at last. "I will reflect on how this contempt should be addressed, assuming it takes place. And I'll listen carefully to arguments." She straightened up. "But I want you to know, Mr. Stern, if you persist, my present intention is to remand you to the custody of the marshal, and I will leave it to the court of appeals to determine whether my order should be stayed while they consider the matter. And I also caution you that I will not terminate your grand jury appearance. You will have to go on answering the prosecutors' questions, or refusing, as the case may be."

Judge Winchell had fixed him with her icy tough-guy look. No friendship. No bullshit. No symphony intermissions. They were now in the heartland of Moira Winchell's judicial existence—her rightful authority. Sharing this look with considerable apprehension, Stern managed to nod.

In silence, the party proceeded back down the street to the new federal building. A block away, Stan broke off. He had a luncheon speech to deliver. No doubt it disappointed him not to be there to see the marshals clap on the cuffs, but there were at least forty-five minutes more and Stan, always precise, did not have the time. He said a word or two to Klonsky and left them to proceed ensemble in the noontime heat, the sounds of downtown construction and traffic banging about them.

Outside the grand jury room, the jurors were lounging, drinking coffee, gabbing, smoking their cigarettes. Sonny raised a hand to round them up.

She stood with Stern and Marta before the door.

"I know this is a matter of principle for you," she said to Stern. She put her hand on his, a mildly shocking gesture in the surroundings. "But I think this is a mistake. Please reconsider."

In the grand jury room, Stern resumed his seat. Klonsky read the first question from her notes: Was he in possession of the safe?

"I am."

She studied her pad again.

"Leaving aside client communications, does Mr. Stern—strike that—do you know of anything removed from the safe since the time the subpoena, G.J. 89-86 Exhibit 192, was first served upon you?"

"I decline to answer."

Sonny peered at him, pale, grim.

"State the grounds."

They were quickly finished. The grand jurors groaned when Klonsky called another recess.

Marta was standing immediately outside the door. "Shit," she said as it opened.

Klonsky asked Barney Hill, the grand jury clerk, to call Judge Winchell's secretary to tell her they were on the way back. The four of them headed out onto the street. Marta lagged behind with Stern, and spoke to him heatedly.

"Now I'm going to beg and plead. I'll use everything—thirty years of service in this court, Mommy's death, everything. And I don't want any back talk. Do you hear me?"

He nodded to her, smiling a bit, and marched down the street, shockingly free of apprehension or doubt.

The judge's staff knew what was transpiring and went quiet as soon as they entered. The secretary called in to the judge to announce their return, but the door to the chambers remained closed, and the four of them—Stern and his daughter, Klonsky and the court reporter—waited in the judge's anteroom. Sonny, if anything, appeared paler. She took the lone seat across from Stern, her lips drawn into her mouth, her jaw gripped firmly, while she stared into space. She was, Stern thought to himself, in a kind of remote observation, so terribly pretty. Then Bud Bailey, one of the deputy marshals, blundered through the door, a sweet bald-headed oaf, with his gun and uniform and jangling keys. His arrival jarred Stern, like a note of music misplayed.

Bailey greeted both Stern and Klonsky by name, then looked at the judge's secretary. "She rang?" Sonny had sat up tensely with Bailey's appearance.

The secretary sent Bailey in first. He could be getting instructions about taking Stern into custody. Stern had imagined all this and felt well girded. He would be escorted to the marshal's lockup, a mesh-fenced holding pen on the third floor which looked much like a birdcage for human beings. He would sit there for an hour or two. If the motion judge in the court of appeals did not rule promptly, he would be transported by jail van to the federal correctional center. There he would be asked to disrobe completely, then searched from head to toe and made to bend over while the guard examined his anus with the beam of a flashlight. Afterwards, he would be given a blue jumpsuit. He would not be inside long. They had drafted the petition for a stay last night; Marta had it with her and would go at once to the twelfth floor to file it. Marta and he had contacted George Mason, president of the county bar association, a figure of prominence, who promised to attempt to get his Board of Governors to file an *amicus* brief. In any event, Mason would organize dozens of lawyers who would join in a petition to the court of appeals. The court, most surely, would order Stern's release and set an expedited schedule for briefing and arguments. To proceed with the appeal, Marta had already insisted on deferring to Mason, a decision with which Stern agreed. The question, of course—the real question—was what he would do once the court of appeals ruled against him and he was required to respond in the grand jury or return to jail.

Klonsky suddenly spoke up in the silent office.

"You still want to write a brief for Judge Winchell?" she asked Marta.

"Sure."

"I think you should write a brief," said Sonny. "I think our discussions have persuaded me that there are serious issues."

Marta blinked once. "Sure," she said again.

Stern began to speak. What discussions, he was going to say, but his daughter dug her hand into his sleeve and spun about with a harsh look that bordered on violence. She mouthed words distinctly: Shut Up.

Stern turned from her. "Sennett will fire you," he told Sonny. "God*damn* it!" said Marta.

"This whole thing is sick," Sonny said. The remark was directed to no one in particular: a final conclusion. Stern had no idea who it was that she meant to condemm, but her judgment was firm. She focused on Stern. "You were right, you know. Do you understand me?"

He did not at first. Then it came to him: the informant. That was what had upset her—seeing Sennett's duplicity, his mean, clever game.

The door to the judge's chambers opened then. Bud Bailey was standing behind Moira Winchell.

"Sandy," she said, even before the company was over the threshold, "Bud will go with you to the grand jury. When you're done, he'll keep you in custody in his office until the court of appeals rules on your petition for a stay. That's the best I can do." Even Moira Winchell, firm and unflappable, was somewhat undone. Her head moved about in the loose wobble of an old lady as she told him she could do no more.

Marta spoke up then. She and Klonsky, after discussion, had agreed there were serious issues. The government now would agree to a week's adjournment in order to allow Stern to file a brief.

"Oh, really?" said Judge Winchell. She turned to Klonsky. "Mr. Sennett had seemed so intent."

"He may not agree with me," said Sonny. "If he doesn't I won't be here next week." She smiled vaguely at her own irony.

"Do you want to speak with him?" asked the judge.

"He can't be reached," she said.

"I see," said the judge. Moira knew she was getting a message of some kind. "Off the record," she said. "What's the deal?"

Stern, his daughter, Sonny exchanged looks among themselve. No one answered the judge.

"Your brief Monday, response Wednesday, a reply if you wish when you appear Thursday morning, 10 a.m.," said the judge, pointing at Marta, Sonny, then Marta again. She looked once more at the three silent lawyers, then shrugged at Bailey, the marshal. "It's a secret," she said.

45

As a child, Peter was a sleepwalker. These were horrifying occasions. Because Clara tended to turn in early, it was usually Stern who had to deal with the situation. Once, Stern found him about to head out wearing his hat and mittens, although they were in the steamy depths of summer. Another night, Peter came down and practiced the clarinet. One other time, Stern heard the bathwater running. Assuming it was Clara, he only happened to peek in to find Peter lying in the tub in his pajamas. He remained fully asleep, the water a shining frame about his dark, serene face. The advice in those years—probably still today—was not to rouse him. Stern pulled him from the water gently, stripped off his clothes, and dried the lean young body, then dressed his son again. In these states, Peter responded to instruction like a magician's assistant in a trance. Walk. Turn left. Turn right. He was, however, incapable of speech. It was a disturbing sight. Like waking the dead. The private theater of dream and sleep were not stage enough to relieve Peter's inner forces. They needed, literally, to be acted out. After the bathtub episode, Peter reported he had dreamed he was dirty.

It was the thought that Peter ought to be allowed to share his burdens which had brought Stern, late Thursday afternoon, to the rehab'ed apartment building where his son lived. After his adventures in the grand jury, he found himself too distracted for work. He was concerned about Klonsky, who, in her dismay over Sennett's high-handed tactics, might have placed a black mark on a promising career, while emotionally Stern felt some need to take advantage of his reprieve. Eventually, his mind turned to Peter. Near three, he had called his son's office, where the staff reminded Stern that Peter had no hours on Thursdays. Next he tried him at home. He was there apparently—the line was busy—and after failing to get through on a number of tries, Stern decided to go ahead while his courage remained high. He wanted no confrontation. No fussing. His manifest assumption was to be that Peter was well-meaning and bound by professional obligations. But Stern had decided it was best to get this out in the open. He preferred to have no other distractions when he proceeded to the calamitous showdown that he was headed for sooner or later with John and Kate. That one, he feared, might blow the Stern family to smithereens; they would float through space like an asteroid belt, pieces of the same matter, within the same orbit, but no longer attached. Only Marta might see things her father's way in the end, and even she would be somewhat divided.

Stern stood in the lobby's dim light, attempting to correlate the name with a button. "4B P. Stern." There. In Stern's opinion, this was a desolate part of town, south along the river. It had been formerly the habitat of skid-row bums and mission houses, until the developers had arrived here in force about five years ago. The old churches, the printing plants, even the unused former train station were turned into loft apartments, but the area did not quite catch on. The streets were empty; there was little planting, no children. A few of the reprobate bums would get soused and return here out of habit or confusion and lie in the sandblasted doorways, their grey heads against the shining brass kickplates of the refinished doors. Apparently, the denizens here were all like Peter, young and childless, happy to trade the convenience of a location adjoining the Center City for other amenities.

A pretty young woman came into the lobby. She carried her cleaning and was dressed in full urban regalia—a blue suit, aerobic shoes for the walk from the office, and yellow headphones. The inner lobby door was activated by some electronic-card pass which she drew out of her handbag. Stern pressed the button for Peter's apartment and, as the young woman held the door, entered. Climbing the stairs—none of these buildings had elevators—he once more prepared himself. No scenes, he promised himself. He knocked on his son's door. After a moment, Peter's face appeared in the seam allowed by the chain lock between the frame and the paneled door.

"Dad." All the usual emotions swam across Peter's face: discomfiture, surprise. Oh God, *this*—this eternal nuisance.

"May I come in?"

Peter did not answer. Instead, he closed the door to sweep aside the chain. Was there the sound of movement inside? There was no one else when Peter threw the door wide. The young man himself was dressed in a spandex cycling outfit—a garish top and black knickers, with lime blocks of reflective material running down his flanks, and little low shoes. Peter's blondish hair was rumpled after his ride. His bike, with the black headgear strung along the handlebars, was propped near the doorway, as much a part of the furnishings as anything else.

"Jesus, Dad, why didn't you call?"

He explained that he could not get through. "There are matters," said Stern, "that I wish to discuss."

"Matters?" asked Peter. They were still standing near the doorway and Stern looked into the apartment hopefully and actually took a step farther inside. It was only a little better than a studio. The kitchen and dining room and living area were merged, with a single bedroom and bath behind the common wall. The decoration was modest—opera posters and bright furniture filled with polyfoam, inexpensive modern stuff. Peter still did not invite him to sit. "What kind of matters?"

"Concerning your mother," said Stern. "I am hoping to have a candid discussion with you."

Peter virtually winced. Perhaps it was the subject—or more likely the notion of an open exchange with his father. Ignoring his son's lack of hospitality, Stern wandered farther into the living room, looking about. "Very nice," he said. He had been here only once, after the closing, when the place was empty and entirely white.

"Look, Dad," said Peter, "I'm kind of into something right now."

"I do not anticipate a lengthy discussion, Peter. I suspect I shall have rather more to say than you, and that is not very much."

"What about?"

Stern, at last, helped himself to a seat on the foam sofa.

"Peter, I have long suspected that you were concerned for more than your own emotional well-being when you urged me not to allow an autopsy of your mother."

Peter stared straight at him, his blue eyes and gaunt face still.

"Frankly, I was thrown off when I visited you at your office," said Stern. "You seemed so easily convinced that I had come there because a new partner of mine had this problem. I realize now that your theory was that I had been infected before, sub-clinically, and was the one who had actually passed this on to my new acquaintance. That was why you insisted on such a rigorous course of testing."

Watching with a frantic, disbelieving look, Peter suddenly held up both hands.

"Dad, not now."

"I am not here to criticize you. On the contrary, I believe—"

Peter leaned down to his father and spoke with a determined clarity.

"Dad, there's somebody here. I have a guest."

With that, on cue, a distinct cough was emitted from the bedroom. There was no mistaking the sound, either.

It was a man.

"I see," said Stern. He stood up at once. As resolved as he was to resist this, a response of dizziness, sickness gripped him. This lifestyle, choice—whatever it was called—remained beyond him. Not the acts, but the very philosophy. Stern, in truth, did not care much for men. They were rough, sometimes vicious, and generally unreliable. Women were far better, except, of course, they frightened him. "Well, we must speak soon," said Stern. He attempted to look at his son, but failed by a fair margin and instead let his eyes fall to the toe of his shoe. There he saw a briefcase, the visitor's no doubt, resting against the block of laminate that passed for the coffee table. The case was zippered, blue vinyl, with a large brass tag hanging from it. Stern had seen the case before. With that realization, he felt an outbreak of something else—panic, riot, emotion out of control: the man was someone he knew.

"Look, we'll have dinner," said Peter.

"This evening?"

"Not tonight. But I'll call." Peter rested a hand on his elbow.

It was, of course, weak and sick. There were secrets he could live without knowing, were there not? Life's compulsions were hopeless. Obliquely, Stern glanced back at the briefcase. The tag was an enlargement of the man's business card—Stern had seen these items before—but it was not visible from here. He let Peter lead him two steps to the door.

"Sometime this week," said Stern. "Soon after, I may be in jail."

"Jail?"

"An interesting story."

Peter at once waved a hand. He did not want to know—or to have his visitor hear it. With that, that clue, there was a sudden pulse of alarm. Stern let his eyes shift to the case again. With the gift of farsightedness, the tag might be legible.

And it was. Not the name, actually. He recognized the crest. When he did, Stern pulled his arm free from Peter's grasp and bent to be sure he had made no mistake.

"Oh, shit," said Peter behind him.

Stern stood up and covertly pulled on the hem to straighten his jacket, a courtroom gesture that he used before confronting a difficult witness.

"Agent Horn," said Stern loudly. "Show yourself."

"Oh, shit," Peter said again, more despairingly.

Stern did not bother to look back at his son. He was watching the bedroom door.

"How do you say it, Agent? 'Don't make me come in there to get you'?"

Kyle Horn, in his sport coat and white shoes, stepped into the living room. He was chewing gum, trying to smile.

"Hey, Sandy," he said.

When Stern finally glanced about, Peter had taken a seat on his sofa and was looking out the window toward the far distance, where he no doubt wished to be. Horn, shameless, had continued smiling. Stern was erect as a soldier.

"Please tell the distinguished United States Attorney for me that it will be a most interesting set of motions."

Horn at once shook his head.

"We didn't do anything wrong. Nobody's rights got violated. You can just cool it."

"I shall not 'cool it.' Any person of decent sensibility will be deeply offended. To use counsel's son—the target's nephew—as an informant?"

"It was all done right," said Horn. He approached Stern briefly and snatched his case from near Stern's shoes. "You'll see."

"I shall never see," said Stern.

Horn was near the door. He pointed to Peter, a form of goodbye.

"Stay in touch," he told Peter.

"What can I say, Kyle? 'Shit happens'?"

"Hey," said Horn as he opened the door. He actually winked. "Life," he told Peter, "is full of surprises."

46

"I'm not sorry," Peter said to his father. "It was the right thing to do. So don't give me your disdainful look."

Peter held his father's eye a second, then moved away. From his refrigerator, he removed a bottle of soda, pulled off the cap, and sat alone at the small butcher-block table, where he drank down the contents. When he belched he covered his mouth, then appeared to concentrate on the wall.

Stern eventually followed him into the kitchen, a narrow whitewashed space built with typical late-century efficiency, the toaster and microwave slotted beneath the cabinets. Stern swung his dark suit jacket over the back of the wire-mesh chair opposite Peter's and sat. His son glanced at him once or twice.

"Peter, I believe I am representing an innocent man."

Peter removed something from his tongue and stared at his fingers.

"He hasn't told you anything, has he?"

Stern reflected. "Very little."

"That figures. I couldn't imagine you were holding back for tactical reasons." He was still not looking at his father. "I was pretty sure you didn't know."

"I know enough, Peter, to believe you have been spreading lies."

Peter turned to him then.

"Don't make judgments," he said. "You don't understand how it happened."

Neither spoke. The compressor clicked on in the refrigerator and a bus wheezed by down in the street. Peter flexed his jaw about ruminatively.

"About five or six weeks before Mom died," said Peter, "Kate comes to see me. One morning, before school. She's forty-five minutes in traffic and as soon as she gets here she does a beeline for the john and I hear her retching. So the great diagnostician says, 'You know, maybe you're pregnant.' And she answers, 'I am. That's why I came. I need the name of a decent place to get an abortion.'

"I'm like, what? And so she tells me this long, involved story. About John. How he thinks he'll never be anything that matters. How inferior he feels in this family. You know, everything we've all thought to ourselves a million times. And how, because of that, and because of her, too, he's done something really stupid at work. Really, really stupid.

"He had his heart set on becoming a floor trader. I guess his idea was that if he could show some ability, he was going to ask you and Mom to put up the money so he could rent a seat. But Uncle Dixon wouldn't really let him near the pits. John kept asking. But Dixon thought the same thing about him as everybody else: dumb as a post. And he's not. He really is not."

"Apparently not," said Stern. Peter, absorbing his father's dry tone, actually smiled.

Kate, Peter said, believed no one would take John seriously until he could demonstrate that he had made money trading. So she suggested they open an account at MD. He was right there on the central desk. He could put in his own orders. It would be almost as if he were in the pits. Kate signed the forms. They both knew that employees of member firms weren't supposed to trade, but it was a minor infraction, Peter said. Everyone did it.

"And they call it Wunderkind because that's what he is, you know, in their heads, that's who they figure he'll be." Peter dwelled on the thought. "I guess he'd promised her he could scrape together $5,000 to get started, but neither one of them is making much money, and so, eventually, he got another idea."

The idea was trading ahead. He'd put in small orders here when he knew that big orders were going to be executed in Chicago or New York. And he'd learned enough when he'd worked in MD's operational areas to know how to use the house error and Wunderkind accounts to hide the profits.

"He promised himself that he was only going to do it once or twice, just to get himself started. Famous last words from the penal colony, right?" Peter asked.

"Those," said Stern, "and 'Just one more time.'"

"Right." Peter actually laughed for a second. Then he sobered himself and went on. "Obviously, the front-running worked. But when he traded, the money was gone like that." Peter snapped his fingers. "He decided he didn't have enough capital to handle the ups and downs in the market. What he needed was real money. So he traded ahead again, say thirty times, and picked up $300,000 in a month."

"And why did he simply not buy his seat on the Exchange at this point?" asked Stern.

"Why didn't he do a lot of things?" Peter smiled, in a way. "I think basically he was afraid to. He couldn't explain to anybody where the money came from. And, frankly, he still didn't know his ass from a hole in the ground as a trader. He'd have lost the seat in a week. He wanted to try to stay even for a couple of months."

"And how much, may I ask, did your sister know about this?"

"Kate?" Peter leveled a hand. "Obviously, she knew about the Wunderkind account. But she didn't know where the initial money came from. Not yet."

"Not yet," said Stern, mostly to himself.

Peter removed two more bottles of soda from the refrigerator, and plunked one, uncapped, in front of his father. It was French mineral water, a brand Stern had never heard of, savored with a rose-petal aroma. Stern asked for a glass.

"I take it John lost the $300,000?"

"Right. He did a little better, but eventually it was gone."

"And so he stole again."

"If that's what you call it."

"That is what I call it," said Stern. "That is what a prosecutor would call it. And that is what a judge would call it when he or she committed John to the penitentiary."

Peter, in front of the white cabinets, turned about.

"Look, Dad, I spent summers down there. I'm not making excuses for him, but it's like nothing really exists. It's all numbers on a scoreboard. That's all. You trade ahead of customers, in ten or twenty lots, you don't hurt a soul. Not really. It's against the rules because if everybody did it the customers would get maimed. But one guy? No harm. It was found money. And it's money that a lot of people down there have found. You think Dixon never traded ahead of a customer?"

"No one has ever cited Dixon as a moral exemplar."

"That's for sure," said Peter with a flash of the same hard light he had shown when he said he wasn't sorry.

Stern told his son to go on.

It was at this point, Peter said, that Kate found out. There was a confession, said Peter, lots of tears.

"She makes him promise that he won't do it again. He's ripped off another 275 K by now, and he reassures her. No way. No chance. He'll never have to do it again. And promptly goes right into the dumper in the market. So he's down to his last twenty, thirty thousand, and he makes The Big Mistake. He hears all these rumors about left-handed sugar. You know about that?"

"Enough," said Stern.

"John thinks he's got inside dope—he bets the ranch that the world sugar market is going to collapse. And he gets creamed. Destroyed. The market goes up so fast he can't even get out. When the smoke clears, not only has he lost every penny in the Wunderkind account, he now owes MD $250,000 to pay for the losses in the value of the positions over and above his equity."

"Enter Dixon?" asked Stern.

"Almost," said Peter. "First, John panics. You can say anything you want to about what he did, but it was low risk. Different Exchanges? And the best bean counter in America couldn't follow the paper trail between the error account and the Wunderkind account without someone to help him. But now, with a quarter-million-dollar deficit, he's in deep. Obviously, they have no money. And he can't like come to the family for a loan. So he takes what seems to be the only alternative. He starts trashing all the records that show who owns the account—you know, the idea is that way they can't find him. He zaps the computer system, he cleans out the files here. He fries up the microfiche. Unfortunately, the duplicate fiche is in Chicago. John had actually called a clerk there with some bullshit and had him ready to send the dupes, but the clerk asked what's-her-name first. Who's in charge there?"

"Margy Allison."

"That's it." Margy, Peter said, called Dixon, who by then had heard from MD's accounting department about the Wunderkind account and its sizable deficit balance. Dixon told Margy to send him the records John had requested. When he summoned John to his office two days later, Dixon had the pages he'd printed out off the fiche and the account statements spread across his desk.

"He had John sit down in one of those Corbusier chairs he's got, the deep square ones with the stainless-steel frames? Then he gets hold of John by the tie, puts his knee in his chest, and beats the living crap out of him. Quite a scene, apparently. Dixon's big, but he's not John's size. But John lies there like a lump, bleeding and crying, just sort of begging."

Peter grabbed a bit at his rumpled hair. Dixon by then had written his own check for the deficit in the Wunderkind account. He preferred that to admitting to his best customers, the ones who had placed the large orders John had traded ahead of, that no one noticed while an employee—worse yet, a relation—had stolen them blind. And he couldn't simply write off the debit without drawing a great deal of attention from his in-house accountants. It was all one pocket or the other, anyway, and to cover himself with the customers, Dixon preferred to keep this quiet.

"But, of course," said Peter, "Uncle Dixon was tear-ass. John's fouled his nest, put the whole business in jeopardy, and Uncle Dixon announces that John's going to pay for it, Dixon-style. Big speech. 'You are now my fucking slave.'" Peter thrust his elbows out in imitation of Dixon and rumbled on; he was an able mimic. "'You've seen your last raise or bonus in this century, and you'll do anything I decide you'll do, whenever I want. You'll be a floor runner or a window washer or the guy who cleans the latrines, if that's what I say. And if you ever think about leaving, or so much as crap crooked, I'll ruin you. I'll take the hit with the customers, and I'll call the CFTC , the FBI, George Bush, anybody I can think of, and I'll tell them this has been laying heavy on my soul, and I'll beg them to fry your ass.' And to back it up, Dixon makes a big show of taking all the account records and throwing them in his personal safe and telling John that they're always going to be there."

"John believed Dixon would carry through?"

"You bet your life."

Stern thought about Margy's story and the legend of Dixon's wrath murmured among his employees. Dixon, no doubt, was convincing when he bragged about his own cruelty.

"In fact, Uncle Dixon says, on second thought, he *will* turn John in. He's going to turn him in tomorrow. Tomorrow comes and he says it'll be the day after that. Then he's back on the fence. And so this is John's life. He works on the order desk. Then, when everybody's gone, Dixon finds something humiliating for him to do, like sort the trash. And then every other day Dixon says he's thought it over, the best course for him is just to drop the dime on John. One day he calls John to his office, while he phones the CFTC Enforcement Division and has this long chat about error accounts. He gets hold of a photo of John and draws bars across it. He even gives John the draft of a letter that Dixon says he's sent to the U.S. Attorney. Every day, it's something else. My beloved uncle is practicing extreme mental cruelty. Hard to believe of him, of course."

Stern, tempted to comment, said nothing at all.

"So that's where this thing is when Kate comes to see me. John is in Uncle Dixon's prison, which by now, he figures, is ten times worse than the real thing. At this point, Kate and he have decided the only thing John can do is bite the bullet: John will call the FBI and confess and go to prison, and Kate will terminate her pregnancy. This is their life plan. And nobody's kidding. All right?"

Peter finished his soda and burped again. He nodded to his father.

"Did you think perhaps," said Stern after a moment, "that I might be helpful in an arena in which I have worked for most of my life?"

"First of all, Dixon was your client, which means he was an object of religious worship. And second, what the hell would you do?"

"Obviously, I would speak with Dixon."

"And how would you prevent him from going to the FBI? That's what he said he'd do. That would leave John without even the benny of having turned himself in."

"I would ask Dixon not to do so."

"And he's always done just what you wanted, right?" His son had lifted his face to a haughty angle. Peter was an angry young man, no doubt about that. Life deeply dissatisfied him—people failed him in all respects. He was not gay, Stern suddenly thought. He was, rather, oddly misanthropic. He rendered help out of some sense of superiority or noble duty, but he expected—perhaps even enjoyed—disappointment, time and again. He had full faith in no one. In this, Stern realized, to a greater measure than he wished, Peter was his son.

"I thought about this for a long time. I went to dinner out there and I talked to Kate and John all night. I took Dixon's little letter to the U.S. Attorney home with me, where he'd laid out the whole scam. I kept going over the details. And then, of course, I figured out the answer. The obvious fucking answer: John *should* go to the FBI. But..." Peter, maestro-like, had lifted both hands.

"Yes?"

"But blame Dixon. Say it was *all* Dixon's show. John was minorly involved, just the flunky."

They looked intently at one another.

"Very clever," said his father at last.

"I thought so." Peter smiled stiffly, for effect. "Of course, there were a few problems. For one thing, John could never carry this off. Not on his own. He didn't have the nerve left to walk down the street by himself, let alone bullshit the FBI."

"So you volunteered?"

"Yes."

"You became his representative."

"Right."

"His defense lawyer," said Stern.

Peter did not answer; it was clear, however, that he had never thought of it this way.

"Is that truly, Peter, how you imagine this business is conducted?"

"Oh, spare me," he said. "I sat at your dinner table too long. How many people have you gotten immunity for who were lying their asses off and blaming whoever the government wanted to hear about?"

"Far fewer than you apparently imagine, Peter. And in any event, whatever fictions were spoken I had not created."

"No? Were they 'fictions' you really believed? I know. You're just the lawyer. If the client has the balls—or the brains—not to tell you he's lying, you pass him along without comment. And how many of those little fairy tales have you helped shape?"

Peter was the son. He knew his father's life well.

"There are distinctions, Peter. I think as little of your presumption in this matter as you would, were I to perform open heart surgery."

"Look," said Peter. "It was my sister." He resumed once more his aspect of inspired anger. The challenge was there: my sister. Your child. They stared again at each other.

"So you called the FBI," said Stern.

Peter met Kyle Horn in the lobby of a downtown hotel. They adjourned to the men's room and searched one another for electronic devices. Then Peter made his proposal. He was uninvolved himself, but he knew a man. The man had a boss who was one of the biggest names at the KCFE. There was a scam. The man was involved—at the bottom, not the top—and he was scared.

He would tell all—but only for immunity and a promise that Peter's part in arranging this would never be revealed. Take it or leave it, Peter told him.

"And the government agreed?"

"Not at first. I had to meet Sennett. They made me go over the whole thing about four times. Finally, I let them interview John in person. All hush-hush, since they wanted John to be able to stay undercover. But I could see they would go for it from the day I gave them Dixon's name. They actually made jokes about RICO'ing the place and calling it Maison Stan."

Maison Stan, thought Stern.

"Did they know you were my son?"

"I told them."

"They must have been very amused."

"I suppose. Mostly, they were concerned. None of us knew for sure who Dixon would use as his lawyer, but once you showed up I got all kinds of bulletins and memos and guidelines and crap about never discussing the case with you. Which I've followed. For the last three weeks they've been telling me I've got to stay away from Marta, too, and I have.

"We all sort of panicked when what's-her-name, Margy, sent out that memo saying you were going to talk to the people on the order desk. But Sennett had figured for a while that they were going to have to subpoena John to keep his cover, so they did it then and told you that you couldn't represent him. Pretty cute, huh?" Peter smiled faintly. Stern did as well. All deserved. They had run rings around him.

"I take it that Mr. Tooley was another player in your farce?"

"More or less. I suggested him and Sennett thought that was great. I think at one point Stan told Mel not to ask too many questions, which was fine with him. He's not your biggest fan."

"Indeed not," said Stern. Peter had located all his father's foremost antagonists and joined league with them. In the midst of everything else, Stern was stung by the thought, and he stood, walking across the tiny kitchen to the counter. For some reason he found himself recalling the early years, when the children were piled with pillows and blankets into the back of the current sedan and the entire family went to the drive-in for a movie. Only Peter of the three children remained awake. Even at the age of six or seven, he would watch the entire show, entertaining his parents with his curiosity about the world of adults, while the girls pressed their tiny hands to their faces and slept.

"You know you have inflicted terrible misery on your uncle."

Peter's eyes lighted on him briefly, holding the same hard gleam.

"I told you I wasn't sorry."

"You believe Dixon deserved this? For what—his treatment of John?"

"For lots of things. He's lived a piggish life."

"I see," said Stern. "For what other grave sins of Dixon's were you attempting to deliver retribution?"

Peter was silent. Eventually, he looked away.

"Help me with the chronology, Peter. When, exactly, did Nate Cawley tell you about your mother's condition? Clearly, it was near the time of these events."

Peter, using his thumb, peeled the paper wrapper off his soda bottle. He was worrying his head somewhat, disappointed about something.

"Nate told me last week he talked to you about Mom. He swore he kept me out of it."

"He did not mention your name," said Stern. "As I said when I arrived, I have been mulling over the circumstances."

Peter shrugged indifferently. He was not certain he believed his father, but that was beside the point.

"He felt someone in the family had to know, because of the

state she was in. He figured I was another doctor, you know. He wanted me to keep an eye out and my mouth shut. Needless to mention," said Peter, glancing fleetingly at his father, "He thinks he made a rather serious error."

"Nate has been hardest on himself, Peter. He even believed that I might sue him. Did you know that?"

"I knew." Peter nodded. "I thought it was possible, frankly. He you got the whole story. I figured you'd regard it as the height of irresponsibility that he involved me rather than you."

Stern meditated an instant on Peter's dim hopes for him. They expected, inalterably, the worst of each other.

"On the contrary, I believe it was prudent. I am certain you did your utmost. You were a devoted son, Peter, to your mother."

Peter puckered his lips a bit at the final words, but said no more.

"And how had you divined what Dixon's role was in your mother's illness?"

Peter looked up. "I'd taken a medical history from him. Remember? I was his doctor. After I talked to Nate, I checked my notes. The dates matched. He had gonorrhea, too, in Korea, did you know that?"

It had not come up in discussion, said Stern.

"He thinks it made him sterile," Peter said. It was a thought, a professional observation. With it, he walked into the other room and sat down on the blue foam sofa. His bravery, his moral certitude seemed to be flagging. His look was turning abject.

"So, when you heard about John's dilemma, it was not entirely accidental that you began to consider how this might be turned back against Dixon." Peter did not answer. Stern approached from the kitchen. "It was gallant of you, Peter, to fight your mother's battles. Not to mention mine." Stern, standing, took a moment to turn a dark countenance on his son, then moved to the window. Evening was coming through a great rosy sky. The last of the near-town commuters were in the street now, a stream of isolated persons carrying home, from various fancy shops, dinners which they would eat in silence, alone. "And may I now demand the last piece, Peter?"

"Which is?"

"How was it that your mother came to learn of this scheme to accuse Dixon?"

In his surprise, Peter let forth a brief sound—part laughter, part groan.

"You're smart," Peter said to him. "I'll always give you that."

Stern dipped his head in appreciation. "And the answer?"

"She could see how distraught Kate was. She knew something was wrong. Finally, she pried some of it out of her. Kate told her what John had done at MD. And that I was trying to work it out. No details."

"And of her pregnancy Kate said what?"

"Nothing. Not a word. She still wasn't positive she wouldn't have to terminate."

Slowly, Stern nodded. That would fit.

"Anyway, so Mom came to see me, to find out what was going on. I told her she shouldn't worry about it. But naturally that didn't satisfy her."

"And so you informed her what you had done?"

"Yeah. Eventually."

"Thinking what? That she would be delighted? That she, of all people, would share your desire for vengeance on Dixon?"

"You don't have to try to make it sound so ludicrous."

"Oh, I see your logic, Peter. You carried in Dixon like a cat out mousing and laid him at your mother's feet. And her reaction—shall I guess?—was horror."

"Horror," said Peter. "I tried to explain it to her. You know. That it was the best thing for everybody in the end, but she wouldn't hear it."

"And how far along had your plan proceeded by then?"

"Pretty far. Sennett'd met John. It was just about a done deal. I'd refused to let him take a lie detector, but we'd agreed that he'd stay undercover at MD and wear a hidden tape recorder—what do they call it? Wear a wire."

"On Dixon?" By the window, Stern was still. "And what was to happen when your uncle was tape-recorded denying any role in the scheme?"

Peter looked at him at length. "You still don't get it, do you?"

Weary of being derided, Stern closed his eyes for an instant and searched in himself for restraint.

"I had to explain it to Mom, too. The idea wasn't to get Uncle Dixon for what John did. I mean, he didn't do it, after all. I knew he would deny it. He'd say it was all John's doing. And John would say Dixon was scared and was trying to save his skin by blaming the whole thing on him. It would be a pissing contest in the end, a flatfooted fucking tie. There'd be nobody to prosecute because the government would never know which version was true. Everybody'd just go on. With no jail. And no torture. It was a decent solution for both of them."

"But?"

"But he kept his mouth shut. Uncle Dixon did."

"Why?"

Peter threw both hands in the air.

"You ask me? You're his lawyer. I don't know what's going on. I sit awake at night. I just can't believe it's gone as far as it has. Have you got any idea?"

Stern pondered, reluctant to speak.

"I have suspected for a few days now that he is assuming blame that properly lies with John and Kate. I cannot imagine what would move him to do that, particularly given what you tell me." He turned back to the old double-hung window, the frame lumpy with generations of paint. "And what happened to this plan to tape-record Dixon?"

"That's why they were trying to subpoena him. In March? They were sure he'd go running for John as soon as he was served. It was a setup. John was wearing the equipment for two weeks. But the agents could never find Dixon. And once they did, he wouldn't talk to John. I mean, not even hello or goodbye. There hasn't been word one between them in months. Uncle Dixon just gives him his killer look—John is still terrified. Sennett figures you'd warned Dixon not to go near him."

"Need I ask, Peter, how Agent Horn was finally able to find your uncle to serve him that day?"

"No, you needn't ask. They were supposed to catch up with him outside, as he came in."

Stern shook his head. How pitiful it was. He returned to the kitchen for his suit coat.

"You've placed yourself in enormous jeopardy, Peter. If the government is ever able to piece this together, you will join your brother-in-law in prison."

"Oh, I was scared at first. But the three of us talked about what would happen if it all went to shit." Peter smiled wanly. "How do they prove I knew John was lying?"

Peter had learned a good deal in those years sitting at his father's dinner table with his bored, superior look. When his children were young, Stern would look at them, arrayed at that table, with such gratitude—they were all clever, all healthy, all pleasing to the eye. They had every good fortune, he thought.

"They were never really skeptical," said Peter. "After they went out to the bank and confirmed that Dixon had written the check to cover the debit on the Wunderkind account. They never seemed to figure there could be any other reason he might do it. And, of course, Dixon had the records that showed who owned the account, and was hiding them. And what's-her-name even lied for him in the grand jury. It looked pretty convincing," said Peter.

"You are referring to Margy?"

"Yeah. Kyle says that after the indictment they'll give her a chance to 'refresh her recollection.'" He made the quotation marks in the air.

Stern straightened the sleeves on his coat. His son, reconsidering everything, sat with his head in his hands. Occasionally, Stern was called upon to represent young people—sixteen, seventeen, eighteen years old, children really—who had taken part in events so heinous that they would be tried as adults. The most recent example was Robert Fouret, a sulky college freshman who, stoned on something, had put his father's Porsche in drive rather than reverse and crushed his waiting girlfriend against the garage wall, killing her. In these circumstances Stern always felt for the parents, wealthy people who had retained him in the hope that he could repair all damage, and who discovered in time that not even a favorable sentence would still the reverberations of great wrongs. It was the parents who saw clearly, helplessly, the way the excesses and impulses of youth, stupid empty-headed acts, childish compulsions acted out in an instant, could burden and even extinguish the opportunities of a young life. Stern saw this, too. But he spared himself, at least for the moment, that anguish.

For the moment, all that made itself clear was that his son and he had reached a point of termination. Within, in his own emotional theater, some final curtain had come splashing down. No doubt he had responsibilities here; he would suffer intensely when it came time to assess blame. But for now he knew that the years—the virtual half of an adult lifetime—of recriminations, of ambivalent efforts with Peter were past. He would greet his son always with absolute cordiality—he owed his mother's memory that much—and he knew that they would forever regard one another with pain. But something essential was over; he was done, he saw, awaiting improvement, acceptance, or change.

He was ready to leave now, but he had learned in the law that the pronouncement of judgments mattered, perhaps more than anything else.

"Peter, I shall say this once. What you have done is unforgivable. It is wholly immoral. And, as important, you have risked unlimited misery for everyone in this family."

Peter took this in quietly, but finally made a sound to himself and once or twice bobbed his head.

"That's what Mom thought. She was terrified. It was the dumbest move of my life, telling her." Peter looked up. "I'm sure it was the last straw." His face was divided by a visible palsy, a tremor of contained emotion. It came to Stern then, a clear realization that, whatever the impact of the awful judgments which Peter applied to others, he afflicted them most severely on himself. He had bid his mother, the dearest soul in his life, farewell for eternity, with her parting expression one of withered hope and dashed beliefs. There was no denying biology. Stern found himself terribly moved by his son and his now interminable anguish.

He stepped toward the door.

"What are you going to do, Dad? What's going to happen?"

Peter, like sons always, still wanted to believe that his father was a man of infinite resources, perfect solutions. Just now, however, Stern had no ideas at all.

47

Marta returned home sometime after ten. From his recliner in the solarium, Stern heard her enter, humming faintly, off-key. Alone among the Stern family, Marta had had a good day. She came back from the courthouse ebullient. 'Even she couldn't stand it,' said Marta about Klonsky. She was thrilled to think she had converted a prosecutor. Back at the office, she had called George Mason with the news, then dictated their brief to Judge Winchell. Finished with that, Marta asked, offhandedly, if there were cases around the office on which she could lend a hand while she was looking for a job. Pay by the hour. Stern, after a moment's reflection, decided his thought was too hopeful and referred her to Sondra.

By the afternoon Marta had set herself up in the one empty office and was examining the flood of files recently received in connection with the new government fraud case, writing longhand or chatting happily on the telephone whenever Stern wandered by. Marta seemed to live her life like an appliance. Plug her in anywhere and she operated on full current. His daughter amazed him, but his soul still soared at the thought of having her company. They would continue this way for some weeks. He would be himself, and hold his breath. And would this prospect even have been possible had Clara lived? No, he decided after an instant, not really. There were many reasons Marta suddenly found the tri-cities attractive, and not the least of them, in all likelihood, was the fact that her mother was gone. So, he thought, goes the heartsore arithmetic of human events. Loss and gain.

Now, in the solarium, he closed his eyes when he heard her

approach. "Are you asleep?" she whispered. He could feel her creep close, but did not stir. Tonight he was not prepared for any further commerce with his children, even Marta. He remained inert, listening as she trod the stairs. He had no thought of sleep, no inclination. Around one, he moved to the kitchen and sat under the green glass shade over the breakfast table, sipping sherry, as he had the night Clara was discovered. He was past judgments for the time being. Nor was he absorbed yet with the trigonometries of possible solutions. Instead, he sat, deliberating, taking stock, mourning again, up to his chin in the heavy glop of something like heartbreak, which held him fast as quicksand.

Near 5:30 a.m., he crept upstairs, showered, and dressed. He percolated coffee and warmed a roll from the freezer. Then he headed downtown, to the refuge of work and the office. He entered through the back door and stood still. There was, once more, some faint sign of disturbance.

Dixon was back.

He was on the sofa in Stern's office, upright this time, but asleep. His fancy loafers were off, carefully paired, not far from where the safe still remained, and he had slept with his legs crossed at the ankle. He wore a raw-silk sport coat—the air conditioning had apparently been left on high overnight and the room was chilled—and his arms were thrown out wide along the top of the nubby off-white fabric of the sofa cushions. His chin rested on the bold pattern of his tropical shirt.

Stern stood before the dark glass of his desk, silently lifting the stacks of papers from his attaché case.

"You must have thought that was pretty goddamn funny the other day." Dixon spoke clearly, but he had not moved. "That bullshit with the safe? 'You deceive me, Dixon.'" He opened his eyes. "Like you're some fucking oracle." Putting a hand to his neck, he craned his head about. "You must have been laughing your ass off. Since you'd already pawed through the thing."

"Ah," said Stern. Silvia. A breach of security.

"I got a bill from the guy who fixed the back door. You should have heard your sister. 'Oh, that's from Alejandro.' La di da." He had briefly adopted a falsetto. "Like, Oh, didn't I mention that my brother hired a goon to kick the door in. Four hundred bucks, by the way. I expect you to pay."

Dixon had his fearsome, lightless look and a haggard appearance. He was unshaven and visibly weary; his eyes seemed shrunken within the dark orbits. Reminded, he asked Stern to dial his home. Stern pressed a button on the speed dial and handed him the phone, while he left to put up coffee in the small kitchen down the hall. When he returned, Dixon was just bidding Silvia goodbye.

"Your sister says you and I have to stop meeting like this." Dixon laughed. Silvia's humor was awkward, but Dixon adored it. "I see you're not in jail."

Stern lifted both hands to show off his entire large form.

"I called Marta," said Dixon. "She said your girlfriend there, what's-her-name, saved your ass."

"For the time being," said Stern. "Festivities will resume next week. Will you come to visit me?"

"Visit you," muttered Dixon. "What's your game, Stern?"

"My game?" He revolved fully to consider his brother-in-law, a courtroom turn. "Have you found another lawyer, Dixon?"

"I don't want another lawyer. I changed my mind."

"You need another attorney, Dixon. A lawyer and client must have confidence in one another."

"I have confidence in you."

"But I, Dixon, have no confidence in you—in your character or your motives. You are a vain, disloyal, deceitful man. You are a terrible client and, if you care, a wretched friend."

Dixon blinked a bit and rubbed his eyes.

"I'm not a friend," said Dixon finally. He still had no idea what was going on, and he smiled weakly. "I'm a relation. You can't get rid of me."

"On the contrary. I am exhausted by the mysteries of your affairs. And your disdain for me."

"Disdain?"

"Among the legion of resentments I bear you, Dixon, I believe that none is greater than this: there is no person in the world who has better insight into Clara's death than you. And you have kept those details to yourself. Undoubtedly for your own good, to serve some misbegotten and bewildering personal agenda."

"You're jerked off because I didn't mention that check she gave me."

Stern did not answer.

"And there's really a simple explanation."

"Dixon, you are about to lie to me again."

"No," he said, with his frozen innocent look.

"Yes."

"Stern," he said.

"You owe me some regard, Dixon."

"I have a lot of regard for you."

"Dixon, I may be befuddled for the remainder of my lifetime about your motivations, but I have no doubts about Clara's. I am one of those Jews who can do arithmetic. Almost $600,000 stolen by trading ahead and $250,000 plus lost in the deficit in the Wunderkind account equal somewhat more than $850,000, which is the amount of the check Clara wrote against her investment account at River National. My wife was paying the debts her son-in-law incurred in the brokerage account her daughter had opened. And I would be pleased if you would not affront me by denying what is obvious."

"All right." He nodded once and began to pace, his mind clearly racing. "She knew John and I were both involved. She thought maybe I'd be willing to take all the heat myself. And she offered to pay the costs."

"A lie!" Stern slammed shut his case. Long-suffering, pusillanimous, he was suddenly on the rim of a smoking volcanic rage with Dixon. "Dixon, you may have convinced Margy long ago with that folderol about how you and John were secret conspirators and that you deserved all the blame, but I am well aware that you were never involved in this crime."

"Margy?" Dixon stopped. "I thought she was high on your shit-list."

"I have reevaluated." Stern was tempted to add a further word in her defense, having spoken in error about her when he and Dixon last met, but he remained convinced that somewhere along she had agreed to follow Dixon's bidding in what she told Stern. 'Leave the kid out.' He could hear Dixon saying it. "You may as well know, Dixon, that I have heard the entire tale: how you decided to spare your business and impose punishment yourself, and how you were informed against as a result."

Dixon waited, stood still, then finally retreated to the sofa to assess this new development. He removed his sport coat and threw it down there and, after further reflection, sat down beside it himself.

"As you conceived of matters originally, Dixon, how long was John intended to remain in your purgatory?"

Dixon jiggled a hand, as if something were in it. He was still manifestly uncertain about telling the truth.

"No time limits," he said at last. "As a matter of fact, I told him straight out that two or three years from now I'd probably go to the government and burn him, anyway."

"Apparently, he believed you."

"He should have," said Dixon. He gave his brother-in-law another direct and lightless look, the smoke of the conflagration still darkening his expression until he broke it off in order to reach for a cigarette. He tamped the filter repeatedly on the glass of the desk. "Of course, the big jerk never told me his wife was pregnant."

"Would that have made a difference?"

Dixon shifted his shoulders, not certain. "Probably. I might have thought a little more about the corner I was painting him into."

"And Clara?" asked Stern. "I would like to hear about your last meeting with her. How long before she died did it occur?"

"Three days? Four?" Dixon looked at his cigarette. "There's nothing special to tell. She showed up with that check. Like you say, she wanted to pay his debts. I told her not to bother. I wasn't having any. I wanted his ass, not a check. That's all. She insisted on leaving it. So I threw it in the safe. That's the whole story."

"That's hardly the whole story, Dixon."

"Yes, it is."

"No, Dixon. You were tempted to surrender John to the prosecutors. And not only lost your nerve but stood mute while his freedom was traded for yours. A remarkable transition."

Dixon Hartnell had come of age in the regions where the pressure of the earth had transformed organic wastes into something black and shining and nearly hard as stone. He had taken that lesson to heart—he had his look in place now, as dark and adamantine as if he derived his power to persist from the center of the earth. Transported from the coal lands to the heart of the markets, he had learned that his will was vast, and it was all imposed now. He had no more to say.

"Tell me about your hearing this morning. You really going to the pokey for my sake?"

"If need be. There are enough members of my family bearing witness against you." Dixon absorbed the remark with the same unyielding expression. "Do I take it correctly that Clara informed you of Peter's role in all this?"

Dixon smoked his cigarette without comment.

"Another lawyer, Dixon, might help you mount an excellent motion directed against the grand jury proceedings and the government's conduct *vis à vis* Peter. You would not even have to comment on the veracity of the information he's given them."

A flare of some interest arose in Dixon's face.

"Would I win?"

"In my judgment? No. You would be granted a hearing to determine that there had been no infringement of your right to counsel. Certainly, you could delay Mr. Sennett's steamroller. But I doubt a court would find outrageous governmental conduct or a violation of your rights. The government is more or less constrained to take its witnesses and informants where it finds them. It simply found this one in a rather inconvenient locale."

Dixon shrugged. He was not surprised. Stern again urged him to seek another lawyer's opinion, but Dixon waved a hand.

"I'll take your word for it." He stood then and roamed to the English cabinets. On one shelf, there were pictures, photographs of the family. Clara. The children. If the truth were told—and today once again the truth was required—Stern seldom examined these portraits. They were obligatory items, appropriate decoration. But Dixon paused to consider each photograph, holding them up, one by one, by their frames. Stern gave him the moment, until he was ready himself.

"And now, Dixon, if you please, I should like to know what happened when you met last with Clara. You may be brief. I shall settle for the high points. There is no need," said Stern, with sudden glottal thickness, "for you to dwell on that which you least wish to tell or which I frankly least wish to know."

Dixon wheeled about, maintaining considerable poise, to his credit, but Stern could see that he was wide-awake now. His eyes were larger, his posture almost militarily correct. If Dixon were to accept these rules, this terrain would always remain unexplored between them. After great reflection, Stern had decided he preferred that accord. But Dixon, alas, was who he was, a guts

player to the end. He blinked and looked at Stern straight on.
"Whatta you mean?" he asked.

"What do I mean?" Stern teetered for an instant, and then
toppled down into the smoking heart of his rage. He picked up
his attaché case and slammed it back down on the desktop.
"Shall I draw you pictures, Dixon! Shall we engage in a
dispassionate colloquy about the mortal hazards of sexually
transmitted disease? I refer, Dixon, to your relations with my
wife."

Dixon's grayish eyes did not move. When Stern glanced to the
desktop, he saw that it had cracked, a bullet-like impression at
the point of impact and a single silver line that skated from there
all the way across the smoky surface to the green beveled edge.
The desk, of course, had never been his taste.

"Do you expect me to explain?" Dixon asked. He had moved
behind his brother-in-law, and Stern chose not to face him.

"No."

"Because I can't. I really am a no-good son of a bitch."

"Are you trying to charm me, Dixon?"

"No," he said. "It was a long time ago, Stern."

"I am aware."

"It was an accident."

"Oh, please!"

"Wrong word." He heard Dixon's fingers snap. "Unintended."
When Stern pivoted, Dixon had come close and with an eager,
servile look had the humidor extended. "Cigar?"

Stern grabbed the whole box from him at once.

"Keep your hands off, Dixon!" The humidor ended caught up
in his arms. Stern removed a cigar and lit it, then snapped down
the lid with a round clap somewhat deadened by the felt liner.
He glowered at his brother-in-law while Dixon retreated to the
sofa, where he brought his lighter to another cigarette.

"It was all my fault, you know," he said. "You don't need me to
tell you that. I pestered her for years," he said. "Years." Some
image offered itself, of Dixon at a family gathering emerging
from shadows in the kitchen or the hall and placing his hands
suggestively on Clara's hips. Repelled. Rebuked. Something clear
and uncompromising, so that he would have feared disclosure.
But with her silence, Dixon, being himself, would have been
emboldened. He knew there was some small shining point of

interest he had ignited. Step by step, gesture, nod, and touch, year by year, he had kindled the firepoint, knowing that this possibility of passion was one more treasure to Clara, one more secret. Stern, inclined to imagine more, called a halt. Enough, he told himself. Enough. "I admired her," said Dixon. For the first time, he dared to look at Stern. "She was a woman to admire."

"Dixon. You have no conscience."

"No." He shook his head. "I'm curious. I've always wanted to do what other people wouldn't."

"I believe that is called evil, Dixon."

Dixon put out his cigarette. His mouth seemed to quiver like the muzzle of a dog. Dixon Hartnell was going to cry. His face was flushed near the eyes and he peered downward.

"I really never connected any of it with you."

"I find that hard to credit."

"I mean it."

"You are pathological, Dixon."

"Okay, then that's what I am." He was finally growing impatient with Stern. Self-criticism was not in Dixon's repertoire. He went forward in life, seldom looking back.

"May I ask, Dixon, when this interlude occurred?"

Dixon's face reared up; he was baffled. "What time of day?"

"Please, Dixon. When in the history of humankind did these events take place?"

"I don't know. It was right after Kate went to college. Clara was at the end of things. Very depressed. Swimming through all kinds of dark shit. You were on your big case in Kansas City. Busy, busy, busy."

"Is that your excuse, Dixon?"

Dixon eyed him as he removed another cigarette.

"I told you, I took advantage. She couldn't have cared less about anything. It was an act of despair," Dixon said. "Fucking despair."

"Thank you, Dixon, for your important psychological insight."

"She was destroying her life. She was getting even with you."

"Again," said Stern.

For the first time, he felt, absurdly, that it was likely he might cry. This was not what he wanted to hear, Dixon revealing to him Clara's hidden sides. Did Dixon really have it right? Close enough, probably. Clara had taken her reprisals, hoping that in what was most forbidden some dark magic might be found. She would soil and abase herself, pray for release, and if worst came to worst, she at least would have cause for her misery, her contempt for herself.

"It was *A* night and *A* day. And it was a complete bust," said Dixon. "A zero. I'm not just saying that now. If she hadn't come up with that problem, you could have said nothing happened."

"If," said Stern.

"Obviously, I hadn't noticed," said Dixon. "I'll never forget. She handed me a note at some family shindig. I still remember it. One line. She never wasted words. Not even Dear Asshole. Just 'I am being treated for...' " Dixon circled a hand to fill in the blank. "I had no idea. And then when I told your sister she had to be examined, she promptly tossed me out on my duff. And went to cry on Clara's shoulder. Talk about fucked up."

This drama, all of the play, had transpired entirely out of his presence. He roamed offstage in Kansas City. In the arms of his own jealous mistress. Absorbed in the role he liked best, he had managed to miss the signal events of his lifetime.

He smoked his cigar for some time then. The night without sleep had taken its toll. His eyes felt raw and his limbs, after the rush of anger, were now burning and weak. As for the cigar, he was shocked to find that its taste was no longer pleasing. He would finish it, of course. He had begun to smoke cigars in Henry Mittler's office when he could not really afford them, usually limiting himself to the ones Henry reluctantly supplied, and with a cigar in his hand he still experienced mixed sensations of absolute triumph and parched frugality. But he would have no difficulty, Stern thought, not picking up another. His life, after all, had changed.

"She came to my office," Dixon said. "Just showed up."

"Clara?"

"No, the man in the moon." He had lain down completely on Stern's sofa. "I knew why she had to be there. She hadn't said more to me than 'Pass the beans' for years."

"And?"

"And she came in, she sat down, and she cried. Jesus, did she cry." Dixon lay there a moment with the thought. "Not a dry eye in the house. Anyway, I heard the whole fucking story. Peter. John. Doctors. Treatment. What got me was the money. When she handed over the check, like she thought money—" Dixon lifted a hand, suddenly rheumy-eyed again, hurt once more to think Clara believed dollars might persuade him. In his own mind, of course, Dixon had no price.

"And what was her thought, Dixon? What did she want?"

"Want! What you'd think a mother would want. She wanted her children to be safe. She wanted me to figure a way out. That was the reason for the check. She thought maybe I could repay everybody, MD, all the customers, and wash it all out."

"And what did you tell her?"

"It was too frigging late for that. Peter had already started playing junior G-man."

"Did you understand that Peter's theory was that no one would be charged?"

"Yeah, I understood. That was strictly nuts. I figured if I opened my mouth, John and he would end up drawn and quartered. I thought even those jerks in the U.S. Attorney's Office could see through this. What's my motive, for Chrissake. I'm going to fuck around stealing nickels and dimes?"

"Did you tell Clara that?"

"She was a bright lady. She knew what the risks were. She was scared to death for all of them."

"And so?"

"And so what?"

"How did your conversation end, Dixon?"

"Oh, I don't know. The other reason she'd come was because of her medical condition. She wanted me to know that she might have to let you know the score. I mean, she wasn't worried for my sake—she was concerned Silvia would find out. Anyway, after she got through that, she put on this very composed look and said, 'Dixon, I am really not certain that I am able to carry on.' It was the scariest fucking moment of my life. I didn't have to ask what she was talking about."

"And how did you respond?"

"How the fuck do you think I responded? I begged her not to do it. For about half an hour. I gave her every reason I could think of. She kept talking about the children. Peter and Kate. And John. And you. A lot about you. She was completely unglued. You know, I tried to reassure her. I told her Peter and Kate and John would be okay," said Dixon. "But what could I really say to convince her of that?" He shrugged. "So I promised."

It was like everything else. Everything else. Like forms in the clouds. He had seen it but never made out the shape.

"You promised Clara," said Stern, "that you would stand mute when accused and accept the blame."

Dixon, on the sofa, let his arm dangle down. He flicked his ashes toward the ashtray and missed by a considerable margin. He sat up then and ground the heels of his palms against both eyes.

"May I ask why, Dixon?"

"I just told you why. Because I owed it to her. Look, I'm not you, Stern. I'm not wise or good. I can't help what I do. I can only be sorry afterwards. That's the story of my life. But I clean up my own messes."

They sat together for some time.

"I release you, Dixon."

"What?"

"I release you from this bargain. It was truly valorous. You were dealing for Clara's life, but in spite of your brave efforts, you failed. You may be released."

Dixon shook his head.

"I promised her."

"Dixon."

"I promised."

"I cannot permit this, Dixon."

"I didn't ask for your permission."

"I have thought about this at length, Dixon. I believe that John and Peter must be allowed to play their hands. Speak up. Hire another lawyer and through him tell the truth. See if the prosecutors end up confounded, as Peter calculated they would."

"And what happens if Sennett gets hit by lightning and actually believes me? If he turns on those two, it'll make what he's planning for me look like a party game."

Stern allowed his shoulders to move—his weary, mystical, foreign look. There were no words.

"Listen," said Dixon, "I've held my breath all the way along. I've hoped for months that those creeps would drop the ball over there. Fuck things up, or lose interest, or have doubts. But I won't play it that way. John will never make it. I've seen him when someone turns up the bright lights. In a courtroom, or with somebody really banging away at him, he'll fold. You mark my words. And he'll take Peter down with him. Maybe even Kate."

Dixon was correct—no question of that. He had thought this out carefully. John would be wearing wires on the entire family by the time Sennett was through with him.

"That was the risk Peter chose, Dixon."

"Oh, screw that. They're children."

Stern sat down on the sofa beside him. With a single finger, he actually touched Dixon's hand.

"Dixon, I understand your object. I recognize that you are attempting to settle accounts with me—that you wish to see the rest of my family remain intact. But I absolve you."

Dixon glared at him, rankled—no, more: outraged.

"Can't you just show some fucking gratitude and shut up?" He got to his feet. "I'm pleading guilty, Stern. And I want you to arrange it."

"I shall not."

"Don't give me that 'shall not' crap. This is the right thing."

"It is a fraud, Dixon."

"Oh, stow it, Stern. Don't start boasting with me about your honor. I've known you too long. You've whored around plenty for reasons worse than this. I'm talking about your children."

"No."

"Yes. You think you're the only one in this family with the right to be noble?"

"Silvia—"

"Silvia will be fine. She'll have you to take care of her. She'll see me on the weekends. You'll get me into some country club. I'll do that time standing on my head."

Dixon's primary talents were still in the arena of sales. Pacing here, he had taken on his urgent salesman's bearing. It was all bluster—Stern knew that. Dixon's haggard look and fitful nights were not due to the welcome prospect of country-club living. But Dixon had once been a soldier. He knew that courage was not the absence of fear but the ability to carry on with dignity in spite of it. At this instant he was oddly reminiscent of the young man Stern had met, with his strong chin and wavy brass-toned hair, wearing his uniform like a trophy and willing himself to glory—a perfect specimen of what Stern then believed to be the most enviable species on the planet, a true American.

"Dixon, it is wrong."

"Oh, fuck principle, Stern. Fuck your honor! Don't you understand, you sanctimonious asshole, that this was exactly why she was afraid to come to you?" In great heat, Dixon smote the desk once with his fist. The glass broke through with an odd tone—a clear snap and a whiny ringing. Both men moved at once. Stern rushed to his own side and, like Dixon, held the two pieces together. Along the crack, one edge was now barely below the other. The heaps of papers had tumbled and Stern's cigar had jumped out of the ashtray and lay in the cleft, still burning.

"Will it fall?" Dixon asked.

Stern was not certain. He finally swiveled his desk chair about and propped it beneath the separated halves. Slowly, Dixon removed his hands. The desk sagged barely, perceptibly, but moved no farther.

It required a second for Stern to recollect where they had been. The hammer fall of Dixon's observation had been lost in the commotion; for the moment, he was saved. He knew that Dixon had pondered this matter at length and was once more correct. Clara had doubted her husband's pragmatism, his willingness to yield his scruples, especially in a contest with his son. For the time being, however, he could put that thought aside; the suffering would come later, when he was alone. Right now, he felt a different curiosity, one that had arisen yesterday, with a remark of Peter's.

"Why am I your lawyer, Dixon? Now. In this matter?"

"Where else would I go? And besides, you might have thought something was up if I hired a different attorney."

"But you say you feared my principles."

"You weren't going to find out."

"Is that why you left the safe with me for so long?"

"It was locked."

"Nevertheless."

"Listen, you scared the shit out of me with that song-and-dance about search warrants. I believed you. I thought it was the best place for it."

"But you did not even take the precaution of destroying the check Clara had brought you."

"How could I? I figured the bankers would go look for it. Or the lawyer for the estate. I had my whole routine planned when they got here: 'She wanted to open a new investment account for the kids, died before we finished the papers, boy, am I glad to see you, sign right here.'" Dixon smiled at himself.

"Yet you must have recognized some risk that I might piece it together?"

Dixon leaned over the broken desktop.

"They're your children, Stern. You may give me all your high-minded advice about turning them in, but I don't see you banging down the prosecutor's door. You'd never do it." Dixon, with his canny, handsome face, his weary eyes, regarded his brother-in-law. "You'll do what I want. You've got to."

"You couldn't resist the game, Dixon, could you?"

Dixon shrugged. "Competitive instincts," he said.

"Why do you feel so improved by my weakness? You love to see me bend, Dixon."

They were still across from one another. But the traces of some forgotten laughter already sneaked through Dixon's expression in spite of his most disciplined efforts at suppressing it. He was wonderfully amused, tickled pink.

"I want to plead guilty," he said. He knew he had won, as he knew all along he would, if it came to this.

Stern went down the hall and returned with coffee for both of them. It was, he admitted, an opportune time to negotiate. Sennett would be reluctant to confront a motion concerning the government's relationship with Peter. While he would ultimately prevail, Sennett knew he'd be seriously criticized along the way. The judges would chastise him for his zeal and the defense bar would protest vehemently. The papers might say unpleasant things. Sennett would be eager to avoid the damage to his reputation.

"Sure," said Dixon, quick to agree.

"But I shall not let them stampede us in the interval. Sennett may seek to use the proceedings concerning me as leverage against you. I shall not negotiate from weakness. If they must hold me in contempt—"

"Fine, fine," said Dixon, "we can take adjoining cells." He handed Stern the phone.

It was before eight; the secretaries were not in. But they were in luck. Sennett picked up the line himself.

48

Sennett agreed to see him at four. The U.S. Attorney was cagey on the phone and asked what their meeting might concern, but Stern said merely that it was imperative that they speak. Sennett was at an obvious disadvantage, too apprehensive to ask him to elaborate. The idea came to Stern while they were still speaking. That brittle unyielding edge in Sennett's voice suddenly riled him, but before placing the call, he waited to see Dixon off, and to attend to a few matters on Remo's case, scheduled to start trial a week from Tuesday. By then, it was close to noon.

"Would you have a few minutes for lunch?" He had reached her directly.

"I'm not eating," Sonny said. "The heat's sort of got me." She hung on the line, waiting for something, probably an explanation. "If it's about your meeting with Stan, I won't be there."

More a personal matter, Stern responded. He would welcome a moment of her time. "Could you meet me at the Morgan Towers Club in twenty minutes?"

"Oh, Sandy, I hate those private clubs. I'm dressed like a bag lady. You know, with the heat." As always, the air conditioning in the new federal building had failed.

"I prefer a neutral locale." Away from her office, he meant. "For your sake. I promise there will be no fashion commentary."

"My sake?"

"When we meet," he responded.

He feared at first that she would not come. He sat in one of the overstuffed club chairs across from the elevators, watching the polished steel doors open and close and the business types disembarking. When Sonny arrived, she looked rosy and agitated and, as she herself was the first to acknowledge, out of place, dressed in a simple sleeveless maternity frock better for a country outing. Sonny seemed to have reached that point in her pregnancy where the premium was on merely surviving. There was a vague ungainly roll as she walked. Approaching, she removed a broad slouch hat, with a pink satin ribbon, which she had worn to protect herself from the sun.

"Here." Stern had raised a hand in greeting. He complimented her appearance, and asked again about lunch or a drink.

"I couldn't." She put a hand on her stomach and made a face. "And I'm on the run. Come on, Sandy. What's this about?"

On second thought, he led her down a hall to a rear cloakroom, a small space paneled in red oak, unused in the summer. The banging of the kitchen went on behind the wall, and the vegetable and meat smells of luncheon cooking emerged through the air returns. The place had a vague secret feel.

"I apologize for this maneuvering. I suspect Sennett might criticize you for meeting with me."

She made another face in response: Who cared?

"Sonny, I am deeply grateful for your act yesterday, but it was ill-advised. I am certain that the United States Attorney was displeased."

"I wouldn't call him cheerful."

"No doubt."

She was looking around for a chair. Her legs hurt, she said—she had walked over too quickly. He found a round back card chair in a corner. She put herself down in front of the empty coatrack and fanned herself with her hat. Stern remained standing.

"Sandy, what's the point?"

"Go to Stan, today. Tell him you have thought the matter over and that you are prepared to proceed with full vigor."

"I'm not ready to proceed with full vigor. And today he doesn't care, anyway. He's flipped out over the fact that you found out about"—she dropped a beat—"about the informant. He had four assistants in the library last night until two doing legal research. That's Stan. It's always this macho crap: it's okay because I say so. Then when it hits the fan he wants to call out the Marines to cover his derriere." She stopped abruptly. He knew that as usual she felt she had spoken too freely. "I had no idea, by the way,"

Sonny said. "You know, who it was. I finally asked Stan three days ago. Right after we got off the phone. I think it's sick."

"Sonny, I would not pretend I am not deeply chagrined, but I shall tell you in the privacy of this room that I do not believe the government's conduct in this matter was unlawful."

"Probably not," she said. "But it's shitty. If Stan didn't have a smirk on his face, it wouldn't bother me as much. It's not disembodied principles to him. It's a grudge."

"Sonny, there are no disembodied principles in the practice of law." He spoke with some weight. "There are human beings in every role, in every case. Personalities will always matter."

"It was over the line. The way he handled it." She fingered the ribbon on her hat. "Listen, Sandy, I wasn't doing you a special favor. At least, I don't think I was. I just got really uneasy with the idea of enforcing a subpoena based on that kind of information if we hadn't disclosed the source. I could just see it: the judge locks you up and then finds out there was a sensitive issue which the government never mentioned. She could land on us with both feet. I thought if you wrote a brief, maybe you'd raise it, maybe we would. It would give me a chance to talk to Stan again."

Stern nodded. Her reasoning had been cautious, sound. More thoughtful—more lawyerly—than her boss's.

"Don't think I'm not still pissed at you," Sonny said. "I am. That was an ugly little charade out in the country—asking me questions about those account papers, like you'd never seen them in your life."

"I had not seen them," he said simply. "Ever in my life."

She studied him intently, trying to figure it out, whether he was telling the truth, and if he was, how it could be.

"I really don't understand," she said, then raised a hand. "I know. You've got your confidences, right?"

"Correct."

"It must be a hell of a story." She shrugged. "I suppose that's why you don't want to tell it to the grand jury."

For an instant, he said nothing.

"Sonny, when we were in the country you shared as much as you could with me out of a sense of fairness. I would like to respond in kind. Speaking with Stan this morning, I am sure I left him with the impression that I wished to meet in order to complain about the government's use of my son as an informant. No question, I shall do a good deal of that. But assuming that Mr. Sennett is willing to make the concessions he ought to in the circumstances, I would expect our discussion to lead eventually to an agreement for Dixon to enter a guilty plea."

She took that in and then tipped her head admiringly.

"Nice timing," she said.

"I believe so." They both lingered with the thought of how far Sennett would go to prevent Stern from causing a stir about the government's tactics with Peter. "So, you see, there will be no further grand jury investigation or contempt proceedings."

She smiled when she made the connection.

"You want me to kiss and make up with Stan before he knows? Right?" Sonny laughed out loud. "Oo, that's sneaky," she said. "And, boy, does he deserve it."

Stern smiled with her, but did not speak. Sonny fanned herself again with her hat.

"Look, Sandy, I'm okay with him. He didn't fire me. He knew he should have clued me in a long time before on something this delicate. And besides, he's political enough to figure out the angles. An Assistant out there criticizing him on the issue? No way he can have that. He has to keep me inside the tent. He just took me off the case. He said I'm not objective about you." With that, due to the heat perhaps, or what she had said, or one of the many bodily quirks of pregnancy, her color rose again—her cheeks grew bright, so that for all the world he had the impression of a flower unfolding. "Which I'm not," she added quickly, showing a swift, rueful smile and allowing her eyes to drift to him, where they remained.

It was, Stern thought, a sweet look they shared.

"I think I might have run away with you that night," she said quietly, "if you had asked."

"And I was so close to asking," he answered. Until he heard himself, it did not occur to him that they both had spoken of something in the past, but now, for the first time, that seemed to suit him just as well. Speaking, he had found some touch of grace, a perfect note, so that neither she nor he nor anyone passing would ever know precisely where the meter fell, how much of even one syllable was uttered in the kindliest jest or the truest lost ardor. "Regrettably," he continued, "you are married."

She placed both hands on her stomach. "Lucky for me."

"Just so," he answered.

"I told Charlie we got married so we could be crazy together, so we just have to go on that way." She laughed at herself, flipped her hat, took her feet. "Tell me you approve."

"I do," he said.

"That makes one of us."

He laughed out loud.

"Sonny, you have inspired me," he said. He took a step closer, and she averted her face slightly, giving him her cheek. But he did not kiss her. Instead, moved or, as he would have it, inspired, he placed one of his soft hands on each of her bare shoulders, and then in some peculiar ceremony, standing just a few inches from her, let them travel down her arms, a strange would-be embrace. He grasped her above the elbows, on the forearms, at last her hands. She had raised her face by then to greet him, eye to eye.

"When I grow up," she said, "I want to be like Sandy Stern."

49

So that was life, thought Stern. He descended in the Morgan Towers elevators, blinking off the presence of this young woman as if he were emerging from strong light. For an instant he was full of doubt. On another day, when he was less weakened by lack of sleep, might there have been a different outcome? The doors fell open to the noon sun blazing through the lobby's enormous plate-glass windows, and as he stepped forward, eyes stinging, light-headed, he was amazed to find again that he felt more positively himself than he had in months. The core things—not simply the safe items, but matters of faith and influence—remained in place, impervious to the stamp of failure. He touched the center button on his suit jacket and lifted his chin properly, as he so often did. Mr. Alejandro Stern.

He did not return to the office. Instead, he drove home and went immediately to bed. He would rise and re-dress in time for his appointment with Sennett. But right now he needed solemn contemplation. One of the philosophers, Descartes, Stern believed, had chosen his bed as the site for intense reflection, and for unknown reasons Stern had long followed his example. Most of his closing arguments were composed here, with a bed tray beside him amply laid with food and a yellow pad. He wrote down very little. Instead, he weaved the arguments and phrases in his mind—the same sentences, the same notions, again and again, until his consciousness was little more than the passionate speech he was going to deliver. Today it was Clara. Her last hours now belonged to him.

Stern had known a number of suicides. It was one more sad facet of his practice—so many of his clients were intent on doing harm to themselves one way or the other. He had stopped asking himself why decades ago. For too many of them, the answers were obvious: the self-negation, the willful personal abuse, the deficits, shames, the scars. In the late fifties, when he was starting out, Stern had defended the drug case brought against a local rock 'n' roll star who went by the name of Harky Malarky. Harky was full of the untamed moonstruck bleakness of an Irish bard and always danced along the precipice. Morphine addiction. Destructive women. Violent friends. He died, blind drunk, on a motorcycle he purposely raced from the roadside into a magnificent Utah canyon.

And there were others, not as vivid as Harky, but they all had the same unshakable belief that they were doomed. And Clara had it, too. He had always known that. A terrible hard-bitten pessimism, an absolute gloom. She never foresaw a future in which she was included. A psychiatrist he had met over the years, Guy Pleace, confessed to Stern one night at a private moment, during a party at the Cawleys', that he wrestled with the impulse to commit suicide each day. He got up every morning and it was a task as certain as shaving and going to the office: he must not kill himself. That night, Pleace said, he had seen a goblin of sorts beckoning to him from a lamppost. He had driven around the block three times to be certain it was not there. His wife, who was accustomed to this, took it calmly, knowing that he would have to satisfy himself. Eventually, three years ago, Guy had played a losing game of Russian roulette, one round in the chambers—he had, apparently, let the goblins take their shot.

In the midst of his unnerving, half-drunk confession, Pleace had laughed, because some famous depth psychologist, probably Freud, had commented that human beings cannot grasp the reality of their own deaths. That was not true of Guy; and probably not of Clara, or most others who make a deliberate departure. The cup is always half empty or half full. For most of us—certainly for Stern—the concern was over how much remained. Since the time of his fortieth birthday, in his inevitable greedy way, he had remained irritated by the feeling that the serving had been slight to start with. Here, at home, under his covers, alone with the afternoon sounds of the neighborhood and the air conditioning recirculating the still air of the household, he recognized how frightened Clara's death had left him. We stand in line with certain recognizable figures. Her turn. Now yours.

But for Clara, a bit like Guy, the moment must never have been far away. Nate, in fact, said she had told him as much. To Clara it was always a brief ride to a known destination. She meant to be of service along the way. But a sense of futility that went beyond any psychological name—depression or anomie— no doubt often overcame her. What was the point in waiting, given the aeons, the eternity in which she would never take part? And in this frame of mind she had faced her final choices. Dixon's magnificent, grandiose act in the end must have only complicated her overwrought state. There was not a bearable alternative on the horizon. Could she actually stand by and watch as Dixon undertook this gruesome act of self-sacrifice? Could she reveal her problems, and the past, to her husband, devastating him and, in all likelihood—given the odd explosive chain effect of anger and grief—Silvia, too? That would be a poor reward for Dixon, who, in the circumstance, might even lose the will and strength to see his promise through. Could she instead bear the rest of it and also watch her children march off to the penitentiary? It was not suicide, thought Stern. Not in her eyes. It was euthanasia in the face of mortal heartbreak.

Could he have saved her? Was it the cheapest lie, the glossiest balm for his soul to think that if the same two persons had married today, in a franker era, this would not have taken place? They had assigned one another roles at a time when their own ambitions for each other allowed for more unexplored geography. Now there were counselors and meddlers and self-help aids to force couples to walk within each other's fence. He had respected boundaries that, with just a bit more strength or attention or nerve, he might have been able to surmount. His every effort, though, would have been against her will.

Thirty-odd years ago, Clara Mittler had drafted a composition, called it Clara Stern, and remained intent on playing it to the end. It was a woodwind part of austere and unwavering beauty, and he was the uncritical audience, one set of hands clapping when he took the time to occupy his seat. The quiet precision of this performance hid from all—but most significantly herself—a terrible banging turmoil. Somewhere, well beyond her power to bring it forth, there must have been a thunderous rage. She knew it only as disorganized sound. The noise, she had told Nate, the crashing dissonance of anxiety and unending disappointment, was always with her. Ultimately the noise had come from all directions, at unendurable volume, and Clara bowed to the aesthete's inevitable grief that Beauty would not be her.

He knew for some reason just now what he had not before—how it was done. He had never understood why she had chosen the car. But today that was clear. She had triggered the ignition and then slipped a cassette into the player. The police, of course, had not even looked. It would have been Mozart, certainly, but Stern felt a stitch of a keen frustrated grief that he would never know which selection. The *Requiem*? The *Jupiter*? But the remainder he could imagine. The volume had been turned up considerably—the woodwinds lowed with lost sounds of the soul and the plangent violins engulfed the small space, so that even a fine ear could not detect the engine's rumble, and she lay back, eyes already closed, no doubt, while the magnificent music rose in great waves toward that perfect moment at the end of every piece when there was silence.

50

When Helen called, Stern was dreaming: Dixon had accosted him on a street corner. He was smoking one of Stern's cigars and in his usual joking manner was pointing out that he had gone bald. He circled his hand over his crown and with considerable satisfaction turned about so that Stern could see the large spot where the straight black hair had actually fallen away. As Helen spoke, the dream and its difficult feelings still swam within him and for just the barest instant he was convinced his dreaming had gone on.

"What?" He was lost. Was she crying?

"I need you." She seemed short of breath. When he had answered—as in the office, 'Stern here'—she had said repeatedly she was sorry to be calling. Sorry. Sorry. "I need you here. Please."

"Yes, yes. I shall be there momentarily."

In the bathroom, he felt unbalanced by the light. He splashed water on his face and gave up the thought of shaving. The line of a sheet was impressed on his cheek. Had she even mentioned the problem? One of her children, he imagined. The boy in college. He crept down to the garage.

When he started the Cadillac, the digital clock flashed on. It was almost three; early Friday morning. He had been asleep since a little after nine, having gotten only an hour or two on Wednesday night. Marta had kept him awake, demanding that he share in advance every thought and nuance that would go into the closing argument in *U.S.* v. *Cavarelli*. Stern had delivered this argument at ten yesterday morning, then waited with poor Remo most of the day for the jury, which returned near five

o'clock. Not guilty. With the verdict, Judge Winchell had fixed
Remo with a sour look, but her sole comment had been to Moses
Appleton: 'Better luck next time.' Marta, who had assisted her
father throughout, even cross-examined one of the surveillance
agents, was eager to celebrate. Gracious to the core, Moses had
insisted on buying both of them a drink. After a single soda
water, Stern had left Marta and Appleton for the sleep of the old
and weary. Why were triumph and exultation always so fleeting?
He drove through the night streets now, toward Helen's, waking
gradually and increasingly alarmed.

Facing him, in Helen's drive, a van had been backed to the
paneled door of the garage. In his own headlights Stern could
read the lettering, reversed to be legible in rearview mirrors :

 AMBULANCE

QUIK—ALERT

PARAMEDICS

Not again, he thought, God, not again. He ran up the walk, his
change and keys jumping in his pockets; he did not have to ring
the bell. Helen, by the door, swept it open and was in his arms at
once, weeping and thanking him for coming. He had caught her
face for just a second, but it was a sight. She had been fully made
up when she started crying. A mess of liner was clumped along
her cheeks, and the tears had washed away the cosmetics in
streaks below her eyes. A tuft of her hair stood on end. In his
arms, in spite of the heavy robe, he could tell that she was
otherwise unclad, and all of this—the sight of her, the feeling
now, her voice and breath, her urgent clinging—unloosed in him
a tremendous wallop of sensation. His poor heart. It was like a
barnacle drifting through the sea and ready to attach itself to
any prominence. And still how welcome all this was, her ardor,
her presence, her declared need. Lord, what a dear person Helen
Dudak was to him. For this instant he felt amazing gratitude.
"What? Please?" He held her hands.

She tossed her head about.

"I'm so sorry I had to call you. You were the only person I
could think of. Sandy, please..." She did not finish; a retching
sound escaped her. She pressed her folded hand to her mouth
and once more leaned against him.

"Lady, hey. Sir?" A *latino* in the ambulance service's brown
uniform was on the landing of the staircase, beckoning down to

both of them. "His no good." The man slowly shook his head.
Helen wailed, a brief wavering sound.

Stern was already on the way up, following the attendant, who
had retraced his way along the staircase and was headed down
the hall. In Helen's bedroom there was a terrible stink. The bed
was unmade. And a man was in it, a crippled, still figure,
unclothed, his face beneath the plastic form of an oxygen mask.
In extremity, he had apparently lost control of his bowels. There
was a second attendant here, a young white man, and both of
them were busy with the equipment which they had at the
bedside, two large green cast-iron tanks and a cart with wires
and various apparatuses. On one corner of the king-sized bed,
entirely unexplained, stood a small wooden end table. The
latino, the one Stern had seen on the stairs, gestured to Stern in
the doorway. He was removing the last lead from the man's
chest.

"EKG?" He whistled and drew a smooth line in space. "No
good. They'll pronounce him at Riverside. Okay I use the phone?
I got to call the cops." Before he moved on, the attendant leaned
over and removed the air mask from the man in the bed and
stopped to close his eyes, a quick stroke with his forefinger and
his thumb. Even from the doorway, Stern could tell.

"Oh, dear God," he said out loud. Helen had arrived beside
him. Stern was holding on to the doorjamb. "Who is it?" he asked
her, moved by some impulse of propriety or hope. Helen had not
looked at him directly since he had arrived. She gripped Stern's
hand with both of hers and bowed her head a bit, so that her
forehead rested against his shoulder. "Helen, please tell me that
is not Dixon."

As before, she merely shook her head, the washed-out tousles
of fox-colored hair. She had no words for the moment. And in
any event, what Stern wanted was something she could never
say.

*   *   *

With the attendants' consent, it was Stern who summoned the
police. He called Division 4 Homicide and insisted they rouse the
lieutenant at home. When he called back, Stern put him on the
line with the attendants. At the lieutenant's instruction, they

were relieved, told to go on their way and to leave the body to
the police. Stern saw the two out as they bumped their tanks and
cart over the threshold. Helen was seated right there, on a low,
upholstered bench positioned by the doorway to collect mail or
packages or wraps. She remained downcast, looking into a
snifter of brandy. Stern sat beside her and she passed him the
glass.

"I'm sorry I had to call," she said again.

"Please, do not—" A hand drummed in the air. The words did
not need to be spoken. "In the act?"

She nodded with emphasis.

Dead with his boots on. Dixon Hartnell in his many lost vain
moments would be abundantly pleased. Stern attempted without success to smile.

"And how long has this been going on?"

"Going on?"

"This," said Stern decidedly.

Helen glanced up.

"Sandy, please don't take that tone with me. He called. Did I
do something wrong?"

Stern worked against the weight of various judgments, too
shocked, it seemed, to follow his customary instinct for
reticence.

"He is married, Helen."

"I'm not."

"No," Stern agreed.

"Do you think this was aimed at you somehow?"

Did he? God knows what he felt. He looked back up the stairs,
where Dixon's body now lay beneath an old blue sheet, like some
shrouded piece of statuary.

"He called me. The week you left me high and dry, as a matter
of fact. And I enjoyed his company. That's all."

"Very well," said Stern.

"He was very romantic," said Helen. Her face was harsh with
unconcealed ire. "He'd call, he'd come by at any hour. He was
charming."

"Yes, I see," said Stern. No need now to ask where Dixon was
roaming to at night. His next utterance would be 'Enough.'

They sat in silence. Stern could hear the clocks tick, the
appliances. The headlights of another car swept into the drive.

"The policeman," Stern said.

Helen tightened the belt on her robe, preparing to tell the story.

Radczyk, alone, in his rumpled sport coat and an old fedora, approached the doorway. Stern shooed Helen into the living room, then let him in.

"Always sad occasions, Lieutenant."

"My business," said Radczyk, and laughed in his inoffensive, hickish way, amused by himself. His blotchy face was red from sleep. He raked the straying hair over his head and clutched his hat.

Stern introduced Helen, who in a few brief strokes said what she had to. They were making love, she said. Radczyk stood in the living room with his tiny pad, making notes.

"So, let's see," he said. "This guy and this gal—" He nodded in a courteous way to Helen, who was standing right there. "This guy—"

"My client," said Stern.

"Your client," said Radczyk. He hitched his chin finally and invited Stern to walk farther down the hall.

"I take it this fella wasn't the gentleman of the house."

"Ms. Dudak is unmarried. He was my brother-in-law," said Stern. "My sister's husband."

"Okay," said Radczyk. He nodded a number of times. He got it now.

"This will be terrible for her."

"Sure, sure. So wha'dya got in mind?" He knew there was something, because Stern had told him on the phone he would ask a favor. He wished to spare his sister, Stern said now. Radczyk listened. It was nothing to him, one way or the other.

"Let me look around, be sure it's kosher," Radczyk said. He was matter-of-fact. It was his job.

Upstairs, he examined the body, touched the chest, rolled Dixon a bit from side to side. Radczyk held his nose. "P.U.," he said. "Stroke or heart attack, you figure?"

"Heart," said Stern. That was the paramedics' diagnosis. Radczyk thought so, too. "Looks okay. No marks or anything. I ain't got a problem, if you're sure that's what you want to do."

Stern said it was.

"I gotta make a call or two," said Radczyk. "Get somebody to

hit the wrong key on the computer." He winked. At the doorway
to the bedroom, Radczyk grabbed Stern's arm, lowered his voice.
"What about the table?" He hitched a shoulder toward the
corner of the bed where the small end table had remained.
Stern only shrugged.

* * *

While Radczyk was on the phone, Stern returned to Helen. She
had not moved. She was still in her robe, still pale and stricken,
barefoot, with her thin calves looking white without hosiery. The
brandy glass was beside her. Stern took it up again and told her
what he planned.

"It will be much easier this way for Silvia," said Stern. Dixon
and he were to have lunch with her today. Stern would drive out
to the house and together they were going to tell her—that
Dixon was going to plead guilty to two counts of mail fraud next
week, and soon after would be confined in a federal penitentiary,
probably the one in Minnesota, for a year, ten months, actually,
with good time. It had not been a task he had been looking
forward to, and in a peculiar way the notion that he had already
shouldered some ominous duty toward his sister made the
thought of what was now at hand easier by some bare measure.

"Silvia," said Helen. With that realization she started crying
again. "I *was* trying to get even with you, I suppose."

"You were entitled."

She wiped her nose on her sleeve before Stern could get out
his hanky.

"I *was*," said Helen, as only she could, in her frank, emphatic
way. "I was so hurt, Sandy. I feel. Felt. Shit." She lowered her
head and laughed and cried at once. "He would have dropped
me, anyway. He hadn't come by for days and he told me tonight
that he'd decided we had to break it off. I couldn't believe it.
Jilted by the replacement, too." Helen smiled a bit, but then the
thought of something, the moment probably, came back to her
and she wrapped her arms about herself and closed her eyes.
"He was trying to comfort me," she said.

She took a second.

"I should have known better. I tried to get even with Miles,
too, after I found out about him. Did you know that? That I had

an affair before I left him?"

"No. Should I?"

"I always felt everyone knew. Didn't you? I was certain you did, that night."

Stern looked at her blankly. "What night?"

"When Nate dropped by," said Helen. "At your house? I'd brought dinner?"

He absorbed this, too.

"I do not approve," Stern said suddenly. "I understand. But I do not approve of any of this."

This utterance amazed him. Not so much the judgment as its sudden force. He realized that he stood revealed, a man of harsh opinions, which he ordinarily kept to himself. It seemed that he spoke mostly out of confusion, but the significance was not lost on Helen. She looked at him bravely, knowing, apparently, with her strong intuitions of him, that it was necessary that something be denounced.

"Of course not," she said.

Radczyk returned then.

"Okey-doke," he said. "All set. No report, no nothin. This here never happened." He nodded politely to Helen. "I'll give you a hand," he said to Stern.

Dixon's clothes were strewn about the room. Stern gathered the items, but Radczyk took them from his hands. "Here, here, let me," he said. "Homicide dick is half an undertaker."

When Dixon was dressed again, they carried him out. Radczyk took the ankles and Stern grasped Dixon's hands, clammy to the touch and strangely firm. The feel was like nothing human; cool, almost chilled. Dead weight, they said. It was a considerable task. Helen walked away at the sight of the body. They rested Dixon on a sofa in the small den off the kitchen and then Stern backed his car into the garage. Together, they laid Dixon out in the back seat and covered him with the same washed-out sheet.

"I'll meet you down there," Radczyk said. "I gotta make a call, then I'll be there."

Stern insisted it was not necessary, but Radczyk would not hear of it.

"You gonna go walkin round Center City with a stiff, better have a badge along. Could get pretty peculiar, otherwise."

Radczyk drove off, and Stern returned to Helen, who had sat

again on the bench, her place of contemplation for the night. She had dressed in the interval, a black top and stretch pants, and had washed her face clean of any makeup. She looked plain, drawn but composed. He had been pondering his outburst, haunted now by embarrassment. Something—that high-and-mighty tone—was so wildly hypocritical. He began to apologize.

"Please, Sandy," she said.

He sighed at length.

"You must understand," he said. And so he told her, more directly than he ever could have imagined, about Clara: she and Dixon had had a brief affair some years ago. As he spoke, it occurred to him that there was nothing in the world he could not say to Helen Dudak.

"Oh, Sandy." She covered her open mouth with one hand.

"So you see," he said.

"Yes, of course." She closed her eyes. Then she took his hand. "He must have envied you terribly."

"Envied me?"

"Don't you see?"

The thought was breathtaking.

They sat together on the bench in silence. He would have to move along, he thought, meet Radczyk. She continued to hold his hand, and now Stern was reluctant to depart.

"How's your friend?" she asked presently.

He did not understand.

"Your new friend," Helen said.

"Oh, that." He smiled to himself. "Well past. Temporary insanity," he said. "I seem to have grown up again."

They were both quiet. Eventually, Helen slumped and held her face in her hands in her familiar, youthful manner.

"Do you believe," she asked, "that we're doomed to repeat the same mistakes all our lives?"

"There is that tendency," he said. But, of course, if he believed that the soul would forever be a slave to its private fetishes, why had he come to the U.S.? Why did he cry out for justice for those who were most often unredeemable? What, indeed, had he spent these months trying to transcend? "But I also believe in second chances."

"So do I," said Helen, and reached over again to take his hand.

* * *

After he married Helen the following spring, Stern told her on a number of occasions that it had all been foregone from the moment they had sat together on that bench. But this was not really true. For months after, he remained uncertain about many things, particularly himself, the limits of his strength and the exact form of his wishes. But as he rose to leave that night, he took her once more in his arms—Helen, who had been in bed with Dixon a few hours ago, and Stern, who had his body in the back seat of his car—and felt, as he embraced her in these impossible circumstances, if only for an instant, the clear bright light of desire. It was what he had felt when he greeted her tonight, but the events that had unfolded since had added a new urgency. What was it? He could never explain, but as he had absorbed her peculiar confession, he had been full of strong emotion. In her disorder, her confusion, her hasty admission that she, like the rest of us, was still, for all her effort, partly invisible to herself, he adored her. So he held her another moment and told her a bit more of the story. About the latest turn of events with Dixon. And the fact that his children were involved. He did not say how. Helen, he knew, would want to share every secret, to tell each of hers and to hear from him everything he told no one else. And in time, he realized, he would probably do that. It was that moment, those discoveries, he would be talking about the following spring.

Then Mr. Alejandro Stern, heavy with thought and feeling, drove through the night, eerily aware of the presence behind him. At every light, he tilted down the rearview mirror so that he could look at the form in the back seat. "My God, Dixon," he said out loud at one point. Envied him. Envied, Helen said. For what? He was a fat man with a foreign accent. The respect he claimed, esteem, was nothing, minor, transitory. What, really, were his achievements? A disordered family life? Poor Dixon. His cravings were unending. Great men, thought Stern, had great appetites. Had someone said that? He was not certain, nor was he sure what name he would put to Dixon. Great something, was the thought tonight.

Radczyk's car, an old Reliant, was in the loading zone behind the building. Stern took the door handle and was ready to alight when he was struck again with that sensation, clear as *déjà vu*, that none of this had happened, that this actual moment was not occurring. Not this or anything of the last week, weeks, months. He was someone else, somewhere else. This was all the concoction of some stupefied wreck in the corner cot of a distant bedlam. He stared at the amber circles thrown down by the crane-necked street lamps and returned gradually to his life.

They carried Dixon under the sheet. Radczyk propped the building's front doors open with pieces of cardboard and they hauled Dixon around to the back service elevator. In a building tenanted principally by lawyers, someone was likely to be here, even at 5:45 in the morning. In the dirty elevator, they kept Dixon, taller than both of them, between them, under his pale blue sheet. Radczyk held the body upright with a hand on Dixon's belt.

In Stern's office, they attempted to position him, as he had been on those two recent nights, on the sofa. Stern crossed Dixon's legs, and with that the body rolled slowly forward, collapsing by stages, until it arrived with a heavy helpless thump on the floor.

Stern covered his face. It could not be avoided. Both Radczyk and he laughed out loud.

Then they placed him once more on the sofa, holding him there. Stern unbuttoned Dixon's jacket, lifted his hands. He was like a store mannequin now. When Stern bent Dixon's legs to position his feet, Dixon's head fell backward, his mouth open, agape, in an unmistakable pose of death.

Neither Radczyk nor he moved for a moment.

"How may I thank you, Lieutenant?" Stern asked as Radczyk started to leave.

"No need," said Radczyk, He looked at Stern sadly. "I owed you. I told ya. Never woulda straightened myself out otherwise."

Radczyk had said he owed him forty times if he had said it once, and Stern had never caught the meaning. But now he did. There was a reason Radczyk sat through each of Marvin's meetings with Stern. A reason for his nervous garrulousness. He and Marvin, after all, were raised as brothers. They had shared many things. Too many. Radczyk, given a reprieve and the opportunity for reform, had seized it; Marvin took the more familiar course. Stern shared a look with Radczyk, this man whom he barely knew—they possessed many of each other's most terrible secrets. Then Stern simply nodded, a compact of confidence, gratitude, renewal.

Stern saw the policeman to the outer door and then, on second thought, went back to retrieve the sheet. He wanted no telltale signs when the others arrived here this morning. Then he returned to his office and was alone with the body of his brother-in-law, Dixon Hartnell. There was no comfortable place to sit. The sofa clearly was out, and his desk chair was still beneath the broken glass, which had not been removed or replaced, given the spell of busy activity for Remo's trial. Stern was required to use one of the upholstered pull-up chairs, cut a bit too narrowly for him. He hauled the chair about to face the body. How sad Dixon looked, how fully depleted. His color was unnatural, that dark gray veinous shade. The spirit had fled.

"Does good always win, Dixon?" Stern asked. "It does on TV."

He had no idea how the words came to him or why, with them, he began to cry. The tears had been in the offing for some days now; that he knew. He was puzzled merely by the moment. But there was no point in holding back. The storm blew up and through him. He covered his mouth with his hanky and pressed his fist to his lips at moments to suppress his howl.

"My God, Dixon," he kept repeating when he spoke.

When he was done, he stood, approached the sofa, and decided to pray. He had never been certain what it was he believed. On High Holidays he attended shul and engaged the Lord in direct address. The rest of the year he seemed agnostic. But at this point, he called on his talent for sincerity, since he was his finest self, an advocate not speaking on his own behalf.

Accept, dear God, the soul of Dixon Hartnell, who made his own amends, and who traveled his own way. He failed, as we all fail, and perhaps more often than some. Yet he recognized fundamental things. Not that we are evil; for we are not. But that, by whatever name—self-interest, impulse, anger, lust, or greed—we are inclined that way; and that it is our tragedy to know this can never change; our duty to try at every moment to overcome it; and our glory occasionally to succeed.

An extra suit hung behind the office door, and Stern quickly changed. He had a tie and shirt in a drawer, and a razor. He would not have his attaché case, but in the confusion no one would notice. He went down the hall to shave, returned, and sat before the telephone. When he heard the first stirring of someone else within the office, he would call Silvia to tell her he had just found Dixon, here where he had spent many recent nights, intent, obsessed with assembling his defense.

From this side of the desk, he faced the shelves of the walnut cabinet where the framed photographs of his family remained, the ones Dixon had lingered with last week. They were free. Totally. John. Kate. Even Peter. That thought had not occurred to him until now. With Dixon's death, the entire matter was over. The events—their shame—would recede into the past. With Clara's fortune, they were now even prosperous. The three of them would have their second chances, too. He tried to envision their futures and his with them, but nothing came—murky shades, something bleak. Then he recalled. There would be a baby—a child. Children always drew a family together. Even his, he supposed. He had some vision, like a vaguely surreal painting, the strange conjunctions of a dream, of all of them drawn close to this pink, unknown infant in a kind of halo radiance, each face alight with that wonderful instinctive glee. They would surround this child and be, each of them, someone new: parents, grandparent, uncle, aunts. New responsibilities. Fantasies. Dreams. Mistakes, of course, would be made. Bad habits would be repeated and, worse, taught anew. They would succumb, each of them in some measure, to folly, to the grasp of unwanted portions of the dark, indomitable past. Nonetheless. We go on.

In the outer office there was the sound of someone arriving; he reached at once for the phone. When he heard his sister's voice, he spoke her name and, in spite of the qualm of grief which unexpectedly rifled through him, began. Yet again, he said, a terrible blow. She knew at once.

"We must manage these burdens together," he told her. "I am able to help."

NOTE

I have been fortunate to draw on the specialized knowledge of many friends in writing this book. Dr. John Weiss provided invaluable advice about medical matters, as did Dr. Robert Stein, the Cook County Examiner, and my father Dr. David Turow. I am grateful to Nadya Walsh for sharing her recollections of Argentina and to Steve Senderowitz for discussing with me various questons of commodities law. My partners Jim Ferguson and Tom Opferman were of great help on other legal points.

I also should note that Gabriel Turow is the author of most of the good lines in Chapter 29.

Finally, to my friends on the commodity futures exchanges, particularly Frank and Brian Gelber Group Inc., I am especially indebted.

The aid of these persons undoubtedly prevented many factual errors. Any that remain are solely my responsibility.